Big Planet

Big Planet is Jack Vance's first major sf novel, and in the words of the *Encyclopedia of Science Fiction*, 'provided an sf model for the planetary romance which has been of significant use for forty years'. The huge world of the title is home to a range of colourfully detailed and imaginative human societies, which Vance explores with the zest and humour which are hallmarks of his work.

The Blue World

Over twelve generations the descendants of a space crash on a world completely covered in water had managed to adapt to their marine culture. Living in villages built on giant clumps of sea plants, they survived on the flora and fauna of the sea. But they have always been at the mercy of the kragen – gigantic squid-like monsters that prey on their fish flocks, and on them. The biggest of these is King Kragen, with whom the colonists can communicate, who has to be appeased. But one man has had enough of a life of slavery and sacrifice. But how can he convince his fellow men that King Kragen must be killed? And how can that be achieved in a world without weapons?

The Dragon Masters and Other Stories

The race of man is growing old, but it's not yet ready to die – not while there are dragons still to kill! The cross-bred dragon armies of the Men of Aerlith are the most appalling horrors ever to threaten the sanity of our future:

Termagents ~ three hundred reptilian giants with six legs apiece, the most fecund breeders of them all.

Jugglers ~ eighteen of them, growling amongst themselves, waiting for an opportunity to snap off a leg from any unwary groom.

Murderers (striding and long-horned) ~ eighty-five of each, with scaly tails and eyes like crystals.

Fiends ~ fifty-two powerful monsters, their tails tipped with spike steel balls. Blue Horrors, Basics, Spider Dragons ... the enemy has no chance.

Also By Jack Vance

The Dying Earth
The Dying Earth (1950) (aka
Mazirian the Magician)
Cugel the Clever (1966) (aka The Eyes
of the Overworld)
Cugel's Saga (1966) (aka Cugel: The
Skybreak Spatterlight)
Rhialto the Marvellous (1984)

Big Planet
Big Planet (1952)
The Magnificent Showboats (1975)
(aka The Magnificent Showboats of
the Lower Vissel River, Lune XXII
South, Big Planet) (aka Showboat
World)

Demon Princes
The Star King (1964)
The Killing Machine (1964)
The Palace of Love (1967)
The Face (1979)
The Book of Dreams (1981)

Planet of Adventure
The Chasch (1968) (City of the
Chasch)
The Wannek (1969) (Servants of the
Wankh)
The Dirdir (1969)
The Pnume (1970)

Durdane
The Anome (1973)
The Brave Free Men (1973)
The Asutra (1974)

Alastor Cluster
Trullion: Alastor 2262 (1973)
Marune: Alastor 933 (1975)
Wyst: Alastor 1716 (1978)

Lyonesse
Suldrun's Garden (1983) (aka Lyonesse)

The Green Pearl (1985)
Madouc (1990)

Cadwal Chronicles
Araminta Station (1988)
Ecce and Old Earth (1991)
Throy (1992)

Gaean Reach
The Domains of Koryphon (1974)
(aka The Gray Prince)
Maske: Thaery (1976)

Other Novels
Vandals of the Void (1953)
The Rapparee (The Five Gold Bands/
The Space Pirate) (1953)
Clarges (To Live Forever) (1956)
The Languages of Pao (1958)
Gold and Iron (Slaves of the Klau/
Planet of the Damned) (1958)
Space Opera (1965)
The Blue World (1966)
Emphyrio (1969)
The Dogtown Tourist Agency (aka
Galactic Effectuator) (1980)

Collections
The World-Thinker and Other
Stories
The Potters of Firsk and Other Stories
(aka Gadget Stories)
Son of the Tree and Other Stories
Golden Girl and Other Stories
The Houses of Iszm and Other Stories
The Dragon Masters and Other
Stories
The Moon Moth and Other Stories

Autobiography
This is Me, Jack Vance (2009)

Jack Vance

SF GATEWAY OMNIBUS

BIG PLANET
THE BLUE WORLD
THE DRAGON MASTERS
AND OTHER STORIES

GOLLANCZ

LONDON

First published in Great Britain in 2013 by
Gollancz
An imprint of the Orion Publishing Group
Orion House, 5 Upper St Martin's Lane,
London WC2H 9EA

An Hachette UK Company

A CIP catalogue record for this book is
available from the British Library

ISBN 978 0 575 10317 7

1 3 5 7 9 10 8 6 4 2

Typeset by Input Data Services Ltd, Bridgwater, Somerset

Printed and bound by CPI Group (UK) Ltd, Croydon, CR0 4YY

The Orion Publishing Group's policy is to use papers
that are natural, renewable and recyclable products and
made from wood grown in sustainable forests. The logging
and manufacturing processes are expected to conform to
the environmental regulations of the country of origin.

www.orionbooks.co.uk
www.gollancz.co.uk

CONTENTS

ENTER THE SF GATEWAY . . .

Towards the end of 2011, in conjunction with the celebration of fifty years of coherent, continuous science fiction and fantasy publishing, Gollancz launched the SF Gateway.

Over a decade after launching the landmark SF Masterworks series, we realised that the realities of commercial publishing are such that even the Masterworks could only ever scratch the surface of an author's career. Vast troves of classic SF & Fantasy were almost certainly destined never again to see print. Until very recently, this meant that anyone interested in reading any of those books would have been confined to scouring second-hand bookshops. The advent of digital publishing changed that paradigm for ever.

Embracing the future even as we honour the past, Gollancz launched the SF Gateway with a view to utilising the technology that now exists to make available, for the first time, the entire backlists of an incredibly wide range of classic and modern SF and fantasy authors. Our plan, at its simplest, was – and still is! – to use this technology to build on the success of the SF and Fantasy Masterworks series and to go even further.

The SF Gateway was designed to be the new home of classic Science Fiction & Fantasy – the most comprehensive electronic library of classic SFF titles ever assembled. The programme has been extremely well received and we've been very happy with the results. So happy, in fact, that we've decided to complete the circle and return a selection of our titles to print, in these omnibus editions.

We hope you enjoy this selection. And we hope that you'll want to explore more of the classic SF and fantasy we have available. These are wonderful books you're holding in your hand, but you'll find much, much more ... through the SF Gateway.

www.sfgateway.com

INTRODUCTION
from The Encyclopedia of Science Fiction

Jack Vance is the working name of US author John Holbrook Vance (1916–), who was educated at the University of California first as a mining engineer, then as a physics major and finally in journalism, though without taking a degree. During World War Two he served in the Merchant Navy, being twice torpedoed, a period during which he wrote his first story, 'The World-Thinker', which he published in *Thrilling Wonder Stories* (Summer 1945). In the late 1940s and early 1950s Vance contributed a variety of short stories and novels to the PULP magazines, primarily *Startling Stories* and *Thrilling Wonder Stories*.

In the meantime, Vance was beginning to compose the kind of story that would eventually make him one of the two or three most deeply influential authors in the sf and fantasy genres after World War Two, an impact greater than that generated by fellow inventors of the modern (post-Edgar Rice Burroughs) Planetary Romance like Leigh Brackett, C. L. Moore or Clark Ashton Smith. The depth and duration of this influence may have something to do with Vance's long prime as a creative figure, for he was writing work of high quality nearly half a century after he came into his own voice, creating an oeuvre whose surface flamboyance never obscured an underlying seriousness. Authors clearly (and often explicitly) influenced by Vance include such widely divergent figures as Jack L. Chalker, Avram Davidson, Terry Dowling, Harlan Ellison, Ursula K. Le Guin, George R. R. Martin, Michael Moorcock, Dan Simmons and Gene Wolfe.

Within the broad remit of the Planetary Romance, Vance created two subgenres, the first being the Dying Earth story that takes its name from his first book, *The Dying Earth* (**1950**). It comprises six previously unpublished tales set on Earth in the far future at a time, long after the wasting away of science, when magic has become the operating principle; after millions of years, the hugely congested tapestry of human civilization – transfigured through genetic engineering and by the drawn-out torsions of evolution – has become an iridescent, deadly maze for its inhabitants. To survive within any genuine Dying Earth requires constant knowing *negotiation,* as there is so much to understand: the whole of human and post-human history. Appropriately, Vance's protagonists tend to make their way through these worlds as an anthropologist might: notating the memedense behaviours typical of the exemplary cultures they inhabit or (especially in later works) visit, and managing in that fashion to survive: deciphering the signals and warning signs given off by an alien world, which is how immigrants avoid despair or death.

Vance's second original sophistication of the Planetary Romance, the big planet story, again takes its name from his first novel to exemplify it: *Big Planet* (**1957**), to which *Showboat World* (**1975**) forms a retroactively conceived sequel (see below). Almost any world depicted in a Vance planetary romance might be linked notionally to Earth by conventional sf explanations (colonisation of other worlds or diaspora, for instance), but the tacitly shared background of most of these tales – they are often described as occupying a vast stretch of the galaxy known as the **Gaean Reach** – is far too loose to be described as comprising a conventional Future History. As noted above, Vance's protagonists, even the more simple-minded of them, are scholars of the worlds they live in. Vance's best work almost always focuses on how humans learn how to come to terms with the splendours and miseries of human cultures, a task that sometimes seems beyond the compass of the naive young protagonists he tended to prefer, many of whom seem too immersed in the revenge plots typical of much of his work to explore the world with the proper dispassionate intensity: but then who better to experience new worlds to the full than an innocent youth ...

As Vance's created worlds became richer and more complex, so too did his style. Always tending towards the baroque, it had developed by the time of *The Dragon Masters* (**1963**) (see below) into an effective high-mannered diction, somewhat pedantic, and almost always saturated with a rich but distanced irony. Vance's talent for naming the people and places in his stories (a mixture of exotic invented terms and obscure or commonplace words with the right resonance) increasingly generated a sense that dream ethnographies were being carved, almost as a gardener would create topiary. Three novels, similar in structure, show these talents at their fullest stretch: *The Blue World* (**1966**) (see below), *Emphyrio* (**1969**) and *The Anome* (**1973**) – it is the first volume of the **Durdane** trilogy – each follow the life of a boy born into and growing up in a static, stratified society, with which he comes into conflict, being driven eventually into rebellion. The invented world in each is particularly carefully thought-out. Both *Emphyrio* and *The Anome* additionally feature some piercing satire of religion.

Vance has written comparatively little short fiction. Apart from those stories already mentioned, the best include 'Telek' (1952 *Astounding*), 'The Moon Moth' (1961 *Galaxy*) and the novella *The Last Castle* (**1967**) (see below). 'The Moon Moth', one of Vance's most elaborate short stories, features the use of music as a secondary form of communication. Music and other arts feature in several other Vance stories, including *Space Opera*

(1965), *Emphyrio, The Anome* **(1973)** and *Showboat World* **(1975)**.

The 1980s saw some slackening in Vance's production, though this might not have been evident to the casual observer, as it was now that much of his earlier short fiction was finally brought out in book form. Beyond continuations of earlier series, his most interesting work in this decade was restricted to two new series. One was the **Lyonesse** sequence of fantasies about Tristan's birthplace off the coast of France, now sunk into the wide funnel of the English Channel: *Suldrun's Garden* **(1983)**, *The Green Pearl* **(1985)** and *Madouc* **(1989)**. Of greater sf interest are the **Cadwal Chronicles** – comprising *Araminta Station* **(1987)**, *Ecce and Old Earth* **(1991)** and *Throy* **(1992)** – expanding the planetary-romance idiom into very long books with a sophisticated, newly plot-wise leisureliness which almost fully warrants their length. Interestingly, the planet Cadwal – effectively the central character of the sequence, in a fashion typical of Vance – is a nature reserve: a level playing field of preserved ecology. None of Vance's novels are exactly Godgames; but the synoptic intensity of the gaze they focus upon the human condition constantly evokes some absent guiding father. At the end of his active career, this luxurious expansiveness became even more evident: in the remarkably complex *Night Lamp* **(1996)**, whose young hero is liberated by a Memory Edit to focus on the fascination of his world and heritage; and in the linked *Ports of Call* **(1998)** and *Lurulu* **(2004)**, in which a mission of revenge is submerged in a blissfully interminable tour through a vast interstellar archipelago of varying societies.

As a landscape artist, a visionary shaper of potential human societies, Vance has been central to both sf and Fantasy. For many of his fellow writers, and for a large audience, he has been for more than half a century the field's central gardener of worlds. In 1984 he received the World Fantasy Award for lifetime achievement; in 1997 he received the SFWA Grand Master Award. He was inducted into the Science Fiction Hall Of Fame in 2001. For his late autobiography, *This is Me, Jack Vance! (or, More Properly, This is 'I')* **(2009)**, he won a Hugo award.

The selections from Vance's work presented here focus on his bright early prime. Before 1950 and *The Dying Earth*, the planetary romance had been generally restricted either to tales which replicated, palely, the work of Edgar Rice Burroughs or to pulp-magazine sf adventures set on worlds which might be colourful but which were at the same time conceived with a fatal thinness. What was lacking was a properly conceived venue sufficient to the needs of romance. In *Big Planet*, the first novel printed here, Vance provided an sf model for the planetary romance which has remained of significant use for half a century. The planet on which the tale is set is a huge world, with an Earthlike climate, and with enough landmass to provide realistic venues in which room for a wide range of social systems. As this Big Planet is significantly low in heavy-metal resources and is therefore less dense than a planet like Earth, gravity is relatively low despite its size; and the lack of minerals justifies Vance's creation of a wide range of low-tech societies. As usual with Vance, the inhabitants of these societies are descended, though remotely, from human stock, and have become exceedingly variegated in ways Vance explores in the ethnographical style he further developed to tell this tale, and which would dominate his work for the rest of his active career. But *Big Planet* is the first, and most purely enjoyable, of his playgrounds.

The second tale printed here is *The Blue World,* which takes place in a planetary colony originally settled (a bit like Australia) by convicts after the spaceship carrying them has crashed. Much time has passed, memories have faded, and the founders' forgotten crimes survive as caste names, with the (manipulative and villainous) priests known as Bezzlers. The planet their ancestors had landed up on is almost all water, and inhabited by serpent-like intelligent natives: the heart of the book deals luminously with the relationship between a conflicted human society and an aquatic race whose God (or ruler) is known as King Kragen.

The two extremely well-known novellas included in the final section here – *The Dragon Masters* (**1963**) and *The Last Castle* (**1967**), which won Vance a Nebula and his second Hugo – are leisurely and swift, dense and alive with action. *The Dragon Masters* is again set, like *The Blue World,* on a distant planet shared, in this case very unwillingly, by two species. Each takes prisoners from the other, and each subjects its victims to breeding experiments, leading to an astonishing richness of diversity, all in several dozen pages. *The Last Castle* (**1967**) is set in the far future where the eponymous Keep houses relics of *Homo sapiens,* who are besieged from within and without; again, mutated species fill the vision as they dance through the 100 pages of this condensed but effortless tale. The two novellas are keys to the vast world of Jack Vance, to visit the realms awaiting.

For a more detailed version of the above, see Jack Vance's author entry in *The Encyclopedia of Science Fiction:* http://sf-encyclopedia.com/entry/vance_jack

Some terms above are capitalised when they would not normally be so rendered; this indicates that the terms represent discrete entries in *The Encyclopedia of Science Fiction.*

BIG PLANET

CHAPTER ONE

Arthur Hidders, he called himself. He wore Earth-style clothes, and, except for the length of his hair and his mustache rings, he looked the complete Earthman – which, in a sense, he was. His age was indeterminate; the exact panel of races which had gone into his make-up was a secret six hundred years gone. He stood an easy five foot six; he was light, with delicate features centered rather too closely in a large round head, which obviously held many brains.

Turning away from the porthole out on space, he fixed old Pianza with a gaze of almost child-like ingenuousness. 'That's all very interesting – but doesn't it seem, well, futile?'

'Futile?' Pianza said with great dignity. 'I'm afraid I don't understand you.'

Hidders made a careless gesture, taking few pains to hide his opinion of Pianza: a well-meaning old man, perhaps a trifle dense. 'Earth-Central has sent commissions to Big Planet once a generation for the last five hundred years. Sometimes the commission returns alive, more often not. In either case nothing is accomplished. A few investigators lose their lives, much money is spent, Big Planet tempers – forgive me – are ruffled, and things go on, regrettably, as before.'

Pianza, certainly well-meaning, not at all dense, reflected that Hidders' air of naïveté comported poorly with his professed occupation of fur-trading. Also, thought Pianza, how could a Big Planet fur-trader – a naïve fur-trader – accumulate the exchange necessary to buy passage to Earth? He answered gravely. 'What you say is true, but this time perhaps events will turn out differently.'

Hidders raised his eyebrows, spread out his hands. 'Has Big Planet changed? Has Earth-Central changed?'

Pianza looked uneasily around the lounge – empty except for the nun who sat statue-quiet, the visible section of her thin white face rapt in meditation. Big Planet lay close ahead; the Bajarnum of Beaujolais could not possibly know of their approach. Pianza committed an indiscretion.

'Conditions are different,' he admitted. 'A great deal different. The former commissions were sent out to – well, let us say, to soothe Earth consciences. We knew there was murder, torture, terror on Big Planet; we knew something had to be done.' He smiled sadly. 'The easiest gesture was to send out commissions. The commissions invariably made the same report: nothing

3

could be done that was not being done already at the Enclave – unless Earth-Central wanted to expand, to take full responsibility for Big Planet.'

'Interesting,' said Hidders. 'You have the gift of expressing complicated ideas in simple language. And now?'

Pianza eyed him doubtfully. The butter had become a little thick. 'Now there's something new on Big Planet: the Bajarnum of Beaujolais.'

'Yes, yes – I've frequently traveled through his realms.'

'Well, on Big Planet there are probably hundreds of rulers no less cruel, arrogant, arbitrary – but the Bajarnum, as you certainly must be aware, is expanding his empire, his range of activities, and not only on Big Planet but elsewhere.'

'Ah,' said Hidders. 'So you come to investigate Charley Lysidder, Bajarnum of Beaujolais.'

'Yes,' muttered Pianza. 'You might say so. And this time we have the authority to act.'

'If he learns of your plans, he will no doubt react with rancor and violence.'

'We realize that,' stammered Pianza, wishing now that he could disavow the conversation. 'But I'm sure he won't learn until we're ready.'

'Perhaps you're right,' said Hidders gravely. 'Let us hope so.'

A dark-skinned man of medium height came into the lounge. His muscles lay close under his skin; he moved quickly, with sharp definite motions. This was Claude Glystra, Executive Chairman of the commission.

Glystra looked swiftly around the lounge, ice-colored glances, hard, searching, just short of suspicious. He joined Hidders and Pianza at the porthole, pointed to a flaming yellow sun close ahead. 'There's Phaedra, we'll be on Big Planet in a few hours.'

A gong rang. 'Lunch,' said Pianza, rising with a feeling of relief. The purpose of the commission was hardly a secret to anyone aboard the ship; however, he had been uncomfortably explicit in his talk with Hidders. He was glad to push the whole matter to the back of his mind.

Glystra led the way from the saloon, pausing at the door to let the nun sweep ahead in a billow of black vestments.

'Peculiar creature,' muttered Pianza.

Glystra laughed. 'There's no one on Big Planet but peculiar people; that's why they're there. If she wants to convert them to her own private peculiarity, that's her privilege.'

Hidders nodded with lively emphasis. 'Perfect democracy on Big Planet, eh Mr. Glystra?'

Pianza watched expectantly; Glystra was nothing if not outspoken. Glystra did not fail him.

'Perfect anarchy, Mr. Hidders.'

In silence they descended the spiral to the dining saloon, took their places. One by one the other members of the commission entered. First was Cloyville, big, booming, florid; then Ketch, dark, drawn and saturnine, like the 'Before' in a laxative advertisement. Next came Bishop, the youngest man on the commission, sheep-faced and seal-smooth, with a brain full of erudition and a tendency toward hypochondria. He satisfied the one with a portable microfilm library, the other with a portable medicine chest. Behind him, and last, was Darrot, erect and military with carrot-colored hair, lips compressed as if against an imminent outburst of temper.

The meal was placid, but overhung with a sense of excitement, almost tension, which persisted, grew stronger all afternoon as the bulk of Big Planet spread across the field of vision. Horizons belled out, blotted Phaedra from the sky, and the spaceship settled into the darkness.

There was a shock, a lurch, a perceptible change of direction. Glystra spun away from the window. The lights flickered, died, then glowed weakly. Glystra ran up the spiral toward the bridge. At the top landing stood a squat man in ship's uniform – Abbigens, the radio operator and purser. Lank blond hair hung down his forehead. He watched Glystra's approach with narrow eyes set far apart.

'What's the trouble?' Glystra demanded sharply. 'What's going on?'

'Don't know, Mr. Glystra. I tried to get in myself; I found the door locked.'

'The ship feels out of control, as if we're going to crash!'

'Don't worry your head about that, Mr. Glystra. We've got emergency landing gear to set us down – automatic stuff. There may be a bit of a thump, but if we sit quiet in the saloon we're safe enough.'

Gently he took Glystra's arm. Glystra shook him off, returned to the door. Solid as a section of the wall.

He ran back down the steps, railing at himself for not taking precautions against just such a chance. To land anywhere on Big Planet except Earth Enclave meant tragedy, debacle, cataclysm. He stood in the saloon doorway; there was a babble of voices, white faces turned to him. Cloyville, Darrot, Pianza, Bishop, Ketch, Hidders and the nun. All there. He ran to the engine room; the door opened under his hands. Corbus, the easygoing chief engineer, pushed him back.

'We've got to get to the life-boats,' barked Glystra.

'No more life-boats.'

'*No more life-boats!* What's happened to them?' Glystra demanded.

'They've been ejected. It's stick by the ship, there's nothing else to do.'

'But the captain, the mate—'

'They don't answer the telephone.'

'But what on earth happened?'

Corbus' reply was drowned by a siren which filled the air, already made mad by the flickering light, with clangor.

Abbigens came into the saloon. He looked around with an air of triumph, nodded toward someone. Who? Glystra twisted his head. Too late. White faces, open mouths. And now – a picture he would never forget: the door swung open, the mate staggered in, his hand held as if he were rubbing his throat. His face was the color of raw potato; ghastly dark ribbons striped the front of his jumper. He pointed a terrible trembling finger at Abbigens. Blood rasped in his lungs, his knees folded, he fell to the deck. His hand slipped to show a second mouth under his chin.

Glystra stared at the squat man with the blond hair falling thickly down his forehead.

Dark shadows rushed up past the saloon ports. A monstrous splintering instant: the floor of the saloon struck up. The lights went out; there was a hoarse crying.

Glystra crawled up the floor. He sensed walls toppling; he saw a sudden dark motion, heard jarring thunder, and then felt an instant of pain . . .

Glystra rose toward consciousness like a waterlogged timber. He opened his eyes; vision reached his brain.

He lay on a low bed at the rear of a plank-walled cottage. With a feverish movement he half-raised on the cot, propped himself on an elbow, stared out the open door, and it seemed that he was seeing the most wonderful sight of his life.

He looked out on a green slope, spangled with yellow and red flowers, which rose to a forest. The gables of a village showed through the foliage, quaint gables of carved dark-brown timber. The entire landscape was drenched in a tingling golden-white radiance; every color shone with jewel-like clarity.

Three girls in peasant dress moved across the field of his vision; they were dancing a merry jig which flung their belled blue and red skirts back and forth, side to side. Glystra could hear music, the drone of a concertina, tinkle of mandolin and guitar.

He slumped back to the cot, closed his eyes. A picture from the golden ages. A beautiful dream.

The thud of footsteps roused him. Watching under half-cracked eyelids he saw Pianza and Cloyville enter the cottage: the one tidy, gray, quiet; the other puffing, red-faced, effusive. Behind came a fresh-faced girl with blonde pigtails, carrying a tray.

Glystra struggled up on his elbows again. Pianza said soothingly, 'Relax, Claude. You're a sick man.'

Glystra demanded, 'Was anyone killed?' He was surprised to find his voice so weak.

There was a moment's silence.

'Well? Who got it?'

'The stewards. They had gone to hide in the shell. And the nun. Apparently she went into her cabin just before the crash. It's twenty feet underground now. Of course the captain and the mate, both with their throats cut.'

Glystra closed his eyes. 'How long has it been?'

'About four days.'

He lay passive a few seconds, thinking. 'What's been happening?'

'The ship's a total loss,' said Cloyville. He pulled out a chair, seated himself. 'Broken in three pieces. A wonder any of us came out alive.'

The girl laid the tray on the bed, knelt, prepared to feed Glystra with a horn spoon.

Glystra looked up ruefully. 'Is this what's been going on?'

'You had to be taken care of,' said Pianza. He patted the girl's head. 'This is Natilien-Thilssa. Nancy for short. She's an excellent nurse.'

Cloyville winked slyly. 'Lucky dog.'

Glystra moved back from the spoon. 'I can feed myself,' he said shortly. He looked up at Pianza. 'Where are we?'

Pianza frowned slightly, as if he had hoped to avoid serious discussion. 'The village of Jubilith – somewhere near the northeastern tip of Beaujolais.'

Glystra pressed his lips together. 'It could hardly be worse. Naturally they planned to drop us closer to Grosgarth, right into the Bajarnum's lap.' He struggled up on his elbow. 'I'm astonished we haven't been taken up already.'

Pianza looked out the door. 'We're rather isolated, and naturally there are no communications ... We've been nervous, I'll admit.'

The last terrible scene in the saloon rose before Glystra's mind. 'Where's Abbigens?'

'Abbigens? Oh, he's gone. Disappeared.'

Glystra groaned under his breath. Pianza looked uneasily at Cloyville, who frowned.

'Why didn't you kill him?' Glystra moaned.

All Pianza could do was shake his head. Cloyville said, 'He got away.'

'There was someone else too,' said Glystra weakly.

Pianza leaned forward, his eyes sharp and gray. 'Someone else? Who?'

'I don't know. Abbigens slaughtered the captain and the mate, the other sabotaged the motors, discharged the life-boats.' He heaved restlessly on the couch. The girl put a cool hand on his forehead. 'I've been unconscious four days. Extraordinary.'

'You've been sedated,' said Pianza, 'to keep you resting. For a while you were out of your head, climbing out of bed, fighting, yelling.'

CHAPTER TWO

Glystra sat up against Nancy's restraining hand, felt the base of his skull. He tried to rise to his feet. Cloyville jumped up. 'For Heaven's sake, Claude, take it easy,' he admonished.

Glystra shook his head. 'We've got to get out of here. Fast. Think. Where's Abbigens? He's gone to report to Charley Lysidder, the Bajarnum.' He stood swaying. Nancy came to cajole him back to the cot, but instead, leaning on her shoulder, he went to the door and stood in the wash of golden-white sunlight, the Big Planet panorama before him. Pianza brought a chair, Glystra sank into it.

The cottage, the forest, the village were situated halfway up the face of a slope, vast beyond Earthly conception. Above, Glystra could see no sharp termination or ridge; the land melted into pale blue distance. Below was a vista so grand and airy that after the first few miles the eye could sense only the spread of territory, meadows and forests becoming a green, blue, beige blur.

Cloyville stretched his heavy arms out into the warmth. 'Here's where I'm coming in my old age.' He yawned. 'We never should have wasted Big Planet on the freaks.'

Nancy slipped into the house with a stiff back.

Cloyville chuckled. 'I guess she thought I was calling her a freak.'

'You'll never have an old age,' said Glystra, 'if we don't clear out of here.' He looked up and down the slope. 'Where's the ship?'

'Up in the forest a little bit.'

'And how far are we from Beaujolais?'

Cloyville looked southwest diagonally up the slope. 'The borders of Beaujolais are vague. Over the top of the slope is a deep valley, apparently volcanic. Full of hot springs, fumaroles, geysers, so they tell me – the valley of the Glass-Blowers. Last year the Bajarnum moved in with his troops, and now the valley is part of Beaujolais. To date he hasn't sent officials or tax-collectors to Jubilith, but they're expected every day, together with a garrison.'

'Why a garrison? To keep order?'

Cloyville gestured down the slope. 'Protection against the nomads – gypsies, they call 'em.'

'Mmmph.' Glystra looked up at the village. 'They don't seem to have suffered too much ... How far is Grosgarth?'

'As near as I can make it, two hundred miles south. There's a garrison town – Montmarchy, they call it – about fifty miles southeast along the slope.'

'Fifty miles.' Glystra considered. 'That's probably where Abbigens headed for ...' A heavy metallic crash sounded from the forest. Glystra looked questioningly at Pianza.

'They're cutting up the ship. It's the most metal they've seen in their lives. We've made them all millionaires.'

'Until the Bajarnum confiscates the whole thing,' said Cloyville.

'We've got to get out,' Glystra muttered, twisting in his chair. 'We've got to get to the Enclave – somehow ...'

Pianza pursed his lips doubtfully. 'It's around the planet, forty thousand miles.'

Glystra struggled up to his feet. 'We've got to get out of here. We're sitting ducks. If we're caught, it's our lives. Charley Lysidder will make an example of us ... Where's the rest of the ship's company?'

Pianza nodded toward the village. 'We've been given a big house. Hidders has gone.'

'Gone? Where to?'

'Grosgarth.' He added hastily, 'He says he'll take a barge to Marwan Gulf and join one of the beach caravans to Wale.'

'Hmmm. The stewards dead, the captain and mate dead, the nun dead, Abbigens gone, Hidders gone—' he counted on his fingers '—that leaves eight: the commission and two engine room officers. You'd better bring them all down here and we'll have a council of war.'

Eyes troubled, Glystra watched Pianza and Cloyville climbing to the village, then turned his attention down the slope. Beaujolain soldiers approaching during the daylight would be visible for many miles. Glystra gave thanks for the non-metallic crust of Big Planet. No metal, no machinery, no electricity, no long-distance communication.

Nancy appeared from the cottage. She had changed her puffed blue skirt for a parti-colored coverall, a harlequin suit of red and orange motley. Over her hair she wore a close-fitting cap, set with two-inch spines of hair waxed to golden points.

Glystra stared a moment. Nancy whirled before him, pirouetted on one toe, with the other leg bent at the knee.

Glystra said, 'Are all the girls at Jubilith as lovely as you are?'

She smiled, tilted her face to the sun. 'I'm not from Jubilith ... I'm an outlander.'

'So? From where?'

She gestured to the north. 'From Veillevaux Forest. My father had the gift, and for many miles people came to ask the future – even some who might have made the pilgrimage to Myrtlesee Fountain.'

'Myrtlesee Fountain?' Glystra opened his mouth to inquire, then reflected that any explanation would be couched in the intricacies of a strange culture, and closed his mouth. Best to listen, to observe, let knowledge come in manageable doses.

'My father grew rich,' continued Nancy. 'He trained me in the crafts. I traveled to Grosgarth and Calliope and Wale and through the Stemvelt Canals, and I went outland as a troubadour, with fine companies, and we saw many towns and castles and beautiful sights.' She shuddered. 'And evil also. Much evil, at Glaythree ...' Tears welled into her eyes, her shoulders sagged. She said forlornly, 'When I returned to Veillevaux Forest I found ruin and desolation. The gypsies from North Heath had raided the village and burnt the house of my father with all my family inside. And I wandered here to Jubilith to learn to dance, that I might dance away my grief ...'

Glystra studied her closely. Marvellous mobility of feature – sparkle of eye, lilt of voice when she spoke of joy – a mouth that was never quite in repose. And when she dwelt on her grief her eyes became large and wistful, and the nervous beauty of her face and body seemed to become less explicit, glowing from some wonderful region inside her mind, as light shines from the inner part of a star.

'And how is it that you were selected to nurse me?'

She shrugged, studied the backs of her hands. 'I'm an outlander; I know the methods of Grosgarth – some of which have been learned from Earth books. *Naisuka.*'

Glystra looked up in puzzlement, repeated the word. 'What is that?'

'It's a Beaujolais word.' She settled herself to the ground at his feet, leaned back against the wall, stretched with the easy looseness of a kitten. 'It means – well, it's what makes a person decide to do things for no reason whatever.'

He pointed down the slope. 'What country is that nestled down there?'

She turned half on her side, propped herself on one elbow. 'The Jubilith claiming ends at the Tsalombar Woods.' She indicated a far line of forest. 'The tree-people live there, above the tritchsod.'

Another idiom unfamiliar to Glystra.

Up by the village the Earthmen appeared. Glystra watched their approach. Guilt in any one of them seemed as remote as guilt in Nancy. But someone had helped Abbigens, someone had burnt out the motors. Of course it might have been Arthur Hidders, and he was gone.

'Sit down,' said Glystra. They took seats on the turf. Glystra looked doubtfully at Nancy. She smiled up cheerfully, made no move to rise; indeed, settled herself more comfortably, stretching her legs, pointing her toes – exotic as a rare bird in her parti-colored motley.

Glystra hesitated, then turned back to the men. 'We're in a tough spot, although I suppose I don't need to belabor the point.'

No one spoke.

'We're shipwrecked with no possibility of getting help from Earth. As far as technical superiority goes, we're no better off than the people of the village. Maybe worse. They understand their tools, their materials; we don't. If we had unlimited time, we might be able to patch up some kind of radio and call the Enclave. We don't have that time. Any minute we can expect soldiers to take us to Grosgarth ... In Grosgarth the Bajarnum will make an example of us. He doesn't want interference, he'll make sure we're aware of it. We've got one chance, that's to get out of Beaujolais, put miles behind us.'

He paused, looked from face to face. Pianza was mild, non-committal; Cloyville's big forehead was creased in a heavy frown, Ketch was petulantly digging at the ground with a bit of sharp gravel. Bishop's face was faintly troubled, with little puckers like inverted V's over his eyes. Darrot ran a hand through his sparse red hair, muttered something to Ketch, who nodded. Corbus the chief engineer sat quietly, as if unconcerned. Vallusser the second engineer glared, as if Glystra were the cause of his difficulties. He said in a thick voice, 'What happens when we escape? Where do we escape to? There's nothing out there—' he waved his hand down the slope '—but wild men. They'll kill us. Some of them are cannibals.'

Glystra shrugged. 'You're free to do whatever you like, save your skin the best way you can. Personally I see one way out. It's hard, it's long, it's dangerous. Maybe it's impossible. It's close to certain not all of us will make it. But we want to escape with our lives, we want to go home. That means—' he accented his words heavily '—one place on Big Planet. The Enclave. We've got to get to the Enclave.'

'Sounds good,' said Cloyville. 'I'm all for it. How do we do it?'

Glystra grinned. 'The only means of locomotion we've got – our feet.'

'Feet?' Cloyville's voice rose.

'Sounds like a pretty stiff hike,' said Darrot.

Glystra shrugged. 'There's no use fooling ourselves. We've got one chance to get back to Earth – that's make Earth Enclave. The only way to get there is to start.'

'But forty thousand miles?' Cloyville protested plaintively. 'I'm a big man, hard on my feet.'

'We'll pick up pack animals,' said Glystra. 'Buy them, steal them, we'll get them somehow.'

'But forty thousand miles,' muttered Cloyville.

Glystra nodded. 'It's a long way. But if we find the right kind of river, we'll float. Or maybe we can angle down to the Black Ocean, find a ship, sail around the coast.'

'Can't be done,' said Bishop. 'The Australian Peninsula reaches down, curves back east. We'd have to wait till we reached Henderland, then cut down, around the Blackstone Cordillera, to the Parmarbo. And, according to the Big Planet Almanac, the Parmarbo is virtually unnavigable due to reefs, pirates, carnivorous sea anemones and weekly hurricanes.'

Cloyville groaned again. Glystra heard a sound from Nancy, and looking down, saw her mouth quivering in efforts to restrain a giggle. He rose to his feet, and Pianza watched him doubtfully. 'How do you feel, Claude?'

'I'm weak. But tomorrow I'll be as good as new. Nothing wrong with me a little exercise won't cure. One thing we can be thankful for—'

'What's that?' asked Cloyville.

Glystra motioned to his feet. 'Good boots. Waterproof, wearproof. We'll need them.'

Cloyville ruefully inspected his big torso. 'I suppose the paunch will work off.'

Glystra glanced around the circle. 'Any other ideas? You, Vallusser?'

Vallusser shook his head. 'I'll stay with the crowd.'

'Good. Now here's the program. We've got to make up packs. We want all the metal we can conveniently carry; it's precious on Big Planet. Each of us ought to be able to manage fifteen pounds. Tools and knives would be best, but I suppose we'll have to take what we can salvage ... Then we'll want clothes, a change apiece. Ship's chart of Big Planet, if available. A compass. Everyone had better find himself a good knife, a blanket, and most important – hand weapons. Has anyone checked the ship?'

Corbus put his hand in his blouse, displayed the black barrel of an ion-discharge pistol. 'This belonged to the Captain. I helped myself.'

'I've got my two,' said Cloyville.

'There should be one in my cabin aboard ship,' said Pianza. 'There was no way in yesterday, but maybe I can squeeze in somehow.'

'There's another in mine,' said Glystra. He put his hands on the arm of the chair, rose to his feet. 'We'd better get started.'

'You'd better rest,' said Darrot gruffly. 'You'll need all your strength. I'll see that your pack is made up.'

Glystra relaxed without embarrassment. 'Thanks. Maybe we'll make better time.'

The seven men filed uphill, into the forest of silky blue–green trees. Glystra watched them from the doorway.

Nancy rose to her feet. 'Best now that you should sleep.'

He went inside, lowered himself to the cot, put his hands under his head, lay staring at the beams. Nancy stood looking down at him. 'Claude Glystra.'

'What?'

'May I come with you?'

He turned his head, stared up in astonishment. 'Come where?'

'Wherever you're going.'

'Around the planet? Forty thousand miles?'

'Yes.'

He shook his head decisively. 'You'd be killed with the rest of us. This is a thousand to one chance.'

'I don't care ... I die only once. And I'd like to see Earth. I've wandered far and I know many things ...' She hesitated.

Glystra put the spur to his brain. It was tired and failed to react. Something was out of place. Would a girl choose such a precarious life from pure wanderlust? Of course, Big Planet was not Earth; human psychology was unpredictable. And yet – he searched her face; was it a personal matter? Infatuation? She colored.

'You blush easily,' Glystra observed.

'I'm strong,' said Nancy. 'I can do as much work as either Ketch or Bishop.'

'A pretty girl can cause a lot of trouble.'

She shrugged. 'There are women everywhere on Big Planet. No one need be alone.'

Glystra sank back on the couch, shaking his head. 'You can't come with us, Nancy.'

She bent over; he felt her breath on his face, warm, moist. 'Tell them I'm a guide. Can't I come as far as the forest?'

'Very well. As far as the forest.'

She ran outside, into the golden radiance of the day. Glystra watched her run up the flowered slope. 'There goes trouble.' He turned his face to the wall.

CHAPTER THREE

He slept an hour, two hours, soaking the rest into his bones. When he awoke, afternoon sunlight was slanting in through the doorway, a flood of richest saffron. Up the slope, the village merry-making was in full swing. Lines of girls and young men, in parti-colored motley like Nancy's, capered back and forth in a dance of light-hearted buffoonery. To his ears came a shrill jig played on fiddles, concertinas, guitars, rhapsodiums. Back, forth, across his vision ran the dancers, bounding in a kind of prancing goose-step.

Pianza and Darrot looked in through the doorway. 'Awake, Claude?' asked Pianza.

Glystra swung his feet over the edge of the cot, sat up. 'Good as new.' He stood up, stretched, patted the back of his head; the soreness had nearly disappeared. 'Everything ready?'

Pianza nodded, 'Ready to go. We found your ion-shine, also a heat-gun belonging to the mate.' He looked at Glystra half-sidewise, an expression of mild calculation on his face. 'I understand Nancy has been included in the expedition.'

'No,' said Glystra, with some irritation. 'I told her she might come as far as the forest, that's only two or three hours away.'

Pianza looked doubtful. 'She's made herself up a pack. Says she's going with us.'

Darrot gave his head a terse shake. 'I don't like it, Claude.' He had a rough baritone voice. It sounded harsh and grating now. 'This march is no place for a girl. Bound to be friction, inconvenience.'

Darrot's cast of mind was peculiarly prim, thought Glystra. In a conciliatory voice he said, 'I'm in full agreement with you. I refused her point blank.'

'But she's all packed,' said Pianza.

Glystra said tartly, 'Well, if she insists on going, if she follows a hundred yards to the rear, I don't see how we can stop her short of physical constraint.'

Pianza blinked. 'Well naturally ...' His voice trailed off.

Darrot was unconvinced. His square face wore a look of mulish displeasure. 'She's traveled widely, she's been to Grosgarth. Suppose she's one of the Bajarnum's secret agents? I understand they're everywhere, even on the other side of the planet, even on Earth.'

'It's possible,' admitted Glystra. 'Anything's possible. For all I know, you work for the Bajarnum yourself. Someone does.'

Darrot snorted, turned away.

'Don't worry,' said Glystra, slapping him on the shoulder. 'When we get to the forest, we'll send her back.' He went to the door, stepped outside. Much of his strength had returned, although his legs felt limp and lax.

Pianza said, 'Bishop salvaged the ship's first-aid kit, and all his food pills and vitamins. They may be useful; our food won't always be the best.'

'Good.'

'Cloyville found his camping equipment, and we're taking along the stove and the water-maker.'

'Any spare power units for the ion-shines?'

'No.'

Glystra chewed his lip. 'That's bad ... Find the nun's body?'

Pianza shook his head. 'Her cabin is on the bottom.'

'Too bad,' said Glystra, although he felt little real remorse. The woman had hardly existed as a human being: he had been conscious of a thin white face, a black robe, a black headdress, an air of intensity, and all was now gone.

Down from the village came the Earthmen, and around them circled the dancers, gay, exalted, aware only of their own motion and color. Ketch, Corbus, Vallusser, Cloyville, Bishop – and Nancy. She stood a little apart, watching the dancing with an air of serene detachment, as if she had renounced whatever ties bound her to Jubilith.

An elder of the village came down the slope, a thin brown man in a heavy loose smock of horizontal brown, gray and white stripes. The rhythm was still in his ears; he jigged to the music following him down the hill.

He spoke to Cloyville, remonstrated; Cloyville pointed to Glystra. The old man jigged to where Glystra stood waiting. He sang out, 'Surely you won't leave us now? The day is at its close; night drifts over the massif and our merriment is not yet upon us.'

Glystra held out his arms while Pianza helped him into his pack. He said with a grin, 'Dance a couple sets for me.'

'You'll be a-dark!'

'We'll be a-dark more times than this once.'

'Inauspicious, importunate.' He broke into a chant such as children might sing at their games. 'The hop-legged sprites abound in the dark; skin to skin they will weld your legs. Bone to bone, flesh to flesh, and all your life shall be hop-step-one, hop-step-one ...'

Nancy caught Glystra's eye, shook her head slightly. Glystra turned away, looked out over Big Planet, already flooded in light of a darker gold. Behind him were the dancers in groups of five, wheeling, kicking out their legs at the knee, wagging their heads drolly, and the music waxed shrill and happy. Looking down the vast slope, Glystra suddenly felt weak before the immensity of the journey ahead. Jubilith seemed warm and secure. Almost like home. And ahead – distance. Sectors and sections, extents and expanses. Looking to where Earth's horizon would lie, he could lift his eyes and see lands reaching far on out: pencil lines of various subtle colors, each line a plain or a forest, a sea, a desert, a mountain range ... He took a step forward, looked over his shoulder. 'Let's go.'

For a long time the merry music followed their backs, and only when the sun passed behind the slope and mauve dusk came down from the sky did the sounds dwindle to the silence of distance.

The way led across the bracken, a thick resilient mat of gray stalks beaded with dull green nodules. The slope was gentle and uniform, and the coming of Big Planet night brought no difficulties; it was only necessary to walk down the fall of the ground.

Cloyville and Darrot strode together at the head of the group; then came Glystra, with Nancy at one elbow and Pianza at the other. To their left walked Ketch a little apart, and behind came Bishop, eyes on the ground. At the rear, twenty paces behind, walked Corbus, striding easily, and Vallusser, picking his way as if his feet hurt.

Twilight waned and stars appeared. Now there was nothing in the world but darkness, the sky, the breast of the planet and their own infinitesimal persons.

Nancy had been carefully quiet, but now in the dark, she pressed closer to Glystra. Glystra, expecting various wiles and persuasions, grinned to himself and prepared to withstand an assault on his senses.

She spoke in a soft low voice. 'Tell me, Claude, which of those stars is Old Sun?'

Glystra scanned the heavens. The constellations were strange and made no particular pattern.

He remembered that on leaving Earth for Big Planet, Cetus was astern till they arrived at Index ... There was Spica, and nearby the black bulge of the Porridge Pot. 'I think that's the Sun there – right above the bright white star, in toward that big blot of fog.'

She stared wide-eyed into the sky. 'Tell me about Earth.'

'It's home,' said Glystra. He looked for several seconds up at the white star. 'I'd like to be there ...'

'Is Earth more beautiful than Big Planet?'

'That's a hard question to answer. Offhand – no. Big Planet is – big. Impressive. The Himalayas on Earth are foothills beside the Sklaemon Range or the Blackstone Cordillera.'

'Where are they?' Nancy asked.

Glystra's mind had been wandering. He looked at her blankly. 'Where are what?'

'Those mountain ranges? Here on Big Planet?'

'The Sklaemons are about thirty thousand miles northwest, in a part of Big Planet called Matador. The Ski-men live there, I believe. The Blackstone Cordillera is to the southeast, about five thousand miles, above the Australian Peninsula, in Henderland.'

'There's so much to be learned ... So many places to see ...' Her voice broke a trifle. 'The Earthmen know more about us than we know ourselves. It isn't fair. You keep us in mental shackles ...'

Glystra laughed sourly. 'Big Planet is a compromise of many people's ideas. Nobody thinks it's right.'

'We grow up barbarians,' she said passionately. 'My father—'

Glystra looked at her quizzically. 'A barbarian is not aware that he is a barbarian.'

'—was murdered. Everywhere is murder and death ...'

Glystra tried to hold his voice at a dispassionate level. 'It's not your fault that this is so – but it's not the fault of the Earth people either. We've never attempted to exercise authority past Virginis Reef. Anyone passing through is on his own – and his children pay the price.'

Nancy shook her head – a kind of personal little jerk with head cocked sidewise, indicating incomplete conviction.

Glystra tried to think. There was little he could say to her that was concrete and definite. He detested human pain and misery as whole-heartedly as she did. He was equally convinced that Earth could maintain authority only through a finite volume of space. It was likewise impossible to prevent people who so desired to pass the boundaries and declare themselves free of supervision. He also admitted that in such a case, many might suffer from the mistakes of a few. It was an injustice arising from the very nature of human beings. Nancy had known the injustice – the murder, the grief, the anger, the aberrations which, reinforcing and building up down the generations now infected tribes, peoples, races, continents, the entire world. These immediacies would be in the forefront of her mind; his problem was to convey a sense of more-and-less relationships, to endow these vaguenesses and conditionals with enough power to counter the force of her emotion.

'On Earth, Nancy, ever since our first archaic histories, the race has graduated into levels. Some people have lived in complete harmony with their times, others have in their core a non-conformist independence – an apparently built-in trait, a basic emotion like hunger, fear, affection. These people are unhappy and insecure in a rigid society; through all the ages they have been the unclassifiables: the pioneers, explorers, flagpole-sitters; the philosophers, the criminals, the prophets of doom, and the progenitors of new cultural complexes. Akhnaton – Brigham Young – Wang Tsi-po – John D'Arcy ...'

They walked on through the dark. The matted bracken crackled underfoot, muffled voices sounded ahead and behind them. The air was cool and warm at once – balmy, soothing, smelling of a peppery lavender from the bracken.

Nancy, still watching Old Sun, said, 'But these people, whoever they were, they have nothing to do with Big Planet.'

'Jubilith,' said Glystra, 'was founded by a ballet troupe who apparently desired solitude and peace to perfect their art. Perhaps they only intended to come out for a year or two, but they stayed. The first settlers, almost six hundred years ago, were nudists – people who dislike the wearing of clothes. Convention on Earth forbids nudity. So they bought a ship and went exploring past the edge of the System. They found Big Planet. At first they thought it too big to be habitable—'

'Why should that be?'

'Gravity,' said Glystra. 'The larger a planet is, the stronger the pull of its gravity. But Big Planet is made of light materials with a specific gravity only a third of Earth's. Earth is a very dense planet, with abundant metals and heavy elements, and so the gravity works out about the same – although there's thirty times the volume here ... The nudists liked Big Planet. It was paradise: sunny, bright, with a mild climate and – most essential – it had an organic complex similar to that of Earth. In other words Big Planet proteins were not incompatible with Earth protoplasm. They settled here, and sent back to Earth for their friends.

'There was room for other minorities – endless room. Out they migrated – all the cults, misanthropic societies, primitivists, communists, religious monasteries, and just people in general. Sometimes they built towns, sometimes they lived by themselves – a thousand, two thousand, five thousand miles from their nearest neighbor. Useful ore deposits are non-existent on Big Planet; technical civilization never had a chance to get started, and Earth refused to allow the export of modern weapons to Big Planet. So Big Planet evolved into a clutter of tiny states and cities, with stretches of open country in between.'

Nancy started to speak, but Glystra anticipated her. 'Yes, we might have organized Big Planet and given it System law. But – in the first place – it is beyond the established boundaries of the System. Secondly, we would thereby have been defeating the purpose of those people who sacrificed their place on the civilized worlds for independence – a perfectly legitimate aim in itself. Thirdly, we would be denying refuge to other restless souls, with the effect of sending them out seeking other worlds, almost inevitably less propitious. So we let Big Planet become the System's Miscellaneous File. We established Earth Enclave, with the university and trade school, for those who wish to return to Earth. But very few apply.'

'Of course not,' said Nancy scornfully. 'It's forbidden. A place of maniacs.'

'Why do you say that?'

'It is well known. Once a Bajarnum of Beaujolais went to the Enclave; he attended the school, and he came back a different man. He freed all the slaves, and stopped all the punishment ordeals. When he declared the land-hold system void, the College of Dukes rose up and killed him, because clearly he was mad.'

Glystra smiled wanly. 'He was the sanest man on the planet ...'

She sniffed.

'Yes,' said Glystra. 'Very few apply to the Enclave. Big Planet is home. It's free – open – limitless. A man can find any kind of life he wants, even if he may be killed almost any minute. Anyone with Big Planet in his blood never feels loose on the civilized worlds. On Earth and the other planets of the System we have a rigid society with precise conventions. It's smooth and easy now; most of the misfits have gone to Big Planet.'

'Dull,' said Nancy. 'Stupid and dull.'

'Not entirely,' said Glystra. 'After all, there are five billion people on Earth, and no two of them are identical.'

Nancy was silent a moment, then, almost as a taunt: 'What of the Bajarnum of Beaujolais? He plans to conquer the planet. He's already expanded Beaujolais threefold.'

Glystra looked straight ahead, down through the infinite Big Planet night. 'If the Bajarnum of Beaujolais or the Nomarch of Skene or the Gaypride Baron or the Nine Wizards or anyone else dominates Big Planet, then the inhabitants of Big Planet have lost their freedom and flexibility even more certainly than if the System organized a federal government. Because then they would be obliged to adapt their lives to aberrations different from their own, and not merely to a few rules and regulations essentially rational.'

She was not convinced. 'I'm surprised that the System considered the Bajarnum important enough to worry about.'

Glystra smiled thinly. 'Just the fact of our being here tells you something about the Bajarnum. He's got spies and agents everywhere – including Earth. He regularly violates our number one law – the embargo on weapons and metal to Big Planet.'

'A man is killed just as surely with a birkwood sword as with a shaft of light.'

Glystra shook his head. 'You are considering only one aspect of the subject. Where do these weapons come from? The System prohibits unlicensed manufacture of weapons. It's very difficult establishing a modern factory in secret, and therefore most of the Bajarnum's weapons are stolen or pirated. Ships and depots are ripped open, men killed or herded into slave-bins, bound out for the One-man Heavens.'

'One-man Heavens? What are they?'

'Among these five billion I mentioned a minute ago are some very strange people,' said Glystra thoughtfully. 'Not all the odd ones have migrated to Big Planet. We have over-rich over-ripe creatures on Earth with too much self-indulgence and not enough conscience. Many of them have found a little world somewhere off in the cluster and set themselves up as gods. The pirates sell them slaves and out on their little domains there's no kind of indulgence or whimsicality they can't allow themselves. After two or three months they return to the System and function as respectable citizens for a period. Then they tire of the cosmopolis, and it's back to their One-man Heaven out in the star-stream.'

CHAPTER FOUR

Nancy remained silent. 'What's that got to do with Charley Lysidder?'

Glystra looked at her sidewise, and she saw his face as a white mask in the darkness. 'How does the Bajarnum pay for his smuggled weapons? They're expensive. Lots of blood and pain is spent on every ion-shine.'

'I don't know ... I never thought of it.'

'There's no metal on Big Planet, few jewels. But there's trade-goods more valuable.'

Nancy said nothing.

'Girls and boys.'

'Oh ...' in a remote voice.

'Charley Lysidder is like a carrier of the plague and he infects half the universe.'

'But – what can you do?'

'I don't know – now. Events have not gone according to plan.'

'You are only eight men. Futile against the Beaujolais army.'

Glystra smiled. 'We never intended to fight.'

'You have no weapons, no plans, no documents—'

'Just brains.'

Nancy subsided into a silence of a quality which caused Glystra to peer at her quizzically. 'You're not impressed?'

'I don't know. I'm – very inexperienced.'

Glystra once more sought her face through the darkness, this time to make sure she was serious. 'We form a team. Each man is a specialist. Pianza here—' he nodded to the gray shape at his left '—is an organizer and administrator. Ketch records our findings on his camera and sonographs. Darrot is an ecologist—'

'What's that?'

Glystra looked ahead to where Cloyville and Darrot walked, and the sound of their footsteps came as a regular double thud-crackle. They were now entering a country clumped with great trees, and ahead loomed the Tsalombar Woods, a line of black heavier than the sky. 'Ecology,' said Glystra, 'is ultimately concerned with keeping people fed. Hungry people are angry and dangerous.'

In a subdued voice Nancy said, 'The gypsies are always hungry ... They killed my father ...'

'Well, to go on, Cloyville is our mineralogist. I'm coordinator and propagandist.' Anticipating her question, he asked, 'Why is the Bajarnum able to conquer his neighbors?'

'Because he has a stronger army ... He's very crafty.'

'Suppose his army no longer obeyed him. Suppose no one on Big Planet paid any attention to his orders. What could he do?'

'Nothing. He'd be powerless.'

'Propaganda at its maximum effectiveness accomplishes just that. I work with Bishop. Bishop is a student of culture – human society. He can look at an arrowhead and tell you whether the man who made it had six wives or shared a wife with six men. He can study the background of people and discover their racial aberrations, their push-buttons – the ideas that make them react like herds of—' he was about to say "sheep" but remembered that Big Planet harbored no sheep '—herds of pechavies.'

She looked at him half-smiling. 'And you can make people behave like pechavies?'

Glystra shook his head. 'Not exactly. Or I should say, not all the time.'

They marched onward down the slope. The trees loomed in closer and they entered Tsalombar Forest. Around him marched eight dark shapes. There were forty thousand miles to travel – and one of these shapes wished him evil. He said under his breath to Nancy, 'Someone here – I don't know who – is my enemy. Somehow, I've got to learn who he is ...'

She had stopped breathing. 'Are you sure?' she asked in a hushed voice.

'Yes.'

'What will he do?'

'If I knew, I'd watch for it.'

'The Magic Fountain at Myrtlesee could tell you who he is. He knows everything.'

Glystra searched his mind. Myrtlesee – a word on a map. 'Where's Myrtlesee?'

She gestured. 'Far to the east. I've never been there; it's a dangerous journey unless you ride the monoline, and that costs much metal. My father told me of the oracle at the Fountain. He babbles in a frenzy and answers any questions asked and then he dies whereupon the Dongmen select a new oracle.'

Glystra was skeptical. 'There have been similar oracles on Earth. They are drugged and their ravings are interpreted as prophecy.'

'It's rather strange ...'

Ahead of them Cloyville and Darrot stopped short. 'Quiet!' hissed Darrot. 'There's a camp ahead. Fires.'

The sighing branches of Tsalombar Forest shut off the sky and the darkness was near-complete. Ahead a tiny spark of red flickered past the ranked tree trunks.

'Would it be the tree-men?' Glystra asked Nancy.

She said doubtfully, 'No … They never come down from the trees. And they never build fires; they're deathly afraid of fire …'

'Then,' said Glystra, 'it is probably a party sent out to capture us.'

'Or gypsies,' said Nancy.

Glystra said, 'Everybody come here, close.' Dark shapes stepped forward.

Glystra said in a low hurried voice, 'I'm going ahead to reconnoiter. I want everyone to stay together. This is emphatic. No one is to move from this group or make a sound until I return. Nancy, you stand at the center; the rest of you stand with your elbows touching. Make sure who is on either side of you, make sure he doesn't move.'

He circled the group. 'Everybody touching two others? Good. Count off.' The names came softly across the darkness.

'I'll be back as soon as possible,' said Glystra. 'If I need help – I'll yell. So keep your ears open.'

The matted bracken crackled under his feet as he stole down the slope.

It was a large fire, a roaring blaze fed by logs, in the center of a clearing. Fifty or sixty men sprawled around the fire, completely at their ease. They wore a loose blue uniform of baggy breeches triced below the knee, smocks gathered at the waist by a black sash. On their chest they wore a red insignia, a triangle apex-down. They carried knives and catapults in their sash; squat baskets heavy with darts hung at their backs. Some of the men wore hats of black felt, bent, twisted, creased in flamboyant flaps and bellies; others went bare-headed with their hats laid nearby on the ground.

They were a rough crew – short and stocky with flat brown faces, little spade beards, narrow-lidded eyes, hooked noses. They had eaten and now were drinking from black kidney-shaped leather sacks. Discipline at the moment was lax.

A little apart, back turned to the noise, stood a man in a black uniform. Glystra saw with unreasonable surprise that it was Abbigens. He conversed with a man evidently the officer-in-charge, apparently instructing him, emphasizing points with motions of his big pale hands. The officer listened, nodded.

Not far from Glystra a train of odd-looking beasts waited restlessly, swinging their long necks, snapping at the air, mumbling and moaning. They were narrow-shouldered, high in the back with six powerful legs and a narrow untrustworthy-looking head, a composite of camel, horse, goat, dog, lizard. The driver had not bothered to remove their packs. With sudden interest, Glystra examined the loads they bore.

One carried three metal cylinders, another a squat barrel and a bundle of metal rods. Glystra recognized the mechanism: a knock-down ion-blast, a field-piece capable of smashing Jubilith flat. It was of Earth manufacture, captured in a merciless little skirmish on an outer world, bought in blood, sold for young flesh ... Glystra looked behind, through the trees, suddenly uneasy. Strange that no sentries had been posted.

A flurry of activity at one side of the clearing caught his attention. A dozen soldiers stood with craned necks, looking up, pointing, talking excitedly. Glystra followed their gaze. A hundred feet overhead was a village – a network of rude trestles, walkways swung on vines, pendant huts swaying like oriole nests. No light showed, the huts were dark, but over the side of the trestles peered several dozen white faces framed in a tousle of brown hair. They made no sound, moved but little, and then like squirrels, quickly, abruptly. Apparently the Beaujolais soldiers had not previously noticed the village. Glystra peered up again. They had found a girl – whey-faced, bleary-eyed, but still a girl. They shouted up taunts and jocularities, to which the tree-men made no response.

Glystra eyed the pack animals with interest, estimating the chances of leading them into the forest while attention was diverted by the girl in the tree-village. He decided they were scant. Perhaps when they bedded down for the night ... For the night? Why should they bed down for the night? Jubilith was three or four hours up-slope. More likely they had camped here to await nightfall before venturing out on the moors where they could be seen from the village.

Where the soldiers were baiting the tree-men there was further activity. A young swaggerer with a spike mustache was climbing a rude ladder toward the hut from which hung the head of the slatternly girl. The way was easy; where a branch angled up, steps were cut into the wood. The soldier, spurred by the approving hoots of his comrades, ran up the trunk, paused on a rude platform. Here he was partly veiled by the branches, camouflaged by the flickering firelight shadows. There was a motion, a swishing sound, a thud, a sound of disturbed branches. A sprawling twisting body plunged down from the shadows, landed with a heavy thump.

Glystra jerked back, startled. The event had taken him unaware. He looked up; there was no motion from the tree-village. The faces stared down as before. Apparently the soldier had sprung a trap. A poised weight had swept down, struck him from the platform. Now he lay moaning, writhing. His fellows stood around him, watching dispassionately. There were glances turned up at the tree-men, but without apparent animus or hostility. There was no clamor for revenge, no threats, no fury. The event had occurred; it was fate ...

Abbigens and the officer strode over, stood looking down at the fallen man. He choked back his groans, lay silent, staring up white-faced. The officer spoke; Glystra could hear the tone of his voice but could not distinguish the words. The soldier on the ground made a reply, tried to rise to his feet, an anguished effort. But his leg lay out at a curious angle; tilting his chin, gritting his teeth, he lay back.

The officer spoke to Abbigens; Abbigens looked up to the tree-men. They watched from the walkways with wary interest. Abbigens spoke, gesturing up at the tree-village. The officer shrugged, turned aside, made a motion to one of the soldiers, turned away.

The soldier looked down at his comrade on the ground, muttered resentfully. He drew his sword from the sheath, stabbed the fallen man through the chest, the neck, finally up through the eye-socket.

Behind the tree Glystra swallowed the lump in his throat. After a moment he was once more able to see the clearing.

The officer strode back and forth through the camp, barking orders, and the words were loud enough for Glystra to hear: 'Up, up on your feet. Form ranks, double-quick, we've overstayed. Driver, see to your beasts—'

Abbigens came forward, spoke briefly to the officer. The officer nodded, crossed the clearing. Glystra could not hear his orders, but the soldier who was tending the pack animals led aside the two beasts bearing the knock-down ion-blast. He removed the packs, assembled the weapon.

Glystra watched with narrow eyes. Was the ion-blast to be used against the tree-village? He looked up. The faces were as before, white blotches peering down from the walkways. One of them looked at him, stared closely a moment, then turned his head back to the clearing without further attention.

The ion-blast was assembled, mounted on its tripod. Firelight glinted on the smooth metal barrel. The cannoneer swivelled the tube back and forth to test the bearing, rocked it up and down checking the balance. He threw off the safety, set the valve, pulled the trigger. A line of violet light lanced from the nozzle, power cracked down the lane of ionized air, spattered into the turf.

Testing. The weapon was ready for use.

The cannoneer set the safety, went to the line of pack animals, selected the strongest beast, yanked at the straps holding the pack to its back. The driver came forward angrily and the two fell into dispute.

Glystra moved, hesitated, started up, fell back. He gathered himself angrily. Boldness. Take a chance. He stepped forward, heart in mouth, moved out into the firelight. He swung the weapon around, opened the nozzle into a narrow gape, threw off the safety. It was so simple as to be ridiculous.

One of the soldiers noticed him, uttered a sharp cry, pointed.

'Stand still!' Glystra called out in a loud clear voice. 'If anyone moves – I'll burn him in two.'

CHAPTER FIVE

Around the clearing shapes froze, startled faces looked in his direction. Yelling in fury, the cannoneer sprang forward. Glystra pulled the trigger; the fan of violet light spread out, power crackled along the conductive air. The cannoneer was shattered and with him five others in the spread of the blaster's fan.

Glystra lifted his voice. 'Pianza! Cloyville!'

No reply.

He called again, as loudly as he could, and waited, watching across the sights of the blaster.

None of the soldiers moved. Abbigens stared with his pasty face flat, his eyes like a pair of olives.

There was a rustle of footsteps behind. 'Who is it?' asked Glystra.

'Will Pianza – and the rest of us.'

'Good. Get around to the side, where you'll be out of range.' He raised his voice. 'Now – you Beaujolains. Move to the center, this side of the fire ... *Quick!*' He charged his voice with the push-button crackle of authority.

Glumly the soldiers sidled into the center of the clearing. Abbigens took three quick steps along with them, but Glystra's voice halted him.

'Abbigens – put your hands on your head, walk backwards toward me. Quick, now ...'

Glystra said aside to Pianza, 'Get his weapon.' He snapped to the officer who was quietly shifting toward the rear of the cluster of men. 'You – come forward, hands on your head.' From the corner of his mouth: 'One of you – Corbus – search him.'

Corbus stepped forward. Vallusser made as if to follow. Glystra snapped, 'You others stand where you are ... This is ticklish.'

Abbigens carried an ion-shine, the officer a rocket-pistol.

Glystra said, 'Put the guns on the ground, tie 'em up with pack ropes.'

Abbigens and the officer lay helpless. The soldiers stood swaying, muttering in the center of the clearing.

'Nancy,' called Glystra over his shoulder.

'Yes,' – in a tight breathless voice.

'Do exactly as I say. Pick up those two weapons – by their barrels. Bring them to me. Don't walk between the blaster and the soldiers. I don't want to kill you.'

Nancy walked across the clearing to where the weapons glittered on the ground, bent.

'*By the barrel!*' rasped Glystra.

She hesitated, turned him an odd wide-eyed look, the skin below the ridge of her cheek-bones tight and pale. Glystra watched her stonily. Trust no one. She gingerly picked up the guns, brought them to him. He dropped them into his pouch, looking warily into the faces of his companions. Behind one of the faces was furious scheming ... Behind which face? Now was a critical moment. Whoever it was would seek to get behind him, pull him away from the blaster ...

He gestured. 'I want all of you to stand over there, to the side.' He waited till all his companions stood to the side of the clearing. 'Now,' he said to the soldiers. 'One at a time, cross the clearing ...'

Half an hour later the soldiers squatted in a tight circle facing inward, a sullen slack-faced group. Abbigens and the officer lay where they had been tied, Abbigens watching Glystra with expressionless eyes. Glystra watched Abbigens also, watched the direction of his glances. Would they seek out his ally?

Pianza looked doubtfully across at the clot of prisoners. 'This poses quite a problem ... What are you planning to do with them?'

Glystra, standing behind the blaster, relaxed a trifle, stretched. 'Well – we can't let them loose. If we can keep the news of this episode away from the Bajarnum, we gain a big head-start.' Together they surveyed the prisoners, and above the rumpled blue uniforms eyes fearfully reflected back the firelight. 'It becomes a choice of killing them or taking them with us.'

Pianza snapped his head around in alarm. 'Take them with us? Is that – feasible?'

'Down the slope a few miles begins the steppe. Nomadland. If there's any fighting to be done, perhaps we can persuade them to do it for us.'

'But – we have the blaster. We don't need swords and darts.'

'What good is a blaster if we're ambushed? Jumped from two or three sides at once? The blaster is a fine weapon when you can see your target.'

Pianza shrugged. 'It may be difficult to manage them.'

'I've considered that. Through the forest we'll tie them together. Once out on the steppes they can march ahead of the blaster. Naturally we'll have to be careful.'

He set the safety on the blaster, nosed the barrel down into the bracken, then strolled to where Abbigens lay. He looked down. 'Think it's about time to talk?'

Abbigens drew back the corners of his wide flat mouth. 'Sure, I'll talk. What do you want to know?'

Glystra smiled thinly. 'Who helped you aboard the *Vittorio*?'

Abbigens looked down the line of faces: Pianza, placid, attentive; the bristling Darrot; Bishop, solemn, a man ludicrously out of place; Ketch;

Corbus; Vallusser; and lastly Nancy, standing wide-eyed by Glystra's left elbow.

'Pianza,' said Abbigens. 'That's the man.'

Pianza raised his mild white eyebrows in startled protest. Somewhere else along the line of faces there was a change of expression – a flicker so faint as to be gone even as it manifested itself.

Glystra abruptly turned away. From the corner of his eye he sensed dark shapes disappearing into the trees. The Beaujolais soldiers! How many? Two, three, four? Taking advantage of the Earthman's preoccupation they had slipped across the clearing, disappeared into the woods.

Glystra cursed. If even one got away, the advantage of their head-start was diminished. He snatched the ion-shine from his pouch, slowly replaced it. It would be foolish wasting power on the tree trunks. The footsteps died in the distance, and then there was silence.

Glystra stood still, trying to collect his wits. At the moment there was only one person he was sure of – himself.

He pointed to Darrot and Corbus. 'You two man the blaster. Neither of you trust the other. There's an enemy among us, we don't know who he is, and we can't give him the opportunity to destroy us all.' He took a step backwards, held his ion-shine ready. 'I want to locate the weapons in the crowd. Pianza, you have an ion-shine?'

'Yes. One of Cloyville's.'

'Turn your back on me, lay it on the ground.'

Pianza did so, without remonstrance. Glystra stepped forward, ran his hand over Pianza's body, into his pouch. He found no other weapon.

In a similar fashion Glystra took the ion-shine from Cloyville, the mate's heat-gun from Ketch. Vallusser and Bishop carried only knives. Nancy carried no weapon of any sort.

Tucking the weapons into his pouch he stepped behind the blaster, took the ion-shine from Corbus. Five ion-shines, counting Abbigens', and the mate's heat-gun.

'Now we're as toothless as possible, and I think we ought to try for some sleep. Ketch, you and Vallusser take a couple of swords, stand on each side of the clearing. Make a triangle with the blaster. Don't get in between the blaster and the soldiers, because if anything happens – you're gone.' He turned to Darrot and Corbus. 'Hear that? Use that blaster if there's even a hint of an excuse.'

'Right,' said Corbus. Darrot nodded.

He looked at Nancy, Pianza, Bishop. 'We'll try for some sleep now and stand the second watch ... Right there by the fire is a good place, out of range of the blaster.'

The bracken was soft and comfortable under the blanket where the firelight had warmed it. Glystra stretched himself down, and fatigue came rising from his bones and muscles, and for an instant he was almost dazed by the pleasant ache of relaxation.

He lay ruminating, hands under his head. Above him the white blotches still peered over the walkways, and for all he could see they had not moved since he had seen them first.

Bishop settled himself nearby, sighed. Glystra eyed him with a moment's pity. Bishop was a student, fastidious, with no natural inclination for roughing it ... Nancy returned from the forest. Glystra had watched her go with an instant suspicion and then had relaxed. It was impractical to supervise every waking moment of everyone. He must remember, he told himself, to send her home to Jubilith the first thing in the morning. He closed his eyes, opened them a crack. Languor came at him in billows, delightful warmth leaching his consciousness. He lay on his side, one arm thrown over his eyes. It was difficult keeping himself awake.

'Awake or dead,' Glystra thought. 'Awake or dead.' And he forced his eyes open. Darrot, Corbus, Ketch, Vallusser. It was not that he trusted them the less, but that he was instinctively sure of Nancy, Pianza and Bishop.

There was no sound in the clearing other than the low mutter from the cluster of soldiers. Darrot and Corbus stood stiff behind the ionic blaster, Ketch paced slowly along one side of the clearing, Vallusser along the other. Behind him Nancy lay still and warm, Bishop slept like a baby, Pianza tossed fretfully.

All in all, quiet and peaceful. But the air was heavy with someone's private tension – his misgivings, fear, vacillation. The tension permeated the clearing, held Glystra's languor at bay.

The tension grew and Glystra tried to place it objectively. In Corbus' tight alertness, in Darrot's rigidity? In the feel of Nancy at his back? Some subtle wrongness in the breathing of Bishop or Pianza? ... What had aroused him he could not determine, but he sensed a focus of action forming. As soon as someone could summon the courage. He tried to see whom Abbigens might be watching, without success.

Minutes passed, a quarter hour, a half hour. The air was brittle as ice.

Ketch took a couple of steps toward the blaster, signaled, muttered a few words, backed off into the woods. Glystra watched without seeming to watch as Ketch attended the needs of his body. The soldiers, noting Ketch's momentary preoccupation, reacted with a small ripple of motion. A curt monosyllable from Darrot froze them.

Ketch returned, and now Vallusser stepped into the woods. Again from the captives the quiver of alertness, and again Darrot's soft command and the slow subsidence of blue-clad shoulders, the sinking of the grotesque black felt hats.

A sudden shape behind the blaster, a sweep of sword, a startled cry, a bubble of pure pain ... Then a stamp of feet, a stabbing flash of steel.

Teeth grinding together, Glystra leapt to his feet, ion-shine in his hand.

At the blaster there was now but one man, crouching, swinging the tube toward Glystra. Glystra saw it coming, saw the elbows tense ... He squeezed the handle of his ion-shine. Crackling electric streaks down the violet ray. Man's head charred, shriveled; blaster smashed, flung askew. Glystra sprang about facing the soldiers. They had raised to their feet, stood poised, undecided whether to attack or flee.

'*Sit down!*' said Glystra, his voice rasping, deadly. The soldiers slumped instantly.

Glystra reached in his pouch, tossed weapons to Pianza, Bishop. 'Watch 'em from here; we don't have any more blasters.'

He strode to the shattered field weapon. Three bodies. Corbus was still alive. Darrot lay with his dead face turned up, frozen in rage. Vallusser's body, with the head like an oversized black walnut, sprawled across Darrot's legs.

Glystra looked down at the bent little body. 'So it was Vallusser the man-hater. I wonder what they bought him with.'

Ketch had unpacked the first-aid kit and they knelt beside Corbus. A thrust through the side of his neck was bleeding profusely. Glystra applied a clotting agent, antiseptic and sprayed an elastic film over the wound, which when dry would grip the edges of the cut close together.

He rose to his feet, stood looking down at Abbigens. 'Your usefulness is limited. I've found out what I wanted to know.'

Abbigens shook the thick yellow hair back out of his face. 'Are you going to – kill me?'

'Wait and see.' Glystra turned away. He looked at his watch. 'Twelve o'clock.' He tossed Corbus' ion-shine to Ketch, turned to Pianza and Bishop. 'You two sleep; we'll take it till three.' He felt alive, refreshed. His enemy had been discovered and dealt with; the pressure of his most immediate problem had been lifted off his mind. Of course, tomorrow would bring new problems ...

CHAPTER SIX

Darrot and Vallusser were buried in a common grave with the Beaujolains: the young swaggerer who had fallen from the tree and the six soldiers who had been killed when Glystra had first seized the blaster.

Abbigens heaved a great sigh when earth began to fall on the bodies. Glystra grinned. Evidently Abbigens had expected to be one with the seven.

Shafts of sunlight, heavy and bright as bars of luminex, prodded down at a slant through the foliage. Pale smoke drifted up from the ashes of the campfire. It was almost time to leave.

Glystra looked around the clearing. Where was Nancy? There she stood, by the pack-beasts, as inconspicuous as she was able to make herself. Behind her the tree trunks rose like the columns of a great temple, admitting brief glimpses of the sunlit slope.

Nancy felt Glystra's eye, turned him her quick wide glance, with a hopeful hesitant smile. Glystra felt his heart beating. He looked away. Corbus was watching him with an unreadable expression. He compressed his lips, strode forward.

'You'd better be on your way, Nancy – back to Jubilith.'

Her smile faded slowly, her mouth drooped, her eyes became moist. She looked off into the forest. 'I'm – afraid,' she said in a voice which lacked conviction. 'Those soldiers who escaped may be waiting in the forest ...'

Glystra snorted. 'They're half-way to Montmarchy by now – worse luck. Besides, you can almost see Jubilith from here, straight up the slope. I'm sorry if you're frightened. You can take a catapult and darts if you like ...'

She apparently realized the hopelessness of argument, turned away without a word, crossed the clearing. At the edge of the forest she paused, looked over her shoulder.

Glystra watched silently.

She turned away. He watched her a few moments, moving through the trees. He saw her come out on the sunny bracken, listlessly start up the slope toward Jubilith.

Half an hour later the column got under way. The Beaujolains walked single-file, each tied to the man ahead and behind by ankle ropes. They carried their swords and catapults, but the darts were packed in panniers, on one of the pack-beasts.

The officer led the column; Abbigens was the last man. Then came the pack-beasts, with Corbus on a litter between the first two. He was awake and cheerful, and guarded the rear of the column with the big heat-gun.

The village overhead was awake, watching. As the column passed through the forest, the thud of feet sounded along the walkways, along with the creak of fiber fastenings, sometimes a mutter of voices, a child crying. Presently a ceiling of tangled and tattered vegetation, supported by a patchwork of branches, vines and dried yellow fronds, cut off the sunlight. This second floor to the forest spread to a surprising extent, dank on the bottom, trailing bits and shreds of rotting vegetation.

'What do you make of that?' asked Pianza.

'Offhand,' responded Glystra, 'it looks like a hanging garden ... We don't have an ecologist with us any more. Darrot probably would have known something about it ...'

Shafts of sunlight ahead indicated the end of the suspended field. Glystra went to the head of the line, where the officer walked, looking sullenly straight ahead.

'What's your name?' asked Glystra.

'Morwatz. Leg-leader Zoriander Morwatz, 112th at the Champs-de-Mars Academy.'

'What were your orders?'

The officer hesitated, debating the propriety of answering the questions. He was a short man, with a full round face, protuberant black eyes. He spoke in a slightly different dialect than did his soldiers, and carried himself with a trace of self-importance. Apparently he was a warrior by accident of caste rather than inclination, essentially not a bad fellow, Glystra decided. A man like Abbigens would completely overshadow him, reduce him to vacillation and querulousness.

'What were your orders?' repeated Glystra.

'We were placed at the command of the Earthman.' He jerked his hand back toward Abbigens. 'He carried a cachet from Charley Lysidder, an instrument of great authority.'

Glystra digested the information a moment, then asked, 'An order addressed to you specifically?'

'To the commanding officer of the Montmarchy garrison.'

'Hmmmm.' Where had Abbigens obtained this order, signed by the Bajarnum of Beaujolais? There was a pattern here which as yet he was unable to see in the whole. Certainly the fact of Vallusser's guilt did not explain all the events of the last few days.

He asked further questions, and learned that Morwatz had been born into the Guerdons, a caste of lesser nobility, and was foolishly proud of the distinction. His home was the village of Pellisade, a few miles south of Grosgarth, and he believed Earth to be the home of a mindless robot race, obeying the sound of gongs and bells like machines. 'We'd die here in Beaujolais, before we'd let ourselves be emasculated,' declared Morwatz with fine fire.

Here was the obverse, thought Glystra, to the stereotype in Earth minds of the Big Planeter as a flamboyant, reckless creature, totally without restraint. Grinning he asked, 'Do any of us look as if our powers of free will were lacking?'

'You're the elite. Here in Beaujolais we have a single lord, Charley Lysidder; never such tyranny as you experience on Earth. Oh, we've heard all about it, from people who know best.' He nodded his plump head several times.

Now he looked at Glystra sidelong. 'Why do you smile?'

Glystra laughed. '*Naisuka*. The reason that is no reason at all.'

Morwatz said suspiciously, 'You use an extremely high-caste word. Even I would not feel proper speaking so.'

'Well, well.' Glystra arched his eyebrows. 'You are not allowed to use certain words – but neither do you live under tyranny.'

Morwatz pursed his lips. 'To be sure the Bajarnum is a harsh man, but he is conquering the barbarians and forcing them to live correctly.'

'And they won't be able to use high-caste words either.'

'Precisely. As it should be.' And now Morwatz screwed up his courage to ask a question of his own. 'And what will you do with us?'

'If you obey orders, you'll have the same chances we have. Frankly, I'm counting on you and your men to protect us on our march. Once we arrive at our destination, your life is your own.'

Morwatz said with interest, 'Where do you march for?'

'Earth Enclave.'

Morwatz frowned. 'I don't know the place. How many leagues?'

'Forty thousand miles. Thirteen thousand leagues.'

Morwatz faltered in his stride. 'You are mad!'

Glystra laughed. 'We have the same man to thank for our troubles.' He jerked his thumb. 'Abbigens.'

Morwatz found it difficult to shape his thoughts. 'First there is Nomadland and the gypsies. If they capture us, they'll roast us alive and eat us. They are men of a different race and they detest the Beaujolains.'

'They won't attack fifty men as readily as they might eight.'

Morwatz shook his head despondently. 'Last six-moon Heinzelman the Hellhorse raided deep into Beaujolais, and paved the way with the utmost in terror.'

Glystra looked ahead through the thinning tree trunks, to the open slope ahead. 'There's Nomadland, ahead of us. What lies beyond?'

'After Nomadland?' Morwatz wrinkled his brow. 'First, the River Oust. And then the swamps, and the Ropemakers of Swamp Island. And after the swamps—'

'What?'

'Directly east, I don't know. Wild men, wild animals. Southerly is the land known as Felissima, and Kirstendale, and the monoline to Myrtlesee Fountain and the oracle. Past Myrtlesee is the Land of Stones, but of this I know nothing, since Myrtlesee is far to the east.'

'How many leagues?'

'Several hundred. But it is hard to determine exactly. From here to the river is – five days. To cross you must use the Edelweiss high-line to Swamp Island, or else you must follow the River Oust southwest back toward Beaujolais.'

'Why can't we cross the river in boats?'

Morwatz made a wise face. 'The griamobots.'

'And what are they?'

'Savage river beasts. Horrible creatures.'

'Hm. And after the river? What then? How long to cross the swamps?'

Morwatz calculated. 'If you journey east, four days – if you find a good swamp car. If you choose to bear southerly, you may take the monoline which leads down past the March – the Hibernian March, that is – to Kirstendale. Possibly six days or a week to Kirstendale. Then, if you're able to leave—'

'Why should we not leave Kirstendale?'

'Some do,' said Morwatz with a sly wink. 'Others don't ... From Kirstendale the monoline runs west to Grosgarth, south through the Felissima trade-towns, east to Myrtlesee Fountain.'

'How long to Myrtlesee from Kirstendale?'

'Oh—' Morwatz made a vague gesture '—two days, three days on the monoline. A dangerous trip otherwise, due to the tribesmen down from Eyrie.'

'And beyond Myrtlesee?'

'Desert.'

'And beyond?'

Morwatz shrugged. 'Ask the Magic Fountain. If you are wealthy and pay much metal he will tell you anything you ask.' He spoke with confidence.

Glystra thought it might be well to inquire the best way to convey himself and his comrades to Earth Enclave.

Overhead the foliage thinned and the column broke out into the blinding Big Planet sunlight. The slope fell away ahead, a vast windy moor, rolling slightly concave before them. No human habitation or artifact was in sight, but far to the north a dense pillar of smoke bent eastward in the wind.

Glystra halted the column, regrouped the soldiers, arranging them in a square around the pack-beasts – zipangotes, so Morwatz called them. The beast carrying the darts was guarded by Corbus riding in a litter directly behind. He carried a catapult and dart in his hand, with the heat-gun tucked inside his shirt secure from any swift clutch. Abbigens walked at the right forward corner, Morwatz at the left rear. Flanking as guards to left and right were Pianza and Cloyville with ion-shines; behind came Bishop and Ketch.

Two hours before noon they set forth across the moor, and as they marched the tremendous slope behind them began to lose its bulk. The upper reaches became murked in the haze, the forest became a dark band. The slope was leveling out into the River Oust peneplain.

A mutter from the soldiers reached his ears. They were faltering in their step, the whites showed in their eyes. There was a general nervous motion along the column, a jerking of arms, a tossing of the grotesque black felt hats.

Following their gaze Glystra saw along the horizon a dozen tall hump-backed zipangotes, approaching at a careless pace.

'Who are they? Gypsies?'

Morwatz scanned the column, his face set in rigid lines. 'They're gypsies, but not the Cossacks. These are high-caste warriors, possibly even Polit-buros. Only Politburos ride zipangotes. We can fight off Cossacks, they have little spirit, no discipline, no method, no mind. Only hunger. As soon as there are a few bodies, no matter whose, they are content. But the Politburos ...' His voice faltered, he shook his head.

Glystra prompted him. 'What about the Politburos?'

'They are the great warriors, the leaders. When they appear the gypsies fight like devils. The Cossacks alone are mere robbers. When a Politburo leads them – demons!'

Glystra looked at Bishop. 'Know much about these gypsies, Bish?'

'There's a short chapter in Vendome's *Big Planet Lore* on the gypsies, but the emphasis is on their racial background rather than their culture. The stock was originally a tribe of Kirghiz herdsmen from Earth. Turkestan, I believe. When Cloud Control increased trans-Caucasian rainfall, they moved out to Big Planet, where steppes presumably would remain steppes. They shipped out third-class, and in the same hold were a tribe of old-fashioned gypsies and a brotherhood of Polynesians. On the trip out the gypsy leader, one Panvilsap, killed the Kirghiz headman, married the Poly-nesian matriarch, and when they were discharged on Big Planet, controlled the entire group. The ensuing culture was mingled Kirghiz, Polynesian and Romany, and dominated by the personality of Panvilsap – an enormous man, a killer, a butcher, as ruthless as he was single-minded.'

The column was now less than a mile distant, approaching without haste.

Glystra turned to Morwatz. 'How do these people live?'

'They herd zipangotes, hare-hounds, pechavies, milk-rats. They gather fungus from the cycads in Depression. Spring and autumn they raid into Beaujolais and Kerkaten to the north, Ramspur to the south. The Oust cuts them off from Felissima and the Rebbirs of Eyrie. Ah,' sighed Morwatz, 'what a grateful war that would be, between the Rebbirs and the gypsies.'

'Typical nomadic society,' inserted Bishop. 'Not a great deal different from the ancient Scythians.'

Morwatz said fretfully, 'Why are you so interested in the mannerisms of the race? Tonight, they intend to eat us ...'

CHAPTER SEVEN

The sun was at zenith, and the coiled gray-green vegetation of the steppe gave off a smoky aroma. As the column approached, it was gradually joined by groups of Cossacks, who fell in behind the slow-jogging zipangotes.

Glystra asked Morwatz, 'Is this their usual method of attack?'

Morwatz yanked at his black headgear. 'They observe no usual methods.'

Glystra said, 'Order your men to take five darts apiece from the pack and stand ready for action.'

Morwatz seemed to fill out, expand. His chest and shoulders became rigid, his face tightened. He strode down the front of the square, barking orders. The Beaujolains straightened, formed harder ranks. In groups of five, they passed beside the pack animal which carried the darts, marched back into ranks.

Bishop said dubiously, 'Aren't you afraid that—' he paused.

'I'm afraid to act afraid,' said Glystra. 'They'd be off like jack-rabbits toward the forest. It's a matter of morale. We've got to act as if these gypsies were dirt under our feet.'

'I guess you're right – in theory.'

The mounted column halted a hundred yards across the moor, just out of catapult range. The beasts were heavier than those in the pack train – sleek, seal-brown, soft-padded creatures, with ridged convex backs, long heavy necks. They were decked in trappings of shaggy leather painted with crude designs, and each wore a white rhinoceros-like horn strapped to its snout.

A tall burly man sat on the first of the zipangotes. He wore blue satin trousers, a short black cloak, a peaked leather cap with cusped ear-pieces protruding at either side. A three-inch brass ring hung from each ear, and on each side of his chest he wore a medal of polished iron. He had a round muscular heavy-lidded face; his skin was maroon as if charged with a special strong blood.

Glystra heard Morwatz mutter, 'Heinzelman the Hellhorse!' And his voice was as flat as if he were reading the hour of his own death.

Glystra re-examined the man, noted his complete ease, an indifferent confidence more striking than any arrogance. Behind rode a dozen others similarly garbed, and still further behind skulked a hundred men and women in beribboned and betasselled breeches of dull red, green or blue, heavy fustian blouses, leather skull-caps, some of which were crested by complicated white objects.

Glystra turned to check the formation of the Beaujolains – *thwinggg!*

something sang past his throat like a hornet. He recoiled, ducked, looked full in the flat face of Abbigens, lowering his catapult with a curiously blank expression.

'Morwatz,' said Glystra, 'take the catapult from Abbigens, tie his wrists together, hobble him.'

Morwatz hesitated a fraction of an instant, then turned, spoke to a pair of soldiers.

There was a scuffle which Glystra ignored – for now Heinzelman the Hellhorse and his Politburos had dismounted and were approaching.

Heinzelman halted a few paces distant, half-smiling, toying with his quirt. 'What is your thought encroaching on the land of the gypsies?' His voice was soft and fluent.

'We're heading for Kirstendale, past the swamps,' said Glystra. 'The route crosses Nomadland.'

Heinzelman drew back his lips, displaying teeth marvellously inlaid with minute bits of colored stone. 'You risk your flesh, entering this land of hungry men.'

'The risk is to the hungry men.'

'From the soldiers?' Heinzelman made a contemptuous gesture. 'I will kill each and drink his blood.'

Glystra heard a whimper, a cry. 'Claude – Claude—'

Hot blood pulsed in his brain. He stood swaying, then became conscious of Heinzelman's amused scrutiny. 'Who calls my name?'

Heinzelman looked negligently over his shoulder. 'A woman of the slopes we found by the forest this morning. She will be spitted at this evening's camp.'

Glystra said, 'Bring her forth, I will buy her from you.'

Heinzelman said lazily, 'Then you have wealth? This is a fortunate day for the gypsies.'

Glystra tried to hold his voice steady. 'Bring forth this woman or I'll send a man to take her.'

'A man? One man?' Heinzelman's eyes narrowed. 'What race of man are you? Not Beaujolain, and you are too dark for a Maquir ...'

Glystra casually brought forth his ion-shine – 'I am an electrician' – and grinned at his own joke.

Heinzelman rubbed his heavy chin. 'In what parts live they?'

'It's not a race; it's an occupation.'

'Ah! There are none such among us; we pursue our own business. We are warriors, killers, eaters. And if I gave you the woman, tonight we should go hungry.'

Glystra came to a grim decision. He turned his head. 'Bring out Abbigens.' To Heinzelman: 'Electricians carry death in their every gesture.'

Abbigens had been thrust forward, and stood still as a pillar, his pale mouth sagging.

Glystra said, 'If killing you did not serve a practical purpose, I'd probably march you all the way to Earth Enclave for de-aberration.' He raised the ion-shine. Abbigens' face was like risen dough. He began to laugh wildly. 'What a joke! What a joke on you, Glystra!' The violet ray snapped out, power crackled down the conductive channel. Abbigens was dead.

Heinzelman appeared faintly bored.

'Give me the woman,' said Glystra, 'or I'll bring this same death to you. I give you the corpse in her place.' He used the rasp of authority. '*Quick!*'

Heinzelman looked up in faint surprise, hesitated, then made a motion to his men. 'Let him have her.'

Nancy came limping forward, fell shaking and sobbing at Glystra's knees. He ignored her. 'Take your meat,' he said to Heinzelman. 'Go your way and we go ours.'

Heinzelman had regained whatever composure he had lost. 'I've seen those electrical clubs before. The Bajarnum of Beaujolais brings them down from the sky. But they kill no more certainly than our lances. Especially in the dark, when lances come from many directions and the club points in only one.'

Glystra turned to Morwatz. 'Give the command to march.'

Morwatz stood back, jerked his arm up and down. 'Forward!'

Heinzelman nodded, half-smiling. 'Perhaps we shall meet again.'

The Great Slope was a shadow behind the western haze; the steppe spread as wide as an ocean, carpeted with blue–green bracken except where black–green furze filled the deeper hollows. And behind were the gypsies, a dark clot like flies on stale meat, the Cossacks squatting around the heavier mass of the Politburos on their zipangotes.

In late afternoon a dark shadow appeared in the distance. 'Looks like trees, probably an artesian pond,' said Cloyville.

Glystra looked around the horizon. 'It seems to be the only shelter in sight. We'd better camp for the night.' He looked uneasily toward the dark specks in the rear. 'I'm afraid we're in for more trouble.'

The shadow took on substance, became a copse of a dozen trees. Under-neath was a carpet of blue–white moss and lush herbage. A dozen gypsy women scuttled from the shadows, hulking creatures in dirty black robes, to disappear over the lip of a nearby swale. A moment later a flock of fragile white creatures rose up on translucent wings and wheeled downwind.

At the center of the copse was a small pond bordered by fat rust-colored reeds. A scattering of transparent bubbles, like jellyfish, lay in the mud of the rim. Glystra looked in suspicion at the water, which seemed brackish, but the Beaujolains drank it with relish. Beside the pond was a tall rick full of branches loaded with acorn-like fruit; beside the rick were tubs full of rank beer and a crude still.

The Beaujolains advanced eagerly to investigate the still. Morwatz ran shouting to stop them; reluctantly they turned back.

Glystra took a small cup from one of the packs, gave it to Morwatz. 'Serve a measure to each of your men.'

There was a whoop of approval and a keg was broached. Glystra said to Pianza, 'If we could serve them grog every night we'd never need to guard them.'

Pianza shook his head. 'Just children. Very little emotional control. I hope they don't become boisterous.'

'Liquor or not, we can't relax. You and Cloyville take the first four hours, Bishop, Ketch and I will take the next four. Keep a sharp eye on the beast with the darts.' He went to change the bandage on Corbus' neck but found Nancy there before him.

The Beaujolains, singing now, built a fire, and heaping on quantities of the branches from the rick, breathed in the aromatic smoke. Pianza called to Glystra in a worried voice. 'They're fighting drunk. I hope they don't get any worse.'

Glystra watched in growing apprehension. The Beaujolains were pushing and shouting, trying to shoulder into the densest clouds of smoke, where they stood with faces wreathed in foolish smiles. When they themselves had been pushed aside, immediately they raised angry outcries, cursed, pushed and elbowed a way back into the smoke.

'Must be a narcotic,' said Glystra. 'Big Planet marijuana. Got to put a stop to it.' He stepped forward. 'Morwatz!'

Morwatz, red-eyed and flushed from his own indulgence in the smoke, turned a reluctant face to the call. 'Get your men fed and bedded down; enough of the smoke breathing.'

Morwatz made a slurred acquiescence, and turning on his men, after a volley of curses, succeeded in bringing order to the camp. A tureen of porridge was prepared – wheat flavored with handfuls of dry meat and fungus.

Glystra went to squat beside Morwatz, where he ate a little apart from his troops. 'What is that stuff?' He gestured toward the rick.

Morwatz looked a little sheepish. 'It's called zygage – a very potent drug, very valuable.' He puffed himself up. 'Generally only the lowest castes inhale smoke – very vulgar, the crudest sensations—'

'How do you usually take it then?'

Morwatz breathed heavily. 'Normally I do not take it at all. Far too expensive for a warrior. The Mercantils occasionally brew a potion, but its use leads to debility, so I am told. The soldiers will sleep well tonight, so you will observe. Zygage saps much vitality; smoke, potion or nose-salve, the user pays very dearly for his pleasure ... But look you there, what manner of drug does your man take?'

Glystra turned his head. Bishop was swallowing his customary handful of vitamins.

Glystra grinned. 'That's a different kind of drug. It has little effect – makes Bishop think he's healthy. He'd never know the difference if someone fed him chalk.'

Morwatz was puzzled. 'Another strange and useless Earth custom.'

Glystra rejoined his companions. Nancy had served Corbus, then went to sit by herself among the zipangotes, as inconspicuous as possible. Glystra had not spoken to her since she had run to his feet from behind the Politburos.

From the fire came a sudden tumult of hoarse quarrelling. A soldier had quietly cast a new armful of the zygage branches on the flames, and Morwatz had come forward expostulating. The soldier, stumbling and red-eyed, cursed him back.

Glystra sighed. 'Now it's discipline. Well—' he rose to his feet '—I suppose we've got to make an example.'

Morwatz was pulling the smoking branches from the blaze; the soldier lurched up, kicked him. Morwatz fell face down into the coals.

Cloyville ran forward to pull at the screaming Morwatz; three soldiers leapt on his back, pulled him down. Pianza aimed the ion-shine, but held his fire for fear of shocking Cloyville. Beaujolains came at him from all directions. He aimed, fired: *snap – snap – snap.* Three soldiers fell flat, shrivelled flesh. The others swarmed over him.

The clearing was suddenly alive with wild-eyed men, screaming and savage. One sprang at Ketch, toppled him. Glystra killed him with his ion-shine, then felt viciously strong arms seize him from behind, hurl him to the ground.

The Earthmen lay weaponless, arms lashed behind their backs.

Nearby Morwatz lay moaning from deep in his throat. The soldier who had first kicked him came forward, a tall man with concave cheeks, a pocked forehead, a split nose. He looked down, and Morwatz regarded him with glazing eyes and moans gradually ascending in pitch. The soldier deliberately drew his sword, punctured Morwatz's neck – once, twice, three times, as if he were prodding a rock; Morwatz gurgled, died. He turned, came to look at his captives, tapped Glystra's chin with the reeking sword. He laughed. 'Your death will not be at my hands. It's back to Grosgarth for you, and there'll be a reward to set us up as noblemen ... Let Charley Lysidder have his will with you ...'

'The gypsies!' said Glystra in a choked voice. 'They'll kill us all!'

'Pah. Dirty animals!' He swung his sword in a wild flourish. 'We'll kill them as they come!' He gave a great exultant roar, a wordless drug-addled cry of pure abandon. Leaping to the rick, he threw armful after armful of branches into the blaze. The smoke poured forth, the Beaujolains inhaled it in tremendous racking gulps. Breaking free to gasp for air, they fell to their hands and knees, crawled back to suck up new lungfuls.

Glystra tugged at his bonds, but they had been well-tied, cinched up with no regard for circulation. He craned his neck. Where was Nancy? Nowhere in sight. Had she escaped? Where could she escape to? Glystra ground his teeth. The gypsies would take her and there would be no succor this time ... Unless she could slip back to the forest during the night. She had clearly fled. The copse was too small to conceal her, and she was nowhere within the range of vision. Twilight was drifting down from the Great Slope – a warm achingly beautiful time of luminous violet air with velvety black and gray shadows below ... There was a distant sound that he found himself listening to, a far chanting from the steppe, a stave of four notes on a minor scale, punctuated by a rumbling bellow as of a bass horn.

The breeze shifted. Smoke from the smouldering zygage drifted through the rapt soldiers to float across the bound Earthmen. Twist, turn as they might, avoiding the smoke was impossible. Pungent and sweet, it blossomed up through their nostrils directly into their brains. For a moment they felt nothing; then as one man they lay back, succumbing to the irresistible power of the drug.

The first sensation was double, triple vitality, a thousandfold perceptiveness that saw, heard, felt, smelt with minuscule and catholic exactness. Each leaf on the tree became an identity, each pulse a singular and unique experience. Flitting swarms of pleasant experiences crowded into the mind: triumphs of love, zest of skiing, sailing, space-boating, diving; the joy of colors, the freedom of clouds. At the same time another part of the mind was furiously active; problems became simplicities; hardships – such as the bonds and the prospect of death at the hands of Charley Lysidder – were details hardly worth attention. And off in the distance the chanting waxed louder. Glystra heard it; surely the Beaujolains must hear it likewise ... But if they heard it they heeded it not at all.

The breeze shifted again; the smoke drifted away. Glystra felt an instant resentment; he fought his bonds, looked enviously to the Beaujolains standing quiet, quivering slightly in the rapturous smoke.

The chanting was loud, close at hand. The Beaujolains at last heeded. They stumbled away from the fire, black hats askew, eyes bulging, bloodshot, faces distended, mouths gaping and gasping for air.

The leader raised his head like a wolf, screamed.

The cry pleased the Beaujolains. Each one threw back his head and echoed it. Scream after scream of furious challenge rang out toward the gypsies. Now laughing, crying, they loaded themselves with darts, ran out of the copse toward the gypsy horde.

The leader called out; the soldiers, without halting, ordered themselves into a loose formation, and shrilling the eager challenge, charged into the afterglow.

The copse was quiet. Glystra rolled to his knees, struggled to his feet, looked around for means to loosen his bonds. Pianza called in a husky voice, 'Stand still; I'll see if I can pull the ropes loose.' He rose to his own knees, raised to his feet. He backed against Glystra's hands, fumbled with the thongs.

He gasped in frustration. 'My fingers are numb ... I can't move my hands ...'

The Beaujolains had crossed the twilight; now the gypsy chanting came to a halt, and only the deep bellow of the horn sounded. Detail was blurred in the evening; Glystra could see men falling, then a convulsive Beaujolain charge which plunged into the gypsies like a knife.

The battle was lost in the dusk.

CHAPTER EIGHT

Glystra tried to break loose the knots on Pianza's wrists, without success. His fingers were like sausages, without sensation. He was suddenly weak, lax; his brain felt inert. The aftermath of the drug.

The lid to the gypsy still quivered, raised. Dripping, sodden, Nancy looked out – wide-eyed, white-faced.

'*Nancy!*' cried Glystra. 'Come here, quick!'

She looked at him as if dazed, moved uncertainly forward, paused, looked out across the steppe toward the melee.

The Beaujolain ululations rose shrill, keen, triumphant.

'Nancy! Cut us loose – before they come back and kill us!'

Nancy looked at him with a strange contemplative expression, as if lost in thought. Glystra fell hopelessly silent. The drugged smoke or the fumes of the still had dulled her reason.

A throbbing chorus of bellows, deep-voiced, rich, rang like bells across the air. There was an intermittent thudding sound, and the Beaujolain yelling choked off, ceased. A voice rose above all others: Heinzelman the Hellhorse. 'I kill, I eat your lives! ... I kill, kill, kill ...'

'*Nancy!*' cried Glystra. 'Come here! Untie us! They'll be here any minute. Don't you want to live?'

She sprang forward, took a knife from her sash: *cut, cut, cut.* Earthmen stood about, rubbing their wrists, grimacing at the pain of restored circulation, torpid with zygage hangover.

Glystra muttered, 'At least we need worry no further about guarding the Beaujolains … A load off our minds …'

'The gypsies will eat well tonight,' said Bishop. Alone in the group he appeared alert. Indeed, he was more than alert; he evidently retained the mental edge and physical tone which the others had felt under the influence of the zygage. Glystra wonderingly watched him prance up and down, like a boxer loosening his muscles. His own frame felt like a sack of damp rags.

Ketch bent with the effort of an old man, picked up a shining piece of metal. 'Somebody's ion-shine.'

Glystra searched the clearing, found his own weapon where it had been carelessly flung. 'Here's mine … They were too steamed up to care about anything.' The breeze brought a wisp of smoke into his face; new fingers of delight searched into his brain. '*Whew!* That stuff is powerful …'

Bishop had flung himself to the turf and was doing pushups. Feeling the stares of the others he jumped to his feet. 'I just feel good,' he said, grinning sheepishly. 'That smoke did me good.'

There was silence from the steppes. Overhead in the pale blue–black sky, stars flickered.

The gypsy war-chant rose up, loud, close at hand. Something whickered overhead, slashing through the leaves.

'Down!' hissed Glystra. 'Arrows … Move away from the fire.'

Loud came the chant: four notes on a querulous quavering scale, sung with syllables that carried no meaning.

Loud came Heinzelman's voice. 'Come forth, you strange men, you miserable intruders, come forth. Come crouch at my feet while I kill you, while I drink your blood; come forth … I am Heinzelman the Hellhorse, Heinzelman the life-eater, I eat your life, I am the It, the Pain-maker, Heinzelman …'

They saw his shape silhouetted, and behind him were a string of zipangotes. Glystra sighted along his ion-shine, then hesitated. It was like felling an ancient tree. He called, 'You'd do better leaving us alone, Heinzelman.'

'*Bah!*' A sound of immeasurable disdain. 'You dare not face me higher than your knees. Now I come to kill you; put down your electrical tricks, bow your neck, I come to kill.'

Glystra numbly started to lay down the ion-shine, then blinked, fought off the man's magnetism. He pushed the button. Purple sparks flashed at

Heinzelman, buried into his chest, absorbed, defeated. 'He's grounded!' thought Glystra in sudden panic.

Heinzelman loomed on the afterglow, a heroic figure, larger than life … Bishop ran forward, closed with him. Heinzelman bellowed, a ringing bull-sound. He bent, Bishop twisted, rose up beneath. Heinzelman performed a majestic cartwheel, struck earth with a ponderous jar. Bishop sat casually on him, made play with his hands a moment, then stood up. Glystra approached, still numb. 'What did you do?'

'Tried out a few judo tricks,' said Bishop modestly. 'I had an idea the fellow won his battles with his voice, his hypnotic suggestion. Sure enough he was soft; no muscle around his major chord. I killed him dead as a mackerel, one tap in the right place.'

'I never knew you were a judo expert.'

'I'm not … I read a book on the subject a few years back, and it came to me all at once – my word, all those zipangotes!'

'They must have belonged to the other Politburos that the Beaujolains killed. They're ours now.'

'Where are the other gypsies?'

Glystra listened. There was not a sound to be heard across the steppes. A far bray of the horn? He could not be sure.

'They've gone. Melted away.'

They returned to the copse leading the zipangotes. Glystra said, 'We'd better get going.'

Cloyville stared. 'Now?'

'Now!' Glystra snapped. He was taut with weariness. 'Three Beaujolain soldiers got away last night. They'll take the news to Montmarchy. A new column will be sent out. They'll be mounted on zipangotes, they'll carry metal weapons. We can't take chances. I don't like it any more than you do but—' he pointed to the zipangotes '—at least we can ride.'

Morning, midday, afternoon – the Earthmen slumped on the curved backs of the zipangotes, half-dazed with fatigue. The gait was a smooth rocking pitch, not conducive to sleep. Evening came with a slow dimming of the sky.

A fire was built in a hollow, a pot of wheat porridge boiled and eaten, two-hour sentry watches set, and the column bedded down.

Glystra was too tired to fall asleep. He twisted and turned. He thought of Nancy, raised to his elbow. Her eyes were on him. Sweating, he sank back into the couch. It would be hard indulging what he felt to be a mutual passion without making themselves ridiculous. It would also be inconsiderate … Sighing, Glystra slumped back into his blankets.

The next morning Glystra opened his eyes to observe Bishop running lightly back and forth along the side of the slope. Glystra rubbed his eyes,

yawned, hauled himself to his feet. Feeling dull and liverish he called irritably to Bishop, 'What in the world's come over you? I never knew you to go
in for early morning exercise before.'

A flush mounted Bishop's long homely face. 'I can't understand it myself.
I just feel good. I've never felt so well in my life. Perhaps my vitamins are
taking hold.'

'They never took hold before we got all doped up with that zygage.
Then they took hold like ice-tongs, and you ran out and played hell with
Heinzelman.'

'I can't understand it,' said Bishop, now half-worried. 'Do you think that
drug has permanently affected me?'

Glystra rubbed his chin. 'If it has it seems to be a good thing – but why
did it give the rest of us hangovers? We all ate the same, drank the same
... Except—' He eyed Bishop speculatively. 'I wish we had more of those
branches; I'd make some experiments.'

'What kind of experiments?'

'It occurred to me that you'd crammed yourself with vitamins – just
before the smoke hit us.'

'Well, yes. That's true. So I did. I wonder if possibly there's a connection
... Interesting thought ...'

'If I ever lay my hands on any more of that zygage,' muttered Glystra,
watching Bishop absent-mindedly flexing his arms, 'I'll find out for sure.'

Four days of steady travel passed, from dawn till sunset. They saw no
human being until on the afternoon of the fourth day they came upon a
pair of young gypsy girls, perhaps sixteen or seventeen years old, tending a
score of sluggish animals, yellow-furred, the size of sheep – pechavies. They
wore tattered gray smocks and their feet were tied in rags. The freshness of
youth was still theirs, and they had a wild prettiness in no way diminished
by their complete fearlessness when they found that the men of the column
were not gypsies.

They deserted their animals and ran forward. 'Are you slavers?' asked the
first happily. 'We wish to be slaves.'

'Sorry,' said Glystra dryly. 'We're just travelers. Why are you so anxious?'

The girls giggled, eyeing Glystra as if his question were obtuse. 'Slaves are
fed often and eat from dishes. Slaves may step under a roof when the rain
comes, and I've heard it said that slaves are eaten only if no other food is
available ... We are to be eaten this winter, unless the pechavies fatten past
expectation.'

Glystra looked at them irresolutely. If he set about righting the wrongs of
everyone they met, they would never arrive at Earth Enclave. On the other
hand – a stealthy thought – if the other men in the column were provided
with women, it would be possible for him to advance his own desires. Of

course, camp-followers would slow up the column. There would be added supply problems, emotional flare-ups.

He looked over his shoulder. Corbus caught his eyes as if divining his thoughts.

'I could use a good slave,' he said easily. 'You – what's your name?'

'I'm Motta. She's Wailie.'

Glystra said weakly, 'Anyone else?'

Pianza shook his head. 'I'm much too old. Too old.'

Cloyville snorted, turned away.

This was embarrassing, thought Glystra. Here is where he should display firmness, leadership ... He passed over Ketch, who gloried in his misogyny, and would suffer the pangs of Saint Anthony before yielding so easily.

Bishop said tentatively, 'I'll take her.'

Glystra felt quick relief, vindication of a sort. And the problems of the future could be met as they arose. Now was the present, now was the time containing that sweet union of carbon, oxygen, hydrogen, spirit, will and imagination named Nancy. He met her eyes, as if there had been a signal. She colored faintly, gave an enigmatic jerk of the shoulder, looking away.

Three more days of riding the steppe, each exactly alike. On the fourth day the land changed. The bracken grew taller and harder to ride through, almost like Earthly manzanita. There were occasional flamboyant shrubs six feet tall, with leaves like peacock fans. Ahead appeared a low black blur, which the gypsy girls identified as the bank of the River Oust.

At noon they came upon a fetish post driven into the earth – a round timber eight feet tall, topped by a spherical gourd painted to represent a face.

The gypsy girls made a wide circuit of the post. Wailie said in a hushed voice, 'The Magickers of Edelweiss put that there, and only just now, to warn us away from the river.'

Bishop patiently pointed out that in all the range of vision there was no living creature but themselves.

'Only just now,' declared Wailie stubbornly. 'See the moist dirt.'

'Does look fresh,' Bishop admitted dubiously.

'If you touch the post, you will blacken and die,' cried Motta.

Glystra, reflecting that many folk-beliefs were based on fact, searched the steppe in all directions ... There! A flicker of white? Whatever it was, it disappeared over a distant swale.

In the middle afternoon they came upon Edelweiss, a stockaded fort, with three-story blockhouses at each corner.

Motta explained. 'Sometimes the South Cossacks raid the Magickers. They are not allowed at the Rummage Sale, because the sight of naked knees drives them mad and they run killing-crazy. But they love the gray powder salt which comes up the river from Gammerei and the Magickers have it in stock, and that is why Edelweiss is girt up with such care.'

The town was illumined full-face by the afternoon sun, and across the clear distance appeared as a toy, a miniature, colored dark and light brown, with black windows, light green and black roofs. From the center of town rose a tall pole, with a cupola at the top, like the crow's-nest of a ship.

Motta explained the purpose of the pole. 'The high-wire to Swamp Island is made fast at the top of the pole. And then the Magickers always watch the distance; they read the clouds as signs, and the wise Hags among them see the future.'

'By watching clouds?'

'So it is said. But we know little, being females and raised for use.'

They continued to the river, and with the afternoon sun at their backs stood looking over the tremendous Oust. It flowed from the far north, appearing into sight out of the hazy distance, and proceeded into the equally distant south, curving back toward the west. Cat's-paws vibrated the surface, and at intervals came a roiling-up from below, as if a monster fin had set the water into turbulent motion. The other shore, two or three miles distant, was low and flat, and overgrown with a dense forest of poles two hundred feet tall. These were silvery-green and stood like stripped and dead tree trunks or gigantic asparagus shoots. A few blots of color showed at their base – vermilion, blue, yellow – too far distant to be resolved into detail. A long island overgrown with feathery foliage split the center of the river like a wedge.

'Look!' Cloyville cried hoarsely – unnecessarily, for every eye was straining fascinated. Floating from behind the island came a black monster. Its body was round and sleek, its head was like a frog, split by a vast mouth. The head darted forward as they watched, chewed and champed at something in the water, then lowered lazily, lay flat. The creature circled, drifted out of sight behind the island.

Cloyville released his breath. '*Whew!* That's a devilish thing to have for a neighbor.'

Pianza searched the face of the river with concern. 'I wonder that anyone dares to cross ...'

Corbus pointed. 'They use the high-line.'

It was a thin gray-white cable, swooping from the pole in the village to one of the spines of the forest on the opposite shore. The low point at the center was only fifty feet above the surface of the river.

Glystra snorted in disgust. 'They've got the river-crossing sewed up, and no mistake ... I suppose we'd better apply for transportation.'

'That's how the Magickers acquire their wealth,' said Motta.

Cloyville muttered, 'They'll probably make us pay through the nose ...'

Glystra rubbed his short black thatch. 'It's a case of take it or leave it.

We've got to take it if it breaks us.' He looked back across the steppe. 'I don't see the Beaujolais flying squad. No doubt it's there ... Once we get past the river we can breathe easier ...'

They set out along the lip of the bluff toward the village.

Above them towered the walls of Edelweiss, two-foot timbers, peeled, set into the ground like piles, lashed at the top with coarse fiber and evidently fastened elsewhere with dowels or tree-nails. The wood appeared punky and soft. Glystra thought that anyone determined on entry could easily chop his way in with a hatchet.

They stopped by the gate, which opened at the rear of a rectangular alcove, well buttressed with extra courses of timber. The gate was open, revealing a short passage walled on either side and cut off at the far end by another wall.

'Strange,' said Glystra. 'No guards, no gate-keeper ... In fact – there's no one.'

'They're afraid,' said Wailie. She raised her strident young voice. 'Magickers! Come out and lead us to the high-line!'

There was no overt response. A stealthy rustle sounded behind the walls.

'Come out,' yelled Motta, 'or we'll burn the walls!'

'My God!' muttered Pianza. Bishop wore an agonized expression.

Wailie sought to outdo her companion. 'Come out and give us welcome – or it's the sword for all within!'

Bishop clapped his hand over her mouth. 'Are you crazy?'

Motta shrieked, 'We'll kill the Magickers and burn the Hags, and slide the town into the river!'

There was motion in the passageway. Three old men, bald, feeble, came forward. Their bare feet were blue-veined and bony, they wore only ragged G-strings, the ribs showed like corrugations down their milk-colored bodies.

'Who are you?' quavered the first. 'Go your ways, disturb us not; we have nothing of value.'

'We want to cross the river,' said Glystra. 'Take us across on the high-line and we won't disturb you any further.'

The old men engaged in a wheezing colloquy, watching Glystra suspiciously as they whispered. Then: 'It is too late in the year. You must wait.'

'Wait!' demanded Glystra indignantly. 'Out here?'

The eyes of the old men faltered, fell. A muffled voice came from behind the wall. The spokesman cocked his head, listened, then said in a plaintive voice, 'We are the quiet Magickers, innocent sorcerers and tradespeople. You are men of the Savage Lands, and doubtless you come to loot our valuables.'

'The eight of us? Nonsense. We want to cross the river.'

There were further instructions from within the wall. The old man said in a quavering voice, 'It is impossible.'

Glystra lowered his head ominously. 'Why?'

'It is forbidden.' The old man withdrew. The gate slammed.

Glystra chewed his lip in frustration. 'Why in the devil—'

Corbus pointed to the tower. 'There's a heliograph up there. It's been shooting signals west. My guess is that they've had orders from the Beaujolains.'

Glystra grunted. 'In that case, it's more urgent than ever to get across. Here we're trapped.'

Cloyville advanced to the bank, peered over. 'No boats in sight.'

'Not even material to make a raft,' said Pianza.

'A raft wouldn't help us,' Cloyville pointed out. 'There's no way to propel it, no sails, no sweeps.'

Glystra looked up at the walls of Edelweiss. Corbus grinned. 'Are you thinking the same thoughts I'm thinking?'

'I'm thinking that a piece of that wall – the section running parallel to the river, right there, would make a fine raft.'

'But how would we cross the river?' demanded Cloyville. 'There's a good current out there; we'd be swept all the way down to Marwan Gulf.'

'There's a way staring you in the face.' Glystra made a lasso out of a length of pack-rope. 'I'm going to climb the wall; you cover me from below.'

He tossed the loop around a timber, hauled himself up, cautiously peered over the top, scrambled over.

He looked down. 'There's no one up here. It's a kind of roof. One of you come up – Corbus.'

Corbus joined him. Behind were blank walls and shielded windows, all silent. Glystra looked skeptically at the windows. 'I suppose they're watching, but afraid to show themselves.'

CHAPTER NINE

There was a sound behind them; Ketch hauled himself over the wall. 'Thought I'd see what the place looked like.' He looked over the flat roofs. 'Pretty dingy.'

'Notice the wall,' said Glystra. 'It's lashed along the top with rope, secured along the middle by dowels. If we cut the rope, break the dowels – there, there, there—' he pointed up a vertical crack where the dowels showed through '—and if a man were to shove at each corner, I think we could drop the wall right over into the river.'

'How about those sea-serpents – the griamobots?' Ketch asked.

'They're an unknown quantity. We'll have to take a chance.'

'They might come up under the raft.'

Glystra nodded. 'It's a chance. Would you rather stay here?'

'No.'

Corbus stretched out his long arms. 'Let's get busy.'

Glystra looked at the sky. 'An hour of light. Enough to get us across, if things go well. Ketch, you go back down, take the whole party, zipangotes and all, down to the beach under the bluff. Naturally, keep clear when things start coming. We'll send the wall down; if it lands in the river, make it fast to the shore, so it won't float away.'

Ketch swung himself back down to the ground.

Glystra turned back to the wall. 'We've got to get this over before they figure out what we're up to.' He looked over the side. Twenty feet below was the edge of the bluff, then another fifty feet, almost straight down, to the beach.

'There won't be any toe-hold to the wall. It should go over almost of its own weight.'

'Fifty feet of it ought to be enough,' said Corbus. 'The wood is light stuff.'

'It's not how much we need, it's how much we can get. I don't think they'll stand still when we get to work.'

Along the beach below they saw the string of zipangotes, with Ketch, Pianza, Bishop, Cloyville and the three girls.

Glystra nodded to Corbus, drew his knife, slashed at the fiber rope binding the top of the wall. A sudden outraged screeching came from behind. Apparently from nowhere appeared four old women, white creatures with straggling pink-gray hair, howling and gesticulating. A number of Magicker men, lean, white-skinned, daubed around their shoulders with green paint, appeared behind them.

The coarse rope parted. 'Now,' said Glystra. He aimed his ion-shine, squeezed the button. Once – twice – three times. Three holes down the vertical crack took the place of the pegs. Setting their shoulders to the top of the posts, they pushed out. The wall leaned, creaked, moved no further.

'Below,' panted Glystra. 'There's more lashings halfway down.' He crouched, peered into the dimness under the roof. 'We'll have to shoot blind ... You break your side, I'll do mine.'

Two shafts of pale purple light, crackling power. A tongue of fire licked up the punky side of the timbers, died in a charred smoulder.

The wall sagged, creaked. 'Now,' panted Glystra, 'before they get their army up here ... Don't go over with it!'

The wall lurched, swept grandly out, fell, landed top-down on the beach, stood a second, sagged outward, slapped into the river with a smash of foam.

Glystra caught a glimpse of Ketch scrambling out with a bit of line, then turned to meet the onrush of a line of the Magickers – gaunt men, naked except for the G-string at their loins. They chattered furiously, but danced back like nervous prize-fighters when they met his eye.

The women screeched, bawled, bellowed, wailed, but the men only made tentative movements forward. Glystra threw a glance down to the river. The wall – now a raft – floated free, pulling at the rope Ketch had made fast. Cloyville and Pianza stood on the shore looking up. Glystra yelled down, 'Lead the animals aboard, tie them in the middle.'

Bishop called up something Glystra did not catch; he had been distracted by the scene in the room immediately below the roof where he stood, a room now open to the air where the wall had fallen away. Glystra's throat contracted, his stomach twitched ... Twenty children hung by their hair two feet off the ground. Stone weights were suspended from their feet. Wide-eyed, silent, the children stared from bulging eyes into the new openness, silent except for a hoarse breathing.

'Making tall ones out of short ones,' came Corbus' cool voice.

'Look farther down,' said Glystra in a low voice. 'In the room next lower.'

Corbus threw a glance toward the prancing Magickers, peered down under the roof. 'Can't see too well ... It's confused ... Oh—'

Glystra turned away. The Magickers were stealthily sliding closer. 'Get back! Back!' he said flatly. 'Or I'll cut your legs out from under you.' In a lower voice he said, 'I guess it wouldn't make any difference to you if you've all gone through – that ...'

But his words were not heard, or if heard, not heeded. Goaded by the frenzied calls of the old women, the Magickers, lips drawn back from their long teeth, were prancing forward, a step at a time. One began to scream – a quavering fierce screech – which the entire line picked up. Suddenly they all were brandishing four-foot pikes tipped with black horny barbs.

'Looks like we'll have to kill a few,' said Glystra between tight lips, 'unless they'll scare ...' He aimed the ion-shine at the roof, blasted a hole in the roof at the feet of the nearest Magicker.

The Magicker never shifted his gaze. His eyes had become fixed, saliva bubbled at his mouth.

'They're crazy – hysterics,' muttered Glystra. 'Poor devils, I don't like it ...'

Step by step the Magickers advanced, jerkily, one motion at a time. Behind came the hoarse shrieks of the Hags, and behind – the far glory of Big Planet sunset. Orange, flaring gold.

Too close. Suddenly desperate, Glystra called in a deadly voice, 'Two steps more, I'll kill the lot of you ...'

One step – two steps – pikes raised in gangling arms.

Glystra squeezed the button. Gaunt forms flapped on the roof.

Hags screamed horror, leapt across the roof to the stairs, black warlock silhouettes, with tatters of cloth flying behind.

Glystra went to the edge, looked over. He yelled down, 'Get a line ready, and make it fast to what's coming down next.'

Corbus was looking up the pole. 'We'd better drop the whole works, pole and all. Otherwise the cable will snap past so fast they won't be able to see it. Notice – three of those guy-lines run to the top, three to the buckle-point at the middle. If we cut off the three at the top, the pole should snap off nice and neat.'

Glystra examined the magazine of his ion-shine, squinting in the failing light. 'Got to go easy on the power. There's not too much soup in this one.' He aimed, squeezed the button.

Three gray cables sang, fell twisting like snakes over the roofs of Edelweiss. The pole snapped like a carrot. From the cupola came wild shrieks of fright. 'God!' said Glystra. 'I'd forgotten all about them ...'

The pole crashed almost at their feet; the crying stopped abruptly.

Corbus called over the side, 'Here it comes ... Heads up!'

The tension of the cable dragged the stub across the roof, over the edge of the bluff.

'Lay hold of it!' Glystra yelled. 'Make it fast to the raft!' He started to scramble down the wall, past the strung-up children, past the first floor, where he would not look. Corbus was at his heels. They ran along the bluff, found a place to scramble down to the beach.

'Hurry,' yelled Pianza. 'Our shore line can't take all the strain; it'll go in a minute.'

Glystra and Corbus waded out into the river, scrambled up onto the cool soft timbers. 'Let 'er go.'

The raft drifted free. Behind them the bluff made a black smear across the afterglow, and perched high was Edelweiss, bereft and forlorn with the stump of its broken pole. 'Poor devils,' said Glystra.

The raft floated out on the river, carried downstream by the current but tethered to the opposite shore by the cable of the broken high-line.

'Ah,' sighed Cloyville, dropping his heavy posterior to the logs. 'Peace – quiet – it's wonderful!'

'Wait till you get to the other side before you rejoice,' said Ketch. 'There's still the griamobots.'

Cloyville rose swiftly to his feet. 'I'd forgotten about them. My Lord! Where are they? ... If it's not one thing it's another ...'

Glystra pointed across the glimmering water to the island – a feathery pyramid sharp on the mauve sky to the southeast. 'We won't miss that island far – if at all. And there's not a damn thing we can do about it!'

'Look,' said Bishop in a soft voice. Heads turned as if activated by cams, eyes went to the object inching over the edge of the raft – a flat glisten-ing thing, solid and muscular. It quivered, jerked up on the raft another six inches, becoming round in cross-section.

Another six inches ... Pianza laughed. Bishop moved forward. 'I thought it was the end of a tentacle.'

'It's a big fluke – some sort of leech or sucker.'

'Disgusting thing.' Bishop kicked it back into the river.

The raft gave a sudden lurch, swerved, twisted. Domes of water boiled up around them.

'Something below,' whispered Glystra.

Motta and Wailie began to whimper.

'Quiet!' snapped Glystra. They stifled the sound to a thin whining in their throat.

The motion ceased; the water subsided.

Bishop touched Glystra's arm. 'Look up on the Edelweiss cliff.'

A torch had appeared. It shone, went out, shone, went out – time and time again for varying intervals.

'Code. They're talking to someone. Probably across the river to Swamp Island. Hope no one cuts the cable at that end.'

'Cloyville could swim ashore with a message,' suggested Corbus. Cloyville snorted indignantly, and Corbus chuckled.

From behind the island came the griamobot, its head high, questing. The dark concealed its features; evident only were big segmented eyes. Water swished and gurgled past the black hulk of its body, from which came a visceral growling sound.

The head wove, swayed back and forth, suddenly darted forward.

'It sees us,' muttered Glystra. He drew his ion-shine. 'Perhaps I can damage it or scare it away ... There's not enough power here for real effect if the brute is determined ...'

'Knock the head off,' said Pianza tremulously. 'Then it won't be able to see us.'

Glystra nodded. The violet beam touched the head. It snapped off like a kicked paper bag. But the neck continued to weave, back, forth, back, forth, and the beast never slowed or changed direction.

Glystra aimed at the body, fired. There was a thin ripping sound and a black ragged hole appeared on the dark hide. White objects like viscera seemed to boil up.

Glystra stared, fired again, at the water line. The monster cried out – in a babble of human voices.

The hulk wobbled, wallowed; long white shapes poured out through the hole.

'Duck!' cried Glystra. 'They're throwing at us!'

Thud! A pike plunged quivering into the wood beside him. Another – another – then a sound unlike the others: a shock and a long throaty gasp.

Glystra raised up. '*Ketch!*'

Ketch tore feebly at the shaft in his chest, fell forward on his knees, inched yet further forward, bowed his head, with the shaft grasped between his hands, and in this position he froze to quiet.

'They're boarding us!' yelled Cloyville.

'Stand aside!' cried Pianza. He elbowed past Cloyville. Lavish plumes of orange flame issued from the heat-gun, wreathed the thin shapes who threw up their arms, fell backward into the river.

The griamobot hulk had settled low in the water, drifted down-current, past the raft and away.

Glystra gently laid Ketch on his side. His hands were locked on the shaft.

Glystra stood up, looked across the dusk toward Town Edelweiss; then after a moment, turned back to Ketch. 'Cloyville – help me.'

He laid hold of Ketch's lax ankles. Cloyville bent, took the shoulders, hesitated. 'What are you going to do?'

'Drop him in the river. I'm sorry. We can't afford emotion.'

Cloyville opened his mouth, stuttered, stammered. Glystra waited.

Cloyville finally said in a subdued voice, 'Don't you think we should – well, give him a burial? A decent burial?'

'Where? In the swamp?'

Cloyville bent to the body.

Ketch was gone.

Glystra stood looking up at Town Edelweiss. 'The griamobot was a hoax. A commercial enterprise, to frighten people off the river, to funnel them through the Edelweiss high-line ...'

Night lay heavy over Big Planet, and the shores were dark. There was silence aboard the raft. Little black waves lapped at the timbers. Downstream they floated, borne by the current; cross-stream, pulled by the tether of the one-time high-line.

The spines of Swamp Island towered above them. The chirping and rasping of myriad small insects came to their ears. No lights were visible.

The raft bumped gently into a ledge of mud, halted.

'We'll have to wait for light,' said Glystra. 'Let's try to get some sleep ...'

But all sat staring across the black water, feeling the loss of dour Ketch as a tongue feels the gap left by a drawn tooth.

The River Oust moved quietly past in the dark, and somewhere now to the south was Ketch.

Dawn came to the water, seeping in from nowhere, moth-colored, the softest luminosity conceivable. First the forest was black and the water black and the sky only less black, then the sky was charged with dimness and the river shone like oil; and then the mother-of-pearl light spread from sky to the air to the river, where it reflected back in odd-shaped leaden plats and planes.

There was more air and water and sky than a man's awareness could encompass. The river's far shore was a low black mark and Town Edelweiss a nubbin on the bluff. The air was still, held in an immense cool quiet, smelling of mud and water and a smoke, spice, early-morning scent, which in all the universe was individual to the one spot here on the shore of the River Oust on Big Planet.

To the east the sky flared orange, yellow, behind the black spines of the Swamp Island forest. They were two hundred feet tall, crowding till in some instances the trunks touched.

Motta screamed, a mindless piping. Glystra swung around; his heart expanded, his blood caked. A tremendous black body blotted out the river; overhead swung a barrel-size head, split by a bony mouth. The head swung down, the eyes stared, the neck looped, the head plunged into the water, returned laden with sodden yellow fiber. It gulped, belched, sank out of sight into the river.

Life returned to the raft. Hysterical women ...

Calmness was restored. Glystra released a great pent sigh. 'Evidently the griamobots exist.'

'I will vouch for it at any time,' declared Cloyville.

'But – they're vegetarians. The Magickers arranged that they should be thought carnivorous, and that was all that was necessary to confine river traffic to the high-line ... Well, let's get moving.'

The raft floated flat and vacant on the river. The zipangotes stood loaded and ready on the spongy black humus, raising their feet up and down, swinging their long necks close to the ground.

Glystra walked a little way into the swamp, testing the footing. The round boles, ash-gray overlaid with green luster, prevented a clear vision of more than a hundred feet, but so far as Glystra could see, the ground was uniformly black peat, patched with shallow water. If sight was occluded horizontally, vertically it was wide open; indeed, the upward lines of the trees impelled the eyes to lift along the multitudinous perspectives, up to the little blot of sky far above. Walking gingerly across the black bog, Glystra felt as if he were two hundred feet under water, an illusion heightened by the flying creatures, which moved along the vertical aisles with the ease of fish. Glystra saw two varieties: a long electric-green tape with filmy green wings along its body, rippling through the air like an eel, and little puffs of foam drifting with no apparent organs of locomotion.

Glystra returned to the river. The zipangotes had been arranged in line, each long dog-like head under the hindquarters of the beast ahead. 'Let's go,' said Glystra.

The river fell behind, was quickly lost to sight. The caravan wound like a snake in tall grass – now left, now right, twisting, side-stepping, detouring the puddles of water.

The sun rose, and they rode through shafts and bars of heavy light, and zebra striping lay along the tall spines.

CHAPTER TEN

About noon, there was a sudden opening before them – a lake. Small waves rippled and glinted at their feet; clouds reflected between areas of deep blue. In the distance floated a few low boats with wide double-lateen booms and baggy orange sails; and beyond was Swamp City. It sat up in the air, on top of the forest, like a mirage; somehow it reminded Glystra of an old-world fishing village.

For several moments the party stood staring at the city on stilts ... A shrill squawking startled them: a blue and yellow flying thing, beating slug-gishly through the air.

'For a moment,' said Cloyville, 'I thought the Magickers were upon us.'

Back to the forest – more winding, squeezing, doubling back, occasion-ally a straight run of twenty or thirty feet.

The sun moved across the sky; at last, in the middle afternoon, Glystra saw overhead the walls and houses of the city. Five minutes later the caravan moved into the shadow of the deck.

'A moment, please,' said an unhurried voice. A platoon of warriors stood beside them, stocky men in mulberry coats.

The officer approached Glystra. 'Your business, if you please?'

'No business. We're travelers.'

'Travelers?' The officer glanced at the zipangotes. 'From where?'

'From Jubilith, north of Beaujolais.'

'How did you get those beasts across the river? Certainly not on the high-line; our agent would have reported you.'

'We ferried them over on a raft. Last night.'

The officer fingered his mustache. 'Did not the griamobots—'

Glystra smiled. 'The Magickers have been hoaxing you. The griamobots are vegetarians, harmless. The only dangerous griamobot was one the Mag-ickers built and filled with soldiers.'

The officer swore under his breath. 'Lord Wittelhatch will wish to hear this. Magicker regulations and tariffs have long irked him, especially since he strung up the cable to begin with.'

'The cable interests me,' said Glystra. 'Is it metal?'

'Oh no, by no means.' The officer laughed affably – a handsome young man with an expressive face and a jaunty straw-colored mustache. 'Come, I'll lead you to where your caravan may rest, and along the way you'll see the working of our industry. We are rope-makers to the world; nowhere is cable equal to ours.'

Glystra hesitated. 'Our wish was to continue as far along the way as possible before nightfall. Perhaps you will direct us—'

'A wealthy man in a hurry,' said the officer, thoughtfully eying the three girls, 'would ride the monoline. It would cost much metal, much metal … Best confer with Wittelhatch.'

'Very well.' Glystra motioned to the column; they followed the officer, and a moment later came upon a scene of industry.

A series of rope-walks occupied an area five hundred feet square, which had been partially cleared, leaving only enough spines to support the weight of the city above. Each rope-walk consisted of a series of frames. In the process of formation the rope passed through a hole in the frame and immediately afterward passed through a wheel, which rotated around the rope as an axis. Fixed at regular intervals on the wheel were five fat slugs, and from their positors white strands ran to the rope. As the rope pulled through the frame, the wheel rotated and five new strands were added to the rope.

Glystra sighted up the rope-walk. Each frame had its wheel, and each wheel carried five slugs secreting thread for the rope. 'Very clever,' said Glystra. 'Very clever indeed.'

'Our rope is unexcelled,' said the officer, with a proud twist for his mustache. 'Flexible, weatherproof, strong. We furnish rope for the monolines of Felissima, Bogover, Thelma, also the long line to Grosgarth in Beaujolais and the line out to Myrtlesee Fountain.'

'Hm … And the monolines are fast transportation?'

The officer inspected him smilingly. 'I assure you.'

'Just what is a monoline?'

The officer laughed. 'Now you joke with me. Come, I will take you to Wittelhatch, and he will doubtless feast you at his evening wassail. I understand an excellent conger bakes in his oven this day.'

'But our packs, our luggage! And the zipangotes, they have not eaten yet, there is nothing in this swamp for them to eat!'

The officer signaled; four men stepped forward. 'Service and groom the beasts, feed them well, pluck their sores, wash and bind their feet, set them out each a dram of dympel.' He said to Glystra, 'Your baggage will be secure,

Swamp Island knows no thieves. Merchants and industers we be, but robbers no, it is against our rotes.'

Wittelhatch was a fat man with a round red face, half-petulant, half-jocular, with crafty heavy-lidded eyes. He wore a white blouse embroidered with red and yellow frogs, a red brocade surcingle, tight blue trousers, black boots. In each ear hung a gold ring and each finger was heavy with assorted metals. He sat in a ceremonial chair, apparently having just lowered himself into place, for he was yet wrestling with the folds of his garments.

The officer bowed gracefully, indicated Glystra with a debonair motion. 'A traveler from the west, Lord.'

'From the west?' Wittelhatch, narrow-eyed, rubbed one of his sub-chins. 'I understand that the high-line across the river has been cut. It will be necessary to kite it back into place. How then did you cross?'

Glystra explained the Magicker hoax. Wittelhatch became shrill and angry. 'The long white muckers – and all the business I've sent them out of pity! Hey, but it discourages an honest community to be set so close to rascals!'

Glystra said with restrained impatience, 'Our wish is to proceed on our way. Your officer suggested that we use the monoline.'

Wittelhatch immediately became business-like. 'How many are in your party?'

'Eight, together with our baggage.'

Wittelhatch turned to the officer. 'What do you suggest, Clodleberg? Five singles and a pack?'

The officer squinted thoughtfully. 'Their baggage is considerable. Better might be two packs and two singles. And since they are unused to the trolleys, a guide.'

'Where is your destination?' Wittelhatch inquired.

'As far east as possible.'

'That's Myrtlesee ... Well now.' Wittelhatch calculated. 'I care little to let my trolleys journey to such vast extents; you must pay substantially. If you buy the trolleys outright – ninety ounces of good iron. If you rent – sixty ounces, plus the guide's pay and a reasonable return fee – another ten ounces.'

Glystra haggled politely, and reduced the rental to fifty ounces plus the zipangotes, and Wittelhatch would pay the guide. 'Perhaps, Clodleberg, you would care to lead the party?' Wittelhatch inquired of the young officer.

Clodleberg twisted his blond mustache. 'Delighted.'

'Good,' said Glystra. 'We'll leave at once.'

Wittelhatch rang a hand-bell. A porter appeared. 'Carry the baggage of these people to the take-off deck.'

Wind blew in sails and trolley wheels whispered down the monoline – a half-inch strand of white Swamp Island cable. From the dome at Swamp City the line led from spine to spine across three miles of swamp to a rocky headland, crossed over the rotten basalt with only six feet to spare, swung in a wide curve to the southeast. At fifty-foot intervals L-brackets mounted to poles supported the line, so designed that the trolleys slid across with only a tremor and slight thud of contact.

Clodleberg rode the first trolley, Glystra followed, then came a pair of three-wheel freight-carriers loaded with packs – food, spare clothing, the metal which represented their wealth, Bishop's vitamins, Cloyville's camping gear, odds and ends from the Beaujolain packs. The first of the freight-carriers was manned by Corbus, Motta and Wailie; the second by Nancy, Pianza and Bishop. Cloyville in a one-man trolley brought up the rear.

As he examined the vehicle he rode in, Glystra well understood Wittel-hatch's reluctance to part with it, even temporarily. The wood was shaped and fitted with painstaking precision, and performed as well as any metal machine from the shops of Earth.

The big wheel was laminated from ten separate strips, glued, grooved and polished. Spokes of hardened withe supported the central hub, whose bearings were wrought from a greasy black hardwood. The seat support was a natural tree-crook, connecting to a slatted floor below. Propulsion was achieved by sails, set to a lateen boom. The halyards, outhauls and sheets led to a cleat-board in front of the seat. Within reach was a double hand-crank, offset like the pedals of a bicycle; turning the crank would drive the trolley up any slight slope at the end of a long suspension which momentum and the pressure of the sails were unable to negotiate.

At noon the land changed. Hills heaved up and it became necessary to make portages, which involved carrying the trolleys and all the baggage up to a higher level of line.

At the end of the day they slept in a vacant cottage near one of the portages and the next morning set off through the mountains – the Wicksill Range, according to Clodleberg. The line swooped far across valleys, from ridge to ridge, with the ground sometimes two thousand feet below. The trolleys, starting out across such a valley, fell into the sag of the cable with a stomach-lifting swoop, falling almost free; then out in the middle the speed would slacken and the trolley would coast on momentum up toward the opposite ridge and presently slow almost to a stop. Then the sail would be trimmed to its fullest efficiency and the drive-crank would be put into use, and gradually the trolley would climb up to the high point.

On the evening of the third day Clodleberg said, 'Tomorrow at this time we should be in Kirstendale, and you must be surprised by nothing you see.'

Glystra pressed for further information, but Clodleberg was disposed to be jocular. 'No, no. You will see for yourself. Kirstendale is a city of great fascination. Possibly you may abandon your fantastic journey and settle in Kirstendale.'

'Are the people aggressive, unfriendly?'

'Not in the slightest.'

'Who rules them? What is their government?'

Clodleberg raised his eyebrows thoughtfully. 'Now that you mention it, I have never heard of a ruler in Kirstendale. Indeed, they rule themselves, if their life could be said to be governed by rule.'

Glystra changed the subject. 'How many days from Kirstendale to Myrtlesee Fountain?'

'I've never made the trip,' said Clodleberg. 'It is not entirely pleasant. At certain seasons the Rebbirs come down from the Eyrie to molest the monoline travelers, although the Dongmen of Myrtlesee are Rebbir stock and try to maintain an open avenue of communication.'

'What lies past Myrtlesee Fountain?'

Clodleberg made a gesture of disgust. 'The desert. The land of fire-eating dervishes; scavengers, blood-suckers, so I'm told.'

'And after?'

'Then the Palo Malo Se Mountains and the Blarengorran Lake. From the lake the Monchevior River runs east, and you might float a considerable distance on one of the river boats – how far I am uncertain, because it flows into the obscure and unknown.'

Glystra heaved a thoughtful sigh. By the time the Monchevior River floated them out of Clodleberg's ken, there would still be thirty-nine thousand miles to Earth Enclave.

During the night a rainstorm broke upon the mountain, and there was no escape from the roaring wind. The travelers straggled up under the lee of a boulder and huddled under their blankets while the Big Planet gale drove north.

Wet and cold they saw a bleared gray dawn come and for a time the rain stopped, though clouds fleeted past on the wind almost within hand's-reach overhead. Climbing upon their trolleys they set handkerchiefs of sail and scudded along the monoline with wheels whirring.

For two hours the line led along the ridge, and the wind pressed up and over the mountain like a water-spill. The vegetation, low shrubs with tattered blue-green streamers of leaves, whipped and flapped below. To the left was a dark valley full of gray mist, to the right the clouds hid the panorama, but when they broke and parted, a pleasant broken country could be seen – hills, forests, small lakes, and several times they glimpsed great stone castles.

Clodleberg looked back at Glystra, swept his hand over the land to the right. 'The Galatudanian Valley, with the Hibernian March below. A land of dukes and knights and barons, stealing each other's daughters and robbing one another ... Dangerous country to walk afoot.'

The wind increased, buffeted the travelers until tears flew from their eyes, and a fine driven spume stung their cheeks. Heeling far to the side, the trolleys skimmed southeast at sixty miles an hour, and they might have traveled faster had not Clodleberg constantly luffed wind from his sails.

For an hour they wheeled along the line, swaying and jerking, and then Clodleberg rose in his seat, signaled to furl sail.

The trolleys coasted to a platform from which a line led at a right angle to their course, down into the valley. The far anchor was invisible; all that could be seen was the gradually diminishing swoop of the white cable.

Nancy peered down the line, drew back with a shiver.

Clodleberg grinned. 'This is the easy direction. Coming back, a person must make a two-day portage from the valley floor.'

'Do we slide down – out there?' asked Nancy in a hushed voice.

Clodleberg nodded, enjoying the trepidation which the prospect of the drop aroused in his charges.

'We'll kill ourselves going so fast; it's so – steep!'

'The wind presses on you, brakes your fall. There's nothing to it. Follow me ...'

He turned his trolley down the slanting line, and in an instant was a far dwindling shape vibrating down the wind.

Glystra stirred himself. 'I guess I'm next ...'

It was like stepping out into nothing, like diving head-first over a cliff ... The first mile was almost free fall. The wind buffeted, cloud-wisps whipped past, the land below was an indeterminate blur.

Overhead the wheel sang into high pitch, though it carried almost no weight. The white line stretched out ahead, always curving slightly up, away, out of vision.

Glystra became aware that the whirr of the wheel was decreasing in pitch; the line was flattening out, the ground below was rising to meet him.

Across a green and yellow forest he rolled and he glimpsed below a settlement of log cabins, with a dozen children in white smocks staring up ... Then they were gone and the forest was dark and deep below. Flying insects darted up past his eyes, and then ahead he saw a platform hung in the top of a giant tree, and here waited Clodleberg.

Glystra stiffly climbed to the platform. Clodleberg was watching him with a crafty smile. 'How did you like the swoop?'

'I'd like to move at that speed for three weeks. We'd be at the Enclave.'

The line began to quiver and sing. Looking back up, Glystra saw the freight-carrier with Corbus, Motta and Wailie.

'We might as well start off,' said Clodleberg. 'Otherwise the platform will be overcrowded.' He tested the wind, shook his head. 'Poor, a poor reach. We'll have to trim our sails close-by; the wind blows almost down the line. However fair winds cannot be ours forever – and I believe the line veers presently to the east, and we'll make better time.'

They set off, close-hauled, sailing so near into the eye of the wind that the leach of the sail flapped constantly. The line ran from tree-top to tree-top, and sometimes black–green foliage brushed Glystra's feet ... Clodleberg had doused his sail, was beckoning him urgently.

'What's the trouble?'

Silence, signaled Clodleberg. He pointed ahead. Glystra trundled his trolley forward, up against Clodleberg's. 'What's wrong?'

Clodleberg was fixedly watching something on the ground, through a gap in the foliage. 'This is a dangerous part of the line ... Bands of soldiers, starving forest people, bandits ... Sometimes they wait till a trolley is over a high space, then cut the line, killing the traveler ...'

Glystra saw movement through the leaves, a shifting of white and gray. Clodleberg climbed from the trolley into the branches of the tree, let himself cautiously down a few feet. Glystra watched him quietly. Behind came the quiver of the next trolley. Glystra signaled it to a halt.

Clodleberg was motioning to him. Glystra left his trolley, climbed to the crotch where Clodleberg stood. Through a gap in the leaves he could see the floor of the forest. Behind a low orange bush crouched three boys about ten years old. Bows and arrows ready, they watched the line like cats at a mousehole.

'Here's where they get their early training,' whispered Clodleberg. 'When they grow larger they go to raiding the towns of the March and all the Galatudanian Valley.' He quietly nocked a quarrel into his crossbow.

'What are you going to do?' asked Glystra.

'Kill the biggest ... I'll be saving the lives of many innocent people.'

Glystra struck up his arm; the bolt shattered a branch over the head of the would-be assassins. Glystra saw their white faces, big dark eyes, open frightened mouths; then they were off, scurrying like rabbits.

'Why did you do that?' asked Clodleberg heatedly. 'Those same skulkers may murder me on my way back to Swamp City.'

Glystra could find no words at first. Then he muttered, 'Sorry ... I suppose you're right. But if this were Earth, or any of the System planets, they'd be at their schooling.'

A shaft of pure brilliance plunged down through the sky – Big Planet sunlight. The rain-washed colors of the forest shone with a glowing clarity never seen on Earth: black-greens, reds, yellows, ochers, buffs, the lime-green of low hangworts, the russet of bundle-bush. The wind blew high, blew low, the clouds flew back across the mountains; they sailed in a fresh sunny breeze.

The monoline dropped down out of the forest, stretched across a river valley, over a swift river which Clodleberg named the Thelma. They made a fifty-foot portage up the opposite bank, and set off once more across a land of peaceful farms and stone houses, undistinguished except for the fact that each house carried on its gable an intricate tangle of brambles and spiny leaves.

Glystra called to Clodleberg. 'What on Earth are those bristling thorn-patches?'

'Those are the ghost-catchers,' said Clodleberg easily. 'This section of country abounds with ghosts; there's a ghost for every house, sometimes more; and since they always give a quick jump which takes them to the roof where they can walk back and forth, the traps discourage them sadly ... The very home of ghosts is this Mankelly Parish, and witches too ...'

Glystra thought that no matter how ordinary and uneventful a Big Planet landscape might appear, it was still – Big Planet.

The monoline paralleled a rutted earthen road, and three times the caravan, swinging along briskly with the breeze on the beam, passed big red farm-wains with six-foot wooden wheels, squeaking and groaning like scalded pigs. They were loaded with red melon-bulbs, bundles of orange vine, baskets of green okra. The lads who walked barefoot alongside goading the long-necked zipangotes wore tall conical hats with veils of white cloth about their faces.

'To fool the ghosts?' Glystra asked Clodleberg.

'To fool the ghosts.'

Afternoon wore on; the country became verdant and the ground supported every kind of pleasant growth. The farming region fell behind; they seemed to be traversing a great parkland.

Clodleberg pointed ahead. 'See there, that white aquifer? There is your first glimpse of Kirstendale, the finest city of the Galatudanian Valley ...'

CHAPTER ELEVEN

For several minutes little enough of Kirstendale could be seen: splashes of white through the trees, a pair of stone causeways. The trolleys sailed across a pasture of red–green grass, the trees parted, and there was the city, rising from a grassy plain with blue mountains in the background.

It was the largest and most elaborate settlement the Earthmen had seen on Big Planet, but it was never a city which might have existed on Earth. It reminded Glystra of the cloud-borne castles in fairy-story illustrations.

The line took a sudden turn and they came upon a scene of gay activity, carnival color.

A game was in progress. On the field were fifty men and women in garments of remarkable complexity and elegance: silks, satins, velvets, coarse tasselled weaves – tucked, flared, gored, bedecked, beribboned, covered with tinsel and lace. The field was laid off into squares by lines of colored grasses, cropped and tended with the nicest precision, and each player occupied a single square. Sheets of silk hung at each side from a row of moored balloons. Each sheet glowed a different color: peach–tan, orange–russet, blue, sea-green, rippling, shining in the breeze. A myriad of small colored balls were in use, balls which half-floated, almost as light as air.

The players caught balls in a manner which seemed to depend on the color of the ball, the color of the player's head-ribbon and the square where the player stood. Balls filled the air, little sunlit jewels, and sometimes a player would catch three balls at once and toss them away with great dexterity. When a ball landed in one of the silken curtains, a score was counted to the great jubilation of certain players and spectators who cried, 'Ohé, ohé, ohé!'

Several hundred men and women watched the game from the sidelines. They were dressed in the same extravagant fashion, and in addition wore headgear of fantastic complexity, confections most ingeniously designed and assembled. One young man displayed a shell like an overturned boat, striped in bright green and scarlet. Balls of fluorescent blue clung here and there to the fabric, and tapes of golden taupe fluttered below. A great puff of bright purple veil rose from the top, and imbedded in this veil were globes of red, green, blue, yellow, shining like Christmas tree ornaments ... A young woman – very beautiful, Glystra thought, supple as a kitten, with sleek yellow hair and long yellow eyes – wore a cloche-helmet of soft leather from which rose a tall antenna, and this antenna radiated prongs tipped with spangles of live fire – vermilion, scintillant green, molten gold ... Another – another – another: baroque, unique, incredible ...

The monoline circled the field. The players and spectators glanced up casually, returned to their game with interest for nothing but the multiple flight of the colored balls.

Glystra noticed an attendant rolling a cart arrayed with pink and white pastries. 'Pianza – look what he's wearing ...'

Pianza snorted in surprise and amusement. 'It's a tuxedo. Dinner jacket. Black tie. Stripe down the trousers, patent leather shoes. Wonderful.'

Out on the field a ball fell into the billowing russet–gold curtain, rolled softly to the ground. There was joyous applause from the spectators.

Cloyville yelled up from the rear, 'Wonder how they'd take to football?'

Glystra slacked his sails, his trolley coasted quietly along the line. The freight-flat behind, with Pianza and Bishop, overtook him. Glystra spoke over his shoulder, 'Bishop, what does the Almanac say about Kirstendale? Anything interesting?'

Bishop came up to stand at the forward end of the flat, under the lead wheel. He looked in frowning reflection toward the looping walls. 'Seems as if there's a mystery of sorts – "the Kirstendale Paradox", that's what they called it. It starts to come back to me. A syndicate of millionaires established the town to beat System taxes. A whole colony came out with their servants – twenty or thirty families. Apparently – well.' He waved his hand. 'There's the result.'

The monoline veered once more, the breeze fell astern. Sails spread out like butterfly wings, the caravan plunged through an arch into the city, coasted up to a landing.

Three quiet men in dark livery came forward, wordlessly removed the packs from the trolleys, put them into carts with high spoked wheels. Glystra started to remonstrate, but catching Clodleberg's eye, desisted. 'What's happening?'

'They assume that you are wealthy,' said Clodleberg, 'from the trolleys and the women.'

'Humph,' grunted Glystra. 'Am I supposed to tip them?'

'Do what?'

'Give them money.'

Clodleberg blinked, still perplexed.

'Money. Metal.'

'Ah, metal!' Clodleberg twisted his natty mustache. 'That is as you wish.'

The head porter approached, a tall solemn-faced man with carefully shaved cheeks, long sideburns terminating in a little puff of whiskers: a man comporting himself with immense dignity.

Glystra handed him three small iron washers. 'For you and your men.'

'Thank you, sir ... And where will you have your luggage sent?'

Glystra shrugged. 'What are the choices?'

'Well, there's the Grand Savoyard and the Metropole and the Ritz-Carlton – all excellent, all equally expensive.'

'How expensive?'

The head porter blinked, raised his black eyebrows the faintest trifle. 'Perhaps an ounce a week ... The Traveler's Inn and the Fairmont are likewise expensive, but something quieter ...'

'What is a good inn of moderate rates?'

The head porter clicked his heels. 'I recommend the Hunt Club. This way, sir, to the carriage.'

He led them to a landau mounted on four elliptical springs of laminated golden wood. There were no zipangotes hitched to the front; in fact the carriage appeared innocent of motive power.

The head porter swung open the door with a flourish. Cloyville, in the lead, hesitated, looked quizzically back over his shoulder. 'A joke? After we get in, do you walk away and leave us sitting here?'

'No indeed, sir, by no means.'

Cloyville gingerly climbed up the two steps, lowered himself into the soft seat. The rest of the party followed.

The head porter closed the door with exquisite finesse, signaled. Four men in tight black uniforms stepped forward; each clipped a strap to the front of the carriage, tossed it over his shoulder, and the carriage was underway. Wooden planking rumbled below the wheels, the hangar-like buildings were behind, they drove over granite flags through the heart of the city.

Kirstendale had been laid out with an eye to striking vistas. It was a city clean as new paper, bright with polished stone and glass, gay with flowers. Towers rose everywhere, each circled by a staircase which spiraled up to meet the onion-shaped bulb of the dwelling.

They approached a cylindrical building in the middle of the city, large as a gas-storage tank. A lush growth of blue–green vine with maroon trumpet-flowers, rows of large windows gave a sense of lightness and elegance to an otherwise heavy building.

The carriage passed under a marquee roofed with stained glass, and the Big Planet sunlight, passing through, puddled the flags with gorgeous color. A sign on the marquee read, 'Hotel Metropole'.

'Hm,' said Cloyville. 'Looks like a nice place … After the – well, inconvenience of the journey, I could stand a week or two in the lap of luxury.'

But the carriage continued around the building, presently passed another marquee. This was draped in rich saffron satin, fringed with royal red tassels. A sign read 'Grand Savoyard'.

Next they passed a portico of somewhat classical dignity: columns, Ionic capitals and entablature. Chiseled letters read 'Ritz-Carlton', and again Cloyville looked wistfully over his shoulder as the carriage swept by. 'We'll probably end up in a flop-house on the skid-road.'

They passed a vaguely Oriental entrance: carved dark wood, a slab of the same wood supporting tall green urns. The sign read, 'The Traveler's Inn'.

The carriage continued another hundred feet and stopped under an awning of green, red and white striped canvas. A bold black and white sign announced 'The Hunt Club'.

A doorman stepped forward, helped them to the pavement, then ran ahead, opened the door.

The party of travelers passed through a short corridor pasted with green baize, decorated with black and white landscapes, entered a large central lobby.

Directly opposite, across the lobby, a corridor led outside. Through the door shone the many-colored radiance of stained glass in the sunlight.

Glystra looked around the walls. At intervals other corridors led off like spokes from a hub, all evidently leading to the outside.

Glystra stopped short. Grinning he turned to Pianza. 'The Metropole, the Grand Savoyard, the Ritz-Carlton, the Traveler's Inn, the Hunt Club – they're all the same.'

Clodleberg made an urgent motion. 'Quiet. This is very real to the Kirsters. You will offend them.'

'But—'

Clodleberg said hurriedly, 'I should have informed you; the entrance you chose places you on the social scale. The accommodations are identical, but it is considered smarter and more fashionable to enter through the Metropole.'

Glystra nodded. 'I understand completely. We'll be careful.'

The doorman led them across the lobby to a circular desk with a polished wood counter. Rods wound with spirals of colored cloth rising from the edge of the counter supported a parasol-shaped top. A central pier continued up three feet, then extended in a ten-foot pole of pitted black wood. Around the pole, veering in and out, flew ten thousand fireflies – swooping, circling, settling on the pitted wood of the pole, flying out again in a swift current, ten, twenty, fifty feet from the pole.

The doorman took them to that section of the desk marked off by the Hunt Club colors. Glystra turned around, counted heads, like the father of a troublesome family. Cloyville, ruddy and flushed, was talking to a tired Pianza; Corbus and Bishop stood with Wailie and Motta, the girls excited, vastly impressed; Nancy stood pale and rather tense by his right elbow, Clodleberg at his left. Nine in all.

'Excuse me, sir,' said the desk clerk. 'Are you Mr. Claude Glystra, of Earth?'

Glystra swung around in surprise. 'Why do you ask?'

'Sir Walden Marchion extends his compliments, and begs that you and your party honor him by residing at his villa the period of your stay. He has sent his carriage for your use, if you will so favor him.'

Glystra turned to Clodleberg, spoke in a cold voice. 'How did this Sir Walden Marchion know of our arrival?'

Clodleberg flushed, preened his mustaches furiously.

'Who's been talking?'

Clodleberg said with immense dignity, 'The head porter at the landing inquired your identity ... I saw no reason to conceal it. You had issued no orders to that effect.'

Glystra turned away. If any harm was to result from the indiscretion, the harm was by now done; no benefit would come of dressing down Clodleberg, for whom, in general, he felt a high regard. 'News certainly travels fast in Kirstendale … What is your opinion in regard to the invitation?'

Clodleberg turned to the desk clerk. 'Exactly who is Sir Walden Marchion?'

'One of the wealthiest and most influential men in Kirstendale. A very distinguished gentleman.'

Clodleberg fondled his mustache. 'Unusual, but gratifying …' He surveyed Glystra with a new appraisal. 'I see no reason to decline.'

Glystra said to the desk clerk, 'We'll accept the invitation.'

The desk clerk nodded. 'I'm sure that you'll find your visit pleasant. Sir Walden has served meat at his table on several occasions … The carriage is awaiting. Ah, Manville, if you will …' He signaled to the clerk at the Grand Savoyard sector of the desk. This clerk nodded to a young man in a rich black livery with yellow piping down the sides, who clicked his heels, bowed, stalked out the Grand Savoyard entrance and a moment later reappeared in the Hunt Club corridor. He strode up to Glystra, clicked his heels, bowed.

'Sir Walden's carriage, sir.'

'Thank you.'

Careful not to commit the *faux pas* of leaving by the Traveler's Inn entrance, the party returned outside, climbed into a long low brougham. The doorman closed the door, the carriage driver said, 'Your luggage will be conveyed to Sir Walden's.'

'Such courtesy,' murmured Pianza. 'Such unbelievable punctilio!'

Cloyville sank back in the deep cushioned seats with a sigh. 'I'm afraid that I like it. Guess I'm soft, or possibly an anachronism. I'll have to admit that all this feudalism finds a customer in me.'

'I wonder,' said Glystra, watching out the window, 'what the desk clerk meant when he said that Sir Walden often served meat.'

Clodleberg blew out his cheeks. 'Easily explained. By a peculiar freak the Galatudanian Valley supports no animal life other than zipangotes, whose flesh is so rank as to be inedible. A parasitic insect deadly to creatures with fur, scales or floss is responsible. The zipangote, with his naked hide, is not troubled. The Kirsters therefore subsist on vegetable food, fruits, yeast, fungus, an occasional water-creature, certain varieties of insect, and on rare occasions, meat, imported from Coelanvilli.'

The carriage, drawn by five runners in Sir Walden's black livery, trundled across the pavement. They passed a row of shops. The first displayed delicate creations of gauze and puff, the second sold flagons carved of green chert and mottled blue soapstone. The next booth offered pompoms of twirled green and rose satin, the next was a jewellery, with trays full of glinting lights, next a display of glassware – goblets exceedingly tall and slender, with tiny cups and long fine stems, and the window glittered and glistened in vertical lines and diamond-colored striations.

'I'm rather interested in the economy,' said Cloyville. 'Somewhere these goods are fabricated. Where? By whom? Slaves? It takes lots of production to support this kind of a set-up. Expensive leisure classes – like that.' He pointed to a plaza where men and women in extravagant clothes sat listening to seven young girls playing flutes and singing in clear sweet voices.

Glystra scratched his head. 'I don't see how they do it. They certainly can't be supplied from Earth ...'

'Evidently this is their secret,' said Pianza. 'The Kirstendale Paradox.'

Cloyville said with an air of finality, 'Whatever it is, it seems to suit everybody; everybody seems happy.'

'Everybody in sight,' said Corbus.

Wailie and Motta had been chattering – bright-eyed, excited. Glystra watched them a moment, wondering what was going on in their brains ... They had filled out, their cheeks were no longer hollow, their hair was glossy and well-tended, they were pretty girls. Corbus and Bishop were modestly proud of them. Corbus patted Motta's head. 'See anything you'd like?'

'Oh, yes! Jewels and metal and lovely cloth, and ribbons and spangles and those lovely sandals ...'

Corbus winked at Bishop. 'Clothes, clothes, clothes.'

'*Le plus de la différence, le plus de la même chose,*' said Bishop.

The carriage turned among the towers – graceful spires swooping up to the onion-shaped dwellings.

The carriage halted by a pale green column; a servant swung wide the door. 'The castle of Sir Walden Marchion ...'

CHAPTER TWELVE

The party alighted, the carriage swept off.

'This way if you please ...'

They climbed the stairs, spiraling up to the beetling shape of Sir Walden's castle. Buttress vanes sprang out from the central column, elbowing up and out to the outer flange.

Corbus felt one of the vanes – a parchment-tan material two inches thick. 'Wood ... Looks like it grows right out of the trunk.' He cocked his head up to where the floor swelled out in a smooth curve. 'These things grew here! They're big plants!'

The servant looked back, his black brows in a straight disapproving line. 'This is the castle of Sir Walden, his manse ...'

Corbus winked at Glystra. 'Guess I was wrong; it's not a big acorn after all.'

'Certainly not,' said the servant.

The stairway made one last swoop far out from the central column, apparently supported by its own structural strength; then the party stood on a wide plat, swept by the cool Big Planet breezes.

The servant flung open the door, stood aside. Sir Walden's guests entered the sky-castle.

They stood in a large room, light and airy, decorated with an unobtrusive intricacy. The floor was not level, but flared like a trumpet bell. A pool of water dyed bright blue filled the depression in the center. Insects with white gauzy wings and feelers scuttled and ran back and forth across the surface, trailing V-ripples which sparkled momentarily green. The floor surrounding the pool was covered by a carpet woven from dark- and light-green floss; the walls were bright blue, except where a frieze in sharp black and white, of blank-faced men with owl-insect eyes, occupied one wall.

'Be at your ease,' said the servant. 'Sir Walden is on his way to welcome you; in the meanwhile dispose yourselves as you will. Refreshing ichors are at your disposal, in three vintages: maychee, worm, vervaine; pray be so good as to enjoy them.'

He bowed, withdrew. The travelers were alone.

Glystra sighed heavily. 'Looks like a nice place ... Doesn't seem to be a jail ...'

Five minutes passed before Sir Walden appeared – a tall man, sober-faced, rather gravely beautiful. He apologized for not being on hand to greet them, professing himself delayed beyond remedy elsewhere.

Glystra, when he found opportunity, muttered aside to Pianza, 'Where have we seen him before? Or have we?'

Pianza shook his head. 'Nowhere to my knowledge ...'

Two lads of fourteen and sixteen wearing pink, yellow and green, with curl-toed sandals of remarkable design, entered the room. They bowed. 'At your service, friends from Mother Earth.'

'My sons,' said Sir Walden, 'Thane and Halmon.'

Glystra said, 'We are delighted to enjoy the hospitality of your house, Sir Walden, but – bluntly – may I inquire why it has been extended to us, complete strangers that we are?'

Sir Walden made an elegant gesture. 'Please ... We will chat far and long – but now, you are weary and travel-worn. So you shall be refreshed.' He clapped his hands. 'Servants!'

A dozen men and women appeared. 'Baths for our guests, scented with—'

he kneaded his chin with his hand, as if the matter required the utmost nicety of judgment; he arrived at a decision '—with Nigali No. 29, that will be most suitable, and let there be new garments for their comfort.'

Cloyville sighed. 'A bath ... Hot water ...'

'Thank you,' said Glystra shortly. Sir Walden's hospitality was still a mystery.

A servant stood before him, bowed. 'This way, sir.'

He was conveyed to a pleasant chamber high above the city. An expressionless young man in tight black livery took his clothes. 'Your bath is through this door, Lord Glystra.'

Glystra stepped into a small room with walls of seamless mother-of-pearl. Warm water rose up around his knees, his waist, his chest. Foam, bubbles surged up under his feet, rushed up past his tingling body, burst into his face with a pleasant sharp fragrance. Glystra sighed, relaxed, floated.

The fragrance of the foam shifted, changed, always new, now tart, now sweet. Bubbles kneaded his skin, flushed it free of grime and perspiration, toned, stimulated, and fatigue was gone, leaving behind a pleasant soft weariness.

The water level dropped swiftly, warm air gushed around him. He pushed open the door.

The man had disappeared. A girl carrying a towel on two outstretched arms stood before him smiling. She wore a short black skirt, no more. Her body was tan and lovely, her hair arranged in a stylized loose swirl.

'I am your room-servant. However, if you find me unpleasant or unsuitable, I will go.'

She seemed very sure that he would find her neither. Glystra stood still a moment, then seized the towel, wrapped himself in it.

'Does – um, everyone get a playmate?'

She nodded.

'The women too?'

She nodded again. 'That they may welcome you with renewed pleasure when at last you depart.'

'Mmmph,' snorted Glystra. He wondered about the man now possibly standing before the naked Nancy. 'Mmmph.'

He said with a brusqueness and finality he did not altogether feel, 'Give me my clothes.'

With no change in expression, she brought him Kirstendale garments, assisted him into the intricate folds, tucks and drapes.

At last she pronounced him dressed. He wore a garment of green and blue in which he felt awkward and ridiculous. The first piece of headgear she brought forward, a tall tricorn dangling a dozen wooden sound-blocks, he refused even to allow on his head. The girl insisted that a man without head-ornament would be a spectacle for derision, and finally he allowed her to pull a loose black velvet beret over his cropped black poll, and before he could protest she had fixed a string of scarlet beads so as to hang over one ear.

She stood back, admired him. 'Now my lord is a lord among lords ... Such a presence ...'

'I feel like a lord among jackasses,' muttered Glystra. He went to the door, but the girl was there before him to sweep it open. Glystra frowned, stalked through, wondering if Sir Walden had also arranged to have him fed with a spoon.

He descended to the main hall. Sunset light poured in through the mullioned windows. A pair of lads placed screens of violet and green satin where they would glow to the best advantage. A round table was spread with heavy ivory cloth, and set with fourteen places.

The plates were marble, thin and fragile, apparently carved and worked by hand; the implements were carved from a hard black wood.

One by one Glystra's companions arrived – the men sheepish in their new garments, the girls sparkling and radiant. Nancy wore pale green, pink and white. When she entered the room Glystra hastily sought her eye, hoping to read how she had disposed of the companion assigned her by the painstaking Sir Walden. She looked away, would not meet his eye. Glystra clamped his mouth, scowled toward the blue pool in the center of the room.

Sir Walden appeared and with him his two sons, a daughter, and a tall woman in billows of lavender lace whom he introduced as his wife.

Dinner was a splendid event, course after course, dishes of unfamiliar, odd-tasting food, all elaborately prepared and served: greens, fibers, cereals, fungus, fruits, thistles, succulent stems, prepared in starchy coverings like ravioli, spicy goulashes, croquettes, pastries, jellies, salads. The variety was such that it came as a slight shock when Glystra realized that the meal was entirely vegetarian – with the exception of certain ambiguous hashes, which he took to be of insect origin, and avoided.

After dinner there was oil-smooth liquor and much talk. Glystra's head swam with the dinner wine, and the liquor relaxed him completely. He leaned toward Sir Walden.

'Sir, you have not yet explained your interest in us casual passers-by.'

Sir Walden made a delicate grimace. 'Surely it is a trivial matter. Since I enjoy your company, and you must rest your heads somewhere – what is the difference?'

'It is a matter which disturbs me,' protested Glystra. 'Every human act is the result of some impulse; the nature of the impulse which caused you to send the messenger for us preys on my mind .... I hope you will forgive my insistence ...'

Sir Walden smiled, toyed with a bit of fruit. 'Some of us here in Kirstendale subscribe to the Doctrine of Illogical Substitution, which in many respects disputes your theory of causation. And then there is the Tempofluxion Dogma – very interesting, although I for one cannot entirely accept the implications. Possibly the central postulates are unknown on Earth? The advouters claim that as the river of time flows past and through us, our brains are disturbed – jostled, if you will – by irregularities, eddies, in the flow of the moments. They believe that if it were possible to control the turbulence in the river, it would be possible to manipulate creative ability in human minds. What do you say to that?'

'That I still wonder why you asked us to be your guests.'

Sir Walden laughed helplessly. 'Very well, you might as well learn the inconsequential truth – and learn the inconsequentiality of our lives here in Kirstendale.' He leaned forward, as if resolved on candor. 'We Kirsters love novelty – the new, the fresh, the exciting. You are Earthmen. No Earthmen have passed through Kirstendale for fifty years. Your presence in my house not only affords me the pleasure of new experience, but also adds to my prestige in the town ... You see, I am perfectly frank, even to my disadvantage.'

'I see,' said Glystra. The explanation appeared reasonable.

'I was quick with my invitation. Undoubtedly you would have received a dozen others inside the hour. But I have connections with the depot agent.'

Glystra tried to remember the head porter at the landing, who must have relayed the information almost instantly to Sir Walden.

Sir Walden cared little for answering Glystra's questions; he preferred to discuss contemporary Earth culture, a lead which Glystra followed, to please his host.

The evening passed. Glystra, head spinning from the wine and liquor, was conducted to his room. Waiting to undress him was the girl who had helped him into his clothes. She moved on soundless bare feet, murmuring softly as she unclasped the buckles, untied the hundred and one ribbons, bindings, tassels. Glystra was drowsy. Her voice was warm and heady as mulled wine.

The morning attendant was a thin-faced young man, who dressed Glystra after his morning bath in silence.

Glystra hurried to the main hall, anxious to find Nancy. How had she spent the night? The question throbbed at the back of his mind like a bubble of stagnant blood. But she was not yet in evidence. Pianza and Corbus sat alone at the table, eating pink melon.

Corbus was speaking. '—think I'll trade Motta in on this yellow-haired girl. That's the way to cross a planet, wench by wench!'

Glystra muttered a greeting, sat down. A moment later Nancy entered the room, fresh, blue-eyed, more beautiful than Glystra had ever remembered her. He half-rose to his feet, caught her eye. She nodded casually, dropped into the seat opposite him, began to dip into the pink melon.

Glystra returned to his own food. Big Planet was not Earth. He could not judge a Big Planet girl by Earth standards … During breakfast he tried to fathom her mind. She was pleasant, detached, cool.

One by one the party entered the hall, until at last everyone was present. Except—

'Where's Cloyville?' asked Pianza. 'Doesn't he plan to get up?' He turned to a servant. 'Will you please arouse Mr. Cloyville?'

The servant returned. 'Mr. Cloyville is not in his room.'

Cloyville was not seen all day.

It was possible, said Sir Walden, that he had wished to explore the town on foot. Glystra, with no other hypothesis to offer, concurred politely. If Cloyville had indeed wandered off, he would return when he felt so inclined. If he had been taken against his will, Glystra was unable to formulate a plan to retrieve him. Words would avail nothing … It might be wise, thought Glystra, to leave Kirstendale as soon as possible. He said as much at lunch.

Wailie and Motta were downcast, and toyed with their food sulkily. 'Best we should remain here in Kirstendale,' said Wailie. 'Everyone is gay; there is no beating of the woman, and a great deal of food.'

'Of course there is no meat,' Motta pointed out, 'but who cares? The fabrics and the perfumed water and—' She glanced at Wailie and giggled. They looked at Corbus and Bishop, and giggled again.

Bishop blushed, sipped green fruit juice. Corbus raised his eyebrows sardonically. Glystra chuckled; then, thinking of Nancy, asked himself ruefully, what am I laughing at?

Sir Walden said gravely, 'I have a rather pleasant surprise for you. Tonight, at our evening meal, there will be meat – a dish prepared in honor of our guests.'

He looked from face to face, half-smiling, waiting for the expected enthusiasm. Then: 'But perhaps for you, meat is not the gala event it is for us … Also, I have been asked to convey the invitation of my Lord Sir Clarence Attlewee to a soirée at his castle this evening. It has likewise been planned in your honor, and he hopes you will accept.'

'Thank you,' said Glystra. 'Speaking for myself, I'll be delighted.' He looked around the circle of faces. 'I think we'll all be there … Even Cloyville, if he shows up.'

During the afternoon Sir Walden took them to what he called a 'pressing'. It proved to be a ceremonial squeezing of essence from a vat of flower petals. Two hundred of the aristocrats appeared, wearing green and gray headgear, which Sir Walden described as traditional for the occasion.

Glystra looked about the plaza, along the ranks of gay careless faces. 'A good proportion of the upper classes must be present, I would imagine,' he said idly to Sir Walden.

Sir Walden stared straight ahead, and not a muscle moved on his face. 'There are others, many others.'

'What is the population of Kirstendale, Sir Walden?'

Sir Walden made a non-committal gesture. 'It is at best a speculation. I have no figures.'

'And what is your speculation?'

Sir Walden darted him a brilliant glance. 'We are a proud race, proud and sensitive. And we have our Secret.'

'Excuse me.'

'Of course.'

The booms which radiated like spokes from the press were bedecked like a maypole, and manned by children. Round and round and round, chanting a shrill song – round and round. Flower fumes rose into the air, and a trickle of yellow–green syrup dripped from the spout. Round and round. Essence of white blossoms, lush yellow petals, blue flake-flowers ... The children bore tiny cups through the crowd, each containing a few drops of essence. Sir Walden said, 'Bring your tongue almost to the liquid, but do not quite taste it.'

Glystra bent his head, followed the instructions. A wave of pungent fragrance swept through his throat, his nose, his entire head. His eyes swam, his head reeled, momentarily dizzy in a kind of floral ecstasy.

'Exquisite,' he gasped when he was able to speak.

Sir Walden nodded. 'That was the Baie-Jolie press. Next will be a heavy Purple Woodmint, then a Marine Garden, then a Rose Thyme, and last my favorite, the fascinating Meadow Harvest Sachet.'

CHAPTER THIRTEEN

Through the afternoon the travelers reveled in perfume, and at last, half-intoxicated from gorgeous odors, they returned to Sir Walden's castle.

Inquiry revealed that Cloyville had not yet returned.

Glystra bathed with a troubled mind. Awaiting him with a towel was the same smiling girl who had served him yesterday. Today she wore, in addition to her short black skirt, a string of red coral beads around her neck.

Sighing, half in frustration, Glystra allowed himself to be arrayed in fresh clothes.

Sir Walden was more attentive and gracious than ever this evening; repeatedly he toasted his guests and planet Earth in wines first green, then orange, then red, and Glystra's head was light before the first series of courses was served.

Course after course: hot pickled fruit, slabs of nutty yeast spread with sweet syrups, salads, croquettes garnished with crisp water-weed – and presently a great tureen was wheeled in, a pottery bowl glazed in stripes of brown, black and green.

Sir Walden himself served the meat – slices of pale roast swimming in rich brown gravy.

Glystra found himself replete, without further appetite, and merely toyed with his portion. Sir Walden and his lady ate with silent concentration, for a moment quiet.

Glystra asked suddenly, 'What kind of animal furnishes the meat?'

Sir Walden looked up, wiped his lips with a napkin. 'A rather large beast, seldom seen in these parts. It seems to have wandered down from the north woods; by rare luck we procured it; its meat is superlatively delicious.'

'Indeed,' said Glystra. Looking about he noticed that Pianza and Bishop had likewise left their plates untouched. Corbus and Clodleberg still had appetite, and ate the meat with relish, as did Nancy and the gypsy girls.

At the final course – a rich cheese-like substance – Glystra said suddenly, 'I think, Sir Walden, that tomorrow we will take our leave of Kirstendale.'

Sir Walden paused in his eating. 'What? So soon?'

'We have far to go, and the monoline takes us but a short distance along the way.'

'But – your friend Cloyville?'

'If he is found—' He paused. 'If he returns, he possibly may be able to overtake us. I feel that we had better go before – ah, any of us wander away.'

'You're spoiling us for the tough life we have ahead,' said Pianza. 'Another week here and I couldn't bring myself to leave.'

Sir Walden politely expressed his regret. 'I invited you as curiosities of the moment; now I look upon you as my friends.'

A coach came to convey the party to Sir Clarence Attlewee's soirée. Sir Walden stood back.

'But do you not come with us?' asked Glystra.

'No,' said Sir Walden. 'I will be occupied this evening.'

Glystra slowly took his seat in the carriage. Automatically he felt to his side – but he had left his weapon in his room. He whispered to Corbus, 'Tonight – don't drink too much. I think that we had better keep our heads clear ... For what – I don't know.'

'Right.'

The carriage stopped by a column painted blue–white, and the party was conducted up a spiral staircase much like Sir Walden Marchion's.

Sir Clarence, a man with a heavy chin and snapping eyes, greeted his guests at the head of the stairs. Glystra stared at him. Somewhere, somehow, Sir Clarence's face was familiar to him. He stammered, 'Haven't we met, Sir Clarence? This afternoon at the pressing?'

'I think not,' said Sir Clarence. 'I was otherwise occupied today.'

'I feel I've spoken to you before. Your voice is familiar.'

Sir Clarence shook his head. 'I'm afraid not.' He conducted them into his home. 'Allow me to present my wife.' He did so. 'And Valery, my daughter ...'

Glystra's mouth fell open. Here was the girl who, nearly naked, waited to serve him when he left his bath.

He leaned forward. Or was she? She regarded him with impersonal interest, frowning slightly as if puzzled by his interest. Glystra mumbled, 'Charmed to make your acquaintance,' and she moved away.

Watching the swing of her body in its complicated wrappings of silk and toile and net, Glystra was certain that she was the same girl.

Bishop nudged him. 'There's something rather peculiar—'

'What?'

'Our host Sir Clarence – I've seen him before.'

'So have I.'

'Where? Do you remember?'

'At the Hunt Club?'

Bishop snapped his fingers. 'That's it.'

'Who is he?'

'Sir Clarence is – or was – the doorman at the Hunt Club.'

Glystra stared, first at Bishop, then at Sir Clarence, who now was speaking with Nancy. Bishop was right.

Behind him he heard a booming laugh, a great roar of merriment. 'Haw, haw, haw! Look at that!'

It was Corbus' laugh, and Corbus laughed only rarely.

Glystra whirled. He looked face to face with Cloyville.

Cloyville wore a black livery, with tiny gold epaulettes. He pushed a cart laden with canapés.

Glystra broke into laughter, as did Bishop and Pianza. Cloyville blushed, a tide of red rising up his bull neck, over his cheeks. He darted an appealing glance toward Sir Clarence, who watched him impassively.

'Well, Cloyville,' said Glystra, 'suppose you let us in on it ... Picking up a little spare change during your stay?'

'Care for hors d'oeuvres, sir?' asked Cloyville tonelessly.

'No, damn it. No hors d'oeuvres. Just an explanation.'

'Thank you, sir,' said Cloyville and rolled his cart away.

Glystra turned to Sir Clarence. 'What's going on? What's the joke?'

Sir Clarence wore a puzzled look. 'The man is new to my employ. He came to me well recommended—'

Glystra wheeled, strode after Cloyville, who seemed intent on rolling his cart out of the room.

'Cloyville!' barked Glystra. 'We're going to thrash this thing out right here.'

'Quiet!' hissed Cloyville. 'It's not polite to create such a disturbance.'

'Thank God I'm not an aristocrat then.'

'But I am – and you're hurting my prestige!'

Glystra blinked. 'You? An aristocrat? You're just a flunky pushing around a tray of sandwiches.'

'Everybody's the same way,' said Cloyville dispiritedly. 'Everybody works. Everybody is everybody else's servant. How do you suppose they keep up the front?'

Glystra sat down. 'But—'

Cloyville said savagely, 'I decided I liked it here. I want to stay. I've had enough of tramping across forty thousand miles of jungle, getting killed. I asked Sir Walden if I could stay. He said yes, but he told me I'd have to work like everybody else, and work hard. There's not a more industrious people in space than the Kirsters. They know what they want, they work for it. For every hour of swanking around as an aristocrat they put in two working – in the shops, the factories, in the homes. Usually all three. Instead of living one life, they live two or three. They love it, thrive on it. I like it too. I've decided I'm built the same way. Call me a snob,' he shouted, voice rising angrily. 'I admit it. But while you and the others are rotting your bones out in the muck I'll be living here like a king!'

'That's all right, Cloyville,' said Glystra mildly. 'Or perhaps I should say, Sir Cloyville. Why couldn't you tell me of your plans?'

Cloyville turned away. 'I thought you'd try to argue with me. Or talk about duty, rot like that—'

'Not at all,' said Glystra. 'You're a free agent.' He turned away. 'I wish you luck. I hope you'll like it here. If we ever get to the Enclave I'll send a plane back to pick you up ...' He returned to the main hall.

Early the next morning a carriage called at the castle of Sir Walden Marchion. Scrutinizing the men who pulled the carriage, Glystra recognized one of Sir Clarence's sons.

Wailie and Motta were missing. Glystra asked Bishop, 'Where's your girl friend?'

Bishop shook his head. 'She had breakfast with me.'

'Did she know we were leaving?'

'Well – yes.'

Glystra turned to Corbus. 'How about Motta?'

Corbus looked at Bishop. 'Let's face it.' He grinned. 'We're just not the men these Kirsters are ...'

Glystra could not prevent himself from glancing swiftly toward Nancy. There she was, pale, rather taut – but there she was. He smiled at her, uncertainly. There was still distance between them.

He turned back to Corbus and Bishop. 'Do you want to look for them?'

Corbus shook his head. 'They're better off here.'

'Let's go,' said Bishop.

At the monoline station, the head porter reached into the carriage, unloaded the packs to a cart, wheeled them to the trolleys.

Glystra winked at his fellows. The porter was Sir Walden Marchion.

With a straight face Glystra tipped him once again, three small iron washers.

Sir Walden bowed low. 'Thank you very much, sir.'

Kirstendale dwindled in the west. As before Clodleberg rode in the lead, with Glystra following. Then came the first freight-carrier with Corbus and Nancy, then the second with Bishop and Pianza. Cloyville's trolley had been left behind at Kirstendale.

The party was dwindling. Glystra thought back across the last few weeks. A desperate bloody time. Ketch, Darrot, Vallusser – killed. Cloyville had abandoned the trek. Abbigens, Morwatz, the fifty Beaujolain soldiers – all killed. Heinzelman, the Politburos, the Magickers in the griamobot – killed. A trail of death spreading behind like a wake ... Who would be next?

The thought hung in his mind like a cloud while they sailed along the bank of a quiet river – the East Fork of the Thelma. The countryside was clumped with Earth-type oaks, cypress, elm and hemlock, imported with the first settlers and now well adapted; Big Planet flora: bell-briar, mutus weed, handkerchief trees, with flowers like strips of rag, bronzenbush, wire-aspen, a hundred nameless varieties of low jointed furze. Truck farms and paddies occupied the river meadows; the caravan passed neat rows of thistle and legumes, tended by a moon-faced thick-necked people who paid them no heed whatever.

The river presently bore to the north. The monoline continued east, and the country changed. The green meadows and forest became a dark blur to the left and behind; ahead was dry savannah and a range of blue hills in the far Big Planet distance. Clodleberg pointed. 'The Eyrie.'

At noon on the third day Clodleberg pointed ahead once more. 'We're coming to Lake Pellitante.' Glystra saw the sheen of water, a limpidity in the sky that told of reflection from a large sheet of calm warm water.

The ground became marshy, and presently the monoline swung to the south. For half an hour they crossed dunes sparsely overgrown with dry yellow grass, and the glare off the white sands combined with the normal brilliance of the sunlight made ordinary vision painful.

A high dune passed below, the dry grass licking up at the trolleys like spume at the crest of a wave, and they coasted down toward a lagoon choked with brilliant yellow reeds.

Clodleberg, riding fifty yards ahead, suddenly dropped from sight. The yellow reeds boiled with life; naked men, thin and tall as giraffes, painted in vertical yellow and black stripes, sprang forth. They were immensely tall – eight feet or more – and they came in great bounds. A sharp cry like a bugle-call sounded; the men stopped short, stiffened back to heave spears ... Violet light fanned out, crackling with white sparks. The tall men fell like rags. Three had not been killed, but lay thrashing their long arms and legs like upturned insects.

Clodleberg picked himself up from the ground, stalked across the marsh, stabbed them with their own spears.

The swamp was quiet. Nothing could be heard but a rustle of the breeze in the reeds, the warm hum of insects. Glystra looked at the power-bank of his ion-shine, shook his head. 'Done for.' He started to toss it to the ground, then remembered the value of metal and tucked it under the seat.

Clodleberg returned to his trolley, still muttering and bristling. 'The plague-taken reed-demons, they cut the line!' Evidently, in Clodleberg's register of evils, this was the most depraved crime of all.

'What race are these people?' asked Bishop, who had clambered down one of the line standards to inspect the bodies.

Clodleberg shrugged, and said in a disinterested tone, 'They call themselves the Stanezi ... They're a great nuisance to travelers, since they gain nothing from the monoline by way of trade.'

Bishop nudged one of the scrawny forms over on its back, peered into the open mouth. 'Filed teeth. Hamitic physiognomy ... A Shilluk tribe emigrated to Big Planet from the Sudan about four hundred years ago – an irredentist group who chose exile rather than submission to World Government. Very possibly here are their descendants.' He looked across the reeds, the dunes, the hot sheen of Lake Pellitante. 'The terrain is much like the one they left.'

'From the swamps of the Nile to the swamps of Lake Pellitante,' apostrophized Pianza.

From the tool-box in his trolley Clodleberg brought a block-and-tackle, and under his direction the broken parts of the monoline were heaved together. Sitting on top of one of the standards Clodleberg was able to sink barbed splints into both ends and secure the splice with three whippings of fine cord. Then the tackle was released and the monoline was once more whole.

Clodleberg's trolley was hoisted back up into position; he set his sails and the caravan was once more under way.

As they rounded the elbow of the lagoon Glystra looked back and saw crouching forms steal from the swamp toward the yellow and black-striped bodies ... What a tragedy, thought Glystra. In ten seconds the flower of the tribe wiped out. There would be wailing tonight in the Stanezi village, groveling in the ashes to the fetishes which had failed them, flagellations, penances ...

The monoline took a long gradual slant up into a line of trees bordering Lake Pellitante, and the sudden shade was like darkness. The wind was light, blowing in vagrant puffs, and the trolleys ghosted hardly faster than a man could walk. The lake lay nearly mirror-calm, with a peculiar yellow–gray glisten on the surface, like a film of spiderweb. The opposite shore was lost in the haze; far out three or four boats were visible, manned, according to Clodleberg, by fishermen of a tribe who held the land in superstitious dread, and never in the course of their lives set foot ashore.

An hour later they passed a village of house-boats – a triple row of barges floating a hundred yards offshore. The central row was covered with vegetation, apparently a community kitchen garden. There was an air of warmth and contentment to the village, lazy days in the sunlight ...

Late afternoon found the party still drifting through the trees of the lakeshore, and at dusk a party of traders appeared, riding the monoline from the opposite direction.

Clodleberg halted his trolley, the lead man in the opposite caravan trundled cautiously closer, and the two exchanged greetings.

The traders were men of Miramar, in Coelanvilli, to the south of Kirstendale, returning from Myrtlesee Fountain. They were bright-eyed wiry men in white linen suits, wearing red kerchiefs around their heads, which detail of dress invested them with a peculiarly piratical air. Clodleberg, however, appeared to be at his ease and Glystra gradually relaxed.

The trade caravan consisted of fourteen freight trolleys loaded with crystallized sugar. By an established rule, the Earthmen, with only four trolleys, were obligated to drop to the ground and allow the traders freeway.

Evening had seeped lavender–gray across the lake, and Glystra decided to camp for the night. The leader of the traders likewise decided to make night camp.

'These are sad times,' he told Glystra. 'Every hand is turned against the trader, and it is wise to band together as many honest arms as possible.'

Glystra mentioned the Stanezi ambush by the lagoon of yellow reeds, and the trader laughed rather weakly.

'The reed men are cowards; they are hardly resourceful or persistent, and run at any loud sounds. It is different on the Palari Desert, where two days ago we escaped the Rebbirs only because a squall of wind drove us at great speed out of danger.' He prodded the earth with a stick, looked uneasily to the east. 'They are keen as the Blackhelm panthers, as single-minded as fate. It would surprise me not at all to find that a party has followed us down the monoline. For this reason we have kept our sleep short and our sentries double.'

CHAPTER FOURTEEN

It was still too early for sleep. The traders sat by the fire, busy with a game involving a rotating cage full of colored insects. Nancy sat cross-legged, her dark-fringed eyes wide, the pupils big and black. Pianza sat on a log, paring his fingernails; Bishop was frowning over a small notebook. Corbus leaned back against a tree, his spare body relaxed, his eyes alert, watchful. Clodle-berg greased the bearings of the trolleys, humming through his teeth.

Glystra walked down to the shore, to watch evening settle over the lake. Immense quiet enveloped the world, and the faint sounds from the camp only pointed up the stillness. The west was orange, green and gray; the east was washed in tenderest mauve. The wind had died completely. The lake lay flat, with a surface rich as milk.

Glystra picked up a pebble, turned it over in his fingers. 'Round pebble, quartz – piece of Big Planet, washed by Big Planet water, the water of Lake Pellitante, polished by the sands of the Big Planet shore ...' He weighed it in his palm, half-minded to preserve it. All his life it would have the power to recreate for him this particular moment, when peace and solitude and strangeness surrounded him, with Big Planet night about to fall.

Nancy drifted down from among the trees, her hair a mist of pale gold. Thinking of the nights at Kirstendale Glystra felt a pang, a pressure in his throat.

She came close beside him. 'Why did you come out here?'

'Just wandering ... Thinking ...'

'Are you sorry you left Kirstendale?'

He was surprised at the tone of wistful reproach. 'No, of course not.'

'You have been avoiding me,' she said simply, looking at him with wide eyes.

Glystra had the uncomfortable feeling he was about to be put on the defensive. 'No, not at all.'

'Perhaps you found the Kirstendale woman more desirable than me?' Again the tone of sad accusation.

Glystra laughed. 'I hardly spoke to her ... How did you find the Kirstendale man?'

She came close to him. 'How could I think of anyone other than you? My mind was full of jealousy ...'

The weight lifted from Glystra's mind, the pressure eased from his throat ... High from the sky came the deep note of a bell, a sonorous vibrating chime. Glystra looked up in astonishment. 'What on Earth is that?'

'Some kind of night-creature, I suppose.'

The note throbbed once more across the lake, and Glystra thought to see a dark shadow sweeping quietly past.

He settled upon a log, pulled her down beside him. 'After Myrtlesee there's no more monoline.'

'No.'

'I've been considering going back to Kirstendale—'

He felt her stiffen, turn her head.

'—and there build a sail-plane large enough to carry all of us. And then I remember that we can't stay aloft indefinitely; that without proper power to keep us going we might as well stay on the ground ... And then I consider fantastic notions: rockets, kites—'

She caressed his face. 'You worry too much, Claude.'

'One scheme might work – a balloon. A hot-air balloon. Unfortunately the trend of the wind is southeast, and we would very soon be blown out to sea.' He heaved a deep sigh.

Nancy pulled him to his feet. 'Let's walk up the shore, where we're farther away from the camp ...'

When they returned, the traders had brought out a big green bottle of wine, and all were sitting around the fire, flushed and talkative. Glystra and Nancy each drank a small quantity, and presently the fire tumbled into coals and the night air pinched at their bones.

Sentry watches were arranged, and the party turned into their blankets. Sleep, under the great trees by Lake Pellitante ...

Brilliant sunlight flooded the camp. Glystra struggled awake. Why did his mouth taste so vilely? Why had not the last sentry aroused him?

He stared around the camp.

The traders were gone!

Glystra jumped to his feet. Under the monoline lay Pianza, face down – and his neck was ghastly with blood.

The trolleys were gone. Four trolleys, a hundred pounds of metal, clothes, tools ...

And Pianza dead ...

They buried him in a shallow grave in utter silence. Glystra looked up and down the monoline, turned back to his company.

'There's no use fooling ourselves. This is a real blow.'

Clodleberg said sheepishly, 'The wine – we should never have drunk the wine. They rubbed the inside of our glasses with sleep oil. One should never trust traders.'

Glystra shook his head glumly, looked toward Pianza's grave. No more Pianza. It was a real loss. A fine fellow, kind, unassuming, cooperative. A wife and three children awaited his return to Earth, but now they would never see him again. The Earth calcium of his bones would settle into the Big Planet soil ... He turned back to the silent group.

'Clodleberg, there's no reason for you to come any further. The trolleys are gone, our metal is gone. There's nothing for you ahead. You'd best get back to Kirstendale and pick up Cloyville's trolley, and that should get you back to Swamp City.'

There would be Corbus, Bishop, Nancy and himself left in the party. 'Any of you others can do likewise. There's hardship and death ahead of us. Anyone who wants to return to Kirstendale – my good wishes go with him.'

Nancy said, 'Why won't you turn back, Claude? There'll be all our life ahead of us – sooner or later we can get a message to the Enclave.'

'No. I'm going on.'

'I'll stick,' said Bishop.

'I don't like Kirstendale,' said Corbus. 'They work too hard.'

Nancy's shoulders drooped.

'You can go back with Clodleberg,' suggested Glystra.

She looked up at him sorrowfully. 'Do you want me to?'

'I never wanted you to come in the first place.'

She tossed her head. 'I'm not going back now.'

Clodleberg rose to his feet, twisted his blond mustache. He bowed politely. 'I wish you all the best of luck. You'd be wiser to return to Swamp City with me. Wittelhatch is not the worst master in the world.' He looked from face to face. 'No?'

'No.'

'May you reach your destination.'

Glystra watched him as he walked through the trees. His arms swung free. He had left his crossbow on the trolley; the trolley was gone.

'Just a minute,' called Glystra.

Clodleberg turned inquiringly. Glystra gave him the heat-gun. 'This should see you past the Stanezi. Throw off the safety here, press this button. There's very little power left in the bank, don't fire it unless it's absolutely necessary.'

'Thank you,' said Clodleberg. 'Thank you very much.'

'Goodbye.'

They watched him disappear through the trees.

Glystra sighed. 'The two or three charges in that gun might have taken us a few extra miles, or killed a few more Rebbirs. It'll save his life ... Well, let's take an inventory. What's left to us?'

'The commissary packs, with the concentrated foods, my vitamins, our blankets, the water-maker and four ion-shines,' said Bishop. 'Not very much.'

'Makes for easier walking,' said Corbus. 'Let's get moving. We'll go crazy standing around here moping.'

'Good enough,' said Glystra. 'Let's start.'

The lake was forty miles wide – two days' march under the quiet trees. On the evening of the second day a river outflowing from the lake toward the south barred the way, and camp was made on the shore.

Next morning a raft was contrived by cross-piling dead branches. By dint of furious poling and paddling the clumsy construction was forced to the opposite bank, three miles downstream from the monoline.

Climbing up on the bank they looked across the landscape. Looming in the northeast were the crags of the Eyrie, guarded by a wall of great cliffs running north to south.

'Looks like about another three days to the cliffs,' said Bishop, 'and no perceptible gap for the monoline.'

'Perhaps it's just as well we're on foot,' said Corbus. 'Imagine the portage to the top of the cliff!'

Glystra turned his head, looked along the river bank toward the lake, looked again, squinted. He pointed. 'What do you see up there?'

'About a dozen men on zipangotes,' said Corbus.

'The traders spoke of a party of Rebbirs ... Conceivably—' He nodded.

Nancy sighed. 'How nice to ride on one of those beasts instead of walking!'

'The same thought had occurred to me,' said Glystra.

Bishop said dolefully, 'Three months ago I was a civilized human being, never thought I'd turn out a horse-thief.'

Glystra grinned. 'Makes it less astonishing when you remember that five or six hundred years ago the Rebbirs were civilized Earthmen.'

'Well,' said Corbus, 'what do we do? Walk down and murder them?'

'If they'll wait for us,' said Glystra. 'I hope we can do it on less than a macro-watt, because—' he scrutinized the indicator on the ion-shine he had claimed from Pianza's body '—there's only two macro-watts left in the bank.'

'About the same here,' said Bishop.

'I've got about two good kicks in mine,' said Corbus.

'If they ride off peaceably,' said Glystra, 'we'll know they're good citizens and their lives won't be on our consciences. But if—'

'They've seen us!' cried Nancy. 'They're coming!'

It was a race across the stretch of gray plain – men in flapping black cloaks crouched on the thundering zipangotes. These were a species different from the string of beasts they had sold to Wittelhatch; they were larger, heavier, and their heads were bony and white, like skulls.

'Demons!' muttered Nancy under her breath.

The men wore tight helmets of a white shiny substance, ridged over the tip and trailing scarlet plumes behind. Crouched low, knees clamped into the horny black sides of their skull-headed chargers, the foremost flourished swords of gleaming metal.

'Up here, up on the bank,' said Glystra. 'We want to delay the front ones till they're all within range ...'

The horny feet thudded furiously across the plain, the Rebbirs sang out calls of the wildest exultation. The faces of the foremost were clear: bony aquiline visages, jut-nosed, the lips drawn back in strain.

'I count thirteen,' said Glystra. 'Bishop, take four on the left; Corbus four on the right; I'll get five from the middle.'

The riders deployed in a near-perfect line in front of the outcrop where the four stood, as if they had lined up to be killed. Three flickers of violet, a crackling of power. Thirteen Rebbirs lay blasted and smouldering on the ground.

A few minutes later they set off across the plain toward the line of cliffs. They rode the four strongest zipangotes; the others had been set free. The Rebbir swords, knives and metal were secure behind their saddles. They wore black cloaks and white helmets.

Nancy found little pleasure in the disguise. 'The Rebbirs smell like goats.' She made a wry face. 'This cloak is abominable. And the helmet is greasy inside.'

'Wipe it out,' advised Glystra. 'If it gets us to Myrtlesee, it's served its purpose ...'

The land, rising in a long slope, became rocky and barren. The flat-leaved vines and creepers near the lake gave way to stunted thorns of a particularly ugly orange color. The tides of sunlight glared and dazzled, and snow on the Eyrie glittered like white fire.

The region was not without inhabitants. From time to time Glystra, glancing to the side, found white eyes in a pink wizened face staring into his from out of the thorn, and occasionally he saw them running, crouched low, bounding over the rocks.

On the morning of the second day a caravan of six freight-carriers appeared in the distance ahead, sailing swiftly down the wind. From a covert fifty yards off the trail the four travelers watched the caravan whirl past – six swift shapes swinging to the press of white cloth – then they were gone downwind, and soon out of sight toward Lake Pellitante.

On the third day, the escarpment loomed big ahead. The monoline rose in a tremendous swoop, up toward the lip of the cliff.

'That's the way you come down from Myrtlesee,' said Glystra. He turned his head, followed the hang of the cable across the sky, up, up, and along, till it disappeared against the chalky front of the cliff. 'Going up wouldn't be so easy. That's a long portage. But down ... Remember the ride down into the Galatudanian Valley?'

Nancy shivered. 'This would be worse ...'

They came to the landing at the end of the monoline, where the portage must start. The trail led off to the left, slanting up over the basalt detritus of crumbled boulders. Then it cut back, into a way dug out of the very side of the cliff and curbed with cemented masonry. Two hundred yards in one direction, then back, traversing – right, left, right, left – and the shoulders of the zipangotes rubbed the inner wall, so that it was necessary to sit with the inside leg looped over the pommel of the saddle. The zipangotes swept up the trail easily, gliding on six legs with no suggestion of effort.

Up, up, back, forth. The face of Big Planet dropped below, spreading wider and wider, and where an Earthly eye might expect a horizon, with a division into land and sky, there was only land, and then still more land. Lake Pellitante glanced and gleamed in the distance. A feeder river came down from the north, circling out of the Eyrie, and stained the earth yellow with its swamps. The outlet river, which they had crossed on rafts, swept broadly southeast, presently breaking into a series of exaggerated meanders, like a crumpled silver ribbon, and then vanished into the south.

Up, up. Wind drove a scud of clouds at the cliff; suddenly the trail was cloaked in damp gray twilight, and the wind swept up the mountain with the sound of a roaring torrent.

The fog glowed yellow, dispersed in trails and wisps; the sun shone full on their backs. Glystra's beast shoved its horny face over the last hump, surged with its four hind feet, and stood on flat ground.

They halted near the edge of the cliff, with the wind pressing up over the rim. The plateau was bare limestone, scoured and free of dust. Gray-white, featureless, it stretched twenty miles flat as a sheet of cardboard, then became mottled, a region of gray shadows. The intervening area was empty except for the monoline: the standards at fifty-foot intervals and the cable dwindling to nothing, like an exercise in perspective.

'Well,' said Glystra, 'nothing in sight, so—'

'Look,' said Corbus in a flat voice. He pointed north, along the rim of the cliff.

Glystra slumped back into the saddle. 'Rebbirs.'

They came along the verge like a column of ants, still several miles distant. Glystra estimated their number at two hundred. In a thick voice he said, 'We'd better get moving ... We can't kill them all. If we ride along the monoline – not too fast – perhaps they won't bother us ...'

'Let's go!' said Corbus.

At a careless lope the caravan started east, down the copy-book perspective of the monoline. Glystra kept an anxious watch on the company to the north. 'They don't seem to be following—'

'They're coming now,' said Corbus.

A dozen of the cavalry spurted forward out of the ranks, raced out at a slant evidently bent on interception.

Glystra clenched his teeth. 'We've got to run for it.'

He dug his knees into the side of the zipangote. It moaned and mumbled and flung itself ahead, bony face straining against the wind.

Twenty-four heavy feet pounded back the limestone. And behind came the Rebbirs, black cloaks flapping.

CHAPTER FIFTEEN

Nightmare flight, thought Glystra; was he asleep? Nightmare steeds, nightmare riders, the gray–white flat given depth only by the diminishing monoline: a nightmare vista permeated by fear and strangeness and pitilessness ...

He broke free of the sensation, cast it away. Turning, he watched the Rebbirs over his shoulder. The whole army had streamed out, as if stimulated by the excitement of the chase. The first dozen had not gained appreciably; Glystra stroked the horny side of his mount with an emotion almost like affection. 'Go to it, boy ...'

Miles, changeless miles: flat gray plains, thunder of pounding feet. Looking ahead, Glystra saw that they were near the region of mottled shadows – dunes of sand, white as salt, crystalline and bright as broken glass.

The Rebbirs had drawn closer, apparently able to extract the most frantic efforts from their mounts. Ahead – the dunes: sand swept off the flatland and piled in huge rounded domes.

Looking behind, Glystra saw a sight which thrilled him, one which might have been beautiful in other, less personal circumstances. The Rebbirs in the van had risen to their feet, standing in wonderful balance on the backs of their plunging mounts. And each, throwing back his cloak, fitted an arrow to a heavy black bow.

The bows bent; behind the arrows Glystra glimpsed keen faces: eagle cast to nose, forehead, chin. A chilling wonderful sight ... He yelled, 'Duck! They're shooting at us!' And he crouched over the side of his beast.

Thwinggg! The shaft sang over his head. The dunes towered above. Glystra felt the feet of his mount sound with a softer thud, a scuffing, and they were coursing across white sand ... The creature was laboring, breath was seizing in its throat. Very few miles left in the clogged muscles, then they would be at bay, the four of them. Their ion-shines would kill ten, fifteen, twenty, fifty – then there would be a sudden surge of hawk-faced men, a raising of swords, a chopping ...

Over the dunes, down the soft round valleys, up to the milk-white crests. Then looking back to view the surge of black-cloaked riders pouring across the swells, like black surf.

The dunes ended, washed against black obsidian hills. Behind, the rumble of multitudinous feet, hoarse war-calls ... Out of the dunes, into an old watercourse through the flint, where possibly once or twice yearly water foamed. The zipangotes stumbled over chunks of fractured black volcanic glass with sagging necks, bent legs.

To either side gullies opened into the watercourse. Glystra swerved to the left. 'In here!' He was panting, in sympathy with the gasps of the zipangote. 'Quick! If we can lose them, we've got a chance ...'

He plunged into the gully; behind came Nancy, pale, white around the mouth, then Bishop, then Corbus.

'Quiet,' said Glystra. 'Back into the shadows—' He held his breath as if he could control the rattling sobs of his beast.

Thudding sounded out in the main watercourse. Black things hurled past the opening. War-calls sounded now loud, now dim.

There was a sudden slackening to the sounds, an ominous change of pitch. Calls vibrated back and forth – questioning tones, answers. Glystra turned, looked behind. The ravine sloped at a near-impossible angle up to a ridge.

Glystra beckoned to Nancy. 'Start up the hill.' To Bishop and Corbus: 'After her.'

Nancy kneed her mount. It moved, mumbled, stopped short at the slope, lowered its skull, tried to turn.

Nancy hauled the reins, kneed the beast desperately. Coughing and whimpering, it set its first pair of feet above its head on the slope, scrambled up.

'Quick!' said Glystra in a harsh whisper. 'They'll be here any minute!'

Bishop and Corbus followed ... The yelling sounded closer. Glystra turned his mount up the slope. Steps sounded behind him, a snuffling. Silence. Then a cry loud and brilliant, the loudest sound Glystra had ever heard. From all directions came answering calls.

Glystra kneed his mount up the slope. Behind came the Rebbir, leaning forward with his sword outstretched, waving it like an eager antenna.

The gully was choked with hot-eyed men and their horny black beasts. The steep slope was a mass of clawing legs, hulking shoulders.

Nancy breasted over the ridge, then Bishop, then Corbus, then Glystra.

Corbus knew what to do. He laughed, his white teeth shining. His ion-shine was ready. He aimed it at the first Rebbir zipangote, squeezed. The white skull-head shattered into a scarlet crush. The beast threw up its front legs like a praying mantis, poised briefly, swung gradually over backwards, fell into the beasts behind.

A tangle of writhing flesh. White skull-faces, despairing eagle-men, a horrid tangle at the bottom of the slope – a talus of hot jerking flesh, the horny bodies of the zipangotes, the softer sinews of men, clotted together like hiving bees.

Glystra whirled his mount, led the way along the ridge. They rode with all the speed left to their beasts, threading the line of the ridge past the in-cursions of gullies, ravines, gulches. Caves and blow-holes opened under their feet.

After five minutes Glystra turned down one of the gullies, halted behind a heavy wall of vitreous slag.

'They'll be a long time finding us now, if they even bother to look ... We'll be safe until dark, at any rate.'

He looked down at the heaving shoulders of his mount. 'You're not much of a looker – but you've been quite a friend ...'

After nightfall they returned to the ridge and stole eastward through the dark. The ridge broadened and flattened; the flint crumbled into rotten gray rock, disappeared under a dim ocean of sand.

As they started across the flat, from far behind came a call, an eery hooting which might or might not have been human. Glystra halted his zipangote, looked up toward the Big Planet constellations, listened. Silence everywhere.

The zipangote shuffled its feet, snorted softly. The distant call came once more. Glystra shifted in his saddle, kneed the zipangote into motion. 'We'd better put distance between us and the Rebbirs while it's still dark. Or at least until we find concealment of some sort.'

They set off quietly across the glimmering sand. Glystra watched over his shoulder. A spatter of meteorites scratched bright lines down the sky. From far back came the mournful call once more.

Big Planet rolled on through space, twisting its shoulder back toward Phaedra. Dawn came, a pink and orange explosion. By this time the zi-pangotes were barely able to stumble and their heads swung on long necks, sometimes striking the ground.

The light grew stronger. A silhouette, low in the east, appeared – vegetation, waving fronds, bearded stalks, tendrils trailing from splayed branches.

Phaedra burst up into the sky. Plain to be seen now was an island of vegetation ten miles long in a white sea. From the center rose a hemispherical dome, glistening as of pale metal.

'That must be Myrtlesee,' said Glystra. 'Myrtlesee Fountain.'

There was no area of transition. Desert became oasis as sharply as if a knife had trimmed away any extraneous straggles of herbage. Blue moss grew fresh and damp; an inch away the clay lay as dry and arid as any twenty miles to the west.

Passing into the cool gloom was like entering the Garden of Paradise. The air smelled of a hundred floral and leafy essences, damp earth, pungent bark. Glystra slid off his mount, tied the reins to a root, helped Nancy to the ground. Her face was pinched and white, Bishop's long countenance was loose and waxy, Corbus' eyes gleamed like moonstones and his mouth was pulled into a thin pale line.

The zipangotes nosed and snuffled in the moss, lay down, rolled over. Glystra ran to remove the packs before they should be crushed.

Nancy lay at full length in the shade, Bishop slumped beside her.

'Hungry?' asked Glystra.

Nancy shook her head. 'Just tired. It's so peaceful here. And quiet … Listen! Isn't that a bird singing?'

Glystra listened, and said, 'It sounds very much like a bird.' A shadow crossed his face; he frowned, shook his head. He dismissed the odd idea which had suddenly been inserted in his mind. And yet – hmm. Strange.

Corbus opened the commissary pack, mixed vitamin concentrate with food powder, moistened it, stirred it into a heavy paste, scraped it into Cloyville's cooker, squeezed down the lid, waited an instant, lifted the lid and withdrew a cake of hot pastry. He contemplated it gloomily. 'If we ever get back to Earth I'm going to eat for a month. Ice cream, steak, apple pie, Swiss cheese on rye with lots of mustard, strawberry shortcake, corned beef and cabbage, fried chicken, spare-ribs—'

'Stop it,' groaned Bishop. 'I'm sick as it is …'

Glystra lay down on the moss. 'Let's hold a council of war.'

Corbus asked lazily, 'What's the problem?'

Glystra looked up into the blue–green foliage, tracing the white veins of a leaf. 'Survival … There were eight of us that left Jubilith, not counting Nancy. You, Bishop, me, Pianza, Ketch, Darrot, Cloyville and Vallusser. Nancy makes nine. We've come a thousand miles and there's only four of us left. Ahead of us is first of all more desert, the main part of the Palari. Then mountains, then the lake and the Monchevior River, then God knows what-all.'

'Trying to scare us?'

Glystra continued as if he hadn't heard. 'When we left Jubilith, I thought the chances pretty good that we'd all make it. Footsore, bedraggled – but alive. I was wrong. We've lost five men. Our weapons are just about done for. I don't know whether I've got a charge left in mine or not. Big Planet is meaner and tougher than we allowed for. The chances are that we'll be killed if we go on. So – now's the time. Anyone who wants to return to Kirstendale on the monoline has my blessing. There's metal enough in those Rebbir swords to make us all rich men. If any of you feel that you'd rather be a live Kirster than a dead Earthman – now's the chance to make up your minds, and no hard feelings.'

He waited. No one spoke.

Glystra still looked up into the leaves. 'We'll rest here in Myrtlesee a day or so, and then – whoever wants to start east ...' He left the sentence hanging in mid-air. His eyelids were heavy. The warm air, the cool shade, the soft moss, fatigue – all induced drowsiness. He aroused himself with a jerk. Bishop was snoring. Nancy was lying on her side. Corbus sat with his back to a tree, eyes half-closed.

Glystra rose to his feet. 'Looks like we're planning to sleep,' he said to Corbus. 'I'll take first look-out. You can have the second, then Bishop, then Nancy ...'

Corbus nodded, stretched out full length.

Glystra paced up and down, clenching and unclenching his hands. It was as if his brain were a house and knocking on the door was a boy with a barrowful of thoughts. Somehow he could not find the key to the door.

He walked softly across the moss, looked down at his companions. Bishop snored, Corbus slept like an innocent child, Nancy's hands trembled, quivered as if in a nightmare. He thought: the traders had killed Pianza, the man on watch; why had they stopped? It would have been perfectly safe to kill the entire party, and the traders apparently lacked qualms of any sort. The Earthmen wore valuable clothes, with many metal accessories. The ion-shines alone represented fortune beyond dreams. Why had not the entire party been slaughtered in their sleep? Was it that the traders had been prevented by someone who carried enough authority, perhaps in the shape of an ion-shine, to enforce his decisions?

Glystra kneaded his knuckles in his palms ... Why? Had his enemy calculated that without metal, without trolleys, they might turn back to Kirstendale? If Pianza had been killed while someone stood acquiescently by, one of these three sleeping before him was not only a spy and a saboteur, but a murderer.

Glystra turned away, the ache of grief and uncertainty in his throat. He walked back into the grove. The moss was like a deep rug of marvellous softness. The air was murmurous, restful. Big Planet sunlight trickled through layers of leaves and open spaces, fell around him with the richness of light in a fairy-tale forest. Through the air came a sweet trilling, soft, flutelike. The song of a bird – no, probably an insect or a lizard; there were no birds on Big Planet. And from the direction of the dome he heard the mellow chime of a gong.

There was a soft sound beside him. He jerked around. It was Nancy. He sighed in relief. 'You frightened me.'

'Claude,' she whispered, 'let's go back – all of us.' She went on breathlessly, 'I have no right to talk this way, I'm an uninvited guest ... But – you'll surely die, I don't want you to die ... Why can't we live, you and I? If we returned to Kirstendale – we could live out our lives in quiet ...'

He shook his head. 'Don't tempt me, Nancy. I can't go back. But I think that you should.'

She drew away, searched his face with wide blue eyes. 'You don't want me any more?'

He laughed wearily. 'Of course I do. I need you desperately. But – it's a miracle that we've come this far. Our luck can't hold out forever.'

'Of course not!' she cried. 'That's why I want you to turn back!' She put her hands on his chest. 'Claude, won't you give up?'

'No.'

Tears trickled down her cheeks. He stood awkwardly, trying to formulate words of comfort. They stuck in his throat. Finally, for want of anything better, he said, 'You'd better rest,' aware that the words sounded stiff and formal.

'I'll never rest again.'

He looked at her questioningly. But she went to the verge of the oasis, leaned against a tree and stood looking across the white desert.

Glystra turned away, paced up and down the cool blue moss.

An hour passed.

He walked down to look at Nancy. She lay outstretched, head on her arms, asleep. Something in her posture, in the stiff turning-away of the back, intimated to Glystra that never again would their relationship be quite the same.

He went to where Corbus lay asleep, touched his shoulder. Corbus' eyes flicked open instantly.

'Your watch. Call Bishop in an hour.'

Corbus yawned, rose to his feet. 'Right.'

A sound. Hoarse throbbing sound. Glystra was very tired, very comfortable.

A harsh yammering penetrated the world behind his eyelids. It was a distant urgent sound. Danger, he must awake. *He must awake!*

He jumped to his feet, wide awake, clawing at his ion-shine.

Corbus lay beside him, asleep.

Bishop was nowhere in sight. Neither was Nancy.

A crackle of harsh voices. A thud. Another thud. Further voices, dying, fading out.

Glystra ran through the foliage, through vines with heart-shaped leaves, through a clump of red feather-bushes with green flowers. He tripped on a body, stopped short, frozen in terror.

The body was headless. Blood still pumped from the stump. The head was nowhere visible. The body belonged to Bishop's head.

Where was that round head with its brain so full of knowledge? Where was Bishop, where had he gone?

He felt a grasp of his arm. 'Claude!'

He felt a sting on his cheek. He looked into Corbus' face: 'They've killed Bishop.'

'So I see. Where's Nancy?'

'Where's Nancy? *Where's Nancy?*'

He turned to look, then halted his gaze, turned to look at the ground at his feet.

'Whoever killed Bishop took her with him,' said Corbus. 'Looks like her tracks, here in the moss—'

Glystra took a deep breath, another. He looked down at the tracks. Sudden energy fired him. He ran off toward the dome. He passed a circle of slim cypresses, branches laden with golden fruit. He came out on a paved walk, leading straight to the great central dome. The whole face of the building was visible as well as the columned arcades to either side. Neither Nancy nor her captors were in sight.

For an instant Glystra stood stock-still, then started forward once again. He ran through the gardens, past a long marble bench, a fountain spraying up six jets of clear water, down a walkway paved with diamond-shaped blocks of white and blue–gray stone.

An old man in a gray wool smock looked up from where he knelt with a trowel in a flower-bed.

Glystra stopped, demanded harshly, 'Where did they go? The men with the girl?'

The old man gazed blankly at him.

Glystra took a short step forward; the old man cringed.

'Where did they go? Answer me, or—'

Corbus came up behind. 'He's deaf.'

Glystra glared, swung away. A door opened into a wall at the end of the walkway; this was the door Nancy must have been taken through. He ran over, tried it. It was as solid as a section of the stone wall.

He pounded on it, yelling, 'Open up! Open! Open, I say!'

Corbus said, 'Pounding on that door won't get you much but a knife in your neck.'

Glystra stood back, stared at the stone building. The sunlight had lost its tingle, the gardens were drab and dismal. In a bitter voice he said, 'There's nowhere on this planet where a man can walk in peace.'

Corbus shrugged. 'I guess anything goes anywhere – so long as they can get away with it.'

Glystra clenched his teeth; the muscles corded around his mouth. 'There's power in this gun to kill a lot of them, and by heaven, I'll see the color of their blood!'

Corbus' voice was tinged with impatience. 'We'll do better if we go at the matter rationally. First we'd better take care of our beasts before they're stolen.'

Glystra glared defiantly up at the stone wall, then turned away. 'Very well … You're right.'

For a moment they stood by the headless body. 'Poor old Bishop,' said Glystra.

'We probably won't outlive him more than a day,' said Corbus in his flat voice.

The zipangotes stood grunting and growling, bumping the white carapaces of their heads against the tree trunks. Wordlessly Glystra and Corbus loaded the packs, handling the pathetic belongings of Bishop and Nancy with heavy fingers.

Corbus stopped in his work. 'If I was running this outfit, do you know what we'd do?'

'What?'

'We'd ride out of here due east as fast as we could make it.'

Glystra shook his head. 'I can't do it, Corbus.'

'There's something fishy going on.'

'I know it. I've got to make sure what it is. I'm fighting a lost cause now … You can still drift back to Kirstendale.'

Corbus grunted.

They climbed into the saddles, rode toward the dome.

CHAPTER SIXTEEN

The air was full of lazy sounds: the far bird-like trill, a hum of small insects, the rustle of warm wind. They passed a clump of gardenia trees; here stood a girl playing with a diabolo. She had a triangle face, big dark eyes; she wore green satin trousers and red slippers. Wordlessly she watched them pass, mouth a little parted, her toy forgotten; and contemplating her shining cleanliness Glystra became warmly aware of his own bristling filth.

They rode out of range of the girl's curious eyes, past a low wall topped with spheres of polished stone overgrown with colored lichen. Behind came the sound of soft singing. The wall merged into the side of the main dome; skirting the building they rode down a neat lane. A ditch with clean water flowed to the left; to the right was a line of small shops. It was a bazaar like hundreds of others Glystra had passed through while traveling among the stars.

Rugs, shawls, quilts hung over rods; fruits and melons lay heaped in neat pyramids; pottery crocks and vessels lay stacked, their glaze misted by a film of dust; baskets hung from ropes. No one heeded them as they rode past on the moaning zipangotes. In the shadows a few heads were turned and Glystra saw the flash of eyes, but there were no voices raised to greet or sell.

One shop, slightly larger than the others, displayed a wooden sword as a guild-mark. Glystra pulled up his mount. 'I've got an idea.' He slid free a pair of the swords they had taken from the Rebbirs, carried them into the dimness of the shop.

A short fat man leaning against a heavy table looked up. He had a big pale head, black hair shingled with gray, a sharp nose and chin, the face of a Rebbir changed and rendered devious by civilization.

Glystra flung the swords down on the table. 'What are these worth to you?'

The fat man looked at them and his face changed. He did not try to conceal his interest. 'Where did you get these?' He reached out, gingerly felt the metal. 'These are the finest steel ... None but the South Rebbir hetmen carry steel like this.'

'I'll part with them cheap,' said Glystra.

The armourer looked up with quick light in his eye. 'What is your wish? A sack of peraldines? A four-tier helmet, mother-of-pearl perhaps, crowned by a Magic Mountain opal?'

'No,' said Glystra. 'It's easier than that. An hour ago my woman was taken into the big dome, or temple, whatever you call it. I want her back.'

'Two steel swords for a woman?' demanded the merchant incredulously. 'Do you joke? I'll furnish you fourteen virgins beautiful as the morning sun for the two swords.'

'No,' said Glystra. 'I want this particular woman.'

The merchant absent-mindedly felt of his neck, stared into the shadow of his shop. 'In truth, I covet the swords ... And yet I own but one head.' He stroked the shiny metal with a reverent hand. 'Still – each of these blades represents a thousand heads – a thousand bits of iron, melted and annealed, cleared of dross, heated and quenched, honed for half a year.' He picked up one of the swords. 'The Dongmen are unpredictable; at times they seem foolish and old, and then one hears of their craft and cruelty, so that an honest man never knows what to believe ...'

Glystra fidgeted. Time was passing; minutes kneaded dull fingers into his mind. Nancy – his mind wavered sidewise into the possibilities. Then a floor of hardness seemed to rise up under his misgivings. Suppose she were bedded, raped; if that were the worst, there was no irreparable harm done ... Possibly she might be allowed a respite. One hour, two hours? Perhaps bathed, perfumed, clothed? It all depended upon the fastidiousness of her captor.

He became aware of the merchant's calculation. 'Well?'

'Just exactly what do you want of me?'

'I want this woman. She is young and beautiful. I imagine she has been taken to someone's private chamber.'

With an expression of surprise at his ignorance, the merchant shook his head. 'The priests are celibate. Only the herarchs allow themselves the use of women. More likely she has been taken to the pens.'

'I know nothing of the temple,' said Glystra. 'I want the help of someone who does.'

The merchant nodded. 'I see. You want help. You'll risk your own head then?'

'Yes,' said Glystra angrily, 'but drop the idea that you won't be risking yours along with me.'

'I won't,' said the merchant coolly. 'But there is one who will.' He pushed with his foot under the counter. A moment later a chunky young man with a face harder and bonier than his father's entered the room. His eyes fell on the swords; he uttered a sharp exclamation, took a step forward, halted, looked at Glystra.

'My son Nymaster,' said the merchant. He turned to the young man. 'One of the blades is yours. First you must take this man through Nello's crevice into the temple. Wear robes, take an extra robe with you. This man will point out a woman he wants; no doubt she'll be pent in the pens. You will bribe Koromutin. Promise him a porphyry dagger. Bring the woman back outside.'

'Is that the all of it?'

'That's everything.'

'Then the blade is mine?'

'The blade is yours.'

Nymaster turned, motioned to Glystra with an air of calm execution. 'Come.'

'One moment,' said Glystra. He went to the door. 'Corbus.'

Corbus slouched into the room, looked around expressionlessly.

Glystra pointed to the two blades. 'If I return with Nancy, this man receives the two swords. If neither of us returns – kill him.'

The merchant voiced an inarticulate protest. Glystra glared at him. 'Do you think I trust you?'

'Trust?' said the merchant with a puzzled expression. 'Trust? What word is that?' And he tested it several times more.

Glystra gave Corbus a wolfish grin. 'If I don't see you again – good luck. Set yourself up as an emperor somewhere.'

The merchant conferred earnestly with his son, gesticulating with the palm of one hand. The son wore a subdued expression.

Nymaster beckoned to Glystra; they left the shop, walked around the building, entered an alley between two fences over which fern fronds fell. Nymaster stopped at a little shed. He pressed heavily on one foot, the door swung open. He reached in, tossed a bundle to Glystra. 'Wear this.'

It was a white gown with a tall peaked hood. Glystra pulled it over his head. 'Now this,' said Nymaster – a maroon sleeveless smock an inch shorter than the first garment. 'And this' – a loose gown of black still shorter, with a second hood.

Nymaster dressed himself similarly. 'It's the wear of a Dongman Ordinary – a lay priest. Once inside the temple no one will look at us.' He tied a third set of robes into a neat bundle, looked up and down the alley. 'This way – quickly.'

They ran a hundred feet to a portal in the fence, passed through into a rank garden of fern. The ground was marshy and quivered underfoot. The ferns crackled and snapped in the wind.

Nymaster halted, then stole forward carefully, stopped once more, held out a hand admonishing silence. Looking past him, through a screen of wire-vine, Glystra saw a tall spindly man with a gray concave face and a crooked nose standing in the sunlight. He carried a quirt in a long gnarled hand, which he slapped idly against his black boots. A little distance away six children of varying ages squatted in a truck garden, grubbing weeds with sharp sticks. Their ankles were knotted together with greasy twine, their only garment was a loose smock of coarse cloth.

Nymaster leaned back, whispered, 'To reach the wall we've got to pass Nello; we can't let him see us, he will raise an outcry.'

He bent, picked up a clod, flung it hard at the little boy at the end of the line. The boy cried out, then quickly silenced himself, bent furtively to his work.

Nello uncoiled like a lazy python, sauntered yawning across the sunny garden to the quivering boy, and raising his whip, carefully and without haste striped the child's buttocks. Once – twice – three times—

Nymaster pulled at Glystra's arms. 'Now while he's absorbed in his enjoyment ...'

Glystra let himself be pulled across the patch of open space, behind a wall of crumbling stone. Nymaster scurried now at top speed, the skirts of his garment flapping in three-colored flashes.

By a thick cycad with a trunk like the skin of a pineapple he paused, looked in all directions, and finally peered through the fronds at the top of Myrtlesee dome.

'Sometimes a priest stands in the turret watching across the desert. This is when they expect important guests, and wish to ready the oracle.' He peered, squinted. 'Hah, there he is, scanning the wide world.'

Glystra saw the dark shape in a cage atop the dome, standing stiff as a gargoyle.

'No matter,' said Nymaster. 'He will never notice us; his gaze is out in the air-layers.' He climbed the wall, using chinks and crevices in the rock for foot and hand holds. Halfway up he disappeared from view, and Glystra, following him up the wall, came upon a narrow gap invisible from below.

Nymaster's voice came from below. 'The wall was built for show, and hollow. There is an avenue within.'

Glystra heard a clink, a click and sparks flew through the darkness. A line of hot smoulder pulsed as Nymaster blew, burst into a tongue of flame, from which he lit a torch.

Nymaster strode ahead confidently, a lord in his own realm. They walked a hundred yards, two hundred yards, across damp well-packed clay. Then the wall ended against blank stone. At their feet was a pit into which Nymaster lowered himself.

'Careful,' he muttered. 'The footholds are only cut into clay. Get a good toe-grip.'

Glystra descended eight feet, ducked under the foundations of a heavy wall, crawled up a slanting passage.

'Now,' said Nymaster, 'we're under the floor of the Main College. Over there—' he pointed '—is the Veridicarium, where the oracle sits.'

Footfalls sounded above – hasty yet light, with an odd hesitancy. Nymaster cocked his head. 'That's the Sacristy, old Caper. When he was young a malicious slave poisoned her teeth, and when he made demands on her, she bit his thigh. The wound never healed and his leg is no thicker than a wand.'

A second mass of rock barred their way. Nymaster said, 'This is the oracle's pedestal. Now we must be careful. Hold your head away from the light, say nothing. If we are halted and recognized—'

'What then?'

'It depends on who the villain is, and his rank. The most dangerous are the novices in black fringes, who are overzealous, and the herarchs, with gold baubles on their hoods. The ordinaries are less conscientious.'

'What do you plan?'

'This passage leads to the pens where prisoners, slaves and exchanges are pent before processing.'

'Processing? Do you mean serving as an oracle?'

Nymaster shook his head. 'By no means. The oracle needs the wisdom of four men to guide his thoughts, and for every dissertation of an oracle three men beside himself must be processed. He himself serves as fourth man, for the next oracle.'

Glystra, gripped by a sudden impatience, waved his hand. 'Let's hurry.'

'Now – absolute quiet,' warned Nymaster. He led around the rock, up a rude wooden ladder, from which he rolled off onto a shelf. He fixed the torch in a rope socket, and crawled off on his stomach through the darkness. Glystra came after. Overhead a stone floor pressed into his back.

Nymaster stopped and Glystra ran into his feet. Nymaster listened, then jerked forward.

'Follow me, swiftly.'

He disappeared. Glystra almost fell into a dim hole. He swung himself down, stood on a stone floor at Nymaster's back. Vile-smelling water gurgled past his feet. Nymaster strode toward the light, a shaft of feeble yellow shining down a flight of steps. He climbed the steps and without hesitation stepped out into the light.

Glystra followed.

The air was hot and reeked with an oily stench that knotted his stomach. From a wide archway came sounds of industry.

Nymaster marched past without pause. Glystra followed on his heels. He turned his head, looked into a bin – into the blank dead eyes of Bishop.

Glystra made a moaning coughing sound, stopped short. He felt Nymaster's hard arm, heard his petulant voice.

'What's the trouble?'

'That is the head of my friend.'

'Ah.' Nymaster was uninterested. 'Beyond is the extraction room where the head is tapped of its wisdom ... It is a precise art, so I am given to understand, and not easily mastered.' He looked sardonically at Glystra. 'Well?'

Glystra pushed himself away from the wall. 'Yes. Let's get it over with.'

By a heroic effort he restrained his gorge. Nymaster impatiently hurried off down the corridor.

Men in robes passed – two, three, four – without paying them heed. Then Nymaster stopped short. 'There, behind this wall are the pens. Look in through the chinks and pick out your woman.'

Glystra pressed close to the stone wall, peered through an irregular hole at about eye-level. A dozen men and women, completely naked, stood in the middle of the room, or sat limply on stone benches. Their hair had been shaved, and their pates daubed with paint of either blue, green or yellow.

'Well – which one is she?' snapped Nymaster. 'That one at the far end?' This was a long-headed creature with pendant breasts and a yellow wrinkled belly.

'No,' said Glystra. 'She's not here.'

'Ha,' muttered Nymaster. 'Hm, this poses a problem … Very difficult – and I fear past the scope of our agreement.'

'Nonsense!' said Glystra in a deadly voice. 'The agreement was to find the woman and bring her out, wherever she was … So now take me to her, or I'll kill you here and now!'

'I don't know where to look for her,' explained Nymaster in a patient voice.

'Find out then!'

Nymaster frowned. 'I'll ask Koromutin. Wait here—'

'No. I'll come with you.'

Nymaster growled under his breath, and turned off down the passage. He thrust his head into a little chamber. The man within was fat and middle-aged. He wore a spotless white tunic and an immaculate collar of ruffled lace. He appeared soft, pompous, petulant, effeminate, capable of irresponsible spite. He was not surprised to see Nymaster and resentful only to the extent that as an important official his time was valuable.

Nymaster spoke to him in a low voice, which Glystra bent forward to hear. Koromutin's eyes rested on him, probed under his hood.

'—he says she's not in the pen; he won't leave till he finds her. She must own the key to his life; she must be a witch. No woman is worth such effort and expense. But in any event we must have her.'

Koromutin frowned judiciously. 'This woman evidently must be pent up-stairs for personal use. If so – well, how much does your father put forward? Now I mind me of a certain dagger of good Philemon porphyry …'

Nymaster nodded. 'It shall be yours.'

Koromutin rubbed his hands, bounded to his feet, examined Glystra with a new speculation. 'The woman is evidently a rich queen. My dear sir,' he bowed, 'I salute your loyalty. Allow me to assist your search.' He turned, not waiting for Glystra's answer, flounced down the hall.

They climbed a flight of curving stairs. From above came the sound of footsteps descending. Koromutin bowed with vast obsequiousness.

'Bow!' hissed Nymaster. 'The Prefect Superior!'

Glystra bowed low. He saw the hem of priestly robes, exceedingly rich. The white was a silky floss; the red, a fur soft as the pelt of a mole; the black, a heavier fur. A peevish voice said, 'Where are you, Koromutin? An oraculation will shortly be in progress, and where is the wisdom? You are remiss.'

Koromutin spoke resonant apologies. The Prefect Superior returned upstairs. Koromutin trotted back to his cubicle, where he donned a high-collared garment of stiff white brocade embroidered with scarlet spiders and a tall white conical hat with ear flaps and cheek guards which almost hid his face.

'Why the delay?' hissed Glystra.

Nymaster shrugged. 'Old Koromutin holds the post of Inculcator, and that is his ceremonial regalia. We will be delayed.'

Glystra said fretfully, 'We have no time for it; let's get about our business.'

Nymaster shook his head. 'Not possible. Koromutin is bound to the oraculation. In any event, I wish to witness the rite; never have I watched an oracle at his revelations.'

Glystra growled threats but Nymaster could not be moved. 'Wait till Koromutin leads us to the woman. She is not in the pens; you saw as much yourself.'

Glystra, fuming and disquieted, was forced to be content.

CHAPTER SEVENTEEN

Koromutin continued his preparations. From a locked cabinet he brought a jar of a murky yellow fluid, from which he filled a rude hypodermic.

'What's that stuff?' demanded Glystra contemptuously.

'That is wisdom.' Koromutin spoke with unctuous complacency. 'The head glands of four men go into each charge; the material is concentrated sagacity.'

Hormones, pineal fluid, thought Glystra; God only knew what nastiness.

Koromutin replaced the jar of fluid in the cabinet, clamped the hypodermic to the front of his hat like a holy emblem. 'Now – to the Veridicarium.'

He led Nymaster and Glystra down the corridor, up the stairs, along a wide passage to the central hall under the dome – a large twelve-sided room paneled with mother-of-pearl and swimming with pale gray color. In the center rose a dais of black wood holding a single chair.

There were only two dozen priests in the hall, arranged in a semi-circle, chanting a litany of monosyllabic gibberish unintelligible to Glystra, and, he suspected, equally meaningless to the priests.

'Only a score,' muttered Koromutin. 'The Lord Voivode will not be pleased. He bases the value of the oracle's wisdom by the number of priests in the hall ... I must wait here, in the alcove.' His voice came muffled as if from under the robes. 'By custom, I follow the oracle.' He glanced around the hall. 'You two had best go by the Boreal Wall, lest some stripling novice peer under your hood and raise an outcry.'

Nymaster and Glystra took inconspicuous positions against a great carved screen. A moment later an egg-shaped palanquin curtained with peach satin and fringed with blue tassels was borne into the hall. Four black men in red breeches served as porters; two girls followed with a chair of withe and clever pink bladder cushions.

The porters set down the equipage; a red-faced little man hopped out from between the curtains, seated himself in the chair which was hurriedly thrust under him.

He beckoned furiously, to no one in particular, to the world at large. 'Haste, haste!' he wheezed. 'Life is running out! The light leaves my eyes while I sit here!'

The Prefect Superior approached him, bowed his head with nicely calculated respect. 'Perhaps the Lord Voivode would care to refresh himself during the preliminary rites.'

'Devil take the preliminaries!' bawled the Voivode. 'In any event I note but a niggardly score of priests here to honor my presence; such makeshift preliminaries I can well spare. Let us to the oraculating; this time let him be a stalwart in his prime – a Rebbir, a Bode, a Juillard. No more like that senile Delta-man who died two minutes after the spasms left him.'

The prefect bowed. 'We will seek to oblige you, Voivode.' He looked up at a sound. 'The oracle comes.'

Two priests entered the room supporting between them a black-haired man in a white smock. He stared back and forth like a trapped animal, digging his heels into the floor.

The Lord Voivode roared in contempt. 'Is this the creature who is to advise me? Faugh! He appears unable to do more than empty his bowels in fear!'

The prefect spoke with imperturbable suavity. 'Let your misgivings vanish, Lord Voivode. He speaks with the wisdom of four men.'

The wretch in the white smock was hoisted to the chair on the dais, where he sat trembling.

The Lord Voivode watched in ill-concealed disgust. 'I believe I can tell him more than he can tell me, even with his wisdom quadrupled; all he knows is fear. And once again the precious instants of my life are wasted futilely; where will I find just treatment?'

The prefect shrugged. 'The world is wide; perhaps somewhere oracles exist superior to ours here at Myrtlesee Fountain. The Lord Voivode might with advantage put his questions to one of those other omniscients.'

The Voivode spluttered, abruptly lapsed into silence.

Now appeared Koromutin, stately and ceremonious in his stiff gown. He climbed the dais, lifted the hypodermic down from his hat, plunged it home in the oracle's neck. The oracle tensed, arched his back like a bow, flung his elbows out, thrust his chin hard into the air. For a moment he sat rigid, then slumped, limp as seaweed into the chair. He put his head into his hand, rubbing his forehead.

There was dead silence in the chamber. The oracle rubbed his forehead. His foot jerked. His head bobbed. Sounds came from his mouth. He raised his head in bewilderment. His shoulders quivered, his feet jerked again, his nose twitched. A swift babble poured from his mouth, rising in pitch. He yelled, in a hoarse bawling voice. His body quivered, jerked – faster, faster. He was vibrating as if the dais were rocking.

Glystra watched with fascinated eyes. 'Is that the wisdom? I find no sense in this screaming.'

'Quiet.'

The man was in wildest agony. Moisture dripped from his mouth, his face muscles were knotted into ropes, his eyes glared like lamps.

The Lord Voivode leaned forward, smiling and nodding. He turned to the prefect, who bent respectfully, put a query inaudible over the yammer of the oracle. The prefect nodded calmly, straightened, teetered back and forth on his heels, hands behind his back.

The oracle sprang to his feet. His back arched, the breath rattled past lips which were pulled back from teeth ... Then he settled limply into the chair. He sat still, calm and serene, as if agony had purged away all the dross in his soul and left him with a vast meditative coolness.

In the silence the prefect's murmur to the Voivode was clearly distinguishable: 'He's now on the settle. You have perhaps five minutes of wisdom before he dies.'

The Voivode hitched himself forward. 'Oracle, answer well, how long have I to live?'

The oracle smiled wearily. 'You ask triviality – and I shall answer. Why not? So – from the position of your body, from your gait, from certain mental considerations, it is evident that you are eaten by an internal canker. Your breath reeks of decay. I judge your life at a year, no more.'

The Voivode turned a contorted face to the prefect. 'Take him away; he is a liar! I pay good slaves and then he tells me lies ...'

The prefect held up a calm hand. 'Never come to Myrtlesee Fountain for flattery or bolus, Voivode; you will hear only truth.'

The Voivode turned back to the oracle. 'How may I extend my life?'

'I have no certain knowledge. A reasonable regimen would include bland foods, abstinence from stimulating narcotics and gland revitalizers, a program of charitable deeds to ease your mind.'

The Voivode twisted angrily back to the prefect. 'You have gulled me;

this creature voids the most odious nonsense. Why does he not reveal the formula?'

'What formula?' inquired the prefect without concern.

'The mixing of the elixir of eternal life!' roared the Voivode. 'What else?'

The prefect shrugged. 'Ask him yourself.'

The Voivode dictated the question. The oracle listened politely.

'There is no such information in my experience, and insufficient data to synthesize such a formula.'

In more gentle tones the prefect suggested, 'Ask only such information as lies in the realm of the natural. The oracle is no seer, like the Witthorns or the Edelweiss Hags.'

The Voivode's face turned a mottled purple. 'How may I best secure my son his inheritance?'

'In a state isolated from external influence a ruler can rule from tradition, by force or by the desire and acquiescence of his subjects. The last of these guarantees the most stable reign.'

'Go on, go on!' screamed the Voivode. 'Time fleets: you will die at any moment!'

'Strange,' said the oracle with a weary smile, 'when now for the first time I have started to live.'

'Speak!' said the prefect sharply.

'Your dynasty started with yourself when you poisoned the previous voivode; there is no tradition of rule. Your son might therefore maintain himself by force. The process is simple. He must kill all who dispute his leadership. These acts will win him new enemies, and he must kill these likewise. If he is able to kill faster than his enemies are able to gather their strength, he will remain in power.'

'Impossible! My son is a popinjay. I am surrounded by traitors, preening cock-o'-the-walk underlings who wait the time of my death as the signal to rob and pillage.'

'In this case your son must prove himself a ruler so able that no one will desire to be rid of him.'

The Voivode's eyes grew dim. His gaze went far away, perhaps to the face of his son.

'To foster this situation, you must institute a change in your own policies. Examine every act of your officials from the viewpoint of the least privileged members of the state, and modify your policies accordingly; then when you die, your son will be floated on a reservoir of good will and loyalty.'

The Voivode leaned back in his chair, looked quizzically up at the prefect. 'And it is for this that I have paid twenty sound slaves and five ounces of copper?'

The prefect was undisturbed. 'He has outlined a course of action to guide you. He has answered your questions.'

'But,' the Voivode protested, 'he told me nothing pleasant!'

The prefect looked blandly up along the mother-of-pearl paneling. 'At Myrtlesee Fountain you will hear no flattery, no spurious evasions. You hear exactitude and truth.'

The Voivode swelled, puffed, blew out his cheeks.

'Very well, another question. The Delta-men have been raiding all Cridgin Valley and stealing cattle. My soldiers flounder in the mud and reeds. How best may I abate this nuisance? What can I do?'

'Plant bush-vine on the Imsidiption Hills.'

The Voivode sputtered; the prefect said hastily, 'Explain if you please.'

'The Delta-folk subsist by preference on clams. For centuries they have cultivated clam beds. You have grazed your pechavies on the Imsidiption slopes so steadily that the vegetation is gone and the rain washes great quantities of silt into River Pannasic. This silt is deposited on the clam beds, the clams die. In hunger the Delta-men raid the cattle of the valley. To abate the nuisance, remove the cause.'

'They have been impudent and treacherous; I want revenge.'

'You will never achieve your wish,' the oracle said.

The Voivode leapt to his feet. He seized a stone jar from his palanquin, threw it viciously at the oracle, struck him on the chest. The prefect held up an outraged hand; the Voivode darted him a look of black malice, flung aside the girls, jumped into the palanquin. The four black porters silently lifted the poles to their shoulders, started for the door.

The oracle had closed his eyes. His mouth drooped. A tic twisted his lips. He began to gasp – great gulping breaths. His fingers clenched, unclenched. Glystra, watching in fascination, started forward, but Nymaster clutched him, drew him back.

'Are you mad? Do you not value your head?'

Koromutin marched past, motioned significantly. 'Await me in the corridor.'

'Hurry!' said Glystra.

Koromutin gave him a glance of wordless contempt, disappeared down the passage. An endless ten minutes later he returned, wearing his usual white and blue robe. Without a word or glance he turned up steps glowing with vermilion lacquer, which gave on an arcade circling the dome. Through tall arches Glystra could see across the oasis, past the shimmer of the desert to the black hills, now hazy in the afternoon light.

Koromutin turned up another flight of stairs, and they came out into another corridor circling the dome. This time the openings overlooked the hall below. Koromutin turned into a small office. A man almost his twin sat at a desk. Koromutin waved Nymaster and Glystra back, approached the desk, spoke with great earnestness, and presently received an answer of equal import.

Koromutin beckoned to Nymaster. 'This is Gentile, the Steward Ordain. He can help us, if your father will part with a second dagger of workmanship like that I am to receive.'

Nymaster grumbled and cursed. 'It can be so arranged.'

Koromutin nodded and the little man at the desk, as if waiting for the signal, arose, stepped out into the hall.

'He has seen the woman in question,' said Koromutin in a confidential undertone, 'and can take you to her quarters. I leave you in his care. Walk discreetly, for now you tread in high places.'

They continued, with Gentile the steward in the lead – along interminable corridors, up another flight of stairs. Glystra heard a sound which caused him to halt in his tracks – a low-pitched steady hum.

Gentile turned impatiently. 'Come now, I will show you the woman, then my task is done.'

'What causes that sound?' asked Glystra.

'Look through the grating; you will see the source. It is a glass and metal organism that talks in distant voices – a thing of potency, but not of our present interest. Come.'

Glystra peered through the grating. He saw modern electronic equipment arranged and hooked together in a manner that suggested knowledgeable improvisation. A rough table held a speaker, a microphone, a bank of controls, and behind, the twenty parallel fins which carried the printed circuits, served as condensers, resistances, impedances ... Glystra stared, the sight opening an entirely new range of possibilities.

'Come, come, come!' barked the steward. 'I wish to keep my head on my shoulders, even if you care nothing for yours.'

'How much further?' snapped Nymaster. The affair was taking him farther afield than he had bargained for.

'A few steps, no more, then you shall see the woman; but mind you, take care not to make your presence known or else we'll all dangle and our heads will be drained.'

'*What!*' barked Glystra savagely. Nymaster gripped his arm, shook his head urgently. 'Don't antagonize the old fool,' he whispered. 'Otherwise we'll never find her.'

CHAPTER EIGHTEEN

They continued, walking on heavy green carpet along a corridor which constantly curved out of sight ahead. At last Gentile halted at a door of heavy wood. He looked furtively behind, then stooped with the ease of much practice, peered through the crack where the hinges dented the jamb.

He turned, motioned to Glystra. 'Come now, look. Assure yourself of her presence – then we must leave. At any moment the High Dain may appear.'

Glystra, smiling grimly, looked through the crack.

Nancy. She sat in a cushioned chair, head back, eyes half-closed. She wore loose pajamas of dull green brocade; her hair was bright and clean, she looked as if she had only just finished scrubbing herself. Her face was blank, expressionless; or rather, she wore an expression Glystra could not identify.

With his left hand Glystra felt for the latch of the door. In his right hand he held his ion-shine. The fat steward squawked. 'Stand back, stand back! Now we must depart!' He plucked Glystra's sleeve with angry fingers.

Glystra shoved him away. 'Nymaster, take care of this fool.'

The door was not locked. He flung it open, stood square in the doorway.

Nancy looked up with wide eyes. 'Claude ...'

She slowly put her feet to the floor, stood up. She did not rush to him in gladness and relief.

'What's the trouble?' he asked quietly. 'What's happened to you?'

'Nothing.' Her voice was listless. 'I'm all right.'

'Let's get moving. There's not too much time.'

He put an arm around her shoulders, urged her forward. She seemed limp, dazed.

Nymaster held the steward negligently by the nape of the neck. Glystra looked deep into his frightened and outraged countenance. 'Back to the radio room.' The steward jerked around, trotted whimpering back along the amber-lit corridor.

Downstairs, back along vaguely remembered ways. Glystra held his ion-shine in one hand, Nancy's arm in the other.

A hum, an electric susurration.

Glystra pushed into the room. A thin man in a blue smock looked up. Glystra said, 'Stand up, be quiet and you won't get hurt.'

The operator slowly rose to his feet, his eyes on Glystra's ion-shine. He knew it for what it was. Glystra said, 'You're an Earthman.'

'That's right. What of it?'

'You set up this equipment?'

The operator turned a contemptuous glance along the table. 'What there is of it … Anything wrong with that? What's your argument?'

'Get me Earth Enclave.'

'No, sir. I won't do it. I value my life pretty high, mister. If you want Earth Enclave, call it yourself. I can't stop you with that heater on me.'

Glystra took a sinister step forward, but the man's face changed not a flicker. 'Stand against the wall, next to the steward … Nancy!'

'Yes, Claude?'

'Come in here, stand over by the wall, out of the way. Don't move.'

She walked slowly to where he had indicated. She was trembling, her eyes roved around the room, up and down the walls. She licked her lips, started to speak, thought better of it.

Glystra sat down at the table, looked over the equipment. Power from a small pile – a simple short-wave outfit like that owned by a million high-school boys on Earth.

He snapped the 'On' switch. 'What's the Enclave frequency?'

'No idea.'

Glystra opened a file index, flipped to E. 'Earth Enclave, Official Monitor – Code 181933'. The control panel displayed six tuning knobs. Under the first was the symbol '0', under the second '10', under the third '100', and so, by multiples of ten, to the sixth. Evidently, thought Glystra, each knob tuned a decimal place of the frequency. He set the sixth knob to '1', the fifth to '8' – he looked up, listened.

Footsteps sounded along the hall, heavy hard feet, and Nancy wailed, a wordless sound of desperation.

'*Quiet!*' hissed Glystra. He bent to the dials. '1' – '9'—

The door swung open. A heavy black-browed face looked in. Instantly the steward was on his belly. 'Holy Dain, it was never my will, none of my doing …'

Mercodion looked over his shoulder into the corridor. 'Inside. Seize those men.'

Glystra bent to the dials. '3' – one more dial to go. Burly men trooped into the room; Nancy staggered out from the wall, her face drawn and bloodless. She stood in the line of fire. 'Nancy!' cried Glystra. '*Get back!*' He aimed his ion-shine. She stood between him and the High Dain. 'I'm sorry,' whispered Glystra huskily. 'It's bigger than your life …'

He squeezed the button. Violet light, ghastly on white faces. A sigh. The light flickered, went out. No power.

Three men in black robes rushed him. He fought, wild and savage as any Rebbir. The table tottered, toppled. In spite of the operator's frantic efforts the equipment crashed, jangled to the floor. At this point Nymaster bolted from the room. His feet pounded down the corridor.

Glystra was fighting from the corner, using elbows, fists, knees. The black-robed men beat him to the floor, kicked his head, wrenched his arms up hard behind his back, punishing him.

'Truss him well,' said Mercodion. 'Take him down to the pen.'

They marched him along the corridors, down the stairs, along the arcade overlooking the oasis.

A black speck streaked low across the sky. Glystra uttered a hoarse cry. 'There's an air-car! An Earthman!'

He stopped, tried to pull close to the window. 'An Earth air-car!'

'An Earth air-car,' said Mercodion easily, 'but not from Earth. From Grosgarth.'

'Grosgarth?' Glystra's mind worked sluggishly. 'Only one man in Grosgarth would own an air-car—'

'Exactly.'

'Does the Bajarnum know—'

'The Bajarnum knows you're here. Do you think he owns an air-car and no radio?'

He said to the black-robed men, 'Take him to the pens, I must greet Charley Lysidder ... Watch him carefully, he's desperate.'

Glystra stood in the middle of the stone floor, naked, damp, miserable. His clothes had been stripped from him, his head was shaved, he had been drenched in an acrid fluid smelling of vinegar.

These were the pens of Myrtlesee Fountain. The air was gruel-thick with latrine reek and slaughter-house odors, seeping in with the steam from the processing rooms. Glystra breathed through his mouth to escape awareness of the stink. Horrible odor – but it was a poor time to be fastidious. He frowned. Strange. A component of the stench was a heavy, pungent, almost sweet smell which tickled his memory.

He stood quietly, trying to think. Difficult. The stone floor oozed under his bare feet. Four old women crouching beside the wall moaned without pause. A thin red-eyed man vilified a blowsy woman with waist-long blonde hair, which for some reason had not been shaved. She sobbed into her hands, without apparent attention to the curses of the man – guttural throat-catching sobs. Steam and stench poured in from the processing room through chinks and cracks in the stone, likewise bars of yellow light flickering through the steam. With the light and the steam came the sounds of the processing: boiling, pounding, rasping, loud conversation.

Eyes looked in at him, through the hole to the corridor, blinked, passed on ... Unreality. Why was he here? He was waiting to have his head boiled. Like Bishop's head. Pianza was lucky; he lay buried beside the yellow reeds of Lake Pellitante. Cloyville was luckier yet. Cloyville wore a grotesque puff of purple lace on his head, and played at being both master and servant.

This was the low ebb. Nearly the low ebb. Much of a man's dignity went with his hair. There was one more notch to slip – from naked humiliation into the anonymous soup of the processing pots. It was almost foreordained, this last notch. It had been a steady progress down a slope toward lesser and lesser life, morale, power ... A whiff of the pungent sweet odor came from the processing rooms, stronger than ever. It was definitely familiar. Lemon-verbena? Musk? Hair-oil? No. Something clicked in Glystra's mind. *Zygage!* He went to the wall, peered through a chink.

Almost under his face a tray held four neatly arranged heads, with their brain-pans sawed off to display the mottled contents.

Glystra twisted away his gaze. To the right a cauldron bubbled; to the left a bin held acorn-shaped fruits. Zygage, indeed. He watched in fascination. A man, sweating and pallid, in clammy black leather breeches and a blue neckerchief, scooped up a shovelful of the zygage acorns, sprinkled them into the cauldron.

Zygage! Glystra turned away from the hole, thinking hard. If zygage were a constituent of the oracle-serum, why, then, the brain-extracts? Probably no reason whatever; probably they were added only for their symbolic potency. Of course he could not be sure – but it seemed unlikely that pituitary and pineal soup would cause wild contortions like those he had witnessed in the Veridicarium. Much more likely that the zygage was the active ingredient; such would be the parallel with Earth plant-extracts: marijuana, curare, opium, peyote, a dozen others less familiar.

He thought of his own experience with zygage: exhilaration, then hangover. The oracle's reaction was the same, on a vastly exaggerated scale. Glystra pondered the episode. A miserable terrified wretch had undergone torment and catharsis to achieve a magnificent calm and rationality.

It had been an amazing transformation, baring the optimum personality apparently latent in every human being. How did the drug act? Glystra's mind veered around the question: a problem for the scientists. It seemed to achieve the results of the great de-aberration institutes on Earth, possibly by the same essential methods: a churning through the events of a lifetime, the rejection of all subconscious obsessions and irrationality. A pity, thought Glystra, that a man only achieves this supreme state to die. It was like the hangover after his smoke-breathing ... In his brain there was a sudden silence, as if a mental clock had stopped ticking. Bishop had felt no hangover. Bishop had – he recalled Bishop's intensified well-being after the zygage inhalation; apparently his habit of ingesting vitamins had warded off the hangover.

Vitamins ... Perhaps the oracle died from exaggerated vitamin depletion.

And the idea gave Glystra much to think about. He walked slowly back and forth across the damp stone floor.

The woman with the yellow hair watched him dully; the red-eyed man spat.

'*Ssst.*'

Glystra looked toward the wall. Hostile eyes gleamed through the hole. He crossed the room, peered out into the corridor.

It was Nymaster. His tough round face wore an expression of angry discomfort. 'Now you lie in the pen,' he said in a low urgent voice. 'So now you die. What then for my father? Your man will take away the swords, and possibly kill my father, for so you ordered.'

True, thought Glystra. Nymaster had served him faithfully. 'Bring me paper,' he said. 'I will write to Corbus.'

Nymaster handed through a greasy scrap of paper, a bit of sharp graphite.

Glystra hesitated. 'Have you heard anything of—'

'Koromutin says you will be oracle. For Charley Lysidder himself. So the prefect told him while he was beating Koromutin.'

Glystra pondered. 'Can you bribe me free? I have other metal, other swords like yours.'

Nymaster shook his head. 'A ton of iron would effect nothing now. Tonight Mercodion has ordained that you burn up your mind for the Bajarnum.'

The words sank into Glystra's mind; he stared at Nymaster, scratching his cheek with a ruminative finger: 'Can you bring Corbus back with you? For another sword of fine steel?'

'Aye,' said Nymaster grudgingly. 'I can do so ... A mortal risk – but I can do so.'

'Then take him this note, and bring him back with you.'

Now the sounds and the stenches of the pen had no meaning for him. He paced up and down, whistling thinly through his teeth.

Up, down, up, down, looking across the room at each turn, watching for Corbus' face.

A chilly thought struck him. He had guessed something of the mechanics of the plot against him. After Morwatz had failed, after he had eluded the second expedition by crossing the River Oust and dropping the high-line, he had been left to go his own way to Myrtlesee, but all the time, all the weary miles from Swamp City, he had merely been taking himself to a pre-arranged trap. The strategy was clear. He had been left to execute it himself. Suppose Corbus were part of the machinery? At this moment nothing was unthinkable.

'Glystra.'

He looked up, turned to the hole. It was Corbus in priest's robes. Glystra glanced right and left, crossed the room.

Corbus looked in at him quizzically. 'How goes it?'

Glystra pressed close to the hole. 'Did you bring it?' he asked in a whisper.

Corbus passed a little package through the hole. 'And now what?'

Glystra smiled thinly. 'I don't know. If I were you I'd start back down the monoline to Kirstendale. You can't do any more here.'

Corbus said, 'You haven't told me what you plan to do with the vitamins.'

'I plan to eat them.'

Corbus eyed him questioningly. 'They been giving you bum chow?'

'No. Just an idea I've got.'

Corbus glanced up and down the corridor. 'With a big hammer I might make a hole in this wall—'

'No. There'd be a hundred priests out here at the first click. You go back to the swordmaker's, wait till tomorrow. If I'm not there then I'm never coming.'

Corbus said coolly, 'There's one or two charges in the ion-shine. I've been half-hoping—' his eyes glistened '—to meet someone we know.'

Glystra's throat constricted. 'I can't believe it,' he muttered.

Corbus said nothing.

'She never had Bishop killed, I'm sure of it … It was an accident. Or he tried to stop her.'

'No matter how you look at it – she's part of the picture. Four good men killed – Bishop, Pianza, Darrot, Ketch. I'm not counting Vallusser; that little rat was in up to his neck. I've been watching her a long time – ever since she insisted on joining our little suicide club.'

Glystra laughed shortly. 'I thought all the time it was – that she—' He had no words to finish.

Corbus nodded. 'I know. One thing I'll say for her, she put her life on the line alongside ours. She came out on top. She's up there—' he jerked his thumb '—and you're down here. What a stinking hole. What are they cooking?'

'Brains,' said Glystra indifferently. 'They distill out some kind of nerve juice which they mix with zygage and feed the oracles. It works on the oracles like the smoke worked on the Beaujolain soldiers, only a thousand times more.'

'And it kills them?'

'Dead as a mackerel.'

'Tonight you're the oracle.'

Glystra held up the package Corbus had brought him. 'I've got this. I don't know what's going to happen. From here out I'm playing strictly by ear. And,' he added, 'I may be wrong, but I have a hunch there'll be a few unforeseen developments here at Myrtlesee Fountain and I'm not worrying.'

Nymaster appeared behind Corbus. 'Come, there's a prefect on his way down. Come quick.'

Glystra pressed close to the hole. 'So long, Corbus.'

Corbus waved his hand non-committally.

CHAPTER NINETEEN

The sun dropped behind the fronds of Myrtlesee Fountain. A mesh of cirrus clouds flared golden in the sky. Dusk drifted in from eastern lands where night had already fallen over peoples and cities and tribes and castles still unseen.

A marble pavilion extended to the east of Myrtlesee Dome, enclosed by a colonnade of ornate design. Behind the colonnade was a pond of still water, dimly reflecting the afterglow with the fronds and ferns of the grove silhouetted in reverse. Four blond and slender youths bearing torches came from the dome. Their hair was cut in effeminate bangs. They wore skin-tight costumes sewed of red and green diamonds, black satin slippers with curled toes. They set the torches in tripods of dark wood, returned within.

A moment later six men in black kilts carried forth a square table which they placed in the exact center of the pavilion. The blond boys brought chairs, and the men in black kilts marched away in a single file.

The boys spread the table with a gold and brown striped cloth, giggling like girls. At the center they arranged a miniature landscape – Myrtlesee Fountain in exact detail, complete with dome and pavilion, even to a table on the pavilion, where five persons sat to the light of tiny candles.

Flagons of liquor and wine were bedded in ice, trays of crystallized fruits, tablets of insect gland-wax, cakes of pressed flower petals were laid exactly in place, then the boys went to pose under the flaming torches, consciously beautiful.

Minutes passed. The boys fidgeted. Dusk gave way to feather-soft Big Planet night. Stars gleamed. A syrup-smooth breeze drifted through the colonnade to flutter the torches.

Voices sounded from the dome. Out on the pavilion came Mercodion, the High Dain of Myrtlesee Fountain and Charley Lysidder, Bajarnum of Beaujolais. Mercodion wore his richest robes, with a stole woven of pearls and metal. The Bajarnum wore a gray jacket of heavy soft cloth, red breeches, soft gray boots.

Behind came the Prefect Superior and two nobles of the Beaujolais empire.

Charley Lysidder remarked with pleasure at the table, glanced appreciatively at the statue-like youths, seated himself.

Wine was poured, food was served. Charley Lysidder was in high spirits and Mercodion extended himself to laugh graciously at his jovialities. Whenever there was silence a girl blew chords on a flute. When one of the diners spoke, she stopped instantly.

Ices and sorbets were brought in glass goblets, and finally pots of fuming incense were placed before each of the diners.

'Now,' said the Bajarnum, 'now for our oracle, Claude Glystra. Originally I had planned to question him under torture, but the oraculation will prove easier for all concerned. He is a man of wide experience and knowledge; he will have much to impart.'

'A pity that such brief opportunity exists to plumb his wisdom.'

The Bajarnum shook a finger. 'It is a matter you must concern yourself with, Mercodion – the maintenance of longer life in your oracles.'

The High Dain bowed his head. 'It is as you say ... And now I will order the oracle prepared and we will go to the Veridicarium.'

The hall was crowded with the rustling black-gowned priests. By custom, hoods were not worn at night, but the characteristic motivation of reducing individuality to the lowest common denominator was expressed by a white head-cloth banded loosely around the forehead, around the nape of the neck, forward under the chin.

Special ceremonial chants had been ordained. Twelve choirs situated each to a wall mingled their voices in a twelve-part polyphony.

The Bajarnum, Mercodion and their retinue entered the hall, strolled to benches before the oracle's dais. A serious-faced girl with shining blonde hair appeared at a side door. She wore black silk pantaloons and a gray-green blouse. For a moment she paused in the doorway, then slowly crossed the room, the only woman among hundreds of men, a peacock among crows. Eyes covertly followed her, tongues moistened celibate lips.

She stopped beside the Bajarnum, looked down at him with an oddly searching expression. Mercodion bowed politely. The Bajarnum smiled a cold tremble-lipped smile. 'Sit down.'

The expression of intentness vanished, her face became blank. She sat quietly beside the Bajarnum. A whisper, a buzz, a rustle of garments rose from the spectators. By rumor the woman was the new toy of the High Dain. Eyes curiously probed his face, but the sallow skin was set like the rind of a pudding and no emotion appeared.

A sad chime sounded; a second tremor ran through the hall, a shifting of stance, a motion of eyes. The Bajarnum suddenly seemed to become aware of the assemblage; he muttered to the High Dain, who nodded, rose to his feet.

'Clear the hall. All must go.'

Murmuring, dissatisfied, the priests filed out the great doors. The hall was now near-empty, and reverberated with echoes of every movement.

A second chime sounded; the oracle appeared. Two prefects stood by his side, the Inculcator in his stiff white gown and tall hat followed close to the rear.

The oracle was wrapped in a robe of gray and red, and white swathing veiled his head. He walked slowly, but without hesitation. At the dais he paused and was lifted to the oracle's seat.

The silence in the hall was like the inside of an ice-cave. Not a breath, not a sigh, not a whisper could be heard.

The prefects held the oracle's arm, the Inculcator stepped close behind. He took the hypodermic from his hat, he swung his arm.

The High Dain frowned, squinted, jumped to his feet. 'Stop!' His voice was harsh.

The watchers sighed.

'Yes, Dain?'

'Remove the head-swathing; the Bajarnum would look on the man's face.'

The prefect hesitated, then reached forward, slowly unhitched the white burnoose.

The oracle looked straight ahead, down into the eyes of the Bajarnum. He smiled grimly. 'If it isn't my old shipmate, Arthur Hidders, dealer in leather.'

The Bajarnum made a slight inclination of the head. 'More people know me as Charley Lysidder.' He examined Glystra with a narrow scrutiny. 'You appear nervous, Mr. Glystra.'

Glystra laughed, rather shakily. Enormous overdoses of vitamins, amino and nucleic acids were reacting on his motor system like stimulants. 'You do me an honor of which I hardly feel myself worthy—'

'We shall see, we shall see,' said the Bajarnum all too easily.

Glystra's eyes went to Nancy. She met his eyes a moment, then looked away. He frowned. Seen in the new context beside the man he had known as Arthur Hidders, she took on a new identity – one not unfamiliar. 'The nun,' he exclaimed.

Charley Lysidder nodded. 'Rather a clever disguise, don't you think?'

'Clever – but why was it necessary?'

The Bajarnum shrugged. 'A fur-and-leather dealer might conceivably accumulate enough Earth exchange to make the old-world pilgrimage – but hardly likely that he would bring his talented young concubine with him.'

'She's talented all right.'

Charley Lysidder turned his head, examined Nancy with dispassionate appreciation. 'A pity, really, that she had to become a base tool of policy, she is apt at finer things … But that fool Abbigens dropped the ship too far from Grosgarth and I had no one at hand to serve me. Yes, a pity, since I will never use a woman fresh from another man's couch. And now she must find another patron.' He glanced humorously at Mercodion. 'I fancy that she will not need to seek far, eh, Dain?'

Mercodion flushed, darted an angry glance at Lysidder. 'My tastes are perhaps as nice, in some respects, as yours, Bajarnum.'

Charley Lysidder settled back in his seat. 'It's no matter; I have uses for her in Grosgarth. Let us proceed with the oraculation.'

Mercodion waved his hand. 'Continue.'

The Inculcator stepped forward, raised the hypodermic.

The point stung deep into Glystra's neck. There was a feeling of injection, of pressure.

The prefects' grip tightened on his arms, tensing in anticipation of his motion. He noticed that Nancy had turned her face to the floor; the Bajarnum of Beaujolais, however, watched the proceedings with lively interest.

A great dark hand clamped on his brain. His body expanded enormously; his arms felt twenty feet long; his feet were at the bottom of a cliff; his eyes were like two long pipes leading out on the world. The Bajarnum's voice came like a sibilant whisper in a vast cave.

'Ah, now he squirms. Now it takes on him.'

The prefects held Glystra with practiced ease.

'Look!' exclaimed the Bajarnum delightedly. 'Look how he flails about … Ah, he has caused me much trouble, that one. Now he pays the price.'

But Glystra felt no pain. He had passed beyond mere sensation. He was re-living his life, from earliest foetus up through the years, re-living, re-experiencing, re-knowing every detail of his existence. Reviewing these events was a great super-consciousness, like an inspector watching a belt of fruit. As each distorted concept, misunderstanding, fallacy appeared, the hand of the inspector reached down, twitched events into rational perspectives, smoothed out the neural snarls which had clogged Glystra's brain.

Childhood flickered past the super-awareness, then early life on Earth, his training among the planets of the System. Big Planet bulked outside the spaceship port, again he crashed on the Great Slope by Jubilith; again he set out on the long journey to the east. He retraced his route through Tsalombar Woods, Nomadland, past Edelweiss, the River Oust, Swamp Island, down the monoline through the Hibernian March, Kirstendale, across the desert toward Myrtlesee Fountain. Present time loomed ahead; he plunged through like a train coming out of a tunnel. He was once more aware and conscious, with the whole of his life rearranged, all his knowledge ordered into compartments, ready for instant use.

The High Dain's voice came to his ears. 'You see him with his brain purged and clear. Now you must hasten; in a few minutes his life-force dwindles and he dies.'

Glystra opened his eyes. His body was at once warm and cool, tingling with sensitivity. He felt strong as a leopard, agile, flooded with potential.

He looked around the hall, studied the troubled faces of the people before him. Victims they were, the result of their inner warps. Nancy was pale as eggshell, her eyes full and moist. He saw her as she was, divined her motives.

The Bajarnum said doubtfully, 'He looks perfectly happy.'

Mercodion answered, 'That's the common response. For a brief period they float on a sea of well-being. Then their vitality fails and they go. Hurry, Bajarnum; hurry if you wish knowledge.'

Charley Lysidder spoke in a loud voice. 'How can I buy weapons from the System Arms Control? Who can I bribe?'

Glystra looked down at the Bajarnum, at Mercodion, at Nancy. The situation seemed suddenly one of vast humor; he found it hard to control his face.

The Bajarnum repeated the question, more urgently.

'Try Alan Marklow,' said Glystra, as if imparting a precious secret.

The Bajarnum leaned forward, excited in spite of himself. 'Alan Marklow? The chairman of the Control?' He sat back, a pink flush, half-anger, half-anticipation, on his face. 'So Alan Marklow can be bought – the sanctimonious scoundrel.'

'To the same extent as any other member of the Control,' said Glystra. 'That is the reasoning behind my advice: if you plan to bribe any of them, the best person to subvert is the man at the top.'

The Bajarnum stared. The High Dain's eyes narrowed. He jerked upright in his seat.

Glystra said, 'As I understand it, you want weapons so that you may extend your empire; am I right?'

'In essence,' the Bajarnum admitted warily.

'What is the motive behind this desire?'

Mercodion raised his head, started to bellow an order, thought better of it, clamped his mouth in a tight white line.

The Bajarnum reflected. 'I wish to add glory to my name, to make Grosgarth the queen city of the world, to punish my enemies.'

'Ridiculous. Futile.'

Charley Lysidder was nonplussed. He turned to Mercodion. 'Is this a usual manifestation?'

'By no means,' snapped Mercodion. He could contain his fury no longer. He leapt to his feet, black brows bristling. 'Answer the questions directly! What kind of oracle are you, evading and arguing and asserting the ego which you must know has been numbed by the drug of wisdom? I command you, act with greater pliability, for you will die in two minutes and the Bajarnum has much he wants to learn.'

'Perhaps my question was inexact,' said the Bajarnum mildly. He returned to Glystra. 'What is the most practical method for me to acquire metal weapons at a low cost?'

'Join the Star Patrol,' said Glystra waggishly. 'They'll issue you a sheath-knife and an ion-shine free.'

Mercodion exhaled a deep breath. The Bajarnum frowned. The interview was not going at all as he had expected. He tried a third time. 'Is it likely that Earth-Central will forcibly federate Big Planet?'

'Highly unlikely,' said Glystra, with complete honesty. He thought it was almost time to die, and sank limply into the chair.

'Most unsatisfactory,' grumbled Mercodion.

Charley Lysidder chewed his lip, surveying Glystra with his deceptively candid eyes. Nancy stared numbly; for all his sharpened perceptions, Glystra could not fathom her thoughts.

'One more question,' said the Bajarnum. 'How can I best prolong my life?'

Only by the sternest measures could Glystra control his features. He responded in a weak and doleful voice, 'Allow the Inculcator to shoot you full of wisdom-stuff, as he has me.'

'Faugh!' spat Mercodion. 'The creature is insufferable! Were he not three-quarters dead, I swear I would run him through ... Indeed—'

But Glystra had slumped to the dais.

'Drag the hulk to the 'toir-room,' roared Mercodion. He turned to Charley Lysidder. 'A miserable mistake, Bajarnum, and if you wish, a second oracle will be prepared.'

'No,' said the Bajarnum, thoughtfully surveying Glystra's body. 'I wonder only what was his meaning.'

'Aberrated mish-mash,' scoffed Mercodion.

They watched the prefects take the body from the hall.

'Strange,' said Charley Lysidder. 'He seemed completely vital – a man very far from death ... I wonder what he meant ...'

A naked man stole through the night, trailing the odor of death. He came through Nello's garden plot, ducked into the alley, quietly approached the street.

No one was in sight or earshot. He trotted quietly through the shadows to the house of the swordsmith.

Light glowed yellow through the shutters. He knocked.

Nymaster opened the door. He stood stock-still, his eyes bulging. A second man came to look suspiciously over his shoulder – Corbus, who stared a breathless moment. 'Claude,' he said huskily, 'You're – you're—' His voice broke.

Glystra said briskly, 'We've got to hurry. First a bath.'

Corbus nodded wryly. 'You need something of the sort.' He turned to Nymaster. 'Fill a tub. Get some clothes.'

Nymaster turned away wordlessly.

'They hauled me to their abattoir,' said Glystra. 'They threw me in a bin full of corpses. When the head-boiler came with his knife, I jumped out at him, and he went into a fit. I escaped through the wall.'

'Did they pump you full of nerve-juice?'

Glystra nodded. 'It's quite an experience.' During his bath he gave Corbus and Nymaster an account of his adventures.

'And now what?' Corbus asked.

'Now,' said Glystra, 'we do Charley Lysidder one in the eye.'

Half an hour later, slipping through the gardens, they looked out on the marble courtyard where the Bajarnum's air-boat rested. A man in a scarlet tunic and black boots lounged against the hood. An ion-shine hung at his waist.

'What do you think?' whispered Glystra.

'If we can get in it, I can fly it,' said Corbus.

'Good. I'll run around behind him. You attract his attention.' He disappeared.

Corbus waited two minutes, then stepped out into the courtyard, levelled his ion-shine. 'Don't move,' he said.

The guard straightened, blinked angrily. 'What's the—' Glystra appeared behind him. There was a dull sound; the guard sagged. Glystra took his weapon, waved to Corbus. 'Let's go.'

Myrtlesee Fountain dwindled below them. Glystra laughed exultantly. 'We're free, Corbus – we've done it.'

Corbus looked out across the vast dark expanse. 'I won't believe it until I see Earth Enclave below us.'

Glystra looked at him in surprise. 'Earth Enclave?'

Corbus said tartly, 'Do you propose to fly to Grosgarth?'

'No. But think. We're in a beautiful position. Charley Lysidder is marooned at Myrtlesee Fountain – without his air-car, without his radio to call for another, if he owns one.'

'There's always the monoline,' said Corbus. 'That's fast enough. He can be back in Grosgarth in four days.'

'The monoline – exactly. He'll use the monoline. That's where we'll have him.'

'Maybe easier said than done. He won't venture out unless he goes armed to the teeth.'

'I don't doubt it. He might conceivably send someone else back to Grosgarth, but only if he owns another air-car. We'll have to make sure. There's a spot, as I recall, where the monoline passes under a bluff, which should suit us very well.'

Corbus shrugged. 'I don't like to play a string of luck too far—'

'We don't need luck now. We're not the poor hag-ridden fugitives that we were; we know what we're doing. Before, the Bajarnum was hunting us; now we're hunting him. Right down there—' Glystra pointed '—that bald-headed bluff. We'll settle on top and wait out the night. Early tomorrow – if he's coming at all – we should see Charley Lysidder scudding west under full press of sail. He'll want to get back to Grosgarth as soon as possible.'

CHAPTER TWENTY

Some two hours after dawn a white speck of sail came drifting across the desert from the green smudge that was Myrtlesee Fountain.

'Here comes the Bajarnum,' said Glystra, with evident satisfaction.

The trolley drew closer, swinging and swaying with the changing force of the wind. It was a long pack-car, equipped with two long lateen booms, and flew down the line gracefully as a white swan.

With a hum and spin of great wheels the contrivance of wood and canvas slid under them, whirled on into the west. Four men and one woman rode the platform: Charley Lysidder, three Beaujolain nobles in scarlet tunics, elaborate black felt hats and black boots – and Nancy.

Glystra looked after the diminishing sail-car. 'None of them wore pleasant expressions.'

'But they all wore ion-shines,' Corbus pointed out. 'It'll be a risky business going near them.'

'I don't intend to go near them.' Glystra rose to his feet, started back toward the air-car.

Corbus said with mild testiness, 'I don't mind chasing after you if I know what you've got on your mind; but if you ask me you're carrying this superman business a little too far.'

Glystra stopped short. 'Do I really give that impression?' He looked reflectively across the sandy wastes toward the green paradise of Myrtlesee. 'Perhaps it's the normal state of the psyche after such a traumatic shock.'

'What's the normal state?'

'Introversion. Egocentricity.' He sighed. 'I'll try to adjust myself.'

'Maybe I'll take a dose of that poison too.'

'I've been thinking along the same lines. But now – let's catch Charley Lysidder.' He slid into the air-car.

They flew west, over the tortured hills of obsidian, the mounds of white sand, the rock flat, over the verge of the great cliff. They slanted down, skimmed low over the tumble of rock and scrub, already shimmering in the morning heat.

The monoline rising to the lip of the cliff etched a vast flat curve, a spider-web line against the sky. Glystra veered west, flew a mile past the bottom platform, landed under one of the stanchions. 'Here we violate the first of Clodleberg's commandments: we cut the line. In fact we excise a hundred feet – the length between two of the stanchions should be enough.'

He climbed one pole, slashed the line; Corbus did the same at the second.

'Now,' said Glystra, 'we double the line, tie the bight to the under-frame.'

'Here's a swingle-bar; that suit you?'

'Fine. Two round turns and a couple half-hitches should do the trick—' he watched while Corbus made the line fast '—and now we go back to the bottom anchor.'

They returned to the platform from which the monoline rose to the lip of the cliff. Glystra landed the air-car in the shadow of the platform, jumped to the landing. 'Pass up one of those ends from under the boat.'

Corbus pulled one of the trailing lengths clear, tossed it up.

'Now,' said Glystra, 'we make fast to the monoline with a couple of rolling hitches.'

'Ah,' said Corbus. 'I begin to catch on. The Bajarnum won't like it.'

'The Bajarnum is not being consulted ... You get into the car, in case the weight of the monoline starts to drag ... Ready?'

'Ready.'

Glystra cut the monoline at a point four feet past the first of his hitches. The line sang apart, the connection to the air-car took hold, and a long wave swerved up the line and out of sight. The air-car now served as the bottom anchor to the monoline.

Glystra joined Corbus. 'I give them about an hour. A little less if the wind is good.'

Time passed. Phaedra shouldered huge and dazzling into the dark blue Big Planet sky. Off in the brush a few albino savages lurked and peered. Insects like eels with a dozen dragonfly wings slid easily through the air, threading the harsh gray branches. Round pink toads with eyes on antennae hopped among the rocks. At the top of the cliff appeared a spot of white.

'Here they come,' said Corbus.

Glystra nodded. 'The ride of their life coming up.'

The white spot at the top of the cliff dipped over the edge, started down the long curve. Glystra chuckled. 'I'd like to watch the Bajarnum's face.'

He pushed down the power-arm. The car lifted from behind the platform, climbed into the air – up, up, as high as the lip of the cliff. The trolley rolled down into the lowest section of the loop, slowed, hung suspended, helpless. Five black dots were the passengers – agitated, outraged, uncertain.

Glystra flew above the trolley to the monoline landing at the top of the cliff, settled on the platform. The second length of line under the air-car he made fast to that section of the monoline which led over the cliff. He cut it, and now the trolley with its five occupants hung entirely suspended from the air-car.

Glystra peered over the brink. 'There he is, the Bajarnum of Beaujolais, trapped fair and square, and not a hand laid on him.'

'They've still got their guns,' said Corbus. 'No matter where we set 'em down, they still can shoot at us – even if we take them as far as the Enclave.'

'I've considered that. Dousing them in a lake will cool Charley Lysidder's temper as well as short out his ion-shines.'

The Bajarnum's face, as he stood dripping on the sand beach, was pinched and white. His eyes glinted like puddles of hot quicksilver; he looked neither left nor right. His three noble companions somehow contrived to maintain their dignity even while water sucked squashily in their boots. Nancy's hair clung dankly to her cheeks. Her face was blank as a marble mask. She sat shivering, teeth chattering audibly.

Glystra tossed her his cloak. Draping it over her shoulders and turning away, she slipped out of her sodden garments.

Glystra stood holding the ion-shine. 'Now one at a time into the car. Corbus will search you for knives and hooks and like unpleasantness on the way.' He nodded to the Bajarnum. 'You first.'

One by one they passed Corbus, who extracted three daggers, the sodden ion-shines, and a deadly little poison slap-sack from the group.

'Back in the car, gentlemen,' said Glystra, 'as far back as possible.'

The Bajarnum said in a voice soft as the hiss of silk, 'There shall be requiting, if I must live two hundred years to see it.'

Glystra laughed. 'Now you spit nonsense, like an angry cat. Any requiting to be done will be for the hundred thousand children you've sold into space.'

The Bajarnum blinked. 'There has been no such number.'

'Well – no matter. A hundred or a hundred thousand – the crime is the same.'

Glystra climbed up into the seat beside Corbus, sat looking down into the five faces. Charley Lysidder's emotions were clear enough: serpent-spite and fury behind the mask of the small features in the too-big head. The three noblemen were uniformly glum and apprehensive. And Nancy? Her face was rapt, her thoughts were clearly far away. But Glystra saw neither fear, anger, nor doubt. Her brow was clear, the line of her mouth was natural, almost happy; her eyes flickered with the passage of her thoughts like the flash of silver fish in dark water.

Here, thought Glystra in sudden insight, is the conflict of multiple personalities resolved; she has been at war with herself; she has been caught in a flow too strong to resist; she submits with relief. She feels guilt; she knows she will be punished; she awaits punishment with joy.

They were all settled. He turned to Corbus. 'Let's go. Think you can find the Enclave?'

'Hope so.' He rapped his knuckles on a black cabinet. 'We can find our way along the radio-beam after we get around the planet.'

'Good.'

The air-car rose into the air, flew west. The lake vanished astern.

Charley Lysidder wrung water from the hem of his cloak. He had recovered something of his suavity and spoke in a thoughtful voice. 'I think you wrong me, Claude Glystra. So indeed I have sold starving waifs, but as a means to an end. Admittedly the means was uncomfortable, but did not people die before Earth became federated?'

'Then your ambition is to federate Big Planet?'

'Exactly.'

'To what purpose?'

The Bajarnum stared. 'Why – would not there then be peace and order?'

'No, of course not – as you must know very well. Big Planet could never be unified by conquest – certainly not by the Beaujolain army mounted on zipangotes, and not in your lifetime. I doubt if you care for peace and order. You have used your army to invade and occupy Wale and Glaythree, both quiet farm-countries, but the gypsies and the Rebbirs roam, ravage, murder at will.'

Nancy turned, eyed the Bajarnum dubiously. The three nobles glared truculently. Charley Lysidder preened a ring in his mustache.

'No,' said Glystra, 'your conquests are motivated by vanity and egotism. You are merely Heinzelman the Hellhorse in better-looking clothes.'

'Talk, talk, talk,' sneered Charley Lysidder. 'Earth commissions come and go, Big Planet swallows them all; they drown like gnats in Batzimarjian Ocean.'

Glystra grinned. 'This commission is different – what there's left of it. I insisted on complete power before I took the job. I do not recommend; I command.'

The Bajarnum's tight features squeezed even closer together, as if he were tasting something bitter. 'Assuming all this were true – what would you do?'

Glystra shrugged. 'I don't know. I have ideas, but no program. One thing is certain: the slaughter, the slaving, the cannibalism must stop.'

'Hah!' The Bajarnum laughed spitefully. 'So you'll call down Earth war-boats, kill the gypsies, the Rebbirs, the nomads, the steppe-men, all the wandering tribes across Big Planet – you'll build an Earth Empire where I would build a Beaujolain Realm.'

'No,' said Glystra. 'Clearly you do not grasp the crux of the problem. Unity can never be imposed on the peoples of Big Planet, any more than a state could be formed from a population of ants, cats, fish, monkeys, elephants. A thousand years may pass before Big Planet knows a single government. An Earth-dominated Big Planet would be unwieldy, expensive, arbitrary – almost as bad as a Beaujolain Empire.'

'Then what do you plan?'

Glystra shrugged. 'Regional organization, small regional guard-corps ...'

The Bajarnum sniffed. 'The whole decrepit paraphernalia of Earth. In five years your regional commanders become petty tyrants, your regional judges are soliciting bribes, your regional policy-makers are enforcing uniformity on the disparate communities.'

'That indeed,' said Glystra, 'is where we must tread warily ...'

He looked out the window across the sun-drenched Big Planet landscape. An endless vista, forested mountains, green valleys, winding rivers, hot plains.

He heard a muffled nervous cry. He twisted to find two of the men in red tunics on their feet, crouching to leap. He twitched the ion-shine; the men in the damp red tunics sank back.

Charley Lysidder hissed a word Glystra could not hear; Nancy shrank to the side of the boat.

There was ten minutes of acrid silence. Finally the Bajarnum said in a crackling self-conscious voice, 'And, may I ask, what you plan with us?'

Glystra looked out the window again. 'I'll tell you in another couple of hours.'

They flew across an island-dappled sea, a gray desert, a range of mountains with white peaks reaching angrily up into dark blue sky. Over a pleasant rolling country dotted with vineyards, Glystra said to Corbus, 'This is far enough, I think. We'll set down here.'

The air-boat touched ground.

Charley Lysidder hung back, his delicate features working. 'What are you going to do?'

'Nothing. I'm turning you loose. You're on your own. You can try to get back to Grosgarth if you like. I doubt if you'll make it. If you stay here, you'll probably have to work for a living – the worst punishment I could devise.'

Charley Lysidder, the three noblemen, sullenly stepped out into the afternoon sunlight. Nancy hung back. Lysidder gestured angrily. 'I have much to say to you.'

Nancy looked desperately at Glystra. 'Won't you let me out elsewhere ...'

Glystra shut the door. 'Take 'er up, Corbus.' He turned to Nancy. 'I'm not setting you down anywhere,' he said shortly.

Charley Lysidder and his three companions became minute shapes, mannikins in rich-colored clothes; rigid, motionless, they watched the air-car swing across the sky. Charley Lysidder raised his fist, shook it in a frenzy of hate. Glystra turned away, grinning. 'Now there's no more Bajarnum of Beaujolais. Vacancy, Corbus; need a job?'

'I believe I'd make a medium-to-good king ... Come to think of it,' Corbus ruminated, 'I've always wanted a nice little feudal domain in a good wine country ... Fancy uniforms, operettas, beautiful women ...' His voice trailed off. 'Anyway, put my name down for the job.'

'It's yours, if I've anything to say about it – and I have.'

'Thanks. My first official act will be to clean out that den of fakers, Myrtlesee Fountain. Or does my empire run that far?'

'If you want Myrtlesee Fountain you've got to take the Palari Desert and the Rebbirs along with it.'

'Draw the boundary along the River Oust,' said Corbus. 'I know when I'm well off.'

Big Planet landscape, swimming in the halcyon light of late afternoon, slipped astern. Glystra finally found it impossible to ignore the quiet figure in the rear of the car. He stepped down from the control platform, settled upon the seat beside her. 'As far as I'm concerned,' he said gruffly, 'I'm willing to believe that you were an unwilling accessory, and I'll see that—'

She interrupted him in a low and passionate voice. 'I'll never be able to make you believe that we were working for the same things.'

Glystra grinned a wry sad smile, remembering the journey east out of Jubilith. Darrot, Ketch, Pianza, Bishop: all dead, and if not by her direct action, at least with her connivance. An angel with bloody hands. In order to win his confidence she had feigned love, prostituted herself.

'I know what you're thinking,' she said, 'but let me speak – and then you may drop me anywhere, in the middle of the ocean if you like.

'The gypsies burnt my home with all inside,' she added in a dull voice. 'I told you so; it is true. I wandered to Grosgarth, Charley Lysidder saw me at the Midsummer Festival. He was crying crusade against all the outside world, and here, so I thought, was how Big Planet might be made safe and evil beings like the gypsies exterminated. He called me to his chambers; I did not refuse. What girl refuses an emperor? He took me to Earth; on the way back we learned of your plans. Apparently you projected nothing more than the persecution of Charley Lysidder. I was bitter against Earth and all its people. They lived in wealth and security, while on Big Planet the great-grandchildren of Earth were murdered and tormented. Why could they not help us?'

Glystra started to speak; she made a weary gesture. 'I know what you will say: "Earth can only wield authority over a finite volume of space. Anyone who passes through the boundaries forfeits the protection of those within." That might have been valid for the first ones to come out from Earth, but it seems cruel to punish the children of these thoughtless ones forever and ever ... And it seemed that while you would do nothing to help us, you wanted to thwart the only man on Big Planet with vision and power: Charley Lysidder. And much as it hurt me, because—' she darted him a brief look '—I had come to love you, I had to fight you.'

'Why didn't you?' asked Glystra.

She shuddered. 'I couldn't. And I've lived in misery ... I can't understand how you failed to suspect me.'

'When I think back,' said Glystra, his eyes on the past, 'it seems as if I knew all the time, but could not make myself believe it. There were a hundred indications. Morwatz's troopers had us bound and helpless; you refused to cut us loose until it was clear that the Beaujolains were dead and the gypsies were coming. You thought the Fountain insects sounded like birds. There are no birds on Big Planet. And when Bishop was killed—'

'I had nothing to do with that. I tried to slip off to the dome. He came after me and the priests killed him and took his head.'

'And Pianza?'

She shook her head. 'The traders had already killed Pianza. I kept them from killing everyone else. But I let them take the trolleys, because I thought that if you would only return to Kirstendale we could live together safe and happy ...' She looked at him and her mouth drooped. 'You don't believe anything of what I'm saying.'

'No, on the contrary, I believe everything ... I wish I had your courage.'

Corbus' voice came raucously down from the control platform. 'You two are beginning to embarrass me. Clinch and get it over with.'

Glystra and Nancy sat in silence. After a moment Glystra said, 'There's a lot of unfinished business behind us ... On our way back we'll drop in at Kirstendale and hire Sir Cloyville to pull us around the streets in a big carriage.'

'Count me in,' said Corbus. 'I'll bring a long whip.'

THE BLUE WORLD

CHAPTER ONE

Among the people of the Floats caste distinctions were fast losing their old-time importance. The Anarchists and Procurers had disappeared altogether; inter-caste marriages were by no means uncommon, especially when they involved castes of approximately the same social status. Society, of course, was not falling into chaos; the Bezzlers and the Incendiaries still maintained their traditional aloofness; the Advertisermen still could not evade a subtle but nonetheless general disesteem, and where the castes were associated with a craft or trade, they functioned with undiminished effectiveness. The Swindlers comprised the vast majority of those who fished from coracles, and though the once numerous Peculators had dwindled to a handful, they still dominated the dye works on Fay Float. Smugglers boiled varnish, Malpractors pulled teeth. Blackguards constructed the sponge-arbors in every lagoon; the Hoodwinks completely monopolized the field of hood-winking. This last relationship always excited the curiosity of the young, who would inquire, 'Which first: the Hoodwinks or hood-winking?' To which the elders customarily replied: 'When the Ship of Space discharged the Firsts upon these blessed floats, there were four Hoodwinks among the Two Hundred. Later, when the towers were built and the lamps established, there were hoods to wink, and it seemed only appropriate that the Hoodwinks should occupy themselves at the trade. It may well be that matters stood so in the Outer Wildness, before the Escape. It seems likely. There were undoubtedly lamps to be flashed and hoods to be winked. Of course there is much we do not know, much concerning which the Memoria are either silent or ambiguous.'

Whether or not the Hoodwinks had been drawn to the trade by virtue of ancient use, it was now the rare Hoodwink who did not in some measure find his vocation upon the towers, either as a rigger, a lamp-tender, or as a full-fledged hoodwink.

Another caste, the Larceners, constructed the towers, which customarily stood sixty to ninety feet high at the center of the float, directly above the primary stalk of the sea-plant. There were usually four legs of woven or laminated withe, which passed through holes in the pad to join a stout stalk twenty or thirty feet below the surface. At the top of the tower was a cupola, with walls of split withe, a roof of varnished and laminated pad-skin. Yard-arms extending to either side supported lattices, each carrying nine lamps arranged in a square, together with the hoods and trip mechanisms. Within the cupola, windows afforded a view across the water to the neighboring floats – a distance as much as the two miles between Green Lamp and Adelvine, or as little as the quarter-mile between Leumar and Populous Equity.

The Master Hoodwink sat at a panel. At his left hand were nine tap-rods, cross-coupled to lamp-hoods on the lattice to his right. Similarly the tap-rods at his right hand controlled the hoods to his left. By this means the configurations he formed and those he received, from his point of view, were of identical aspect and caused him no confusion. During the daytime the lamps were not lit and white targets served the same function. The hoodwink set his configuration with quick strokes of right and left hands, kicked the release, which thereupon flicked the hoods, or shutters, at the respective lamps or targets. Each configuration signified a word; the mastery of a lexicon and a sometimes remarkable dexterity were the Master Hoodwink's stock in trade. All could send at speeds almost that of speech; all knew at least five thousand, and some six, seven, eight, or even nine thousand configurations. The folk of the floats could in varying degrees read the configurations, which were also employed in the keeping of the archives (against the vehement protests of the scriveners), and in various other communications, public announcements and messages.*

On Tranque Float, at the extreme east of the group, the Master Hoodwink was one Zander Rohan, a rigorous and exacting old man with a mastery of over seven thousand configurations. His first assistant, Sklar Hast, had well over five thousand configurations at his disposal; precisely how many more he had never publicized. There were two further assistants, as well as three apprentices, two riggers, a lamp-tender, and a maintenance withe-weaver, this latter a Larcener. Zander Rohan tended the tower from dusk until middle evening: the busy hours during which gossip, announcements, news, and notifications regarding King Kragen flickered up and down the fifty-mile line of the floats.

---

* The orthography had been adopted in the earliest days and was highly systematic. The cluster at the left indicated the genus of the idea, the cluster at the right denoted the specific. In such a fashion ⠶ at the left, signified *color*; hence:

White	⠶ ·
Black	⠶ .
Red	⠶ ··
Pink	⠶ ·.
Dark Red	⠶ ·:

and so forth.

Sklar Hast winked hoods during the afternoon; then, when Zander Rohan appeared in the cupola, he looked to maintenance and supervised the apprentices. A relatively young man, Sklar Hast had achieved his status by the simplest and most uncomplicated policy imaginable: with great tenacity he strove for excellence, and sought to instill the same standards into the apprentices. He was a positive and direct man, without any great affability, knowing nothing of malice or guile and little of tact or patience. The apprentices resented his brusqueness but respected him; Zander Rohan considered him overpragmatic and deficient in reverence for his betters – which was to say, himself. Sklar Hast cared nothing one way or the other. Zander Rohan must soon retire; in due course Sklar Hast would become Master Hoodwink. He was in no hurry; on this placid, limpid, changeless world where time drifted rather than throbbed, there was little to be gained by urgency.

Sklar Hast owned a small pad of which he was the sole occupant. The pad, a heart-shaped wad of spongy tissue a hundred feet in diameter, floated at the north of the lagoon. Sklar Hast's hut was of standard construction: withe bent and lashed, then sheathed with sheets of pad-skin, the tough near-transparent membrane peeled from the bottom of the sea-plant pad. All was then coated with well-aged varnish, prepared by boiling sea-plant sap until the water was driven off and the resins amalgamated.

Other vegetation grew in the spongy tissue of the pad: shrubs, a thicket of bamboo-like rods yielding good-quality withe, epiphytes hanging from the central spike of the sea-plant. On other pads the plants might be ordered according to aesthetic theory, but Sklar Hast had small taste in these matters, and the center of his pad was little more than an untidy copse of various stalks, fronds, tendrils and leaves, in various shades of black, green and rusty orange.

Sklar Hast knew himself for a fortunate man. There was, unfortunately, an obverse to the picture, for those qualities which had won him prestige, position, a private float, were not those calculated to ease him through the careful routines of float society. Only this afternoon he had become involved in a dispute involving a whole complex of basic float principles. Sitting now on the bench before his hut, sipping a cup of wine, Sklar Hast watched lavender dusk settle over the ocean and brooded upon the headstrong folly of Meril Rohan, daughter to Zander Rohan. A breeze ruffled the water, moved the foliage; drawing a deep breath, Sklar Hast felt his anger loosen and drain away. Meril Rohan could do as she pleased; it was folly to exercise himself – either in connection with her or Semm Voiderveg or anything else. Conditions were as they were; if no one else objected, why should he? With this, Sklar Hast smiled a faint, rather bitter, smile, knowing that he could not fully subscribe to this doctrine ... But the evening was far too soft and soothing for contentiousness. In due course events would right themselves, and looking away toward the horizon, Sklar Hast, in a moment of clarity, thought to see the future, as wide and lucid as the dreaming expanse of water and sky. Presently he would espouse one of the girls whom he currently tested – and forever abandon privacy, he reflected wistfully. There was no need for haste. In the case of Meril Rohan ... But no. She occupied his thoughts merely because of her perverse and headstrong plans in regard to Semm Voiderveg – which did not bear thinking about.

Sklar Hast drained his cup of wine. Folly to worry, folly to fret. Life was good. In the lagoon hung arbors on which grew the succulent spongelike organisms which, when cleaned, plucked and boiled, formed the staple food of the Float folk. The lagoon teemed with edible fish, separated from the predators of the ocean by an enormous net. Much other food was available: spores from the sea-plant fruiting organ, various tendrils and bulbs, as well as the prized flesh of the gray-fish which the swindlers took from the ocean.

Sklar Hast poured himself a second cup of wine and, leaning back, looked up to where the constellations already blazed. Halfway up the southern sky hung a cluster of twenty-five bright stars, from which, so tradition asserted, his ancestors had come, fleeing the persecution of megalomaniac tyrants. Two hundred persons, of various castes, managed to disembark before the Ship of Space foundered in the ocean which spread unbroken around the world. Now, twelve generations later, the two hundred were twenty thousand, scattered along fifty miles of floating sea-plant. The castes, so jealously differentiated during the first few generations, had gradually accommodated themselves to one another and now were even intermingling. There was little to disturb the easy flow of life, nothing harsh or unpleasant – except, perhaps, King Kragen.

Sklar Hast rose, walked to the edge of the float, where only two days before King Kragen had plucked three of his arbors clean. King Kragen's appetite as well as his bulk grew by the year, and Sklar Hast wondered how large King Kragen might eventually become. Was there any limit? During his own lifetime King Kragen had grown perceptibly, and now measured perhaps sixty feet in length. Sklar Hast scowled westward across the ocean, in the direction from which King Kragen customarily appeared, moving with long strokes of his four propulsive vanes in a manner to suggest some vast, grotesquely ugly anthropoid swimming the breast-stroke. There, of course, the resemblance to man ended. King Kragen's body was tough black cartilage, a long cylinder riding a heavy rectangle, from the corners of which extended the vanes. The cylinder comprising King Kragen's main bulk opened forward in a maw fringed with four mandibles and eight palps, aft in an anus. Atop this cylinder, somewhat to the front, rose a turret from which the four eyes protruded: two peering forward, two aft. King Kragen was a terrible force for destruction, but luckily could be placated. King Kragen enjoyed copious quantities of sponges, and when his appetite was appeased, he injured no one and did no damage; indeed he kept the area clear of other marauding kragen, which either he killed or sent flapping and skipping in a panic across the ocean.

Sklar Hast returned to the bench, swung sidewise to where he could watch the winks from Tranque Tower. Zander Rohan was at the hoods; Sklar Hast well knew his touch. It was marked by a certain measured crispness, which very gradually was becoming wooden. To the casual eye Zander Rohan's style was clean and deft; his precision and flexibility were those of a Master Hoodwink. But almost insensibly his speed was falling off, his sense of time was failing; there was a brittle quality to his winking, rather than the supple rhythm of a hoodwink at the height of his powers. Zander Rohan was growing old. Sklar Hast knew that he could outwink Zander Rohan at any time, should he choose to humiliate the old man. This, for all Sklar Hast's bluntness and lack of tact, was the last thing he wished to do. But how long would the old man persist in fulfilling his duties? Even now Zander Rohan had unreasonably delayed his retirement – from jealousy and rancor, Sklar Hast suspected.

The antipathy derived from a whole set of circumstances: Sklar Hast's uncompromising manner, his self-confidence, his professional competence; and then there was the matter of Meril, Zander Rohan's daughter. Five years before, when relations between the two men had been more easy, Rohan had extended a number of not too subtle hints that Sklar Hast might well consider Meril as a possible spouse. By every objective standpoint, the prospect should have aroused Sklar Hast's enthusiasm. Meril was of his own caste, the daughter of a guild-master; Sklar Hast's career could not help but be furthered. They were of the same generation, both Elevenths, a matter of no formal importance but which popularly was regarded as desirable and advantageous. And finally Meril was by no means uncomely, though somewhat leggy and boyishly abrupt of movement. What had given Sklar Hast pause was Meril Rohan's unpredictability and perverse behavior. Like most folk of the floats she could read winks but she also had learned the cursive script of the Firsts. Sklar Hast, with eyes conditioned by the precision and elegance of the hoodwink configurations, considered the script crabbed, sinuous and cryptic; he was annoyed by its lack of uniformity, even though he recognized and was a connoisseur of the unique and individual style that distinguished each Master Hoodwink. On one occasion he had inquired Meril Rohan's motive for learning the script. 'Because I want to read the Memoria,' she told him. 'Because I wish to become a scrivener.'

Sklar Hast had no fault to find with her ambition – he was quite willing that everyone should pursue his own dream – but he was puzzled. 'Why go to such effort? The Analects are given in winks. They teach us the substance of the Memoria and eliminate the absurdities.'

Meril Rohan laughed in a manner Sklar Hast found somewhat strange. 'But it is exactly this which interests me! The absurdities, the contradictions, the allusions – I wonder what they all mean!'

'They mean that the Firsts were a confused and discouraged set of men and women.'

'What I want to do,' said Meril, 'is to make a careful new study of the Memoria. I want to note each of the absurdities and try to understand it, try to relate it to all the other absurdities – because I can't believe that the men who wrote the Memoria considered these passages absurdities.'

Sklar Hast gave a shrug of indifference. 'Incidentally, your father suggested that you might care to be tested. If you like, you can come to my float any time after tomorrow morning – Coralie Vozelle will then be leaving.'

Meril Rohan compressed her lips in mingled amusement and vexation. 'My father is trying to marry me off long before I care to be so dealt with. Thank you, I do not care to be tested. Coralie may exert herself on your behalf yet another week, for all of me. Or another month. Or a year.'

'As you wish,' said Sklar Hast. 'It probably would be time wasted, since we obviously have no community of soul.'

Shortly thereafter Meril Rohan departed Tranque Float for the Scrivener's Academy on Quatrefoil. Sklar Hast had no idea whether or not Meril had mentioned his solicitation to her father, but thereafter the relationship congealed.

In due course Meril Rohan returned to Tranque with her own copies of the Memoria. The years on Quatrefoil had changed her. She was less careless, less flamboyant, less free with her opinions, and had become almost beautiful, though she still ran to leg and a certain indefinable informality of dress and conduct. Sklar Hast twice had offered to test her. On the first occasion she gave him an absentminded negative; on the second – only a day or two before – she had informed him that Semm Voiderveg was planning to espouse her without benefit of testing.

Sklar Hast found the news incredible, disturbing, unacceptable. Semm Voiderveg, a Hooligan by caste, was Tranque Intercessor, with a prestige second only to that of Ixon Myrex, the Float Arbiter. Nevertheless Sklar Hast found a dozen reasons why Meril Rohan should not become spouse to Semm Voiderveg, and he was not at all diffident in imparting them. 'He's an old man! You're hardly more than a girl! He's probably an Eighth! Maybe a Ninth.'

'He's not so old. Ten years older than you, or so I should guess. Also he's a Tenth.'

'Well, you're an Eleventh, and I'm an Eleventh!'

Meril Rohan looked at him, head at a sidelong tilt, and Sklar Hast suddenly became aware of matters he had never noticed before: the clear luminosity of her skin, the richness of her dark curls, the provocative quality that once had seemed boyish abruptness but now was – something else.

'Bah,' muttered Sklar Hast. 'You're both insane, the pair of you. He for wiving without a test, you for flinging yourself into the household of a kragen-feeder. You know his caste? He's only a Hooligan.'

'What a disrespectful attitude!' she exclaimed. 'Semm Voiderveg is Intercessor!'

Sklar Hast peered frowningly at her in an attempt to learn if she were serious. There seemed to be a lightness to her voice, a suppressed levity, which he was unable to interpret. 'What of it?' he asked. 'When you add everything together, the kragen is only a fish. A large fish, true. Still, it seems foolish making so much ceremony over a fish.'

'If he were an ordinary fish, your words would have meaning,' said Meril Rohan. 'King Kragen is not a fish, and he is – extraordinary.'

Sklar Hast made a bitter sound. 'And you're the one who went to Quatrefoil to become a scrivener! How do you think Voiderveg will take to your unorthodox ideas?'

'I don't know.' Meril Rohan gave her head a frivolous toss. 'My father wants me married. As spouse to the Intercessor I'll have time to work on my analysis.'

'Disgusting,' said Sklar Hast, and walked away. Meril Rohan gave her shoulders a shrug and went her own way.

Sklar Hast brooded on the matter during the morning and later in the day approached Zander Rohan: a man as tall as himself, with a great mop of white hair, a neat white beard, a pair of piercing gray eyes, a pinkish complexion, and a manner of constant irascible truculence. In no respect did Meril Rohan resemble her father save in the color of her eyes.

Sklar Hast, who had the least possible facility with tact or subtlety, said, 'I've been speaking to Meril. She tells me you want her to espouse Voiderveg.'

'Yes,' said Zander Rohan. 'What of it?'

'It's a poor match. You know Voiderveg: he's portly, pompous, complacent, obstinate, stupid—'

'Here, here!' exclaimed Rohan. 'He's Intercessor to Tranque Float! He does my daughter great honor by agreeing to test her!'

'Hmm.' Sklar Hast raised his eyebrows. 'She told me he'd waived testing.'

'As to that, I can't say. If so, the honor is even greater.'

Sklar Hast drew a deep breath and made a hard decision. 'I'll marry her,' he growled. 'I'll waive testing. It would be a much better match for her.'

Rohan drew back, lips parted in an unpleasant grin. 'Why should I give her to an assistant hoodwink when she can have the Intercessor? Especially a man who thinks he's too good for her, to begin with!'

Sklar Hast held back his anger. 'I am a Hoodwink, as is she. Do you want her attached to a Hooligan?'

'What difference does it make? He is Intercessor!'

'I'll tell you what difference it makes,' said Sklar Hast. 'He can't do anything except caper for the benefit of a fish. I am Assistant Master Hoodwink, not just an assistant hoodwink. You know my quality.'

Zander Rohan compressed his lips, gave his head a pair of short sharp jerks. 'I know your quality – and it's not all it should be. If you expect to master your craft, you had best strike the keys with more accuracy and use fewer paraphrases. When you meet a word you can't wink, let me know and I will instruct you.'

Sklar Hast clamped his throat upon the words that struggled to come forth. For all his bluntness he had no lack of self-control when circumstances warranted, as they did now. Staring eye to eye with Zander Rohan, he weighed the situation. Should he choose, he might require Zander Rohan to defend his rank, and it almost seemed that Rohan were daring him to challenge: for the life of him Sklar Hast could not understand why – except on the basis of sheer personal antipathy. Such contests, once numerous, now were rare, inasmuch as consideration of dignity made resignation of status incumbent upon the loser. Sklar Hast had no real wish to drive Zander Rohan from his position, and he did not care to be driven forth himself ... He turned his back and walked away from the Master Hoodwink, ignoring the contemptuous snort that came after him.

At the foot of the tower he stood staring bleakly and unseeingly through the foliage. A few yards away was Zander Rohan's ample three-dome cottage, where, under a pergola draped with sweet-tassel, Meril Rohan sat weaving white cloth at the loom – the spare-time occupation of every female from childhood to old age. Sklar Hast went to stand by the low fence of woven withe which separated Rohan's plot from the public way. Meril acknowledged his presence with a faint smile and continued with her weaving.

Sklar Hast spoke with measured dignity. 'I have been talking with your father. I protested the idea of your espousal to Voiderveg. I told him I would marry you myself.' And he turned to look off across the lagoon. 'Without testing.'

'Indeed. And what did he say?'

'He said no.'

Meril, making no comment, continued with her weaving.

'The situation as it stands is ridiculous,' said Sklar Hast. 'Typical of this outlying and backward float. You would be laughed out of countenance on Apprise or even Sumber.'

'If you are unhappy here, why do you not go elsewhere?' asked Meril in a voice of gentle malice.

'I would if I could – I'd leave these insipid floats in their entirety! I'd fly to the far worlds! If I thought they weren't all madhouses.'

'Read the Memoria and find out.'

'Hmf. After twelve generations all may be changed. The Memoria are a pedant's preserve. Why rake around among the ashes of the past? The scriveners are of no more utility than the intercessors. On second thought you and Semm Voiderveg will make a good pair. While he invokes blessings upon King Kragen, you can compile a startling new set of Analects.'

Meril halted her weaving, frowned down at her hands. 'Do you know, I think I will do exactly this?' She rose to her feet, came over to the fence. 'Thank you, Sklar Hast!'

Sklar Hast inspected her with suspicion. 'Are you serious?'

'Certainly. Have you ever known me otherwise?'

'I've never been sure ... How will a new set of Analects be useful? What's wrong with the old ones?'

'When sixty-one books are condensed into three, a great deal of information is left out.'

'Vagueness, ambiguity, introspection: is any of it profitable?'

Meril Rohan pursed her lips. 'The inconsistencies are interesting. In spite of the persecutions the Firsts suffered, all express regret at leaving the Home Worlds.'

'There must have been other sane folk among the madmen,' said Sklar Hast reflectively. 'But what of that? Twelve generations are gone; all may be changed. We ourselves have changed, and not for the better. All we care about is comfort and ease. Appease, assuage, compromise. Do you think the Firsts would have capered and danced to an ocean-beast as is the habit of your prospective spouse?'

Meril glanced over Sklar Hast's shoulder; Sklar Hast turned to see Semm Voiderveg the Intercessor, standing by with arms clasped behind his back, head thrust forward: a man of maturity, portly, but by no means ill-favored, with regular features in a somewhat round face. His skin was clear and fresh, his eyes a dark magnetic brown.

'These are impertinent remarks to make of the Intercessor!' said Semm Voiderveg reproachfully. 'No matter what you think of him as an individual, the office deserves respect!'

'What office? What do you do?'

'I intercede for the folk of Tranque Float; I secure for us all the benevolence of King Kragen.'

Sklar Hast gave an offensive laugh. 'I wonder always if you actually believe your own theories.'

'"Theory" is an incorrect word,' stated Semm Voiderveg. '"Science" or "doxology" is preferable.' He went on in a cold voice, 'The facts are incontrovertible. King Kragen rules the ocean, he lends us protection; in return we gladly tender him a portion of our bounty. These are the terms of the Covenant.'

The discussion was attracting attention among others of the float; already a dozen folk had halted to listen. 'In all certainty we have become soft and fearful,' said Sklar Hast. 'The Firsts would turn away in disgust. Instead of protecting ourselves, we bribe a beast to do the job.'

'Enough!' barked Semm Voiderveg in a sudden cold fury. He turned to Meril, pointed toward the cottage. 'Within – that you need not hear the wild talk of this man! An Assistant Master Hoodwink! Astonishing that he has risen so high in the guild!'

With a rather vague smile Meril turned and went into the cottage. Her submission not only irked Sklar Hast, it astounded him.

With a final indignant glance of admonition Semm Voiderveg followed her within.

Sklar Hast turned away toward the lagoon and his own pad. One of the men who had halted called out. 'A moment, Sklar Hast! You seriously believe that we could protect our own if King Kragen decided to depart?'

'Certainly,' snapped Sklar Hast. 'We could at least make the effort! The intercessors want no changes – why should they?'

'You're a trouble-maker, Sklar Hast!' called a shrill female voice from the back of the group. 'I've known you since you were an infant; you never were less than perverse!'

Sklar Hast pushed through the group, walked through the gathering dusk to the lagoon, ferried himself by coracle to his pad.

He entered the hut, poured himself a cup of wine, and went out to sit on the bench. The halcyon sky and the calm water soothed him, and he was able to summon a grin of amusement for his own vehemence – until he went to look at the arbors plucked bare by King Kragen, whereupon his ill-humor returned.

He watched winks for a few moments, more conscious than ever of Zander Rohan's brittle mannerisms. As he turned away, he noticed a dark swirl in the water at the edge of the net: a black bulk surrounded by glistening cusps and festoons of starlit water. He went to the edge of his float and strained his eyes through the darkness. No question about it: a lesser kragen was probing the net which enclosed Tranque Lagoon!

CHAPTER TWO

Sklar Hast ran across the pad, jumped into his coracle, thrust himself to the central float. He delayed only long enough to tie the coracle to a stake formed of a human femur, then ran at top speed to the hoodwink tower. A mile to the west flickered the Thrasneck lamps, the configurations coming in the unmistakable style of Durdan Farr, the Thrasneck Master Hoodwink: '... thirteen ... bushels ... of ... salt ... lost ... when ... a ... barge ... took ... water ... between ... Sumber ... and ... Adelvine ...'

Sklar Hast climbed the ladder, burst into the cupola. Zander Rohan swung about in a surprise that became truculence when he saw Sklar Hast. The pale pink of his face deepened to rose, his lips thrust out, his white hair puffed and glistened as if angry in its own right. It occurred fleetingly to Sklar Hast that Zander Rohan had been in communication with Semm Voiderveg, the subject under discussion doubtless being himself. But now he pointed to the lagoon. 'A rogue, breaking the nets. I just saw him. Call King Kragen!'

Zander Rohan instantly forgot his resentment, flashed the cut-in signal. His fingers jammed down rods; he kicked the release. 'Call ... King ... Kragen!' he signaled. 'Rogue ... in ... Tranque ... Lagoon!'

On Thrasneck Float Durdan Farr relayed the message to the tower on Bickle Float, and so along the line of floats to Sciona at the far west, which thereupon returned the signal: 'King ... Kragen ... is ... nowhere ... at ... hand.' Back down the line of towers flickered the message, returning to Tranque Float in something short of twelve minutes.

Sklar Hast had not awaited the return message. Descending the ladder, he ran back to the lagoon. The kragen had cut open a section of the net and now hung in the gap, plucking sponges from a nearby arbor. Sklar Hast pushed through the crowd which stood watching in awe. 'Ha! Ho!' cried Sklar Hast, flapping his arms. 'Leave us, you dismal black beast!'

The kragen ignored him and with insulting assurance continued to pluck sponges and convey them to its maw. Sklar Hast picked up a heavy knurled joint from a sea-plant stem, hurled it at the turret, striking the forward eye-tube. The kragen recoiled, worked its vanes angrily. The folk on the float muttered uneasily, though a few laughed in great gratification. 'There's the way to deal with kragen!' exulted Irvin Belrod, a wizened old Advertiser-man. 'Strike another blow!'

Sklar Hast picked up a second joint, but someone grabbed his arm: Semm Voiderveg, who spoke in a sharp voice. 'What ill-conceived acts are you committing?'

Sklar Hast jerked free. 'Watch and you'll see.' He turned toward the kragen, but Voiderveg stepped in his way. 'This is arrogance! Have you forgotten the Covenant? King Kragen has been notified; let him deal with the nuisance. This is his prerogative!'

'While the beast destroys our net? Look!' Sklar Hast pointed across the water to Thrasneck Tower, where the return message now flickered: 'King... Kragen ... is ... nowhere ... to ... be ... seen.'

Semm Voiderveg gave a stiff nod. 'I will issue a notice to all intercessors and King Kragen will be summoned.'

'Summoned how? By calling into the night with lamps held aloft?'

'Concern yourself with hoodwinking,' said Semm Voiderveg in the coldest of voices. 'The intercessors will deal with King Kragen.'

Sklar Hast turned, hurled the second joint, which struck the beast in the maw. It emitted a hiss of annoyance, thrashed with vanes, and breaking wide the net, surged into the lagoon. Here it floated, rumbling and hissing, a beast perhaps fifteen feet in length.

'Observe what you have accomplished!' cried Semm Voiderveg in a ringing voice. 'Are you satisfied? The net is now broken and no mistake.'

All turned to watch the kragen, which swung its vanes and surged through the water, a caricature of a man performing the breast-stroke. Starlight danced and darted along the disturbed water, outlining the gliding black bulk. Sklar Hast cried out in fury: the brute was headed for his arbors, so recently devastated by the appetite of King Kragen! He ran to his coracle, thrust himself to his pad. Already the kragen had extended its palps and was feeling for sponges. Sklar Hast sought for an implement which might serve as a weapon; there was nothing to hand: a few articles fashioned from human bones and fish cartilage, a wooden bucket, a mat of woven fiber.

Leaning against the hut was a boat-hook, a stalk ten feet long, carefully straightened, scraped, and seasoned, to which a hook-shaped human rib had been lashed. He took it up and now from the central pad came Semm Voiderveg's cry of remonstrance. 'Sklar Hast! What do you do?'

Sklar Hast paid no heed. He ran to the edge of the pad, jabbed the boat-hook at the kragen's turret. It scraped futilely along the resilient cartilage. The kragen swung up a palp, knocked the pole aside. Sklar Hast jabbed the pole with all his strength at what he considered the kragen's most vulnerable area: a soft pad of receptor-endings directly above the maw. Behind, he heard Semm Voiderveg's outraged protest: 'This is not to be done! Desist! Desist!'

The kragen quivered at the blow, twisted its massive turret to gaze at Sklar Hast. It swung up its fore-vane, slashing at Sklar Hast, who leaped back with inches to spare. From the central pad Semm Voiderveg bawled, 'By no means molest the kragen; it is a matter for the King! We must respect the King's authority!'

Sklar Hast stood back in fury as the kragen resumed its feeding. As if to punish Sklar Hast for his assault, it passed close beside the arbors, worked its vanes, and the arbors – sea-plant stalk lashed with fiber – collapsed. Sklar Hast groaned. 'No more than you deserve,' called out Semm Voiderveg with odious complacence. 'You interfered with the duties of King Kragen – now your arbors are destroyed. This is justice.'

'"Justice"? Bah!' bellowed Sklar Hast. 'Where is King Kragen? We feed the gluttonous beast; why isn't he at hand when we need him?'

'Come, come,' admonished Semm Voiderveg. 'This is hardly the tone in which to speak of King Kragen!'

Sklar Hast groped through the shadows, retrieved the boat-hook, to find that the bone had broken, leaving a sharp point. With all his power, Sklar Hast thrust this at the kragen's eye. The point slid off the hemispherical lens, plunged into the surrounding tissue. The kragen humped almost double, thrust itself clear of the water, fell with a great splash and, sounding, sank from sight. Waves crossed the lagoon, reflected from the surrounding floats, subsided. The lagoon was quiet.

Sklar Hast went to his coracle, pushed himself to the mainland, joined the group which stood peering down into the water.

'Is it dead?' inquired one Morgan Resly, a Swindler of good reputation.

'No such luck,' growled Sklar Hast. 'Next time—'

'Next time – what?' demanded Semm Voiderveg.

'Next time, I'll kill it.'

'And what of King Kragen, who reserves such affairs to himself?'

'King Kragen doesn't care a fig one way or the other,' said Sklar Hast. 'Except for one matter: if we took to the habit of killing kragen, we might begin to look him over with something of the sort in mind.'

Semm Voiderveg made a guttural sound, threw up his hands, turned, walked rapidly away.

Poe Belrod, nominal Elder of the Belrod clan even though Irvin surpassed him in actual age, asked Sklar Hast, 'Can you really kill a kragen?'

'I don't know,' said Sklar Hast. 'I haven't given the notion any thought – so far.'

'They're a tough beast.' Poe Belrod shook his big, crafty head in doubt. 'And then we'd have the wrath of King Kragen to fear.'

'It's a matter to think about,' said Sklar Hast.

Timmons Valby, an Extorter, spoke. 'How is King Kragen to know? He can't be everywhere at once.'

'He knows, he knows all!' stated a nervous old Incendiary. 'All goes well along the floats; we must not cause grief and woe from pride; remember

Kilborn's Dictum from the Analects: "*Pride goeth before a fall!*"'

'Yes, indeed, but recall Baxter's Dictum: "*There shall no evil happen to the just, but the wicked shall be filled with mischief!*"'

The group stood silent a moment, looking over the lagoon, but the kragen did not reappear.

'He's broken through the bottom and departed,' said Morgan Resly, the Swindler.

The group gradually dispersed, some going to their huts, others to Tranque Inn: a long structure furnished with tables, benches, and a counter where wines, syrups, spice-cake, and pepperfish were to be had. Sklar Hast joined this latter group, but sat morosely to the side while every aspect of the evening's events was discussed. Everyone was vehement in his detestation of the rogue kragen, but some questioned the method used by Sklar Hast. Jonas Serbano, a Bezzler, felt that Sklar Hast had acted somewhat too precipitously. 'In matters of this sort, where King Kragen is concerned, all must consult. The wisdom of many is preferable to the headlong rashness of one, no matter how great the provocation.'

Eyes went to Sklar Hast, but he made no response, and it remained for one of the younger Belrods to remark, 'That's all very well, but by the time everyone argues and debates, the sponges are eaten and gone.'

'Better lose an arbor of sponges than risk the displeasure of King Kragen!' replied Jonas Serbano tartly. 'The sea and all that transpires therein is his realm; we trespass at our peril!'

Young Garth Gasselton, an Extorter by caste though a pad-stripper by trade, spoke with the idealistic fervor of youth. 'If conditions were as they should be, we would be masters of all: float, lagoon, and sea alike! The sponges would then be our own; we would need bow our heads to no one!'

At a table across the room sat Ixon Myrex, the Tranque Arbiter, a Bezzler of great physical presence and moral conviction. To this moment he had taken no part in the conversation, sitting with his massive head averted, thus signifying a desire for privacy. Now he slowly turned and fixed a somewhat baleful stare upon young Garth Gasselton. 'You speak without reflection. Are we then so omnipotent that we can simply wave our hands across the sea and command all to our sway? You must recognize that comfort and plenty are neither natural endowments nor our rightful due, but benefits of the most tentative nature imaginable. In short, we exist by the indulgence of King Kragen, and never must we lose sight of the fact!'

Young Gasselton blinked down at his cup of syrup, but old Irvin Belrod was not so easily abashed. 'I'll tell you one thing that you're forgetting, Arbiter Myrex. King Kragen is as he is because we made him so. At the beginning he was a normal kragen, maybe a bit bigger and smarter than the others. He's what he is today because somebody made the mistake of truckling to him. Now the mistake has been made, and I'll grant you that King Kragen is wise and clever and occasionally serves us by scaring away the rogues – but where will it end?'

Wall Bunce, an old Larcener crippled by a fall from the Tranque tower yard-arms, held up an emphatic finger. 'Never forget Cardinal's Dictum from the Analects: "*Whoever is willing to give will never lack someone to take.*"'

Into the inn came Semm Voiderveg and Zander Rohan. They seated themselves beside Ixon Myrex: the three most influential men of the float. After giving Voiderveg and Rohan greeting, Ixon Myrex returned to Wall Bunce. 'Don't go quoting the Analects to me, because I can quote in return: "*The most flagrant fool is the man who doesn't know when he's well off!*"'

'I give you, "*If you start a fight with your hands in your pockets, you'll have warm hands but a bloody nose!*"' called Wall Bunce.

Ixon Myrex thrust out his chin. 'I don't intend to quote Dicta at you all evening, Wall Bunce.'

'It's a poor way to win an argument,' Irvin Belrod remarked.

'I am by no manner of means conducting an argument,' stated Ixon Myrex ponderously. 'The subject is too basic; it affects the welfare of Tranque and of all the floats. There certainly cannot be two sides to a matter as fundamental as this!'

'Here, now,' protested a young scrivener. 'You beg the question! All of us favor continued prosperity and welfare. We're at odds because we define "welfare" differently.'

Ixon Myrex looked down the bridge of his nose. 'The welfare of Tranque Float is not so abstruse a matter,' he said. 'We require merely an amplitude of food and a respect for institutions established by wise men of the past.'

Semm Voiderveg, looking off into mid-air, spoke in a measured minatory voice. 'Tonight an exceedingly rash act was performed, by a man who should know better. I simply cannot understand a mentality which so arrogantly preempts to itself a decision concerning the welfare of the whole float.'

Sklar Hast at last was stung. He gave a sarcastic chuckle. 'I understand your mentality well enough. If it weren't for King Kragen, you'd have to work like everyone else. You've achieved a sinecure, and you don't want a detail changed, no matter how much hardship and degradation are involved.'

'"Hardship"? There is plenty for all! And "degradation"? Do you dare use the word in connection with myself or Arbiter Myrex or Master Hoodwink Rohan? I assure you that these men are by no means "degraded", and I believe that they resent the imputation as keenly as I do myself!'

Sklar Hast grinned. 'There's a dictum to cover all that: "*If the shoe fits, wear it.*"'

Zander Rohan burst out, 'This caps all! Sklar Hast, you disgrace your caste and your calling! I have no means of altering the circumstances of your birth, but thankfully, I am Guild-Master. I assure you that your career as a hoodwink is at an end!'

'Bah,' sneered Sklar Hast. 'On what grounds?'

'Turpitude of the character!' roared Zander Rohan. 'This is a passage of the bylaws, as well you know!'

Sklar Hast gave Zander Rohan a long slow inspection, as before. He sighed and made his decision. 'There's also a passage to the effect that a man shall be Guild-Master only so long as he maintains a paramount proficiency. I challenge not only your right to pass judgment but your rank as Guild-Master as well.'

Silence held the inn. Zander Rohan spoke in a choked voice. 'You think you can outwink me?'

'At any hour of the day or night.'

'Why have you not made this vaunted ability manifest before?'

'If you want to know the truth, I did not wish to humiliate you.'

Zander Rohan slammed his fist upon the table. 'Very well. We shall see who is to be humiliated. Come: to the tower!'

Sklar Hast raised his eyebrows in surprise. 'You are in haste?'

'You said, "any hour of the day or night".'

'As you wish. Who will judge?'

'Arbiter Myrex, of course. Who else?'

'Arbiter Myrex will serve well enough, provided we have others to keep time and note errors.'

'I appoint Semm Voiderveg; he reads with great facility.'

Sklar Hast pointed to others in the room, persons he knew to be keen of eye and deft at reading winks. 'Rubal Gallager – Freeheart Noe – Herlinger Showalter. I appoint these to read winks and note errors.'

Zander Rohan made no objection; all in the inn arose and crossed to the tower.

The space under the tower was enclosed by a wall of withe and varnished pad-skin. On the first level was a shed given over to practice mechanisms; on the second were stores: spare hoods, oil for the lamps, connection cords and records; the third and fourth levels housed apprentices, assistant hoodwinks on duty and maintenance larceners.

Into the first level trooped Zander Rohan and Sklar Hast, followed by those whom they had appointed judges, and ten or twelve others – as many as the shed could contain. Lamps were turned up, benches pushed back, window shutters raised for ventilation.

Zander Rohan went to the newer of the two practice machines, ran his fingers over the keys, kicked the release. He frowned, thrust out his lip, went to the older of the machines, which was looser and easier but with considerably more backlash. The tighter machine required more effort but allowed more speed. He signaled to the apprentices, who stood looking down from the second level. 'Oil. Lubricate the connections. Is this how you maintain the equipment?'

The apprentices hastened to obey.

Sklar Hast ran his fingers over the keys of both machines and decided to use the newer, if the choice were his. Zander Rohan went to the end of the room where he conferred in quiet tones with Ixon Myrex and Semm Voiderveg. All three turned, glanced at Sklar Hast, who stood waiting impassively. Antagonism hung heavy in the room.

Ixon Myrex and Semm Voiderveg came toward Sklar Hast. 'Do you have any conditions or exceptions to make?'

'Tell me what you propose,' said Sklar Hast. 'Then I'll tell you my conditions or exceptions.'

'We propose nothing unusual – in fact, a test similar to those at the Aumerge Tournament during the Year of Waldemar's Dive.'

Sklar Hast gave a curt nod. 'Four selections from the Analects?'

'Precisely.'

'What selections?'

'Apprentice exercises might be most convenient, but I don't think Master Rohan is particular in this case.'

'Nor I. Apprentice exercises will be well enough.'

'I propose we use tournament weighing: The best score is multiplied by 50, the next by 30, the next by 20, the worst by 10. This ensures that your best effort will receive the greatest weight.'

Sklar Hast reflected. The system of weighting tended to favor the efforts of the nervous or erratic operator, while the steadier and more consistent operator was handicapped. Still, under the present circumstances, it made small difference: neither he nor Zander Rohan were typically given to effulgent bursts of speed. 'I agree. What of miswinks?'

'Each error or miswink to add three seconds to the score.'

Sklar Hast acquiesced. There was further discussion of a technical nature, as to what constituted an error, how the errors should be noted and reckoned in regard to the operation of the clock.

Finally all possible contingencies had been discussed. The texts were selected: Exercises 61, 62, 63, 64, all excerpts from the Analects, which in turn had been derived from the sixty-one volumes of Memoria.

Before assenting to the exercises, Zander Rohan donned the spectacles which he recently had taken to using – two lenses of clear gum, melted, cast and held in frames of laminated withe – and carefully read the exercises. Sklar Hast followed suit, though through his work with the apprentices he was intimately acquainted with them. The contestants might use either machine, and both elected to use the new machine. Each man would wink an exercise in turn, and Zander Rohan signified that he wished Sklar Hast to wink first.

Sklar Hast went to the machine, arranged Exercise 61 in front of him, stretched his brown fingers, tested the action of keys and kick-rods. Across the room sat the judges, while Arbiter Myrex controlled the clock. At this moment the door slid back, and into the shed came Meril Rohan.

Zander Rohan made a peremptory motion, which she ignored. Intercessor Voiderveg frowned and held up an admonitory finger, which she heeded even less. Sklar Hast looked once in her direction, meeting her bright gaze, and could not decide on its emotional content: scorn? detestation? amusement? It made no great difference.

'Ready!' called Ixon Myrex. Sklar Hast bent slightly forward, strong hands and tense fingers poised. 'Set! Wink!'

Sklar Hast's hands struck down at the keys; his foot kicked the release. The first configuration, the second, the third. Sklar Hast winked deliberately, gradually loosening, letting his natural muscular rhythm augment his speed.

– even were we able to communicate with the Home Worlds, I wonder if we would now choose to do so. Ignoring the inevitable prosecution which would ensue (owing to our unique background) – as I say, not even considering this – we have gained here something which none of us have ever known before: a sense of achievement on a level other than what I will call 'social manipulation'. We are, by and large, happy on the floats. There is naturally much homesickness, nostalgia, vain regrets – how could this be avoided? Would they be less poignant on New Ossining? This is a question all of us have argued at length, to no decision. The facts are that we all seem to be facing the realities of our new life with a fortitude and equanimity of which we probably did not suspect ourselves capable.

'End!' called Sklar Hast. Ixon Myrex checked the clock. 'One hundred forty-six seconds.'

Sklar Hast moved back from the machine. A good time, though not dazzling, and by no means his best speed. 'Mistakes?' he inquired.

'No mistakes,' stated Rubal Gallager.

Norm time was one hundred fifty-two seconds, which gave him a percentum part score of 6/152, or 3.95 minus.

Zander Rohan poised himself before the machine and at the signal winked forth the message in his usual somewhat brittle style. Sklar Hast listened carefully, and it seemed as if the Master Hoodwink were winking somewhat more deliberately than usual.

Zander Rohan's time was one hundred forty-five seconds; he made no mistakes, and his score was 4.21 minus. He stepped to the side with the trace of a smile. Sklar Hast glanced from the corner of his eye to Meril Rohan, for no other reason than idle curiosity, or so he told himself. Her face revealed nothing.

He set Exercise 62 before him. Ixon Myrex gave the signal; Sklar Hast's hands struck out the first wink. Now he was easy and loose, and his fingers worked like pistons.

Exercise 62, like 61, was an excerpt from the Memorium of Eleanor Morse:

A hundred times we have discussed what to my mind is perhaps the most astonishing aspect of our new community on the float: the sense of trust, of interaction, of mutual responsibility. Who could have imagined from a group of such diverse backgrounds, with such initial handicaps (whether innate or acquired I will not presume to speculate), there might arise so placid, so ordered and so cheerful a society. Our elected leader, like myself, is an embezzler. Some of our most tireless and self-sacrificing workers were previously peculators, hooligans, goons: one could never match the individuals with their past lives. The situation, of course, is not unanimous, but to an amazing extent old habits and attitudes have been superseded by a positive sense of participation in the life of something larger than self. To most of us it is as if we had regained a lost youth or, indeed, a youth we never had known.

'End!' called Sklar Hast.

Ixon Myrex stopped the clock. 'Time: one hundred eighty-two seconds. Norm: two hundred seconds. Mistakes? None.'

Sklar Hast's score was a solid 9 minus. Zander Rohan winked a blazing-fast but nervous and staccato one hundred seventy-nine seconds but made at least two mistakes. Rubal Gallager and Herlinger Showalter claimed to have detected enough of a waver in one of the corner hoods to qualify as a third error, but Freeheart Noe had not noticed, and both Semm Voiderveg and Ixon Myrex insisted that the configuration had been clearly winked. Nevertheless, with a penalty of six seconds, his time became a hundred eighty-five with a score of 15/200 or 7.50 per cent minus.

Sklar Hast approached the third exercise thoughtfully. If he could make a high score on this third exercise, Zander Rohan, already tense, might well press and blow the exercise completely.

He poised himself. 'Wink!' cried Ixon Myrex. And again Sklar Hast's fingers struck the tabs. The exercise was from the Memorium of Wilson Snyder, a man of unstated caste:

Almost two years have elapsed, and there is no question but what we are an ingenious group.

Alertness, ingenuity, skill at improvisation: These are our characteristics. Or, as our detractors would put it, a low simian cunning.

Well, so be it. Another trait luckily common to all of us (more or less) is a well-developed sense of resignation, or perhaps fatalism is the word, toward circumstances beyond our control. Hence we are a far happier group than might be a corresponding number of, say, musicians, or scientists, or even law-enforcement officers. Not that these professions go unrepresented among our little band. Jora Alvan – an accomplished flautist. James Brunet – professor of physical science at Southwestern University. Howard Gallagher – a high-ranking police official. And myself – but no! I adhere to my resolution, and I'll say nothing of my past life. Modesty? I wish I could claim as much!

'End!' Sklar Hast drew a deep breath and stepped back from the machine. He did not look toward Zander Rohan; it would have been an act of malignant gloating to have done so. For he had driven the machine as fast as its mechanism permitted. No man alive could have winked faster, with a more powerful driving rhythm.

Ixon Myrex examined the clock. 'Time: one hundred seventy-two seconds,' he said reluctantly. 'Norm ... This seems incorrect. Two hundred eight?'

'Two hundred eight is correct,' said Rubal Gallager dryly. 'There were no mistakes.'

Ixon Myrex and Semm Voiderveg chewed their lips glumly. Freeheart Noe calculated the score: 36/208, or a remarkable 17.3 minus!

Zander Rohan stepped forward bravely enough and poised himself before the machine. 'Wink!' cried Ixon Myrex in a voice that cracked from tension. And Zander Rohan's once precise fingers stiffened with his own fear and tension, and his careful rhythm faltered. All in the room stood stiff and embarrassed.

Finally he called: 'End!'

Ixon Myrex read the clock. 'Two hundred and one seconds.'

'There were two mistakes,' said Semm Voiderveg. Rubal Gallager started to speak, then held his tongue. He had noted at least five instances which an exacting observer – such as Zander Rohan himself – might have characterized as error. But the contest was clearly one-sided. Two hundred and one seconds, plus six penalty seconds gave Zander Rohan a score of 1/208 or .48 minus.

The fourth exercise was from the Memorium of Hedwig Swin, who, like Wilson Snyder, maintained reserve in regard to her caste.

Ixon Myrex set the clock with unwilling fingers, called out the starting signal. Sklar Hast winked easily, without effort, and the configurations spilled forth in a swift certain flow:

A soft, beautiful world! A world of matchless climate, indescribable beauty, a world of water and sky, with, to the best of my knowledge, not one square inch of solid ground. Along the equator where the sea-plants grow, the ocean must be comparatively shallow, though no one has plumbed the bottom. Quite certainly this world will never be scarred and soiled by an industrial civilization, which of course is all very well. Still, speaking for myself, I would have welcomed a jut of land or two: a good honest mountain, with rocks and trees with roots gripping the soil, a stretch of beach, a few meadows, fields and orchards. But beggars can't be choosers, and compared with our original destination this world is heaven.

'End!'

Ixon Myrex spoke tersely. 'Time: one hundred forty-one. Norm: one hundred sixty.'

All was lost for Zander Rohan. To win he would have to wink for a score of twenty-five or thirty, or perhaps even higher. He knew he could not achieve this score and winked without hope and without tension and achieved his highest score of the test: a strong 12.05 minus. Nonetheless he had lost, and now, by the guild custom, he must resign his post, and give way to Sklar Hast.

He could not bring himself to speak the words. Meril turned on her heel, departed the building.

Zander Rohan finally turned to Sklar Hast. He had started to croak a formal admission of defeat when Semm Voiderveg stepped quickly forward, took Zander Rohan's arm, pulled him aside.

He spoke in urgent tones while Sklar Hast looked on with a sardonic grin. Ixon Myrex joined the conversation, and pulled his chin doubtfully. Zander Rohan stood less erect than usual, his fine bush of white hair limp and his beard twisted askew. From time to time he shook his head in forlorn but unemphatic objection to Semm Voiderveg's urgings.

But Semm Voiderveg had his way and turned toward Sklar Hast. 'A serious defect in the test has come to light. I fear it cannot be validated.'

'Indeed?' asked Sklar Hast. 'And how is this?'

'It appears that you work daily with these exercises, during your instruction of the apprentices. In short, you have practiced these exercises intensively, and the contest thereby is not a fair one.'

'You selected the exercises yourself.'

'Possibly true. It was nevertheless your duty to inform us of your familiarity with the matter.'

'In sheer point of fact,' said Sklar Hast, 'I am not familiar with the exercises, and had not winked them since I was an apprentice myself.'

Semm Voiderveg shook his head. 'I find this impossible to believe. I for one refuse to validate the results of this so-called contest and I believe that Arbiter Myrex feels much the same disgust and indignation as I do myself.'

Zander Rohan had the grace to croak a protest. 'Let the results stand. I cannot explain away the score.'

'By no means!' exclaimed Semm Voiderveg. 'A Master Hoodwink must be a man of utter probity. Do we wish in this august position one who—'

Sklar Hast said in a gentle voice, 'Be careful of your words, Intercessor. The penalties for slander are strict, as Arbiter Myrex can inform you.'

'Slander exists if truth is absent or malice is the motivation. I am concerned only for the well-being of Tranque Float, and the conservation of traditional morality. Is it slander, then, if I denounce you as a near-approach to a common cheat?'

Sklar Hast took a slow step forward, but Rubal Gallager took his arm. Sklar Hast turned to Arbiter Myrex. 'And what do you say to all this: you who are Arbiter?'

Ixon Myrex's forehead was damp. 'Perhaps we should have used other texts for the test. Even though you had no hand in the selection.'

To the side stood two or three members of the Belrod clan, deep-divers for stalk and withe, of the Advertiserman caste, generally prone to a rude and surly vulgarity. Now Poe Belrod, the Caste Elder, a squat, large-featured man, slapped his hand to his thigh in indignation. 'Surely, Arbiter Myrex, you cannot subscribe to a position so obviously arbitrary and contrived? Remember, you are elected to decide issues on the basis of justice and not orthodoxy!'

Ixon Myrex flew into a rage. 'Do you question my integrity? An abuse was brought to my attention by the Intercessor; it seems a real if unfortunate objection, and I declare the test invalid. Zander Rohan remains Master Hoodwink.'

Sklar Hast started to speak, but now there was a cry from outside the shed: 'The kragen has returned; the kragen swims in the lagoon!'

CHAPTER THREE

Sklar Hast pushed outside, went at a run to the lagoon, followed by all those who had witnessed the test.

Floating in the center of the lagoon was the black hulk of the kragen, vanes restlessly swirling the water. For a moment the forward-looking eyes surveyed the crowd on the main float; then it surged slowly forward, mandibles clicking with a significant emphasis. Whether or not it recognized Sklar Hast was uncertain; nevertheless it swam toward where he stood, then suddenly gave a great thrust of the vanes, plunged full speed ahead to throw a wave up over the edge of the pad. As it struck the edge it flung out a vane and the flat end slashed past Sklar Hast's chest. He staggered back in surprise and shock, to trip on a shrub and fall.

From nearby came Semm Voiderveg's chuckle. 'Is this the kragen you spoke so confidently of killing?'

Sklar Hast regained his feet, and stood looking silently at the kragen. Starlight glinted from the oily black back as if it were covered with satin. It swung to the side and began plucking with great energy at a set of convenient sponge arbors, which, as luck would have it, were the property of the Belrods, and Poe Belrod called out a series of bitter curses.

Sklar Hast looked about him. At least a hundred folk of Tranque Float stood nearby. Sklar Hast pointed. 'The vile beast of the sea plunders us. I say we should kill it, and all other kragen who seek to devour our sponges!'

Semm Voiderveg emitted a high-pitched croak. 'Are you insane? Someone, pour water on this maniac hoodwink, who has too long focused his eyes on flashing lights!'

In the lagoon the kragen tore voraciously at the choicest Belrod sponges, and the Belrods emitted a series of anguished hoots.

'I say, kill the beast!' cried Sklar Hast. 'The King despoils us; must we likewise feed all the kragen of the ocean?'

'Kill the beast!' echoed the younger Belrods.

Semm Voiderveg gesticulated in vast excitement, but Poe Belrod shoved him roughly aside. 'Quiet, let us listen to the hoodwink. How could we kill the kragen? Is it possible?'

'No!' cried Semm Voiderveg. 'Of course it is not possible! Nor is it wise or proper! What of our covenant with King Kragen?'

'King Kragen be damned!' cried Poe Belrod roughly. 'Let us hear the hoodwink. Come then: do you have any method in mind by which the kragen can be destroyed?'

Sklar Hast looked dubiously through the dark toward the great black hulk. 'I think – yes. A method that requires the strength of many men.'

Poe Belrod waved his hand toward those who had come to watch the kragen. 'Here they stand.'

'Come,' said Sklar Hast. He walked back toward the center of the float. Thirty or forty men followed him, mostly Swindlers, Advertisermen, Blackguards, Extorters and Larceners. The remainder hung dubiously back.

Sklar Hast led the way to a pile of poles stacked for the construction of a new storehouse. Each pole, fabricated from withes laid lengthwise and bound in glue, was twenty feet long by eight inches in diameter, and combined great strength with lightness. Sklar Hast selected a pole even thicker – the ridge beam. 'Pull this pole forth, lay it on a trestle!'

While this was being accomplished, he looked about and signaled Rudolf Snyder, a Ninth, though a man no older than himself, of the long-lived Incendiary Caste, which now monopolized the preparation of fiber, the laying of rope and plaits. 'I need two hundred feet of hawser, stout enough to lift the kragen. If there is none of this, then we must double or redouble smaller rope to the same effect.'

Rudolf Snyder took four men to help him and brought rope from the warehouse.

Sklar Hast worked with great energy, rigging the pole in accordance with his plans. 'Now – lift! Carry all to the edge of the pad!'

Excited by his urgency, the men shouldered the pole, carried it close to the lagoon, and at Sklar Hast's direction set it down with one end resting on the hard fiber of a rib. The other end, to which two lengths of hawser were tied, rested on a trestle and almost overhung the water. 'Now,' said Sklar Hast. 'Now we kill the kragen.' He made a noose at the end of a hawser, advanced toward the kragen, which watched him through the rear-pointing eyes of its turret. Sklar Hast moved slowly, so as not to alarm the creature, which continued to pluck sponges with a contemptuous disregard.

Sklar Hast approached the edge of the pad. 'Beast!' he called. 'Ocean brute! Come closer. Come.' He bent, splashed water at the kragen. Provoked, it surged toward him. Sklar Hast waited, and just before it swung its vane, he tossed the noose over its turret. He signaled his men. 'Now!' They heaved on the line, dragged the thrashing kragen through the water. Sklar Hast guided the line to the end of the pole. The kragen surged suddenly forward; in the confusion and the dark the men heaving on the rope fell backward. Sklar Hast seized the slack, and dodging a murderous slash of the kragen's fore-vane flung a hitch around the end of the pole. He danced back. 'Now!' he called. 'Pull, pull! Both lines! The beast is as good as dead!'

On each of the pair of hawsers tied to the head of the pole twenty men heaved. The pole raised on its base; the line tautened around the kragen's turret; the men dug in their heels; the base of the pole bit into the hard rib. The pole raised farther, braced by the angle of the ropes. With majestic deliberation the thrashing kragen was lifted from the water and swung up into the air. From the others who watched passively came a murmurous moan of fascination. Semm Voiderveg, who had been standing somewhat apart, made a gesture of horror and walked swiftly away.

Ixon Myrex the Arbiter, for reasons best known to himself, was nowhere to be seen, nor was Zander Rohan.

The kragen made gulping noises, reached its vanes this way and that, to no avail. Sklar Hast surveyed the creature, somewhat at a loss as to how next to proceed. His helpers were looking at the kragen in awe, uncomfortable at their own daring. Already they stole furtive glances out over the ocean, which, perfectly calm, glistened with the reflections of the blazing constellations. Sklar Hast thought to divert their attention. 'The nets!' he called out to those who watched. 'Where are the hooligans? Repair the nets before we lose all our fish! Are you helpless?'

Certain net-makers, a trade dominated by the Hooligans, detached themselves from the group, went out in coracles to repair the broken net.

Sklar Hast returned to a consideration of the dangling kragen. At his orders the hawsers supporting the tilted pole were made fast to ribs on the surface of the pad; the men now gathered gingerly about the dangling kragen, and speculated as to the best means to kill the creature. Perhaps it was already dead. To test this theory, a lad of the Belrods prodded the kragen with a length of stalk and suffered a broken collar-bone from a quick blow of the fore-vane.

Sklar Hast stood somewhat apart, studying the creature. Its hide was tough; its cartilaginous tissue even tougher. He sent one man for a boat-hook, another for a sharp femur-stake, and from the two fashioned a spear.

The kragen hung limp, the vanes swaying, occasionally twitching. Sklar Hast moved forward cautiously, touched the point of the spear to the side of the turret, thrust with all his weight. The point entered the tough hide perhaps half an inch, then broke. The kragen jerked, snorted, a vane slashed out. Sklar Hast sensed the dark flicker of motion, dodged and felt the air move beside his face. The spear shaft hurtled out over the pond; the vane struck the pole on which the kragen hung, bruising the fibers.

'What a quarrelsome beast!' muttered Sklar Hast. 'Bring more rope; we must prevent such demonstrations.'

From the side came a harsh command: 'You are mad-men; why do you risk the displeasure of King Kragen? I decree that you desist from your rash acts!'

This was the voice of Ixon Myrex, who now had appeared on the scene. Sklar Hast could not ignore Ixon Myrex as he had Semm Voiderveg. He considered the dangling kragen, looked about at the faces of his comrades. Some were hesitating; Ixon Myrex was not a man to be trifled with.

Sklar Hast spoke in a voice which he felt to be calm and reasonable. 'The kragen is destroying our arbors. If the King is slothful about his duties, why should we permit—'

Ixon Myrex's voice shook with wrath. 'That is no way to speak! You violate the Covenant!'

Sklar Hast spoke even more politely than before. 'King Kragen is nowhere to be seen. The intercessors who claim such large power run back and forth in futility. We must act for ourselves; is not this the free will and independence men claim as their basic right? So join us in killing this ravenous beast.'

Ixon Myrex held up his hands, which trembled with indignation. 'Return the kragen to the lagoon, that thereby—'

'That thereby it may destroy more arbors?' demanded Sklar Hast. 'This is not the result I hope for. Nor do you offer the support you might. Who is more important – the men of the Floats or the kragen?'

This argument struck a chord in his comrades, and they all shouted: 'Yes, who is more important – men or kragen?'

'Men rule the floats, King Kragen rules the ocean,' stated Ixon Myrex. 'There is no question of comparing importances.'

'The lagoon is also under the jurisdiction of man,' said Sklar Hast. 'This particular kragen is now on the float. Where is the rope?'

Arbiter Myrex called out in his sternest tones: 'This is how I interpret the customs of Tranque Float: The kragen must be restored to the water, with all haste. No other course is consistent with custom.'

There was a stirring among the men who had helped snare the sea-beast. Sklar Hast said nothing, but taking up the rope, formed a noose. He crawled forward, flipped up the noose to catch a dangling vane, then crawling back and rising to his feet, he circled the creature, binding the dangling vanes. The kragen's motions became increasingly constricted and finally were reduced to spasmodic shudders. Sklar Hast approached the creature from the rear, careful to remain out of reach of mandibles and palps, and made the bonds secure. 'Now – the vile beast can only squirm. Lower it to the pad, and we will find a means to make its end.'

The guy ropes were shifted; the pole tilted and swung; the kragen fell to the surface of the pad, where it lay passive, palps and mandibles moving slightly in and out. It showed no agitation or discomfort; perhaps it felt none: the exact degree of the kragen's sensitivity and ratiocinative powers had never been determined.

In the east the sky was lightening where the cluster of flaring blue and white suns known as Phocan's Cauldron began to rise. The ocean glimmered with a leaden sheen, and the folk who stood on the central pad began to glance furtively along the obscure horizon, muttering and complaining. Some few called out encouragement to Sklar Hast, recommending the most violent measures against the kragen. Between these and others furious arguments raged. Zander Rohan stood by Ixon Myrex, both obviously disapproving of Sklar Hast's activity. Of the Caste Elders only Poe Belrod and Elmar Pronave, Jackleg and Master Withe-weaver, defended Sklar Hast and his unconventional acts.

Sklar Hast ignored all. He sat watching the black hulk with vast distaste, furious with himself as well for having become involved in so perilous a project. What, after all, had been gained? The kragen had broken his arbors; he had revenged himself and prevented more destruction: well enough, but he had also incurred the ill-will of the most influential folk of the float. More seriously, he had involved those others who had trusted him and looked to him for leadership, and toward whom he now felt responsibility.

He rose to his feet. There was no help for it; the sooner the beast was disposed of, the more quickly life would return to normal. He approached the kragen, examined it gingerly. The mandibles quivered in their anxiety to sever his torso; Sklar Hast stayed warily to the side. How to kill the beast?

Elmar Pronave approached, the better to examine the creature. He was a tall man with a high-bridged broken nose and black hair worn in the two ear-plumes of the old Procurer Caste, now no longer in existence save for a few aggressively unique individuals scattered through the floats, who used the caste-marks to emphasize their emotional detachment.

Pronave circled the hulk, kicked at the rear vane, bent to peer into one of the staring eyes. 'If we could cut it up, its parts might be of some use.'

'The hide is too tough for our knives,' growled Sklar Hast. 'There's no neck to be strangled.'

'There are other ways to kill.'

Sklar Hast nodded. 'We could sink the beast into the depths of the ocean – but what to use for weight? Bones? Far too valuable. We could load bags with ash, but there is not that much ash to hand. We could burn every hut on the float as well as the hoodwink tower, and still not secure sufficient. To burn the kragen would require a like mountain of fuel.'

A young Larcener who had worked with great enthusiasm during the trapping of the kragen spoke forth: 'Poison exists! Find me poison, I will fix a capsule to a stick and push it into the creature's maw!'

Elmar Pronave gave a sardonic bark of laughter. 'Agreed; poisons exist, hundreds of them, derived from various sea-plants and animals – but which are sufficiently acrid to destroy this beast? And where is it to be had? I doubt if there is that much poison nearer than Green Lamp Float.'

Phocan's Cauldron, rising into the sky, revealed the kragen in fuller detail. Sklar Hast examined the four blind-seeming eyes in the turret, the intricate construction of the mandibles and tentacles at the maw. He touched the turret, peered at the dome-shaped cap of chitin that covered it. The turret itself seemed laminated, as if constructed of stacked rings of cartilage, the eyes protruding fore and aft in inflexible tubes of a rugose harsh substance. Others in the group began to crowd close; Sklar Hast jumped forward, thrust at a young Felon boat-builder, but too late. The kragen flung out a palp, seized the youth around the neck. Sklar Hast cursed, heaved, tore; the clenched palp was unyielding. Another curled out for his leg; Sklar Hast kicked, danced back, still heaving upon the Felon's writhing form. The kragen drew the Felon slowly forward, hoping, so Sklar Hast realized, to pull him within easier reach. He loosened his grip, but the kragen allowed its palp to sway back to encourage Sklar Hast, who once more tore at the constricting member. Again the kragen craftily drew its captive and Sklar Hast forward; the second palp snapped out once more and this time coiled around Sklar Hast's leg. Sklar Hast dropped to the ground, twisted himself around and broke the hold, though losing skin. The kragen petulantly jerked the Felon to within reach of its mandible, snipped off the young man's head, tossed body and head aside. A horrified gasp came from the watching crowd. Ixon Myrex bellowed, 'Sklar Hast, a man's life is gone, due to your savage obstinacy! You have much to answer for! Woe to you!'

Sklar Hast ignored the imprecation. He ran to the warehouse, found chisels and a mallet with a head of dense sea-plant stem, brought up from a depth of two hundred feet.* The chisels had blades of pelvic bone ground sharp against a board gritted with the silica husks of foraminifera. Sklar Hast returned to the kragen, put the chisel against the pale lamellum between the chitin dome and the foliations of the turret. He tapped; the chisel penetrated; this, the substance of a new layer being added to the turret, was relatively soft, the consistency of cooked gristle. Sklar Hast struck again; the chisel cut deep. The kragen squirmed.

Sklar Hast worked the chisel back out, made a new incision beside the first, then another and another, working around the periphery of the chitin dome, which was approximately two feet in diameter. The kragen squirmed and shuddered, whether in pain or apprehension it alone knew. As Sklar Hast worked around to the front, the palps groped back for him, but he shielded himself behind the turret, and finally gouged out the lamellum completely around the circumference of the turret.

His followers watched in awe and silence; from the others who watched came somber mutters, and occasional whimpers of superstitious dread from the children.

The channel was cut; Sklar Hast handed chisel and mallet back to Elmar Pronave. He mounted the body of the kragen, bent his knees, hooked fingers under the edge of the chitin dome, heaved. The dome ripped up and off, almost unbalancing Sklar Hast. The dome rolled down to the pad, the turret stood like an open-topped cylinder; within were coils and loops of something like dirty gray string. There were knots here, nodes there, on each side a pair of kinks, to the front a great tangle of kinks and loops.

---

* The advertiserman takes below a pulley which he attaches to a sea-plant stalk. By means of ropes, buckets of air are pulled down, allowing him to remain under water as long as he chooses. Using two such systems, alternately lowered, the diver can descend to a depth of two hundred feet, where the sea-plant stalks grow dense and rigid.

Sklar Hast looked down in interest. He was joined by Elmar Pronave. 'The creature's brain, evidently,' said Sklar Hast. 'Here the ganglions terminate. Or perhaps they are merely the termini of muscles.'

Elmar Pronave took the mallet and with the handle prodded at a node. The kragen gave a furious jerk. 'Well, well,' said Pronave. 'Interesting indeed.' He prodded further: here, there. Every time he touched the exposed ganglions the kragen jerked. Sklar Hast suddenly put out his hand to halt him. 'Notice. On the right, those two long loops; likewise on the left. When you touched this one here, the fore-vane jerked.' He took the mallet, prodded each of the loops in turn, and in turn each of the vanes jerked.

'Aha!' declared Elmar Pronave. 'Should we persist, we could teach the kragen to jig.'

'Best we should kill the beast,' said Sklar Hast. 'Day is approaching, and who knows but what ...' From the float sounded a sudden low wail, quickly cut off as by the constriction of breath. The group around the kragen stirred; someone vented a deep sound of dismay. Sklar Hast jumped up on the kragen, looked around. The population on the float were staring out to sea; he looked likewise, to see King Kragen.

King Kragen floated under the surface, only his turret above water. The eyes stared forward, each a foot across: lenses of tough crystal behind which flickered milky films and a pale blue sheen. King Kragen had either drifted close down the trail of Phocan's Cauldron on the water or had approached sub-surface.

Fifty feet from the lagoon nets he let his bulk come to the surface: first the whole of his turret, then the black cylinder housing the maw and the digestive process, finally the great flat sub-body: this, five feet thick, thirty feet wide, sixty feet long. To the sides protruded the propulsive vanes, thick as the girth of three men. Viewed from dead ahead, King Kragen appeared a deformed ogre swimming the breast-stroke. His forward eyes, in their horn tubes, were turned toward the float of Sklar Hast, and seemed fixed upon the hulk of the mutilated kragen. The men stared back, muscles stiff as sea-plant stalk. The kragen which they had captured, once so huge and formidable, now seemed a miniature, a doll, a toy. Through its after-eyes it saw King Kragen and gave a fluting whistle, a sound completely lost and desolate.

Sklar Hast suddenly found his tongue. He spoke in a husky, urgent tone. 'Back. To the back of the float!'

Now rose the voice of Semm Voiderveg the Intercessor. In quavering tones he called out across the water. 'Behold, King Kragen, the men of Tranque Float! Now we denounce the presumptuous bravado of these few heretics! Behold, this pleasant lagoon, with its succulent sponges, devoted to the well-being of the magnanimous King Kragen—' The reedy voice faltered as King Kragen twitched his great vanes and eased forward. The great eyes stared without discernible expression, but behind there seemed to be a leaping and shifting of pale pink and blue lights. The folk on the float drew back as King Kragen breasted close to the net. With a twitch of his vanes, he ripped the net; two more twitches shredded it. From the folk on the float came a moan of dread; King Kragen had not been mollified.

King Kragen eased into the lagoon, approached the helpless kragen. The bound beast thrashed feebly, sounded its fluting whistle. King Kragen reached forth a palp, seized it, lifted it into the air, where it dangled helplessly. King Kragen drew it contemptuously close to his great mandibles, chopped it quickly into slices of gray and black gristle. These he tossed away, out into the ocean. He paused to drift a moment, to consider. Then he surged on Sklar Hast's pad. One blow of his fore-vane demolished the hut, another cut a great gouge in the pad. The after-vanes thrashed among the arbors; water, debris, broken sponges boiled up from below. King Kragen thrust again, wallowed completely up on the pad, which slowly crumpled and sank beneath his weight.

King Kragen pulled himself back into the lagoon, cruised back and forth destroying arbors, shredding the net, smashing huts of all the pads of the lagoon. Then he turned his attention to the main float, breasting up to the edge. For a moment he eyed the population, which started to set up a terrified keening sound, then thrust himself forward, wallowed up on the float, and the keening became a series of hoarse cries and screams. The folk ran back and forth with jerky scurrying steps.

King Kragen bulked on the float like a toad on a lily pad. He struck with his vanes; the float split. The hoodwink tower, the great structure so cunningly woven, so carefully contrived, tottered. King Kragen lunged again, the tower toppled, falling into the huts along the north edge of the float.

King Kragen floundered across the float. He destroyed the granary, and bushels of yellow meal laboriously scraped from sea-plant pistils streamed into the water. He crushed the racks where stalk, withe and fiber were stretched and flexed; he dealt likewise with the rope-walk. Then, as if suddenly in a hurry, he swung about, heaved himself to the southern edge of the float. A number of huts and thirty-two of the folk, mostly aged and very young, were crushed or thrust into the water and drowned.

King Kragen regained the open sea. He floated quietly a moment or two, palps twitching in the expression of some unknowable emotion. Then he moved his vanes and slid off across the calm ocean.

Tranque Float was a devastation, a tangle, a scene of wrath and grief. The lagoon had returned to the ocean, with the arbors reduced to rubbish and the shoals of food-fish scattered. Many huts had been crushed. The hoodwink tower lay toppled. Of a population of four hundred and eighty, forty-three were dead, with as many more injured. The survivors stood blank-eyed and limp, unable to comprehend the full extent of the disaster that had come upon them.

Presently they roused themselves and gathered at the far western edge, where the damage had been the least. Ixon Myrex sought through the faces, eventually spied Sklar Hast sitting on a fragment of the fallen hoodwink tower. He raised his hand slowly, pointed. 'Sklar Hast! I denounce you! The evil you have done to Tranque Float cannot be uttered in words. Your arrogance, your callous indifference to our pleas, your cruel and audacious villainy – how can you hope to expiate them?'

Sklar Hast paid no heed. His attention was fixed upon Meril Rohan, where she knelt beside the body of Zander Rohan, his fine brisk mop of white hair dark with blood.

Ixon Myrex called in a harsh voice: 'In my capacity as Arbiter of Tranque Float, I declare you a criminal of the basest sort, together with all those who served you as accomplices, and most noteworthy Elmar Pronave! Elmar Pronave, show your shameful face! Where do you hide?'

But Elmar Pronave had been drowned and did not answer.

Ixon Myrex returned to Sklar Hast. 'The Master Hoodwink is dead and cannot denounce you in his own terms. I will speak for him: you are Assistant Master Hoodwink no longer. You are ejected from your caste and your calling!'

Sklar Hast wearily gave his attention to Ixon Myrex. 'Do not bellow nonsense. You can eject me from nothing. I am Master Hoodwink now. I was Master Hoodwink as soon as I bested Zander Rohan; even had I not done so, I became Master Hoodwink upon his death. You outrank me not an iota; you can denounce but do no more.'

Semm Voiderveg the Intercessor spoke forth. 'Denunciations are not enough! Argument in regard to rank is footling! King Kragen, in wreaking his terrible but just vengeance, intended that the primes of the deed should die. I now declare the will of King Kragen to be death, by either strangulation or bludgeoning, for Sklar Hast and all his accomplices.'

'Not so fast,' said Sklar Hast. 'It appears to me that a certain confusion is upon us. Two kragen, a large one and a small one, have injured us. I, Sklar Hast, and my friends, are those who hoped to protect the float from depredation. We failed. We are not criminals; we are simply not as strong or as wicked as King Kragen.'

'Are you aware,' thundered Semm Voiderveg, 'that King Kragen reserves to himself the duty of guarding us from the lesser kragen? Are you aware that in assaulting the kragen, you in effect assaulted King Kragen?'

Sklar Hast considered. 'I am aware that we will need more powerful tools than ropes and chisels to kill King Kragen.'

Semm Voiderveg turned away speechless. The people looked apathetically toward Sklar Hast. Few seemed to share the indignation of the elders.

Ixon Myrex sensed the general feeling of misery and fatigue. 'This is no time for recrimination. There is work to be done.' His voice broke with his own deep and sincere grief. 'All our fine structures must be rebuilt, our tower rendered operative, our net rewoven.' He stood quiet for a moment, and something of his rage returned. 'Sklar Hast's crime must not go without appropriate punishment. I ordain a Grand Convocation to take place in three days, on Apprise Float. The fate of Sklar Hast and his gang will be decided by a Council of Elders.'

Sklar Hast walked away. He approached Meril Rohan, who sat with her face in her hands, tears streaming down her cheeks.

'I'm sorry that your father died,' said Sklar Hast awkwardly. 'I'm sorry anyone died – but I'm especially sorry that you should be hurt.'

Meril Rohan surveyed him with an expression he was unable to decipher. He spoke in a voice hardly more than a husky mutter. 'Someday the sufferings of the Tranque folk must lead to a happier future – for all the folk, of all the floats ... I see it is my destiny to kill King Kragen. I care for nothing else.'

Meril Rohan spoke in a clear quiet voice. 'I wish my duty were as plain to me. I, too, must do something. I must expunge or help to expunge whatever has caused this evil that today has come upon us. Is it King Kragen? Is it Sklar Hast? Or something else altogether?' She was musing now, her eyes unfocused, almost as if she were unaware of her father's corpse, of Sklar Hast standing before her. 'It is a fact that the evil exists. The evil has a source. So my problem is to locate the source of the evil, to learn its nature. Only when we know our enemy can we defeat it.'

CHAPTER FOUR

The ocean had never been plumbed. At two hundred feet, the maximum depth attempted by stalk-cutters and pod-gatherers, the sea-plant stems were still a tangle. One Ben Murmen, Sixth, an Advertiserman, half-daredevil, half-maniac, had descended to three hundred feet, and in the indigo gloom noted the stalks merging to disappear into the murk as a single great trunk. But attempts to sound the bottom, by means of a line weighted with a bag of bone chippings, were unsuccessful. How then had the sea-plants managed to anchor themselves? Some supposed that the plants were of great antiquity and had developed during a time when the water was much lower. Others conjectured a sinking of the ocean bottom; still others were content to ascribe the feat to an innate tendency of the sea-plants.

Of all the floats Apprise was the largest and one of the first to be settled. The central agglomeration was perhaps nine acres in extent; the lagoon was bounded by thirty or forty smaller pads. Apprise Float was the traditional site of the convocations, which occurred at approximately yearly intervals and which were attended by the active and responsible adults of the system, who seldom otherwise ventured far from home, since it was widely believed that King Kragen disapproved of travel. He ignored the coracles of swindlers, and also the rafts of withe or stalk which occasionally passed between the floats, but on other occasions he had demolished boats or coracles that had no ostensible business or purpose. Coracles conveying folk to a convocation had never been molested, however, even though King Kragen always seemed aware that a convocation was in progress, and often watched proceedings from a distance of a quarter-mile or so. How King Kragen gained his knowledge was a matter of great mystery: some asserted that on every float lived a man who was a man in semblance only: who inwardly was a manifestation of King Kragen. It was through this man, according to the superstition, that King Kragen knew what transpired on the floats.

For three days preceding the convocation there was incessant flickering along the line of the hoodwink towers; the destruction of Tranque Float was reported in full detail, together with Ixon Myrex's denunciation of Sklar Hast and Sklar Hast's rebuttal. On each of the floats there was intense discussion and a certain degree of debate. Since, in most cases, the arbiter and the intercessor of each float inveighed against Sklar Hast, there was little organized sentiment in his favor.

On the morning of the convocation, early, before the morning sky showed blue, coracles full of folk moved between the floats. The survivors of the Tranque Float disaster, who for the most part had sought refuge on Thrasneck and Bickle, were among the first under way, as were the folk from Almack and Sciona, in the far west.

All morning the coracles shuttled back and forth between the floats; shortly before noon the first groups began to arrive on Apprise. Each group wore the distinctive emblems of its float; and those who felt caste distinction important likewise wore the traditional hair-stylings, forehead plaques, and dorsal ribbons; otherwise all dressed in much the same fashion: shirts and pantalets of coarse linen woven from sea-plant fiber, sandals of rug-fish leather, ceremonial gauntlets and epaulettes of sequins cut from the kernels of a certain half-animal, half-vegetable mollusc.

As the folk arrived they trooped to the famous old Apprise Inn, where they refreshed themselves at a table on which was set forth a collation of beer, pod-cakes, pepperfish and pickled fingerlings; after which the newcomers separated to various quarters of the float, in accordance with traditional caste distinctions.

In the center of the float was a rostrum. On surrounding benches the notables took their places: craft-masters, caste-elders, arbiters and intercessors. The rostrum was at all times open to any person who wished to speak, so long as he gained the sponsorship of one of the notables. The first speakers at the convocations customarily were elders intent on exhorting the younger folk to excellence and virtue; so it was today. An hour after the sun had reached the zenith the first speaker made his way to the rostrum: a portly old Incendiary from Maudelinda Float who had in just such a fashion opened the speaking at the last five convocations. He sought and was perfunctorily granted sponsorship – by now his speeches were regarded as a necessary evil. He mounted the rostrum and began to speak. His voice was rich, throbbing, voluminous; his periods were long, his sentiments well-used, his illuminations unremarkable:

'We meet again. I am pleased to see so many of the faces which over the years have become familiar and well-beloved; and alas there are certain faces no more to be seen, those who have slipped away to the Bourne, many untimely, as those who suffered punishment only these few days past before the wrath of King Kragen, of whom we all stand in awe. A dreadful circumstance thus to provoke the majesty of this Elemental Reality; it should never have occurred; it would never have occurred if all abided by the ancient disciplines. Why must we scorn the wisdom of our ancestors? Those noble and most heroic of men who dared revolt against the tyranny of the mindless helots, to seize the Ship of Space which was taking them to brutal confinement, and to seek a haven here on this blessed world! Our ancestors knew the benefits of order and rigor: they designated the castes and set them to tasks for which they presumably had received training on the Home World. In such a fashion the Swindlers were assigned the task of swindling fish; the Hoodwinks were set to winking hoods; the Incendiaries, among whom I am proud to number myself, wove ropes; while the Bezzlers gave us many of the intercessors who have procured the favor and benevolent guardianship of King Kragen.

'Like begets like; characteristics persist and distill: why then are the castes crumbling and giving way to helter-skelter disorder? I appeal to the youth of today: read the Analects; study the artifacts in the Museum; renew your dedication to the system formulated by our forefathers: you have no heritage more precious than your caste identity!'

The old Incendiary spoke on in such a vein for several minutes further and was succeeded by another old man, a former Hoodwink of good reputation, who worked until films upon his eyes gave one configuration much the look of another. Like the old Incendiary he too urged a more fervent dedication to the old-time values. 'I deplore the sloth of today's youth! We are becoming a race of sluggards! It is sheer good fortune that King Kragen protects us from the gluttony of the lesser kragen. And what if the tyrants of out-space discovered our haven and sought once more to enslave us? How would we defend ourselves? By hurling fish-heads? By diving under the floats in the hope that our adversaries would follow and drown themselves? I propose that each float form a militia, well-trained and equipped with darts and spears, fashioned from the hardest and most durable stalk obtainable!'

The old Hoodwink was followed by the Sumber Float Intercessor, who courteously suggested that should the out-space tyrants appear, King Kragen would be sure to visit upon them the most poignant punishments, the most absolute of rebuffs, so that the tyrants would flee in terror never to return. 'King Kragen is mighty, King Kragen is wise and benevolent, unless his dignity is impugned, as in the detestable incident at Tranque Float, where the willfulness of a bigoted free-thinker caused agony to many.' Now he modestly turned down his head. 'It is neither my place nor my privilege to propose a punishment suitable to so heinous an offense as the one under discussion. But I would go beyond this particular crime to dwell upon the underlying causes; namely the bravado of certain folk, who ordain themselves equal or superior to the accepted ways of life which have served us so well so long ...'

Presently he descended to the float. His place was taken by a somber man of stalwart physique, wearing the plainest of garments. 'My name is Sklar Hast,' he said. 'I am that so-called "bigoted free-thinker" just referred to. I have much to say, but I hardly know how to say it. I will be blunt. King Kragen is not the wise beneficent guardian the intercessors like to pretend. King Kragen is a gluttonous beast who every year becomes more enormous and more gluttonous. I sought to kill a lesser kragen which I found destroying my arbors; by some means King Kragen learned of this attempt and reacted with insane malice.'

'Hist! Hist!' cried the intercessors from below. 'Shame! Outrage!'

'Why does King Kragen resent my effort? After all, he kills any lesser kragen he discovers in the vicinity. It is simple and self-evident. King Kragen does not want men to think about killing kragen for fear they will attempt to kill him. I propose that this is what we do. Let us put aside this ignoble servility, this groveling to a sea-beast, let us turn our best efforts to the destruction of King Kragen.'

'Irresponsible maniac!' 'Fool!' 'Vile-minded ingrate!' called the intercessors.

Sklar Hast waited, but the invective increased in volume. Finally Phyral Berwick, the Apprise Arbiter, mounted the rostrum and held up his hands.

'Quiet! Let Sklar Hast speak! He stands on the rostrum; it is his privilege to say what he wishes.'

'Must we listen to garbage and filth?' called Semm Voiderveg. 'This man has destroyed Tranque Float; now he urges his frantic lunacy upon everyone else.'

'Let him urge,' declared Phyral Berwick. 'You are under no obligation to comply.'

Sklar Hast said, 'The intercessors naturally resist these ideas; they are bound closely to King Kragen and claim to have some means of communicating with him. Possibly this is so. Why else should King Kragen arrive so opportunely at Tranque Float? Now here is a very cogent point: if we can agree to liberate ourselves from King Kragen, we must prevent the intercessors from making known our plans to him, otherwise we shall suffer more than necessary. Most of you know in your hearts that I speak truth. King Kragen is a crafty beast with an insatiable appetite and we are his slaves. You know this truth but you fear to acknowledge it. Those who spoke before me have mentioned our forefathers: the men who captured a ship from the tyrants who sought to immure them on a penal planet. What would our forefathers have done? Would they have submitted to this gluttonous ogre? Of course not.

'How can we kill King Kragen? The plans must wait upon agreement, upon the concerted will to act, and in any event must not be told before the intercessors. If there are any here who believe as I do, now is the time for them to make themselves heard.'

He stepped down from the rostrum. Across the float was silence. Men's faces were frozen. Sklar Hast looked to right and to left. No one met his eye.

The portly Semm Voiderveg mounted the rostrum. 'You have listened to the murderer. He knows no shame. On Tranque Float we condemned him to death for his malevolent acts. According to custom he demanded the right to speak before a convocation; now he has done so. Has he confessed his great crime? Has he wept for the evil he has visited upon Tranque Float? No! He gibbers his plans for further enormities; he outrages decency by mentioning our ancestors in the same breath with his foul proposals! Let the convocation endorse the verdict of Tranque Float; let all those who respect King Kragen and benefit from his ceaseless vigilance raise now their hands in the clenched fist of death!'

'Death!' roared the intercessors and raised their fists. But elsewhere through the crowd there was hesitation and uneasiness. Eyes shifted backwards and forwards; there were furtive glances out to sea.

Semm Voiderveg looked back and forth across the crowd in disappointment. 'I well understand your reluctance to visit violence upon a fellow man, but in this case any squeamishness whatever is misplaced.' He pointed a long, pale finger at Sklar Hast. 'Do you understand the pure concentrated villainy embodied in this man? I will expatiate. Just prior to the offense for which he is on trial, he committed another, against his benefactor and superior, Master Hoodwink Zander Rohan. But this furtive act, this attempt to cheat the Master Hoodwink in a winking contest and thus dislodge the noble Rohan from his office, was detected by Tranque Arbiter Ixon Myrex and myself, and so failed to succeed.'

Sklar Hast roared: 'What? Is there no protection from slander here? Must I submit to venom of this sort?'

Phyral Berwick told him, 'Your recourse is simple. You may let the man speak, then if you can prove slander, the slanderer must face an appropriate penalty.'

Semm Voiderveg spoke with great earnestness. 'Mind you, a harsh truth is not slander. Personal malice must be proved as a motive. And there is no reason why I should feel malice. To continue—'

But Sklar Hast appealed to Phyral Berwick. 'Before he continues, I feel that the matter of slander should be clarified. I wish to prove that this man accuses me from spite.'

'Can you do so?'

'Yes.'

'Very well.' Phyral Berwick motioned to Semm Voiderveg. 'You must delay the balance of your remarks until the matter of slander is settled.'

'You need only request information of Arbiter Myrex,' protested Semm Voiderveg. 'He will assure you that the facts are as I have stated.'

Phyral Berwick nodded to Sklar Hast. 'Proceed: prove slander, if you can.'

Sklar Hast pointed to Second Assistant Hoodwink Vick Caverbee. 'Please stand forth.'

Caverbee, a small sandy-haired man with a wry face, his nose slanted in one direction, mouth in another, stepped somewhat reluctantly forward. Sklar Hast said, 'Voiderveg claims that I outwinked Master Hoodwink Rohan by means of diligent practice of the test exercises. Is this true?'

'No. It's not true. It can't possibly be true. The apprentices have been training on Exercises 1 through 50. When Arbiter Myrex asked for exercises to be used for the contest, I brought the advanced exercises from the locker. He and Intercessor Voiderveg made the selection themselves.'

Sklar Hast pointed to Arbiter Myrex. 'True or false?'

Arbiter Myrex drew a deep breath. 'True, in a technical sense. Still, you had an opportunity to practice the Exercises.'

'So did Master Hoodwink Rohan,' said Sklar Hast with a grim smile. 'Needless to say, I did nothing of the sort.'

'So much is clear,' said Phyral Berwick curtly. 'But as for slander—'

Sklar Hast nodded toward Caverbee. 'He has the answer for that also.'

Caverbee spoke even more reluctantly than before. 'Intercessor Voiderveg wished to espouse the Master Hoodwink's daughter. He spoke of the matter first to the Master Hoodwink, then to Meril Rohan. I could not help but overhear the matter. She gave him a flat refusal. The Intercessor asked the reason, and Meril Rohan said that she planned to espouse the Assistant Hoodwink Sklar Hast, if ever he approached her as if she were something other than a kick-release on a wink machine. Intercessor Voiderveg seemed very much annoyed.'

'Bah!' called Voiderveg, his face flaming pink. 'What of slander now?'

Sklar Hast looked through the crowd. His eyes met those of Meril Rohan. She did not wait to be requested to speak. She rose to her feet. 'I am Meril Rohan. The evidence of the Second Assistant Hoodwink is by and large accurate. At that time I planned to espouse Sklar Hast.'

Sklar Hast turned back to Phyral Berwick. 'There is the evidence.'

'You have made a reasonable case. I adjudicate that Intercessor Semm Voiderveg is guilty of slander. What penalty do you demand?'

'None. It is a trivial matter. I merely want the issues judged on the merits, without the extraneous factors brought forward by Intercessor Voiderveg.'

Phyral Berwick turned to Voiderveg. 'You may continue speaking, but you must refrain from further slander.'

'I will say no more,' said Voiderveg in a thick voice. 'Eventually I will be vindicated.' He stepped down from the rostrum, marched over to sit beside Arbiter Myrex, who somewhat pointedly ignored him.

A tall dark-haired man wearing a richly detailed gown of white, scarlet, and black, asked for the rostrum. This was Barquan Blasdel, Apprise Intercessor. He had a sobriety, an ease, a dignity of manner that lent him vastly more conviction than that exercised by the somewhat over-fervid Semm Voiderveg.

'As the accused admits, the matter of slander is remote to the case, and I suggest that we dismiss it utterly from our minds. Aside from this particular uncertainty, none other exists. The issues are stark – almost embarrassingly clear. The Covenant requires that King Kragen be accorded the justice of the sea. Sklar Hast wantonly, deliberately and knowingly violated the Covenant and brought about the death of forty-three men and women. There can be no argument.' Barquan Blasdel shrugged in a deprecatory manner. 'Much as I dislike to ask the death penalty, I must. So fists high then! Death to Sklar Hast!'

'Death!' roared the intercessors once again, holding high their fists, turning around and gesturing to others in the throng to join them.

Barquan Blasdel's temperate exposition swayed more folk than Voiderveg's accusations, but still there was a sense of hesitation, of uncertainty, as if all suspected that there was yet more to be said.

Barquan Blasdel leaned quizzically forward over the rostrum. 'What? You are reluctant in so clear a case? I cannot prove more than I have.'

Phyral Berwick, the Apprise Arbiter, rose to his feet. 'I remind Barquan Blasdel that he has now called twice for the death of Sklar Hast. If he calls once more and fails to achieve an affirmative vote Sklar Hast is vindicated.'

Barquan Blasdel smiled out over the crowd. He turned a swift almost furtive look of appraisal toward Sklar Hast and without further statement descended to the float.

The rostrum was empty. No one sought to speak. Finally Phyral Berwick himself mounted the steps: a stocky square-faced man with gray hair, ice-blue eyes, a short gray beard. He spoke slowly. 'Sklar Hast calls for the death of King Kragen. Semm Voiderveg and Barquan Blasdel call for the death of Sklar Hast. I will tell you my feelings. I have great fear in the first case and great disinclination in the second. I have no clear sense of what I should do. Sklar Hast, rightly or wrongly, has forced us to a decision. We should consider with care and make no instant judgments.'

Barquan Blasdel jumped to his feet. 'Respectfully I must urge that we hold to the issue under consideration, and this is the degree of Sklar Hast's guilt in connection with the Tranque Float tragedy.'

Phyral Berwick gave a curt nod. 'We will recess for an hour.'

CHAPTER FIVE

Sklar Hast pushed through the crowd to where he had seen Meril Rohan, but when he reached the spot, she had moved away. As he stood searching for her, men and women of various floats, castes, guilds and generations pressed forward to stare at him, to speak to him, tentatively, curiously. A few, motivated by a psychic morbidity, reached out to touch him; a few reviled him in hoarse choked voices. A tall red-haired man, of the Peculator caste by his artfully dyed emblem of five colors, thrust forward an excited face. 'You speak of killing King Kragen: how may this be done?'

Sklar Hast said in a careful voice, 'I don't know. But I hope to learn.'

'And if King Kragen becomes infuriated by your hostility and ravages each of the floats in turn?'

'There might be temporary suffering, but our children and their children would benefit.'

Another spoke: a short clench-jawed woman. 'If it means my toil and my suffering and my death, I would as soon that these misfortunes be shared by those who would benefit.'

'All this is a personal matter, of course,' said Sklar Hast politely. He attempted to sidle away, but was halted by another woman, this one wearing the blue and white sash of Hooligan Preceptress, who shook her finger under the first woman's nose: 'What of the Two Hundred who fled the tyrants? Do you think they worried about risk? No! They sacrificed all to avoid slavery, and we have benefited. Are we immune then from danger and sacrifice?'

'No!' shouted the first woman. 'But we need not urge it upon ourselves!'

An intercessor from one of the outer floats stepped forward. 'King Kragen is our benefactor! What is this foolish talk of risk and slavery and sacrifice? Instead we should speak of gratitude and praise and worship.'

The red-haired Peculator, leaning in front of Sklar Hast, waved his arms impatiently at the intercessor: 'Why don't the intercessors and all of like mind take King Kragen and voyage to a far float and serve him as you please, but leave the remainder of us in peace?'

'King Kragen serves us all,' declared the intercessor with great dignity. 'We would be performing an ignoble act to deprive everyone else of his beneficent guardianship.'

The Hooligan Preceptress had a countering remark, but Sklar Hast managed to step aside, and now he saw Meril Rohan at a nearby booth, where she sipped tea from a mug. He edged through the crowd and joined her. She acknowledged his presence with the coolest of nods.

'Come,' said Sklar Hast, taking her arm. 'Let us move to the side, where the folk do not crush in on us. I have much to say to you.'

'I don't care to talk with you. A display of childish petulance perhaps, but this is the situation.'

'And it is precisely what I wish to discuss with you,' declared Sklar Hast.

Meril Rohan smiled faintly. 'Better that you be contriving arguments to save your neck. The convocation may well decide that your life has continued as long as is desirable.'

Sklar Hast winced. 'And how will you vote?'

'I am bored with the entire proceedings. I will probably return to Quatrefoil.'

Perceiving the situation to be awkward, Sklar Hast departed with as good grace as he could muster.

He went to join Rubal Gallager, who sat under the Apprise Inn pergola. 'The float is in ruins, you have made enemies – still your life is no longer in danger,' said Rubal Gallager. 'At least, this is my opinion.'

Sklar Hast gave a sour grunt. 'Sometimes I wonder if the effort is worthwhile. Still there is much to do. If nothing else, the hoodwink tower must be rebuilt. And I have my office to consider.'

Rubal Gallager gave a ripe chuckle. 'With Semm Voiderveg as Intercessor and Ixon Myrex as Arbiter, your tenure will hardly be one of sheer harmony.'

'The least of my worries,' said Sklar Hast. 'Assuming of course that I leave the convocation alive.'

'I think you may count upon this,' said Rubal Gallager with a somewhat grim overtone to his voice. 'There are many who wish you dead, doubtless – but there are many who do not.'

Sklar Hast considered a moment and gave his head a dubious shake. 'I hardly know what to say. For twelve generations the folk of the floats have lived in harmony, and we think it savage if a man so much as threatens another man with his fist ... Would I want to be the node of contention? Would I want the name "Sklar Hast" to be echoed down the generations as the man who brought strife to the floats?'

Rubal Gallager regarded him in quizzical amusement. 'I have never known you previously to wax philosophical.'

'It is not an occupation I enjoy,' said Sklar Hast, 'though it seems as if more and more it is to be forced upon me.' He looked across the float to the refreshment booth where Meril Rohan sat speaking across a bench with one who was a stranger to Sklar Hast: a thin young man with an intense abrupt-angled face and a habit of nervous gesticulation. He wore neither caste nor guild emblems, but from the green piping at the throat of his smock Sklar Hast deduced him to be from Sankston Float ... His thoughts were interrupted by the return of Phyral Berwick to the rostrum.

'We will now resume our considerations. I hope that all who speak will eschew excitement and emotion. This is a deliberative assembly of reasonable and calm beings, not a mob of fanatics to be incited, and I wish all to remember this. If angry men shout at each other, the purpose of the convocation is defeated, and I will again call a recess. So now, who wishes to speak?'

From the audience a man called: 'Question!'

Phyral Berwick pointed his finger. 'Step forward, state your name, caste, craft, and propound your question.'

It was the thin-faced young man with the intense expression whom Sklar Hast had observed speaking with Meril Rohan. He said, 'My name is Roger Kelso. My lineage is Larcener, although I have departed from caste custom and my craft now is scrivener. My question has this background: Sklar Hast is accused of responsibility for the Tranque Float disaster, and it is the duty of the convocation to measure this responsibility. To do this we first must measure the proximate cause of tragedy. This is an essential element of traditional jurisprudence and if any think otherwise I will quote the Memorium of Lester McManus, where he describes the theoretical elements of Home-world law. This is a passage not included in the Analects and is not widely known. Suffice it to say, the man who establishes a precursory condition for a crime is not necessarily guilty; he must actually, immediately, and decisively cause the event.'

Barquan Blasdel, in his easy, almost patronizing voice, interrupted: 'But this is precisely Sklar Hast's act: he disobeyed King Kragen's statute, and this precipitated his terrible justice.'

Roger Kelso listened with a patience obviously foreign to his nature; he fidgeted, and his dark eyes glittered. He said, 'If the worthy Intercessor allows, I will continue.'

Barquan Blasdel nodded politely and sat down.

'When Sklar Hast spoke, he put forth a conjecture which absolutely must be resolved: namely, did Semm Voiderveg, the Tranque Intercessor, call King Kragen to Tranque Float? This is a subtle question. Much depends upon not only *if* Semm Voiderveg issued the call, but *when*. If he did so when the rogue kragen was first discovered: well and good. If he called after Sklar Hast made his attempt to kill the kragen, then Semm Voiderveg becomes more guilty of the Tranque disaster than Sklar Hast, because he certainly must have foreseen the consequences. What is the true state of affairs? Do the intercessors secretly communicate with King Kragen? And my specific question: did Semm Voiderveg call King Kragen to Tranque Float in order that Sklar Hast and his helpers be punished?'

'Bah!' called Barquan Blasdel. 'This is a diversion, a dialectic trick!'

Phyral Berwick deliberated a moment. 'The question seems definite enough. I personally cannot supply an answer, but I think that it deserves one, if only to clarify matters. Semm Voiderveg: what do you say?'

'I say nothing.'

'Come,' said Phyral Berwick reasonably. 'Your craft is intercessor; your responsibility lies to the men whom you represent and for whom you intercede; certainly not to King Kragen, no matter how fervent your respect. Evasion, secrecy, or stubborn silence can only arouse our distrust and lead away from justice: surely you recognize this much.'

'It is to be understood,' said Semm Voiderveg tartly, 'that even if I did summon King Kragen – and it would violate guild policy to make a definite statement in this regard – my motives were of the highest order.'

'Well, then, did you do so?'

Semm Voiderveg looked toward Barquan Blasdel for support, and the Apprise Intercessor once more rose to his feet. 'Arbiter Berwick, I must insist that we are pursuing a blind alley, far from our basic purpose.'

'What then is our basic purpose?' asked Phyral Berwick.

Barquan Blasdel held out his arms in a gesture of surprise. 'Is there any doubt? By Sklar Hast's own admission he has violated King Kragen's laws and the orthodox custom of the floats. It only remains to us – this and no more – to establish a commensurate punishment.'

Phyral Berwick started to speak, but yielded to Roger Kelso, who had leapt quickly to his feet. 'I must point out an elemental confusion in the worthy Intercessor's thinking. King Kragen's laws are not human laws, and is unorthodoxy a crime? If so, then many more beside Sklar Hast are guilty.'

Barquan Blasdel remained unruffled. 'The confusion lies in another quarter. The laws I refer to stem from the Covenant between ourselves and King Kragen: he protects us from the terrors of the sea; in return he insists that we acknowledge his sovereignty of the sea. And as for orthodoxy, this is no more and no less than respect for the opinions of the arbiters and intercessors of all the floats, who are trained to judiciousness, foresight and decorum. So now we must weigh the exact degree of Sklar Hast's transgressions.'

'Precisely,' said Roger Kelso. 'And to do this, we need to know whether Semm Voiderveg summoned King Kragen to Tranque Float.'

Barquan Blasdel's voice at last took on a harsh edge. 'We must not question the acts of any man when he performs in the role of intercessor! Nor is it permitted to probe the guild secrets of the intercessors!'

Phyral Berwick signaled Barquan Blasdel to silence. 'In a situation like this, when fundamental questions are under consideration, guild secrecy becomes of secondary importance. Not only I, but all the other folk of the floats, wish to know the truth, with a minimum of obscurantism. Secrecy of any sort may not be allowed: This is my ruling. So then, Semm Voiderveg, you were asked: did you summon King Kragen to Tranque Float on the night in question?'

The very air seemed to congeal; every eye turned on Semm Voiderveg. He cleared his throat, raised his eyes to the sky. But he showed no embarrassment in his reply. 'The question seems nothing less than ingenuous. How could I function as intercessor without some means of conveying to King Kragen both the extent of our trust and fidelity, likewise the news of emergency when such existed? When the rogue appeared, it was no less than my duty to summon King Kragen. I did so. The means are irrelevant.'

Barquan Blasdel nodded in profound approval, almost relief. Phyral Berwick drummed his fingers on the rostrum. Several times he opened his mouth to speak, and each time closed it. Finally he asked, rather lamely, 'Are these the only occasions upon which you summon King Kragen?'

Semm Voiderveg made a show of indignation. 'Why do you question me? I am Intercessor; the criminal is Sklar Hast!'

'Easy, then: the questions illuminate the extent of the alleged crime. For instance, let me ask this: do you ever summon King Kragen to feed from your lagoon in order to visit a punishment or a warning upon the folk of your float?'

Semm Voiderveg blinked. 'The wisdom of King Kragen is inordinate. He can detect delinquencies; he makes his presence known—'

'Specifically then, you summoned King Kragen to Tranque Float when Sklar Hast sought to kill the rogue?'

'My acts are not in the balance. I see no reason to answer the question.'

Barquan Blasdel rose majestically to his feet. 'I was about to remark as much.'

'And I!' called Vidal Reach, the Sumber Intercessor.

'And I!' 'And I!' from various other intercessors.

Phyral Berwick spoke to the crowd in a troubled voice. 'There seems no practical way to determine exactly when Semm Voiderveg called King Kragen. If he did so after Sklar Hast had begun his attack upon the rogue, then in my opinion Semm Voiderveg the Intercessor is more immediately responsible for the Tranque disaster than Sklar Hast, and it becomes a travesty to visit any sort of penalty upon Sklar Hast. Unfortunately there seems no way of settling this question.'

Poe Belrod, the Advertiserman Elder, rose to his feet and stood looking sidelong toward Semm Voiderveg. 'I can shed some light on the situation. I was a witness to all which occurred. When the rogue appeared in the lagoon, Semm Voiderveg went to watch with the others. He did not go apart until after Sklar Hast began to kill the beast. I am sure others will be witness to this; Semm Voiderveg made no attempt to conceal his presence.'

Several others who had been at the scene corroborated the testimony of Poe Belrod.

The Apprise Intercessor, Barquan Blasdel, again gained the rostrum. 'Arbiter Berwick, I beg that you sedulously keep to the paramount issue. The facts are these: Sklar Hast and his gang committed an act knowingly proscribed both by Tranque Arbiter Ixon Myrex and by Tranque Intercessor Semm Voiderveg. The consequences stemmed from this act; Sklar Hast is inevitably guilty.'

'Barquan Blasdel,' said Phyral Berwick, 'you are Apprise Intercessor. Have you ever summoned King Kragen to Apprise Float?'

'As Semm Voiderveg and I have incessantly pointed out, Sklar Hast is the criminal at the bar, not the conscientious intercessors of the various floats. By no means may Sklar Hast be allowed to evade his punishment. King Kragen is not lightly to be defied! Even though the convocation will not raise their collective fist to smite Sklar Hast, I say that he must die. It is a matter this serious.'

Phyral Berwick fixed his pale blue eyes upon Barquan Blasdel. 'If the convocation gives Sklar Hast his life, he will not die unless I die before him.'

'Nor I!' called Poe Belrod. 'Nor I!' – this was from Roger Kelso. And now all those men of Tranque Float who had joined Sklar Hast in the killing of the rogue kragen came toward the rostrum, shouting their intention of joining Sklar Hast either in life or death, and with them came others, from various floats.

Barquan Blasdel scrambled up onto the rostrum, held his arms wide, and finally was able to make himself heard. 'Before others declare themselves – look out to sea! King Kragen watches, attentive to learn who is loyal and who is faithless!'

The crowd swung about as if one individual. A hundred yards off the float the water swirled lazily around King Kragen's great turret. The crystal eyes pointed like telescopes toward Apprise Float. Presently the turret sank beneath the surface. The blue water roiled, then flowed smooth and featureless.

Sklar Hast stepped forward, started to mount to the rostrum. Barquan Blasdel the Intercessor halted him. 'The rostrum must not become a shouting place. Stay till you are summoned!' But Sklar Hast pushed him aside, went to face the crowd. He pointed toward the smooth ocean. 'There you have seen the vile beast, our enemy! Why should we deceive ourselves? Intercessors, arbiters, all of us – let us forget our differences, let us join our crafts and our resources! If we do so, we can evolve a method to kill King Kragen! We are men; why should we abase ourselves before anything whatever?'

Barquan Blasdel threw back his head, aghast. He took a step toward Sklar Hast, as if to seize him, then turned to the audience. 'You have heard this madman – twice you have heard him! And also you have observed the vigilance of King Kragen whose force is known to all! Choose therefore – obey either the exhortations of a twitching lunatic, or be guided by our ancient trust in the benevolence of mighty King Kragen. There must be a definite resolution to this matter. We can have no half measures! Sklar Hast must die! So now hold high your fists – each and all! Silence the frantic screamings of Sklar Hast! King Kragen is near at hand! Death to Sklar Hast!' He thrust his fist high into the air.

The intercessors followed suit. 'Death to Sklar Hast!'

Hesitantly, indecisively, other fists raised, then others and others. Some changed their minds and drew down their fists or thrust them high; some raised their fists only to have others pull them down. Altercations sprang up across the float; the hoarse sound of contention began to make itself heard. Barquan Blasdel leaned forward in sudden concern, calling for calm. Sklar Hast likewise started to speak, but he desisted – because suddenly words were of no avail. In a bewildering, almost magical, shift the placid convocation had become a mêlée. Men and women tore savagely at each other, screaming, cursing, raging, squealing. Emotion accumulated from childhood, stored and constrained, now exploded; identical fear and hate prompted opposite reactions. Luckily few weapons were available: clubs of stalk, a bone ax or two, a half dozen stakes, as many knives. Across the float the tide of battle surged, out into the water. Staid Jacklegs and responsible Malpractors sought to drown each other; Advertisermen ignored their low estate and belabored Bezzlers; orthodox Incendiaries kicked, clawed, tore and bit as furiously as any varnish-besotted Smuggler. While the struggle was at its most intense King Kragen once more surfaced, this time a quarter-mile to the north, whence he turned his vast incurious gaze upon the float.

The fighting slowed and dwindled, partly from sheer exhaustion, partly from the efforts of the most responsible; and the combatants were thrust apart. In the lagoon floated half a dozen corpses; on the float lay as many more. Now for the first time it could be seen that those who stood by Sklar Hast were considerably outnumbered, by almost two to one, and also that this group included for the most part the most vigorous and able of the craftsmen, though few of the Masters.

Barquan Blasdel, still on the rostrum, cried out, 'A sorry day indeed, a sorry day! Sklar Hast, see the anguish you have brought to the floats!'

Sklar Hast looked at him, panting and haggard with grief. Blood coursed down his face from the slash of a knife, the garments were ripped from his chest. Ignoring Blasdel, he mounted the rostrum and addressed the two groups: 'I agree with Barquan Blasdel: this is a sorry day – but let there be no mistake: men must rule the ocean beast or be ruled! I now return to Tranque Float, where the great damage must be repaired. As Blasdel the Intercessor has said, there is no turning back now. So be it. Let those who want free lives come to Tranque, where we will take counsel on what to do next.'

Barquan Blasdel made a hoarse peculiarly ugly sound: an ejaculation of bitter amusement rendered glottal and guttural by hate. His ease and facility of manner had deserted him; he crouched tensely over the railing of the rostrum. 'Go then to ruined Tranque! All you faithless, you irreverent ones – get hence and good riddance! Let Tranque be your home, and let Tranque become a name accursed; an evil odor; a vile disease! Only do not scream to King Kragen for aid when the rogues, unchided by the great King, devour your sponges, tear your nets, crush your coracles!'

'The many cannot be as rapacious as the one,' said Sklar Hast. 'Nevertheless, do not be persuaded by the ranting of the Intercessor. Tranque Float is ruined and will support but few folk until the nets are repaired and new arbors seeded. For the present, a migration such as Blasdel suggests is impractical.'

From the red-haired Peculator came a call: 'Let the intercessors take King Kragen and migrate to some far line of floats; then all of us will be suited!'

Blasdel, making no response, jumped down from the rostrum and marched off across the float to his private pad.

CHAPTER SIX

In spite of the strife, or perhaps because it did not seem real, and in spite of the devastation, almost all of the Tranque folk elected to return to their home float. A few, appalled by the circumstances, took up temporary habitancy elsewhere, perhaps at the hut of a caste cousin or guild-fellow, but most decided for better or worse to return to Tranque. So they did, silently rowing their coracles, nursing such aches, bruises or wounds as they had incurred, looking neither left nor right, for fear of staring across the water into the face of friend or neighbor whom they had only just desisted from belaboring.

It was a melancholy voyage, through the gray-violet evening, down along the line of floats, each with its characteristic silhouette, each with its peculiar ambience or quirk of personality, so that a turn of phrase might be noted as typically Aumerge or a bit of carved wood identified immediately and unmistakably as the work of a Leumar Niggler. And now Tranque, of all the floats, was devastated, Tranque alone. It was enough to make tears of grief and bitterness well from the eyes of the Tranque folk. For them all was changed; the old life would never return. The resentments and bitterness might numb and scar over, but the friendships would never again be easy, the trusts whole. Still, Tranque was home. There was no other place to go.

There was small comfort to be found on Tranque. A third of the huts were in ruins. The granary and all the precious flour had been wasted; the proud tower lay in a tangle of splinters and wreckage. Directly across the float, in a great avenue of destruction, could be traced the course of King Kragen.

On the morning after the convocation the folk stood about in groups, working in a desultory fashion, glancing sidewise in surly silence toward persons whom they had known all their lives. Somewhat to Sklar Hast's surprise Semm Voiderveg had returned to the float, though his own cottage had been crushed by King Kragen and now was only a tangle of crushed withe and tattered pad-skin. Semm Voiderveg went to look disconsolately at the mess, poking and prodding here and there, extracting an implement, a pot, a bucket, an article of clothing, a volume of Analects sodden from water which had gushed up from a broken place in the float. Feeling Sklar Hast's gaze upon him, he gave an angry shrug and marched away to the undamaged cottage of Arbiter Myrex, with whom he was lodged.

Sklar Hast continued toward his own destination: the hut of the former Master Hoodwink, which also had suffered destruction, though perhaps in lesser degree. Meril Rohan was hard at work, cutting up the rubbish, stacking usable withe and such varnished pad-skin as might feasibly be re-used. Sklar Hast silently began to help her, and she made no objection.

At last, protected by a toppled cupboard, she found what she sought: sixty-one folios bound in supple gray-fish leather. Sklar Hast carried the volumes to a bench, covered them with a sheet of pad-skin against the possibility of a sudden shower. Meril turned back to the ruined hut, but Sklar Hast took her hand and led her to the bench. She seated herself with-out argument, and Sklar Hast sat beside her. 'I have been anxious to talk to you.'

'I expected as much.'

Sklar Hast found her composure baffling. What did it signify? Love? Hate? Indifference? Frigidity?

She went on to enlighten him. 'I've always had contradicting impulses in regard to you. I admire your energy. Your decisiveness – some call it ruth-lessness – makes me uneasy. Your motives are transparent and do you no discredit, although your recklessness and heedlessness do.'

Sklar Hast was moved to protest. 'I am neither one nor the other! In emer-gencies one must act without vacillation. Indecisiveness and failure are the same.'

Meril nodded toward the ruins. 'What do you call this?'

'Not failure. It is a setback, a misfortune, a tragedy – but how could it have been avoided? Assuming, of course, that we intended to free ourselves from King Kragen.'

Meril Rohan shrugged. 'I don't know the answer. But the decisions which you took alone should have been taken jointly by everyone.'

'No,' said Sklar Hast stubbornly. 'How far would we get, how fast would we be able to react, if at every need for action we were forced to counsel? Think of the outcries and the delay from Myrex and Voiderveg and even your father! Nothing would be accomplished; we would be mired!'

Meril Rohan made restless movements with her hands. Finally she said, 'Very well. This is clear. Also it echoes the Memorium of Lester McManus. I forget his exact phrasing, but he remarks that since we are men, and since most of us prefer to be good, we are constantly looking for absolutes. We want no taint on any of our actions and we can't reconcile ourselves to ac-tions which are in any aspect immoral.'

'Unfortunately,' said Sklar Hast, 'there are very few absolutely moral deeds, except possibly pure passivity – and I am uncertain as to this. It may be there is *no* completely moral act. The more decisive and energetic any act is, the more uncertain will become the chances of its being absolutely moral.'

Meril Rohan was amused. 'This sounds like a certain "principle of uncer-tainty" James Brunet the scientist mentions in his Memorium, but which seems quite incomprehensible to me ... You may be right – from your point of view. Certainly not from Semm Voiderveg's.'

'Nor King Kragen's.'

Meril nodded, a faint smile on her lips and looking at her, Sklar Hast wondered why he ever had thought to test other girls of the float when surely this was the one he wanted. He studied her a moment, trying to decide wherein lay her charm. Her figure was by no means voluptuous, though it was unmistakably feminine. He had seen prettier faces, though Meril's face, with its subtle irregularities and unexpected delicacies of modeling and quick, almost imperceptible quirks and flexibilities, was fascination itself ... Now she was pensive and sat looking east across the water, where the whole line of floats extended, one behind the other, curving to the north just sufficiently to allow all to be seen: Thrasneck, Bickle, Sumber, Adelvine, Green Lamp, Fleurnoy, Aumerge, Quincunx, Fay, all these last merging into the horizon haze, all the others no more than lavender-gray smudges on the dark blue ocean. Above all towered a great billowing white cloud. Sklar Hast sensed something of her thoughts and drew a deep breath. 'Yes ... It's a beautiful world. If only there were no King Kragen.'

She turned impulsively to him, took his arm. 'There are other floats, to east and west. Why don't we go, leave King Kragen behind?'

Sklar Hast gloomily shook his head. 'King Kragen wouldn't let us go.'

'We could wait until he was at the far west, at Almack or Sciona, and sail east. He'd never know.'

'We could do that – and leave King Kragen supreme. Do you think this would be the way of the Firsts?'

Meril reflected. 'I don't know ... After all, they fled the tyrants; they did not return to attack them.'

'They had no choice! The Ship of Space sank in the ocean.'

Meril shook her head. 'They had no intention of attacking anyone. They considered themselves lucky to escape ... Frankly, there is much in the Memoria that puzzles me, allusions I don't comprehend, especially in regard to the tyrants.'

Sklar Hast picked up Meril's concordance to the Memoria, opened the pages. Spelling out the letters with difficulty, for his eyes and mind were attuned to hoodwink configurations, he found the entry entitled 'Kragen'.

Meril, noticing what he read, said, 'The references aren't very explicit.' She ran her finger swiftly along the references, opened books:

'This is Eleanor Morse: "All is peace, all is ideal, save only for one rather horrible aquatic beast: fish? insect? echinoderm? The classifications are meaningless, of course. We've decided to call them 'kragen'." And Paul van Blee writes: "About our only spectator sport is watching the kragen and betting which one of us gets eaten first. We've seen some monstrous specimens,

up to twenty feet in length. Certainly no encouragement for aquatic sports!"
James Brunet, the scientist, says: "The other day Joe Kamy stuck a tender
young kragen, scarcely four feet long, with a sharp stick. Blood – or whatever you wish to call it – ran blue, like some of the terrestrial lobsters and
crabs. I wonder if that indicates a similar internal chemistry. Haemoglobin contains iron, chlorophyll, magnesium; haemocyanin, as in blue lobster
blood, copper. It's a powerful beast, this kragen, and I'd swear intelligent."
That's about all anyone says about the kragen.'

Sklar Hast nodded. 'Something that puzzles me and that I can't get away
from: if the intercessors are able to communicate with the kragen, even to
the extent of summoning it – how do they do it? Through the Master Hoodwink? Does he flash some particular signal? I've never heard of any such
system.'

'Nor I,' said Meril rather stiffly.

'You can't know,' said Sklar Hast, 'because you're not a hoodwink.'

'I know my father never called King Kragen to Tranque Float.'

'Voiderveg admitted that he did so. But how?' He rose to his feet and stood
looking off across the float. 'Well – I must work with the others.' He hesitated a moment, but Meril Rohan offered him no encouragement. 'Is there
anything you need?' he asked presently. 'Remember, I am Guild-Master now
and you are under my protection, so you must call me if there is any lack.'

Meril Rohan gave a terse nod.

'Will you be my spouse, untested?' asked Sklar Hast, rather lamely.

'No.' Her mood had changed once more, and she had become remote.
Sklar Hast wondered why. 'I need nothing,' she said. 'Thank you.'

Sklar Hast turned away and went to join those who disassembled the
old hoodwink tower. He had acted too precipitously, too awkwardly, he
told himself. With Zander Rohan only days dead, Meril undoubtedly still
grieved and could hardly be interested in offers of espousal.

He put her from his mind, and joined the hoodwinks and larceners who
were salvaging such of the old structure as was useful. Broken withe, fragments of torn pad-skin trash, were taken to a 'fire-raft' floating on the lagoon
and burnt, and in short order the look of devastation disappeared.

Hooligans meanwhile had raised the net, and were repairing the damage.
Sklar Hast paused to watch them, then spoke to Roger Kelso the scrivener,
who for reasons of his own had come to Tranque Float. 'Imagine a net of
heavy hawser hanging over the lagoon. King Kragen swims into the lagoon,
anxious to glut himself. The net drops; King Kragen is entangled ...' He
paused.

'And then?' inquired Roger Kelso with a saturnine grin.

'Then we bind him securely, tow him out to sea and bid him farewell.'

Roger Kelso nodded. 'Possible – under optimum conditions. I have two objections. First, his mandibles. He might well cut the net in front of him, extend his palps, draw around more of the net, and cut himself free. Secondly, the intercessors. They would observe the suspended net, guess its purpose, and either warn King Kragen away or invite him to come and punish the criminals who sought to kill him.'

Sklar Hast sadly agreed. 'Whatever means we ultimately fix upon, the intercessors must never learn of it.'

The Master Larcener, Rollo Barnack, had heard the conversation. Now he said, 'I have also given thought to the problem of King Kragen. A solution has occurred to me: a device of innocent appearance which, if all goes well – and mind you, there is no guarantee of this – but as I say, if all goes precisely, King Kragen might well be killed. Best of all, the vigilance of Semm Voiderveg need not be aroused.'

'You interest me extremely,' said Sklar Hast. 'Describe this ingenious device.'

Rollo Barnack started to speak, but noting the approach of Arbiter Ixon Myrex, Intercessor Semm Voiderveg and several others of like conviction, held his tongue.

Arbiter Myrex was spokesman for the group. His voice was clear, firm and unemotional: clearly the confrontation had been discussed and rehearsed. 'Sklar Hast, we speak to you now in a spirit not necessarily of amity, but at least one of compromise.'

Sklar Hast nodded warily. 'Speak on.'

'You will agree that chaos, disorder, destruction and contention must be halted, absolutely and definitely; that Tranque Float must be restored to its former high status and reputation.' He looked at Sklar Hast expectantly.

'Continue,' said Sklar Hast.

'You make no response,' complained Ixon Myrex.

'You asked no question,' said Sklar Hast. 'You merely uttered an asseveration.'

Ixon Myrex made a petulant gesture. 'Do you so agree?'

'Certainly,' said Sklar Hast. 'Do you expect me to argue otherwise?'

Arbiter Myrex ignored the question. 'We must necessarily cooperate. It is impossible that conditions can return to normal unless all of us exert ourselves to this end, and, er, make certain sacrifices.' He paused, but Sklar Hast made no remark. 'Essentially, it seems absurd and paradoxical that you, with your fanatically unorthodox views, should continue in an office which carries great weight and prestige. The best interests of the float are served by your voluntary relinquishment of the office.'

'Indeed. And what sacrifices do you propose to make?'

'We are agreed that if you display a sense of responsibility, relinquish the guild-mastership, make a sober, sincere, profession of orthodoxy, we will remit your delinquencies, and hold them no longer to your discredit.'

'This is magnanimity indeed,' sneered Sklar Hast. 'What sort of blubbering water-sheep do you take me for?'

Ixon Myrex nodded curtly. 'We feared that this might be your response. Now violence is as abhorrent to us as it is to every man and woman of the floats, and therefore we make no threats; nevertheless we require from you a solemn undertaking never again to engage in unorthodox activities, or those which challenge the authority of King Kragen.'

'And if I don't?'

'Then we will ask that you depart Tranque Float.'

'And where do you suggest that I go?'

Semm Voiderveg could contain his passion no longer. He pointed a white quivering finger to the sea. 'We suggest that you and others of your ilk depart! There are other floats; they are mentioned in the Analects; the Firsts saw them when the Ship of Space came down. Go forth then to some other float, and allow us who wish peace to live as we always have.'

Sklar Hast's lip curled. 'What of King Kragen? It seems that you contravene the Covenant, suggesting that I trespass upon his ocean. What of that?'

'The trespass then becomes an issue between you and King Kragen! The affair is none of mine.'

'And if King Kragen follows us to our new domicile, deserting the Home Floats? What would the intercessors do then?'

Semm Voiderveg blinked. The concept clearly took him by surprise. 'If such an exigency arises, be assured that we will know how to deal with it.'

Sklar Hast prepared to return to his work. 'I will not resign my rightful guild-mastership; I promise no fidelity to you or King Kragen; I will not set forth across the ocean.'

Semm Voiderveg started to speak, but Ixon Myrex held up his hand. 'What then do you plan?' he asked cannily.

Sklar Hast stared at him a long moment, with conflicting impulses struggling inside his brain. All prudence and sagacity urged him to dissemble, to feign orthodoxy or at least disinterest, while he arrived at some method to kill King Kragen. But what if he failed in the attempt? Then once again Tranque Float would be devastated and people who wanted nothing to do with the project would be injured, even killed. It seemed only just that he announce his intentions, in order to give those who disapproved a chance to remove themselves. But by so warning Ixon Myrex and Semm Voiderveg he guaranteed himself of their vigilance, their antagonism and possibly their interference. It was simple common sense and good generalship to dissemble, to calm Ixon Myrex and Semm Voiderveg and blunt their suspicions. What if a few innocent persons did get killed? No battles were won without casualties. And Sklar Hast tried to twist his tongue to speak evasion and reassurance, but he could not do it; he was physically unable to put on the necessary mask, and felt a great anger for his own weakness. 'If I were you,' he said roughly, 'I'd depart Tranque Float and stay away. Because there might well be further "unorthodoxy", as you call it.'

'Exactly in what degree?' asked Ixon Myrex crisply.

'I've made no plans. I wouldn't tell you in any event. But now, against my better judgment, I've warned you.'

Semm Voiderveg once more began to speak, but once more Ixon Myrex silenced him. 'I see that our attempt at a harmonious solution is in vain. You warned me; I will warn you. Any attempt to offend King Kragen, any attempt upon his dignity will be regarded as a capital crime. That is my judgment as Arbiter of Tranque Float! You have challenged authority and the majesty of tradition. Beware that your impudence does not bring you to grief!'

One of the others spoke: Gian Recargo, the Bezzler Elder, a man of great gentility, rectitude, and presence. 'Sklar Hast, are you aware of your irresponsibility? You threaten the lives and properties of others who wish no part of your mad antics; do you not feel shame?'

'I have thought at length about the situation,' said Sklar Hast. 'I have concluded that a great evil exists, that inertia and fear press so heavily upon otherwise worthy folk like yourself that you abide this evil. Someone must be willing to take great risks, even with the lives of other people. This is not irresponsibility; it is far more responsibility than I relish. The judgment is not solely my own; I am no monomaniac. Many other sane and responsible folk agree with me that King Kragen must be defeated. Why do you not join us? Once the sea-beast is destroyed, we are free. Is not this worth the risk? We can use the ocean as we please! We need feed the gluttonous maw no longer! The intercessors will be deprived of their sinecures and must then work like the rest of us, which appalls them; hence their antagonism. This is the way the future must go!'

Gian Recargo was silent. Ixon Myrex tugged irritably on his beard. A heavy half-moment went by. Semm Voiderveg looked at them impatiently. 'Why do you not refute this incredible diatribe?'

Gian Recargo turned away to look out over the lagoon. 'I must think at length,' he muttered. 'I do not care to hear such a challenge to my courage.'

'Bah,' said Ixon Myrex uneasily. 'Conditions were well enough in the past. Who wants to sail the ocean? And the sponges consumed by King Kragen are not a staggering tax upon us.'

Semm Voiderveg smote the air with his fist. 'This is superficial! The issue is Sklar Hast's abominable arrogance, his disrespect and irreverence toward our great King Kragen!'

Gian Recargo turned on his heel and walked slowly off across the float.

Semm Voiderveg made another angry gesticulation. Ixon Myrex held his ground a moment longer, turned a searching gaze upon ruined tower, lagoon, Sklar Hast, the others who stood attentively about, then made a nondescript sound and marched away.

The hoodwinks and larceners returned to work. Sklar Hast, with Roger Kelso, went off to confer with Rollo Barnack, to hear his plan for killing King Kragen. Both agreed that if conditions were right, if timing were precise, if the materials were sufficiently tough, King Kragen might well be killed.

CHAPTER SEVEN

Gradually the evidence of disaster disappeared; gradually Tranque Float resumed its normal aspect. The broken huts and shattered timbers were burned on the fire-raft, and the ashes carefully stored for later use in the manufacture of soap, whitewash, fire-brick, the mordanting of cloth, the weighting of sinkers, the clarification of varnish. The corpses, after two weeks' submersion in special receptacles, during which time certain small finned worms stripped the flesh from the bones, were conveyed to a remote part of the float where the hardest bones were removed, and the remainder calcined for lime: a work which traditionally had been the exclusive domain of Advertisermen.

Withe had been cut, seasoned, formed into new huts, covered with padskin and varnished; new sponge arbors had been built, seeded with floss and lowered into the bright blue water.

The hoodwink tower, the most massive and complicated object of the float, was the last structure to be rebuilt. The new tower was even taller than the old, more massive in design, with a site somewhat closer to the lagoon.

The method of construction was also different from the old and elicited considerable comment among the folk of Tranque Float. Customarily each leg descended through a hole in the float to be anchored in the crotch of a sturdy underwater stem. In the new tower these supports terminated in a low platform twenty-five feet square, and from this platform rose the four legs: great poles a hundred feet long fabricated from lengths of withe laid in varnish and whipped. The legs, held rigid by spreaders, gradually converged, to terminate in a frame six feet square.

The proportions of the tower, the mass of the poles and the comparatively small area of the base platform, aroused as much curiosity and criticism as the unconventional method of construction. Ixon Myrex on one occasion taxed Rollo Barnack, the Master Larcener, with unorthodoxy.

'Never have I seen a tower of this sort before!' he complained. 'I see no need for such heavy construction. The posts are as staunch above as they are below: why is this?'

'It lends an added solidity,' declared Rollo Barnack with a wise wink.

'Solid perhaps, but so precariously narrow at the base that a good gust of wind will tip it over and hurl it into the lagoon!'

'Do you really think so?' Rollo Barnack asked earnestly, standing back and inspecting the tower as if this were his first clear view of it.

'I am no larcener,' Ixon Myrex went on, 'and I know little enough of construction, but this is how it appears to me. Especially when the tower house is built aloft and the lamps and hoods hung on the cross-arm! Think of the force, the leverage!'

'You are quite right,' said Rollo Barnack. 'To counteract this force we propose to run guy-lines.'

The Arbiter shook his head in puzzlement. 'Why did you not build in the old manner, with legs sufficiently outspread so that the guy-lines were not needed? This seems overcomplicated to me.'

'We use much less float area,' Rollo Barnack pointed out. 'This is a significant consideration.'

Ixon Myrex shook his head without conviction, but made no further protest.

So the guy-lines were extended. Next the control house was added, then the great yard-arm on which the hoods and lamps hung. This last was constructed with the most meticulous care, from sections of the densest stem obtainable. Ixon Myrex, once again inspecting the construction, was astounded by the mass of the yard-arm. In explanation, Rollo Barnack referred to the consequent lack of vibration and the greater control thus afforded the hoodwinks. 'Have no fear, Arbiter. Every detail in the construction of this tower has been carefully thought out.'

'Like the guy-ropes, I suppose?' Ixon Myrex inquired sarcastically. 'And the manner in which the legs are affixed to the base platform: bound, no less! By ropes! Is this a solid manner in which to build a hoodwink tower?'

'We hope it will fulfill its purpose,' Rollo Barnack said. 'If it does this, we shall ask no more of it.'

And again Ixon Myrex departed, shaking his head.

During this time King Kragen had not appeared in the vicinity of Tranque Float.

From the Thrasneck hoodwink tower came occasional news of his whereabouts: he had been seen cruising to the south of Sankston heading west; he had put in at Populous Equity to feed; he had fed again at Parnassus, the float next west. Thereafter, he submerged and for two days nothing was heard of him.

Tranque was almost back to normal. The sponges were growing large and beginning to burst from their husks; the huts had all been rebuilt; the new hoodwink tower, if somewhat ponderous and top-heavy, stood tall and impressive.

The yard-arm had been a long time in preparation. Each end was tapered to a point and boiled in varnish for three days, then baked over a slow fire, until the stem was hard and dense. Along the lengths were fixed reinforcing struts, and all scraped and buffed and oiled so it shone smooth and glossy.

Finally the yard was hoisted to the top of the tower and secured in place, and again no precaution seemed too great. First it was seated in a socket, then glued, lashed, and pegged.

Once more Ixon Myrex was baffled. 'The tower stands askew!'

'How so?' asked Rollo Barnack mildly.

'Notice how it fronts: not directly upon the Thrasneck Tower as it should, but considerably to the side. The folk on Thrasneck will read all our winks with a squint, sidelong.'

Rollo Barnack nodded judiciously. 'We are not unaware of this condition. It was planned in this manner, for the following reasons. First, it is rumored that the Thrasneck folk are planning a new tower, to be constructed somewhere along the line in which we now face. Second, the configuration of the underwater stems has made it difficult to fix the posts at any other angle than as you see, and we believe that in time there will be a gradual turning and twisting, which will bring the tower more directly to bear upon the current Thrasneck tower.'

Intercessor Semm Voiderveg, who had regained something of his former poise, joined Ixon Myrex's criticisms. 'This seems the least graceful and efficient tower I have ever seen! Notice that long heavy pointed yard-arm, and that narrow, elongated cabin below: has anyone ever seen the like before?'

Rollo Barnack repeated his former remark. 'It looks more than efficient to me. If it fulfills its purpose, we will be more than happy.'

Ixon Myrex shook his head sadly. 'The folk of other floats believe us eccentric and perverse as it is; with this new tower staring blankly to sea, they will consider us lunatics.'

'Correctly, perhaps,' said Sklar Hast with a grin. 'Why don't you and Voiderveg depart?'

'Let us not talk about matters of the past!' muttered Ixon Myrex. 'It all seems a bad dream, as if it never happened.'

'Unfortunately it did,' said Sklar Hast, 'and King Kragen still swims the sea. If only he would die of natural causes, or choke on a surfeit of sponges, or drown!'

Semm Voiderveg studied him levelly. 'You are a man without reverence, without fidelity.'

Ixon Myrex and Semm Voiderveg presently departed. Sklar Hast watched them go. 'What a situation!' he complained to Roger Kelso. 'We cannot act like honorable men; we cannot declare ourselves; instead we must skulk about in this half-brazen, half-furtive pretense.'

'It is pointless to worry about the matter,' said Kelso. 'The choice long since was made; we are now ready to act.'

'And if we fail?'

Roger Kelso shrugged. 'I put our chances of success as one in three. All must go with such exactness, such precision of timing as to make optimism out of the question.'

Sklar Hast said, 'We must warn the folk of the float. This is the very least we can do.'

Rollo Barnack and Roger Kelso argued but without success. Sklar Hast finally had his way, and in the early part of the evening he called a meeting of all the folk of the float.

He spoke briefly and to the point. 'Tranque Float is once more whole. Life seems to be placid and even. It is only fair to announce that this is illusory. Many of us are not reconciled to the overlordship of King Kragen, and we propose to end it. We may be unsuccessful; there may be a new and even more disastrous set of circumstances in the future. So all are warned, and are welcome to leave Tranque for other more orthodox floats.'

Ixon Myrex jumped to his feet. 'Sklar Hast – you may not involve the rest of us in your scheme! It is not right! This is my judgment as Arbiter.'

Sklar Hast made no response.

Semm Voiderveg spoke. 'Naturally I endorse the Arbiter's views! And may I ask how you propose to implement your preposterous schemes?'

'We are evolving a strain of poisonous sponges,' Roger Kelso told him. 'When King Kragen eats, he will become waterlogged and sink.'

Sklar Hast turned away, walked to the edge of the float to look off across the water. Behind him was further wrangling, then by twos and threes and fours, the folk went off to their various huts.

Meril Rohan came to join Sklar Hast, and for a moment both looked off across the twilight. Meril Rohan said, 'This is a difficult time we live in, without clear-cut rights and wrongs, and it is hard to know how to act.'

'An era has come to an end,' said Sklar Hast. 'A Golden Age, an Age of Innocence – it is ended. Violence, hate, turbulence have come to the floats. The world will never be the same again.'

'A new and better world may come of it all.'

Sklar Hast shook his head. 'I doubt it. If King Kragen foundered and sank at this moment, there would still be changes. It seems as if suddenly the time were ripe for change. We must go forward – or go back.'

Meril Rohan was silent. Then she pointed toward Thrasneck. 'Watch the winks.'

'... *King* ... *Kragen* ... *seen* ... *to* ... *the* ... *north* ... *of* ... *Quincunx* ... *proceeding* ... *in* ... *an* ... *easterly* ... *direction* ...'

'The time is not yet,' said Sklar Hast. 'We are not quite ready.'

The next day King Kragen was seen to the north of Tranque Float, drifting idly without apparent purpose. For an hour he floated placidly, eye-tubes fixed on Tranque, then veered close as if in curiosity, and gave Tranque a brief inspection. Semm Voiderveg, arrayed in his ceremonial robes, came forth to stand at the edge of the float, where he performed his ritual postures and beckonings. King Kragen watched a moment or two, then reacting to some unknowable emotion gave a quick jerk and with a surge of his vanes swung about and swam to the west, mandibles scissoring, palps pushing in and out.

Semm Voiderveg made a final genuflection, and watched King Kragen's departure.

Nearby stood Sklar Hast, and as Semm Voiderveg turned to go back to his hut, his gaze met that of Sklar Hast. For a brief moment the two men studied each other, with a hostility in which there existed no understanding. Sklar Hast felt an emotion far different from the simple contempt he felt for Ixon Myrex. It was as if Semm Voiderveg were himself part kragen; as if in his veins flowed a thick indigo ooze instead of red human blood.

A week later King Kragen feasted on Bickle sponges, and the next day did likewise at Thrasneck. On the day following, a hundred yards from the entrance to Tranque lagoon, he slowly surfaced and once more gave Tranque Float a deliberate, almost suspicious, scrutiny.

As Semm Voiderveg ran forth in his ceremonial robes, Sklar Hast mounted the ladder to the hoodwink house; but King Kragen slowly submerged. The water swirled over his domed black turret; the sea lay calm and blue as before.

Sklar Hast came down from the tower to meet Semm Voiderveg returning to his hut. 'King Kragen is vigilant! He knows Tranque Float for the haunt of evil that it is! Beware!' And Semm Voiderveg strode off in a flutter of black. Sklar Hast looked after him, wondering if Semm Voiderveg were perhaps mad. Returning to the open-sided shed, where with a number of apprentices and assistant hoodwinks he was constructing a pair of what he referred to as "practice mechanisms", he discussed the possibility with Ben Kell, the Assistant Master Hoodwink, who had no opinion.

'In Voiderveg's opinion you are mad,' said Kell. 'These are difficult matters to define. In the context of a year ago, Voiderveg is saner than sane.

With conditions as they are now, the question of who is most sane wavers on an edge.'

Sklar Hast grinned sourly. He had lost weight; his cheeks had become a trifle concave, and there was a sprinkle of gray in the hair at his temples. 'Let's take these things outside and give Myrex something new to worry over.'

The mechanisms were carried out and set on the float halfway between the tower and the lagoon, one to the right, one to the left. In the lagoon, broad on the tower, hung a large arbor already ripe with sponges. Twenty feet beyond, apparently by sheer chance, floated a chip of wood. The chip, the two "practice mechanisms" and the tower formed a rough square seventy feet on a side.

Stakes were driven into the substance of the float, the mechanisms were anchored firmly. Upon each was a sighting device, similar to a navigator's pelorus, which Sklar Hast adjusted to bear on the floating chip.

He had prophesied correctly. Almost immediately the Arbiter appeared with his now familiar doubts and criticisms. He began in a tone of weary patience, 'What are these objects?'

'These are practice machines for the apprentices. We will leave them here until suitable accommodation is arranged under the tower.'

'Seemingly you would equip the tower with frames, hoods and lamps before constructing practice machines.'

'Normally we would do so. But we are testing a new linkage system. And it would not be well to allow the apprentices to scamp their practice.'

'In the meantime we can send no messages. We are isolated.'

Sklar Hast pointed to the Thrasneck tower. 'You can read all that transpires elsewhere. Nothing of consequence occurs here.'

'Nevertheless, we should put our system into working order as rapidly as possible.' And he gave the tower a black look. 'Awkward, top-heavy and askew as it is.'

'If it achieves its purpose,' said Sklar Hast, 'it will be the most beautiful object the world has yet seen.'

Arbiter Myrex gave him a sharp glance. 'What is the meaning of that remark?'

Sklar Hast saw that he had gone too far. Ixon Myrex was a slow and rigid man, but not stupid. 'Sheer exuberance, sheer hyperbole.'

Ixon Myrex grunted. 'The structure is an aesthetic disgrace. Already we are the laughingstock of the whole line. When the folk speak of "Quatrefoil" and "Sankston" for extravagance and eccentricity, now they will add "Tranque". I would not be sorry to see it destroyed and another erected in its place.'

'This one will serve,' said Sklar Hast carelessly.

Further days passed. King Kragen dined at Green Lamp, at Fleurnoy and at Adelvine three days running, then swam far west to Granolt. For two days he was seen no more, then appeared far out on the horizon to the south of Aumerge, coasting east. The following day he dined once more at Adelvine, to the near depletion of the Adelvine lagoon, and the following day at Sumber, the third float north from Tranque, with only Thrasneck and Bickle between. On Tranque Float a mood of uneasiness and foreboding manifested itself. People spoke in hushed voices and looked constantly sidelong toward the sea. By some sort of psychic osmosis all knew that a great project was afoot, even though the nature of the project was unknown – to all but about thirty or so of the most secretive men of the float.

Two days after King Kragen dined at Sumber, he appeared in the ocean to the north of Tranque and lay floating for half an hour, twitching his great vanes. At this, certain of the more timorous departed Tranque, conveying themselves, their women and children to Thrasneck.

Semm Voiderveg stormed up to Sklar Hast. 'What is going on? What do you plan?'

'More to the point,' said Sklar Hast, 'what do you plan?'

'What do I plan?' bellowed the portly Intercessor. 'What else do I plan but rectitude? It is you and your accomplices who threaten the fabric of our existence!'

'Calm yourself, Voiderveg,' said Wall Bunce with an insensitive grin. 'Yonder floats the kragen to which you have pledged yourself. If you appear at a disadvantage you forfeit his respect.'

Rudolf Snyder gave a cry of warning. 'He moves! He swims forward!'

Semm Voiderveg made a wild gesture. 'I must go to welcome him. Sklar Hast, I warn you, I implore you, do nothing contrary to the Covenant!'

Sklar Hast made no reply. With a final desperate glare of admonition, the Intercessor marched to the edge of the float and began his ritual gesticulations.

King Kragen moved slowly forward, by small twitches and flicks of the vanes. The eye-tubes studied the float carefully, as if something of the tension and emotion of those on the float had reached him.

King Kragen approached the mouth of the lagoon. Semm Voiderveg signaled his assistants, who drew back the net to allow King Kragen access into the lagoon.

The great black bulk approached. Sklar Hast became conscious of the close attention of Ixon Myrex and several others. It was clear that counsel had been taken and plans made to forestall any action on his part. Sklar Hast had expected something of the sort, and was not perturbed. He went to a bench and seated himself, as if contemptuously disassociating himself from the entire affair. Looking around, he saw that others of orthodox persuasion similarly stood near Roger Kelso and Rubal Gallager, apparently ready to employ forcible restraint, if the necessity arose. Elsewhere about the float, others of the conspiracy were casually going to their places. To Sklar Hast it seemed that the program was blatantly obvious, and he wondered that neither Semm Voiderveg, Ixon Myrex, nor any of those who supported them had perceived it.

There was one who had: Gian Recargo, Elder of the Bezzlers. He came now to the bench and seated himself beside Sklar Hast. 'This is a precarious hour.' He glanced up toward the hoodwink tower. 'I hope, for all our sakes, that all goes well.'

Sklar Hast nodded grimly. 'So do I.'

Time moved with nerve-racking slowness. The sun shone almost perpendicularly upon the ultramarine water. The foliage – black, orange, green, purple, tawny yellow – swayed in the faintest of warm breezes. Into the lagoon swam King Kragen. Semm Voiderveg ran to the edge of the float, and performed his gestures of reverence and invitation.

Sklar Hast frowned, rubbed his chin. Gian Recargo glanced at him sidewise. 'What of Semm Voiderveg?' he asked in the driest of voices.

'I had not considered him,' muttered Sklar Hast. 'A flaw in my thinking ... I will do my best for him.' He rose to his feet, joined Rollo Barnack, who lounged beside one of the practice mechanisms. At the other one stood Ben Kell, the Assistant Master Hoodwink, both in a position where they could sight across their peloruses. 'The Intercessor stands in the way,' Sklar Hast muttered. 'Pay him no heed. I will try to save him.'

'It will be dangerous for you as well.'

Sklar Hast nodded. 'Unfortunately this is so. All of us are running grave risks. Heed neither Semm Voiderveg nor myself. Proceed as if neither of us were imperiled. We will both escape.'

Rollo Barnack nodded. 'As you wish.' And he looked across the pelorus, to see a twitching tip of King Kragen's forward vane.

King Kragen floated quietly ten or twenty seconds, studying Semm Voiderveg. Once again he eased forward, thrust forth his palps, and gave himself a last thrust which pushed him close to the arbor.

King Kragen began to feed.

Rollo Barnack, looking along the points of his pelorus, found the turret slightly to the right of his line of sight. He waited. King Kragen floated a trifle to the left. Rollo Barnack gave a prearranged signal, raising his hand, running his fingers through his hair. Ben Kell, at the other pelorus, was already doing likewise.

At the back of the tower Poe Belrod and Wall Bunce already had cut the bindings that lashed the two rear legs to the stubs rising from the base platform. Rudolf Snyder and Garth Gasselton loosed the rear guy-lines. At each of the fore guy-lines – those leading toward the lagoon – five men pulled as casually and nonchalantly as possible.

The great tower, tall, heavy, narrow-based, pivoted over on the two legs yet bound. The great pointed yard-arm began to sweep out a great arc that would terminate upon King Kragen's turret.

Directly in the path of the falling tower stood Semm Voiderveg, intent at his rituals. Sklar Hast strode forward to thrust the Intercessor out of the way. Others realized that the tower was falling. There came sudden startled screams. Semm Voiderveg looked over his shoulder to see the toppling structure and likewise sensed Sklar Hast lunging at him. He gave a strangled croak, and, trying to run, stumbled with flapping arms. Both men rolled clear. The astounded King Kragen gave a twitch of the vanes. Down like an enormous pick-axe came the tower, and the pointed yard-arm missed the turret dead-center only by the amount of King Kragen's twitch of alarm. Down upon the black barrel came the point, glancing away and burying itself in the black rectangular pad below. From Rollo Barnack and Roger Kelso came groans of disappointment; others screamed in horror and fright. King Kragen himself emitted a fierce, whistling hiss and thrashed out with all four vanes. The yard-arm snapped from the tower; King Kragen surged struggling back into the lagoon. With two of the palps it seized the stump still protruding from its flesh, snatched it forth and brandished it high in the air. Semm Voiderveg, struggling to his feet, called out in a shrill sobbing voice, 'Mercy, King Kragen, a terrible mistake! Mercy, have mercy!'

King Kragen surged close and brought the length of timber vindictively down on Semm Voiderveg, crushing him to the pad. Again he struck, then roaring and hissing hurled the object at Sklar Hast. Then, backing up and accelerating forward, he charged the float.

'Run,' cried Rollo Barnack hoarsely. 'Run for your lives!'

King Kragen was not content with the devastation of Tranque. He likewise wrought havoc upon Thrasneck and Bickle, then fatigued, or perhaps in pain, he propelled himself to sea and disappeared.

CHAPTER EIGHT

A Grand Convocation was called on Apprise Float. Barquan Blasdel, the Apprise Intercessor, was the first to speak. His remarks were predictably bitter, his manner grim. He eulogized Semm Voiderveg at length; he lamented the dead of Tranque, Thrasneck, and Bickle; he described the havoc and disaster; he speculated pessimistically regarding the status of the broken Covenant. 'His comprehensible fury is not yet assuaged, but do the guilty suffer? No. This morning King Kragen attacked and demolished the coracles of four Vidmar swindlers. Who can blame him? To come in good faith, under the terms of the Covenant, to receive his just due, encouraged and welcomed by the Intercessor – and then to experience this murderous attack! King Kragen has demonstrated restraint in not destroying every float of the chain!

'Needless to say, the wretched conspirators who hatched this plot must be punished. The last convocation ended in riot and bloodshed. We must be more controlled, more sagacious on this occasion, but we must definitely act. The conspirators must die.'

Barquan Blasdel did not call for a show of fists, since the accused had not yet spoken in their behalf.

Phyral Berwick, the Apprise Arbiter, hence convocation moderator, looked around the float. 'Who cares to speak?'

'I.' Gian Recargo, Elder of the Tranque Bezzlers, came forward. 'I was not an active conspirator. Initially I was of the orthodox view; then I changed my thinking. It is still changed. The so-called conspirators indeed have brought damage and loss of life to the floats. They grieve for this as much as anyone. But the damage and the deaths are inevitable, because I have come to agree with Sklar Hast. King Kragen must be killed. So let us not revile these men who by dint of great ingenuity and daring almost killed King Kragen. They did as well as they were able to. Sklar Hast risked his own life to save the life of Semm Voiderveg. King Kragen killed the intercessor.'

Barquan Blasdel leaped to his feet and ridiculed Gian Recargo's defense of what he called the 'blasphemous irresponsibility of the conspirators'. After him spoke Archibel Verack, Quincunx Intercessor; then Parensic Mole, the Wyebolt Arbiter; then in succession other arbiters, intercessors, elders and guild-masters.

There was clearly no consensus. It seemed as if approximately a third of those present favored the most drastic penalties for the conspirators; another third, while regretting the destruction and death toll, regretted even more strongly the failure of the plot; while the final third were persons confused, indecisive and fearful who swayed first in one direction, then another.

Sklar Hast, advised by Gian Recargo, did not speak, and only watched and listened stonily as Barquan Blasdel and others heaped opprobrium upon him.

The afternoon drew on, and tempers began to grow short. Barquan Blasdel finally decided to bring matters to a head. In a voice deadly calm he again enumerated the sins of Sklar Hast and his fellows, then pitching his voice at a compelling level, called for a show of fists. 'Peace and the Covenant! All who favor this, raise their fists! We must purge the evil that threatens us! And I say—' he leaned forward, looked menacingly across the float '—that if the convocation does not correctly vote death to the murderers, we right-thinkers and true-believers must organize ourselves into a disciplined group, to make sure that justice is done! The matter is this serious, this basic, this important! Crime may not go unpunished! We vacillated before; see where it took us! So I say to you: vote death to the murderers, or see justice sternly imposed by the mighty force of orthodox anger. So now: fists high against Sklar Hast and the conspirators!'

Fists thrust into the air. An equal number stayed down, though many of these belonged to the confused and undecided. Now began the ominous mutter of argument that had preceded the bloodshed at the last convocation.

Sklar Hast jumped to his feet, strode to the rostrum. 'Clearly we are divided. Some wish to serve King Kragen, others prefer not to do so. We are on the verge of a terrible experience, which by all means must be prevented. There is one simple way to do this. Other floats as fertile as these exist. I propose to depart these beloved Home Floats, and make a new life elsewhere. I naturally will welcome all who wish to join me, though I urge this course upon no one. We will gain freedom. We will serve no King Kragen. Our life will be our own. Undoubtedly there will be initial deprivations, but we shall overcome them and build a life as pleasant as that of Home – perhaps more pleasant because there will be no tyrannical King Kragen. Who then wishes to sail away to a new home?'

A few hands raised, then others, and others still, to represent perhaps a third of those present.

'This is more than I expected,' said Sklar Hast. 'Go then to your floats, load your coracles with tools, pots, varnish, cordage – all your utile goods. Then return here, to Apprise Lagoon. We will await a propitious time to depart, when the sea-beast is known to be at Sciona, should we choose to sail east, or at Tranque, should we sail west. Needless to say, the direction and hour of departure must remain secret. There is no reason to explain why.' He cast an ironic glance toward Barquan Blasdel, who sat like a carved image. 'It is a sad thing to leave an ancestral home, but it is worse to remain and submit to tyranny. The Firsts made this same decision, and it is clear that at least some of us still retain the ideals of our forefathers.'

Barquan Blasdel spoke without rising to his feet: a crass act. 'Don't talk of ideals – merely go. Go gladly. Go with all goodwill. We will not miss you. And never seek to return when the teeming rogues, unchided by the great king, devour your poor sponges, tear your nets, crush your coracles!'

Sklar Hast ignored him. 'All then who will depart these sad Home Floats:

we meet here in two days time. We will then secretly decide our hour of departure.'

Barquan Blasdel laughed. 'You need not fear our interference. Depart whenever you desire; indeed we will facilitate your going.'

Sklar Hast reflected a moment. 'You will not inform King Kragen of our going?'

'No. Of course, he may learn of the fact through his own observation.'

'This will be our plan then. On the evening of the third day, when the wind blows fair to the west, we depart – provided, of course, that King Kragen cruises to the east.'

CHAPTER NINE

Barquan Blasdel the Apprise Intercessor, his spouse and six daughters, oc-cupied a pad on the ocean to the north of the main Apprise float, somewhat isolated and apart. It was perhaps the choicest and most pleasant pad of the Apprise complex, situated where Blasdel could read the hoodwink towers of Apprise; of Quatrefoil and The Bandings to the east; of Granolt to the west. The pad was delightfully overgrown with a hundred different plants and vines: some yielding resinous pods, others capsules of fragrant sap, others crisp tendrils and shoots. Certain shrubs produced stains and pigment; a purple-leaved epiphyte yielded a rich-flavored pith. Other growths were en-tirely ornamental – a situation not too usual along the floats, where space was at a premium and every growing object weighed for its utility. Along the entire line of floats few pads could compare to that of Barquan Blasdel for beauty, variety of plantings, isolation and calm.

In late afternoon of the second day after the convocation, Barquan Blas-del returned to his pad. He dropped the painter of his coracle over a stake of carved bone, gazed appreciatively into the west. The sun had only just departed the sky, which now glowed with effulgent greens, blues, and, at the zenith, a purple of exquisite purity. The ocean, rippling to the first whispers of the evening breeze, reflected the sky. Blasdel felt surrounded, immersed in color ... He turned away, marched to his house, whistling between his teeth. In the lagoon were five hundred coracles, perhaps as many as six hundred, loaded with goods: the property of the most perverse and trouble-some elements of the floats. On the morrow they would depart, and no more would be heard from them. Ever again. And Blasdel's whistling became slow and thoughtful. Although life seemingly flowed smoothly, he had sensed recently the awakening of an uneasiness, a dissatisfaction, which had made itself felt in a hundred different ways. Barquan Blasdel had not been quite so surprised by the attempt upon King Kragen's life as he professed to be. Though for a fact the attempt had approached success more nearly than he would have expected. A clever, unscrupulous fellow, that Sklar Hast. An obstreperous, recalcitrant, skeptical man of great energy, whom Barquan Blasdel was more than happy to have out of the way.

All was working out for the best. Indeed, indeed, indeed! The affair could not have resolved itself more smoothly if he had personally arranged the entire sequence of events! At one stroke all the grumblers, ne'er-do-wells, the covertly insolent, the obstinate hardheads – at one stroke all would disappear, never again to trouble the easy and orthodox way of life!

Almost jauntily Barquan Blasdel ambled up the path to his residence: a group of five semi-detached huts, screened by the garden from the main float, and so providing a maximum of privacy for Blasdel, his spouse and his six daughters. Blasdel halted. On a bench beside the door sat a man. Twilight murk concealed his face. Blasdel frowned, peered. Intruders upon his private pad were not welcome. Blasdel marched forward. The man rose from the bench and bowed: it was Phyral Berwick, the Apprise Arbiter. 'Good evening,' said Berwick. 'I trust I did not startle you.'

'By no means,' said Blasdel shortly. With rank equal to his own, Berwick could not be ignored, although after his extraordinary and equivocal conduct at the two convocations, Blasdel could not bring himself to display more than a minimum of formal courtesy. He said, 'Unfortunately I was not expecting callers and can offer you no refreshment.'

'A circumstance of no moment,' declared Berwick. 'I desire neither food nor drink.' He waved his hand around the pad. 'You live on a pad of surpassing beauty, Barquan Blasdel. Many envy you.'

Blasdel shrugged. 'My conduct is orthodox; I am armored against adverse opinion. But what urgency brings you here? I fear that I must be less than ceremonious; I am shortly due at the hoodwink tower to participate in a coded all-float conference.'

Berwick made a gesture of polite acquiescence. 'My business is of small moment. But I would not keep you standing out here in the dusk. Shall we enter?'

Blasdel grunted, opened the door, allowed Berwick to pass into the hut. From a cupboard he brought luminant fiber, which he set aglow and arranged in a holder. Turning a quick side-glance toward Berwick, he said, 'In all candor I am somewhat surprised to see you. Apparently you were among the most vehement of those dissidents who planned to depart.'

'I may well have given that impression,' Berwick agreed. 'But you must realize that declarations uttered in the heat of emotion are occasionally amended in the light of sober reason.'

Blasdel nodded curtly. 'True enough. I suspect that many other of the ingrates will think twice before joining this hare-brained expedition.' Though he hoped not.

'This is partly the reason for my presence here,' said Berwick. He looked around the room. 'An interesting chamber. You own dozens of valuable artifacts. Where are the others of your family?'

'In the domestic area. This is my sanctum, my workroom, my place of meditation.'

'Indeed.' Berwick inspected the walls. 'Indeed, indeed! I believe I notice certain relics of the forefathers!'

'True,' said Blasdel. 'This small flat object is of the substance called "metal", and is extremely hard. The best bone knife will not scratch it. The purpose of this particular object I cannot conjecture. It is an heirloom. These books are exact copies of the Memoria. Alas! I find much in them beyond my comprehension. There is nothing more of any great interest. On the shelf – my ceremonial head-dresses; you have seen them before. Here is my telescope. It is old; the case is warped, the gum of the lenses has bulged and cracked. It was poor gum, to begin with, but I have little need for a better instrument. My possessions are few. Unlike many intercessors and certain arbiters—' here he cast a meaningful eye at Phyral Berwick '—I do not choose to surround myself with sybaritic cushions and baskets of sweetmeats.'

Berwick laughed ruefully. 'You have touched upon my weaknesses. Perhaps the fear of deprivation has occasioned second thoughts in me.'

'Ha, hah!' Blasdel became jovial. 'I begin to understand. The scalawags who set off to wild new floats can expect nothing but hardship: wild fish, horny sponges, new varnish with little more body than water; in short they will be returning to the life of savages. They must expect to suffer the depredations of lesser kragen, who will swiftly gather. Perhaps in time ...' His voice dwindled; his face took on a thoughtful look.

'You were about to say?' prompted Phyral Berwick.

Blasdel gave a noncommittal laugh. 'An amusing, if far-fetched, conceit crossed my mind. Perhaps in time one of these lesser kragen will vanquish the others, and drive them away. When this occurs, those who flee King Kragen will have a king of their own, who may eventually ...' Again his voice paused.

'Who may eventually rival King Kragen in size and force? The concept is not unreasonable – although King Kragen is already enormous from long feasting, and shows no signs of halting his growth.' An almost imperceptible tremor moved the floor of the hut. Blasdel went to look out the door. 'I thought I felt the arrival of a coracle.'

'Conceivably a gust of wind,' said Berwick. 'Well, to my errand. As you have guessed I did not come to examine your relicts or comment upon the comfort of your cottage. My business is this. Over two thousand folk are leaving the Home Floats. I feel that no one, not even the most violently fanatic intercessor, would wish this group to meet King Kragen upon the ocean. King Kragen, as you are aware, becomes petulant, even wrathful, when he finds men trespassing upon his realm. Now he is more irascible than ever. Perhaps he fears the possibility of the second King Kragen concerning which we speculated. Hence I came to inquire the whereabouts of King Kragen. In the evening the wind blows west, and the optimum location for King Kragen would be at Tranque or Thrasneck.'

Blasdel nodded sagely. 'This, of course, is a question of fortuity, and certainly the emigrants are putting their luck to the test. Should King Kragen chance to be waiting in the west tomorrow evening, and should he spy the flotilla, his wrath might well be excited, to the detriment of the expedition.'

'And where,' inquired Berwick, 'was King Kragen at last notification?'

Barquan Blasdel knit his heavy black eyebrows. 'I believe that I saw some winks to the effect that he had been observed cruising easterly below Adelvine toward Sumber. I might have well misread the flicker – I only noted the configuration from the corner of my eye – but such was my understanding.'

'Excellent,' declared Berwick. 'This is good news. The emigrants should then be able to make their departure safely and without interference.'

'So we hope,' said Blasdel. 'King Kragen of course is subject to unpredictable whims and quirks.'

Berwick made a confidential sign. 'Sometimes – so it is rumored – he responds to signals transmitted in some mysterious manner by the intercessors. Tell me, Barquan Blasdel, is this the case? We are both notables and together share responsibility for the welfare of Apprise Float. Is it true then that the intercessors communicate with King Kragen, as has been alleged?'

'Now then, Arbiter Berwick,' said Blasdel, 'this is hardly a pertinent question. Should I answer yes, then I would be divulging a craft secret. Should I answer no, then it would seem that we intercessors boast of nonexistent capabilities. So you must satisfy yourself with those hypotheses that seem the most profitable.'

'Fairly answered,' said Phyral Berwick. 'However – and in the strictest confidence – I will report to you an amusing circumstance. As you know, at both convocations, I more or less aligned myself with the party of Sklar Hast. I was subsequently accepted into their most intimate counsels. I can inform you with authority – but first, you will assure me of your silence? As under no circumstances would I betray Sklar Hast or compromise the expedition!'

'Certainly, indeed; my lips are sealed as with fourteen-year-old varnish.'

'You will under no circumstances communicate, signal, hint or imply any element of what I am about to confide, to any person or any thing, the prohibition to include written messages, winks, or any other method of communication?'

Barquan Blasdel gave an uneasy, high-pitched laugh – almost a giggle. 'Your charge upon me is not only legalistic, it is portentous in the extreme.'

'Do you agree to the provisions?'

'Certainly! I have already assured you of my reticence!'

'Well then, I take you at your word. This is Sklar Hast's amusing tactic: He has arranged that a group of influential intercessors shall accompany the group. If all goes well, the intercessors live. If not, like all the rest, they will be crushed in the mandibles of King Kragen.' And Phyral Berwick, standing back, watched Barquan Blasdel with an attentive gaze. 'What do you make of that?'

Blasdel stood rigid, fingering his fringe of black beard. He darted a quick glance toward Berwick. 'Which intercessors are to be kidnapped?'

'Aha!' said Berwick. 'That, like your response to the question I put to you, is in the nature of a craft secret. I doubt if lesser men will be troubled, but if I were intercessor for Aumerge or Sumber or Quatrefoil or even Apprise, I believe that I might have cause for caution.'

Blasdel stared at Berwick with mingled suspicion and uneasiness. 'Do you take this means to warn me? If so, I would thank you to speak less ambiguously. Personally I fear no such attack. Within a hundred feet are three stalwarts, testing my daughters for marriage. A loud call would bring instant help from the float, which is scarcely a stick's throw beyond the garden.'

Berwick nodded sagely. 'It seems then that you are quite secure.'

'Still, I must now hurry to the main float,' said Blasdel. 'I am expected at the hoodwink tower for an all-float conference, and the evening grows no younger.'

Berwick bowed and stood aside. 'You will naturally remember to reveal nothing of what I told you, to put forth no oblique warning, to hint nothing – in fact to make no reference to the matter in any way whatever.'

Blasdel made an impatient gesture. 'I will say nothing beyond my original intention, to the effect that the villain Sklar Hast obviously knows no moderation, and that it behooves all notables and craft masters to guard themselves against some form of final vengeance.'

Berwick frowned. 'I hardly think you need go quite so far. Perhaps you could phrase it somewhat differently. In this wise: Sklar Hast and his sturdy band take their leave in the morning; now is the last chance for persons so inclined to cast in their lot with the group; however, you hope that all intercessors will remain at their posts.'

'Pah!' cried Barquan Blasdel indignantly. 'That conveys no sense of imminence! I will say Sklar Hast is desperate; should he decide to take hostages, his diseased mind would select intercessors as the most appropriate persons!'

Berwick made a firm dissent. 'This, I believe, transcends the line I have drawn. My honor is at stake and I can agree to no announcement which baldly states the certainty as a probability. If you choose to make a jocular reference, or perhaps urge that not too many intercessors join the expedition, then all is well: a subtle germ of suspicion has been planted, you have done your duty and my honor has not been compromised.'

'Yes, yes,' cried Blasdel. 'I agree to anything! But I must hurry to the hoodwink tower. While we quibble Sklar Hast and his bandits are kidnapping intercessors!'

'And what is the harm there?' inquired Berwick mildly. 'You state that King Kragen has been observed from Adelvine proceeding west; hence the intercessors are in no danger and presumably will be allowed to return once Sklar Hast is assured that King Kragen is no longer a danger. Conversely, if the intercessors have betrayed Sklar Hast and given information to King Kragen so that he waits at the far west off Sciona Float, then they deserve to die with the rest. It is justice of the most precise and exquisite balance.'

'That is the difficulty,' muttered Blasdel, trying to push past Berwick to the door. 'I cannot answer for the silence of the other intercessors. Suppose one among them has notified King Kragen? Then a great tragedy ensues.'

'Interesting! So you can indeed summon King Kragen when you so desire?'

'Yes, yes, but, mind you, this is a secret. And now—'

'It follows then that you always know the whereabouts of King Kragen. How do you achieve this?'

'There is no time to explain; suffice it to say that a means is at hand.'

'Right here? In your workroom?'

'Yes indeed. Now stand aside. After I have broadcast the warning, I will make all clear. Stand aside then!'

Berwick shrugged and allowed Blasdel to run from the cottage, through the garden to the edge of the pad.

Blasdel stopped short at the water's edge. The coracle had disappeared. Where previously Apprise Float had raised its foliage and its hoodwink tower against the dusk, there was now only blank water and blank sky. The pad floated free; urged by the west wind of evening it already had left Apprise Float behind.

Blasdel gave an inarticulate sound of fury and woe. He turned to find Berwick standing behind him. 'What has happened?'

'It seems that while we talked, advertisermen cut through the stem of your pad. At least this is my presumption.'

'Yes, yes,' grated Blasdel. 'So much is obvious. What else?'

Berwick shrugged. 'It appears that, willy-nilly, whether we like it or not, we are part of the great emigration. Now that such is the case, I am relieved to know that you have a means to determine the whereabouts of King Kragen. Come. Let us make use of this device and reassure ourselves.'

Blasdel made a harsh, throaty sound. He crouched and for a moment seemed on the point of hurling himself at Phyral Berwick. From the shadows of the verdure appeared another man. Berwick pointed. 'I believe Sklar Hast himself is at hand.'

'You tricked me,' groaned Barquan Blasdel between clenched teeth. 'You have performed an infamous act, which you shall regret.'

'I have done no such deed, although it appears that you may well have misunderstood my position. But the time for recrimination is not now. We share a similar problem, which is how to escape the malevolence of King Kragen. I suggest that you now proceed to locate him.'

Without a word Blasdel turned, proceeded to his cottage. He entered the main room, with Berwick and Sklar Hast close behind. He crossed to the wall, lifted a panel to reveal an inner room. He brought more lights; all entered. A hole had been cut in the floor, and through the pad, the spongy tissue had been painted with a black varnish to prevent its growing together. A tube fashioned from fine yellow stalk perhaps four inches in diameter led down into the water. 'At the bottom,' said Blasdel curtly, 'is a carefully devised horn, of exact shape and quality. The end is four feet in diameter and covered with a diaphragm of seasoned and varnished pad-skin. King Kragen emits a sound to which this horn is highly sensitive.' He went to the tube, put down his ear, listened, slowly turned the tube around a vertical axis. He shook his head. 'I hear nothing. This means that King Kragen is at least ten miles distant. If he is closer I can detect him. He passed to the west early today; presumably he swims somewhere near Vidmar or Leumar or Populous Equity.'

Sklar Hast laughed quietly. 'Urged there by the intercessors?'

Blasdel gave a sour shrug. 'As to that I have nothing to say.'

'How then do you summon King Kragen?'

Blasdel pointed to a rod rising from the floor, the top of which terminated in a crank. 'In the water below is a drum. Inside this drum fits a wheel. When the crank is turned, the wheel, working in resin, rubs against the drum and emits a signal. King Kragen can sense this sound from a great distance – once again about ten miles. Assume he is at, say, Sankston, and is needed at Bickle. The Intercessor at The Bandings calls him, until the horn reveals him to be four or five miles distant, whereupon the Intercessor at Quatrefoil calls him, then the Hastings Intercessor, and so forth until he is within range of the Intercessor at Bickle Float.'

'I see,' said Sklar Hast. 'In this fashion Semm Voiderveg called King Kragen to Tranque. Whereupon King Kragen destroyed Tranque Float and killed forty-three persons.'

'That is the case.'

'And you have the hypocrisy to call us murderers!'

Blasdel once more shrugged and said nothing.

Phyral Berwick said, 'Perhaps it is fortunate that Semm Voiderveg is already dead. He would have been selected to accompany the emigration, and his lot would not have been a happy one.'

'This is unreasonable!' Barquan Blasdel declared heatedly. 'He was as faithful to his convictions as Sklar Hast is to his own! After all, Voiderveg did not enjoy the devastation of Tranque Float. It was his home. Many of those who were killed were his friends. He gave his faith and his trust utterly to King Kragen. And, in return, was killed.'

Sklar Hast swung around. 'And what of you?'

Blasdel shook his head sadly. 'I am a man who thinks at many levels.'

Sklar Hast turned away in disgust. He spoke to Berwick. 'What should we do with this apparatus? Destroy it? Or preserve it?'

Berwick considered. 'We might on some occasion wish to listen for King Kragen. I doubt if we will ever desire to summon him.'

Sklar Hast gave a sardonic jerk of his head. 'Who knows? To his death perhaps.' He turned to Blasdel. 'What persons are aboard the float in addition to us?'

'My spouse – in the cottage two roofs along. Three young daughters who weave ornaments for the Star-cursing Festival. Three older daughters who prove themselves to three stalwarts. All are unaware that their pad floats on the deep ocean.' His voice quavered. 'None wish to become emigrants to a strange line of floats.'

Sklar Hast said, 'No more do any of the rest of us – but we were forced to choose. I feel no pity for them, or for you. There will be work for all hands. Indeed, we may formulate a new guild: the Kragen-killers. If rumor is accurate, they infest the ocean.'

He left the room, went out into the night. Blasdel stood rigid, numbed by the alteration in his circumstances. He slowly turned, cast a rancorous glare at Phyral Berwick, who stolidly returned the gaze. Blasdel gave an angry snort of sheer frustration. He went to listen once more at the detecting horn. Then he also left the room.

Berwick followed and lowered the panel. Both joined Sklar Hast at the edge of the pad, where now several coracles were tied. A dozen men stood in the garden. Sklar Hast turned to Blasdel. 'Summon your spouse, your daughters and those who test them. Explain the circumstances, and gather your belongings. The evening breeze is at hand and blows us west. We journey east.'

Blasdel departed, accompanied by Berwick. Sklar Hast and the others entered the workroom, carried everything of value or utility to the coracles, including the small metal relict, the sixty-one books, the listening horn and the summoning drum. Then all embarked in the coracles, and Barquan Blasdel's beautiful pad was left to drift solitary upon the ocean.

CHAPTER TEN

Morning came to the ocean and with it the breeze from the west. Sails were rigged and the oarsmen rested. The floats could no longer be seen; the ocean was a ruffled blue mirror in all directions. Sklar Hast lowered Blasdel's horn into the water, listened. Nothing could be heard. Barquan Blasdel did the same and agreed that King Kragen was nowhere near.

There were perhaps six hundred coracles in the flotilla, each carrying from three to six persons, with as much gear, household equipment and tools as possible, together with sacks of food and water.

Two or three hours after sunrise the breeze died. The sails were lowered and oars alone propelled the coracles. At noon the sun burned brightly down, and awnings were rigged overhead to fend away the glare.

Late in the day several medium-sized floats were seen ahead and slightly to the north. The Home Floats and King Kragen were still too close at hand to make the idea of permanent habitation attractive or feasible, but as the evening breeze would soon be rising, to blow the coracles back to the west, the flotilla headed toward the floats in order to tie up and save the oarsmen the effort of rowing into the wind. After twenty-four hours in the coracles, a chance to disembark, to stretch the legs and walk back and forth would be more than welcome.

With the sun low in the west, shining over the backs of the voyagers, the coracles approached the strange floats. They were similar in general appearance to the Home Floats, but wild and less ordered, with vegetation rampant, so that the central spike was almost a pyramid of foliage. The breeze, blowing from the floats, brought an odor that astonished Sklar Hast. He called to Roger Kelso, who rowed in a nearby coracle. 'Do you smell what I think I smell?'

Roger Kelso tested the air, raised his eyebrows. 'I'm not sure. I smell something ... Perhaps just rubbish, or a dead fish.'

'Perhaps.' Sklar Hast, standing in the coracle, looked carefully through the tangle, but could see nothing. Other folk in other coracles likewise had scented the stench from the float, and were likewise looking uneasily into the foliage. But nothing moved and no sounds were to be heard. The first coracle nosed up to the edge of the float; the youth in the bow jumped ashore with a stake and painter; others did likewise, and presently all the coracles were tied up, either to the float or to one another.

Not everyone alighted, and those who did remained close to the coracles. Presently one of the young men came upon the source of the odor: an area littered with refuse. Nearby was a charred area, where coals still glowed among ashes and smoldering sponge husks. The floats were inhabited.

'By whom?' whispered Meril Rohan. 'Who can they be?'

Sklar Hast called out to the jungle: 'Come forth, show yourselves! We mean no harm!'

There was silence, except for the rustle of the wind in the foliage. The sun was now gone, and the afterglow began to darken over the float.

'Look here!' This was the call of a young niggler who had ventured a few hundred yards around the edge of the float. He came running back holding an object which he gave to Phyral Berwick: a necklace, or at least a circular cord from which was suspended a number of glossy reddish chunks of metal.

Sklar Hast looked with awe toward the foliage. 'Come forth! We wish to speak with you!'

He received no answer.

'Savages, probably filthy and naked,' muttered Phyral Berwick. 'But they have what we don't have – metal. Where do they get it?'

From the tangle now came a screech, a terrible quavering sound full of rage and menace, and at the same time a number of sticks came hurtling down from the sky.

'We're not welcome,' said Sklar Hast. 'This is clear. Back to our boats.'

The voyagers re-embarked, with much more celerity than they had gone ashore. From the foliage came another screech, this time of exultation and mirth, and a series of mad hoots, which raised the hair on the necks of the voyagers.

The coracles were cast off and drifted into the lee of the floats, a hundred yards offshore. In the dusk the voyagers saw a number of pallid shapes emerge from the foliage to run back and forth along the shore, prancing and capering. Their faces and physiognomy could not be discerned.

Sklar Hast rowed his coracle a cautious few yards closer, but was greeted by a new shower of sticks and once again retreated.

Darkness fell, and the coracles waited out the evening breeze. On the float a fire was kindled, and two or three dozen man-like creatures emerged to stand in the flicker.

Roger Kelso spoke to Sklar Hast across the water: 'Somewhere I have read of a group of Second or Third folk who committed unorthodox acts and were "banished" – a word that well may mean "sent away". If so, and if they came in this direction, these must be their descendants.'

'It is chilling to contemplate how little is the distance between us and savagery,' said Sklar Hast. 'Still – they have copper, and we do not.'

'How is this?' demanded Rubal Gallager. 'Where does it come from?'

No one made a response, and all looked back across the dark water at the floats, now silhouetted against the sky.

With the end of dusk and the coming of the constellations the wind died, and once more the flotilla proceeded east, across water calm and smooth. All night some rowed while others slept, until finally the first amber flush to the east brought with it a whisper of the welcome wind from the west. Sails were raised; into the dawn scudded the coracles, over a bright, empty sea.

The second day was like the first, with a brief rain squall halfway through the afternoon, which served to replenish the jugs. Swindlers netted various edible sea-creatures, and while the coracles carried ample food, this demonstrated ability to subsist, if necessary, from the ocean was reassuring, and there was singing and badinage between the coracles.

On the morning of the third day a small kragen was observed. It approached from the north, swimming its lunging breast-stroke, and halted a hundred yards distant to watch the flotilla pass. It twitched its vanes, darted forward, almost as if in an effort to alarm the voyagers, then sank abruptly below the surface. A moment later certain of the swindlers gazing down through a water-box saw it pass below – a great sprawling, writhing shadow. A quarter-mile to the south it surfaced and lay floating quietly, then presently disappeared.

Toward the end of the fourth day a line of floats was observed ahead, as rich and beautiful as the Home Floats, though perhaps half as numerous. From the voyagers came rapturous murmurs. Sklar Hast stood up in his coracle, signaled for a conference, and all the other coracles drew close, to form a great raft drifting and rocking on the water.

Sklar Hast said, 'Here are the first floats we have encountered, aside from the floats of the savages. We move slowly. King Kragen can swim three times our speed. In a single day and night – if he so chose, and if he knew our whereabouts – he could come to find us. I feel that we should not consider landing here, but should proceed till we come to at least one other line of floats.'

Murmurs of disappointment arose, for these floats, lush and heavy with black, green, orange and gold vegetation, after four days on the ocean, seemed visions of Arcadia.

There was discussion, a certain amount of argument and some grumbling to the effect that King Kragen would never see fit to swim this far, either from curiosity or vindictive rage. Phyral Berwick sided with Sklar Hast, as did most of the caste-elders and guild-masters, and finally amid soft cries of regret the floats were left behind. Again the flotilla sailed out upon the empty sea.

At noon on the sixth day another line of floats was sighted, and all knew that here was to be the new home. All were now happy that the first line had been passed. These were as extensive, as spacious, and even more numerous than the Home Floats, with myriads of the prized small pads upon which a family could build and cultivate to its own taste.

The flotilla landed at a large float near the center of the line. There were no evidences of occupation, by savages or otherwise. The coracles were unloaded and moved to a cove where they could not be seen from the sea.

In the evening, after a festive supper, there was an informal council of the guild-masters and caste-elders.

'Our two immediate problems,' said Phyral Berwick, 'aside from the inevitable toil of establishing ourselves in comfort and security, are the disposition of our hostages, and our organization. These are both problems of some complexity. The matter of organizing ourselves into a responsible group is perhaps the simplest. The problem is this: looking around me, I see eight Master Hoodwinks, six Master Larceners, sixteen Master Advertisers, and so on. Naturally all cannot be masters. My suggestion is that the various guild-masters confer and select one of their number as grand-master, by lot, by seniority, or by any other means. Then we can function with more decisiveness. This can be a temporary arrangement at least, until we settle other of the floats.

'Secondly – what of those whom we have with us? What of them? They have served their purpose, but now what? We can't kill them, we can't keep them in a pen, we can't let them return to the Home Floats – at least not yet. We must consider the matter carefully.'

All turned to look toward the group of intercessors, who sat with their families somewhat to the side. The intercessors themselves evinced glumness and dissatisfaction in varying degrees. The spouses and older children appeared less concerned, while the very young, romping with others of their own age, were in the best of spirits.

Barquan Blasdel, noticing that his case was under discussion, scowled, started to rise, then thought better of it and muttered something to the Parnassus Intercessor Luke Robinet.

Roger Kelso said, 'If we could trust them to leave us in peace, then there would be no problem. We could give them coracles, stores and wish them well. But as sure as we sit here, as soon as they returned to the Home Floats, there would be plots and schemes. Blasdel for one would like nothing better than to bring King Kragen across the water to punish us.'

'We must destroy the beast,' said Sklar Hast in a voice of absolute dedication.

'Easier said than done. Though I expect that long years will pass before King Kragen again ventures near a hoodwink tower.'

'In the meantime – the intercessors may not return,' said Phyral Berwick. 'This is a distasteful situation. The act of placing restraints upon anyone violates our most cherished traditions – but it must be. The question becomes: how to enforce these restraints without inflicting harshness?'

The problem was debated at length and finally a solution was achieved. Most of the coracles were to be taken to a distant float and hidden, where the intercessors could not find them. Only sufficient coracles to serve the needs of swindlers and blackguards and hooligans, at their respective tasks of fish-swindling, arbor-building and net-emplacement, would be retained. These would be moved to a location forbidden to the intercessors on pain of incarceration in a withe cage. To guarantee that coracles would not be stolen by night, oars and sails would be impounded in a locked and guarded case. Also – and this stratagem was propounded in a low voice by Roger Kelso, so that the intercessors might not hear – to the keel of each coracle, below the waterline, a line would be attached. This line would run underneath the float and communicate with an alarm of some kind. When the swindlers used a coracle, they would discreetly detach the line, and restore it when they returned. Sklar Hast suggested that four or five young swindlers be appointed to guard the coracles and to make sure that the alarm lines were at all times attached when the coracles were not in use.

The system was accepted as that which imposed the least rigor upon the intercessors. Barquan Blasdel, when the prohibitions were explained, waxed indignant. 'First you kidnap us and bundle us across perilous seas, then you perform the infamy of proscribing to our feet certain portions of the float! What do you expect of us?'

'We expect cooperation,' said Sklar Hast in the driest of voices. 'Also work. Here, on the New Floats, everyone works, including intercessors, because here there is no need for intercession.'

'You show no more humility or spiritual sense than a six-barb conger,' said Barquan Blasdel evenly.

Sklar Hast shrugged. 'Eventually we will kill King Kragen, then you may walk where you will, and be humble where you will – but until the loathsome beast settles dead to the ocean's floor you must keep a circumspect distance between yourself and our coracles.'

Barquan Blasdel stared at Sklar Hast a full ten seconds. 'You have further designs upon the life of King Kragen?'

'Who knows what the future holds?' said Sklar Hast.

On the following day the great task of altering the wild new float began. Pads at the center of the float were designated for removal, in order to form a lagoon. Nigglers stripped away the surface skin, which would serve a great variety of purposes. The pulp below was cut into strips, which when dry and stiff would serve as insulation and planking; or when plucked and shredded became cushioning, fuel, or an ingredient of the coarse paper produced by scriveners. The ribs and tubes of the pads were put aside to season, and the lower membrane, this of the fine transparent quality suitable for windows, was taken. Below were the great cantilever ribs, from which coracle keels and sponge arbors were constructed, and below this the stems, over which sleeves were now fitted to extend above the water level. Sap exuding was collected in buckets, boiled and aged to make varnish. Later, perhaps in a month or two when the sap had stopped flowing, the stem would be cut by advertisermen, stripped of fiber for ropes and cordage, and woody strips for withe.

The aperture thus left vacant would become the float lagoon: an anchorage for coracles, a pond for captive food-fish, a source of scenic delight and a locale for water sports.

While the nigglers stripped pad-skin from the future lagoon, others cleared away waste vegetation, which was burned for ash. Boys climbed the central spikes with buckets, to collect pollen from the great fruiting pods and this when tested proved to be a quality even finer and more fragrant than the famed Maudelinda yield, which was a cause for great rejoicing.

As soon as withes had been seasoned larceners and felons set to work constructing huts, while the bezzlers, traditionally the monitors of sanitation, cleanliness and the purity of the water supply, constructed reservoirs to store the afternoon rainfall. At all these tasks the intercessors, their spouses and children, assisted with more or less good grace, and gradually became divided into two groups: those who gave over their initial resentment and began to adapt themselves to the new life, and those others – about half – who would not be reconciled and held themselves dourly aloof. Of the latter group Barquan Blasdel was the most notable representative, and he made no secret of his continuing resentment. All were careful to observe the restraints put upon their movements, and night after night the coracle alarm remained undisturbed.

One evening Sklar Hast joined Roger Kelso and Meril Rohan at a bench where they were comparing the Sixty-one Memoria which had been confiscated from Barquan Blasdel with those that Meril Rohan had copied for herself. 'I presume there are differences?' Sklar Hast asked.

'Indeed,' said Kelso. 'It's inevitable. The Firsts, whatever their other talents, had few literary skills; some of the books contain much repetition and dullness, others are vainglorious and devote pages to self-encomium. Others are anxious to explain in great detail the vicissitudes that led to their presence on the Ship of Space. Some of this is inevitably omitted in the copying, so that every new edition, in a sense, becomes a set of analects.' He tapped Barquan Blasdel's books. 'These are very old, and are the most complete of my experience.' He opened one of the books, looked along the pages. 'The Firsts were of course a very mixed group, derived from a social structure far more complicated than our own. Apparently they might belong to several different castes at once. There are hints of this situation that I do not even profess to understand.'

'According to my reading of the Analects,' said Sklar Hast, 'all describe the Home Worlds as a place of maniacs.'

'We have to take some of this with caution. Never forget that the Firsts were human beings very little different from ourselves. Some were of the most respected castes of the Home World society, until, as they explain it, persons in authority turned on them and instituted a savage persecution, ending as we know in our ancestors seizing control of the Ship of Space and fleeing here.'

'It is all very confusing,' said Sklar Hast. 'None seems to have much contemporary application. For instance, they do not tell us how they boiled varnish on the Home World, or how they propelled their coracles. Do creatures like the kragen infest the Home Worlds? If so, how do the Home Folk deal with them? Do they kill them or feed them sponges? The Firsts, to my knowledge, are silent on these points.'

'Evidently they are not overly concerned,' said Kelso reflectively. 'Otherwise they would have dealt with these matters at length. There is much that they fail to make clear. As in our own case, the various castes seemed trained to explicit trades. Especially interesting are the memoirs of James Brunet. Like the others, he professes several castes: Scientist, Forger, Caucasoid. All are extinct among us, as the Forgers have all become scriveners. A part of his Memorium consists of rather conventional exhortations to virtue, but at the beginning of the book he says this.' Here Kelso opened a book and read:

To those who follow us, to our children and grandchildren, we can leave no tangible objects of value. We brought nothing to the world but ourselves and the wreckage of our lives. We will undoubtedly die here – a fate probably preferable to New Ossining, but by no means the destiny any of us had planned for ourselves. There is no way to escape. Of the entire group I alone have a technical education, most of which I have forgotten. And to what end could I turn it? This is a soft world. It consists of ocean, air, sunlight and seaweed. There is land nowhere. To escape – even if we had the craft to build a new ship, which we do not – we need metal and metal there is none. Even to broadcast a radio signal we need metal. None … no clay to make pottery, no silica for glass, no limestone for concrete, no ore from which to smelt metal. Still, on reflection, all is not hopeless. Ash is similar chemically to fire clay. The shells of foraminifera are silica. Our own bones become a source of lime. A very high-melt, if low-quality, glass could result if the three were fused in the proper proportion. Presumably the ocean carries various salts, but how to extract the metal without electricity? There is iron in our blood: how to extract it? A strange helpless sensation to live on this world where the hardest substance is our own bone! We have, during our lives, taken so many things for granted, and now it seems that no one can evoke something from nothing … This is a problem on which I must think. An ingenious man can work wonders, and I, a successful forger – or rather, almost successful – am certainly ingenious.

Roger Kelso paused in his reading. 'This is the end of the chapter.'

'He seems to have been a man of no great force,' mused Sklar Hast. 'It is true that metal can be found nowhere, except where the savages contemptuously discard it.' On the bench before them was the bit of metal which had once graced the workroom of Barquan Blasdel. Sklar Hast lifted it, hefted it. 'Obdurate stuff indeed.' He reached for the crude copper necklace which they had found on the wild floats. 'Here is the great mystery: where, how, do the savages derive this?'

Roger Kelso heaved a deep sigh, shook his head in perplexity. 'Eventually we will learn.' He returned to the book. 'He writes his next chapter after a lapse of months:

Before I proceed I must provide as best I can a picture of the way the universe works, for it is clear that none of my colleagues are in any position to do so, excellent fellows though they are. Please do not suspect me of whimsey: our personalities and social worth undoubtedly vary with the context in which we live.

Here Kelso looked up. 'I don't quite understand all of his implications. Does he mean that his colleagues are *not* excellent fellows? Or were not? Why should he say this? His own caste doesn't seem to be the highest … I suppose that the matter is unimportant.' He turned the pages. 'He now goes into an elaborate set of theorizations regarding the nature of the world, which, I confess, I find overcomplex, even artificial. There is no consistency to his beliefs. Either he knows nothing, or is confused, or the world essentially is inconsistent. He claims that all matter is composed of less than a hundred "elements", joined together in "compounds". The elements are constructed of smaller entities: "electrons", "protons", "neutrons", and others, which are not necessarily matter, but forces, depending on your point of view. When electrons move the result is an electric current: a substance or condition – he is not clear here – of great energy and many capabilities. Too much electricity is fatal; in smaller quantities we use it to control our bodies. According to Brunet all sorts of remarkable things can be achieved with electricity.'

'Let us provide ourselves an electric current then,' said Sklar Hast. 'This may become our weapon against the kragen.'

'The matter is not so simple. In the first place, the electricity must be channeled through metal wires.'

'Here is metal,' said Sklar Hast, examining the fragments before him, 'though this is hardly likely to be sufficient.'

'The electricity must also be generated,' said Kelso. 'On the Home Planet this seems to be a complicated process, requiring a great deal of metal.'

'Then how do we get metal? Are we so backward that even the savages strew it around like sponge-husk, while we have none?'

Kelso tilted his head dubiously sidewise. 'On other planets there seems to be no problem. Ore is refined and shaped into a great variety of tools. Here we have no ore. In other cases, metals are extracted from the sea, once again using electricity.'

Sklar Hast made a sound of disgust. 'This is like chasing oneself around a pole. To procure metal, we need electricity. To obtain electricity, metal is required. How does one break into this closed circle? The savages are more adept than we. Do they also wield electricity? Perhaps we should send someone to learn from them.'

'Not I,' said Kelso. He returned to the book. 'Brunet mentions various means to generate electricity. There is the "voltaic cell", where two metals are immersed in acid. He describes a means to derive the acid, using rain-water, sea-brine and electricity. Then there is thermo-electricity, photo-electricity, chemical electricity, electricity produced by cataphoresis, electricity generated by moving a wire near another wire in which electricity flows. He states that all living creatures produce small quantities of electricity.'

'What of metal?' asked Sklar Hast. 'Does he indicate any simple methods to secure metal?'

Kelso turned pages, paused to read. 'He mentions that blood contains a small quantity of iron. He suggests a method for extracting it, by using a high degree of heat. But he also points out that there is at hand no substance capable of serving as a receptacle under such extremes of heat. He states that on the Home World many plants concentrate metallic compounds, and suggests that certain of our own sea-plants might do the same. But again either heat or electricity is needed to secure the pure metal.'

Sklar Hast ruminated. 'Our first and basic problem, as I see it, is self-protection. We need a weapon to kill King Kragen in the event that he tracks us across the sea. It might be a device of metal – or it might be a larger and more savage kragen, if such exist ...' He considered. 'Perhaps you should make production of metal and electricity your goal, and let no other pursuits distract you. I am sure that the council will agree, and put at your disposal such helpers as you may need.'

'I would be pleased to do my best.'

'And I,' said Sklar Hast, 'I will reflect upon the kragen.'

CHAPTER ELEVEN

Three days later a kragen was seen, a beast of not inconsiderable size, perhaps twenty feet in length. It came cruising along the edge of the float, and observing the men, stopped short. For twenty minutes it floated placidly, swirling water back and forth with its vanes. Then slowly it swung about and continued along the line of floats.

A month passed, during which the community achieved a rude measure of comfort. A large quantity of stalk and withe had been cut, scraped and racked, as well as a heap of root-wisp, which now that a rope-walk had been rigged, was being twisted into rope. Three large pads had been cut from the side and center of the float, creating a large lagoon with a relatively narrow mouth – this at the request of Sklar Hast. Arbors were constructed, seeded with sponge-floss, and lowered into the water.

During this period four kragen had passed by. The fourth occurrence seemed to be a return visit of the first. On this fourth visit the kragen paused, inspected the lagoon with care. It tentatively nudged the net, which had just been set in place, then backed away and presently floated off.

Sklar Hast watched the occurrence. Then he went to inspect the new-cut stalk, which now was sufficiently cured. He laid out a pattern, and work began. First a wide base was built near the narrow mouth of the lagoon, with a substructure extending down to the main stem of the float. On this base was erected an A-frame derrick of glued withe, seventy feet tall, with integral braces, the entire structure whipped tightly with strong line and varnished. Another identical derrick was built to overhang the ocean. Before either of the derricks were completed, a small kragen broke through the net to feast upon the yet unripe sponges. 'At your next visit, you will not fare so well,' Sklar Hast called to the beast. 'May the sponges rot in your stomach!'

The kragen swam lazily off down the line of floats, unperturbed by the threat. It returned two days later. This time the derricks were guyed and in place, but not yet fitted with tackle. Again Sklar Hast reviled the beast, which this time ate with greater fastidiousness, plucking only those sponges which like popcorn had overgrown their husks. The men worked far into the night installing the strut which, when the derrick tilted out over the water, thrust high the topping-halyard to provide greater leverage.

On the next day the kragen returned and entered the lagoon with insulting assurance: a beast somewhat smaller than that which Sklar Hast had captured on Tranque Float, but nonetheless a creature of respectable size. Standing on the float, a stalwart old swindler flung a noose around the creature's turret, and on the pad a line of fifty men marched away with a heavy rope. The astonished kragen was towed to the outward-leaning derrick, swung up and in. The dangling vanes were lashed; it was lowered to the float. As soon as the bulk collapsed the watching folk, crying out in glee, shoved forward, almost dancing into the gnashing mandibles. 'Back, fools!' roared Sklar Hast. 'Do you want to be cut in half? Back!' He was largely ignored. A dozen chisels hacked at the horny hide; clubs battered at the eyes. 'Back!' raged Sklar Hast. 'Back! What do you achieve by antics such as this? Back!' Daunted, the vengeful folk moved aside. Sklar Hast took chisel and mallet and as he had done on Tranque Float, cut at the membrane joining dome to turret. He was joined by four others; the channel was swiftly cut and a dozen hands ripped away the dome. Again, with pitiless outcry, the crowd surged forward. Sklar Hast's efforts to halt them were fruitless. The nerves and cords of the creature's ganglionic center were torn from the turret, while the kragen jerked and fluttered and made a buzzing sound with its mandibles. The turret was plucked clean of the wet-string fibers as well as other organs, and the kragen lay limp. Sklar Hast moved away in disgust. Rollo Barnack jumped up on the hulk. 'Halt now! No more senseless hacking! If the kragen has bones harder than our own, we will want to preserve them for use. Who knows what use can be made of a kragen's cadaver? The hide is tough; the mandibles are harder than the deepest stalk. Let us proceed intelligently!'

Sklar Hast watched from a little distance as the crowd examined the dead beast. He had no further interest in the kragen. A planned experiment had been foiled almost as soon as the hate-driven mob had rushed forward. But there would be more kragen for his derricks; hopefully they could be noosed by the sea-derrick before they broke into the lagoon. In years to come, strong-boats or barges equipped with derricks might even go forth to hunt the kragen ... He approached the kragen once again, peered into the empty turret, where now welled a puddle of viscous dark blue blood. The sight stirred something deep in his brain: a response, a recollection, a reference. In the Analects? It came to him: the blood of certain sea-creatures of Earth also ran blue: lobsters and king crab, whatever these might be.

Kelso shared a similar interest in the dark blue fluid. He brought buckets with which he bailed out the blood and conveyed it to a barrel. Sklar Hast watched with interest. 'What do you propose?'

'Nothing definite. I am collecting substances. The savages found metal somewhere. If I collect enough materials and try various methods of extraction on all, perhaps I will be able to achieve what the savages have already done.'

'The savages are proving a great inspiration,' said Sklar Hast. 'I wonder what other wonders and accomplishments they could teach?'

'Here would be a good use to make of the intercessors,' observed Rollo Barnack. 'So far they have showed little enthusiasm for the new life.'

'The death of the kragen has made them very glum,' said Wall Bunce jocularly. 'Hey, intercessors! What do you think now?'

The intercessors, who had watched the killing of the kragen from a distance, turned away in contempt and disgust. Sklar Hast strolled over to where they stood talking in low voices. 'Do you still think that we need fear harassment by the kragen?' he asked.

Luke Robinet spoke in a voice quivering with detestation: 'These are small fry and not King Kragen. Someday he will find you and punish you for breaking the Covenant. Then all your ropes and pulleys and derricks will be of no avail whatever!'

Sklar Hast nodded dolefully. 'It would be a sad affair. King Kragen should have been killed when he first appeared, as we have killed the sea-beast today. Think how much easier life would have been for all of us! Instead he was fed and fawned upon, and now he looms over all our lives.'

Barquan Blasdel said in his even, easy voice: 'You are an insensitive man, Sklar Hast. You see only what is before your nose; you are ignorant of the spiritual benefits to be derived from self-abasement.'

'Absolutely true,' said Sklar Hast. 'I fear I have suffered serious disadvantages in this respect.'

The Wyebolt Intercessor, a thin hot-eyed old man with an undisciplined mop of white hair, rasped: 'Your sarcastic fleers and flaunts will avail little when King Kragen at last demands an accounting!'

Sklar Hast noted certain uneasy movements and grimaces among the intercessors. 'How do you expect that this will come to pass?'

The Wyebolt Intercessor ignored the wry looks of his fellows, or perhaps, sensing them, he modified his reply. 'What will be, will be. It certainly must be assumed that King Kragen will not allow his intercessors to be so misused.'

'The beast neither knows nor cares,' scoffed Sklar Hast, hoping to infuriate the Wyebolt Intercessor to the point where he might make an indiscreet revelation.

Barquan Blasdel performed a large, almost indulgent gesture. 'This conversation is footless. You have us at a disadvantage. Eventually these poor folk will tire of your crass materialism and reject all that you represent. Until then we must be patient.' With a quick but monitory glance around the circle of intercessors, he crossed to his hut and entered.

Sklar Hast moved on, across the float to where Meril Rohan had established what she called a 'school' for the instruction of children. This was an institution not absolutely unknown on the Home Floats – in fact, the Quatrefoil Academy for the training of scriveners was notable – but children usually were educated through guild agencies.

Meril had watched the landing of the kragen but had taken no part in the frenzied death-rite. Instead, turning her back, she had gone to her 'school', which, of course, had been vacated by reason of the excitement at the other side of the float.

Here Sklar Hast, coming through the still heavy tangle of vines, found her, sitting on a bench looking out across the blue water. He approached and sat beside her. 'What are you thinking about?'

She was silent a moment. 'I was thinking about the times to come, and wondering what is to befall us.'

Sklar Hast laughed. 'I can't allow myself to wonder. The problems of Now are too great. If I wondered where all was to lead, I'd be halted.'

Meril, making no reply, nodded slowly as if at some profound inner discovery. 'And where does all your wondering take you?' Sklar Hast asked.

'No single place. We are of the Eleventh generation; already there are Twelfths and Thirteenths. It seems that over all these years we have been living dreams. The Floats were so easy and fertile that no one has ever been forced to work or think or suffer. Or fight.'

Sklar Hast nodded gloomily. 'Undoubtedly you are right – but now we have been forced, and we are fighting. Today we won our first victory.'

'But such a cheap victory. And what is the fight for? Merely that the kragen should not eat our sponges, that we should be allowed to continue this dreaming placid life, that it might go on forever … I am not proud of myself. I was sickened by the death of the kragen. We fled the Home Floats. It was the right thing to do – but is this the end of our ambitions? A life of lagoons and sunlight, without even King Kragen to worry us? It frightens me somehow, and I wonder if this is all my life is to be: something without achievement or victory or meaning of any kind whatever.'

Sklar Hast frowned. 'I have never thought exactly in these terms. Always the immediate problems seem urgent.'

'I imagine that this would always be the case, no matter how trivial the problems. In her Memorium Eleanor Morse speaks of her "goals", and how they moved further and further into the distance and so to achieve them she forced herself to become a Bezzler. This has no particular meaning for us, except that it illustrates how ambition forces folk to better themselves. So I have been trying to form some goals for myself, that I might just possibly hope to achieve.'

'What are they?'

'You won't mock me? Or laugh?' Meril turned grave eyes upon him.

'No.' Sklar Hast took her hand, held it.

Meril looked around the array of crude benches. 'I attended the Scriveners Academy on Quatrefoil. There are four large structures furnished for study, a refectory and two dormitories. I want to bring such an academy into being here. Not just a place for scriveners, but an academy for the advancement of all knowledge. There are hints of what is to be learned in the Memoria ... This is my goal: to establish this academy, where the young people learn their guild skills, learn the Memoria, but most important learn the same dissatisfaction that I feel, so that they too shall have goals.'

Sklar Hast was silent. Then he said, 'You shall certainly have all my help ... And you shame me. I ask myself, what are my own goals? I am sorry to say that they were satisfied, at least in part, when the derrick lifted the kragen from the water. I had thought no farther ahead. True, I want this float to be prosperous and happy ...' He frowned. 'I have a goal. Two goals. First: I want you for my spouse. I want no other. Second: I want to destroy King Kragen.' He took her other hand. 'What do you say to this?'

'Destroy King Kragen, by all means.'

'And what of the first goal?'

'I would think it is – attainable.'

A hand shook Sklar Hast. He awoke to see a dark form standing above him, black against the stars. 'Who is it? What do you want?'

'I am Julio Rile; I guard the coracles. I want you to come with me.'

Sklar Hast lurched to his feet, pulled on a cloak, slipped his feet into sandals. 'What happens? Are they stealing our boats?'

'No. There is a strange noise coming from the water.'

Sklar Hast went with the youth to the edge of the float. Kneeling, putting his head close to the water, he heard an odd sound: a groaning, scraping, wheezing sound, unlike all that Sklar Hast had ever heard before. There was one that had been similar ... Sklar Hast turned, went at a lope to the hut that housed the horn taken from Barquan Blasdel's pad at Apprise Float. He brought it forth, carried it to the edge of the float, lowered it into the water. The sound was startlingly loud. Sklar Hast turned the horn, noted the direction from which the sound reached a maximum intensity. He grinned a sudden angry grin. 'Go, awake Phyral Berwick and Rollo Barnack and Rubal Gallager. Make haste. Bring them here.'

Sklar Hast awoke Poe Belrod and Roger Kelso. The whole group listened at the horn and looked in the direction from which the sound seemed to emanate: the hut occupied by Barquan Blasdel.

Sklar Hast whispered: 'Someone will be watching at the front; let us approach from the rear.'

They moved quietly through the shadows, around to the rear of Barquan Blasdel's hut. Sklar Hast brought out a knife, slit the pad-skin, pushed through into the interior.

A lamp on a shelf lit the room dimly. Kneeling around a hole in the floor were Barquan Blasdel and Luke Robinet. They manipulated a contrivance of wood, leather and cord, which extended through the hole into the black water. To the side was a plug to fill the hole during the day.

Barquan Blasdel slowly rose to his feet, as did Luke Robinet. Into the room came Phyral Berwick, Rollo Barnack, and the others.

No one spoke. There was clearly nothing to be said. Sklar Hast went to the hole, lifted out the sound-producing mechanism, replaced the plug.

There were hurried footsteps in the outer room. A voice spoke through the door. 'Caution; halt the sounds. Folk are astir.'

Sklar Hast flung wide the door, seized the speaker, Vidal Reach, formerly Sumber Intercessor, and drew him into the room. Quietly he went to the front door. No one else could be seen. In all likelihood the entire group of intercessors were concerned with the plot, but only these three could be directly charged.

From the first Barquan Blasdel had made no pretense of satisfaction with his altered circumstances. His former rank counted nothing, and in fact aroused antagonism among his float-fellows. Blasdel grudgingly adapted himself to his new life, building sponge-arbors and scraping withe. His spouse, who on Apprise Float had commanded a corps of four maidens and three garden-men, at first rebelled when Blasdel required her to bake pan-golay, as the bread-stuff baked from pollen was known, and core sponges 'like any low-caste slut', as she put it. Finally she surrendered to the protests of her empty stomach. Her daughters adapted themselves with better grace, and indeed the four youngest participated with great glee at the slaughter of the kragen. The remaining two stayed in the background, eyebrows raised at the vulgar fervor of their sisters.

These then were the circumstances of Barquan Blasdel's existence at the time of his ill-founded concept of summoning King Kragen. Luke Robinet and Vidal Reach lived under similar conditions, with no restraints except in regard to the coracles.

On the morning after their apprehension, the three conspirators were brought before a judicial assembly of guild-masters and caste-elders. Inasmuch as Phyral Berwick had participated in the actual apprehension of the persons accused, Gian Recargo served as Arbiter.

The morning sun shone bright on the float. At the entrance to the lagoon lay the bulk of the kragen, still in the process of being flensed by apprentice nigglers and advertisers. The assembly sat in near silence, conversing in whispers.

From the hut where they had spent the night came Barquan Blasdel, Luke Robinet, and Vidal Reach, blinking in the glare of the sun. In utter silence they were marched to a bench and ordered to sit.

Phyral Berwick arose and described the circumstances of the previous night. 'It is evident that they intended to attract the attention of King Kragen, if by some chance he were cruising near.'

Gian Recargo leaned forward. 'Have they admitted as much?'

The Arbiter looked at the accused. 'What have you to say?'

'So far as I am concerned, nothing,' said Barquan Blasdel.

'You admit the charges?'

'I have no statement to make. Things are as they are.'

'Do you deny or repudiate any of Phyral Berwick's testimony?'

'No.'

'You must be aware that this is an extremely serious charge.'

'From your point of view.'

'Did you have reason to believe that King Kragen is, or was, in the vicinity? Or did you produce this noise merely in the hope of attracting his attention if he should chance to be nearby?'

'I repeat, I have no statement to make.'

'You put forward no defense?'

'It would obviously be futile.'

'You do not deny the acts?'

'I have no statement to make. Things are as they are.'

Luke Robinet and Vidal Reach were similarly taciturn. The Arbiter took statements from Sklar Hast, Julio Rile, and Rollo Barnack. He said, 'Clearly the accused are guilty of the most vindictive intentions. I am at a loss as to what penalty to impose. There is absolutely no precedent, to my knowledge.'

Phyral Berwick spoke. 'Our problem is how to make ourselves secure. We can kill these men. We might maroon them on a lonely float, even the Savage Floats, or we can guard them more carefully. I even feel a certain sympathy for them. If I shared the fervor of their convictions, I might act similarly in a similar situation. I say, give them the sternest of warnings, but give them their lives.'

No one dissented. Gian Recargo turned to the three criminals. 'We give you your lives. All shall be as before. I suspect that this is more than you would do for us, but no matter. We are not you. But remember, for our own security, we can show no more mercy! Consider that you are now living a new life, and make the best possible use of it! Go. Return to your work. Try to make yourselves deserving of the trust we have placed in you.'

'We did not ask to be brought here,' said Barquan Blasdel in his easy voice.

'Your presence here is a direct consequence of your original treachery, when you attempted to arrange that King Kragen should intercept our flotilla. In retrospect, it seems that we are unreasonably merciful. Still, this is the nature of the life we hope to lead – and you are the unworthy beneficiaries. Go, and remember that mercy will not be extended a third time.'

Luke Robinet and Vidal Reach were somewhat subdued, but Barquan Blasdel sauntered away undaunted. Sklar Hast and Roger Kelso watched him depart. 'There is a man who knows only hate,' said Sklar Hast. 'Forbearance has not won his gratitude. He will bear the most vigilant watch!'

'We are not preparing ourselves fast enough,' said Kelso.

'For what?'

'For the inevitable confrontation. Sooner or later King Kragen will find us. The intercessors seem to feel that he swims this far afield. If he comes, we have no means of escape, and certainly no means to repel him.'

Sklar Hast somberly agreed. 'All too true. We do not feel enough urgency; this is indeed a false security. By some means we must formulate a system by which we can protect ourselves. Weapons! Think of a great harpoon, launched by a hundred men, tipped with hard metal ... But we have no metal.'

'But we do,' said Kelso. He brought forth a gray pellet the size of a baby's tooth. 'This is iron.'

Sklar Hast took it, turned it back and forth in his fingers. 'Iron! From where did it come?'

'I produced it.'

'By the system the savages use?'

'As to that, I can't say.'

'But how? What is its source? The air? The sea? The fruit of the float?'

'Come to Outcry Float tomorrow, somewhat before noon. I will explain all.'

'Including the provenance of the name "Outcry"?'

'All will be explained.'

CHAPTER TWELVE

In order to work undisturbed, with a minimum of interference from casual passers-by and elderly guild-masters with well-meant advice, Kelso had pre-empted for his investigations the float next to the west, and this, for reasons arising from his activities, became known as Outcry Float. For helpers and assistants and fellow researchers, Kelso had recruited several dozen of the most alert young men and women available, who worked with an energy and enthusiasm surprising even to themselves.

Only three hundred yards separated the two floats, and as Sklar Hast paddled the intervening distance, he already envisaged hoodwink towers transmitting messages between the two. A vagrant thought came to him: Best set up practice machines, so that old hoodwinks should not lose their reflexes, that apprentices might be instructed, that the craft might be kept alive.

Arriving at Outcry Float, he tied the coracle to the rude dock which Kelso had caused to be built. A path led around a tall clump of banner-bush into a central area beside the central spike, which was now scrupulously cleared of vegetation, and as a result the pad surface had become a liverish purple-brown.

Kelso was hard at work on an intricate contrivance the purpose of which Sklar Hast could not fathom. A rectangular frame of stalk rose ten feet in the air, supporting a six-foot hoop of woven withe in a plane parallel to the surface of the float. To the hoop was glued a large sheet of first-quality pad-skin, which had been scraped, rubbed, and oiled until it was almost perfectly transparent. Below, Kelso now arranged a box containing ashes. As Sklar Hast watched, he mixed in a quantity of water and some gum, enough to make a gray dough, which he worked with his fingers and knuckles, to leave a saucer-shaped depression.

The sun neared the zenith; Kelso signaled two of his helpers. One climbed the staging; the other passed up buckets of water. The first poured these upon the transparent membrane, which sagged under the weight.

Sklar Hast watched silently, giving no voice to his perplexity. The membrane, now brimming, seemed to bulge perilously. Kelso, at last satisfied with his arrangements, joined Sklar Hast. 'You are puzzled by this device; nevertheless it is very simple. You own a telescope?'

'I do. An adequately good instrument, though the gum is clouded.'

'The purest and most highly refined gum discolors, and even with the most careful craftsmanship lenses formed of gum yield distorted images, of poor magnification. On the Home World, according to Brunet, lenses are formed of a material called "glass".'

The sun reached the zenith; Sklar Hast's attention was caught by a peculiar occurrence in the box of damp ash. A white-hot spot had appeared; the ash began to hiss and smoke. He drew near in wonderment. 'Glass would seem a useful material,' Kelso was saying. 'Brunet describes it as a mixture of substances occurring in ash which he calls "fluxes", together with a compound called "silica" which is found in ash, but also occurs in husks of sea-ooze: "plankton", as Brunet calls it. Here I have mixed ash and sea-ooze; I have constructed a water-lens to condense sunlight. I am trying to make glass ...' He peered into the box, then lifted it a trifle, bringing the image of the sun to its sharpest focus. The ash glowed red, orange, yellow; suddenly it seemed to slump. With a rod Kelso pushed more ash into the center, until the wooden box gave off smoke, whereupon Kelso pulled it aside and gazed anxiously at the molten matter in the center. 'Something has happened; exactly what we will determine when the stuff is cool.' He turned to his bench, brought forward another box, this half-full of powdered charcoal. In a center depression rested a cake of black-brown paste.

'And what do you have there?' asked Sklar Hast, already marveling at Kelso's ingenuity.

'Dried blood. I and my men have drained ourselves pale. It is an operation conducive of woe, hence "Outcry Float".'

'But why should you bleed yourself?' demanded Sklar Hast.

'Again I must refer you to the scientist Brunet. He reveals that human blood is colored red by a substance called "haemoglobin". This is composed of much carbon, oxygen, and hydrogen and a single particle of iron. Carbon is the main ingredient of char; oxygen gives to air its invigorating quality; with hydrogen oxygen makes water. But today we seek only that extremely small quantity of iron. So here is blood. I will burn away the various unstable fluids, gases, and oozes, to discover what remains. If all goes well, we will again find unyielding iron.' Kelso thrust the box under the lens. The dried blood smoldered and smoked, then burst into flame which gave off a nauseous odor. Kelso squinted up at the sun. 'The lens burns well only when the sun is overhead, so our time is necessarily limited.'

'Rather than water, transparent gum might be used, which then would harden, and the sun could be followed across the sky.'

'Unfortunately no gum is so clear as water,' said Kelso regretfully. 'Candle-plant sap is yellow. Bindlebane seep holds a blue fog.'

'What if the two were mixed, so that the blue defeated the yellow? And then the two might be filtered and boiled. Or perhaps water can be coagulated with tincture of bone.'

Kelso assented. 'Possibly feasible, both.'

They turned to watch the blood, now a glowing sponge which tumbled into cinders and then, apparently consumed, vanished upon the surface of the blazing charcoal. Kelso snatched the crucible out from under the lens. 'Your blood seems not overrich,' Sklar Hast noted critically. 'It might be wise to tap Barquan Blasdel and the intercessors; they appear a hearty lot.'

Kelso clapped a cover upon the box. 'We will know better when the charcoal goes black.' He went to his bench, brought back another box. In powdered charcoal stood another tablet, this of black paste. 'And what substance is this?' inquired Sklar Hast.

'This,' said Kelso, 'is kragen blood, which we boiled last night. If man's blood carries iron, what will kragen blood yield? Now we discover.' He thrust it under the lens. Like the human blood, it began to smoulder and burn, discharging a smoke even more vile than before. Gradually the tablet flaked and tumbled to the surface of the charcoal; as before, Kelso removed it and covered it with a lid. Going to his first box, he prodded among the cinders with a bit of sharp bone, scooped out a congealed puddle of fused material which he laid on the bench. 'Glass. Beware. It is yet hot.'

Sklar Hast, using two pieces of bone, lifted the object. 'So this is glass. Hmm. It hardly seems suitable for use as a telescope lens. But it may well prove useful otherwise. It seems dense and hard – indeed, almost metallic.'

Kelso shook his head in deprecation. 'I had hoped for greater transparency. There are probably numerous impurities in the ash and sea-ooze. Perhaps they can be removed by washing the ash or treating it with acid, or something of the sort.'

'But to produce acid, electricity is necessary, or so you tell me.'

'I merely quote Brunet.'

'And electricity is impossible?'

Kelso pursed his lips. 'That we will see. I have hopes. One might well think it impossible to generate electricity using only ash, wood, water, and sea-stuff – but we shall see. Brunet offers a hint or two. But first, as to our iron ...'

The yield was small: a nodule of pitted gray metal like the first, half the size of a pea. 'That bit represents three flasks of blood,' Kelso remarked glumly. 'If we bled every vein on the float we might win sufficient iron for a small pot.'

'This is not intrinsically an unreasonable proposal,' said Sklar Hast. 'We can all afford a flask of blood, or two, or even more, during the course of months. To think – we have produced metal entirely on our own resources!'

Kelso wryly inspected the iron nodule. 'There is no problem to burning the blood under the lens. If every day ten of the folk come to be bled, eventually we will sink the pad under the accumulated weight of the iron.' He removed the lid from the third box. 'But observe here! We have misused our curses! The kragen is by no means a creature to be despised!'

On the charcoal rested a small puddle of reddish-golden metal, three times as large as the iron nodule. 'This metal must be copper, or one of its alloys. Brunet describes copper as a dark red metal, very useful for the purpose of conducting electricity.'

Sklar Hast lifted the copper from the coals, tossed it back and forth till it was cool. 'The savages have copper, in chunks larger than this. Do they kill kragen and burn their blood? It seems incredible! Those distorted furtive half-men!'

Kelso chewed reflectively at his lip. 'The kragen must ingest its copper from some source. Perhaps the savages know the source.'

'Metal!' murmured Sklar Hast reverently. 'Metal everywhere! Nicklas Rile has been hacking apart the kragen for its bones. He is discarding the internal organs, which are black as snuff-flower. Perhaps they should also be burned under the lens.'

'Convey them here, I will burn them. And then, after we burn the kragen's liver or whatever the organ, we might attempt to burn snuff-flower as well. Who knows? Perhaps all black substances yield copper, all red substances iron. Though Brunet never makes so inclusive a generalization.'

The kragen's internal organs yielded further copper. The snuff-flowers produced only a whitish-yellow ash which Kelso conscientiously stored in a tube labeled: *ash of snuff-flower.*

Four days later the largest kragen seen so far appeared. It came swimming in from the west, paralleling the line of floats. A pair of swindlers, returning to the float with a catch of gray-fish, were the first to spy the great black cylinder surmounted by its four-eyed turret. They bent to their oars, shouting the news ahead. A well-rehearsed plan now went into effect. A team of four young swindlers ran to a lightweight coracle, shoved off, paddled out to intercept the kragen. Behind the coracle trailed two ropes, each controlled by a gang of men. The kragen, lunging easily through the water, approached, swimming fifty yards off the float. The coracle eased forward, rowed by two of the men, with one named Bade Beach going forward to stand on the gunwales. The kragen stopped the motion of its vanes, to drift and eye the coracle and the derricks with flinty suspicion.

The two swindlers at the oars thrust the coracle closer. Bade Beach stood tensely, twitching a noose. The fourth man controlled the lines to the float. The kragen, contemptuous of attack, issued a few nonplussed clicks of the mandibles, twitched the tips of its vanes, to create four whirlpools. The coracle eased closer, to within a hundred feet – eighty – sixty feet. Bade Beach bent forward.

The kragen decided to punish the men for their provocative actions. It thrust sharply forward. When it was but 30 feet distant, Bade Beach tossed a noose toward the turret – and missed. From the float came groans of disappointment. One of the gangs hastily jerked the coracle back. The kragen swerved, turned, made a second furious charge which brought it momentarily to within five feet of the coracle, whereupon Bade Beach dropped the noose over its turret. From the float came a cheer; both gangs hauled on their lines, one snatching the coracle back to safety, the other tightening the noose and pulling the kragen aside, almost as it touched the coracle.

Thrashing and jerking the kragen was dragged over to the sea-leaning derrick and hoisted from the water in the same fashion as the first. This was a large beast: the derrick creaked, the float sagged; before the kragen heaved clear from the water sixty-five men were tugging on the end of the lift. The derrick tilted back, the kragen swung in over the float. The vanes were lashed, the beast lowered. Again the onlookers surged forward, laughing, shouting, but no longer exemplifying the fury with which they had attacked the first kragen.

Chisels and mallets were plied against the kragen turret; the dome was pried loose, the nerve-nodes destroyed. Fiber buckets were brought, the body fluids were scooped out and carried off to evaporation trays.

Sklar Hast had watched from the side. This had been a large beast – about the size of King Kragen when first he had approached the Old Floats, a hundred and fifty years previously. Since they had successfully dealt with this creature, they need have small fear of any other – except King Kragen. And Sklar Hast was forced to admit that the answer was not yet known. No derrick could hoist King Kragen from the water. No line could restrain the thrust of his vanes. No float could bear his weight. Compared to King Kragen, this dead hulk was a pygmy ... From behind came a rush of feet; a woman tugged at his elbow, gasping and gulping in the effort to catch her breath. Sklar Hast, startled, scanning the float, could see nothing to occasion her distress. Finally she was able to blurt: 'Barquan Blasdel has taken to the sea, Barquan Blasdel is gone!'

'What!' cried Sklar Hast.

CHAPTER THIRTEEN

Barquan Blasdel, his spouse, his two older daughters and their lovers, together with Luke Robinet and Vidal Reach, were missing, as was a sturdy coracle. Their plans had been daring, carefully laid and precisely executed. For weeks they had secreted stores in a tangled nook to the far side of the float, near Meril Rohan's school. Secretly oars had been fabricated as well as a mast and a sail. Then they had awaited the capture of a second kragen, assuming correctly that the attention of everyone would be diverted.

The two young men, spouses to Blasdel's daughters, made off with the coracle. Even with a kragen dangling in mid-air the sight of Barquan Blasdel in a coracle might well have attracted attention. The two young men were more inconspicuous. They untied the coracle, paddled it around to the south side of the float. The stores were loaded aboard, all embarked, oars were shipped and the coracle sent scudding away from New Home Float. By sheer bad luck a woman rendered squeamish by pregnancy had put the breadth of the float between her and the landing of the kragen, and had seen the coracle disappearing around Outcry Float.

Phyral Berwick despatched ten coracles in instant pursuit, but by this time evening was at hand, with an unusually brisk wind. What with the sail, all hands at the oars, the dusk, and dozens of floats to hide among, there was small chance that the fugitive coracle could be overtaken. Barquan Blasdel might even choose to veer north or south and so lose himself the more completely.

The search coracles stayed out all night. Eight searched among the floats, ghosting back and forth along the starlit channels; two struck west as fast and hard as the most stalwart swindlers could take them. When dawn came to throw a pearl-colored light over the sea, the new floats were almost invisible to the east, but the searchers were alone on the sea. Barquan Blasdel's coracle was nowhere to be seen. Those searching among the floats fared no better. All returned to New Home Float on the dawn wind.

A convocation of the councillors was called to consider the situation. Some bemoaned the leniency which had been extended the fugitive intercessors. 'Why did we allow our qualms to conquer us?' moaned Robin Magram. 'We should have made a clean job and strangled the lot.'

Phyral Berwick nodded patiently. 'You may be right. Still, I for one could not bring myself to commit murder, even though it would have been to our best interests.'

Magram jerked his thumb toward the huts in which lurked the remaining intercessors. 'What of them? Each wishes us evil. Each is now planning the same despicable act as that performed by Blasdel. Let us kill them now – quietly, without malice, but with a beautiful finality!'

Sklar Hast made a morose objection. 'This would do no good. We would become murderers in all truth. The fat is now in the fire. In fact, we would do better by turning them free – giving them a coracle and sending them off.'

'Not so fast!' protested Rollo Barnack. 'Barquan Blasdel may never reach the Home Floats!'

'He need merely sail on the night wind and paddle west,' said Sklar Hast. 'But very well, let us wait till we know for sure what has eventuated.'

Robin Magram growled, 'If Barquan Blasdel returns to the old floats, one eventuation is sure. We must expect hostile actions. The man is a vessel of malice.'

'Not necessarily,' argued Phyral Berwick. 'Remember, the folk of the floats are by and large sensible. They are our caste-brothers, our friends, our relatives. And what do they gain by attacking us?'

'We have escaped King Kragen; we acknowledge no overlord,' said Sklar Hast pessimistically. 'Misery brings jealousy and resentment. The intercessors can whip them to a sullen fury.' He pitched his voice to a nasal falsetto. '"Those insolent fugitives! How dare they scamp their responsibility to noble King Kragen? How dare they perform such bestial outrages against the lesser kragen? Everyone to the coracles! We go to punish the iconoclasts!"'

'Possibly correct,' said Kelso. 'But the intercessors are by no means the only influential folk of the floats. The arbiters will hardly agree to any such schemes.'

'In essence,' said Phyral Berwick, 'we have no information. We speculate in a void. Barquan Blasdel may lose himself on the ocean and never return to the Old Floats. He may be greeted with apathy or with excitement. We talk without knowledge. It seems to me that we should take steps to inform ourselves as to the true state of affairs: in short, that we send spies to derive this information for us.'

Phyral Berwick's proposal ultimately became the decision of all. It was further decided that the remaining intercessors be guarded more carefully, until it was definitely learned whether or not Barquan Blasdel had returned to the Old Floats. If such were the case, the location of the New Floats was no longer a secret, and the consensus was that the remaining intercessors should likewise be allowed to return, should they choose to do so. Robin Magram considered the decision soft-headed. 'Do you think they would warrant us like treatment in a similar situation? Remember, they planned that King Kragen should waylay us!'

'True enough,' said Arrel Sincere wearily, 'but what of that? We can either kill them, hold them under guard, or let them go their way, the last option being the least taxing and the most honorable.'

Robin Magram made no further protest, and the council then concerned itself with the details of the projected spy operation. None of the coracles at hand were considered suitable, and it was decided to build a coracle of special design – long, light, low to the water, with two sails of fine weave to catch every whisper of wind. Three men were named to the operation, all originally of Almack Float, a small community far to the east, in fact next to Sciona, at the end of the chain. None of the three had acquaintance on Apprise and so stood minimal chance of being recognized.

The coracle was built at once. A light keel of laminated and glued withe was shaped around pegs driven into the float; ribs were bent and lashed into place; diagonal ribs were attached to these, then the whole was covered with four layers of varnished pad-skin.

At mid-morning of the fourth day after Barquan Blasdel's flight, the coracle, almost a canoe, departed to the west, riding easily and swiftly over the sunny water. In its gear was included the horn taken from Barquan Blasdel's old workroom on Apprise Float. For three hours it slid along the line of floats, each an islet bedecked in blue, green, purple, orange and black verdure, surmounted by the arching fronds of the prime plant, each surrounded by its constellation of smaller pads. The coracle reached the final float of the group and struck out to the west, water swirling and sparkling behind the long oars. Afternoon waned; the rain clouds formed and swept across the sky, with black brooms hanging below. After the rain came sunset, making a glorious display among the broken clouds. The breeze began to blow; the sails were raised; the men pulled in their oars and rested. The coracle thrust swiftly west, with a chuckling of bow-wave and wake. Then came the mauve dusk with the constellations appearing and then night with the stars blazing down on the glossy black water. The men took turns sleeping, and the night passed. Before dawn the adverse wind rose; the men, saving their strength, rowed only with enough force to maintain headway.

The second day passed in a like manner. The first line of floats met by the flotilla fell behind, somewhat to the north. Another day went by. The floats of the savages failed to appear; presumably they had been passed in the night. Just before dawn of the fourth day the men lowered the horn into the water and listened.

Silence.

The men stood erect, looked into the west. Allowing for the increased speed of their passage, Tranque Float should be near at hand. But only a blank horizon could be seen.

At noon the men, increasingly dubious, ceased paddling and once more searched the horizon. As before, there was nothing visible save the line dividing dark blue from bright blue. The floats by now should be well within sight. Had they veered too far north or too far south?

The men deliberated and decided that while their own course had generally been true west, the original direction of flight might have been something south of east. In validation of this view was the fact that they had passed the intervening line of floats to the south. Hence the Old Floats in all probability lay behind the northern horizon. They agreed to paddle four hours to the north, then if nothing were seen, to return to the south.

Toward the waning of afternoon, with the rain clouds piling up, far smudges showed themselves. Now they halted, lowered the horn, to hear *crunch crunch crunch* with startling loudness. The men twisted the tube to detect the direction of the sound. It issued from the north. Crouching low, they listened, ready to paddle hastily away if the sound grew louder. But it seemed to lessen, and the direction veered to the east. Presently it died to near-inaudibility, and the men proceeded.

The floats took on substance, extending both east and west; soon the characteristic profiles could be discerned, and then the hoodwink towers.

Dead ahead was Aumerge, with Apprise Float yet to the west.

So they paddled up the chain, the floats with familiar and beloved names drifting past, floats where their ancestors had lived and died: Aumerge, Quincunx, Fay, Hastings, Quatrefoil, with its curious cloverleaf shape, and then the little outer group, The Bandings, and beyond, after a gap of a mile, Apprise Float.

The sun set, the hoodwink towers began to flicker, but the configurations could not be read. The men paddled the coracle toward Apprise. Verdure bulked up into the sky; the sounds and odors of the Old Floats wafted across the water, inflicting nostalgic pangs upon each of the men. They landed in a secluded little cove which had been described to them by Phyral Berwick, and covered the coracle with leaves and rubbish. According to the plan, two remained by the coracle, while the third, one Henry Bastaff, went off across the float toward the central common and Apprise Market.

Hundreds of people were abroad on this pleasant evening, but Henry Bastaff thought their mood to be weary and even a trifle grim. He went to the ancient Apprise Inn, which claimed to be the oldest building of the floats: a long shed beamed with twisted old stalks, reputedly cut at the astounding depth of three hundred feet. Within was a long buffet constructed of laminated strips, golden-brown with wax and use. Shelves to the rear displayed jars and tubes of arrack, beer, and spirits of life, together with various delicacies and sweetmeats. To the front wide eaves thatched with garwort frond shaded several dozen tables and benches where travelers rested and lovers kept rendezvous. Henry Bastaff seated himself where he could watch both the Apprise hoodwink tower and that of Quatrefoil to the east. The serving maid approached; he ordered beer and nut wafers. As he drank and ate, he listened to conversations at nearby tables and read the messages which flickered up and down the line of floats.

The conversations were uninformative; the hoodwink messages were the usual compendium of announcements, messages, banter. Then suddenly in mid-message came a blaze, all eighteen lights together, to signal news of great importance. Henry Bastaff sat up straight on the bench.

'Important ... information! ... This ... afternoon ... several ... of ... the ... intercessors ... kidnapped ... by ... the ... rebels ... returned ... to ... the ... Floats ... They ... are ... Barquan ... Blasdel ... of ... Apprise ... with ... his ... spouse ... and ... several ... dependants ... Vidal ... Reach ... of ... Sumber ... Luke ... Robinet ... of ... Parnassus ... They ... have ... a ... harrowing ... tale ... to ... tell ... The ... rebels ... are ... established ... on ... a ... float ... to ... the ... east ... where ... they ... kill ... kragen ... with ... merciless ... glee ... and ... plan ... a ... war ... of ... extermination ... upon ... the ... folk ... of ... the ... Old ... Floats ... The ... intercessors ... escaped ... and ... after ... an ... unnerving ... voyage ... across ... the ... uncharted ... ocean ... late

... today ... landed ... on ... Green ... Lamp ... Float ... Barquan ... Blasdel
... has ... called ... for ... an ... immediate ... convocation ... to ... consider
... what ... measures ... to ... take ... against ... the ... rebels ... who ... daily
... wax ... in ... arrogance.'

CHAPTER FOURTEEN

Six days later Henry Bastaff reported to the Council of New Home Float. 'Our arrival was precarious, for our initial direction took us many miles to the south of the Old Floats. Next time we must keep to the north of the floats intervening, whereupon we should make an easy landfall. Apparently the Blasdel coracle experienced even worse difficulties, for they reached Green Lamp Float about the same time we landed on Apprise. Possibly they delayed on one of our floats until they felt that we had given up pursuit. I sat at the Old Tavern when the news came, and I saw great excitement. The people seemed more curious than vindictive, even somewhat wistful. I heard no talk of King Kragen except one remark, somewhat ambiguous, to the effect that the rebels were perfectly welcome to attempt the slaughter of certain local kragen. A convocation was called for the following day. Since the folk of Almack Float would attend, I thought it best that Maible and Barway remain hidden. I stained my face swindler color, shaved away most of my eyebrows, pulled my hair forward, and wore a swindler's hood. I seemed the most inept of swindlers: half goon, half advertiser. At the convocation I looked eye to eye with my uncle Fodor the withe-peeler, who never turned for a second glance.

'The convocation was vehement and lengthy. Barquan Blasdel resumed his rank of Apprise Intercessor, without a moment's hesitation or as much as a by-your-leave. In my opinion Vrink Smathe, who had succeeded to the post, found no joy in Blasdel's return. He sat three rows back, bereft of his gown and nosepiece, frowning and blinking every time Barquan Blasdel spoke, which was almost continually.

'With great earnestness Blasdel called for a punitive expedition. He spoke of those who had departed as "iconoclasts", "monsters", "vicious scum of the world, which it was the duty of all decent folk to expunge".

'A certain number were stimulated, mostly those whom I would call the lowest element: folk of low prestige, unskilled, unknowledgeable and jealous of their betters. But these were few. In general he aroused only lukewarm attention. No one of importance showed heart for the project. The new intercessors in particular were less than enthusiastic. Clearly they covet their new posts, which they would lose if the old intercessors returned.

'Blasdel, seeing that he had aroused no vast sympathy for his wrongs, almost lost his temper, which is a rare thing to see in Barquan Blasdel. He accused those who were reluctant of cowardice and complacence, and so aroused antagonism. Everyone knows the temper of Emacho Feroxibus, Elder of the Quatrefoil Bezzlers. He is highly orthodox; still he is no poltroon. Very brusquely he instructed Blasdel to speak with a less pointed tongue. "No one questions your zeal, but let it be applied to constructive purposes! What avail is there in destroying these folk? They are gone; good riddance. We shall maintain our ancient ways with more dedication because the dissidents have departed! I, for one, do not care to hear any further rabble-rousing!"

'I must say that Barquan Blasdel was not at all cowed. He said, "It is all very well to temporize, and no one enjoys attempting an arduous and uncomfortable task such as the one I propose. Nevertheless these are unregenerates, creatures of the most depraved sort."

'Feroxibus laughed in his face. "If they are this evil, how did they allow you to live? Why did they not drown you?"

'Barquan Blasdel was taken aback. But he said, "It is clear enough. They feared discovery by King Kragen and planned that if the worst occurred, we would intercede in their behalf."

'Emacho Feroxibus said no more, nor did Barquan Blasdel, and the convocation ended without any decisive acts.

'But this was only the convocation: the overt situation. I doubt if Barquan Blasdel was surprised by the lack of response. His last act was to call a meeting of all intercessors at the cottage of Vrink Smathe that evening.

'I went back to the coracle and conferred with Barway and Maible. Barway is a deep-diver. With this attribute in mind, and recalling the typical arrangement of an intercessor's workroom, we evolved a means to secure more information. Barway can tell you what occurred better than I.'

Barway now made his report. He was a year or two younger than Henry Bastaff, an expert oarsman and a deep-diver of great endurance. He was an Advertiserman by caste, but had taken as a spouse the daughter of an Incendiary, and was generally held in high esteem. He spoke modestly, in a subdued manner.

'We made our plans while the sun was still high. I took a bearing on Smathe's hut, put on my goggles, ducked under the float. I don't know how many of you have swum under a float, but it's a beautiful sight. The water is deep blue, overhead is the white subskin and down below go the stems until finally they disappear into the depths.

'Smathe's hut was about seventy-five yards from the edge. This is a distance I can swim easily. But there and back: no. I would run out of air and drown under the float, unless I could find a hole like the one we found in Blasdel's hut. I trailed a rope so that I could be hauled back and revived if I failed to find the hut.

'But there was no problem. Seventy-five yards from the edge of the float I saw the dark hole above and the horn. I rose and floated in the hole. The plug was off. I was able to breathe.

'No one was in the workroom. In an outer chamber I heard voices, which seemed to be those of Vrink Smathe and his spouse. They were jointly lamenting the return of Barquan Blasdel. In fact, Smathe's spouse was upbraiding him for submitting so tamely to Barquan Blasdel's resumption of his position, and speaking in language quite unbecoming a woman of the Bezzlers, as I believe her caste to be.

'I did not linger. I made my rope fast to the horn, so that after dark I could find my way back. Then I returned to the coracle.

'We waited until evening. Henry Bastaff went back to Apprise Inn and listened to the talk, but heard nothing of consequence. As soon as we observed intercessors entering Smathe's hut, I took to the water, and guiding myself by the rope returned to the hole in the Smathes' workroom.'

At this the members of the council all gave a small shudder, since the under-water by night was a region of superstitious dread, especially under the pad: the locale of children's horror tales.

Barway continued. 'I was early. The intercessors continued to come in as I waited. Vrink Smathe came to listen at the horn, and I was forced to submerge. I had taken little air and began to feel strain. Smathe turned the horn about, and I was forced to draw back when it pointed toward me. It stopped – and I realized that Smathe could hear my heartbeats. I swam to the other side of the hole and looked up through the water. Smathe was listening with his ear down and eyes turned away. I surfaced, took air and went below once more.' Barway laughed. The councilors responded with wry grimaces. Barway was understating the drama of the moment, as all knew.

'Smathe left the horn. I surfaced. I heard him say, "For a moment I heard a curious pounding sound: a thump thump thump. But it went away." Someone suggested that the sound was probably due to someone jumping on the float, and Smathe agreed to this. And then Blasdel came into the room.'

Barquan Blasdel looked around the circle of intercessors, all of whom wore ceremonial black gowns with float emblems. He spoke first to Vrink Smathe: 'Guards are posted against eavesdroppers?'

'Four apprentices stand outside the hut, with lanterns. No one may approach.'

'Good. What we discuss now is of the utmost gravity and must not be disclosed, by deed or action.

'First of all, the intercessors now present must be ratified in their posts. Vidal Reach, Luke Robinet, and I relinquish our posts as Intercessors for Sumber, Parnassus, and Apprise, and now become Central Authorities. I hereby accede to the urgent suggestions made by many of you and will become Supreme Presiding Intercessor for all the floats. Luke Robinet and Vidal Reach will become my Chief Manciples.

'Now, to our main business. In spite of the timidity and inertia of the population, we cannot allow the rebels to continue in a state of insubordination. The reasons for this are many. First, they dared to attack King Kragen and to attempt his death: a deed of horror. Secondly, they kidnapped fifteen intercessors, a most heinous act. Third, even now they kill kragen with ever greater facility and already are preparing an assault upon King Kragen. Fourthly, even if they chose to remain quietly on their new floats, they represent a challenge to King Kragen's rule and thus to our authority. Fifthly, they have subjected me, Vidal Reach, Luke Robinet, and all the rest to the most repugnant indignities, thus by extension attacking the whole institution of Intercessorship: which is to say ourselves. We must destroy them. Before I proceed, do I have your unanimous approval and endorsement of the viewpoints I have just presented?'

Endorsement was somewhat cautious but unanimous.

'These then are my proposals. We will organize a militia, to be called "The Defenders", or "King Kragen's Admonitors", or "The Peoples' Protectors", or something similar. The able-bodied men of the New Floats number less than a thousand. Probably not more than five hundred would be fit to fight.

'To secure absolute and overwhelming strength we must recruit a force of at least a thousand active, strong and zealous young men. We shall train them in the use of weapons, and more importantly, wash from their minds all compunction, pity or qualms against violence, and likewise do so in ourselves. I realize we thus contradict our oldest and most cherished tradition, but it is in a worthy cause.

'When the force is trained and equipped, we will embark in a suitable fleet of coracles, go forth and subdue the rebels. The most vicious and recalcitrant we must deal with definitely and finally; the rest shall be brought back in shame to the main floats and reduced to a new and low caste. Thus shall the lesson be driven home! Thus shall the power and benevolence of King Kragen be asserted! Thus shall we maintain and augment our own prestige!'

Barway reported the exhortations of Barquan Blasdel in as careful detail as he was able, in addition to the discussion that followed. No one had offered serious opposition to Barquan Blasdel's plan; there had only been a questioning as to ways and means.

'Did they announce a time schedule?' asked Phyral Berwick.

'I gather that they will begin immediately.'

'I would expect as much.' Phyral Berwick heaved a deep sigh. 'Thus fear and pain and brutality come to the floats. It seems as if even in spite of our heritage we are little better than the folk of the Outer Worlds.'

Sklar Hast said, 'We must contrive counter-measures. First, there is no further point in keeping the intercessors captive. Better if now we give them a coracle and send them home. In this way they will learn nothing of our plans.'

'What are our plans?' Arrel Sincere asked bleakly.

Sklar Hast considered. 'We have a number of alternatives. We could train a militia of our own and trust to our own skill and strength. Ultimately, after much bloodshed, I fear we would be defeated. We could pack our belongings and flee once again, to seek a new far set of floats. This is not an appealing idea. We can try to kill King Kragen – but they would still attack us. Or we can defeat our enemies by a strategy which so far I am unable to define ... In the meantime we must continue a close observation of the Home Floats.'

CHAPTER FIFTEEN

On the world which had no name, there were no seasons, no variations of climate except those to be found by traversing the latitudes. Along the equatorial doldrums, where floats of sea-plant grew in chains and clots, each day was like every other, and the passage of a year could be detected only by watching the night sky. Though the folk had small need for accurate temporal distinctions, each day was numbered and each year named for some significant event. A duration of twenty-two years was a 'surge', and was also reckoned by number. Hence a given date might be known as the 349th day in the Year of Malvinon's Deep Dive during the Tenth Surge. Time reckoning was almost exclusively the province of the scriveners. To most of the folk life was as pellucid and effortless as the glassy blue sea at noon.

King Kragen's attack upon Tranque Float occurred toward the year's end, which thereupon became the Year of Tranque's Abasement, and it was generally assumed that the following year would be known as the Year of the Dissenters' Going.

As the days passed and the year approached its midpoint, Barquan Blasdel, instead of allowing the memory of his kidnapping to grow dim, revived it daily with never-flagging virulence. Each evening saw a memorandum from Barquan Blasdel flicker up and down the chain of floats: 'Vigilance is necessary! The dissidents are led by men of evil energy! They flout the majesty of King Kragen; they despise the folk who maintain old traditions and most especially the intercessors. They must be punished and taught humility. Should they dare to attack us, which is not beyond the limits of their megalomaniac viciousness, they must be hurled into the sea. To this end – King Kragen's Exemplary Corps!'

At a conclave of notables he made a speech of great earnestness, depicting the goals of the rebels in the most serious light, in which he was supported by those intercessors who had been liberated and who had made their way back to the Home Floats.

'Do we wish to see their detestable philosophy transplanted here?' demanded Barquan Blasdel. 'A thousand times no! King Kragen's Exemplary Corps will act as one man to destroy the invading rebels, or, if a policy of cauterization is decided upon, to wipe out the central node of sepsis!'

Emacho Feroxibus, Elder of the Quatrefoil Bezzlers, was not moved by Barquan Blasdel's vehemence. 'Let them be,' he growled. 'I have had long association with many of these folk, who are persons of high caste and good character. They obviously do not plan to invade the Home Floats; such a thought is absurd, and so long as they do not molest us, why should we molest them? No one should risk drowning for so dismal a cause.'

Barquan Blasdel, containing his temper, explained carefully. 'The matter is more complex than this. Here is a group who have fled in order to avoid paying their just due to King Kragen. If they are allowed to prosper, to make profit of their defection, then other folk may be tempted to wonder, why do we not do likewise? If the sin of kragen-killing becomes vulgar recreation, where is reverence? Where is continuity? Where is obedience to High Authority?'

'This may be true,' stated Providence Dringle, Chief Hoodwink for the Populous Equity Float. 'Nonetheless in my opinion the cure is worse than the complaint. And to risk a heretical opinion, I must say the benefits we derive from High Authority no longer seem commensurate with the price we pay.'

Blasdel swung about in shock, as did the other intercessors. 'May I ask your meaning?' Blasdel inquired icily.

'I mean that King Kragen consumes from six to seven bushels of choice sponges daily. He maintains his rule in the water surrounding the floats, true, but what do we need fear from the lesser kragen? By your own testimony the dissidents have developed a method to kill the kragen with facility.'

Blasdel said with frigid menace, 'I cannot overlook the fact that your remarks are identical to the preposterous ravings of the dissidents, who so rightly shall be obliterated.'

'Do not rely on my help,' said Providence Dringle.

'Nor mine,' said Emacho Feroxibus. 'I must also make note of the fact that while heretofore each float maintained the establishment of one intercessor, now there are two, not even to mention this corps of uniformed ruffians you are training.'

'It is a distressing sight,' said Barquan Blasdel in a voice quietly sad, 'to see a man once effective and orthodox decline so suddenly into verbose senility. Emacho Feroxibus, speak on! Be sure that we will listen to you with the respect your advanced age and long career of service deserve! Talk as you will!'

Emacho Feroxibus's face was purple with rage. 'You mealy-mouthed scoundrel! I'd teach you senility with my bare hands, were it not for my detestation of violence!'

The conclave shortly thereafter was adjourned.

King Kragen's Exemplary Corps was one thousand strong. Their barracks and training area was Tranque Float, which never had been restored to habitation. They wore a smart uniform, consisting of a gown somewhat like the intercessors' formal robes, black in front and white in back, with an emblem representing King Kragen sewed on the chest. They wore helmets of laminated pad-skin and rug-fish leather well-varnished, with the varnished dorsal fin of the gray-fish for a crest. For weapons they carried pikes of fine straight withe tipped with a blade of the hardest stem-wood, and daggers of similar quality. They lacked bows and arrows only because none of the materials found on the floats or in the sea offered the necessary resilience. A dart thrower, on the order of an atlatl, was tested, but accuracy was so poor that it was discarded.

The Exemplary Corps, though it included men of every caste and guild, was mainly comprised of those whose careers were not proceeding with celerity, or who disliked toil with unusual vehemence. The other folk of the floats regarded the Exemplars with mixed emotions. They imposed something of a strain upon the normal functioning of the economy, for they ate a great deal and produced none of their own food. Meanwhile King Kragen daily seemed to wax in size and appetite. The need for such a large corps – or any corps at all – was continually questioned. Few accepted the intercessors' contention that the dissidents planned an attack on the Home Floats.

Nevertheless the corps made a brave, if somewhat sinister show, parading in platoons of twenty with lances aslant over their shoulders, or rowing their new twelve-man coracles at great speed across the ocean whenever King Kragen was not about. For the intercessors, dubious of King Kragen's attitude, had kept from him the knowledge of the Exemplary Corps – though no one considered it likely that he would forbid the organization if he knew of its aims.

Barquan Blasdel was Commandant of the corps and wore a uniform even more striking than that of the Exemplars: a split black and white gown, tied at his ankles, with buttons of polished bindlebane, purple epaulettes carved to represent kragen mandibles, a purple helmet with a crest simulating King Kragen's maw, with palps and mandibles outspread: a fearsome sight.

Daily the corps drilled: running, jumping, thrusting lances into dummies, springing in and out of their boats. Daily they heard Barquan Blasdel discourse upon the infamy of the rebels and the vileness of their habits. Daily the corps performed a ritual expressing homage and devotion to King Kragen and absolute obedience to those who interceded with him. Most of the float notables in private expressed disapprobation of the corps, and Emacho Feroxibus began to prepare an official sanction against the corps. Immediately King Kragen appeared at Quatrefoil Float, where Emacho Feroxibus was caste-elder, and remained four days, eating with great appetite. The Quatrefoil arbors were barren of sponges, and finally the folk of the float in desperation prevailed upon Emacho Feroxibus to modify his stand. He vented a great curse upon Barquan Blasdel, another upon the Exemplars, and a final objurgation against King Kragen, to the awe of all. Then he turned, a feeble and embittered man, and walked slowly to his hut.

King Kragen departed Quatrefoil Float. Three days later the body of Emacho Feroxibus was found floating in the lagoon, an apparent suicide, though many refuted this notion and claimed that in his grief he must have wandered blindly into the water. A few hinted of circumstances even more grim, but made no public assertion of their beliefs, since, if they were right, the message was clear.

The day arrived when in Barquan Blasdel's opinion King Kragen's Exemplary Corps was ready to perform the duty for which it was intended. Across Tranque Float went the word: 'A week from today!'

A week later the sun went down and Tranque Float was taut with expectation. Barquan Blasdel, resplendent in his uniform, addressed the massed corps by torch-light.

'Brave members of the invincible Exemplar Corps! The time has come! The detestable vermin who live across the water pose a threat we can no longer tolerate. Already along these beautiful floats of our own, voices are whispering an envious desire for the depraved ease of the rebels! We must win them back to the right way, the orthodox way! By persuasion if possible, by force if necessary! All bodes well! King Kragen has graciously given us leave to trespass upon his ocean and now relaxes near Helicon. So now – load boats! Rack pikes! Embark all! We sail to the east!'

A great hoarse cheer rose from the Exemplars. With a will the coracles were loaded; with rehearsed agility the Exemplars sprang aboard, thrust away from Tranque Float. Oars dug into the water; with another great guttural call the coracles surged toward the east.

Dawn came; water reflected the color of silver ash, then ruffled to the morning breeze. Big plum-blue square-sails were hoisted. They bellied; oars were shipped. The Exemplars rested. Ninety boats sailed the morning ocean: long low boats painted black and purple, with a white-and-black kragen blazoned on each straining sail. In each boat crouched twelve men in black-and-white gowns and black helmets with the spined crest.

Directly into the dazzle of the rising sun they sailed, and the glare served to conceal the boats that waited for them. When the breeze died and the sun had lifted, these boats were only a quarter-mile to the east: ten boats of strange design. They were twice as long as the twelve-man coracles, and each carried about twenty men. They waited in a line across the course of the Exemplar boats. The center boat, propelled by sixteen oars, advanced. In the bow stood Sklar Hast.

He hailed the leading boat of the Exemplars. 'What boats are you, and where are you bound?'

Barquan Blasdel rose to his feet. 'Sklar Hast! You dare bring your boats so close to the Home Floats?'

'We sailed forth to meet you.'

'Then you have sailed your last. We are bound to the new floats, to visit justice upon you.'

'Turn back,' said Sklar Hast. 'Take warning! If you come farther, you are all dead men!'

Barquan Blasdel made a gesture to the other boats. 'Forward! Pikes to hand! Board, kill, capture!'

'Stand back!' roared Sklar Hast. 'Take warning, fools! Do you think we are helpless? Go back to the Home Floats and save your lives!'

The Exemplar coracles sped forward. That one in which Barquan Blasdel stood moved over to the side, to where Barquan Blasdel could command the battle. With only a hundred feet between, men in the waiting boats suddenly rose to their feet, holding bows fashioned from kragen-turret splines.

They aimed, discharged arrows with flaming globular tips. The arrows struck into the black coracles, broke to spread flaming oil.

In the first volley twenty of the black-and-purple boats were aflame. In the second volley, forty burnt. In the third volley, sixty. The withe and varnished pad-skin burned like tinder; fear-crazed Exemplars leaped into the sea. The thirty boats yet whole backed water, turned aside. Barquan Blasdel's boat already was out of range.

Sklar Hast steeled his heart, signaled. Another volley of flaming arrows set another ten boats aflame, and with an almost miraculous swiftness the proud black fleet of King Kragen's Exemplary Corps was destroyed.

'Forward!' Sklar Hast ordered. 'One more volley. We must make a total end to this business!'

Reluctantly – for further action now seemed sheer slaughter – the archers lobbed a final volley of fire-arrows, and now, whether because the range was great or because the archers had no more will to attack, only eight boats were struck.

The water seethed with swimming shapes. As the coracles burned and collapsed, cases of stores floated loose, and the Exemplars clung to these.

Sklar Hast gave an order; the boats from New Float backed away from the scene of the battle. Cautiously those coracles still afloat returned. Stores and weapons were thrown overboard to lighten ship; swimming Exemplars were taken aboard to the limits of capacity, and ropes were thrown out to those yet floating.

Sluggishly, towing the men still in the water, the overloaded coracles returned across the sea toward Tranque Float.

Of the ninety proud black-and-purple boats which had set forth, twenty still floated.

Of a thousand Exemplars, five hundred survived.

Sklar Hast listened to the underwater horn and could detect nothing to indicate the proximity of King Kragen. He gave an order to his oarsmen, and the New Float boats followed the wallowing Exemplar fleet back to Tranque. To complete Barquan Blasdel's utter humiliation, when the black boats were a hundred yards from Tranque, the New Float boats moved in close, discharged two final volleys of fire-arrows, to destroy all the Exemplar coracles. All, Barquan Blasdel included, were forced to swim the last hundred yards to Tranque Float.

The following day a convocation was called on Apprise Float. There were none of the usual rambling introductory remarks. Morse Swin, the Apprise Arbiter, Phyral Berwick's one-time assistant, a big blond slow-spoken man, went to the rostrum. 'Yesterday occurred a great tragedy, a futile useless tragedy, and all our wisdom is needed to resolve the situation. One thing is certain: reproaches are futile. The folly of attempting to attack the New Float has been made utterly evident, and it is high time that these so-called Exemplars put aside their pretensions or ideals or vanities – whatever one wishes to call them; I have heard each word used, as well as others – in any event, it is time that these idle men doff their uniforms and return to work.'

Barquan Blasdel jumped to his feet. 'Do I hear aright?' he called in a voice icily cold.

Morse Swin looked at him in surprise. 'Intercessor, if you please, I am speaking from the rostrum. When I am finished, you may have your turn.'

'But I will not permit you to spout arrant nonsense. I thought to hear an impassioned urge for all men to rededicate themselves to what now must be our single concentrated goal: the absolute destruction of the rebels!'

'Intercessor, if you will restrain yourself, I wish to continue my remarks. I definitely take a less vehement view of the situation. We have our problems to solve; let us leave the folk of New Float to theirs.'

Barquan Blasdel would not be quelled. 'And what if they attack us?'

'They have shown no disposition to do so. They defended themselves and defeated you. If they planned an attack, they would never have allowed you to return to Tranque Float with your survivors. You should give thanks for your life and adjust yourself to the realities of the situation. I for one will hear of no further such ventures. The Exemplars must be disbanded and return to earning their living. This is my feeling, and I ask the approval of the convocation. Who agrees?'

There was vigorous assent.

'Who disagrees?'

In response came a sound of much lesser volume but much greater emotion. It issued from the throats of the intercessors and from the Exemplars themselves, who, wearing their uniforms and helmets, stood in four carefully ordered groups.

Morse Swin nodded his big, heavy head. 'The verdict of the convocation seems definite; still, anyone who wishes is entitled to speak.'

Barquan Blasdel came to the rostrum. He put his hands on the rail, turned his dark brooding gaze over the convocation. 'You people who assented to the view of Morse Swin did so after only the most superficial attention. Shortly I will ask you to vote again.

'I wish to make three points.

'First, the setback of yesterday was unimportant. We shall win. Of that there is no doubt. Do we not have King Kragen on our side? We withdrew after sustaining losses, it is true. Do you know why this was made necessary? Because upon these floats, perhaps here at the convocation, at this very moment, there are spies. Furtive, skulking creatures of the most perverted and amoral attitudes imaginable! We expected no serious opposition; we set sail – but the spies had sent word ahead! The rebels prepared a dastardly and cruel ambush. What fiends these rebels are, to hurl fire at defenseless boats! Our drowned comrades will not go unavenged, I assure you! Do I speak truth, comrade Exemplars?'

From the uniformed groups came an impassioned shout: 'Truth!'

Barquan Blasdel looked slowly around the convocation. 'Morse Swin spoke of realities. He is the man who is not realistic. King Kragen is benevolent, but he is now wrathful. His is the might, his is the force! We cannot deny him! He has ordained that his Exemplars act, he has given them sharp weapons fashioned from the hardest stem, he has given them his endorsement! The Exemplars act on King Kragen's behalf. They are men of true faith; they are forbearing and benevolent, as is King Kragen; but like King Kragen, they are terrible in their wrath. King Kragen's Exemplary Corps must not be contravened! They know the path of rectitude, which is derived from the will of King Kragen; they will not be denied! When an Exemplar speaks, he speaks with the voice and the will of King Kragen! Do not oppose, nor contradict, nor fail to obey! Because first to be feared are the sharp weapons, the daggers and pikes, and second, the source of all awe and majesty, King Kragen himself. I, his Intercessor, and Chief Exemplar, assure you of the "reality" of this situation. Who should know better?

'We now enter a time of emergency! All must look as with a single gaze to the east, toward the float of the rebels. All must harden their minds, put aside the soft ways of ease, until the rebels are destroyed and the emergency is ended.

'During this emergency we require a strong authority, a central coordinating mind to ensure that all proceeds with efficiency. I have attempted to withdraw myself from a post of such responsibility, but all insist that I take this terrible burden upon myself. I can only, with humility, profess my readiness to make this personal sacrifice, and I now so proclaim this emergency and this assumption of absolute authority. I will be pleased to hear a unanimous and hearty endorsement.'

From the Exemplars and the intercessors came a great call. Elsewhere were frozen faces and indignant mutters.

'Thank you,' said Barquan Blasdel. 'The unanimity of the endorsement will be duly noted in the records. The convocation is now adjourned. When circumstances warrant, when the emergency is at an end, I will announce the fact and call another convocation. All may now return to your home floats. Instructions as to how you best may serve King Kragen will be forthcoming.'

Sputtering with anger, Morse Swin jumped to his feet. 'One moment! Are you insane? This is not traditional procedure! You did not call for adverse voices!'

Barquan Blasdel made a small, quiet signal to a nearby group of Exemplars. Ten of these stalked forward, seized Morse Swin by the elbows, hustled him away. He struggled and kicked; one of the Exemplars struck him on the back of the head with the haft of his dagger.

Barquan Blasdel nodded placidly. 'I did not call for adverse voices because there was obvious unanimity. The convocation is adjourned.'

CHAPTER SIXTEEN

Henry Bastaff described the convocation to a silent conclave of notables on New Home Float. 'There was no core of opposition, no firmness. Old Emacho Feroxibus was dead, Morse Swin had been dragged off. The folk were stunned. The situation was too fantastic to be credible. No one knew whether to laugh or scream or tear the Exemplars apart with their bare hands. They did nothing. They dispersed and went back to their huts.'

'And now Barquan Blasdel rules the floats,' said Phyral Berwick.

'With the most exacting rigor.'

'So then we must expect another attack.'

Henry Bastaff agreed. 'Without any doubt whatever.'

'But how? Surely they won't attempt another raid!'

'As to this, I can't say. They might build boats with shields to divert fire-arrows, or evolve a system to throw fire-arrows of their own.'

'Fire-arrows we can tolerate,' said Sklar Hast. 'We can build our boats with kragen-hide rather than pad-skin; this is no great threat ... I can't imagine how Blasdel hopes to attack us. Yet undoubtedly he does so intend.'

'We must continue our surveillance,' said Phyral Berwick. 'So much is evident.' He looked at Henry Bastaff. 'Are you willing to return?'

Bastaff hesitated. 'The risk is great. Blasdel knows that we spy on him. The Exemplars will be very much on the alert ... I suspect that the best information will be gained from under the pad, under the Intercessor's hut. If Barway and Maible will return, I will accompany them.'

Phyral Berwick clapped him on the shoulder. 'You have the admiration and gratitude of us all! Because now our very lives depend upon information!'

Four days later Roger Kelso took Sklar Hast to Outcry Float, where he pointed out a contrivance whose function or purpose Sklar Hast could not fathom. 'You will now see electricity produced,' said Roger Kelso.

'What? In that device?' Sklar Hast inspected the clumsy apparatus. A tube of hollow stalk five inches in diameter, supported by a scaffold, rose twenty feet into the air. The base was held at one end of a long box containing what appeared to be wet ashes. The far end of the box was closed by a slab of compressed carbon, into which were threaded copper wires. At the opposite end, between the tube and the wet ashes, was another slab of compressed carbon.

'This is admittedly a crude device, unwieldy to operate and of no great efficiency,' said Kelso. 'It does however meet our peculiar requirements: which is to say, it produces electricity without metal, through the agency of water pressure. Brunet describes it in his Memorium. He calls it the "Rous machine" and the process "cataphoresis". The tube is filled with water, which is thereby forced through the mud, which here is a mixture of ashes and sea-slime. The water carries an electric charge which it communicates to the porous carbon as it seeps through. By this means a small but steady and quite dependable source of electricity is at our hand. As you may have guessed, I have already tested the device and so can speak with confidence.' He turned, signaled his helpers. Two clamped shut the box of mud, others mounted the scaffold, carrying buckets of water which they poured into the tube. Kelso connected the wires to a coil of several dozen revolutions. He brought forward a dish. On a cork rested a small rod of iron.

'I have already "magnetized" this iron,' said Kelso. 'Note how it points to the north? It is called a "compass" and can be used as a navigational device. Now – I bring it near the end of the coil. See it jerk! Electricity is flowing in the wire!'

Sklar Hast was much impressed. Kelso spoke on. 'The process is still in a crude state. I hope eventually to build pumps propelled by the wind to raise the water, or even a generator propelled by the wind, when we have much more metal than we have now. But even this Rous machine implies a dramatic possibility. With electricity we can disassociate sea-water to produce the acid of salt, and a caustic of countering properties as well. The acid can then be used to produce more highly concentrated streams of electricity – if we are able to secure more metal. So I ask myself, where do the savages procure their copper? Do they slaughter young kragen? I am so curious that I must know, and I plan to visit the Savage Floats to learn their secret.'

'No,' said Sklar Hast. 'When they killed you, who would build another Rous machine? No, Roger Kelso. What was MacArthur's Dictum: "*No man is indispensable*"? It is incorrect. You are too important to risk. Send your helpers, but do not venture yourself into danger. The times are too troubled for you to indulge yourself in the luxury of dying.'

Kelso gave a grudging acquiescence. 'If you really believe this.'

Sklar Hast returned to New Home Float, where he sought out Meril Rohan. He enticed her aboard a small coracle, and rowed east along the line of floats. Upon a little pad floating somewhat to the south of the line, they halted and went ashore, and sat under a thicket of wild sugar-stem. 'Here,' said Meril, 'is where we can build our home, and this is where we shall have our children.'

Sklar Hast sighed. 'It is so peaceful, so calm, so beautiful ... Think how things must be on the Home Floats, where that madman rules!'

'If only all could be peaceful ... Perhaps chaos is in our nature, in the nature of man!'

'It would seem,' said Sklar Hast, chewing on a stalk of sugar-stem, 'that we of the floats should by all rationality be less prone to these qualities. The Firsts fled the Outer Worlds because they were subjected to oppression; hence it would seem that their mildness and placidity after twelve generations would be augmented in us.'

Meril gave a mischievous laugh. 'Let me tell you my theory regarding the Firsts.' She did, and Sklar Hast was first amused, then incredulous, finally indignant. 'What a thing to say! These are the Firsts! Our ancestors! You are an iconoclast in all truth! Is this what you teach the children? In any event, it is all so ridiculous!'

'I don't think so. So many things are explained. So many curious passages become clear, so many ambiguous musings and what would seem irrational regrets are clarified.'

'I refuse to believe this! Why – it's ...' Words deserted him. Then he said, 'I look at you and I watch your face, and I think you are a product of the Firsts, and I know what you say is impossible.'

Meril Rohan laughed in great merriment. 'But just think, if it's so, then perhaps the Outer Worlds would not be such dreadful places as we have previously believed.'

Sklar Hast shrugged. 'We'll never be sure – because we can never leave this world.'

'Do you know what someday we'll do? Not you or I, but perhaps our children or their children. They'll find the Ship of Space, they'll dive or send down grapples and raise it to the surface. Then they'll study it very carefully. Perhaps there'll be much to learn, perhaps nothing ... But just think! Suppose they could contrive a way to fly space once more, or at the very least to send out some sort of message!'

'Anything is possible,' said Sklar Hast. 'If your violently unorthodox theory is correct, if the Firsts were as you seem to believe, then this might be a desirable goal.' He sighed once more. 'You and I will never see it; we'll never know the truth of your theories – which perhaps is just as well.'

A coracle manned by Carl Snyder and Roble Baxter, two of Roger Kelso's helpers, sailed west to the Savage Floats. Nine days later they returned, gaunt, sunburned but triumphant. Carl Snyder reported to the Council of Elders: 'We waited offshore until dark. The savages sat around a fire, and using a telescope I could see them clearly. They are a wretched folk: dirty, naked, ugly. When they were asleep we approached and found a spot where we could hide the coracle and ourselves. Three days we watched the savages. There are only twenty or thirty. They do little more than eat, sleep, copulate, and smelt copper. First they heat the husks of their sponges to a char. This char they pulverize and put into a pot to which a bellows is attached. As they work the bellows, the charcoal glows in many colors, and finally dissipates, and the copper remains.'

'And to think that for twelve generations we have thrown sponge husks into the sea!' cried Kelso in anguish.

'It would seem,' reflected Sklar Hast, 'that the kragen derive the copper of their blood from sponges. Where then is the source of iron in our own blood? It must be found in some article of our own diet. If the source was found, we would not need to drain ourselves pale to obtain pellets.'

'We test every substance we can lay our hands on,' said Kelso. 'We have created a white powder and a yellow powder, but no metal. Naturally we continue with our tests.'

Several days later Kelso once more invited Sklar Hast to Outcry Float. Under four long open-sided sheds fifty men and women worked at retorts fashioned from ash cemented with sea-ooze. Bellows puffed, charcoal glowed, fumes billowed up and drifted away through the foliage.

Kelso showed Sklar Hast a container of copper pellets. Sklar Hast reverently trickled the cold, clinking shapes through his fingers. 'Metal! All from kragen blood?'

'From kragen blood and organs, and from the husks of sponges. And here – here is our iron!' He showed Sklar Hast a container holding a much smaller quantity of iron: a handful. 'This represents a hundred bleedings. But we have found iron elsewhere: in glands of the gray-fish, in the leaves of bindlebane, in purple-weed pith. Small quantities, true, but before we had none.'

Sklar Hast hefted the iron. 'In my imagination I see a great engine constructed of iron. It floats on the water and moves faster than any coracle. King Kragen sees it. He is awed, he is taken aback, but in his arrogance he attacks. The engine thrusts forth an iron knife; iron hooks grip King Kragen, and the iron knife hacks him in two.' Once again Sklar Hast let the pellets of iron sift through his fingers. He shook his head ruefully. 'We might bleed every man, woman, and child dry a hundred times, a thousand times, and still lack iron to build such a kragen-killing engine.'

'Unfortunately true,' said Roger Kelso. 'The engine you suggest is out of our reach. Still, using our wits, perhaps we can contrive something almost as deadly.'

'We had better make haste. Because Barquan Blasdel and his Exemplars think only of bringing some terrible fate to us.'

Whatever the fate Barquan Blasdel planned for the folk of New Home Float, he kept his own counsel. Perhaps he had not yet perfected the plan; perhaps he wished to consolidate the authority of the Exemplars; perhaps he suspected that spies gauged his every move. In this latter conjecture he was accurate. Henry Bastaff, in the role of an itinerant spice-grinder, frequented Apprise Inn with ears angled toward the Exemplars who customarily relaxed from their duties here.

He learned little. The Exemplars spoke in large voices, hinting of portentous events, but it was clear that they knew nothing.

Occasionally Barquan Blasdel himself would appear, wearing garments of new and elaborate style. Over a tight black coverall he wore a jacket, or surplice, of embroidered purple strips, looped around shoulders, chest, waist and thighs. From his shoulders extended a pair of extravagantly wide epaulettes, from which hung a black cloak, which flapped and billowed as he walked. His headdress was even more impressive: an elaborate bonnet of pad-skin cusps and prongs, varnished and painted black and purple: a symbolic representation of King Kragen's countenance.

Barquan Blasdel's dark gaunt face was sober and harsh these days, though his voice, when he spoke, was as easy and relaxed as ever, and generally he managed a slight smile, together with an earnest forward inclination of the head, which gave the person to whom he spoke a sense of participation in affairs of profound importance.

Barway and Maible had taken elaborate precautions against the vigilance of the Exemplars. Their coracle was submerged and tucked under the edge of the float; working from underwater, they had cut rectangular niches up into the pulp of the float, with a bench above water-level and ventilation holes up through the top surface into the shadow of a hessian bush. In these niches they lay during daylight hours, making occasional underwater visits to the hole in Vrink Smathe's workroom. By night they came forth to eat the food brought by Henry Bastaff.

Like Henry Bastaff, they had learned nothing. Barquan Blasdel and the Exemplars seemed to be marking time. King Kragen made his usual leisurely circuit of the floats. Twice Henry Bastaff saw him and on each occasion marveled at his size and might. On the evening after the second occasion, sitting at his usual place to the back of Apprise Inn, he heard a brief snatch of conversation which he considered significant. Later in the evening he reported to Barway and Maible: 'This may mean something or nothing; it is hard to judge. I personally feel that something is afoot. In any event these are the circumstances. A pair of blackguards had come in from Sumber, and a Felon Elder asked regarding Thrasneck and Bickle. The blackguards replied that all the previous month they had worked at Thrasneck Lagoon, building sponge-arbors in profusion: enough to serve not only Thrasneck, but Tranque, Bickle, Sumber, Adelvine and Green Lamp as well. These arbors were of a new design, heavier and more durable, and buoyed by bundles of withe rather than bladders. The Felon Elder then spoke of sponge barges his guild brothers were building on Tranque: a project supposedly secret, but why maintain secrecy about a set of sponge barges? It wasn't as if they were attack boats for the Exemplars. Here a group of Exemplars came into the inn and the conversation halted.'

'Sponge arbors and barges,' mused Maible. 'Nothing immediately sinister here.'

'Not unless the intent is to provision a new expeditionary force.'

'Something is in the wind,' said Henry Bastaff. 'Intercessors both new and old are arriving at Apprise, and there's talk of a conclave. You two keep your ears on Smathe's workroom, and I'll try to catch a word or two of what's happening.'

Mid-morning of the following day Henry Bastaff walked by the hessian bush under which lay Barway and Maible. Squatting, pretending to tie the thongs of his sandals, he muttered: 'Bastaff here. Today is the conclave, highly important, beside the hoodwink tower. I'm going to try to hide behind a stack of hood-facings; I may or may not be successful. One of you swim to where the tower posts go through the float. There's a gap of a few inches where you can breathe and possibly hear – especially if you chisel away some of the pulp.'

From under the fronds of the hessian bush came a muffled voice. 'Best that you keep your distance; they'll be on the alert for spies. We'll try to hear the proceedings from below.'

'I'll do whatever looks safe,' said Henry Bastaff. 'I'm going. There's an Exemplar watching me.'

In their niche below the pad, Maible and Barway heard his retreating footsteps and, a moment later, another leisurely tread, as someone, presumably the Exemplar, strolled by.

The footsteps moved away; Barway and Maible relaxed.

After consultation, Barway slipped from the shelf into the water, and after taking his bearings, swam to where the poles of the hoodwink tower passed through the float. Here, as Bastaff had stated, were gaps at which, after a certain amount of cutting and chiseling, Barway could either put his mouth and nose or his ear, but not both at once.

Henry Bastaff went about his business of spice-grinding, and after an hour or so walked past the hoodwink tower. The pile of hood-facings was as before. Henry Bastaff looked in all directions. No one appeared to be observing him. He squatted, shifted the facings this way and that and contrived an opening into which he inserted himself.

Time passed. The longer Henry Bastaff sat the more uneasy he became. The pile of facings suddenly seemed over-provident. The area had been too conveniently deserted. Could it be that the facings had been arranged to serve as a spy-trap?

Hurriedly Bastaff wriggled back out, and after a quick look around, took himself off.

A half hour later intercessors began to gather on the scene. Six Exemplar Selects came to stand guard, and to prevent unauthorized persons from pressing too close.

At last Barquan Blasdel appeared, walking slowly, his black cloak drifting and billowing behind. Three Exemplars of the Fervent category marched at his back. He passed near the stack of facings, and turned them a quick glance. They had been disarranged, slightly moved. Barquan Blasdel's lips tightened in a small secret smile. He turned, spoke to the Fervent Exemplars, who took up positions beside the pile of facings.

Barquan Blasdel faced the assembled intercessors. He raised his hands for silence.

'Today begins a new phase of our preparations,' he said. 'We expect to achieve two purposes: to systematize our relations with King Kragen, and to establish a necessary pre-condition to our great project. Before I go into details, I wish to make some comments in regard to espionage. No creature is as vile as a spy, especially a spy from the Dissident Floats. If apprehended, he can expect but small mercy at our hands. So now I inquire: have all present been vigilant in this regard?'

The assembled intercessors nodded their heads and gave witness that, indeed, they had exercised meticulous caution.

'Good!' declared Barquan Blasdel heartily. 'Still, the dissident spies are clever and viciously militant. They know no more fear than a spurgeon, and even less guilt for their misdeeds. But we are more clever than these spies. We know how to smell them out! In fact, the rank odor of an unmitigated spy issues from behind that stack of hood-facings. Fervents! Take the necessary measures!'

The Exemplar Fervents tore into the stack of facings. Barquan Blasdel came to watch. The Fervents found nothing. They looked at Barquan Blasdel, who pulled at his lip in annoyance. 'Well, well,' said Blasdel. 'A vigilance too extreme is preferable to carelessness.'

Below, where the pole passed through the float, Barway, by dint of taking a deep breath and holding his ear to the crevice, had heard the last remark. But now Barquan Blasdel returned to his previous place, and his words became muffled and incomprehensible.

Barquan Blasdel spoke for several minutes. All listened attentively, including the six Exemplars Barquan Blasdel had put on guard, to such an extent that presently they stood at the last row of the intercessors. Barquan Blasdel finally noticed and waved them back. One of these, more punctilious than the others, retreated past the edge of the hoodwink supply shed, where a man stood listening. 'Ho!' called the Exemplar. 'What do you do here?'

The man so detected gave a wave of all-indulgent tolerance and staggered drunkenly away.

'Halt!' cried the Exemplar. 'Return and declare yourself!' He jumped forward and dragged the man forth into the open area. All examined him with

245

attention. His skin was dark, his face was bland and bare of hair; he wore the nondescript snuff-colored smock of a Peculator or Malpractor.

Barquan Blasdel marched forward. 'Who are you? Why do you lurk in these forbidden precincts?'

The man staggered again and made a foolish gesture. 'Is this the tavern? Pour out the arrack, pour for all! I am a stranger on Apprise – I would know the quality of your food and drink.'

Vrink Smathe snorted. 'The fool is a spice-grinder and drunk. I have seen him often. Direct him to the inn.'

'No!' roared Blasdel, jerking forward in excitement. 'This is a dissident, this is a spy! I know him well! He has shaved his head and his face, but never can he defeat my acuity! He is here to learn our secrets!'

The group turned their attention upon the man, who blinked even more vehemently. 'A spy? Not I. I seek only a cup of arrack.'

Blasdel sniffed the air in front of the captive's face. 'There is no odor: neither beer nor arrack nor spirits of life. Come! All must satisfy themselves as to this so that there will be no subsequent contradictions and vacillations.'

'What is your name?' demanded Vogel Womack, the Adelvine Intercessor. 'Your float and your caste? Identify yourself!'

The captive took a deep breath, cast off his pretense of drunkenness. 'I am Henry Bastaff. I am a dissident. I am here to find if you plan evil against us. That is my sole purpose.'

'A spy!' cried Barquan Blasdel in a voice of horror. 'A self-confessed spy.'

The intercessors set up a chorus of indignant hoots. Barquan Blasdel said, 'He is guilty of at least a double offense: first, the various illegalities entering into his dissidence; and second, his insolent attempt to conspire against us, the staunch, the faithful, the true! As Chief Exemplar, I am compelled to demand the extreme penalty.'

Vogel Womack tried to temper Barquan Blasdel's wrath. 'Let us delay our judgment,' he remarked uneasily. 'Presently the man's deed may not appear so grave.'

Barquan Blasdel ignored him. 'This man is a vile dissident, an agent of turmoil and a spy. He must suffer an extreme penalty! To this declaration there will be allowed no appeal!'

Henry Bastaff was taken to Vrink Smathe's dwelling which stood nearby and confined in the workroom, with four Exemplars surrounding him and never for an instant taking away their gaze.

Henry Bastaff surveyed the surroundings. To right and left were shelves; at the back a screen concealed the hole through the float.

Henry Bastaff spoke to the Exemplars. 'I heard Blasdel's program. Are you men interested in what is to happen?'

None responded.

Henry Bastaff smiled wanly and looked toward the quarter of the room in which was the hole. 'Blasdel intends to lead King Kragen to the new floats, so that King Kragen may express his displeasure against the dissidents, and may also destroy whatever dissident boats stand in the way.'

No one spoke.

'To this end,' said Henry Bastaff in a clear and distinct voice, 'he has built floating sponge arbors to guarantee King Kragen an ample ration during the voyage, together with barges for more sponges, boats for the necessary advertisermen and a force of Exemplars to occupy New Home Float.'

The four men in uniform merely stared at him. After a few minutes Henry Bastaff repeated the information. He added: 'I may never see the New Floats again, but I hope I have helped us to freedom. Farewell to the men of the New Floats; I wish only that they could be warned of the evil which Barquan Blasdel plans to bring to them.'

'Silence!' spoke one of the Exemplars. 'You have ranted enough.'

CHAPTER SEVENTEEN

On the following day an alteration was made in the method by which King Kragen was tendered his oblation. Previously, when King Kragen approached a lagoon with the intent of feasting, arbors overgrown with sponges were floated to the edge of the net, for King Kragen to pluck with his palps. Now the sponges were plucked by advertisermen, heaped upon a great tray and floated forth between a pair of coracles. When the tray was in place, Barquan Blasdel went to Vrink Smathe's workroom, where he seemed not to see Henry Bastaff. He listened at the horn. King Kragen was close at hand; the scraping of his chitin armor sounded loud in the earpiece. Blasdel turned the crank which sent forth the summoning rattle. King Kragen's scraping ceased, then began once more, increasing in intensity. King Kragen was approaching.

He appeared from the east, turret and massive torso riding above the surface, the great rectangular platform gliding through the ocean on easy strokes of his vanes.

The forward eyes noted the offering. He eased forward, inspected the tray, and with his forward palps began to scoop the sponges into his maw.

From the float folk watched in somber speculation. Barquan Blasdel came forth to stand on the edge of the pad, to bow and gesticulate ritual approval as King Kragen ate.

The tray was empty. King Kragen made no move to depart. Blasdel swung about, called to a Fervent Exemplar. 'The sponges – how many were offered?'

'Seven bushels. King Kragen usually eats no more.'

'Today he seems to hunger. Are others plucked?'

'Those for the market: another five bushels.'

'They had best be tendered King Kragen; it is not well to stint.'

While King Kragen floated motionless, the coracles were pulled to the float. Another five bushels were poured upon the tray, and the tray thrust back toward King Kragen. Again he ate, consuming all but a bushel or two. Then, replete, he submerged till only his turret remained above water. And there he remained, moving sluggishly a few feet forward, a few feet backward.

Nine days later Maible and Barway, haggard as much from horror as privation, reported to the folk of New Float. 'On the following day King Kragen had not yet moved. It was clear that the new method of feeding had impressed him favorably. So at noon the tray was again filled, with at least ten bushels of sponge, and again King Kragen devoured the lot.

'During this time Henry Bastaff was moved from Smathe's workroom, and we could not learn of his new place of incarceration. This saddened us for we had intended to attempt his rescue through the horn hole.

'On the third day Blasdel made an announcement which went across the hoodwink towers, to the effect that King Kragen had demanded the privilege of executing the dissident spy who had sinned so grievously against him. At noon the tray went out. At the very top was a wide board supporting a single great sponge; and below, the usual heap. King Kragen had not moved fifty yards for three days. He approached the tray, reached for the topmost sponge. It seemed fastened to the board. King Kragen jerked, and so decapitated Henry Bastaff, whose head had been stuffed into the sponge. It was a horrible sight, with the blood spouting upon the pile of sponges. King Kragen seemed to devour them with particular relish.

'With Henry Bastaff dead, we no longer had reason to delay – except for curiosity. King Kragen showed no signs of moving, of visiting other floats. It was clear that he found the new feeding system to his liking. On the fourth day his meal was furnished by Granolt Float and ferried to Apprise by coracle. On the fifth day the sponges were brought from Sankston. It appears that King Kragen is now a permanent guest at Apprise Float – which is the essential first part of Blasdel's plan.'

There was a moment or two of silence. Phyral Berwick made a sound of revulsion. 'It is a situation which we must change.' He looked at Sklar Hast. 'How far advanced are your preparations?'

Sklar Hast pointed at Roger Kelso. 'Ask the man who smelts our metal.'

'Our resources are multiplying,' said Kelso. 'We have bled everyone on the float, twice or three times; this blood has yielded ten pounds of iron, which we have hammered and refined. It is now hard and tough beyond all belief – but still there is only ten pounds. The kragen and the sponge husks have given us much more copper: fifty or sixty pounds at a guess. Our electrical device has produced twenty-four flasks of acid of salt, which we maintain in bottles blown in our glass shop. This is now an establishment completely separated from the smelting.'

'Encouraging and interesting,' said Robin Magram, the Master Incendiary, a man not too imaginative, 'but how will it avail against King Kragen?'

'We haven't completed our experiments,' said Kelso. 'I can't give you a definite answer – yet. We need a live kragen, and they've been giving us a wide berth. Perhaps we'll be forced to go hunting.'

'Meanwhile,' said Sklar Hast, 'we can disrupt Blasdel's timetable.'

A month later, in the dead of night, with only starlight to guide them, six black coracles approached Tranque Float. It showed a barren unfamiliar silhouette, denuded of all verdure save for the central spikes and their attendant fronds. At the eastern end of the float were low barracks and a flat area apparently used as an exercise ground; at the western end was a bleak construction area, where the skeletons of sponge arbors glimmered white in the starlight.

The net across the lagoon mouth was cut. The coracles drifted into the lagoon, where were ranked long arbor after arbor, each bulging with ripe sponges. The men made silent play with knives, cutting away the withe floats and the anchor ropes; the arbors submerged, disappeared; the water of the lagoon rippled blank and vacant.

The coracles departed as stealthily as they had come. They circled the float. From the eastern side of Tranque, toward Thrasneck Float, extended six floating fingers to which were moored twelve double-hulled barges. Oil was poured into each hull, torches were flung; great flames thrust high into the sky, and angry cries came from the barracks. The black boats, with the men in black straining to the paddles, fled eastward across the ocean. For an hour the orange flames licked the sky, then slowly dwindled and died.

Two months later, a scout coracle, after a cautious reconnaissance, returned to report that the docks had been repaired, that new barges were nearly complete, that new arbors were in place, and that the area was patrolled continuously by Exemplars armed with pikes and swords.

CHAPTER EIGHTEEN

The year, which subsequently became known as the Year of the Exemplars, came to an end. Shortly after the beginning of the new year, three swindlers, working the water to the east of Tranque Float, sighted a fleet approaching from the east. The two younger swindlers made a hurried motion to haul in their lines, but the elder halted them. 'Our business is swindling; no more. Let the boats go by; they will not molest us.'

So the swindlers sat back and watched the flotilla pass. There were twelve galleys, rather high of freeboard, sheathed with a dull black membrane. Each carried a crew of thirty who sat low and rowed through holes in the hull, and thus were protected from missiles. They wore casques and corselets of the same black membrane that sheathed the hulls, and beside each was a bow, a dozen arrows with fire-bulb tips, a long lance with a tang of orange metal. The galleys accompanied a strange rectangular barge riding on three hulls. Platforms fore and aft supported a pair of bulky objects concealed by tarpaulins, with beside each a tub. In each of the three hulls were rows of squat glass vats, two hundred and ten in all, each of two quarts capacity, each two-thirds full of pale liquid. Like the galleys, the barge was propelled by oarsmen sitting low in the hulls and protected from hostile missiles by the screen of black membrane.

The Exemplars on Tranque Float observed the flotilla, and hoodwink towers flickered an alarm: *The ... dissidents ... are ... returning ... in ... force! ... They ... come ... in ... strange ... black ... canoes ... and ... an ... even ... more ... peculiar ... black ... barge ... They ... show ... no ... fear.*

Returning came instruction in a code unintelligible to those of the flotilla. They could now see the Tranque docks where the new barges floated and where already the laden arbors had been brought forth to be attached and towed astern. The docks swarmed with Exemplars, ready to defeat any attempt to destroy the barges a second time. But the flotilla sailed past, and the hoodwink towers flickered once again: *The ... dissidents ... proceed ... west ... They ... are ... passing ... Tranque ... Float ... It ... is ... difficult ... to ... conjecture ... their ... intent.* And back came coded instructions, evidently advising cautious observation, for the Exemplars boarded coracles and rowed on a course parallel to the flotilla, keeping a cautious two hundred yards between.

The flotilla continued up the line of floats: Thrasneck, Bickle, Green Lamp; at last Fay, Quatrefoil, and finally Apprise.

In the water before the lagoon lolled King Kragen – a bloated monstrous King Kragen, dwarfing the entire flotilla.

King Kragen became aware of the boats. He swung about, the monstrous vanes sucking whirlpools into the ocean. The eyes with opalescent films shifting back and forth fixed upon the black sheathing of galleys, armor, and barge, and he seemed to recognize the substance of kragen hide, for he emitted a snort of terrible displeasure. He jerked his vanes, and the ocean sucked and swirled.

The barge swung sidewise to King Kragen. The tarpaulins were jerked away from the platforms at either end, to reveal massive crossbow-like mechanisms fashioned from laminated stalk and kragen chitin, with cables woven from strips of kragen-leather. Two teams of men turned a windlass hauling back the great cross-arms. Into the channels were placed iron harpoons smelted from human blood. In the holds other men lowered four thousand plates of iron and copper into the glass vats.

King Kragen sensed menace. Why else should men be so bold? He twitched his vanes, inched forward – to within a hundred feet. Then he lunged. Vanes dug the water; with an ear-shattering shriek King Kragen charged, mandibles snapping.

The men at the crossbows were pale as sea-foam; their fingers twitched. Sklar Hast turned to call: 'Fire!' but his voice caught in his throat and what he intended for an incisive command came forth as a startled stammer. The command was nevertheless understood. The left crossbow thudded, snapped; the harpoon, trailing a black cable, sprang at King Kragen's turret, buried itself. King Kragen hissed.

The right crossbow thudded, snapped: the second harpoon stabbed deep into the turret. Sklar Hast motioned to the men in the hold. 'Connect!' The men joined copper to copper. In the hold two hundred and ten voltaic cells, each holding ten thin-leaved cathodes and ten thin-leaved anodes, connected first in series of seventy, and these series in parallel, poured a gush of electricity along the copper cables wrapped in varnished pad-skin leading to the harpoons. Into and through King Kragen's turret poured the energy, and King Kragen went stiff. His vanes protruded at right angles to his body. Sklar Hast laughed – an explosion of nervous relief. 'King Kragen is amenable, no less than the smaller kragen.'

'I never doubted,' said Roger Kelso.

They dove into the water, along with twenty others. They swam to King Kragen, clambered up the rigid subsurface platform; with mallets and copper chisels they attacked the lining between dome and turret wall.

On Apprise Float a great throng had gathered. One man, running back and forth, was Barquan Blasdel. He leaped into one of the coracles and, screaming orders, led the Exemplars against the Dissident flotilla.

Fire-arrows cut arcs across the sky; seven coracles burst into flames, and the Exemplars plunged into the water. The others swerved aside. Barquan Blasdel issued the most strenuous commands, but the Exemplars made no new sorties.

King Kragen floated stiff and still – eyes staring, palps protruding. His turret was thirty feet in circumference, but twenty-two men hacked with chisels, and now the lining was broken. Bars were inserted into the crack, all heaved. With a splitting sound the dome was dislodged. It slid over and in falling pulled away one of the harpoons. The circuit was broken; King Kragen once more owned his self-control.

For one galvanic instant he lay quiescent, trembling. Then he gave vent to an appalling scream, a sound which sent the folk on the float to their knees.

King Kragen hurled himself out of the water. The men who had hacked away his turret were flung far and wide, all except three who had managed to reach into the turret and cling to the knotted gray cords. One of these was Sklar Hast. While King Kragen lunged and thrashed, he slashed at the nerve nodes with his iron knife. Again King Kragen screamed, and thrust himself into the ocean. Water crashed down into the turret; two men were washed away. Sklar Hast, with arms and legs clenched among the strands, alone remained in place. The salt water on the exposed brain caused King Kragen great discomfort, and he sprang back out of the water, bent double. Sklar Hast hewed and hacked; the vanes, palps and mandibles jerked, contracted, twisted, snapped in accordance. King Kragen's vehemence lessened; he floated moaning with vanes dangling limp. Some of the men who had been flung away swam back; in a ceremony both dreadful and exalted King Kragen's nerve nodes were torn out and cast into the sea.

King Kragen floated limp, a lifeless hulk. The men plunged into the sea to wash themselves, swam back to the barge. The flotilla now eased toward Apprise Float. Sklar Hast stood on the forward platform. Barquan Blasdel cried to the folk: 'To arms! Stakes, chisels, mallets, knives, bludgeons! Smite the miscreants!'

Sklar Hast called to the throng: 'King Kragen is dead. What do you say to this?'

There was silence; then a faint cheer, and a louder cheer, and finally uproarious celebration.

Sklar Hast pointed a finger at Barquan Blasdel. 'That man must die. He organized the Exemplars. He murdered Henry Bastaff. He has fed your food to the vile King Kragen. He would have continued doing so until King Kragen overgrew the entire float.'

Barquan Blasdel cried to his Exemplars: 'Weapons at ready! Any who attack – kill!'

Sklar Hast called to the Exemplars: 'Throw down your weapons! You are finished. King Kragen is dead. You are Exemplars only to a dead sea-beast.'

Barquan Blasdel looked quickly in all directions. His Exemplars, outnumbered by the men of the float, showed no disposition to fight. Barquan Blasdel laughed brassily and turned away. 'Hold!' called Morse Swin, the Apprise Arbiter. 'Barquan Blasdel, return! You must face the verdict of a convocation!'

'Never! Not I!' Barquan Blasdel tried to push through the throng, and this was a mistake, for it triggered the counter-impulse to halt him. When he was touched, he smote, and again he erred, for the blow brought a counter-blow and Barquan Blasdel was presently torn to pieces. The crowd now turned upon the Exemplars, and all those who were unable to escape to the coracles shared Barquan Blasdel's fate. Those who fled in the coracles were intercepted by the black galleys, herded into a clot, where they surrendered themselves.

'Come ashore, men of the New Floats; deliver us the Exemplars, that they may be served like their fellows!' cried one from the float.

Another voice cried, 'Come greet your old friends, who long have been saddened at your absence!'

And another voice called, 'Tonight the arrack will flow; come drink your share! Tonight the yellow lamps will burn; we will play the pipes and dance; come dance in the light of our yellow lamps!'

Sklar Hast considered a moment, then he replied, 'We will come ashore, and we will deliver the prisoners. Let us have no more frantic bloodshed, however. Those who have committed crimes, let them face a convocation and be punished or freed according to our ancient traditions. Is it agreed? Otherwise we must return to New Floats!'

Morse Swin called out, 'We agree in all respects! Enough blood has been spilled; we want no more!'

'Then we come ashore, to rejoice with you!'

And the black boats of the New Floats landed upon Apprise; the men went ashore to greet old friends, caste-fellows and guild-brothers.

The corpse of King Kragen floated in the ocean, a desolate hulk. Already dusk had come; the hoodwink towers flickered in all earnest; from Tranque in the east to Almack and Sciona in the far west flashed the news. Intercessors stared mournfully across the water. Exemplars divested themselves of their uniforms and sheepishly mingled with those whom so recently they had treated with arrogance. They were derided and vilified, but none were injured; the mood of the folk was too rich and full. Before every hut yellow lamps flared; the oldest arrack, the most mellow spirits of life were brought forth; old friends drank together. All night, under the white constellations, there was revelry and joy and great thanksgiving that never again need the folk of the floats serve King Kragen or another like him.

THE DRAGON MASTERS
AND OTHER STORIES

The Miracle Workers

CHAPTER ONE

The war party from Faide Keep moved eastward across the downs: a column of a hundred armored knights, five hundred foot soldiers, a train of wagons. In the lead rode Lord Faide, a tall man in his early maturity, spare and cat-like, with a sallow dyspeptic face. He sat in the ancestral car of the Faides, a boat-shaped vehicle floating two feet above the moss, and carried, in add-ition to his sword and dagger, his ancestral side weapons.

An hour before sunset a pair of scouts came racing back to the column, their club-headed horses loping like dogs. Lord Faide braked the motion of his car. Behind him the Faide kinsmen, the lesser knights, the leather-capped foot soldiers halted; to the rear the baggage train and the high-wheeled wagons of the jinxmen creaked to a stop.

The scouts approached at breakneck speed, at the last instant flinging their horses sidewise. Long shaggy legs kicked out, padlike hooves plowed through the moss. The scouts jumped to the ground, ran forward. 'The way to Ballant Keep is blocked!'

Lord Faide rose in his seat, stood staring eastward over the gray–green downs. 'How many knights? How many men?'

'No knights, no men, Lord Faide. The First Folk have planted a forest be-tween North and South Wildwood.'

Lord Faide stood a moment in reflection, then seated himself, pushed the control knob. The car wheezed, jerked, moved forward. The knights touched up their horses; the foot soldiers resumed their slouching gait. At the rear the baggage train creaked into motion, together with the six wagons of the jinxmen.

The sun, large, pale and faintly pink, sank in the west. North Wildwood loomed down from the left, separated from South Wildwood by an area of stony ground, only sparsely patched with moss. As the sun passed behind the horizon, the new planting became visible: a frail new growth connecting the tracts of woodland like a canal between two seas.

Lord Faide halted his car, stepped down to the moss. He appraised the landscape, then gave the signal to make camp. The wagons were ranged in a circle, the gear unloaded. Lord Faide watched the activity for a moment, eyes sharp and critical, then turned and walked out across the downs through the lavender and green twilight. Fifteen miles to the east his last enemy awaited him: Lord Ballant of Ballant Keep. Contemplating tomorrow's battle, Lord

Faide felt reasonably confident of the outcome. His troops had been tempered by a dozen campaigns; his kinsmen were loyal and single-hearted. Head Jinxman to Faide Keep was Hein Huss, and associated with him were three of the most powerful jinxmen of Pangborn: Isak Comandore, Adam McAdam and the remarkable Enterlin, together with their separate troupes of cabalmen, spellbinders and apprentices. Altogether, an impressive assemblage. Certainly there were obstacles to be overcome: Ballant Keep was strong; Lord Ballant would fight obstinately; Anderson Grimes, the Ballant Head Jinxman, was efficient and highly respected. There was also this nuisance of the First Folk and the new planting which closed the gap between North and South Wildwood. The First Folk were a pale and feeble race, no match for human beings in single combat, but they guarded their forests with traps and deadfalls. Lord Faide cursed softly under his breath. To circle either North or South Wildwood meant a delay of three days, which could not be tolerated.

Lord Faide returned to the camp. Fires were alight, pots bubbled, orderly rows of sleep-holes had been dug into the moss. The knights groomed their horses within the corral of wagons; Lord Faide's own tent had been erected on a hummock, beside the ancient car.

Lord Faide made a quick round of inspection, noting every detail, speaking no word. The jinxmen were encamped a little distance apart from the troops. The apprentices and lesser spellbinders prepared food, while the jinxmen and cabalmen worked inside their tents, arranging cabinets and cases, correcting whatever disorder had been caused by the jolting of the wagons.

Lord Faide entered the tent of his Head Jinxman. Hein Huss was an enormous man, with arms and legs heavy as tree trunks, a torso like a barrel. His face was pink and placid, his eyes were water-clear; a stiff gray brush rose from his head, which was innocent of the cap jinxmen customarily wore against the loss of hair. Hein Huss disdained such precautions: it was his habit, showing his teeth in a face-splitting grin, to rumble, 'Why should anyone hoodoo me, old Hein Huss? I am so inoffensive. Whoever tried would surely die, of shame and remorse.'

Lord Faide found Huss busy at his cabinet. The doors stood wide, revealing hundreds of mannikins, each tied with a lock of hair, a bit of cloth, a fingernail clipping, daubed with grease, sputum, excrement, blood. Lord Faide knew well that one of these mannikins represented himself. He also knew that should he request it Hein Huss would deliver it without hesitation. Part of Huss' *mana* derived from his enormous confidence, the effortless ease of his power. He glanced at Lord Faide and read the question in his mind. 'Lord Ballant did not know of the new planting. Anderson Grimes has now informed him, and Lord Ballant expects that you will be delayed.

Grimes has communicated with Gisborne Keep and Castle Cloud. Three hundred men march tonight to reinforce Ballant Keep. They will arrive in two days. Lord Ballant is much elated.'

Lord Faide paced back and forth across the tent. 'Can we cross this planting?'

Hein Huss made a heavy sound of disapproval. 'There are many futures. In certain of these futures you pass. In others you do not pass. I cannot ordain these futures.'

Lord Faide had long learned to control his impatience at what sometimes seemed to be pedantic obfuscation. He grumbled, 'They are either very stupid or very bold planting across the downs in this fashion. I cannot imagine what they intend.'

Hein Huss considered, then grudgingly volunteered an idea. 'What if they plant west from North Wildwood to Sarrow Copse? What if they plant west from South Wildwood to Old Forest?'

'Then Faide Keep is almost ringed by forest.'

'And what if they join Sarrow Copse to Old Forest?'

Lord Faide stood stock-still, his eyes narrow and thoughtful. 'Faide Keep would be surrounded by forest. We would be imprisoned ... These plantings, do they proceed?'

'They proceed, so I have been told.'

'What do they hope to gain?'

'I do not know. Perhaps they hope to isolate the keeps, to rid the planet of men. Perhaps they merely want secure avenues between the forests.'

Lord Faide considered. Huss' final suggestion was reasonable enough. During the first centuries of human settlement, sportive young men had hunted First Folk with clubs and lances, eventually had driven them from their native downs into the forests. 'Evidently they are more clever than we realize. Adam McAdam asserts that they do not think, but it seems that he is mistaken.'

Hein Huss shrugged. 'Adam McAdam equates thought to the human cerebral process. He cannot telepathize with the First Folk, hence he deduces that they do not "think". But I have watched them at Forest Market, and they trade intelligently enough.' He raised his head, appeared to listen, then reached into his cabinet, delicately tightened a noose around the neck of one of the mannikins. From outside the tent came a sudden cough and a whooping gasp for air. Huss grinned, twitched open the noose. 'That is Isak Comandore's apprentice. He hopes to complete a Hein Huss mannikin. I must say he works diligently, going so far as to touch its feet into my footprints whenever possible.'

Lord Faide went to the flap of the tent. 'We break camp early. Be alert, I may require your help.' Lord Faide departed the tent.

Hein Huss continued the ordering of his cabinet. Presently he sensed the approach of his rival, Jinxman Isak Comandore, who coveted the office of Head Jinxman with all-consuming passion. Huss closed the cabinet and hoisted himself to his feet.

Comandore entered the tent, a man tall, crooked and spindly. His wedge-shaped head was covered with coarse russet ringlets; hot red–brown eyes peered from under his red eyebrows. 'I offer my complete rights to Keyril, and will include the masks, the headdress, the amulets. Of all the demons ever contrived he has won the widest public acceptance. To utter the name Keyril is to complete half the work of a possession. Keyril is a valuable property. I can give no more.'

But Huss shook his head. Comandore's desire was the full simulacrum of Tharon Faide, Lord Faide's oldest son, complete with clothes, hair, skin, eyelashes, tears, excrement, sweat and sputum – the only one in existence, for Lord Faide guarded his son much more jealously than he did himself. 'You offer convincingly,' said Huss, 'but my own demons suffice. The name Dant conveys fully as much terror as Keyril.'

'I will add five hairs from the head of Jinxman Clarence Sears; they are the last, for he is now stark bald.'

'Let us drop the matter; I will keep the simulacrum.'

'As you please,' said Comandore with asperity. He glanced out the flap of the tent. 'That blundering apprentice. He puts the feet of the mannikin backwards into your prints.'

Huss opened his cabinet, thumped a mannikin with his finger. From outside the tent came a grunt of surprise. Huss grinned. 'He is young and earnest, and perhaps he is clever, who knows?' He went to the flap of the tent, called outside. 'Hey, Sam Salazar, what do you do? Come inside.'

Apprentice Sam Salazar came blinking into the tent, a thick-set youth with a round florid face, overhung with a rather untidy mass of straw-colored hair. In one hand he carried a crude pot-bellied mannikin, evidently intended to represent Hein Huss.

'You puzzle both your master and myself,' said Huss. 'There must be method in your folly, but we fail to perceive it. For instance, this moment you place my simulacrum backwards into my track. I feel a tug on my foot, and you pay for your clumsiness.'

Sam Salazar showed small evidence of abashment. 'Jinxman Comandore has warned that we must expect to suffer for our ambitions.'

'If your ambition is jinxmanship,' Comandore declared sharply, 'you had best mend your ways.'

'The lad is craftier than you know,' said Hein Huss. 'Look now.' He took the mannikin from the youth, spit into its mouth, plucked a hair from his head, thrust it into a convenient crevice. 'He has a Hein Huss mannikin, achieved at very small cost. Now, Apprentice Salazar, how will you hoodoo me?'

'Naturally, I would never dare. I merely want to fill the bare spaces in my cabinet.'

Hein Huss nodded his approval. 'As good a reason as any. Of course you own a simulacrum of Isak Comandore?'

Sam Salazar glanced uneasily sidewise at Isak Comandore. 'He leaves none of his traces. If there is so much as an open bottle in the room, he breathes behind his hand.'

'Ridiculous!' exclaimed Hein Huss. 'Comandore, what do you fear?'

'I am conservative,' said Comandore dryly. 'You make a fine gesture, but some day an enemy may own that simulacrum; then you will regret your bravado.'

'Bah. My enemies are all dead, save one or two who dare not reveal themselves.' He clapped Sam Salazar a great buffet on the shoulder. 'Tomorrow, Apprentice Salazar, great things are in store for you.'

'What manner of great things?'

'Honor, noble self-sacrifice. Lord Faide must beg permission to pass Wildwood from the First Folk, which galls him. But beg he must. Tomorrow, Sam Salazar, I will elect you to lead the way to the parley, to deflect deadfalls, scythes and nettle-traps from the more important person who follows.'

Sam Salazar shook his head and drew back. 'There must be others more worthy; I prefer to ride in the rear with the wagons.'

Comandore waved him from the tent. 'You will do as ordered. Leave us; we have had enough apprentice talk.'

Sam Salazar departed. Comandore turned back to Hein Huss. 'In connection with tomorrow's battle, Anderson Grimes is especially adept with demons. As I recall, he has developed and successfully publicized Pont, who spreads sleep; Everid, a being of wrath; Deigne, a force of fear. We must take care that in countering these effects we do not neutralize each other.'

'True,' rumbled Huss. 'I have long maintained to Lord Faide that a single jinxman – the Head Jinxman in fact – is more effective than a group at cross-purposes. But he is consumed by ambition and does not listen.'

'Perhaps he wants to be sure that should advancing years overtake the Head Jinxman other equally effective jinxmen are at hand.'

'The future has many paths,' agreed Hein Huss. 'Lord Faide is well-advised to seek early for my successor, so that I may train him over the years. I plan to assess all the subsidiary jinxmen, and select the most promising. Tomorrow I relegate to you the demons of Anderson Grimes.'

Isak Comandore nodded politely. 'You are wise to give over responsibility. When I feel the weight of my years I hope I may act with similar forethought. Good night, Hein Huss. I go to arrange my demon masks. Tomorrow Keyril must walk like a giant.'

'Good night, Isak Comandore.'

Comandore swept from the tent, and Huss settled himself on his stool. Sam Salazar scratched at the flap. 'Well, lad?' growled Huss. 'Why do you loiter?'

Sam Salazar placed the Hein Huss mannikin on the table. 'I have no wish to keep this doll.'

'Throw it in a ditch, then.' Hein Huss spoke gruffly. 'You must stop annoying me with stupid tricks. You efficiently obtrude yourself upon my attention, but you cannot transfer from Comandore's troupe without his express consent.'

'If I gain his consent?'

'You will incur his enmity; he will open his cabinet against you. Unlike myself, you are vulnerable to a hoodoo. I advise you to be content. Isak Comandore is highly skilled and can teach you much.'

Sam Salazar still hesitated. 'Jinxman Comandore, though skilled, is intolerant of new thoughts.'

Hein Huss shifted ponderously on his stool, examined Sam Salazar with his water-clear eyes. 'What new thoughts are these? Your own?'

'The thoughts are new to me, and for all I know new to Isak Comandore. But he will say neither yes nor no.'

Hein Huss sighed, settled his monumental bulk more comfortably. 'Speak then, describe these thoughts, and I will assess their novelty.'

'First, I have wondered about trees. They are sensitive to light, to moisture, to wind, to pressure. Sensitivity implies sensation. Might a man feel into the soul of a tree for these sensations? If a tree were capable of awareness, this faculty might prove useful. A man might select trees as sentinels in strategic sites, and enter into them as he chose.'

Hein Huss was skeptical. 'An amusing notion, but practically not feasible. The reading of minds, the act of possession, televoyance, all similar interplay, require psychic congruence as a basic condition. The minds must be able to become identities at some particular stratum. Unless there is sympathy, there is no linkage. A tree is at opposite poles from a man; the images of tree and man are incommensurable. Hence, anything more than the most trifling flicker of comprehension must be a true miracle of jinxmanship.'

Sam Salazar nodded mournfully. 'I realize this, and at one time hoped to equip myself with the necessary identification.'

'To do this you must become a vegetable. Certainly the tree will never become a man.'

'So I reasoned,' said Sam Salazar. 'I went alone into a grove of trees, where I chose a tall conifer. I buried my feet in the mold, I stood silent and naked – in the sunlight, in the rain; at dawn, noon, dusk, midnight. I closed my mind to man-thoughts, I closed my eyes to vision, my ears to sound. I took no nourishment except from rain and sun. I sent roots forth from my feet and branches from my torso. Thirty hours I stood, and two days later another thirty hours, and after two days another thirty hours. I made myself a tree, as nearly as possible to one of flesh and blood.'

Hein Huss gave the great inward gurgle which signalized his amusement. 'And you achieved sympathy?'

'Nothing useful,' Sam Salazar admitted. 'I felt something of the tree's sensations – the activity of light, the peace of dark, the coolness of rain. But visual and auditory experience – nothing. However, I do not regret the trial. It was a useful discipline.'

'An interesting effort, even if inconclusive. The idea is by no means of startling originality, but the empiricism – to use an archaic word – of your method is bold, and no doubt antagonized Isak Comandore, who has no patience with the superstitions of our ancestors. I suspect that he harangued you against frivolity, metaphysics and inspirationalism.'

'True,' said Sam Salazar. 'He spoke at length.'

'You should take the lesson to heart. Isak Comandore is sometimes unable to make the most obvious truth seem credible. However, I cite you the example of Lord Faide who considers himself an enlightened man, free from superstition. Still, he rides in his feeble car, he carries a pistol sixteen hundred years old, he relies on Hellmouth to protect Faide Keep.'

'Perhaps – unconsciously – he longs for the old magical times,' suggested Sam Salazar thoughtfully.

'Perhaps,' agreed Hein Huss. 'And you do likewise?'

Sam Salazar hesitated. 'There is an aura of romance, a kind of wild grandeur to the old days – but of course,' he added quickly, 'mysticism is no substitute for orthodox logic.'

'Naturally not,' agreed Hein Huss. 'Now go; I must consider the events of tomorrow.'

Sam Salazar departed, and Hein Huss, rumbling and groaning, hoisted himself to his feet. He went to the flap of his tent, surveyed the camp. All now was quiet. The fires were embers, the warriors lay in the pits they had cut into the moss. To north and south spread the woodlands. Among the trees and out on the downs were faint flickering luminosities, where the First Folk gathered spore-pods from the moss.

Hein Huss became aware of a nearby personality. He turned his head and saw approaching the shrouded form of Jinxman Enterlin, who concealed his face, who spoke only in whispers, who disguised his natural gait with a stiff stiltlike motion. By this means he hoped to reduce his vulnerability to hostile jinxmanship. The admission carelessly let fall of failing eyesight, of stiff joints, forgetfulness, melancholy, nausea might be of critical significance in controversy by hoodoo. Jinxmen therefore maintained the pose of absolute health and virility, even though they must grope blindly or limp doubled up from cramps.

Hein Huss called out to Enterlin, lifted back the flap to the tent. Enterlin entered; Huss went to the cabinet, brought forth a flask, poured liquor into a pair of stone cups. 'A cordial only, free of overt significance.'

'Good,' whispered Enterlin, selecting the cup farthest from him. 'After all, we jinxmen must relax into the guise of men from time to time.' Turning his back on Huss, he introduced the cup through the folds of his hood, drank. 'Refreshing,' he whispered. 'We need refreshment; tomorrow we must work.'

Huss issued his reverberating chuckle. 'Tomorrow Isak Comandore matches demons with Anderson Grimes. We others perform only subsidiary duties.'

Enterlin seemed to make a quizzical inspection of Hein Huss through the black gauze before his eyes. 'Comandore will relish this opportunity. His vehemence oppresses me, and his is a power which feeds on success. He is a man of fire, you are a man of ice.'

'Ice quenches fire.'

'Fire sometimes melts ice.'

Hein Huss shrugged. 'No matter. I grow weary. Time has passed all of us by. Only a moment ago a young apprentice showed me to myself.'

'As a powerful jinxman, as Head Jinxman to the Faides, you have cause for pride.'

Hein Huss drained the stone cup, set it aside. 'No. I see myself at the top of my profession, with nowhere else to go. Only Sam Salazar the apprentice thinks to search for more universal lore; he comes to me for counsel, and I do not know what to tell him.'

'Strange talk, strange talk!' whispered Enterlin. He moved to the flap of the tent. 'I go now,' he whispered. 'I go to walk on the downs. Perhaps I will see the future.'

'There are many futures.'

Enterlin rustled away and was lost in the dark. Hein Huss groaned and grumbled, then took himself to his couch, where he instantly fell asleep.

CHAPTER TWO

The night passed. The sun, flickering with films of pink and green, lifted over the horizon. The new planting of the First Folk was silhouetted, a sparse stubble of saplings, against the green and lavender sky. The troops broke camp with practiced efficiency. Lord Faide marched to his car, leaped within; the machine sagged under his weight. He pushed a button, the car drifted forward, heavy as a waterlogged timber.

A mile from the new planting he halted, sent a messenger back to the wagons of the jinxmen. Hein Huss walked ponderously forward, followed by Isak Comandore, Adam McAdam and Enterlin. Lord Faide spoke to Hein Huss. 'Send someone to speak to the First Folk. Inform them we wish to pass, offering them no harm, but that we will react savagely to any hostility.'

'I will go myself,' said Hein Huss. He turned to Comandore. 'Lend me, if you will, your brash young apprentice. I can put him to good use.'

'If he unmasks a nettle-trap by blundering into it, his first useful deed will be done,' said Comandore. He signaled to Sam Salazar, who came reluctantly forward. 'Walk in front of Head Jinxman Hein Huss that he may encounter no traps or scythes. Take a staff to probe the moss.'

Without enthusiasm Sam Salazar borrowed a lance from one of the foot soldiers. He and Huss set forth along the low rise that previously had separated North from South Wildwood. Occasionally outcroppings of stone penetrated the cover of moss; here and there grew bayberry trees, clumps of tarplant, ginger-tea and rosewort.

A half-mile from the planting Huss halted. 'Now take care, for here the traps will begin. Walk clear of hummocks, these often conceal swing-scythes; avoid moss which shows a pale blue; it is dying or sickly and may cover a deadfall or a nettle-trap.'

'Why cannot you locate the traps by clairvoyance?' asked Sam Salazar in a rather sullen voice. 'It appears an excellent occasion for the use of these faculties.'

'The question is natural,' said Hein Huss with composure. 'However you must know that when a jinxman's own profit or security is at stake his emotions play tricks on him. I would see traps everywhere and would never know whether clairvoyance or fear prompted me. In this case, that lance is a more reliable instrument than my mind.'

Sam Salazar made a salute of understanding and set forth, with Hein Huss stumping behind him. At first he prodded with care, uncovering two traps, then advanced more jauntily; so swiftly indeed that Huss called out in exasperation, 'Caution, unless you court death!'

Sam Salazar obligingly slowed his pace. 'There are traps all around us, but I detect the pattern, or so I believe.'

'Ah, ha, you do? Reveal it to me, if you will. I am only Head Jinxman, and ignorant.'

'Notice. If we walk where the spore-pods have recently been harvested, then we are secure.'

Hein Huss grunted. 'Forward then. Why do you dally? We must do battle at Ballant Keep today.'

Two hundred yards further, Sam Salazar stopped short. 'Go on, boy, go on!' grumbled Hein Huss.

'The savages threaten us. You can see them just inside the planting. They hold tubes which they point toward us.'

Hein Huss peered, then raised his head and called out in the sibilant language of the First Folk.

A moment or two passed, then one of the creatures came forth, a naked humanoid figure, ugly as a demon-mask. Foam-sacs bulged under its arms, orange-lipped foam-vents pointed forward. Its back was wrinkled and loose, the skin serving as a bellows to blow air through the foam-sacs. The fingers of the enormous hands ended in chisel-shaped blades, the head was sheathed in chitin. Billion-faceted eyes swelled from either side of the head, glowing like black opals, merging without definite limit into the chitin. This was a representative of the original inhabitants of the planet, who until the coming of man had inhabited the downs, burrowing in the moss, protecting themselves behind masses of foam exuded from the underarm sacs.

The creature wandered close, halted. 'I speak for Lord Faide of Faide Keep,' said Huss. 'Your planting bars his way. He wishes that you guide him through, so that his men do not damage the trees, or spring the traps you have set against your enemies.'

'Men are our enemies,' responded the autochthon. 'You may spring as many traps as you care to; that is their purpose.' It backed away.

'One moment,' said Hein Huss sternly. 'Lord Faide must pass. He goes to battle Lord Ballant. He does not wish to battle the First Folk. Therefore it is wise to guide him across the planting without hindrance.'

The creature considered a second or two. 'I will guide him.' He stalked across the moss toward the war party.

Behind followed Hein Huss and Sam Salazar. The autochthon, legs articulated more flexibly than a man's, seemed to weave and wander, occasionally pausing to study the ground ahead.

'I am puzzled,' Sam Salazar told Hein Huss. 'I cannot understand the creature's actions.'

'Small wonder,' grunted Hein Huss. 'He is one of the First Folk, you are human. There is no basis for understanding.'

'I disagree,' said Sam Salazar seriously.

'Eh?' Hein Huss inspected the apprentice with vast disapproval. 'You engage in contention with me, Head Jinxman Hein Huss?'

'Only in a limited sense,' said Sam Salazar. 'I see a basis for understanding with the First Folk in our common ambition to survive.'

'A truism,' grumbled Hein Huss. 'Granting this community of interests with the First Folk, what is your perplexity?'

'The fact that it first refused, then agreed to conduct us across the planting.'

Hein Huss nodded. 'Evidently the information which intervened, that we go to fight at Ballant Keep, occasioned the change.'

'This is clear,' said Sam Salazar. 'But think—'

'You exhort me to think?' roared Hein Huss.

'—here is one of the First Folk, apparently without distinction, who makes an important decision instantly. Is he one of their leaders? Do they live in anarchy?'

'It is easy to put questions,' Hein Huss said gruffly. 'It is not as easy to answer them.'

'In short—'

'In short, I do not know. In any event, they are pleased to see us killing one another.'

CHAPTER THREE

The passage through the planting was made without incident. A mile to the east the autochthon stepped aside and without formality returned to the forest. The war party, which had been marching in single file, regrouped into its usual formation. Lord Faide called Hein Huss and made the unusual gesture of inviting him up into the seat beside him. The ancient car dipped and sagged; the power-mechanism whined and chattered. Lord Faide, in high good spirits, ignored the noise. 'I feared that we might be forced into a time-consuming wrangle. What of Lord Ballant? Can you read his thoughts?'

Hein Huss cast his mind forth. 'Not clearly. He knows of our passage. He is disturbed.'

Lord Faide laughed sardonically. 'For excellent reason! Listen now, I will explain the plan of battle so that all may coordinate their efforts.'

'Very well.'

'We approach in a wide line. Ballant's great weapon is of course Volcano. A decoy must wear my armor and ride in the lead. The yellow-haired apprentice is perhaps the most expendable member of the party. In this way we will learn the potentialities of Volcano. Like our own Hellmouth, it was built to repel vessels from space and cannot command the ground immediately under the keep. Therefore we will advance in dispersed formation, to regroup two hundred yards from the keep. At this point the jinxmen will impel Lord Ballant forth from the keep. You no doubt have made plans to this end.'

Hein Huss gruffly admitted that such was the case. Like other jinxmen, he enjoyed the pose that his power sufficed for extemporaneous control of any situation.

Lord Faide was in no mood for niceties and pressed for further information. Grudging each word, Hein Huss disclosed his arrangements. 'I have prepared certain influences to discomfit the Ballant defenders and drive them forth. Jinxman Enterlin will sit at his cabinet, ready to retaliate if Lord Ballant orders a spell against you. Anderson Grimes undoubtedly will cast a demon – probably Everid – into the Ballant warriors; in return, Jinxman Comandore will possess an equal or a greater number of Faide warriors with the demon Keyril, who is even more ghastly and horrifying.'

'Good. What more?'

'There is need for no more, if your men fight well.'

'Can you see the future? How does today end?'

'There are many futures. Certain jinxmen – Enterlin for instance – profess to see the thread which leads through the maze; they are seldom correct.'

'Call Enterlin here.'

Hein Huss rumbled his disapproval. 'Unwise, if you desire victory over Ballant Keep.'

Lord Faide inspected the massive jinxman from under his black saturnine brows. 'Why do you say this?'

'If Enterlin foretells defeat, you will be dispirited and fight poorly. If he predicts victory, you become overconfident and likewise fight poorly.'

Lord Faide made a petulant gesture. 'The jinxmen are loud in their boasts until the test is made. Then they always find reasons to retract, to qualify.'

'Ha, ha!' barked Hein Huss. 'You expect miracles, not honest jinxmanship. I spit—' he spat. 'I predict that the spittle will strike the moss. The probabilities are high. But an insect might fly in the way. One of the First Folk might rise through the moss. The chances are slight. In the next instant there is only one future. A minute hence there are four futures. Five minutes hence, twenty futures. A billion futures could not express all the possibilities of tomorrow. Of these billion, certain are more probable than others. It is true that these probable futures sometimes send a delicate influence into the jinxman's brain. But unless he is completely impersonal and disinterested, his own desires overwhelm this influence. Enterlin is a strange man. He hides himself, he has no appetites. Occasionally his auguries are exact. Nevertheless, I advise against consulting him. You do better to rely on the practical and real uses of jinxmanship.'

Lord Faide said nothing. The column had been marching along the bottom of a low swale; the car had been sliding easily downslope. Now they came to a rise, and the power-mechanism complained so vigorously that Lord Faide was compelled to stop the car. He considered. 'Once over the crest we will be in view of Ballant Keep. Now we must disperse. Send the least valuable man in your troupe forward – the apprentice who tested out the moss. He must wear my helmet and corselet and ride in the car.'

Hein Huss alighted, returned to the wagons, and presently Sam Salazar came forward. Lord Faide eyed the round, florid face with distaste. 'Come close,' he said crisply. Sam Salazar obeyed. 'You will now ride in my place,' said Lord Faide. 'Notice carefully. This rod impels a forward motion. This arm steers – to right, to left. To stop, return the rod to its first position.'

Sam Salazar pointed to some of the other arms, toggles, switches and buttons. 'What of these?'

'They are never used.'

'And these dials, what is their meaning?'

Lord Faide curled his lip, on the brink of one of his quick furies. 'Since their use is unimportant to me, it is twenty times unimportant to you. Now. Put this cap on your head, and this helmet. See to it that you do not sweat.'

Sam Salazar gingerly settled the magnificent black and green crest of Faide on his head, with a cloth cap underneath.

'Now this corselet.'

The corselet was constructed of green and black metal sequins, with a pair of scarlet dragon-heads at either side of the breast.

'Now the cloak.' Lord Faide flung the black cloak over Sam Salazar's shoulders. 'Do not venture too close to Ballant Keep. Your purpose is to attract the fire of Volcano. Maintain a lateral motion around the keep, outside of dart range. If you are killed by a dart, the whole purpose of the deception is thwarted.'

'You prefer me to be killed by Volcano?' inquired Sam Salazar.

'No. I wish to preserve the car and the crest. These are relics of great value. Evade destruction by all means possible. The ruse probably will deceive no one; but if it does, and if it draws the fire of Volcano, I must sacrifice the Faide car. Now – sit in my place.'

Sam Salazar climbed into the car, settled himself on the seat.

'Sit straight,' roared Lord Faide. 'Hold your head up! You are simulating Lord Faide! You must not appear to slink!'

Sam Salazar heaved himself erect in the seat. 'To simulate Lord Faide most effectively, I should walk among the warriors, with someone else riding in the car.'

Lord Faide glared, then grinned sourly. 'No matter. Do as I have commanded.'

CHAPTER FOUR

Sixteen hundred years before, with war raging through space, a group of space captains, their home-bases destroyed, had taken refuge on Pangborn. To protect themselves against vengeful enemies, they built great forts armed with weapons from the dismantled spaceships.

The wars receded, Pangborn was forgotten. The newcomers drove the First Folk into the forests, planted and harvested the river valleys. Ballant Keep, like Faide Keep, Castle Cloud, Boghoten and the rest, overlooked one of these valleys. Four squat towers of a dense black substance supported an enormous parasol roof, and were joined by walls two-thirds as high as the towers. At the peak of the roof a cupola housed Volcano, the weapon corresponding to Faide's Hellmouth.

The Faide war party advancing over the rise found the great gates already secure, the parapets between the towers thronged with bowmen. According to Lord Faide's strategy, the war party advanced on a broad front. At the center rode Sam Salazar, resplendent in Lord Faide's armor. He made, however, small effort to simulate Lord Faide. Rather than sitting proudly erect, he crouched at the side of the seat, the crest canted at an angle. Lord Faide watched with disgust. Apprentice Salazar's reluctance to be demolished was understandable; if his impersonation failed to convince Lord Ballant, at least the Faide ancestral car might be spared. For a certainty Volcano was being manned; the Ballant gun-tender could be seen in the cupola, and the snout protruded at a menacing angle.

Apparently the tactic of dispersal, offering no single tempting target, was effective. The Faide war party advanced quickly to a point two hundred yards from the keep, below Volcano's effective field, without drawing fire; first the knights, then the foot soldiers, then the rumbling wagons of the magicians. The slow-moving Faide car was far outdistanced; any doubt as to the nature of the ruse must now be extinguished.

Apprentice Salazar, disliking the isolation, and hoping to increase the speed of the car, twisted one of the other switches, then another. From under the floor came a thin screeching sound; the car quivered and began to rise. Sam Salazar peered over the side, threw out a leg to jump. Lord Faide ran forward, gesturing and shouting. Sam Salazar hastily drew back his leg, returned the switches to their previous condition. The car dropped like a rock. He snapped the switches up again, cushioning the fall.

'Get out of that car!' roared Lord Faide. He snatched away the helmet, dealt Sam Salazar a buffet which toppled him head over heels. 'Out of the armor; back to your duties!'

Sam Salazar hurried to the jinxmen's wagons, where he helped erect Isak Comandore's black tent. Inside the tent a black carpet with red and yellow patterns was laid; Comandore's cabinet, his chair and his chest were carried in, and incense set burning in a censer. Directly in front of the main gate Hein Huss superintended the assembly of a rolling stage, forty feet tall and sixty feet long, the surface concealed from Ballant Keep by a tarpaulin.

Meanwhile, Lord Faide had dispatched an emissary, enjoining Lord Ballant to surrender. Lord Ballant delayed his response, hoping to delay the attack as long as possible. If he could maintain himself a day and a half, reinforcements from Gisborne Keep and Castle Cloud might force Lord Faide to retreat.

Lord Faide waited only until the jinxmen had completed their preparations, then sent another messenger, offering two more minutes in which to surrender.

One minute passed, two minutes. The envoys turned on their heels, marched back to the camp.

Lord Faide spoke to Hein Huss. 'You are prepared?'

'I am prepared,' rumbled Hein Huss.

'Drive them forth.'

Huss raised his arm; the tarpaulin dropped from the face of his great display, to reveal a painted representation of Ballant Keep.

Huss retired to his tent, pulled the flaps together. Braziers burnt fiercely, illuminating the faces of Adam McAdam, eight cabalmen and six of the most advanced spellbinders. Each worked at a bench supporting several dozen dolls and a small glowing brazier. The cabalmen and spellbinders worked with dolls representing Ballant men-at-arms; Huss and Adam McAdam employed simulacra of the Ballant knights. Lord Ballant would not be hoodooed unless he ordered a jinx against Lord Faide – a courtesy the keep-lords extended each other.

Huss called out: 'Sebastian!'

Sebastian, one of Huss' spellbinders, waiting at the flap to the tent, replied, 'Ready, sir.'

'Begin the display.'

Sebastian ran to the stage, struck fire to a fuse. Watchers inside Ballant Keep saw the depicted keep take fire. Flame erupted from the windows, the roof glowed and crumbled. Inside the tent the two jinxmen, the cabalmen and the spellbinders methodically took dolls, dipped them into the heat of the braziers, concentrating, reaching out for the mind of the man whose doll they burnt. Within the keep men became uneasy. Many began to imagine burning sensations, which became more severe as their minds grew more sensitive to the idea of fire. Lord Ballant noted the uneasiness. He signaled to his chief jinxman Anderson Grimes. 'Begin the counterspell.'

Down the front of the keep unrolled a display even larger than Hein Huss', depicting a hideous beast. It stood on four legs and was shown picking up two men in a pair of hands, biting off their heads. Grimes' cabalmen meanwhile took up dolls representing the Faide warriors, inserted them into models of the depicted beast, closed the hinged jaws, all the while projecting ideas of fear and disgust. And the Faide warriors, staring at the depicted monster, felt a sense of horror and weakness.

Inside Huss' tent the braziers reeked and dolls smoked. Eyes stared, brows glistened. From time to time one of the workers gasped – signaling the entry of his projection into an enemy mind. Within the keep warriors began to mutter, to slap at burning skin, to eye each other fearfully, noting each other's symptoms. Finally one cried out, and tore at his armor. 'I burn! The cursed witches burn me!' His pain aggravated the discomfort of the others; there was a growing sound throughout the keep.

Lord Ballant's oldest son, his mind penetrated by Hein Huss himself, struck his shield with his mailed fist. 'They burn me! They burn us all! Better to fight than burn!'

'Fight! Fight!' came the voices of the tormented men.

Lord Ballant looked around at the twisted faces, some displaying blisters, scaldmarks. 'Our own spell terrifies them; wait yet a moment!' he pleaded.

His brother called hoarsely, 'It is not your belly that Hein Huss toasts in the flames, it is mine! We cannot win a battle of hoodoos; we must win a battle of arms!'

Lord Ballant cried desperately, 'Wait, our own effects are working! They will flee in terror; wait, wait!'

His cousin tore off his corselet. 'It's Hein Huss! I feel him! My leg's in the fire, the devil laughs at me. Next my head, he says. Fight, or I go forth to fight alone!'

'Very well,' said Lord Ballant in a fateful voice. 'We go forth to fight. First – the beast goes forth. Then we follow and smite them in their terror.'

The gates to the keep swung suddenly wide. Out sprang what appeared to be the depicted monster: legs moving, arms waving, eyes rolling, issuing evil sounds. Normally the Faide warriors would have seen the monster for what it was: a model carried on the backs of three horses. But their minds had been influenced; they had been infected with horror; they drew back with arms hanging flaccid. From behind the monster the Ballant knights galloped, followed by the Ballant foot soldiers. The charge gathered momentum, tore into the Faide center. Lord Faide bellowed orders; discipline asserted itself. The Faide knights disengaged, divided into three platoons, engulfed the Ballant charge, while the foot soldiers poured darts into the advancing ranks.

There was the clatter and surge of battle; Lord Ballant, seeing that his sally had failed to overwhelm the Faide forces, and thinking to conserve his own forces, ordered a retreat. In good order the Ballant warriors began to back up toward the keep. The Faide knights held close contact, hoping to win to the courtyard. Close behind came a heavily loaded wagon pushed by armored horses, to be wedged against the gate.

Lord Faide called an order; a reserve platoon of ten knights charged from the side, thrust behind the main body of Ballant horsemen, rode through the foot soldiers, fought into the keep, cut down the gate-tenders.

Lord Ballant bellowed to Anderson Grimes, 'They have won inside; quick with your cursed demon! If he can help us, let him do so now!'

'Demon-possession is not a matter of an instant,' muttered the jinxman. 'I need time.'

'You have no time! Ten minutes and we're all dead!'

'I will do my best. Everid, Everid, come swift!'

He hastened into his workroom, donned his demon-mask, tossed handful after handful of incense into the brazier. Against one wall stood a great form: black, slit-eyed, noseless. Great white fangs hung from its upper palate; it stood on heavy bent legs, arms reached forward to grasp. Anderson Grimes swallowed a cup of syrup, paced slowly back and forth. A moment passed.

'Grimes!' came Ballant's call from outside. 'Grimes!'

A voice spoke. 'Enter without fear.'

Lord Ballant, carrying his ancestral side-arm, entered. He drew back with an involuntary sound. 'Grimes!' he whispered.

'Grimes is not here,' said the voice. 'I am here. Enter.'

Lord Ballant came forward stiff-legged. The room was dark except for the feeble glimmer of the brazier. Anderson Grimes crouched in a corner, head bowed under his demon-mask. The shadows twisted and pulsed with shapes and faces, forms struggling to become solid. The black image seemed to vibrate with life.

'Bring in your warriors,' said the voice. 'Bring them in five at a time, bid them look only at the floor until commanded to raise their eyes.'

Lord Ballant retreated; there was no sound in the room.

A moment passed; then five limp and exhausted warriors filed into the room, eyes low.

'Look slowly up,' said the voice. 'Look at the orange fire. Breathe deeply. Then look at me. I am Everid, Demon of Hate. Look at me. Who am I?'

'You are Everid, Demon of Hate,' quavered the warriors.

'I stand all around you, in a dozen forms ... I come closer. Where am I?'
'You are close.'

'Now I am you. We are together.'

There was a sudden quiver of motion. The warriors stood straighter, their faces distorted.

'Go forth,' said the voice. 'Go quietly into the court. In a few minutes we march forth to slay.'

The five stalked forth. Five more entered.

Outside the wall the Ballant knights had retreated as far as the gate; within, seven Faide knights still survived, and with their backs to the wall held the Ballant warriors away from the gate mechanism.

In the Faide camp Huss called to Comandore, 'Everid is walking. Bring forth Keyril.'

'Send the men,' came Comandore's voice, low and harsh. 'Send the men to me. I am Keyril.'

Within the keep twenty warriors came marching into the courtyard. Their steps were cautious, tentative, slow. Their faces had lost individuality, they were twisted and distorted, curiously alike.

'Bewitched!' whispered the Ballant soldiers, drawing back. The seven Faide knights watched with sudden fright. But the twenty warriors, paying them no heed, marched out the gate. The Ballant knights parted; for an instant there was a lull in the fighting. The twenty sprang like tigers. Their swords glistened, twinkling in water-bright arcs. They crouched, jerked, jumped; Faide arms, legs, heads were hewed off. The twenty were cut and battered, but the blows seemed to have no effect.

The Faide attack faltered, collapsed. The knights, whose armor was no protection against the demoniac swords, retreated. The twenty possessed warriors raced out into the open toward the foot soldiers, running with great strides, slashing and rending. The Faide foot soldiers fought for a moment, then they too gave way and turned to flee.

From behind Comandore's tent appeared thirty Faide warriors, marching stiffly, slowly. Like the Ballant twenty their faces were alike – but between the Everid-possessed and the Keyril-possessed was the difference between the face of Everid and the face of Keyril.

Keyril and Everid fought, using the men as weapons, without fear, retreat, or mercy. Hack, chop, cut. Arms, legs, sundered torsos. Bodies fought headless for moments before collapsing. Only when a body was minced, hacked to bits, did the demoniac vitality depart. Presently there were no more men of Everid, and only fifteen men of Keyril. These hopped and limped and tumbled toward the keep where Faide knights still held the gate. The Ballant knights met them in despair, knowing that now was the decisive moment. Leaping, leering from chopped faces, slashing from tireless arms, the warriors cut a hole into the iron. The Faide knights, roaring victory cries, plunged after. Into the courtyard surged the battle, and now there was no longer doubt of the outcome. Ballant Keep was taken.

Back in his tent Isak Comandore took a deep breath, shuddered, flung down his demon-mask. In the courtyard the twelve remaining warriors dropped in their tracks, twitched, gasped, gushed blood and died.

Lord Ballant, in the last gallant act of a gallant life, marched forth brandishing his ancestral side-arm. He aimed across the bloody field at Lord Faide, pulled the trigger. The weapon spewed a brief gout of light; Lord Faide's skin prickled and hair rose from his head. The weapon crackled, turned cherry-red and melted. Lord Ballant threw down the weapon, drew his sword, marched forth to challenge Lord Faide.

Lord Faide, disinclined to unnecessary combat, signaled to his soldiers. A flight of darts ended Lord Ballant's life, saving him the discomfort of formal execution.

There was no further resistance. The Ballant defenders threw down their arms, marched grimly out to kneel before Lord Faide, while inside the keep the Ballant women gave themselves to mourning and grief.

CHAPTER FIVE

Lord Faide had no wish to linger at Ballant Keep, for he took no relish in his victories. Inevitably, a thousand decisions had to be made. Six of the closest Ballant kinsmen were summarily stabbed and the title declared defunct. Others of the clan were offered a choice: an oath of lifelong fealty together with a moderate ransom, or death. Only two, eyes blazing hate, chose death and were instantly stabbed.

Lord Faide had now achieved his ambition. For over a thousand years the keep-lords had struggled for power; now one, now another gaining ascendancy. None before had ever extended his authority across the entire continent – which meant control of the planet, since all other land was either sun-parched rock or eternal ice. Ballant Keep had long thwarted Lord Faide's drive to power; now – success, total and absolute. It still remained to chastise the lords of Castle Cloud and Gisborne, both of whom, seeing opportunity to overwhelm Lord Faide, had ranged themselves behind Lord Ballant. But these were matters that might well be assigned to Hein Huss.

Lord Faide, for the first time in his life, felt a trace of uncertainty. Now what? No real adversaries remained. The First Folk must be whipped back, but here was no great problem; they were numerous, but no more than savages. He knew that dissatisfaction and controversy would ultimately arise among his kinsmen and allies. Inaction and boredom would breed irritability; idle minds would calculate the pros and cons of mischief. Even the most loyal would remember the campaigns with nostalgia and long for the excitement, the release, the license, of warfare. Somehow he must find means to absorb the energy of so many active and keyed-up men. How and where, this was the problem. The construction of roads? New farmland claimed from the downs? Yearly tournaments-at-arms? Lord Faide frowned at the inadequacy of his solutions, but his imagination was impoverished by the lack of tradition. The original settlers of Pangborn had been warriors, and had brought with them a certain amount of practical rule-of-thumb knowledge, but little else. The tales they passed down the generations described the great spaceships which moved with magic speed and certainty, the miraculous weapons, the wars in the void, but told nothing of human history or civilized achievement. And so Lord Faide, full of power and success, but with no goal toward which to turn his strength, felt more morose and saturnine than ever.

He gloomily inspected the spoils from Ballant Keep. They were of no great interest to him. Ballant's ancestral car was no longer used, but displayed behind a glass case. He inspected the weapon Volcano, but this could not be moved. In any event it was useless, its magic lost forever. Lord Faide now knew that Lord Ballant had ordered it turned against the Faide car, but that it had refused to spew its vaunted fire. Lord Faide saw with disdainful amusement that Volcano had been sadly neglected. Corrosion had pitted the metal, careless cleaning had twisted the exterior tubing, undoubtedly diminishing the potency of the magic. No such neglect at Faide Keep! Jambart the weapon-tender cherished Hellmouth with absolute devotion. Elsewhere were other ancient devices, interesting but useless – the same sort of curios that cluttered shelves and cases at Faide Keep. (Peculiar, these ancient men! thought Lord Faide: at once so clever, yet so primitive and impractical. Conditions had changed; there had been enormous advances since the dark ages sixteen hundred years ago. For instance, the ancients had used intricate fetishes of metal and glass to communicate with each other. Lord Faide need merely voice his needs; Hein Huss could project his mind a hundred miles to see, to hear, to relay Lord Faide's words.) The ancients had contrived dozens of such objects, but the old magic had worn away and they never seemed to function. Lord Ballant's side-arm had melted, after merely stinging Lord Faide. Imagine a troop armed thus trying to cope with a platoon of demon-possessed warriors! Slaughter of the innocents!

Among the Ballant trove Lord Faide noted a dozen old books and several reels of microfilm. The books were worthless, page after page of incomprehensible jargon; the microfilm was equally undecipherable. Again Lord Faide wondered skeptically about the ancients. Clever of course, but to look at the hard facts, they were little more advanced than the First Folk: neither had facility with telepathy or voyance or demon-command. And the magic of the ancients: might there not be a great deal of exaggeration in the legends? Volcano, for instance. A joke. Lord Faide wondered about his own Hellmouth. But no – surely Hellmouth was more trustworthy; Jambart cleaned and polished the weapon daily and washed the entire cupola with vintage wine every month. If human care could induce faithfulness, then Hellmouth was ready to defend Faide Keep!

Now there was no longer need for defense. Faide was supreme. Considering the future, Lord Faide made a decision. There should no longer be keep-lords on Pangborn; he would abolish the appellation. Habitancy of the keeps would gradually be transferred to trusted bailiffs on a yearly basis. The former lords would be moved to comfortable but indefensible manor houses, with the maintenance of private troops forbidden. Naturally they must be allowed jinxmen, but these would be made accountable to himself – perhaps through some sort of licensing provision. He must discuss the matter with Hein Huss. A matter for the future, however. Now he merely wished to settle affairs and return to Faide Keep.

There was little more to be done. The surviving Ballant kinsmen he sent to their homes after Hein Huss had impregnated fresh dolls with their essences. Should they default on their ransoms, a twinge of fire, a few stomach cramps would more than set them right. Ballant Keep itself Lord Faide would have liked to burn – but the material of the ancients was proof to fire. But in order to discourage any new pretenders to the Ballant heritage Lord Faide ordered all the heirlooms and relics brought forth into the courtyard, and then, one at a time, in order of rank, he bade his men choose. Thus the Ballant wealth was distributed. Even the jinxmen were invited to choose, but they despised the ancient trinkets as works of witless superstition. The lesser spellbinders and apprentices rummaged through the leavings, occasionally finding an overlooked bauble or some anomalous implement. Isak Comandore was irritated to find Sam Salazar staggering under a load of the ancient books. 'And what is your purpose with these?' he barked. 'Why do you burden yourself with rubbish?'

Sam Salazar hung his head. 'I have no definite purpose. Undoubtedly there was wisdom – or at least knowledge – among the ancients; perhaps

I can use these symbols of knowledge to sharpen my own understanding.'

Comandore threw up his hands in disgust. He turned to Hein Huss, who stood nearby. 'First he fancies himself a tree and stands in the mud; now he thinks to learn jinxmanship through a study of ancient symbols.'

Huss shrugged. 'They were men like ourselves, and, though limited, they were not entirely obtuse. A certain simian cleverness is required to fabricate these objects.'

'Simian cleverness is no substitute for sound jinxmanship,' retorted Isak Comandore. 'This is a point hard to overemphasize; I have drummed it into Salazar's head a hundred times. And now, look at him.'

Huss grunted noncommittally. 'I fail to understand what he hopes to achieve.'

Sam Salazar tried to explain, fumbling for words to express an idea that did not exist. 'I thought perhaps to decipher the writing, if only to understand what the ancients thought, and perhaps to learn how to perform one or two of their tricks.'

Comandore rolled up his eyes. 'What enemy bewitched me when I consented to take you as apprentice? I can cast twenty hoodoos in an hour, more than any of the ancients could achieve in a lifetime.'

'Nevertheless,' said Sam Salazar, 'I notice that Lord Faide rides in his ancestral car, and that Lord Ballant sought to kill us all with Volcano.'

'I notice,' said Comandore with feral softness, 'that my demon Keyril conquered Lord Ballant's Volcano, and that riding on my wagon I can outdistance Lord Faide in his car.'

Sam Salazar thought better of arguing further. 'True, Jinxman Comandore, very true. I stand corrected.'

'Then discard that rubbish and make yourself useful. We return to Faide Keep in the morning.'

'As you wish, Jinxman Comandore.' Sam Salazar threw the books back into the trash.

CHAPTER SIX

The Ballant clan had been dispersed, Ballant Keep was despoiled. Lord Faide and his men banqueted somberly in the great hall, tended by silent Ballant servitors.

Ballant Keep had been built on the same splendid scale as Faide Keep. The great hall was a hundred feet long, fifty feet wide, fifty feet high, paneled in planks sawed from pale native hardwood, rubbed and waxed to a rich honey color. Enormous black beams supported the ceiling; from these hung candelabra, intricate contrivances of green, purple and blue glass, knotted with ancient but still bright light-motes. On the far wall hung portraits of all the lords of Ballant Keep – one hundred and five grave faces in a variety of costumes. Below, a genealogical chart ten feet high detailed the descent of the Ballants and their connections with the other noble clans. Now there was a desolate air to the hall, and the one hundred and five dead faces were meaningless and empty.

Lord Faide dined without joy, and cast dour side-glances at those of his kinsmen who reveled too gladly. Lord Ballant, he thought, had conducted himself only as he himself might have done under the same circumstances; coarse exultation seemed in poor taste, almost as if it were disrespect for Lord Faide himself. His followers were quick to catch his mood, and the banquet proceeded with greater decorum.

The jinxmen sat apart in a smaller room to the side. Anderson Grimes, erstwhile Ballant Head Jinxman, sat beside Hein Huss, trying to put a good face on his defeat. After all, he had performed creditably against four powerful adversaries, and had no cause to feel a diminution of *mana*. The five jinxmen discussed the battle, while the cabalmen and spellbinders listened respectfully. The conduct of the demon-possessed troops occasioned the most discussion. Anderson Grimes readily admitted that his conception of Everid was a force absolutely brutal and blunt, terrifying in its indomitable vigor. The other jinxmen agreed that he undoubtedly succeeded in projecting these qualities; Hein Huss however pointed out that Isak Comandore's Keyril, as cruel and vigorous as Everid, also combined a measure of crafty malice, which tended to make the possessed soldier a more effective weapon.

Anderson Grimes allowed that this might well be the case, and that in fact he had been considering such an augmentation of Everid's characteristics.

'To my mind,' said Huss, 'the most effective demon should be swift enough to avoid the strokes of the brute demons, such as Keyril and Everid. I cite my own Dant as example. A Dant-possessed warrior can easily destroy a Keyril or an Everid, simply through his agility. In an encounter of this sort the Keyrils and Everids presently lose their capacity to terrify, and thus half the effect is lost.'

Isak Comandore pierced Huss with a hot russet glance. 'You state a presumption as if it were fact. I have formulated Keyril with sufficient craft to counter any such displays of speed. I firmly believe Keyril to be the most fearsome of all demons.'

'It may well be,' rumbled Hein Huss thoughtfully. He beckoned to a steward, gave instructions. The steward reduced the light a trifle. 'Behold,' said Hein Huss. 'There is Dant. He comes to join the banquet.' To the side of the room loomed the tiger-striped Dant, a creature constructed of resilient metal, with four terrible arms, and a squat black head which seemed all gaping jaw.

'Look,' came the husky voice of Isak Comandore. 'There is Keyril.' Keyril was rather more humanoid and armed with a cutlass. Dant spied Keyril. The jaws gaped wider, it sprang to the attack.

The battle was a thing of horror; the two demons rolled, twisted, bit, frothed, uttered soundless shrieks, tore each other apart. Suddenly Dant sprang away, circled Keyril with dizzying speed, faster, faster; became a blur, a wild coruscation of colors that seemed to give off a high-pitched wailing sound, rising higher and higher in pitch. Keyril hacked brutally with his cutlass, then seemed to grow feeble and wan. The light that once had been Dant blazed white, exploded in a mental shriek; Keyril was gone and Isak Comandore lay moaning.

Hein Huss drew a deep breath, wiped his face, looked about him with a complacent grin. The entire company sat rigid as stones, staring, all except the apprentice Sam Salazar, who met Hein Huss' glance with a cheerful smile.

'So,' growled Huss, panting from his exertion, 'you consider yourself superior to the illusion; you sit and smirk at one of Hein Huss' best efforts.'

'No, no,' cried Sam Salazar. 'I mean no disrespect! I want to learn, so I watched you rather than the demons. What could they teach me? Nothing!'

'Ah,' said Huss, mollified. 'And what did you learn?'

'Likewise, nothing,' said Sam Salazar, 'but at least I do not sit like a fish.'

Comandore's voice came soft but crackling with wrath. 'You see in me the resemblance to a fish?'

'I except you, Jinxman Comandore, naturally,' Sam Salazar explained.

'Please go to my cabinet, Apprentice Salazar, and fetch me the doll that is your likeness. The steward will bring a basin of water, and we shall have some sport. With your knowledge of fish you perhaps can breathe under water. If not – you may suffocate.'

'I prefer not, Jinxman Comandore,' said Sam Salazar. 'In fact, with your permission, I now resign your service.'

Comandore motioned to one of his cabalmen. 'Fetch me the Salazar doll. Since he is no longer my apprentice, it is likely indeed that he will suffocate.'

'Come now, Comandore,' said Hein Huss gruffly. 'Do not torment the lad. He is innocent and a trifle addled. Let this be an occasion of placidity and ease.'

'Certainly, Hein Huss,' said Comandore. 'Why not? There is ample time in which to discipline this upstart.'

'Jinxman Huss,' said Sam Salazar, 'since I am now relieved of my duties to Jinxman Comandore, perhaps you will accept me into your service.'

Hein Huss made a noise of vast distaste. 'You are not my responsibility.'

'There are many futures, Hein Huss,' said Sam Salazar. 'You have said as much yourself.'

Hein Huss looked at Sam Salazar with his water-clear eyes. 'Yes, there are many futures. And I think that tonight sees the full amplitude of jinxman-ship ... I think that never again will such power and skill gather at the same table. We shall die one by one and there shall be none to fill our shoes ... Yes, Sam Salazar. I will take you as apprentice. Isak Comandore, do you hear? This youth is now of my company.'

'I must be compensated,' growled Comandore.

'You have coveted my doll of Tharon Faide, the only one in existence. It is yours.'

'Ah, ha!' cried Isak Comandore leaping to his feet. 'Hein Huss, I salute you! You are generous indeed! I thank you and accept!'

Hein Huss motioned to Sam Salazar. 'Move your effects to my wagon. Do not show your face again tonight.'

Sam Salazar bowed with dignity and departed the hall.

The banquet continued, but now something of melancholy filled the room. Presently a messenger from Lord Faide came to warn all to bed, for the party returned to Faide Keep at dawn.

CHAPTER SEVEN

The victorious Faide troops gathered on the heath before Ballant Keep. As a parting gesture Lord Faide ordered the great gate torn off the hinges, so that ingress could never again be denied him. But even after sixteen hundred years the hinges were proof to all the force the horses could muster, and the gates remained in place.

Lord Faide accepted the fact with good grace and bade farewell to his cousin Renfroy, whom he had appointed bailiff. He climbed into his car, settled himself, snapped the switch. The car groaned and moved forward. Behind came the knights and the foot soldiers, then the baggage train, laden with booty, and finally the wagons of the jinxmen.

Three hours the column marched across the mossy downs. Ballant Keep dwindled behind; ahead appeared North and South Wildwood, darkening all the sweep of the western horizon. Where once the break had existed, the First Folk's new planting showed a smudge lower and less intense than the old woodlands.

Two miles from the woodlands Lord Faide called a halt and signaled up his knights. Hein Huss laboriously dismounted from his wagon, came forward.

'In the event of resistance,' Lord Faide told the knights, 'do not be tempted into the forest. Stay with the column and at all times be on your guard against traps.'

Hein Huss spoke. 'You wish me to parley with the First Folk once more?'

'No,' said Lord Faide. 'It is ridiculous that I must ask permission of savages to ride over my own land. We return as we came; if they interfere, so much the worse for them.'

'You are rash,' said Huss with simple candor.

Lord Faide glanced down at him with black eyebrows raised. 'What damage can they do if we avoid their traps? Blow foam at us?'

'It is not my place to advise or to warn,' said Hein Huss. 'However, I point out that they exhibit a confidence which does not come from conscious weakness; also, that they carried tubes, apparently hollow grasswood shoots, which imply missiles.'

Lord Faide nodded. 'No doubt. However, the knights wear armor, the soldiers carry bucklers. It is not fit that I, Lord Faide of Faide Keep, choose my path to suit the whims of the First Folk. This must be made clear, even if the exercise involves a dozen or so First Folk corpses.'

'Since I am not a fighting man,' remarked Hein Huss, 'I will keep well to the rear, and pass only when the way is secure.'

'As you wish.' Lord Faide pulled down the visor of his helmet. 'Forward.'

The column moved toward the forest, along the previous track, which showed plain across the moss. Lord Faide rode in the lead, flanked by his brother, Gethwin Faide and his cousin, Mauve Dermont-Faide.

A half-mile passed, and another. The forest was only a mile distant. Overhead the great sun rode at zenith; brightness and heat poured down; the air carried the oily scent of thorn and tarbush. The column moved on, more slowly; the only sound the clanking of armor, the muffled thud of hooves in the moss, the squeal of wagon wheels.

Lord Faide rose up in his car, watching for any sign of hostile preparation. A half-mile from the planting the forms of the First Folk, waiting in the shade along the forest's verge, became visible. Lord Faide ignored them, held a steady pace along the track they had traveled before.

The half-mile became a quarter-mile. Lord Faide turned to order the troops into single file and was just in time to see a hole open suddenly into the moss and his brother, Gethwin Faide, drop from sight. There was a rattle, a thud, the howling of the impaled horse; Gethwin's wild calls as the horse kicked and crushed him into the stakes. Mauve Dermont-Faide, riding beside Gethwin, could not control his own horse, which leaped aside from the pit and blundered upon a trigger. Up from the moss burst a tree trunk studded with foot-long thorns. It snapped, quick as a scorpion's tail; the thorns punctured Mauve Dermont-Faide's armor, his chest, whisked him from his horse to carry him suspended, writhing and screaming. The tip of the scythe pounded into Lord Faide's car, splintered against the hull. The car swung groaning through the air. Lord Faide clutched at the windscreen to prevent himself from falling.

The column halted; several men ran to the pit, but Gethwin Faide lay twenty feet below, crushed under his horse. Others took Mauve Dermont-Faide down from the swaying scythe, but he, too, was dead.

Lord Faide's skin tingled with a gooseflesh of hate and rage. He looked toward the forest. The First Folk stood motionless. He beckoned to Bernard, sergeant of the foot soldiers. 'Two men with lances to try out the ground ahead. All others ready with darts. At my signal spit the devils.'

Two men came forward, and marching before Lord Faide's car, probed at the ground. Lord Faide settled in his seat. 'Forward.'

The column moved slowly toward the forest, every man tense and ready. The lances of the two men in the vanguard presently broke through the moss, to disclose a nettle-trap – a pit lined with nettles, each frond ripe with globes of acid. Carefully they probed out a path to the side, and the column filed around, each man walking in the other's tracks.

At Lord Faide's side now rode his two nephews, Scolford and Edwin. 'Notice,' said Lord Faide in a voice harsh and tight. 'These traps were laid since our last passage; an act of malice.'

'But why did they guide us through before?'

Lord Faide smiled bitterly. 'They were willing that we should die at Ballant Keep. But we have disappointed them.'

'Notice, they carry tubes,' said Scolford.

'Blowguns possibly,' suggested Edwin.

Scolford disagreed. 'They cannot blow through their foam-vents.'

'No doubt we shall soon learn,' said Lord Faide. He rose in his seat, called to the rear. 'Ready with the darts!'

The soldiers raised their crossbows. The column advanced slowly, now only a hundred yards from the planting. The white shapes of the First Folk moved uneasily at the forest's edges. Several of them raised their tubes, seemed to sight along the length. They twitched their great hands.

One of the tubes was pointed toward Lord Faide. He saw a small black object leave the opening, flit forward, gathering speed. He heard a hum, waxing to a rasping, clicking flutter. He ducked behind the windscreen; the projectile swooped in pursuit, struck the windscreen like a thrown stone. It fell crippled upon the forward deck of the car – a heavy black insect like a wasp, its broken proboscis oozing ocher liquid, horny wings beating feebly, eyes like dumbbells fixed on Lord Faide. With his mailed fist, he crushed the creature.

Behind him other wasps struck knights and men; Corex Faide-Battaro took the prong through his visor into the eye, but the armor of the other knights defeated the wasps. The foot soldiers, however, lacked protection; the wasps half-buried themselves in flesh. The soldiers called out in pain, clawed away the wasps, squeezed the wounds. Corex Faide-Battaro toppled from his horse, ran blindly out over the heath, and after fifty feet fell into a trap. The stricken soldiers began to twitch, then fell on the moss, thrashed, leaped up to run with flapping arms, threw themselves in wild somersaults, forward, backward, foaming and thrashing.

In the forest, the First Folk raised their tubes again. Lord Faide bellowed, 'Spit the creatures! Bowmen, launch your darts!'

There came the twang of crossbows, darts snapped at the quiet white shapes. A few staggered and wandered aimlessly away; most, however, plucked out the darts or ignored them. They took capsules from small sacks, put them to the end of their tubes.

'Beware the wasps!' cried Lord Faide. 'Strike with your bucklers! Kill the cursed things in flight!'

The rasp of horny wings came again; certain of the soldiers found courage enough to follow Lord Faide's orders, and battered down the wasps. Others struck home as before; behind came another flight. The column became a tangle of struggling, crouching men.

'Footmen, retreat!' called Lord Faide furiously. 'Footmen back! Knights to me!'

The soldiers fled back along the track, taking refuge behind the baggage wagons. Thirty of their number lay dying, or dead, on the moss.

Lord Faide cried out to his knights in a voice like a bugle. 'Dismount, follow slow after me! Turn your helmets, keep the wasps from your eyes! One step at a time, behind the car! Edwin, into the car beside me, test the footing with your lance. Once in the forest there are no traps! Then attack!'

The knights formed themselves into a line behind the car. Lord Faide drove slowly forward, his kinsman Edwin prodding the ground ahead. The First Folk sent out a dozen more wasps, which dashed themselves vainly against the armor. Then there was silence ... cessation of sound, activity. The First Folk watched impassively as the knights approached, step by step.

Edwin's lance found a trap, the column moved to the side. Another trap – and the column was diverted from the planting toward the forest. Step by step, yard by yard – another trap, another detour, and now the column was only a hundred feet from the forest. A trap to the left, a trap to the right: the safe path led directly toward an enormous heavy-branched tree. Seventy feet, fifty feet, then Lord Faide drew his sword.

'Prepare to charge, kill till your arms tire!'

From the forest came a crackling sound. The branches of the great tree trembled and swayed. The knights stared, for a moment frozen into place. The tree toppled forward, the knights madly tried to flee – to the rear, to the sides. Traps opened; the knights dropped upon sharp stakes. The tree fell; boughs cracked armored bodies like nuts; there was the hoarse yelling of pinned men, screams from the traps, the crackling subsidence of breaking branches. Lord Faide had been battered down into the car, and the car had been pressed groaning into the moss. His first instinctive act was to press the switch to rest position; then he staggered erect, clambered up through the boughs. A pale unhuman face peered at him; he swung his fist, crushed the faceted eye-bulge, and roaring with rage scrambled through the branches. Others of his knights were working themselves free, although almost a third were either crushed or impaled.

The First Folk came scrambling forward, armed with enormous thorns, long as swords. But now Lord Faide could reach them at close quarters. Hissing with vindictive joy he sprang into their midst, swinging his sword with both hands, as if demon-possessed. The surviving knights joined him and the ground became littered with dismembered First Folk. They drew back slowly, without excitement. Lord Faide reluctantly called back his knights. 'We must succor those still pinned, as many as still are alive.'

As well as possible branches were cut away, injured knights drawn forth. In some cases the soft moss had cushioned the impact of the tree. Six knights were dead, another four crushed beyond hope of recovery. To these Lord Faide himself gave the *coup de grâce*. Ten minutes further hacking and chopping freed Lord Faide's car, while the First Folk watched incuriously from the forest. The knights wished to charge once more, but Lord Faide ordered retreat. Without interference they returned the way they had come, back to the baggage train.

Lord Faide ordered a muster. Of the original war party, less than two-thirds remained. Lord Faide shook his head bitterly. Galling to think how easily he had been led into a trap! He swung on his heel, strode to the rear of the column, to the wagons of the magicians. The jinxmen sat around a small fire, drinking tea. 'Which of you will hoodoo these white forest vermin? I want them dead – stricken with sickness, cramps, blindness, the most painful afflictions you can contrive!'

There was general silence. The jinxmen sipped their tea.

'Well?' demanded Lord Faide. 'Have you no answer? Do I not make myself plain?'

Hein Huss cleared his throat, spat into the blaze. 'Your wishes are plain. Unfortunately we cannot hoodoo the First Folk.'

'And why?'

'There are technical reasons.'

Lord Faide knew the futility of argument. 'Must we slink home around the forest? If you cannot hoodoo the First Folk, then bring out your demons! I will march on the forest and chop out a path with my sword!'

'It is not for me to suggest tactics,' grumbled Hein Huss.

'Go on, speak! I will listen.'

'A suggestion has been put to me, which I will pass to you. Neither I nor the other jinxmen associate ourselves with it, since it recommends the crudest of physical principles.'

'I await the suggestion,' said Lord Faide.

'It is merely this. One of my apprentices tampered with your car, as you may remember.'

'Yes, and I will see he gets the hiding he deserves.'

'By some freak he caused the car to rise high into the air. The suggestion is this: that we load the car with as much oil as the baggage train affords, that we send the car aloft and let it drift over the planting. At a suitable moment, the occupant of the car will pour the oil over the trees, then hurl down a torch. The forest will burn. The First Folk will be at least discomfited; at best a large number will be destroyed.'

Lord Faide slapped his hands together. 'Excellent! Quickly, to work!' He called a dozen soldiers, gave them orders; four kegs of cooking oil, three buckets of pitch, six demijohns of spirit were brought and lifted into the car. The engines grated and protested, and the car sagged almost to the moss.

Lord Faide shook his head sadly. 'A rude use of the relic, but all in good purpose. Now, where is that apprentice? He must indicate which switches and which buttons he turned.'

'I suggest,' said Hein Huss, 'that Sam Salazar be sent up with the car.'

Lord Faide looked sidewise at Sam Salazar's round, bland countenance. 'An efficient hand is needed, a seasoned judgment. I wonder if he can be trusted?'

'I would think so,' said Hein Huss, 'inasmuch as it was Sam Salazar who evolved the scheme in the first place.'

'Very well. In with you, Apprentice! Treat my car with reverence! The wind blows away from us; fire this edge of the forest, in as long a strip as you can manage. The torch, where is the torch?'

The torch was brought and secured to the side of the car.

'One more matter,' said Sam Salazar. 'I would like to borrow the armor of some obliging knight, to protect myself from the wasps. Otherwise—'

'Armor!' bawled Lord Faide. 'Bring armor!'

At last, fully accoutered and with visor down, Sam Salazar climbed into the car. He seated himself, peered intently at the buttons and switches. In truth he was not precisely certain as to which he had manipulated before

... He considered, reached forward, pushed, turned. The motors roared and screamed; the car shuddered, sluggishly rose into the air. Higher, higher, twenty feet, forty feet, sixty feet – a hundred, two hundred. The wind eased the car toward the forest; in the shade the First Folk watched. Several of them raised tubes, opened the shutters. The onlookers saw the wasps dart through the air to dash against Sam Salazar's armor.

The car drifted over the trees; Sam Salazar began ladling out the oil. Below, the First Folk stirred uneasily. The wind carried the car too far over the forest; Sam Salazar worked the controls, succeeded in guiding himself back. One keg was empty, and another; he tossed them out, presently emptied the remaining two, and the buckets of pitch. He soaked a rag in spirit, ignited it, threw it over the side, poured the spirit after.

The flaming rag fell into leaves. A crackle, fire blazed and sprang. The car now floated at a height of five hundred feet. Salazar poured over the remaining spirits, dropped the demijohns, guided the car back over the heath, and fumbling nervously with the controls dropped the car in a series of swoops back to the moss.

Lord Faide sprang forward, clapped him on the shoulder. 'Excellently done! The forest blazes like tinder!'

The men of Faide Keep stood back, rejoicing to see the flames soar and lick. The First Folk scurried back from the heat, waving their arms; foam of a peculiar purple color issued from their vents as they ran, small useless puffs discharged as if by accident or through excitement. The flames ate through first the forest, then spread into the new planting, leaping through the leaves.

'Prepare to march!' called Lord Faide. 'We pass directly behind the flames, before the First Folk return.'

Off in the forest the First Folk perched in the trees, blowing out foam in great puffs and billows, building a wall of insulation. The flames had eaten half across the new planting, leaving behind smouldering saplings.

'Forward! Briskly!'

The column moved ahead. Coughing in the smoke, eyes smarting, they passed under still blazing trees and came out on the western downs.

Slowly the column moved forward, led by a pair of soldiers prodding the moss with lances. Behind followed Lord Faide with the knights, then came the foot soldiers, then the rumbling baggage train, and finally the six wagons of the jinxmen.

A thump, a creak, a snap. A scythe had broken up from the moss; the soldiers in the lead dropped flat; the scythe whipped past, a foot from Lord Faide's face. At the same time a plaintive cry came from the rear guard. 'They pursue! The First Folk come!'

Lord Faide turned to inspect the new threat. A clot of First Folk, two hundred or more, came across the moss, moving without haste or urgency. Some carried wasp-tubes, others thorn-rapiers.

Lord Faide looked ahead. Another hundred yards should bring the army out upon safe ground; then he could deploy and maneuver. 'Forward!'

The column proceeded, the baggage train and the jinxmen's wagons pressing close up against the soldiers. Behind and to the side came the First Folk, moving casually and easily.

At last Lord Faide judged they had reached secure ground. 'Forward, now! Bring the wagons out, hurry now!'

The troops needed no urging; they trotted out over the heath, the wagons trundling after. Lord Faide ordered the wagons into a close double line, stationed the soldiers between, with the horses behind and protected from the wasps. The knights, now dismounted, waited in front.

The First Folk came listlessly, formlessly forward. Blank white faces stared; huge hands grasped tubes and thorns; traces of the purplish foam showed at the lips of their underarm orifices.

Lord Faide walked along the line of knights. 'Swords ready. Allow them as close as they care to come. Then a quick charge.' He motioned to the foot soldiers. 'Choose a target ... !' A volley of darts whistled overhead, to plunge into white bodies. With chisel-bladed fingers the First Folk plucked them out, discarded them with no evidence of vexation. One or two staggered, wandered confusedly across the line of approach. Others raised their tubes, withdrew the shutter. Out flew the insects, horny wings rasping, prongs thrust forward. Across the moss they flickered, to crush themselves against the armor of the knights, to drop to the ground, to be stamped upon. The soldiers cranked their crossbows back into tension, discharged another flight of darts, caused several more First Folk casualties.

The First Folk spread into a long line, surrounded the Faide troops. Lord Faide shifted half his knights to the other side of the wagons.

The First Folk wandered closer. Lord Faide called for a charge. The knights stepped smartly forward, swords swinging. The First Folk advanced a few more steps, then stopped short. The flaps of skin at their backs swelled, pulsed; white foam gushed through their vents; clouds and billows rose up around them. The knights halted uncertainly, prodding and slashing into the foam but finding nothing. The foam piled higher, rolling in and forward, pushing the knights back toward the wagons. They looked questioningly toward Lord Faide.

Lord Faide waved his sword. 'Cut through to the other side! Forward!' Slashing two-handed with his sword, he sprang into the foam. He struck something solid, hacked blindly at it, pushed forward. Then his legs were seized; he was upended and fell with a spine-rattling jar. Now he felt the grate of a thorn searching his armor. It found a crevice under his corselet and pierced him. Cursing he raised on his hands and knees, plunged blindly forward. Enormous hard hands grasped him, heavy forms fell on his shoulders. He tried to breathe, the foam clogged his visor; he began to smother. Staggering to his feet he half-ran, half-fell out into the open air, carrying two of the First Folk with him. He had lost his sword, but managed to draw his dagger. The First Folk released him and stepped back into the foam. Lord Faide sprang to his feet. Inside the foam came the sounds of combat; some of his knights burst into the open; others called for help. Lord Faide motioned to the knights. 'Back within; the devils slaughter our kinsmen! In and on to the center!'

He took a deep breath. Seizing his dagger he thrust himself back into the foam. A flurry of shapes came at him: he pounded with his fists, cut with his dagger, stumbled over a mass of living tissue. He kicked the softness, and stepped on metal. Bending, he grasped a leg but found it limp and dead. First Folk were on his back, another thorn found its mark; he groaned and thrust himself forward, and once again fell out into the open air.

A scant fifty of his knights had won back into the central clearing. Lord Faide cried out, 'To the center; mount your horses!' Abandoning his car, he himself vaulted into a saddle. The foam boiled and billowed closer. Lord Faide waved his arm. 'Forward, all; at a gallop! After us the wagons – out into the open!'

They charged, thrusting the frightened horses into the foam. There was white blindness, the feel of forms underneath, then the open air once again. Behind came the wagons, and the foot soldiers, running along the channel cut by the wagons. All won free – all but the knights who had fallen under the foam.

Two hundred yards from the great white clot of foam, Lord Faide halted, turned, looked back. He raised his fist, shook it in a passion. 'My knights, my car, my honor! I'll burn your forests, I'll drive you into the sea, there'll be no peace till all are dead!' He swung around. 'Come,' he called bitterly to the remnants of his war party. 'We have been defeated. We retreat to Faide Keep.'

CHAPTER EIGHT

Faide Keep, like Ballant Keep, was constructed of a black, glossy substance, half metal, half stone, impervious to heat, force and radiation. A parasol roof, designed to ward off hostile energy, rested on five squat outer towers, connected by walls almost as high as the lip of the overhanging roof.

The homecoming banquet was quiet and morose. The soldiers and knights ate lightly and drank much, but instead of becoming merry, lapsed into gloom. Lord Faide, overcome by emotion, jumped to his feet. 'Everyone sits silent, aching with rage. I feel no differently. We shall take revenge. We shall put the forests to the torch. The cursed white savages will smother and burn. Drink now with good cheer; not a moment will be wasted. But we must be ready. It is no more than idiocy to attack as before. Tonight I take council with the jinxmen, and we will start a program of affliction.'

The soldiers and knights rose to their feet, raised their cups and drank a somber toast. Lord Faide bowed and left the hall.

He went to his private trophy room. On the walls hung escutcheons, memorials, deathmasks, clusters of swords like many-petaled flowers; a rack of side-arms, energy pistols, electric stilettos; a portrait of the original Faide, in ancient spacefarer's uniform, and a treasured, almost unique, photograph of the great ship that had brought the first Faide to Pangborn.

Lord Faide studied the ancient face for several moments, then summoned a servant. 'Ask the Head Jinxman to attend me.'

Hein Huss presently stumped into the room. Lord Faide turned away from the portrait, seated himself, motioned to Hein Huss to do likewise. 'What of the keep-lords?' he asked. 'How do they regard the setback at the hands of the First Folk?'

'There are various reactions,' said Hein Huss. 'At Boghoten, Candelwade and Havve there is distress and anger.'

Lord Faide nodded. 'These are my kinsmen.'

'At Gisborne, Graymar, Castle Cloud and Alder there is satisfaction, veiled calculation.'

'To be expected,' muttered Lord Faide. 'These lords must be humbled; in spite of oaths and undertakings, they still think rebellion.'

'At Star Home, Julian-Douray and Oak Hall I read surprise at the abilities of the First Folk, but in the main disinterest.'

Lord Faide nodded sourly. 'Well enough. There is no actual rebellion in prospect; we are free to concentrate on the First Folk. I will tell you what is in my mind. You report that new plantings are in progress between Wildwood, Old Forest, Sarrow Copse and elsewhere – possibly with the intent of surrounding Faide Keep.' He looked inquiringly at Hein Huss, but no comment was forthcoming. Lord Faide continued. 'Possibly we have underestimated the cunning of the savages. They seem capable of forming plans and acting with almost human persistence. Or, I should say, more than human persistence, for it appears that after sixteen hundred years they still consider us invaders and hope to exterminate us.'

'That is my own conclusion,' said Hein Huss.

'We must take steps to strike first. I consider this a matter for the jinxmen. We gain no honor dodging wasps, falling into traps, or groping through foam. It is a needless waste of lives. Therefore, I want you to assemble your jinxmen, cabalmen and spellbinders; I want you to formulate your most potent hoodoos—'

'Impossible.'

Lord Faide's black eyebrows rose high. '"Impossible"?'

Hein Huss seemed vaguely uncomfortable. 'I read the wonder in your mind. You suspect me of disinterest, irresponsibility. Not true. If the First Folk defeat you, we suffer likewise.'

'Exactly,' said Lord Faide dryly. 'You will starve.'

'Nevertheless, the jinxmen cannot help you.' He hoisted himself to his feet, started for the door.

'Sit,' said Lord Faide. 'It is necessary to pursue this matter.'

Hein Huss looked around with his bland, water-clear eyes. Lord Faide met his gaze. Hein Huss sighed deeply. 'I see I must ignore the precepts of my trade, break the habits of a lifetime. I must explain.' He took his bulk to the wall, fingered the side-arms in the rack, studied the portrait of the ancestral Faide. 'These miracle workers of the old times – unfortunately we cannot use their magic! Notice the bulk of the spaceship! As heavy as Faide Keep.' He turned his gaze on the table, teleported a candelabra two or three inches. 'With considerably less effort they gave that spaceship enormous velocity, using ideas and forces they knew to be imaginary and irrational. We have advanced since then, of course. We no longer employ mysteries, arcane constructions, wild nonhuman forces. We are rational and practical – but we cannot achieve the effects of the ancient magicians.'

Lord Faide watched Hein Huss with saturnine eyes. Hein Huss gave his deep rumbling laugh. 'You think that I wish to distract you with talk? No, this is not the case. I am preparing to enlighten you.' He returned to his seat, lowered his bulk with a groan. 'Now I must talk at length, to which I am not accustomed. But you must be given to understand what we jinxmen can do and what we cannot do.

'First, unlike the ancient magicians, we are practical men. Naturally there is difference in our abilities. The best jinxman combines great tele-pathic facility, implacable personal force, intimate knowledge of his fellow humans. He knows their acts, motives, desires and fears; he understands the symbols that most vigorously represent these qualities. Jinxmanship in the main is drudgery – dangerous, difficult and unromantic – with no mystery except that which we employ to confuse our enemies.' Hein Huss glanced at Lord Faide to encounter the same saturnine gaze. 'Ha! I still have told you nothing; I still have spent many words talking around my inability to con-found the First Folk. Patience.'

'Speak on,' said Lord Faide.

'Listen then. What happens when I hoodoo a man? First I must enter into his mind telepathically. There are three operational levels: the conscious, the unconscious, the cellular. The most effective jinxing is done if all three levels are influenced. I feel into my victim, I learn as much as possible, supplementing my previous knowledge of him, which is part of my stock in trade. I take up his doll, which carries his traces. The doll is highly useful but not indispensable. It serves as a focus for my attention; it acts as a pattern, or a guide, as I fix upon the mind of the victim, and he is bound by his own telepathic capacity to the doll which bears his traces.

'So! Now! Man and doll are identified in my mind, and at one or more levels in the victim's mind. Whatever happens to the doll the victim feels to be happening to himself. There is no more to simple hoodooing than that, from the standpoint of the jinxman. But naturally the victims differ greatly. Susceptibility is the key idea here. Some men are more susceptible than others. Fear and conviction breed susceptibility. As a jinxman succeeds he becomes ever more feared, and consequently the more efficacious he becomes. The process is self-generative.

'Demon-possession is a similar technique. Susceptibility is again essential; again conviction creates susceptibility. It is easiest and most dramatic when the characteristics of the demon are well known, as in the case of Comandore's Keyril. For this reason, demons can be exchanged or traded among jinxmen. The commodity actually traded is public acceptance and familiarity with the demon.'

'Demons then do not actually exist?' inquired Lord Faide half-incredulously.

Hein Huss grinned vastly, showing enormous yellow teeth. 'Telepathy works through a superstratum. Who knows what is created in this superstratum? Maybe the demons live on after they have been conceived; maybe they now are real. This of course is speculation, which we jinxmen shun.

'So much for demons, so much for the lesser techniques of jinxmanship. I have explained sufficient to serve as background to the present situation.'

'Excellent,' said Lord Faide. 'Continue.'

'The question, then, is: How does one cast a hoodoo into a creature of an alien race?' He looked inquiringly at Lord Faide. 'Can you tell me?'

'I?' asked Lord Faide surprised. 'No.'

'The method is basically the same as in the hoodooing of men. It is necessary to make the creature believe, in every cell of his being, that he suffers or dies. This is where the problems begin to arise. Does the creature think – that is to say, does he arrange the processes of his life in the same manner as men? This is a very important distinction. Certain creatures of the universe use methods other than the human nerve-node system to control their environments. We call the human system "intelligence" – a word which properly should be restricted to human activity. Other creatures use different agencies, different systems, arriving sometimes at similar ends. To bring home these generalities, I cannot hope to merge my mind with the corresponding capacity in the First Folk. The key will not fit the lock. At least, not altogether. Once or twice when I watched the First Folk trading with men at Forest Market, I felt occasional weak significances. This implies that the First Folk mentality creates something similar to human telepathic impulses. Nevertheless, there is no real sympathy between the two races.

'This is the first and the least difficulty. If I were able to make complete telepathic contact – what then? The creatures are different from us. They have no words for "fear", "hate", "rage", "pain", "bravery", "cowardice". One may deduce that they do not feel these emotions. Undoubtedly they know other sensations, possibly as meaningful. Whatever these may be, they are unknown to me, and therefore I cannot either form or project symbols for these sensations.'

Lord Faide stirred impatiently. 'In short, you tell me that you cannot efficiently enter these creatures' minds; and that if you could, you do not know what influences you could plant there to do them harm.'

'Succinct,' agreed Hein Huss. 'Substantially accurate.'

Lord Faide rose to his feet. 'In that case you must repair these deficiencies. You must learn to telepathize with the First Folk; you must find what influences will harm them. As quickly as possible.'

Hein Huss stared reproachfully at Lord Faide. 'But I have gone to great lengths to explain the difficulties involved! To hoodoo the First Folk is a monumental task! It would be necessary to enter Wildwood, to live with the First Folk, to become one of them, as my apprentice thought to become a tree. Even then an effective hoodoo is improbable! The First Folk must be susceptible to conviction! Otherwise there would be no bite to the hoodoo! I could guarantee no success. I would predict failure. No other jinxman would dare tell you this, no other would risk his *mana*. I dare because I am Hein Huss, with life behind me.'

'Nevertheless we must attempt every weapon at hand,' said Lord Faide in a dry voice. 'I cannot risk my knights, my kinsmen, my soldiers against these pallid half-creatures. What a waste of good flesh and blood to be stuck by a poison insect! You must go to Wildwood; you must learn how to hoodoo the First Folk.'

Hein Huss heaved himself erect. His great round face was stony; his eyes were like bits of water-worn glass. 'It is likewise a waste to go on a fool's errand. I am no fool, and I will not undertake a hoodoo which is futile from the beginning.'

'In that case,' said Lord Faide, 'I will find someone else.' He went to the door, summoned a servant. 'Bring Isak Comandore here.'

Hein Huss lowered his bulk into the chair. 'I will remain during the interview, with your permission.'

'As you wish.'

Isak Comandore appeared in the doorway, tall, loosely articulated, head hanging forward. He darted a glance of swift appraisal at Lord Faide, at Hein Huss, then stepped into the room.

Lord Faide crisply explained his desires. 'Hein Huss refuses to undertake the mission. Therefore I call on you.'

Isak Comandore calculated. The pattern of his thinking was clear: he possibly could gain much *mana*; there was small risk of diminution, for had not Hein Huss already dodged away from the project? Comandore nodded. 'Hein Huss has made clear the difficulties; only a very clever and very lucky jinxman can hope to succeed. But I accept the challenge, I will go.'

'Good,' said Hein Huss. 'I will go, too.' Isak Comandore darted him a sudden hot glance. 'I wish only to observe. To Isak Comandore goes the responsibility and whatever credit may ensue.'

'Very well,' said Comandore presently. 'I welcome your company. Tomorrow morning we leave. I go to order our wagon.'

Late in the evening Apprentice Sam Salazar came to Hein Huss where he sat brooding in his workroom. 'What do you wish?' growled Huss.

'I have a request to make of you, Head Jinxman Huss.'

'Head Jinxman in name only,' grumbled Hein Huss. 'Isak Comandore is about to assume my position.'

Sam Salazar blinked, laughed uncertainly. Hein Huss fixed wintry-pale eyes on him. 'What do you wish?'

'I have heard that you go on an expedition to Wildwood, to study the First Folk.'

'True, true. What then?'

'Surely they will now attack all men?'

Hein Huss shrugged. 'At Forest Market they trade with men. At Forest Market men have always entered the forest. Perhaps there will be change, perhaps not.'

'I would go with you, if I may,' said Sam Salazar.

'This is no mission for apprentices.'

'An apprentice must take every opportunity to learn,' said Sam Salazar. 'Also you will need extra hands to set up tents, to load and unload cabinets, to cook, to fetch water and other such matters.'

'Your argument is convincing,' said Hein Huss. 'We depart at dawn; be on hand.'

CHAPTER NINE

As the sun lifted over the heath the jinxmen departed Faide Keep. The high-wheeled wagon creaked north over the moss, Hein Huss and Isak Comandore riding the front seat, Sam Salazar with his legs hanging over the tail. The wagon rose and fell with the dips and mounds of the moss, wheels wobbling, and presently passed out of sight behind Skywatcher's Hill.

Five days later, an hour before sunset, the wagon reappeared. As before, Hein Huss and Isak Comandore rode the front seat, with Sam Salazar perched behind. They approached the keep, and without giving so much as a sign or a nod, drove through the gate into the courtyard.

Isak Comandore unfolded his long legs, stepped to the ground like a spider; Hein Huss lowered himself with a grunt. Both went to their quarters, while Sam Salazar led the wagon to the jinxmen's warehouse.

Somewhat later Isak Comandore presented himself to Lord Faide, who had been waiting in his trophy room, forced to a show of indifference through considerations of position, dignity and protocol. Isak Comandore stood in the doorway, grinning like a fox. Lord Faide eyed him with sour dislike, waiting for Comandore to speak. Hein Huss might have stationed himself an entire day, eyes placidly fixed on Lord Faide, awaiting the first word; Isak Comandore lacked the absolute serenity. He came a step forward. 'I have returned from Wildwood.'

'With what results?'

'I believe that it is possible to hoodoo the First Folk.'

Hein Huss spoke from behind Comandore. 'I believe that such an undertaking, if feasible, would be useless, irresponsible and possibly dangerous.' He lumbered forward.

Isak Comandore's eyes glowed hot red–brown; he turned back to Lord Faide. 'You ordered me forth on a mission; I will render a report.'

'Seat yourselves. I will listen.'

Isak Comandore, nominal head of the expedition, spoke. 'We rode along the river bank to Forest Market. Here was no sign of disorder or of hostility. A hundred First Folk traded timber, planks, posts and poles for knife blades, iron wire, and copper pots. When they returned to their barge we followed them aboard, wagon, horses and all. They showed no surprise—'

'Surprise,' said Hein Huss heavily, 'is an emotion of which they have no knowledge.'

Isak Comandore glared briefly. 'We spoke to the barge-tenders, explaining that we wished to visit the interior of Wildwood. We asked if the First

Folk would try to kill us to prevent us from entering the forest. They professed indifference as to either our well-being or our destruction. This was by no means a guarantee of safe conduct; however, we accepted it as such, and remained aboard the barge.' He spoke on with occasional emendations from Hein Huss.

They had proceeded up the river, into the forest, the First Folk poling against the slow current. Presently they put away the poles; nevertheless the barge moved as before. The mystified jinxmen discussed the possibility of teleportation, or symbological force, and wondered if the First Folk had developed jinxing techniques unknown to men. Sam Salazar, however, noticed that four enormous water beetles, each twelve feet long with oil-black carapaces and blunt heads, had risen from the river bed and pushed the barge from behind – apparently without direction or command. The First Folk stood at the bow, turning the nose of the barge this way or that to follow the winding of the river. They ignored the jinxmen and Sam Salazar as if they did not exist.

The beetles swam tirelessly; the barge moved for four hours as fast as a man could walk. Occasionally, First Folk peered from the forest shadows, but none showed interest or concern in the barge's unusual cargo. By mid-afternoon the river widened, broke into many channels and became a marsh; a few minutes later the barge floated out into the open water of a small lake. Along the shore, behind the first line of trees appeared a large settlement. The jinxmen were interested and surprised. It had always been assumed that the First Folk wandered at random through the forest, as they had originally lived in the moss of the downs.

The barge grounded; the First Folk walked ashore, the men followed with the horses and wagon. Their immediate impressions were of swarming numbers, of slow but incessant activity, and they were attacked by an overpoweringly evil smell.

Ignoring the stench the men brought the wagon in from the shore, paused to take stock of what they saw. The settlement appeared to be a center of many diverse activities. The trees had been stripped of lower branches, and supported blocks of hardened foam three hundred feet long, fifty feet high, twenty feet thick, with a space of a man's height intervening between the underside of the foam and the ground. There were a dozen of these blocks, apparently of cellular construction. Certain of the cells had broken open and seethed with small white fishlike creatures – the First Folk young.

Below the blocks masses of First Folk engaged in various occupations, in the main unfamiliar to the jinxmen. Leaving the wagon in the care of Sam Salazar, Hein Huss and Isak Comandore moved forward among the First Folk, repelled by the stench and the pressure of alien flesh, but drawn by curiosity. They were neither heeded nor halted; they wandered everywhere about the settlement. One area seemed to be an enormous zoo, divided into a number of sections. The purpose of one of these sections – a kind of range two hundred feet long – was all too clear. At one end three or four First Folk released wasps from tubes; at the other end a human corpse hung on a rope – a Faide casualty from the battle at the new planting. Certain of the wasps flew straight at the corpse; just before contact they were netted and removed. Others flew up and away or veered toward the First Folk who stood along the side of the range. These latter also were netted and killed at once.

The purpose of the business was clear enough. Examining some of the other activity in this new light, the jinxmen were able to interpret much that had hitherto puzzled them.

They saw beetles tall as dogs with heavy saw-toothed pincers attacking objects resembling horses; pens of insects even larger, long, narrow, segmented, with dozens of heavy legs and nightmare heads. All these creatures – wasps, beetles, centipedes – in smaller and less formidable form were indigenous to the forest; it was plain that the First Folk had been practicing selective breeding for many years, perhaps centuries.

Not all the activity was warlike. Moths were trained to gather nuts, worms to gnaw straight holes through timber; in another section caterpillars chewed a yellow mash, molded it into identical spheres. Much of the evil odor emanated from the zoo; the jinxmen departed without reluctance, and returned to the wagon. Sam Salazar pitched the tent and built a fire, while Hein Huss and Isak Comandore discussed the settlement.

Night came; the blocks of foam glowed with imprisoned light; the activity underneath proceeded without cessation. The jinxmen retired to the tent and slept, while Sam Salazar stood guard.

The following day Hein Huss was able to engage one of the First Folk in conversation: the first attention of any sort given to them.

The conversation was long; Hein Huss reported only the gist of it to Lord Faide. (Isak Comandore turned away, ostentatiously disassociating himself from the matter.)

Hein Huss first of all had inquired as to the purpose of the sinister preparations: the wasps, beetles, centipedes and the like.

'We intend to kill men,' the creature had reported ingenuously. 'We intend to return to the moss. This has been our purpose ever since men appeared on the planet.'

Huss had stated that such an ambition was shortsighted, that there was ample room for both men and First Folk on Pangborn. 'The First Folk,' said Hein Huss, 'should remove their traps and cease their efforts to surround the keeps with forest.'

'No,' came the response, 'men are intruders. They mar the beautiful moss. All will be killed.'

Isak Comandore returned to the conversation. 'I noticed here a significant fact. All the First Folk within sight had ceased their work; all looked toward us, as if they, too, participated in the discussion. I reached the highly important conclusion that the First Folk are not complete individuals but components of a larger unity, joined to a greater or less extent by a telepathic phase not unlike our own.'

Hein Huss continued placidly, 'I remarked that if we were attacked, many of the First Folk would perish. The creature showed no concern, and in fact implied much of what Jinxman Comandore had already induced: "There are always more in the cells to replace the elements which die. But if the community becomes sick, all suffer. We have been forced into the forests, into a strange existence. We must arm ourselves and drive away the men, and to this end we have developed the methods of men to our own purposes!"'

Isak Comandore spoke. 'Needless to say, the creature referred to the ancient men, not ourselves.'

'In any event,' said Lord Faide, 'they leave no doubt as to their intentions. We should be fools not to attack them at once, with every weapon at our disposal.'

Hein Huss continued imperturbably. 'The creature went on at some length. "We have learned the value of irrationality." "Irrationality" of course was not his word or even his meaning. He said something like "a series of vaguely motivated trials" – as close as I can translate. He said, "We have learned to change our environment. We use insects and trees and plants and water-slugs. It is an enormous effort for us who would prefer a placid life in the moss. But you men have forced this life on us, and now you must suffer the consequences." I pointed out once more that men were not helpless, that many First Folk would die. The creature seemed unworried. "The community persists." I asked a delicate question, "If your purpose is to kill men, why do you allow us here?" He said, "The entire community of men will be destroyed." Apparently they believe the human society to be similar to their own, and therefore regard the killing of three wayfaring individuals as pointless effort.'

Lord Faide laughed grimly. 'To destroy us they must first win past Hell-mouth, then penetrate Faide Keep. This they are unable to do.'

Isak Comandore resumed his report. 'At this time I was already convinced that the problem was one of hoodooing not an individual but an entire race. In theory this should be no more difficult than hoodooing one. It requires no more effort to speak to twenty than to one. With this end in view I ordered the apprentice to collect substances associated with the creatures. Skinflakes, foam, droppings, all other exudations obtainable. While he did so, I tried to put myself in rapport with the creatures. It is difficult, for their telepathy works across a different stratum than ours. Nevertheless, to a certain extent I have succeeded.'

'Then you can hoodoo the First Folk?' asked Lord Faide.

'I vouchsafe nothing until I try. Certain preparations must be made.'

'Go then; make your preparations.'

Comandore rose to his feet and with a sly side-glance for Hein Huss left the room. Huss waited, pinching his chin with heavy fingers. Lord Faide looked at him coldly. 'You have something to add?'

Huss grunted, hoisted himself to his feet. 'I wish that I did. But my thoughts are confused. Of the many futures, all seem troubled and angry. Perhaps our best is not good enough.'

Lord Faide looked at Hein Huss with surprise; the massive Head Jinxman had never before spoken in terms so pessimistic and melancholy. 'Speak then; I will listen.'

Hein Huss said gruffly, 'If I knew any certainties I would speak gladly. But I am merely beset by doubts. I fear that we can no longer depend on logic and careful jinxmanship. Our ancestors were miracle workers, magicians. They drove the First Folk into the forest. To put us to flight in our turn the First Folk have adopted the ancient methods: random trial and purposeless empiricism. I am dubious. Perhaps we must turn our backs on sanity and likewise return to the mysticism of our ancestors.'

Lord Faide shrugged. 'If Isak Comandore can hoodoo the First Folk, such a retreat may be unnecessary.'

'The world changes,' said Hein Huss. 'Of so much I feel sure: the old days of craft and careful knowledge are gone. The future is for men of cleverness, of imagination untroubled by discipline; the unorthodox Sam Salazar may become more effective than I. The world changes.'

Lord Faide smiled his sour dyspeptic smile. 'When that day comes I will appoint Sam Salazar Head Jinxman and also name him Lord Faide, and you and I will retire together to a hut on the downs.'

Hein Huss made a heavy fateful gesture and departed.

CHAPTER TEN

Two days later Lord Faide, coming upon Isak Comandore, inquired as to his progress. Comandore took refuge in generalities. After another two days Lord Faide inquired again and this time insisted on particulars. Comandore grudgingly led the way to his workroom, where a dozen cabalmen, spellbinders and apprentices worked around a large table, building a model of the First Folk settlement in Wildwood.

'Along the lakeshore,' said Comandore, 'I will range a great number of dolls, daubed with First Folk essences. When this is complete I will work up a hoodoo and blight the creatures.'

'Good. Perform well.' Lord Faide departed the workroom, mounted to the topmost pinnacle of the keep, to the cupola where the ancestral weapon Hellmouth was housed. 'Jambart! Where are you?'

Weapon-tender Jambart, short, blue-jowled, red-nosed and big-bellied, appeared. 'My lord?'

'I come to inspect Hellmouth. Is it prepared for instant use?'

'Prepared, my lord, and ready. Oiled, greased, polished, scraped, burnished, tended – every part smooth as an egg.'

Lord Faide made a scowling examination of Hellmouth – a heavy cylinder six feet in diameter, twelve feet long, studded with half-domes interconnected with tubes of polished copper. Jambart undoubtedly had been diligent. No trace of dirt or rust or corrosion showed; all was gleaming metal. The snout was covered with a heavy plate of metal and tarred canvas; the ring upon which the weapon swiveled was well-greased.

Lord Faide surveyed the four horizons. To the south was fertile Faide Valley; to the west open downs; to north and east the menacing loom of Wildwood.

He turned back to Hellmouth and pretended to find a smear of grease. Jambart boiled with expostulations and protestations; Lord Faide uttered a grim warning, enjoining less laxity, then descended to the workroom of Hein Huss. He found the Head Jinxman reclining on a couch, staring at the ceiling. At a bench stood Sam Salazar surrounded by bottles, flasks and dishes.

Lord Faide stared balefully at the confusion. 'What are you doing?' he asked the apprentice.

Sam Salazar looked up guiltily. 'Nothing in particular, my lord.'

'If you are idle, go then and assist Isak Comandore.'

'I am not idle, Lord Faide.'

'Then what do you do?'

Sam Salazar gazed sulkily at the bench. 'I don't know.'

'Then you are idle!'

'No, I am occupied. I pour various liquids on this foam. It is First Folk foam. I wonder what will happen. Water does not dissolve it, nor spirits. Heat chars and slowly burns it, emitting a foul smoke.'

Lord Faide turned away with a sneer. 'You amuse yourself as a child might. Go to Isak Comandore; he can find use for you. How do you expect to become a jinxman, dabbling and prattling like a baby among pretty rocks?'

Hein Huss gave a deep sound: a mingling of sigh, snort, grunt and clearing of the throat. 'He does no harm, and Isak Comandore has hands enough. Salazar will never become a jinxman; that has been clear a long time.'

Lord Faide shrugged. 'He is your apprentice, and your responsibility. Well, then. What news from the keeps?'

Hein Huss, groaning and wheezing, swung his legs over the edge of the couch. 'The lords share your concern, to greater or less extent. Your close allies will readily place troops at your disposal; the others likewise if pressure is brought to bear.'

Lord Faide nodded in dour satisfaction. 'For the moment there is no urgency. The First Folk hold to their forests. Faide Keep of course is impregnable, although they might ravage the valley ...' He paused thoughtfully. 'Let Isak Comandore cast his hoodoo. Then we will see.'

From the direction of the bench came a hiss, a small explosion, a whiff of acrid gas. Sam Salazar turned guiltily to look at them, his eyebrows singed. Lord Faide gave a snort of disgust and strode from the room.

'What did you do?' Hein Huss inquired in a colorless voice.

'I don't know.'

Now Hein Huss likewise snorted in disgust. 'Ridiculous. If you wish to work miracles, you must remember your procedures. Miracle-working is not jinxmanship, with established rules and guides. In matters so complex it is well that you take notes, so that the miracles may be repeated.'

Sam Salazar nodded in agreement and turned back to the bench.

CHAPTER ELEVEN

Late during the day, news of new First Folk truculence reached Faide Keep. On Honeymoss Hill, not far west of Forest Market, a camp of shepherds had been visited by a wandering group of First Folk, who began to kill the sheep with thorn-swords. When the shepherds protested they, too, were attacked, and many were killed. The remainder of the sheep were massacred.

The following day came other news: four children swimming in Brastock River at Gilbert Ferry had been seized by enormous water-beetles and cut into pieces. On the other side of Wildwood, in the foothills immediately below Castle Cloud, peasants had cleared several hillsides and planted them to vines. Early in the morning they had discovered a horde of black disk-like flukes devouring the vines – leaves, branches, trunks and roots. They set about killing the flukes with spades and at once were stung to death by wasps.

Adam McAdam reported the incidents to Lord Faide, who went to Isak Comandore in a fury. 'How soon before you are prepared?'

'I am prepared now. But I must rest and fortify myself. Tomorrow morning I work the hoodoo.'

'The sooner the better! The creatures have left their forest; they are out killing men!'

Isak Comandore pulled his long chin. 'That was to be expected; they told us as much.'

Lord Faide ignored the remark. 'Show me your tableau.'

Isak Comandore took him into his workroom. The model was now complete, with the masses of simulated First Folk properly daubed and sensitized, each tied with a small wad of foam. Isak Comandore pointed to a pot of dark liquid. 'I will explain the basis of the hoodoo. When I visited the camp I watched everywhere for powerful symbols. Undoubtedly there were many at hand, but I could not discern them. However, I remembered a circumstance from the battle at the planting: when the creatures were attacked, threatened with fire and about to die, they spewed foam of dull purple color. Evidently this purple foam is associated with death. My hoodoo will be based upon this symbol.'

'Rest well, then, so that you may hoodoo to your best capacity.'

The following morning Isak Comandore dressed in long robes of black, set a mask of the demon Nard on his head to fortify himself. He entered his workroom, closed the door.

An hour passed, two hours. Lord Faide sat at breakfast with his kin, stubbornly maintaining a pose of cynical unconcern. At last he could contain himself no longer and went out into the courtyard where Comandore's underlings stood fidgeting and uneasy. 'Where is Hein Huss?' demanded Lord Faide. 'Summon him here.'

Hein Huss came stumping out of his quarters. Lord Faide motioned to Comandore's workshop. 'What is happening? Is he succeeding?'

Hein Huss looked toward the workshop. 'He is casting a powerful hoodoo. I feel confusion, anger—'

'In Comandore, or in the First Folk?'

'I am not in rapport. I think he has conveyed a message to their minds. A very difficult task, as I explained to you. In this preliminary aspect he has succeeded.'

'"Preliminary"? What else remains?'

'The two most important elements of the hoodoo: the susceptibility of the victim and the appropriateness of the symbol.'

Lord Faide frowned. 'You do not seem optimistic.'

'I am uncertain. Isak Comandore may be right in his assumption. If so, and if the First Folk are highly susceptible, today marks a great victory, and Comandore will achieve tremendous *mana!*'

Lord Faide stared at the door to the workshop. 'What now?'

Hein Huss' eyes went blank with concentration. 'Isak Comandore is near death. He can hoodoo no more today.'

Lord Faide turned, waved his arm to the cabalmen. 'Enter the workroom! Assist your master!'

The cabalmen raced to the door, flung it open. Presently they emerged supporting the limp form of Isak Comandore, his black robe spattered with purple foam. Lord Faide pressed close. 'What did you achieve? Speak!'

Isak Comandore's eyes were half-closed, his mouth hung loose and wet. 'I spoke to the First Folk, to the whole race. I sent the symbol into their minds—' His head fell limply sidewise.

Lord Faide moved back. 'Take him to his quarters. Put him on his couch.' He turned away, stood indecisively, chewing at his drooping lower lip. 'Still we do not know the measure of his success.'

'Ah,' said Hein Huss, 'but we do!'

Lord Faide jerked around. 'What is this? What do you say?'

'I saw into Comandore's mind. He used the symbol of purple foam; with tremendous effort he drove it into their minds. Then he learned that purple foam means not death – purple foam means fear for the safety of the community, purple foam means desperate rage.'

'In any event,' said Lord Faide after a moment, 'there is no harm done. The First Folk can hardly become more hostile.'

Three hours later a scout rode furiously into the courtyard, threw himself off his horse, ran to Lord Faide. 'The First Folk have left the forest! A tremendous number! Thousands! They are advancing on Faide Keep!'

'Let them advance!' said Lord Faide. 'The more the better! Jambart, where are you?'

'Here, sir.'

'Prepare Hellmouth! Hold all in readiness!'

'Hellmouth is always ready, sir!'

Lord Faide struck him across the shoulders. 'Off with you! Bernard!'

The sergeant of the Faide troops came forward. 'Ready, Lord Faide.'

'The First Folk attack. Armor your men against wasps, feed them well. We will need all our strength.'

Lord Faide turned to Hein Huss. 'Send to the keeps, to the manor houses, order our kinsmen to join us, with all their troops and all their armor. Send to Bellgard Hall, to Boghoten, Camber and Candelwade. Haste, haste, it is only hours from Wildwood.'

Huss held up his hand. 'I have already done so. The keeps are warned. They know your need.'

'And the First Folk – can you feel their minds?'

'No.'

Lord Faide walked away. Hein Huss lumbered out the main gate, walked around the keep, casting appraising glances up the black walls of the squat towers, windowless and proof even against the ancient miracle-weapons. High on top the great parasol roof Jambart the weapon-tender worked in the cupola, polishing that which already glistened, greasing surfaces already heavy with grease.

Hein Huss returned within. Lord Faide approached him, mouth hard, eyes bright. 'What have you seen?'

'Only the keep, the walls, the towers, the roof, and Hellmouth.'

'And what do you think?'

'I think many things.'

'You are noncommittal; you know more than you say. It is best that you speak, because if Faide Keep falls to the savages you die with the rest of us.'

Hein Huss' water-clear eyes met the brilliant black gaze of Lord Faide. 'I know only what you know. The First Folk attack. They have proved they are not stupid. They intend to kill us. They are not jinxmen; they cannot afflict us or force us out. They cannot break in the walls. To burrow under, they must dig through solid rock. What are their plans? I do not know. Will they succeed? Again, I do not know. But the day of the jinxman and his orderly array of knowledge is past. I think that again we must grope for miracles, blindly and foolishly, like Salazar pouring liquids on foam.'

A troop of armored horsemen rode in through the gates: warriors from nearby Bellgard Hall. And as the hours passed contingents from other keeps came to Faide Keep, until the courtyard was dense with troops and horses.

Two hours before sunset the First Folk were sighted across the downs. They seemed a very large company, moving in an undisciplined clot with a number of stragglers, forerunners and wanderers out on the flanks.

The hot-bloods from outside keeps came clamoring to Lord Faide, urging a charge to cut down the First Folk; they found no seconding voices among the veterans of the battle at the planting. Lord Faide, however, was pleased to see the dense mass of First Folk. 'Let them approach only a mile more – and Hellmouth will take them! Jambart!'

'At your call, Lord Faide.'

'Come, Hellmouth speaks!' He strode away with Jambart after. Up to the cupola they climbed.

'Roll forth Hellmouth, direct it against the savages!'

Jambart leaped to the glistening array of wheels and levers. He hesitated in perplexity, then tentatively twisted a wheel. Hellmouth responded by twisting slowly around on its radial track, to the groan and chatter of long-frozen bearings. Lord Faide's brows lowered into a menacing line. 'I hear evidence of neglect.'

'Neglect, my lord, never! Find one spot of rust, a shadow of grime, you may have me whipped!'

'What of the sound?'

'That is internal and invisible – none of my responsibility.'

Lord Faide said nothing. Hellmouth now pointed toward the great pale tide from Wildwood. Jambart twisted a second wheel and Hellmouth thrust forth its heavy snout. Lord Faide, in a voice harsh with anger, cried, 'The cover, fool!'

'An oversight, my lord, easily repaired.' Jambart crawled out along the top of Hellmouth, clinging to the protuberances for dear life, with below only the long smooth sweep of roof. With considerable difficulty he tore the covering loose, then grunting and cursing, inched himself back, jerking with his knees, rearing his buttocks.

The First Folk had slowed their pace a trifle, the main body only a half-mile distant.

'Now,' said Lord Faide in high excitement, 'before they disperse, we exterminate them!' He sighted through a telescopic tube, squinting through the dimness of internal films and incrustations, signaled to Jambart for the final adjustments. 'Now! Fire!'

Jambart pulled the firing lever. Within the great metal barrel came a sputter of clicking sounds. Hellmouth whined, roared. Its snout glowed red, orange, white, and out poured a sudden gout of blazing purple radiation – which almost instantly died. Hellmouth's barrel quivered with heat, fumed, seethed, hissed. From within came a faint pop. Then there was silence.

A hundred yards in front of the First Folk a patch of moss burnt black where the bolt had struck. The aiming device was inaccurate. Hellmouth's bolt had killed perhaps twenty of the First Folk vanguard.

Lord Faide made feverish signals. 'Quick! Raise the barrel. Now! Fire again!'

Jambart pulled the firing arm, to no avail. He tried again, with the same lack of success. 'Hellmouth evidently is tired.'

'Hellmouth is dead,' cried Lord Faide. 'You have failed me. Hellmouth is extinct.'

'No, no,' protested Jambart. 'Hellmouth rests! I nurse it as my own child! It is polished like glass! Whenever a section wears off or breaks loose, I neatly remove the fracture, and every trace of cracked glass.'

Lord Faide threw up his arms, shouted in vast inarticulate grief, ran below. 'Huss! Hein Huss!'

Hein Huss presented himself. 'What is your will?'

'Hellmouth has given up its fire. Conjure me more fire for Hellmouth, and quickly!'

'Impossible.'

'Impossible!' cried Lord Faide. 'That is all I hear from you! Impossible, useless, impractical! You have lost your ability. I will consult Isak Comandore.'

'Isak Comandore can put no more fire into Hellmouth than can I.'

'What sophistry is this? He put demons into men, surely he can put fire into Hellmouth!'

'Come, Lord Faide, you are overwrought. You know the difference between jinxmanship and miracle-working.'

Lord Faide motioned to a servant. 'Bring Isak Comandore here to me!'

Isak Comandore, face haggard, skin waxy, limped into the courtyard. Lord Faide waved peremptorily. 'I need your skill. You must restore fire to Hellmouth.'

Comandore darted a quick glance at Hein Huss, who stood solid and cold. Comandore decided against dramatic promises that could not be fulfilled. 'I cannot do this, my lord.'

'What! You tell me this, too?'

'Remark the difference, Lord Faide, between man and metal. A man's normal state is something near madness; he is at all times balanced on a knife-edge between hysteria and apathy. His senses tell him far less of the world than he thinks they do. It is a simple trick to deceive a man, to possess him with a demon, to drive him out of his mind, to kill him. But metal is insensible; metal reacts only as its shape and condition dictates, or by the working of miracles.'

'Then you must work miracles!'

'Impossible.'

Lord Faide drew a deep breath, collected himself. He walked swiftly across the court. 'My armor, my horse. We attack.'

The column formed, Lord Faide at the head. He led the knights through the portals, with armored footmen behind.

'Beware the foam!' called Lord Faide. 'Attack, strike, cut, draw back. Keep your visors drawn against the wasps! Each man must kill a hundred! Attack!'

The troop rode forth against the horde of First Folk, knights in the lead. The hooves of the horses pounded softly over the thick moss; in the west the large pale sun hung close to the horizon.

Two hundred yards from the First Folk the knights touched the club-headed horses into a lope. They raised their swords and, shouting, plunged forward, each man seeking to be first. The clotted mass of First Folk separated: black beetles darted forth and after them long segmented centipede creatures. They dashed among the horses, mandibles clicking, snouts slashing. Horses screamed, reared, fell over backwards; beetles cut open armored knights as a dog cracks a bone. Lord Faide's horse threw him and ran away; he picked himself up, hacked at a nearby beetle, lopped off its front leg. It darted forward, he lopped off the leg opposite; the heavy head dipped, tore up the moss. Lord Faide cut off the remaining legs, and it lay helpless.

'Retreat,' he bellowed. 'Retreat!'

The knights moved back, slashing and hacking at beetles and centipedes, killing or disabling all which attacked.

'Form into a double line, knights and men. Advance slowly, supporting each other!'

The men advanced. The First Folk dispersed to meet them, armed with their thorn-swords and carrying pouches. Ten yards from the men they reached into the pouches, brought forth dark balls which they threw at the men. The balls broke and spattered on the armor.

'Charge!' bawled Lord Faide. The men sprang forward into the mass of First Folk, cutting, slashing, killing. 'Kill!' called Lord Faide in exultation. 'Leave not one alive!'

A pang struck him, a sting inside his armor, followed by another and another. Small things crawled inside the metal, stinging, biting, crawling. He looked about: on all sides were harassed expressions, faces working in anguish. Sword arms fell limp as hands beat on the metal, futilely trying to scratch, rub. Two men suddenly began to tear off their armor.

'Retreat,' cried Lord Faide. 'Back to the keep!'

The retreat was a rout, the soldiers shedding articles of armor as they ran. After them came a flight of wasps – a dozen or more, and half as many men cried out as the poison prongs struck into their backs.

Inside the keep stormed the disorganized company, casting aside the last of their armor, slapping their skin, scratching, rubbing, crushing the ferocious red mites that infested them.

'Close the gates,' roared Lord Faide.

The gates slid shut. Faide Keep was besieged.

CHAPTER TWELVE

During the night the First Folk surrounded the keep, forming a ring fifty yards from the walls. All night there was motion, ghostly shapes coming and going in the starlight.

Lord Faide watched from a parapet until midnight, with Hein Huss at his side. Repeatedly, he asked, 'What of the other keeps? Do they send further reinforcements?' to which Hein Huss each time gave the same reply: 'There is confusion and doubt. The keep-lords are anxious to help but do not care to throw themselves away. At this moment they consider and take stock of the situation.'

Lord Faide at last left the parapet, signaling Hein Huss to follow. He went to his trophy room, threw himself into a chair, motioned Hein Huss to be seated. For a moment he fixed the jinxman with a cool, calculating stare. Hein Huss bore the appraisal without discomfort.

'You are Head Jinxman,' said Lord Faide finally. 'For twenty years you have worked spells, cast hoodoos, performed auguries – more effectively than any other jinxman of Pangborn. But now I find you inept and listless. Why is this?'

'I am neither inept nor listless. I am unable to achieve beyond my abilities. I do not know how to work miracles. For this you must consult my apprentice Sam Salazar, who does not know either, but who earnestly tries every possibility and many impossibilities.'

'You believe in this nonsense yourself! Before my very eyes you become a mystic!'

Hein Huss shrugged. 'There are limitations to my knowledge. Miracles occur – that we know. The relics of our ancestors lie everywhere. Their methods were supernatural, repellent to our own mental processes – but think! Using these same methods the First Folk threaten to destroy us. In the place of metal they use living flesh – but the result is similar. The men of Pangborn, if they assemble and accept casualties, can drive the First Folk back to Wildwood – but for how long? A year? Ten years? The First Folk plant new trees, dig more traps – and presently come forth again, with more terrible weapons: flying beetles, large as a horse; wasps strong enough to pierce armor, lizards to scale the walls of Faide Keep.'

Lord Faide pulled at his chin. 'And the jinxmen are helpless?'

'You saw for yourself. Isak Comandore intruded enough into their consciousness to anger them, no more.'

'So then – what must we do?'

Hein Huss held out his hands. 'I do not know. I am Hein Huss, jinxman. I watch Sam Salazar with fascination. He learns nothing, but he is either too stupid or too intelligent to be discouraged. If this is the way to work miracles, he will work them.'

Lord Faide rose to his feet. 'I am deathly tired. I cannot think, I must sleep. Tomorrow we will know more.'

Hein Huss left the trophy room, returned to the parapet. The ring of First Folk seemed closer to the walls, almost within dart-range. Behind them and across the moors stretched a long pale column of marching First Folk. A little back from the keep a pile of white material began to grow, larger and larger as the night proceeded.

Hours passed, the sky lightened; the sun rose in the east. The First Folk tramped the downs like ants, bringing long bars of hardened foam down from the north, dropping them into piles around the keep, returning into the north once more.

Lord Faide came up on the parapet, haggard and unshaven. 'What is this? What do they do?'

Bernard the sergeant responded. 'They puzzle us all, my lord.'

'Hein Huss! What of the other keeps?'

'They have armed and mounted; they approach cautiously.'

'Can you communicate our urgency?'

'I can, and I have done so. I have only accentuated their caution.'

'Bah!' cried Lord Faide in disgust. 'Warriors they call themselves! Loyal and faithful allies!'

'They know of your bitter experience,' said Hein Huss. 'They ask themselves, reasonably enough, what they can accomplish which you who are already here cannot do first.'

Lord Faide laughed sourly. 'I have no answer for them. In the meantime we must protect ourselves against the wasps. Armor is useless; they drive us mad with mites ... Bernard!'

'Yes, Lord Faide.'

'Have each of your men construct a frame two-feet square, fixed with a short handle. To these frames should be sewed a net of heavy mesh. When these frames are built we will sally forth, two soldiers to guard one half-armored knight on foot.'

'In the meantime,' said Hein Huss, 'the First Folk proceed with their plans.'

Lord Faide turned to watch. The First Folk came close up under the walls carrying rods of hardened foam. 'Bernard! Put your archers to work! Aim for the heads!'

Along the walls bowmen cocked their weapons. Darts spun down into the First Folk. A few were affected, turned and staggered away; others plucked away the bolts without concern. Another flight of bolts, a few more First Folk were disabled. The others planted the rods in the moss, exuded foam in great gushes, their back-flaps vigorously pumping air. Other First Folk brought more rods, pushed them into the foam. Entirely around the keep, close under the walls, extended the mound of foam. The ring of First Folk now came close and all gushed foam; it bulked up swiftly. More rods were brought, thrust into the foam, reinforcing and stiffening the mass.

'More darts!' barked Lord Faide. 'Aim for the heads! Bernard – your men, have they prepared the wasp-nets?'

'Not yet, Lord Faide. The project requires some little time.'

Lord Faide became silent. The foam, now ten feet high, rapidly piled higher. Lord Faide turned to Hein Huss. 'What do they hope to achieve?'

Hein Huss shook his head. 'For the moment I am uncertain.'

The first layer of foam had hardened; on top of this the First Folk spewed another layer, reinforcing again with the rods, crisscrossing, horizontal and vertical. Fifteen minutes later, when the second layer was hard the First Folk emplaced and mounted rude ladders to raise a third layer. Surrounding the keep now was a ring of foam thirty feet high and forty feet thick at the base.

'Look,' said Hein Huss. He pointed up. The parasol roof overhanging the walls ended only thirty feet above the foam. 'A few more layers and they will reach the roof.'

'So then?' asked Lord Faide. 'The roof is as strong as the walls.'

'And we will be sealed within.'

Lord Faide studied the foam in the light of this new thought. Already the First Folk, climbing laboriously up ladders along the outside face of their wall of foam, were preparing to lay on a fourth layer. First – rods, stiff and dry, then great gushes of white. Only twenty feet remained between roof and foam.

Lord Faide turned to the sergeant. 'Prepare the men to sally forth.'

'What of the wasp-nets, sir?'

'Are they almost finished?'

'Another ten minutes, sir.'

'Another ten minutes will see us smothering. We must force a passage through the foam.'

Ten minutes passed, and fifteen. The First Folk created ramps behind their wall: first, dozens of the rods, then foam, and on top, to distribute the weight, reed mats.

Bernard the sergeant reported to Lord Faide. 'We are ready.'

'Good.' Lord Faide descended into the courtyard. He faced the men, gave them their orders. 'Move quickly, but stay together; we must not lose ourselves in the foam. As we proceed, slash ahead and to the sides. The First Folk see through the foam; they have the advantage of us. When we break through, we use the wasp-nets. Two foot soldiers must guard each knight. Remember, quickly through the foam, that we do not smother. Open the gates.'

The gates slid back, the troops marched forth. They faced an unbroken blank wall of foam. No enemy could be seen.

Lord Faide waved his sword. 'Into the foam.' He strode forward, pushed into the white mass, now crisp and brittle and harder than he had bargained for. It resisted him; he cut and hacked. His troops joined him, carving a way into the foam. First Folk appeared above them, crawling carefully on the mats. Their back flaps puffed, pumped; foam issued from their vents, falling in a cascade over the troops.

Hein Huss sighed. He spoke to Apprentice Sam Salazar. 'Now they must retreat, otherwise they smother. If they fail to win through, we all smother.'

Even as he spoke the foam, piling up swiftly, in places reached the roof. Below, bellowing and cursing, Lord Faide backed out from under, wiped his face clear. Once again, in desperation, he charged forward, trying at a new spot.

The foam was friable and cut easily, but the chunks detached still blocked the opening. And again down tumbled a cascade of foam, covering the soldiers.

Lord Faide retreated, waved his men back into the keep. At the same moment First Folk crawling on mats on the same level as the parapet over the gate laid rods up from the foam to rest against the projecting edge of the roof. They gushed foam; the view of the sky was slowly blocked from the view of Hein Huss and Sam Salazar.

'In an hour, perhaps two, we will die,' said Hein Huss. 'They have now sealed us in. There are many men here in the keep, and all will now breathe deeply.'

Sam Salazar said nervously, 'There is a possibility we might be able to survive – or at least not smother.'

'Ah?' inquired Hein Huss with heavy sarcasm. 'You plan to work a miracle?'

'If a miracle, the most trivial sort. I observed that water has no effect on the foam, nor a number of other liquids: milk, spirits, wine, or caustic. Vinegar, however, instantly dissolves the foam.'

'Aha,' said Hein Huss. 'We must inform Lord Faide.'

'Better that you do so,' said Sam Salazar. 'He will pay me no heed.'

CHAPTER THIRTEEN

Half an hour passed. Light filtered into Faide Keep only as a dim gray gloom. Air tasted flat, damp and heavy. Out from the gates sallied the troops. Each carried a crock, a jug, a skin, or a pan containing strong vinegar.

'Quickly now,' called Lord Faide, 'but careful! Spare the vinegar, don't throw it wildly. In close formation now – forward.'

The soldiers approached the wall, threw ladles of vinegar ahead. The foam crackled, melted.

'Waste no vinegar,' shouted Lord Faide. 'Forward, quickly now; bring forward the vinegar!'

Minutes later they burst out upon the downs. The First Folk stared at them, blinking.

'Charge,' croaked Lord Faide, his throat thick with fumes. 'Mind now, wasp-nets! Two soldiers to each knight! Charge, double-quick. Kill the white beasts.'

The men dashed ahead. Wasp-tubes were leveled. 'Halt!' yelled Lord Faide. 'Wasps!'

The wasps came, wings rasping. Nets rose up; wasps struck with a thud. Down went the nets; hard feet crushed the insects. The beetles and the lizard-centipedes appeared, not so many as of the last evening, for a great number had been killed. They darted forward, and a score of men died, but the insects were soon hacked into chunks of reeking brown flesh. Wasps flew, and some struck home; the agonies of the dying men were unnerving. Presently the wasps likewise decreased in number, and soon there were no more.

The men faced the First Folk, armed only with thorn-swords and their foam, which now came purple with rage.

Lord Faide waved his sword; the men advanced and began to kill the First Folk, by dozens, by hundreds.

Hein Huss came forth and approached Lord Faide. 'Call a halt.'

'A halt? Why? Now we kill these bestial things.'

'Far better not. Neither need kill the other. Now is the time to show great wisdom.'

'They have besieged us, caught us in their traps, stung us with their wasps! And you say halt?'

'They nourish a grudge sixteen hundred years old. Best not to add another one.'

Lord Faide stared at Hein Huss. 'What do you propose?'

'Peace between the two races, peace and cooperation.'

'Very well. No more traps, no more plantings, no more breeding of deadly insects.'

'Call back your men. I will try.'

Lord Faide cried out, 'Men, fall back. Disengage.'

Reluctantly the troops drew back. Hein Huss approached the huddled mass of purple-foaming First Folk. He waited a moment. They watched him intently. He spoke in their language.

'You have attacked Faide Keep; you have been defeated. You planned well, but we have proved stronger. At this moment we can kill you. Then we can go on to fire the forest, starting a hundred blazes. Some of the fires you can control. Others not. We can destroy Wildwood. Some First Folk may

314

survive, to hide in the thickets and breed new plans to kill men. This we do not want. Lord Faide has agreed to peace, if you likewise agree. This means no more death-traps. Men will freely approach and pass through the forests. In your turn you may freely come out on the moss. Neither race shall molest the other. Which do you choose? Extinction – or peace?'

The purple foam no longer dribbled from the vents of the First Folk. 'We choose peace.'

'There must be no more wasps, beetles. The death-traps must be disarmed and never replaced.'

'We agree. In our turn we must be allowed freedom of the moss.'

'Agreed. Remove your dead and wounded, haul away the foam rods.'

Hein Huss returned to Lord Faide. 'They have chosen peace.'

Lord Faide nodded. 'Very well. It is for the best.' He called to his men. 'Sheathe your weapons. We have won a great victory.' He ruefully surveyed Faide Keep, swathed in foam and invisible except for the parasol roof. 'A hundred barrels of vinegar will not be enough.'

Hein Huss looked off into the sky. 'Your allies approach quickly. Their jinxmen have told them of your victory.'

Lord Faide laughed his sour laugh. 'To my allies will fall the task of removing the foam from Faide Keep.'

CHAPTER FOURTEEN

In the hall of Faide Keep, during the victory banquet, Lord Faide called jovially across to Hein Huss. 'Now, Head Jinxman, we must deal with your apprentice, the idler and the waster Sam Salazar.'

'He is here, Lord Faide. Rise, Sam Salazar, take cognizance of the honor being done you.'

Sam Salazar rose to his feet, bowed.

Lord Faide proffered him a cup. 'Drink, Sam Salazar, enjoy yourself. I freely admit that your idiotic tinkerings saved the lives of us all. Sam Salazar, we salute you, and thank you. Now, I trust that you will put frivolity aside, apply yourself to your work, and learn honest jinxmanship. When the time comes, I promise that you shall find a lifetime of employment at Faide Keep.'

'Thank you,' said Sam Salazar modestly. 'However, I doubt if I will become a jinxman.'

'No? You have other plans?'

Sam Salazar stuttered, grew faintly pink in the face, then straightened himself, spoke as clearly and distinctly as he could. 'I prefer to continue what you call my frivolity. I hope I can persuade others to join me.'

'Frivolity is always attractive,' said Lord Faide. 'No doubt you can find other idlers and wasters, runaway farm boys, and the like.'

Sam Salazar said staunchly, 'This frivolity might become serious. Undoubtedly the ancients were barbarians. They used symbols to control entities they were unable to understand. We are methodical and rational; why can't we systematize and comprehend the ancient miracles?'

'Well, why can't we?' asked Lord Faide. 'Does anyone have an answer?'

No one responded, although Isak Comandore hissed between his teeth and shook his head.

'I personally may never be able to work miracles; I suspect it is more complicated than it seems,' said Sam Salazar. 'However, I hope that you will arrange for a workshop where I and others who might share my views can make a beginning. In this matter I have the encouragement and the support of Head Jinxman Hein Huss.'

Lord Faide lifted his goblet. 'Very well, Apprentice Sam Salazar. Tonight I can refuse you nothing. You shall have exactly what you wish, and good luck to you. Perhaps you will produce a miracle during my lifetime.'

Isak Comandore said huskily to Hein Huss, 'This is a sad event! It signalizes intellectual anarchy, the degradation of jinxmanship, the prostitution of logic. Novelty has a way of attracting youth; already I see apprentices and spellbinders whispering in excitement. The jinxmen of the future will be sorry affairs. How will they go about demon-possession? With a cog, a gear and a push-button. How will they cast a hoodoo? They will find it easier to strike their victim with an axe.'

'Times change,' said Hein Huss. 'There is now the one rule of Faide on Pangborn, and the keeps no longer need to employ us. Perhaps I will join Sam Salazar in his workshop.'

'You depict a depressing future,' said Isak Comandore with a sniff of disgust.

'There are many futures, some of which are undoubtedly depressing.'

Lord Faide raised his glass. 'To the best of your many futures, Hein Huss. Who knows? Sam Salazar may conjure a spaceship to lead us back to home-planet.'

'Who knows?' said Hein Huss. He raised his goblet. 'To the best of the futures!'

The Dragon Masters

CHAPTER ONE

The apartments of Joaz Banbeck, carved deep from the heart of a limestone crag, consisted of five principal chambers, on five different levels. At the top were the reliquarium and a formal council chamber: the first a room of somber magnificence housing the various archives, trophies and mementos of the Banbecks; the second a long narrow hall, with dark wainscoting chest-high and a white plaster vault above, extending the entire width of the crag, so that balconies overlooked Banbeck Vale at one end and Kergan's Way at the other.

Below were Joaz Banbeck's private quarters: a parlor and bedchamber, then next his study and finally, at the bottom, a workroom where Joaz permitted none but himself.

Entry to the apartments was through the study, a large L-shaped room with an elaborate groined ceiling, from which depended four garnet-encrusted chandeliers. These were now dark; into the room came only a watery gray light from four honed-glass plates on which, in the manner of a *camera obscura*, were focused views across Banbeck Vale. The walls were paneled with lignified reed; a rug patterned in angles, squares and circles of maroon, brown and black covered the floor.

In the middle of the study stood a naked man, his only covering the long fine brown hair which flowed down his back, the golden torc which clasped his neck. His features were sharp and angular, his body thin; he appeared to be listening, or perhaps meditating. Occasionally he glanced at a yellow marble globe on a nearby shelf, whereupon his lips would move, as if he were committing to memory some phrase or sequence of ideas.

At the far end of the study a heavy door eased open. A flower-faced young woman peered through, her expression mischievous, arch. At the sight of the naked man, she clapped her hands to her mouth, stifling a gasp. The naked man turned – but the heavy door had already swung shut.

For a moment he stood deep in frowning reflection, then slowly went to the wall on the inside leg of the L. He swung out a section of the bookcase, passed through the opening. Behind him the bookcase thudded shut. Descending a spiral staircase he came out into a chamber rough-hewn from the rock: Joaz Banbeck's private workroom. A bench supported tools, metal shapes and fragments, a bank of electromotive cells, oddments of circuitry: the current objects of Joaz Banbeck's curiosity.

The naked man glanced at the bench, picked up one of the devices, inspected it with something like condescension, though his gaze was as clear and wondering as that of a child.

Muffled voices from the study penetrated to the workroom. The naked man raised his head to listen, then stooped under the bench. He lifted a block of stone, slipped through the gap into a dark void. Replacing the stone, he took up a luminous wand, and set off down a narrow tunnel, which presently dipped to join a natural cavern. At irregular intervals luminous tubes exuded a wan light, barely enough to pierce the murk. The naked man jogged forward swiftly, the silken hair flowing like a nimbus behind him.

Back in the study the minstrel-maiden Phade and an elderly seneschal were at odds. 'Indeed I saw him!' Phade insisted. 'With these two eyes of mine, one of the sacerdotes, standing thus and so, as I have described.' She tugged angrily at his elbow. 'Do you think me bereft of my wits, or hysterical?'

Rife the seneschal shrugged, committing himself neither one way nor the other. 'I do not see him now.' He climbed the staircase, peered into the sleeping parlor. 'Empty. The doors above are bolted.' He peered owlishly at Phade. 'And I sat at my post in the entry.'

'You sat sleeping. Even when I came past you snored!'

'You are mistaken; I did but cough.'

'With your eyes closed, your head lolling back?'

Rife shrugged once more. 'Asleep or awake, it is all the same. Admitting that the creature gained access, how did he leave? I was wakeful after you summoned me, as you must agree.'

'Then remain on guard, while I find Joaz Banbeck.' Phade ran down the passage which presently joined Bird Walk, so called for the series of fabulous birds of lapis, gold, cinnabar, malachite and marcasite inlaid into the marble. Through an arcade of green and gray jade in spiral columns she passed out into Kergan's Way, a natural defile which formed the main thoroughfare of Banbeck Village. Reaching the portal, she summoned a pair of lads from the fields. 'Run to the brooder, find Joaz Banbeck! Hasten, bring him here; I must speak with him.'

The boys ran off toward a low cylinder of black brick a mile to the north.

Phade waited. With the sun Skene at its nooning, the air was warm; the fields of vetch, bellegarde, spharganum, gave off a pleasant odor. Phade went to lean against a fence. Now she began to wonder about the urgency of her news, even its basic reality. 'No!' she told herself fiercely. 'I saw! I saw!'

At either side tall white cliffs rose to Banbeck Verge, with mountains and crags beyond, and spanning all the dark sky flecked with feathers of cirrus. Skene glittered dazzling bright, a minuscule flake of brilliance.

Phade sighed, half-convinced of her own mistake. Once more, less vehemently, she reassured herself. Never before had she seen a sacerdote; why should she imagine one now?

The boys, reaching the brooder, had disappeared into the dust of the exercise pens. Scales gleamed and winked; grooms, dragon masters, armorers in black leather moved about their work.

After a moment Joaz Banbeck came into view. He mounted a tall thin-legged Spider, urged it to the full extent of its head-jerking lope, pounded down the track toward Banbeck Village.

Phade's uncertainty grew. Might Joaz become exasperated, would he dismiss her news with an unbelieving stare? Uneasily she watched his approach. Coming to Banbeck Vale only a month before she still felt unsure of her status. Her preceptors had trained her diligently in the barren little valley to the south where she had been born, but the disparity between teaching and practical reality at times bewildered her. She had learned that all men obeyed a small and identical group of behaviors; Joaz Banbeck, however, observed no such limits, and Phade found him completely unpredictable.

She knew him to be a relatively young man, though his appearance provided no guide to his age. He had a pale austere face in which gray eyes shone like crystals, a long thin mouth which suggested flexibility, yet never curved far from a straight line. He moved languidly; his voice carried no vehemence; he made no pretense of skill with either saber or pistol. He seemed deliberately to shun any gesture which might win the admiration or affection of his subjects. Yet he had both.

Phade originally had thought him cold, but presently changed her mind. He was, so she decided, a man bored and lonely, with a quiet humor which at times seemed rather grim. But he treated her without discourtesy, and Phade, testing him with all her hundred and one coquetries, not infrequently thought to detect a spark of response.

Joaz Banbeck dismounted from the Spider, ordered it back to its quarters. Phade came diffidently forward, and Joaz turned her a quizzical look. 'What requires so urgent a summons? Have you remembered the nineteenth location?'

Phade flushed in confusion. Artlessly she had described the painstaking rigors of her training; Joaz now referred to an item in one of the classifications which had slipped her mind.

Phade spoke rapidly, excited once more. 'I opened the door into your study, softly, gently. And what did I see? A sacerdote, naked in his hair! He did not hear me. I shut the door, I ran to fetch Rife. When we returned – the chamber was empty!'

Joaz's eyebrows contracted a trifle; he looked up the valley. 'Odd.' After a moment he asked, 'You are sure that he saw nothing of you?'

'No. I think not. Yet, when I returned with stupid old Rife he had disappeared! Is it true that they know magic?'

'As to that, I cannot say,' replied Joaz.

They returned up Kergan's Way, traversed tunnels and rock-walled corridors, finally came to the entry chamber.

Rife once more dozed at his desk. Joaz signaled Phade back, and going quietly forward, thrust aside the door to his study. He glanced here and there, nostrils twitching. The room was empty.

He climbed the stairs, investigated the sleeping-parlor, returned to the study. Unless magic were indeed involved, the sacerdote had provided himself a secret entrance. With this thought in mind, he swung back the bookcase door, descended to the workshop, and again tested the air for the sour-sweet odor of the sacerdotes. A trace? Possibly.

Joaz examined the room inch by inch, peering from every angle. At last, along the wall below the bench, he discovered a barely perceptible crack, marking out an oblong.

Joaz nodded with dour satisfaction. He rose to his feet, returned to his study. He considered his shelves: what was here to interest a sacerdote? Books, folios, pamphlets? Had they even mastered the art of reading? When next I meet a sacerdote I must inquire, thought Joaz vaguely; at least he will tell me the truth. On second thought, he knew the question to be ludicrous; the sacerdotes, for all their nakedness, were by no means barbarians, and in fact had provided him his four vision-panes – a technical engineering feat of no small skill.

He inspected the yellowed marble globe which he considered his most valued possession: a representation of mythical Eden. Apparently it had not been disturbed. Another shelf displayed models of the Banbeck dragons: the rust-red Termagant; the Long-horned Murderer and its cousin the Striding Murderer; the Blue Horror; the Fiend, low to the ground, immensely strong, tail tipped with a steel barbel; the ponderous Jugger, skull-cap polished and white as an egg. A little apart stood the progenitor of the entire group – a pearl-pallid creature upright on two legs, with two versatile central members, a pair of multi-articulated brachs at the neck. Beautifully detailed though these models might be, why should they pique the curiosity of a sacerdote? No reason whatever, when the originals could be studied daily without hindrance.

What of the workshop, then? Joaz rubbed his long pale chin. He had no illusions about the value of his work. Idle tinkering, no more. Joaz put aside conjecture. Most likely the sacerdote had come upon no specific mission, the visit perhaps being part of a continued inspection. But why?

A pounding at the door: old Rife's irreverent fist. Joaz opened to him.

'Joaz Banbeck, a notice from Ervis Carcolo of Happy Valley. He wishes to confer with you, and at this moment awaits your response on Banbeck Verge.'

'Very well,' said Joaz. 'I will confer with Ervis Carcolo.'

'Here? Or on Banbeck Verge?'

'On the Verge, in half an hour.'

CHAPTER TWO

Ten miles from Banbeck Vale, across a wind-scoured wilderness of ridges, crags, spines of stone, amazing crevasses, barren fells and fields of tumbled boulders lay Happy Valley. As wide as Banbeck Vale but only half as long and half as deep, its bed of wind-deposited soil was only half as thick and correspondingly less productive.

The Chief Councilor of Happy Valley was Ervis Carcolo, a thick-bodied short-legged man with a vehement face, a heavy mouth, a disposition by turns jocose and wrathful. Unlike Joaz Banbeck, Carcolo enjoyed nothing more than his visits to the dragon barracks, where he treated dragon masters, grooms and dragons alike to a spate of bawled criticism, exhortation, invective.

Ervis Carcolo was an energetic man, intent upon restoring Happy Valley to the ascendancy it had enjoyed some twelve generations before. During those harsh times, before the advent of the dragons, men fought their own battles, and the men of Happy Valley had been notably daring, deft and ruthless. Banbeck Vale, the Great Northern Rift, Clewhaven, Sadro Valley, Phosphor Gulch: all acknowledged the authority of the Carcolos.

Then down from space came a ship of the Basics, or grephs, as they were known at that time. The ship killed or took prisoner the entire population of Clewhaven; attempted as much in the Great Northern Rift, but only partially succeeded; then bombarded the remaining settlements with explosive pellets.

When the survivors crept back to their devastated valleys, the dominance of Happy Valley was a fiction. A generation later, during the Age of Wet Iron, even the fiction collapsed. In a climactic battle Goss Carcolo was captured by Kergan Banbeck and forced to emasculate himself with his own knife.

Five years of peace elapsed, and then the Basics returned. After depopulating Sadro Valley, the great black ship landed in Banbeck Vale, but the inhabitants had taken warning and had fled into the mountains. Toward nightfall twenty-three of the Basics sallied forth behind their precisely trained warriors: several platoons of Heavy Troops, a squad of Weaponeers – these hardly distinguishable from the men of Aerlith – and a squad of Trackers: these emphatically different. The sunset storm broke over the Vale, rendering the flyers from the ship useless, which allowed Kergan Banbeck to perform the amazing feat which made his name a legend on Aerlith. Rather than joining the terrified flight of his people to the High Jambles, he assembled sixty warriors, shamed them to courage with jeers and taunts.

It was a suicidal venture – fitting the circumstances.

Leaping from ambush they hacked to pieces one platoon of the Heavy Troops, routed the others, captured the twenty-three Basics almost before they realized that anything was amiss. The Weaponeers stood back frantic with frustration, unable to use their weapons for fear of destroying their masters. The Heavy Troopers blundered forward to attack, halting only when Kergan Banbeck performed an unmistakable pantomime to make it clear that the Basics would be the first to die. Confused, the Heavy Troopers drew back; Kergan Banbeck, his men and the twenty-three captives escaped into the darkness.

The long Aerlith night passed; the dawn storm swept out of the east, thundered overhead, retreated majestically into the west; Skene rose like a blazing storm. Three men emerged from the Basic ship: a Weaponeer and a pair of Trackers. They climbed the cliffs to Banbeck Verge, while above flitted a small Basic flyer, no more than a buoyant platform, diving and veering in the wind like a poorly-balanced kite. The three men trudged south toward the High Jambles, a region of chaotic shadows and lights, splintered rock and fallen crags, boulders heaped on boulders. It was the traditional refuge of hunted men.

Halting in front of the Jambles the Weaponeer called out for Kergan Banbeck, asking him to parley.

Kergan Banbeck came forth, and now ensued the strangest colloquy in the history of Aerlith. The Weaponeer spoke the language of men with difficulty, his lips, tongue and glottal passages more adapted to the language of the Basics.

'You are restraining twenty-three of our Revered. It is necessary that you usher them forth, in all humility.' He spoke soberly, with an air of gentle melancholy, neither asserting, commanding, nor urging. As his linguistic habits had been shaped to Basic patterns, so with his mental processes.

Kergan Banbeck, a tall spare man with varnished black eyebrows, black hair shaped and varnished into a crest of five tall spikes, gave a bark of humorless laughter. 'What of the Aerlith folk killed, what of the folk seized aboard your ship?'

The Weaponeer bent forward earnestly, himself an impressive man with a noble aquiline head. He was hairless except for small rolls of wispy yellow fleece. His skin shone as if burnished; his ears, where he differed most noticeably from the unadapted men of Aerlith, were small fragile flaps. He wore a simple garment of dark blue and white, carried no weapons save a small multi-purpose ejector. With complete poise and quiet reasonableness he responded to Kergan Banbeck's question: 'The Aerlith folk who have been killed are dead. Those aboard the ship will be merged into the understratum, where the infusion of fresh outside blood is of value.'

Kergan Banbeck inspected the Weaponeer with contemptuous deliberation. In some respects, thought Kergan Banbeck, this modified and carefully inbred man resembled the sacerdotes of his own planet, notably in the clear fair skin, the strongly modeled features, the long legs and arms. Perhaps telepathy was at work, or perhaps a trace of the characteristic sour-sweet odor had been carried to him: turning his head he noticed a sacerdote standing among the rocks not fifty feet away – a man naked except for his golden torc and long brown hair blowing behind him like a pennant. By the ancient etiquette, Kergan Banbeck looked through him, pretended that he had no existence. The Weaponeer after a swift glance did likewise.

'I demand that you release the folk of Aerlith from your ship,' said Kergan Banbeck in a flat voice.

The Weaponeer smilingly shook his head, bent his best efforts to the task of making himself intelligible. 'These persons are not under discussion; their—' he paused, seeking words '—their destiny is ... parceled, quantum-type, ordained. Established. Nothing can be said more.'

Kergan Banbeck's smile became a cynical grimace. He stood aloof and silent while the Weaponeer croaked on. The sacerdote came slowly forward, a few steps at a time. 'You will understand,' said the Weaponeer, 'that a pattern for events exists. It is the function of such as myself to shape events so that they will fit the pattern.' He bent, and with a graceful sweep of arm seized a small jagged pebble. 'Just as I can grind this bit of rock to fit a round aperture.'

Kergan Banbeck reached forward, took the pebble, tossed it high over the tumbled boulders. 'That bit of rock you shall never shape to fit a round hole.'

The Weaponeer shook his head in mild deprecation. 'There is always more rock.'

'And there are always more holes,' declared Kergan Banbeck.

'To business then,' said the Weaponeer. 'I propose to shape this situation to its correct arrangement.'

'What do you offer in exchange for the twenty-three grephs?'

The Weaponeer gave his shoulder an uneasy shake. The ideas of this man were as wild, barbaric and arbitrary as the varnished spikes of his hair-dress. 'If you desire I will give you instruction and advice, so that—'

Kergan Banbeck made a sudden gesture. 'I make three conditions.' The sacerdote now stood only ten feet away, face blind, gaze vague. 'First,' said Kergan Banbeck, 'a guarantee against future attacks upon the men of Aerlith. Five grephs must always remain in our custody as hostages. Second – further to secure the perpetual validity of the guarantee – you must deliver me a spaceship, equipped, energized, armed, and you must instruct me in its use.'

The Weaponeer threw back his head, made a series of bleating sounds through his nose.

'Third,' continued Kergan Banbeck, 'you must release all the men and women presently aboard your ship.'

The Weaponeer blinked, spoke rapid hoarse words of amazement to the Trackers. They stirred, uneasy and impatient, watching Kergan Banbeck sidelong as if he were not only savage, but mad. Overhead hovered the flyer; the Weaponeer looked up and seemed to derive encouragement from the sight. Turning back to Kergan Banbeck with a firm fresh attitude, he spoke as if the previous interchange had never occurred. 'I have come to instruct you that the twenty-three Revered must be instantly released.'

Kergan Banbeck repeated his own demands. 'You must furnish me a spaceship, you must raid no more, you must release the captives. Do you agree, yes or no?'

The Weaponeer seemed confused. 'This is a peculiar situation – indefinite, unquantizable.'

'Can you not understand me?' barked Kergan Banbeck in exasperation. He glanced at the sacerdote, an act of questionable decorum, then performed in a manner completely unconventional: 'Sacerdote, how can I deal with this blockhead? He does not seem to hear me.'

The sacerdote moved a step nearer, his face as bland and blank as before. Living by a doctrine which proscribed active or intentional interference in the affairs of other men, he could make to any question only a specific and limited answer. 'He hears you, but there is no meeting of ideas between you. His thought-structure is derived from that of his masters. It is incommensurable with yours. As to how you must deal with him, I cannot say.'

Kergan Banbeck looked back to the Weaponeer. 'Have you heard what I asked of you? Did you understand my conditions for the release of the grephs?'

'I heard you distinctly,' replied the Weaponeer. 'Your words have no meaning, they are absurdities, paradoxes. Listen to me carefully. It is ordained, complete, a quantum of destiny, that you deliver to us the Revered. It is irregular, it is not ordainment that you should have a ship, or that your other demands be met.'

Kergan Banbeck's face became red; he half-turned toward his men but restraining his anger, spoke slowly and with careful clarity. 'I have something you want. You have something I want. Let us trade.'

For twenty seconds the two men stared eye to eye. Then the Weaponeer drew a deep breath. 'I will explain in your words, so that you will comprehend. Certainties – no, not certainties: definites ... Definites exist. These are units of certainty, quanta of necessity and order. Existence is the steady succession of these units, one after the other. The activity of the universe can be expressed by reference to these units. Irregularity, absurdity – these are like half a man, with half a brain, half a heart, half of all his vital organs. Neither are allowed to exist. That you hold twenty-three Revered as captives is such an absurdity: an outrage to the rational flow of the universe.'

Kergan Banbeck threw up his hands, turned once more to the sacerdote. 'How can I halt his nonsense? How can I make him see reason?'

The sacerdote reflected. 'He speaks not nonsense, but rather a language you fail to understand. You can make him understand your language by erasing all knowledge and training from his mind, and replacing it with patterns of your own.'

Kergan Banbeck fought back an unsettling sense of frustration and unreality. In order to elicit exact answers from a sacerdote, an exact question was required; indeed it was remarkable that this sacerdote stayed to be questioned. Thinking carefully, he asked, 'How do you suggest that I deal with this man?'

'Release the twenty-three grephs.' The sacerdote touched the twin knobs at the front of his golden torc: a ritual gesture indicating that, no matter how reluctantly, he had performed an act which conceivably might alter the course of the future. Again he tapped his torc, and intoned, 'Release the grephs; he will then depart.'

Kergan Banbeck cried out in unrestrained anger. 'Who then do you serve? Man or greph? Let us have the truth! Speak!'

'By my faith, by my creed, by the truth of my *tand* I serve no one but myself.' The sacerdote turned his face toward the great crag of Mount Gethron and moved slowly off; the wind blew his long fine hair to the side.

Kergan Banbeck watched him go, then with cold decisiveness turned back to the Weaponeer. 'Your discussion of certainties and absurdities is interesting. I feel that you have confused the two. Here is certainty from my viewpoint! I will not release the twenty-three grephs unless you meet my terms. If you attack us further, I will cut them in half, to illustrate and realize your figure of speech, and perhaps convince you that absurdities are possible. I say no more.'

The Weaponeer shook his head slowly, pityingly. 'Listen, I will explain. Certain conditions are unthinkable, they are unquantized, un-destined—'

'Go,' thundered Kergan Banbeck. 'Otherwise you will join your twenty-three revered grephs, and I will teach you how real the unthinkable can become!'

The Weaponeer and the two Trackers, croaking and muttering, turned, retreated from the Jambles to Banbeck Verge, descended into the valley. Over them the flyer darted, veered, fluttered, settled like a falling leaf.

Watching from their retreat among the crags, the men of Banbeck Vale presently witnessed a remarkable scene. Half an hour after the Weaponeer had returned to the ship, he came leaping forth once again, dancing, cavorting. Others followed him – Weaponeers, Trackers, Heavy Troopers and eight more grephs – all jerking, jumping, running back and forth in distracted steps. The ports of the ship flashed lights of various colors, and there came a slow rising sound of tortured machinery.

'They have gone mad!' muttered Kergan Banbeck. He hesitated an instant, then gave an order. 'Assemble every man; we attack while they are helpless!'

Down from the High Jambles rushed the men of Banbeck Vale. As they descended the cliffs, a few of the captured men and women from Sadro Valley came timidly forth from the ship and meeting no restraint fled to freedom across Banbeck Vale. Others followed – and now the Banbeck warriors reached the valley floor.

Beside the ship the insanity had quieted; the out-worlders huddled quietly beside the hull. There came a sudden mind-shattering explosion: a blankness of yellow and white fire. The ship disintegrated. A great crater marred the valley floor; fragments of metal began to fall among the attacking Banbeck warriors.

Kergan Banbeck stared at the scene of destruction. Slowly, his shoulders sagging, he summoned his people and led them back to their ruined valley. At the rear, marching single-file, tied together with ropes, came the twenty-three grephs, dull-eyed, pliant, already remote from their previous existence. The texture of Destiny was inevitable: the present circumstances could not apply to twenty-three of the Revered. The mechanism must therefore adjust to insure the halcyon progression of events. The twenty-three, hence, were something other than the Revered: a different order of creature entirely. If this were true, what were they? Asking each other the question in sad croaking undertones, they marched down the cliff into Banbeck Vale.

CHAPTER THREE

Across the long Aerlith years the fortunes of Happy Valley and Banbeck Vale fluctuated with the capabilities of the opposing Carcolos and Banbecks. Golden Banbeck, Joaz's grandfather, was forced to release Happy Valley from clientship when Uttern Carcolo, an accomplished dragon-breeder, produced the first Fiends. Golden Banbeck, in his turn, developed the Juggers, but allowed an uneasy truce to continue.

Further years passed; Ilden Banbeck, the son of Golden, a frail ineffectual man, was killed in a fall from a mutinous Spider. With Joaz yet an ailing child, Grode Carcolo decided to try his chances against Banbeck Vale. He failed to reckon with old Hendel Banbeck, grand-uncle to Joaz and Chief Dragon Master. The Happy Valley forces were routed on Starbreak Fell; Grode Carcolo was killed and young Ervis gored by a Murderer. For various reasons, including Hendel's age and Joaz's youth, the Banbeck army failed to press to a decisive advantage. Ervis Carcolo, though exhausted by loss of blood and pain, withdrew in some degree of order, and for further years a suspicious truce held between the neighboring valleys.

Joaz matured into a saturnine young man who, if he excited no enthusiastic affection from his people, at least aroused no violent dislike. He and Ervis Carcolo were united in a mutual contempt. At the mention of Joaz's study, with its books, scrolls, models and plans, its complicated viewing-system across Banbeck Vale (the optics furnished, it was rumored, by the sacerdotes), Carcolo would throw up his hands in disgust. 'Learning? Pah! What avails all this rolling in bygone vomit? Where does it lead? He should have been born a sacerdote; he is the same sort of sour-mouthed cloud-minded weakling!'

An itinerant, one Dae Alvonso, who combined the trades of minstrel, child-buyer, psychiatrist and chiropractor, reported Carcolo's obloquies to Joaz, who shrugged. 'Ervis Carcolo should breed himself to one of his own Juggers,' said Joaz. 'He would thereby produce an impregnable creature with the Jugger's armor and his own unflinching stupidity.'

The remark in due course returned to Ervis Carcolo, and by coincidence, touched him in a particularly sore spot. Secretly he had been attempting an innovation at his brooders: a dragon almost as massive as the Jugger with the savage intelligence and agility of the Blue Horror. But Ervis Carcolo worked with an intuitive and over-optimistic approach, ignoring the advice of Bast Givven, his Chief Dragon Master.

The eggs hatched; a dozen spratlings survived. Ervis Carcolo nurtured them with alternate tenderness and objurgation. Eventually the dragons matured. Carcolo's hoped-for combination of fury and impregnability was realized in four sluggish irritable creatures, with bloated torsos, spindly legs, insatiable appetites. ('As if one can breed a dragon by commanding it: "Exist!"' sneered Bast Givven to his helpers, and advised them: 'Be wary of the beasts; they are competent only at luring you within reach of their brachs.')

The time, effort, facilities and provender wasted upon the useless hybrid had weakened Carcolo's army. Of the fecund Termagants he had no lack; there was a sufficiency of Long-horned Murderers and Striding Murderers, but the heavier and more specialized types, especially Juggers, were far from adequate to his plans. The memory of Happy Valley's ancient glory haunted his dreams; first he would subdue Banbeck Vale, and often he planned the ceremony whereby he would reduce Joaz Banbeck to the office of apprentice barracks-boy.

Ervis Carcolo's ambitions were complicated by a set of basic difficulties. Happy Valley's population had doubled but rather than extending the city by breaching new pinnacles or driving tunnels, Carcolo constructed three new dragon-brooders, a dozen barracks and an enormous training compound. The folk of the valley could choose either to cram the fetid existing tunnels or build ramshackle dwellings along the base of the cliff. Brooders, barracks, training compounds and huts encroached on Happy Valley's already inadequate fields. Water was diverted from the pond to maintain the brooders; enormous quantities of produce went to feed dragons. The folk of Happy Valley, undernourished, sickly, miserable, shared none of Carcolo's aspirations, and their lack of enthusiasm infuriated him.

In any event, when the itinerant Dae Alvonso repeated Joaz Banbeck's recommendation that Ervis Carcolo breed himself to a Jugger, Carcolo seethed with choler. 'Bah! What does Joaz Banbeck know about dragon-breeding? I doubt if he understands his own dragon-talk.' He referred to the means by which orders and instructions were transmitted to the dragons: a secret jargon distinctive to every army. To learn an opponent's dragon-talk was the prime goal of every dragon master, for he thereby gained a certain degree of control over his enemies' forces. 'I am a practical man, worth two of him,' Carcolo went on. 'Can he design, nurture, rear and teach dragons? Can he impose discipline, teach ferocity? No. He leaves all this to his dragon masters, while he lolls on a couch eating sweetmeats, campaigning only against the patience of his minstrel-maidens. They say that by astrological divination he predicts the return of the Basics, that he walks with his neck cocked, watching the sky. Is such a man deserving of power and a prosperous life? I say no! Is Ervis Carcolo of Happy Valley such a man? I say yes, and this I will demonstrate!'

Dae Alvonso judiciously held up his hand. 'Not so fast. He is more alert than you think. His dragons are in prime condition; he visits them often. And as for the Basics—'

'Do not speak to me of Basics,' stormed Carcolo. 'I am no child to be frightened by bugbears!'

Again Dae Alvonso held up his hand. 'Listen. I am serious, and you can profit by my news. Joaz Banbeck took me into his private study—'

'The famous study, indeed!'

'From a cabinet he brought out a ball of crystal mounted on a black box.'

'Aha!' jeered Carcolo. 'A crystal ball!'

Dae Alvonso went on placidly, ignoring the interruption. 'I examined this globe, and indeed it seemed to hold all of space; within it floated stars and planets, all the bodies of the cluster. "Look well," said Joaz Banbeck, "you will never see the like of this anywhere. It was built by the olden men and brought to Aerlith when our people first arrived."

'"Indeed," I said. "And what is this object?"

'"It is a celestial armamentarium," said Joaz. "It depicts all the nearby stars, and their positions at any time I choose to specify. Now—" here he pointed "—see this white dot? This is our sun. See this red star? In the old almanacs it is named Coralyne. It swings near us at irregular intervals, for such is the flow of stars in this cluster. These intervals have always coincided with the attacks of the Basics."

'Here I expressed astonishment; Joaz assured me regarding the matter. "The history of men on Aerlith records six attacks by the Basics, or grephs as they were originally known. Apparently as Coralyne swings through space the Basics scour nearby worlds for hidden dens of humanity. The last of these was long ago during the time of Kergan Banbeck, with the results you know about. At that time Coralyne passed close in the heavens. For the first time since, Coralyne is once more close at hand." This,' Alvonso told Carcolo, 'is what Joaz Banbeck told me, and this is what I saw.'

Carcolo was impressed in spite of himself. 'Do you mean to tell me,' demanded Carcolo, 'that within this globe swim all the stars of space?'

'As to that, I cannot vouch,' replied Dae Alvonso. 'The globe is set in a black box, and I suspect that an inner mechanism projects images or perhaps controls luminous spots which simulate the stars. Either way it is a marvelous device, one which I would be proud to own. I offered Joaz several precious objects in exchange, but he would have none of them.'

Carcolo curled his lip in disgust. 'You and your stolen children. Have you no shame?'

'No more than my customers,' said Dae Alvonso stoutly. 'As I recall, I have dealt profitably with you on several occasions.'

Ervis Carcolo turned away, pretended to watch a pair of Termagants exercising with wooden scimitars. The two men stood by a stone fence behind which scores of dragons practiced evolutions, dueled with spears and swords, strengthened their muscles. Scales flashed, dust rose up under splayed stamping feet; the acrid odor of dragon-sweat permeated the air.

Carcolo muttered, 'He is crafty, that Joaz. He knew you would report to me in detail.'

Dae Alvonso nodded. 'Precisely. His words were – but perhaps I should be discreet.' He glanced slyly toward Carcolo from under shaggy white eyebrows.

'Speak,' said Ervis Carcolo gruffly.

'Very well. Mind you, I quote Joaz Banbeck. "Tell blundering old Carcolo that he is in great danger. If the Basics return to Aerlith, as well they may, Happy Valley is absolutely vulnerable and will be ruined. Where can his people hide? They will be herded into the black ship, transported to a cold new planet. If Carcolo is not completely heartless he will drive new tunnels, prepare hidden avenues. Otherwise—"'

'Otherwise what?' demanded Carcolo.

'Otherwise there will be no more Happy Valley, no more Ervis Carcolo.'

'Bah,' said Carcolo in a subdued voice. 'The young jackanapes barks in shrill tones.'

'Perhaps he extends an honest warning. His further words – but I fear to offend your dignity.'

'Continue! Speak!'

'These are his words – but no, I dare not repeat them. Essentially he considers your efforts to create an army ludicrous; he contrasts your intelligence unfavorably to his own; he predicts—'

'Enough!' roared Ervis Carcolo, waving his fists. 'He is a subtle adversary, but why do you lend yourself to his tricks?'

Dae Alvonso shook his frosty old head. 'I merely repeat, with reluctance, that which you demand to hear. Now then, since you have wrung me dry, do me some profit. Will you buy drugs, elixirs, wambles or potions? I have here a salve of eternal youth which I stole from the Demie Sacerdote's personal coffer. In my train are both boy and girl children, obsequious and handsome, at a fair price. I will listen to your woes, cure your lisp, guarantee a placidity of disposition – or perhaps you would buy dragon eggs?'

'I need none of those,' grunted Carcolo. 'Especially dragon's eggs which hatch to lizards. As for children, Happy Valley seethes with them. Bring me a dozen sound Juggers and you may depart with a hundred children of your choice.'

Dae Alvonso shook his head sadly, lurched away. Carcolo slumped against the fence, staring across the dragon pens.

The sun hung low over the crags of Mount Despoire; evening was close at hand. This was the most pleasant time of the Aerlith day, when the winds ceased, leaving a vast velvet quiet. Skene's blaze softened to a smoky yellow, with a bronze aureole; the clouds of the approaching evening storm gathered, rose, fell, shifted, swirled; glowing and changing in every tone of gold, orange–brown, gold–brown and dusty violet.

Skene sank; the golds and oranges became oak-brown and purple; lightning threaded the clouds and the rain fell in a black curtain. In the barracks men moved with vigilance, for now the dragons became unpredictable: by turns watchful, torpid, quarrelsome. With the passing of the rain, evening became night, and a cool quiet breeze drifted through the valleys. The dark sky began to burn and dazzle with the stars of the cluster. One of the most effulgent twinkled red, green, white, red, green.

Ervis Carcolo studied this star thoughtfully. One idea led to another, and presently to a course of action which seemed to dissolve the entire tangle of uncertainties and dissatisfactions which marred his life. Carcolo twisted his mouth to a sour grimace; he must make overtures to that popinjay Joaz Banbeck – but if this were unavoidable: so be it!

Hence, the following morning, shortly after Phade the minstrel-maiden discovered the sacerdote in Joaz's study, a messenger appeared in the Vale, inviting Joaz Banbeck up to Banbeck Verge for a conference with Ervis Carcolo.

CHAPTER FOUR

Ervis Carcolo waited on Banbeck Verge with Chief Dragon Master Bast Givven and a pair of young fuglemen. Behind, in a row, stood their mounts: four glistening Spiders, brachs folded, legs splayed at exactly identical angles. These were of Carcolo's newest breed and he was immoderately proud of them. The barbs surrounding the horny visages were clasped with cinnabar cabochons; a round target enameled black and studded with a central spike covered each chest. The men wore the traditional black leather breeches, with short maroon cloaks, black leather helmets with long flaps slanting back across the ears and down to the shoulders.

The four men waited, patient or restless as their natures dictated, surveying the well-tended length of Banbeck Vale. To the south stretched fields of various food-stuffs: vetch, bellegarde, moss-cake, a loquat grove. Directly opposite, near the mouth of Clybourne Crevasse, the shape of the crater created by the explosion of the Basic ship could still be seen. North lay more fields, then the dragon compounds, consisting of black-brick barracks, a brooder, an exercise field. Beyond lay Banbeck Jambles – an area of wasteland where ages previously a section of the cliff had fallen, creating a wilderness of tumbled rock similar to the High Jambles under Mount Gethron, but smaller in compass.

One of the young fuglemen rather tactlessly commented upon the evident prosperity of Banbeck Vale, to the implicit deprecation of Happy Valley. Ervis Carcolo listened glumly a moment or two, then turned a haughty stare toward the offender.

'Notice the dam,' said the fugleman. 'We waste half our water in seepage.'

'True,' said the other. 'That rock facing is a good idea. I wonder why we don't do something similar.'

Carcolo started to speak, thought better of it. With a growling sound in his throat, he turned away. Bast Givven made a sign; the fuglemen hastily fell silent.

A few moments later Givven announced: 'Joaz Banbeck has set forth.'

Carcolo peered down toward Kergan's Way. 'Where is his company? Does he ride alone?'

'So it seems.'

A few minutes later Joaz Banbeck appeared on Banbeck Verge riding a Spider caparisoned in gray and red velvet. Joaz wore a loose lounge cloak of soft brown cloth over a gray shirt and gray trousers, with a long-billed hat of blue velvet. He held up his hand in casual greeting; brusquely Ervis Carcolo returned the salute, and with a jerk of his head sent Givven and the fuglemen off out of earshot.

Carcolo said gruffly, 'You sent me a message by old Alvonso.'

Joaz nodded. 'I trust he rendered my remarks accurately?'

Carcolo grinned wolfishly. 'At times he felt obliged to paraphrase.'

'Tactful old Dae Alvonso.'

'I am given to understand,' said Carcolo, 'that you consider me rash, ineffectual, callous to the best interests of Happy Valley. Alvonso admitted that you used the word "blunderer" in reference to me.'

Joaz smiled politely. 'Sentiments of this sort are best transmitted through intermediaries.'

Carcolo made a great show of dignified forbearance. 'Apparently you feel that another Basic attack is imminent.'

'Just so,' agreed Joaz, 'if my theory, which puts their home by the star Coralyne, is correct. In which case, as I pointed out to Alvonso, Happy Valley is seriously vulnerable.'

'And why not Banbeck Vale as well?' barked Carcolo.

Joaz stared at him in surprise. 'Is it not obvious? I have taken precautions. My people are housed in tunnels, rather than huts. We have several escape

routes, should this prove necessary, both to the High Jambles and to Banbeck Jambles.'

'Very interesting.' Carcolo made an effort to soften his voice. 'If your
theory is accurate – and I pass no immediate judgment – then perhaps I
would be wise to take similar measures. But I think in different terms. I
prefer attack, activity, to passive defense.'

'Admirable,' said Joaz Banbeck. 'Important deeds are done by men such
as you.'

Carcolo became a trifle pink in the face. 'This is neither here nor there,'
he said. 'I have come to propose a joint project. It is entirely novel, but carefully thought out. I have considered various aspects of this matter for several
years.'

'I attend you with great interest,' said Joaz.

Carcolo blew out his cheeks. 'You know the legends as well as I, perhaps
better. Our people came to Aerlith as exiles during the War of the Ten Stars.
The Nightmare Coalition apparently had defeated the Old Rule, but how the
war ended—' he threw up his hands '—who can say?'

'There is a significant indication,' said Joaz. 'The Basics revisit Aerlith and
ravage us at their pleasure. We have seen no men visiting except those who
serve the Basics.'

'"Men"?' Carcolo demanded scornfully. 'I call them something else.
Nevertheless, this is no more than a deduction, and we are ignorant as to
the course of history. Perhaps Basics rule the cluster; perhaps they plague
us only because we are weak and weaponless. Perhaps we are the last men;
perhaps the Old Rule is resurgent. And never forget that many years have
elapsed since the Basics last appeared on Aerlith.'

'Many years have elapsed since Aerlith and Coralyne were in such convenient apposition.'

Carcolo made an impatient gesture. 'A supposition, which may or may
not be relevant. Let me explain the basic axiom of my proposal. It is simple
enough. I feel that Banbeck Vale and Happy Valley are too small a compass
for men such as ourselves. We deserve larger scope.'

Joaz agreed. 'I wish it were possible to ignore the practical difficulties
involved.'

'I am able to suggest a method to counter these difficulties,' asserted
Carcolo.

'In that case,' said Joaz, 'power, glory and wealth are as good as ours.'

Carcolo glanced at him sharply, slapped his breeches with the gold-
beaded tassel to his scabbard. 'Reflect,' he said. 'The sacerdotes inhabited
Aerlith before us. How long no one can say. It is a mystery. In fact, what
do we know of the sacerdotes? Next to nothing. They trade their metal and
glass for our food, they live in deep caverns, their creed is disassociation,

reverie, detachment, whatever one may wish to call it – totally incomprehensible to one such as myself.' He challenged Joaz with a look; Joaz merely fingered his long chin. 'They put themselves forward as simple metaphysical cultists; actually they are a very mysterious people. Has anyone yet seen a sacerdote woman? What of the blue lights, what of the lightning towers, what of the sacerdote magic? What of weird comings and goings by night, what of strange shapes moving across the sky, perhaps to other planets?'

'The tales exist, certainly,' said Joaz. 'As to the degree of credence to be placed in them—'

'Now we reach the meat of my proposal!' declared Ervis Carcolo. 'The creed of the sacerdotes apparently forbids shame, inhibition, fear, regard for consequence. Hence, they are forced to answer any question put to them. Nevertheless, creed or no creed, they completely befog any information an assiduous man is able to wheedle from them.'

Joaz inspected him curiously. 'Evidently you have made the attempt.'

Ervis Carcolo nodded. 'Yes. Why should I deny it? I have questioned three sacerdotes with determination and persistence. They answered all my questions with gravity and calm reflection, but told me nothing.' He shook his head in vexation. 'Therefore, I suggest that we apply coercion.'

'You are a brave man.'

Carcolo shook his head modestly. 'I would dare no direct measures. But they must eat. If Banbeck Vale and Happy Valley co-operate, we can apply a very cogent persuasion: hunger. Presently their words may be more to the point.'

Joaz considered a moment or two. Ervis Carcolo twitched his scabbard tassel. 'Your plan,' said Joaz at last, 'is not a frivolous one, and is ingenious – at least at first glance. What sort of information do you hope to secure? In short, what are your ultimate aims?'

Carcolo sidled close, prodded Joaz with his forefinger. 'We know nothing of the outer worlds. We are marooned on this miserable world of stone and wind while life passes us by. You assume that Basics rule the cluster, but suppose you are wrong? Suppose the Old Rule has returned? Think of the rich cities, the gay resorts, the palaces, the pleasure-islands! Look up into the night sky, ponder the bounties which might be ours! You ask how can we implement these desires? I respond, the process may be so simple that the sacerdotes will reveal it without reluctance.'

'You mean—'

'Communication with the worlds of men! Deliverance from this lonely little world at the edge of the universe!'

Joaz Banbeck nodded dubiously. 'A fine vision, but the evidence suggests a situation far different, namely the destruction of man, and the Human Empire.'

Carcolo held out his hands in a gesture of open-minded tolerance. 'Perhaps you are right. But why should we not make inquiries of the sacerdotes? Concretely I propose as follows: that you and I agree to the mutual cause I have outlined. Next, we request an audience with the Demie Sacerdote. We put our questions. If he responds freely, well and good. If he evades, then we act in mutuality. No more food to the sacerdotes until they tell us plainly what we want to hear.'

'Other valleys, vales, and gulches exist,' said Joaz thoughtfully.

Carcolo made a brisk gesture. 'We can deter any such trade by persuasion or by the power of our dragons.'

'The essence of your idea appeals to me,' said Joaz, 'but I fear that all is not so simple.'

Carcolo rapped his thigh smartly with the tassel. 'And why not?'

'In the first place, Coralyne shines bright in the sky. This is our first concern. Should Coralyne pass, should the Basics not attack – then is the time to pursue this matter. Again – and perhaps more to the point – I doubt that we can starve the sacerdotes into submission. In fact, I think it highly unlikely. I will go farther. I consider it impossible.'

Carcolo blinked. 'In what wise?'

'They walk naked through sleet and storm; do you think they fear hunger? And there is wild lichen to be gathered. How could we forbid this? You might dare some sort of coercion, but not I. The tales told of the sacerdotes may be no more than superstition – or they may be understatement.'

Ervis Carcolo heaved a deep disgusted sigh. 'Joaz Banbeck, I took you for a man of decision. But you merely pick flaws.'

'These are not flaws, they are major errors which would lead to disaster.'

'Well then. Do you have any suggestions of your own?'

Joaz fingered his chin. 'If Coralyne recedes and we are still on Aerlith – rather than in the hold of the Basic ship – then let us plan to plunder the secrets of the sacerdotes. In the meantime I strongly recommend that you prepare Happy Valley against a new raid. You are over-extended, with your new brooders and barracks. Let them rest, while you dig yourself secure tunnels!'

Ervis Carcolo stared straight across Banbeck Vale. 'I am not a man to defend. I attack!'

'You will attack heat-beams and ion-rays with your dragons?'

Ervis Carcolo turned his gaze back to Joaz Banbeck. 'Can I consider us allies in the plan I have proposed?'

'In its broadest principles, certainly. However I don't care to co-operate in starving or otherwise coercing the sacerdotes. It might be dangerous, as well as futile.'

For an instant Carcolo could not control his detestation of Joaz Banbeck;

337

his lip curled, his hands clenched. 'Danger? Pah! What danger from a handful of naked pacifists?'

'We do not know that they are pacifists. We do know that they are men.'

Carcolo once more became brightly cordial. 'Perhaps you are right. But – essentially at least – we are allies.'

'To a degree.'

'Good. I suggest that in the case of the attack you fear, we act together, with a common strategy.'

Joaz nodded distantly. 'This might be effective.'

'Let us coordinate our plans. Let us assume that the Basics drop down into Banbeck Vale. I suggest that your folk take refuge in Happy Valley, while the Happy Valley army joins with yours to cover their retreat. And likewise, should they attack Happy Valley, my people will take refuge in Banbeck Vale.'

Joaz laughed in sheer amusement. 'Ervis Carcolo, what sort of lunatic do you take me for? Return to your valley, put aside your foolish grandiosities, dig yourself protection. And fast! Coralyne is bright!'

Carcolo stood stiffly. 'Do I understand that you reject my offer of alliance?'

'Not at all. But I cannot undertake to protect you and your people if you will not help yourselves. Meet my requirements, satisfy me that you are a fit ally – then we shall speak further of alliance.'

Ervis Carcolo whirled on his heel, signaled to Bast Givven and the two young fuglemen. With no further word or glance he mounted his splendid Spider, goaded him into a sudden leaping run across the Verge, and up the slope toward Starbreak Fell. His men followed, somewhat less precipitously.

Joaz watched them go, shaking his head in sad wonder. Then, mounting his own Spider, he returned down the trail to the floor of Banbeck Vale.

CHAPTER FIVE

The long Aerlith day, equivalent to six of the old Diurnal Units, passed. In Happy Valley there was grim activity, a sense of purpose and impending decision. The dragons exercised in tighter formation, the fuglemen and cornets called orders with harsher voices. In the armory bullets were cast, powder mixed, swords ground and honed.

Ervis Carcolo drove himself with dramatic bravado, wearing out Spider after Spider as he sent his dragons through various evolutions. In the case of the Happy Valley forces, these were for the most part Termagants – small active dragons with rust-red scales, narrow darting heads, chisel-sharp fangs. Their brachs were strong and well-developed: they used lance, cutlass or mace with equal skill. A man pitted against a Termagant stood no chance, for the scales warded off bullets as well as any blow the man might have strength enough to deal. On the other hand a single slash of fang, the rip of a scythe-like claw, meant death to the man.

The Termagants were fecund and hardy and throve even under the conditions which existed in the Happy Valley brooders; hence their predominance in Carcolo's army. This was a situation not to the liking of Bast Givven, Chief Dragon Master, a spare wiry man with a flat crooked-nosed face, eyes black and blank as drops of ink on a plate. Habitually terse and tight-lipped, he waxed almost eloquent in opposition to the attack upon Banbeck Vale. 'Look you, Ervis Carcolo, we are able to deploy a horde of Termagants, with sufficient Striding Murderers and Long-horned Murderers. But Blue Horrors, Fiends and Juggers – no! We are lost if they trap us on the fells!'

'I do not plan to fight on the fells,' said Carcolo. 'I will force battle upon Joaz Banbeck. His Juggers and Fiends are useless on the cliffs. And in the matter of Blue Horrors we are almost his equal.'

'You overlook a single difficulty,' said Bast Givven.

'And what is this?'

'The improbability that Joaz Banbeck plans to permit all this. I allow him greater intelligence.'

'Show me evidence!' charged Carcolo. 'What I know of him suggests vacillation and stupidity! So we will strike – hard!' Carcolo smacked fist into palm. 'Thus we will finish the haughty Banbecks!'

Bast Givven turned to go; Carcolo wrathfully called him back. 'You show no enthusiasm for this campaign!'

'I know what our army can do and what it cannot do,' said Givven bluntly. 'If Joaz Banbeck is the man you think he is, we might succeed. If he has even the sagacity of a pair of grooms I listened to ten minutes ago, we face disaster.'

In a voice thick with rage, Carcolo said, 'Return to your Fiends and Juggers. I want them quick as Termagants.'

Bast Givven went his way. Carcolo jumped on a nearby Spider, kicked it with his heels. The creature sprang forward, halted sharply, twisted its long neck about to look Carcolo in the face. Carcolo cried, 'Hust, hust! Forward at speed, smartly now! Show these louts what snap and spirit mean!' The Spider jumped ahead with such vehemence that Carcolo tumbled over backward, landing on his neck, where he lay groaning. Grooms came running, assisted him to a bench where he sat cursing in a steady low voice. A surgeon examined, pressed, prodded, recommended that Carcolo take to his couch, and administered a sedative potion.

Carcolo was carried to his apartments beneath the west wall of Happy Valley, placed under the care of his wives, and so slept for twenty hours. When he awoke the day was half gone. He wished to arise, but found himself too stiff to move, and groaning, lay back. Presently he called for Bast Givven, who appeared and listened without comment to Carcolo's adjurations.

Evening arrived; the dragons returned to the barracks. There was nothing to do now but wait for daybreak.

During the long night Carcolo underwent a variety of treatments: massage, hot baths, infusions, poultices. He exercised with diligence, and as the night reached its end, he declared himself fit. Overhead the star Coralyne vibrated poisonous colors: red, green, white, by far the brightest star of the cluster. Carcolo refused to look up at the star, but its radiance struck through the corners of his eyes whenever he walked on the valley floor.

Dawn approached. Carcolo planned to march at the earliest moment the dragons were manageable. A flickering to the east told of the oncoming dawn storm, still invisible across the horizon. With great caution the dragons were mustered from their barracks and ordered into a marching column. There were almost three hundred Termagants; eighty-five Striding Murderers; as many Long-horned Murderers; a hundred Blue Horrors; fifty-two squat, immensely powerful Fiends, their tails tipped with spiked steel balls; eighteen Juggers. They growled and muttered evilly among themselves, watching an opportunity to kick each other or to snip a leg from an unwary groom. Darkness stimulated their latent hatred for humanity, though they had been taught nothing of their past, nor the circumstances by which they had become enslaved.

The dawn lightning blazed and crackled, outlining the vertical steeples, the astonishing peaks of the Malheur Mountains. Overhead passed the storm, with wailing gusts of wind and thrashing banks of rain moving on toward Banbeck Vale. The east glowed with a gray–green pallor, and Carcolo gave the signal to march. Still stiff and sore he hobbled to his Spider, mounted, ordered the creature into a special and dramatic curvet. Carcolo had miscalculated; malice of the night still gripped the mind of the dragon. It ended its curvet with a lash of the neck which once again dashed Carcolo to the ground, where he lay half-mad with pain and frustration.

He tried to rise, collapsed; tried again, fainted. Five minutes he lay unconscious, then seemed to rouse himself by sheer force of will. 'Lift me,' he whispered huskily. 'Tie me into the saddle. We must march.' This being manifestly impossible, no one made a move. Carcolo raged, finally called hoarsely for Bast Givven. 'Proceed; we cannot stop now. You must lead the troops.'

Givven nodded glumly. This was an honor for which he had no stomach.

'You know the battle-plan,' wheezed Carcolo. 'Circle north of the Fang, cross the Skanse with all speed, swing north around Blue Crevasse, then south along Banbeck Verge. There Joaz Banbeck may be expected to discover you. You must deploy so that when he brings up his Juggers you can topple them back with Fiends. Avoid committing our Juggers, harry him with Termagants; reserve the Murderers to strike wherever he reaches the edge. Do you understand me?'

'As you explain it, victory is certain,' muttered Bast Givven.

'And so it is, unless you blunder grievously. Ah, my back! I can't move. While the great battle rages I must sit by the brooder and watch eggs hatch! Now go! Strike hard for Happy Valley!'

Givven gave an order; the troops set forth. Termagants darted into the lead, followed by silken Striding Murderers and the heavier Long-horned Murderers, their fantastic chest-spikes tipped with steel. Behind came the ponderous Juggers, grunting, gurgling, teeth clashing together with the vibration of their steps. Flanking the Juggers marched the Fiends, carrying heavy cutlasses, flourishing their terminal steel balls as a scorpion carries his sting; then at the rear came the Blue Horrors, who were both massive and quick, good climbers, no less intelligent than the Termagants. To the flanks rode a hundred men: dragon masters, knights, fuglemen and cornets. They were armed with swords, pistols and large-bore blunderbusses.

Carcolo, on a stretcher, watched till the last of his forces had passed from view, then commanded himself carried back to the portal which led into the Happy Valley caves. Never before had the caves seemed so dingy and shallow. Sourly he eyed the straggle of huts along the cliff, built of rock, slabs of resin-impregnated lichen, canes bound with tar. With the Banbeck campaign at an end, he would set about cutting new chambers and halls into the cliff. The splendid decorations of Banbeck Village were well-known; Happy Valley would be even more magnificent. The halls would glow with opal and nacre, silver and gold ... and yet, to what end? If events went as planned, there was his great dream in prospect. And then, what consequence a few paltry decorations in the tunnels of Happy Valley?

Groaning, he allowed himself to be laid on his couch and entertained himself picturing the progress of his troops. By now they should be working down from Dangle Ridge, circling the mile-high Fang. He tentatively stretched his arms, worked his legs. His muscles protested, pain shot back and forth along his body – but it seemed as if the injuries were less than before. By now the army would be mounting the ramparts which rimmed that wide area of upland fell known as the Skanse. The surgeon brought Carcolo a potion; he drank and slept, to awake with a start. What was the time? His troops might well have joined battle!

He ordered himself carried to the outer portal; then, still dissatisfied, commanded his servants to transport him across the valley to the new dragon brooder, the walkway of which commanded a view up and down the valley. Despite the protests of his wives, here he was conveyed, and made as comfortable as bruises and sprains permitted.

He settled himself for an indeterminate wait, but news was not long in coming.

Down the North Trail came a cornet on a foam-bearded Spider. Carcolo sent a groom to intercept him, and heedless of aches and pains raised himself from his couch. The cornet threw himself off his mount, staggered up the ramp, sagged exhausted against the rail.

'Ambush!' he panted. 'Bloody disaster!'

'Ambush?' groaned Carcolo in a hollow voice. 'Where?'

'As we mounted the Skanse Ramparts. They waited till our Termagants and Murderers were over, then charged with Horrors, Fiends and Juggers. They cut us apart, drove us back, then rolled boulders on our Juggers! Our army is broken!'

Carcolo sank back on the couch, lay staring at the sky. 'How many are lost?'

'I do not know. Givven called the retreat; we withdrew in the best style possible.'

Carcolo lay as if comatose; the cornet flung himself down on a bench.

A column of dust appeared to the north, which presently dissolved and separated to reveal a number of Happy Valley dragons. All were wounded; they marched, hopped, limped, dragged themselves at random, croaking, glaring, bugling. First came a group of Termagants, darting ugly heads from side to side; then a pair of Blue Horrors, brachs twisting and clasping almost like human arms; then a Jugger, massive, toad-like, legs splayed out in weariness. Even as it neared the barracks it toppled, fell with a thud to lie still, legs and talons jutting into the air.

Down from the North Trail rode Bast Givven, dust-stained and haggard. He dismounted from his drooping Spider, mounted the ramp. With a wrenching effort, Carcolo once more raised himself on the couch.

Givven reported in a voice so even and light as to seem careless, but even the insensitive Carcolo was not deceived. He asked in puzzlement: 'Exactly where did the ambush occur?'

'We mounted the Ramparts by way of Chloris Ravine. Where the Skanse falls off into the ravine a porphyry outcrop juts up and over. Here they awaited us.'

Carcolo hissed through his teeth. 'Amazing.'

Bast Givven gave the faintest of nods.

Carcolo said, 'Assume that Joaz Banbeck set forth during the dawn-storm, an hour earlier than I would think possible; assume that he forced his troops at a run. How could he reach the Skanse Ramparts before us even so?'

'By my reckoning,' said Givven, 'ambush was no threat until we had crossed the Skanse. I had planned to patrol Barchback, all the way down Blue Fell, and across Blue Crevasse.'

Carcolo gave somber agreement. 'How then did Joaz Banbeck bring his troops to the Ramparts so soon?'

Givven turned, looked up the valley, where wounded dragons and men still straggled down the North Trail. 'I have no idea.'

'A drug?' puzzled Carcolo. 'A potion to pacify the dragons? Could he have made bivouac on the Skanse the whole night long?'

'The last is possible,' admitted Givven grudgingly. 'Under Barch Spike are empty caves. If he quartered his troops there during the night, then he had only to march across the Skanse to waylay us.'

Carcolo grunted. 'Perhaps we have underestimated Joaz Banbeck.' He sank back on his couch with a groan. 'Well then, what are our losses?'

The reckoning made dreary news. Of the already inadequate squad of Juggers, only six remained. From a force of fifty-two Fiends, forty survived and of these five were sorely wounded. Termagants, Blue Horrors and Murderers had suffered greatly. A large number had been torn apart in the first onslaught, many others had been toppled down the Ramparts to strew their armored husks through the detritus. Of the hundred men, twelve had been killed by bullets, another fourteen by dragon attack; a score more were wounded in various degree.

Carcolo lay back, his eyes closed, his mouth working feebly.

'The terrain alone saved us,' said Givven. 'Joaz Banbeck refused to commit his troops to the ravine. If there were any tactical error on either side, it was his. He brought an insufficiency of Termagants and Blue Horrors.'

'Small comfort,' growled Carcolo. 'Where is the balance of the army?'

'We have good position on Dangle Ridge. We have seen none of Banbeck's scouts, either man or Termagant. He may conceivably believe we have retreated to the valley. In any event his main forces were still collected on the Skanse.'

Carcolo, by an enormous effort raised himself to his feet. He tottered across the walkway to look down into the dispensary. Five Fiends crouched in vats of balsam, muttering, sighing. A Blue Horror hung in a sling, whining as surgeons cut broken fragments of armor from its gray flesh. As Carcolo watched, one of the Fiends raised itself high on its anterior legs, foam gushing from its gills. It cried out in a peculiar poignant tone, fell back dead into the balsam.

Carcolo turned back to Givven. 'This is what you must do. Joaz Banbeck surely has sent forth patrols. Retire along Dangle Ridge, then taking all concealment from the patrols, swing up into one of the Despoire Cols

– Tourmaline Col will serve. This is my reasoning. Banbeck will assume that you are retiring to Happy Valley, so he will hurry south behind the Fang, to attack as you come down off Dangle Ridge. As he passes below Tourmaline Col, you have the advantage and may well destroy Joaz Banbeck there with all his troops.'

Bast Givven shook his head decisively. 'What if his patrols locate us in spite of our precautions? He need only follow our tracks to bottle us into Tourmaline Col, with no escape except over Mount Despoire or out on Starbreak Fell. And if we venture out on Starbreak Fell his Juggers will destroy us in minutes.'

Ervis Carcolo sagged back down upon the couch. 'Bring the troops back to Happy Valley. We will await another occasion.'

CHAPTER SIX

Cut into the cliff south of the crag which housed Joaz's apartments was a large chamber known as Kergan's Hall. The proportions of the room, the simplicity and lack of ornament, the massive antique furniture contributed to the sense of lingering personality, as well as an odor unique to the room. This odor exhaled from naked stone walls, the petrified moss parquetry, old wood – a rough ripe redolence which Joaz had always disliked, together with every other aspect of the room. The dimensions seemed arrogant in their extent, the lack of ornament impressed him as rude, if not brutal. One day it occurred to Joaz that he disliked not the room but Kergan Banbeck himself, together with the entire system of overblown legends which surrounded him.

The room nevertheless in many respects was pleasant. Three tall groined windows overlooked the vale. The casements were set with small square panes of green–blue glass in muntins of black ironwood. The ceiling likewise was paneled in wood, and here a certain amount of the typical Banbeck intricacy had been permitted. There were mock pilaster capitals with gargoyle heads, a frieze carved with conventionalized fern-fronds. The furniture consisted of three pieces: two tall carved chairs and a massive table, all polished dark wood, all of enormous antiquity.

Joaz had found a use for the room. The table supported a carefully detailed relief map of the district, on a scale of three inches to the mile. At the center was Banbeck Vale, on the right hand Happy Valley, separated by a turmoil of crags and chasms, cliffs, spikes, walls and five titanic peaks:

Mount Gethron to the south, Mount Despoire in the center, Barch Spike, the Fang and Mount Halcyon to the north.

At the front of Mount Gethron lay the High Jambles, then Starbreak Fell extended to Mount Despoire and Barch Spike. Beyond Mount Despoire, between the Skanse Ramparts and Barchback, the Skanse reached all the way to the tormented basalt ravines and bluffs at the foot of Mount Halcyon.

As Joaz stood studying the map, into the room came Phade, mischievously quiet. But Joaz sensed her nearness by the scent of incense, in the smoke of which she had steeped herself before seeking out Joaz. She wore a traditional holiday costume of Banbeck maidens: a tight-fitting sheath of dragon intestine, with muffs of brown fur at neck, elbows and knees. A tall cylindrical hat, notched around the upper edge, perched on her rich brown curls, and from the top of this hat soared a red plume.

Joaz feigned unconsciousness of her presence; she came up behind him to tickle his neck with the fur of her neckpiece. Joaz pretended stolid indifference; Phade, not at all deceived, put on a face of woeful concern. 'Must we all be slain? How goes the war?'

'For Banbeck Vale the war goes well. For poor Ervis Carcolo and Happy Valley the war goes ill indeed.'

'You plan his destruction,' Phade intoned in a voice of hushed accusation. 'You will kill him! Poor Ervis Carcolo!'

'He deserves no better.'

'But what will befall Happy Valley?'

Joaz Banbeck shrugged idly. 'Changes for the better.'

'Will you seek to rule?'

'Not I.'

'Think!' whispered Phade. 'Joaz Banbeck, Tyrant of Banbeck Vale, Happy Valley, Phosphor Gulch, Glore, the Tarn, Clewhaven and the Great Northern Rift.'

'Not I,' said Joaz. 'Perhaps you would rule in my stead?'

'Oh! Indeed! What changes there would be! I'd dress the sacerdotes in red and yellow ribbons. I'd order them to sing and dance and drink May wine; the dragons I'd send south to Arcady, except for a few gentle Termagants to nursemaid the children. And no more of these furious battles. I'd burn the armor and break the swords, I'd—'

'My dear little flutterbug,' said Joaz with a laugh. 'What a swift reign you'd have indeed!'

'Why swift? Why not forever? If men had no means to fight—'

'And when the Basics came down, you'd throw garlands around their necks?'

'Pah. They shall never be seen again. What do they gain by molesting a few remote valleys?'

'Who knows what they gain? We are free men – perhaps the last free men in the universe. Who knows? And will they be back? Coralyne is bright in the sky!'

Phade became suddenly interested in the relief map. 'And your current war – dreadful! Will you attack, will you defend?'

'This depends on Ervis Carcolo,' said Joaz. 'I need only wait till he exposes himself.' Looking down at the map he added thoughtfully, 'He is clever enough to do me damage, unless I move with care.'

'And what if the Basics come while you bicker with Carcolo?'

Joaz smiled. 'Perhaps we shall all flee to the Jambles. Perhaps we shall all fight.'

'I will fight beside you,' declared Phade, striking a brave attitude. 'We will attack the great Basic spaceship, braving the heat-rays, fending off the power-bolts. We will storm to the very portal, we will pull the nose of the first marauder who shows himself!'

'At one point your otherwise sage strategy falls short,' said Joaz. 'How does one find the nose of a Basic?'

'In that case,' said Phade, 'we shall seize their—' She turned her head at a sound in the hall. Joaz strode across the room, flung back the door. Old Rife the porter sidled forward. 'You told me to call when the bottle either overturned or broke. Well, it's done both and irreparably, not five minutes ago.'

Joaz pushed past Rife, ran down the corridor. 'What means this?' demanded Phade. 'Rife, what have you said to disturb him?'

Rife shook his head fretfully. 'I am as perplexed as you. A bottle is pointed out to me. "Watch this bottle day and night" – so I am commanded. And also, "When the bottle breaks or tips, call me at once." I tell myself that here in all truth is a sinecure. And I wonder, does Joaz consider me so senile that I will rest content with a make-work task such as watching a bottle? I am old, my jaws tremble, but I am not witless. To my surprise the bottle breaks! The explanation admittedly is workaday: a fall to the floor. Nevertheless, without knowledge of what it all means, I obey orders and notify Joaz Banbeck.'

Phade had been squirming impatiently. 'Where then is this bottle?'

'In the studio of Joaz Banbeck.'

Phade ran off as swiftly as the tight sheath about her thighs permitted: through a transverse tunnel, across Kergan's Way by a covered bridge, then up at a slant toward Joaz's apartments.

Down the long hall ran Phade, through the anteroom where a bottle lay shattered on the floor, into the studio, where she halted in astonishment. No one was to be seen. She noticed a section of shelving which stood at an angle. Quietly, timorously, she stole across the room, peered down into the workshop.

The scene was an odd one. Joaz stood negligently, smiling a cool smile, as across the room a naked sacerdote gravely sought to shift a barrier which had sprung down across an area of the wall. But the gate was cunningly locked in place, and the sacerdote's efforts were to no avail. He turned, glanced briefly at Joaz, then started for the exit into the studio.

Phade sucked in her breath, backed away.

The sacerdote came out into the studio, started for the door.

'Just a moment,' said Joaz. 'I wish to speak to you.'

The sacerdote paused, turned his head in mild inquiry. He was a young man, his face bland, blank, almost beautiful. Fine transparent skin stretched over his pale bones. His eyes – wide, blue, innocent – seemed to stare without focus. He was delicate of frame, sparsely fleshed; his hands were thin, with fingers trembling in some kind of nervous imbalance. Down his back, almost to his waist, hung the mane of long light-brown hair.

Joaz seated himself with ostentatious deliberation, never taking his eyes from the sacerdote. Presently he spoke in a voice pitched at an ominous level. 'I find your conduct far from ingratiating.' This was a declaration requiring no response, and the sacerdote made none.

'Please sit,' said Joaz. He indicated a bench. 'You have a great deal of explaining to do.'

Was it Phade's imagination? Or did a spark of something like wild amusement flicker and die almost instantaneously in the sacerdote's eyes? But again he made no response. Joaz, adapting to the peculiar rules by which communication with the sacerdotes must be conducted, asked, 'Do you care to sit?'

'It is immaterial,' said the sacerdote. 'Since I am standing now, I will stand.'

Joaz rose to his feet and performed an act without precedent. He pushed the bench behind the sacerdote, rapped the back of the knobby knees, thrust the sacerdote firmly down upon the bench. 'Since you are sitting now,' said Joaz, 'you might as well sit.'

With gentle dignity the sacerdote regained his feet. 'I shall stand.'

Joaz shrugged. 'As you wish. I intend to ask you some questions. I hope that you will cooperate and answer with precision.'

The sacerdote blinked owlishly.

'Will you do so?'

'Certainly. I prefer, however, to return the way I came.'

Joaz ignored the remark. 'First,' he asked, 'why do you come to my study?'

The sacerdote spoke carefully, in the voice of one talking to a child. 'Your language is vague; I am confused and must not respond, since I am vowed to give only truth to anyone who requires it.'

Joaz settled himself in his chair. 'There is no hurry. I am ready for a long

discussion. Let me ask you then: did you have impulses which you can explain to me, which persuaded or impelled you to come to my studio?'

'Yes.'

'How many of these impulses did you recognize?'

'I don't know.'

'More than one?'

'Perhaps.'

'Less than ten?'

'I don't know.'

'Hmm ... Why are you uncertain?'

'I am not uncertain.'

'Then why can't you specify the number as I requested?'

'There is no such number.'

'I see ... You mean, possibly, that there are several elements of a single
motive which directed your brain to signal your muscles in order that they
might carry you here?'

'Possibly.'

Joaz's thin lips twisted in a faint smile of triumph. 'Can you describe an
element of the eventual motive?'

'Yes.'

'Do so, then.'

There was an imperative against which the sacerdote was proof. Any
form of coercion known to Joaz – fire, sword, thirst, mutilation – these to
a sacerdote were no more than inconveniences; he ignored them as if they
did not exist. His personal inner world was the single world of reality; either
acting upon or reacting against the affairs of the Utter Men demeaned him;
absolute passivity, absolute candor were his necessary courses of action.
Understanding something of this, Joaz rephrased his command: 'Can you
think of an element of the motive which impelled you to come here?'

'Yes.'

'What is it?'

'A desire to wander about.'

'Can you think of another?'

'Yes.'

'What is it?'

'A desire to exercise myself by walking.'

'I see ... Incidentally, are you trying to evade answering my questions?'

'I answer such questions as you put to me. So long as I do so, so long as I
open my mind to all who seek knowledge – for this is our creed – there can
be no question of evasion.'

'So you say. However, you have not provided me an answer that I find
satisfactory.'

The sacerdote's reply to the comment was an almost imperceptible widening of the pupils.

'Very well then,' said Joaz Banbeck. 'Can you think of another element to this complex motive we have been discussing?'

'Yes.'

'What is it?'

'I am interested in antiques. I came to your study to admire your relicts of the old worlds.'

'Indeed?' Joaz raised his eyebrows. 'I am lucky to possess such fascinating treasures. Which of my antiques interests you particularly?'

'Your books. Your maps. Your great globe of the Arch-world.'

'The Arch-world? Eden?'

'This is one of its names.'

Joaz pursed his lips. 'So you come here to study my antiques. Well then, what other elements to this motive exist?'

The sacerdote hesitated an instant. 'It was suggested to me that I come here.'

'By whom?'

'By the Demie.'

'Why did he so suggest?'

'I am uncertain.'

'Can you conjecture?'

'Yes.'

'What are these conjectures?'

The sacerdote made a small bland gesture with the fingers of one hand. 'The Demie might wish to become an Utter Man, and so seeks to learn the principles of your existence. Or the Demie might wish to change the trade articles. The Demie might be fascinated by my descriptions of your antiques. Or the Demie might be curious regarding the focus of your vision-panels. Or—'

'Enough. Which of these conjectures, and of other conjectures you have not yet divulged, do you consider most probable?'

'None.'

Joaz raised his eyebrows once more. 'How do you justify this?'

'Since any desired number of conjectures can be formed, the denominator of any probability-ratio is variable and the entire concept becomes arithmetically meaningless.'

Joaz grinned wearily. 'Of the conjectures which to this moment have occurred to you, which do you regard as the most likely?'

'I suspect that the Demie might think it desirable that I come here to stand.'

'What do you achieve by standing?'

'Nothing.'

'Then the Demie does not send you here to stand.'

To Joaz's assertion, the sacerdote made no comment.

Joaz framed a question with great care. 'What do you believe that the Demie hopes you will achieve by coming here to stand?'

'I believe that he wishes me to learn how Utter Men think.'

'And you learn how I think by coming here?'

'I am learning a great deal.'

'How does it help you?'

'I don't know.'

'How many times have you visited my study?'

'Seven times.'

'Why were you chosen specially to come?'

'The synod has approved my *tand*. I may well be the next Demie.'

Joaz spoke over his shoulder to Phade. 'Brew tea.' He turned back to the sacerdote. 'What is a *tand*?'

The sacerdote took a deep breath. 'My *tand* is the representation of my soul.'

'Hmm. What does it look like?'

The sacerdote's expression was unfathomable. 'It cannot be described.'

'Do I have one?'

'No.'

Joaz shrugged. 'Then you can read my thoughts.'

Silence.

'Can you read my thoughts?'

'Not well.'

'Why should you wish to read my thoughts?'

'We are alive in the universe together. Since we are not permitted to act, we are obliged to know.'

Joaz smiled skeptically. 'How does knowledge help you, if you will not act upon it?'

'Events follow the Rationale, as water drains into a hollow and forms a pool.'

'Bah!' said Joaz, in sudden irritation. 'Your doctrine commits you to non-interference in our affairs, nevertheless you allow your "Rationale" to create conditions by which events are influenced. Is this correct?'

'I am not sure. We are a passive people.'

'Still, your Demie must have had a plan in mind when he sent you here. Is this not correct?'

'I cannot say.'

Joaz veered to a new line of questioning. 'Where does the tunnel behind my workshop lead?'

'Into a cavern.'

Phade set a silver pot before Joaz. He poured, sipped reflectively. Of contests there were numberless varieties; he and the sacerdote were engaged in a hide-and-seek game of words and ideas. The sacerdote was schooled in patience and supple evasions, to counter which Joaz could bring pride and determination. The sacerdote was handicapped by an innate necessity to speak truth; Joaz, on the other hand, must grope like a man blindfolded, unacquainted with the goal he sought, ignorant of the prize to be won. Very well, thought Joaz, let us continue. We shall see whose nerves fray first. He offered tea to the sacerdote, who refused with a shake of the head so quick and of such small compass as to seem a shudder.

Joaz made a gesture signifying it was all the same to him. 'Should you desire sustenance or drink,' he said, 'please let it be known. I enjoy our conversation so inordinately that I fear I may prolong it to the limits of your patience. Surely you would prefer to sit?'

'No.'

'As you wish. Well then, back to our discussion. This cavern you mentioned – is it inhabited by sacerdotes?'

'I fail to understand your question.'

'Do sacerdotes use the cavern?'

'Yes.'

Eventually, fragment by fragment, Joaz extracted the information that the cavern connected with a series of chambers, in which the sacerdotes smelted metal, boiled glass, ate, slept, performed their rituals. At one time there had been an opening into Banbeck Vale, but long ago this had been blocked. Why? There were wars throughout the cluster; bands of defeated men were taking refuge upon Aerlith, settling in rifts and valleys. The sacerdotes preferred a detached existence and had shut their caverns away from sight. Where was this opening? The sacerdote seemed vague, indefinite. Somewhere to the north end of the valley. Behind Banbeck Jambles? Possibly. But trading between men and sacerdotes was conducted at a cave entrance below Mount Gethron. Why? A matter of usage, declared the sacerdote. In addition this location was more readily accessible to Happy Valley and Phosphor Gulch. How many sacerdotes lived in these caves? Uncertainty. Some might have died, others might have been born. Approximately how many this morning? Perhaps five hundred.

At this juncture the sacerdote was swaying and Joaz was hoarse. 'Back to your motive – or the elements of your motives – for coming to my studio. Are they connected in any manner with the star Coralyne, and a possible new coming of the Basics, or the grephs, as they were formerly called?'

Again the sacerdote seemed to hesitate. Then: 'Yes.'

'Will the sacerdotes help us against the Basics, should they come?'

'No.' This answer was terse and definite.

'But I assume that the sacerdotes wish the Basics driven off?'

No answer.

Joaz rephrased his words. 'Do the sacerdotes wish the Basics repelled from Aerlith?'

'The Rationale bids us stand aloof from affairs of men and non-men alike.'

Joaz curled his lip. 'Suppose the Basics invaded your caves, dragged you off to the Coralyne planet. Then what?'

The sacerdote almost seemed to laugh. 'The question cannot be answered.'

'Would you resist the Basics if they made the attempt?'

'I cannot answer your question.'

Joaz laughed. 'But the answer is not no?'

The sacerdote assented.

'Do you have weapons, then?'

The sacerdote's mild blue eyes seemed to droop. Secrecy? Fatigue? Joaz repeated the question.

'Yes,' said the sacerdote. His knees sagged, but he snapped them tight.

'What kind of weapons?'

'Numberless varieties. Projectiles, such as rocks. Piercing weapons, such as broken sticks. Cutting and slashing weapons such as cooking utensils.' His voice began to fade as if he were moving away. 'Poisons: arsenic, sulfur, triventidum, acid, black-spore. Burning weapons, such as torches and lenses to focus the sunlight. Weapons to suffocate: ropes, nooses, slings, cords. Cisterns, to drown the enemy ...'

'Sit down, rest,' Joaz urged him. 'Your inventory interests me, but its total effect seems inadequate. Have you other weapons which might decisively repel the Basics should they attack you?'

The question, by design or chance, was never answered. The sacerdote sank to his knees, slowly, as if praying. He fell forward on his face, then sprawled to the side. Joaz sprang forward, yanked up the drooping head by its hair. The eyes, half-open, revealed a hideous white expanse. 'Speak!' croaked Joaz. 'Answer my last question! Do you have weapons – or a weapon – to repel a Basic attack?'

The pallid lips moved. 'I don't know.'

Joaz frowned, peered into the waxen face, drew back in bewilderment. 'The man is dead.'

CHAPTER SEVEN

Phade looked up from drowsing on a couch, face pink, hair tossed. 'You have killed him!' she cried in a voice of hushed horror.

'No. He has died – or caused himself to die.'

Phade staggered blinking across the room, sidled close to Joaz, who pushed her absently away. Phade scowled, shrugged and then, as Joaz paid her no heed, marched from the room.

Joaz sat back, staring at the limp body. 'He did not tire,' muttered Joaz, 'until I verged upon secrets.'

Presently he jumped to his feet, went to the entry hall, sent Rife to fetch a barber. An hour later the corpse, stripped of hair, lay on a wooden pallet covered by a sheet, and Joaz held in his hands a rude wig fashioned from the long hair.

The barber departed; servants carried away the corpse. Joaz stood alone in his studio, tense and light-headed. He removed his garments, to stand naked as the sacerdote. Gingerly he drew the wig across his scalp and examined himself in the mirror. To a casual eye, where the difference? Something was lacking: the torc. Joaz fitted it about his neck, once more examined his reflection, with dubious satisfaction.

He entered the workshop, hesitated, disengaged the trap, cautiously pulled away the stone slab. On hands and knees he peered into the tunnel and, since it was dark, held forward a glass vial of luminescent algae. In the faint light the tunnel seemed empty. Irrevocably putting down his fears, Joaz clambered through the opening. The tunnel was narrow and low; Joaz moved forward tentatively, nerves thrilling with wariness. He stopped often to listen, but heard nothing but the whisper of his own pulse.

After perhaps a hundred yards the tunnel broke out into a natural cavern. Joaz stopped, stood indecisively, straining his ears through the gloom. Luminescent vials fixed to the walls at irregular intervals provided a measure of light, enough to delineate the direction of the cavern, which seemed to be north, parallel to the length of the valley. Joaz set forth once again, halting to listen every few yards. To the best of his knowledge the sacerdotes were a mild unaggressive folk, but they were also intensely secretive. How would they respond to the presence of an interloper? Joaz could not be sure, and proceeded with great caution.

The cavern rose, fell, widened, narrowed. Joaz presently came upon evidences of use: small cubicles, hollowed into the walls, lit by candelabra holding tall vials of luminous stuff. In two of the cubicles Joaz came upon sacerdotes, the first asleep on a reed rug, the second sitting cross-legged, gazing fixedly at a contrivance of twisted metal rods. They gave Joaz no attention; he continued with a more confident step.

The cave sloped downward, widened like a cornucopia, suddenly broke into a cavern so enormous that Joaz thought for a startled instant that he had stepped out into the night. The ceiling reached beyond the flicker of the myriad of lamps, fires and glowing vials. Ahead and to the left smelters and forges were in operation; then a twist in the cavern wall obscured something of the view. Joaz glimpsed a tiered tubular construction which seemed to be some sort of workshop, for a large number of sacerdotes were occupied at complicated tasks. To the right was a stack of bales, a row of bins containing goods of unknown nature.

Joaz for the first time saw sacerdote women: neither the nymphs nor the half-human witches of popular legend. Like the men they seemed pallid and frail, with sharply defined features; like the men they moved with care and deliberation; like the men they wore only their waist-long hair. There was little conversation and no laughter: rather an atmosphere of not unhappy placidity and concentration. The cavern exuded a sense of time, use and custom. The stone floor was polished by endless padding of bare feet; the exhalations of many generations had stained the walls.

No one heeded Joaz. He moved slowly forward, keeping to the shadows, and paused under the stack of bales. To the right the cavern dwindled by irregular proportions into a vast horizontal funnel, receding, twisting, telescoping, losing all reality in the dim light.

Joaz searched the entire sweep of vast cavern. Where would be the armory, with the weapons of whose existence the sacerdote, by the very act of dying, had assured him? Joaz turned his attention once more to the left, straining to see detail in the odd tiered workshop which rose fifty feet from the stone floor. A strange edifice, thought Joaz, craning his neck; one whose nature he could not entirely comprehend. But every aspect of the great cavern – so close beside Banbeck Vale and so remote – was strange and marvelous. Weapons? They might be anywhere; certainly he dared seek no further for them.

There was nothing more he could learn without risk of discovery. He turned back the way he had come: up the dim passage, past the occasional side cubicles, where the two sacerdotes remained as he had found them before: the one asleep, the other intent on the contrivance of twisted metal. He plodded on and on. Had he come so far? Where was the fissure which led to his own apartments? Had he passed it by, must he search? Panic rose in his throat, but he continued, watching carefully. There, he had not gone wrong! There it opened to his right, a fissure almost dear and familiar. He plunged into it, walked with long loping strides, like a man under water, holding his luminous tube ahead.

An apparition rose before him, a tall white shape. Joaz stood rigid. The gaunt figure bore down upon him. Joaz pressed against the wall. The figure stalked forward, and suddenly shrank to human scale. It was the young sacerdote whom Joaz had shorn and left for dead. He confronted Joaz, mild blue eyes bright with reproach and contempt. 'Give me my torc.'

With numb fingers Joaz removed the golden collar. The sacerdote took it, but made no move to clasp it upon himself. He looked at the hair which weighted heavy upon Joaz's scalp. With a foolish grimace Joaz doffed the disheveled wig, proffered it. The sacerdote sprang back as if Joaz had become a cave-goblin. Sidling past, as far from Joaz as the wall of the passage allowed, he paced swiftly off down the tunnel. Joaz dropped the wig to the floor, stared down at the unkempt pile of hair. He turned, looked after the sacerdote, a pallid figure which soon became one with the murk. Slowly Joaz continued up the tunnel. There – an oblong blank of light, the opening to his workshop. He crawled through, back to the real world. Savagely, with all his strength, he thrust the slab back in the hole, slammed down the gate which originally had trapped the sacerdote.

Joaz's garments lay where he had tossed them. Wrapping himself in a cloak he went to the outer door, looked forth into the anteroom where Rife sat dozing. Joaz snapped his fingers. 'Fetch masons, with mortar, steel and stone.'

Joaz bathed with diligence, rubbing himself time after time with emulsion, rinsing and re-rinsing himself. Emerging from the bath he took the waiting masons into his workshop, ordered the sealing of the hole.

Then he took himself to his couch. Sipping a cup of wine, he let his mind rove and wander. Recollection became reverie, reverie became dream. Joaz once again traversed the tunnel, on feet light as thistle-down, down the long cavern, and the sacerdotes in their cubicles now raised their heads to look after him. At last he stood in the entrance to the great underground void, and once more looked right and left in awe. Now he drifted across the floor, past sacerdotes laboring earnestly over fires and anvils. Sparks rose from retorts, blue gas flickered above melting metal.

Joaz moved beyond to a small chamber cut into the stone. Here sat an old man, thin as a pole, his waist-long mane of hair snow-white. The man examined Joaz with fathomless blue eyes, and spoke, but his voice was muffled, inaudible. He spoke again; the words rang loud in Joaz's mind.

'I bring you here to caution you, lest you do us harm, and with no profit to yourself. The weapon you seek is both non-existent and beyond your imagination. Put it outside your ambition.'

By great effort Joaz managed to stammer, 'The young sacerdote made no denial; this weapon must exist!'

'Only within the narrow limits of special interpretation. The lad can speak no more than the literal truth, nor can he act with other than grace. How can you wonder why we hold ourselves apart? You Utter folk find purity incomprehensible; you thought to advantage yourself, but achieved nothing but an exercise in rat-like stealth. Lest you try again with greater boldness I must abase myself to set matters correct. I assure you, this so-called weapon is absolutely beyond your control.'

First shame, then indignation came over Joaz; he cried out, 'You do not understand my urgencies! Why should I act differently? Coralyne is close; the Basics are at hand. Are you not men? Why will you not help us defend the planet?'

The Demie shook his head, and the white hair rippled with hypnotic slowness. 'I quote you the Rationale: passivity, complete and absolute. This implies solitude, sanctity, quiescence, peace. Can you imagine the anguish I risk in speaking to you? I intervene, I interfere, at vast pain of the spirit. Let there be an end to it. We have made free with your studio, doing you no harm, offering you no indignity. You have paid a visit to our hall, demeaning a noble young man in the process. Let us be quits, let there be no further spying on either side. Do you agree?'

Joaz heard his voice respond, quite without his conscious prompting; it sounded more nasal and shrill than he liked. 'You offer this agreement now when you have learned your fill of my secrets, but I know none of yours.'

The Demie's face seemed to recede and quiver. Joaz read contempt, and in his sleep he tossed and twitched. He made an effort to speak in a voice of calm reason: 'Come, we are men together; why should we be at odds? Let us share our secrets, let each help the other. Examine my archives, my cases, my relics at your leisure, and then allow me to study this existent but nonexistent weapon. I swear it shall be used only against the Basics, for the protection of both of us.'

The Demie's eyes sparkled. 'No.'

'Why not?' argued Joaz. 'Surely you wish us no harm?'

'We are detached and passionless. We await your extinction. You are the Utter Men, the last of humanity. And when you are gone, your dark thoughts and grim plots will be gone; murder and pain and malice will be gone.'

'I cannot believe this,' said Joaz. 'There may be no men in the cluster, but what of the universe? The Old Rule reached far! Sooner or later men will return to Aerlith.'

The Demie's voice became plangent. 'Do you think we speak only from faith? Do you doubt our knowledge?'

'The universe is large. The Old Rule reached far.'

'The last men dwell on Aerlith,' said the Demie. 'The Utter Men and the sacerdotes. You shall pass; we will carry forth the Rationale like a banner of glory, through all the worlds of the sky.'

'And how will you transport yourselves on this mission?' Joaz asked cunningly. 'Can you fly to the stars as naked as you walk the fells?'

'There will be a means. Time is long.'

'For your purposes, time needs to be long. Even on the Coralyne planets there are men. Enslaved, reshaped in body and mind, but men. What of them? It seems that you are wrong, that you are guided by faith indeed.'

The Demie fell silent. His face seemed to stiffen.

'Are these not facts?' asked Joaz. 'How do you reconcile them with your faith?'

The Demie said mildly, 'Facts can never be reconciled with faith. By our faith, these men, if they exist, will also pass. Time is long. Oh, the worlds of brightness: they await us!'

'It is clear,' said Joaz, 'that you ally yourselves with the Basics and that you hope for our destruction. This can only change our attitudes toward you. I fear that Ervis Carcolo was right and I wrong.'

'We remain passive,' said the Demie. His face wavered, seemed to swim with mottled colors. 'Without emotion, we will stand witness to the passing of the Utter Men, neither helping nor hindering.'

Joaz spoke in fury, 'Your faith, your Rationale – whatever you call it – misleads you. I make this threat: if you fail to help us, you will suffer as we suffer.'

'We are passive, we are indifferent.'

'What of your children? The Basics make no difference between us. They will herd you to their pens as readily as they do us. Why should we fight to protect you?'

The Demie's face faded, became splotched with fog, transparent mist; his eyes glowed like rotten meat. 'We need no protection,' he howled. 'We are secure.'

'You will suffer our fate,' cried Joaz, 'I promise you this!'

The Demie collapsed suddenly into a small dry husk, like a dead mosquito; with incredible speed, Joaz fled back through the caves, the tunnels, up through his workroom, his studio, into his bed chamber where now he jerked upright, eyes starting, throat distended, mouth dry.

The door opened; Rife's head appeared. 'Did you call, sir?'

Joaz raised himself on his elbows, looked around the room. 'No. I did not call.'

Rife withdrew. Joaz settled back on the couch, lay staring at the ceiling. He had dreamed a most peculiar dream. Dream? A synthesis of his own imaginings? Or, in all verity, a confrontation and exchange between two minds? Impossible to decide, and perhaps irrelevant; the event carried its own conviction.

Joaz swung his legs over the side of the couch, blinked at the floor. Dream or colloquy, it was all the same. He rose to his feet, donned sandals and a robe of yellow fur, limped morosely up to the Council Room and stepped out on a sunny balcony.

The day was two-thirds over. Shadows hung dense along the western cliffs. Right and left stretched Banbeck Vale. Never had it seemed more prosperous or more fruitful, and never before unreal: as if he were a stranger to the planet. He looked north along the great bulwark of stone which rose sheer to Banbeck Verge. This too was unreal, a façade behind which lived the sacerdotes. He gauged the rock face, superimposing a mental projection of the great cavern. The cliff toward the north end of the vale must be scarcely more than a shell!

Joaz turned his attention to the exercise field, where Juggers were thudding briskly through defensive evolutions. How strange was the quality of life which had produced Basic and Jugger, sacerdote and himself. He thought of Ervis Carcolo, and wrestled with sudden exasperation. Carcolo was a distraction most unwelcome at the present time. There would be no tolerance when Carcolo was finally brought to account. A light step behind him, the pressure of fur, the touch of gay hands, the scent of incense. Joaz's tensions melted. If there were no such creatures as minstrel-maidens, it would be necessary to invent them.

Deep under Banbeck Scarp, in a cubicle lit by a twelve-vial candelabra, a naked white-haired man sat quietly. On a pedestal at the level of his eyes rested his *tand*, an intricate construction of gold rods and silver wire, woven and bent seemingly at random. The fortuitousness of the design, however, was only apparent. Each curve symbolized an aspect of Final Sentience; the shadow cast upon the wall represented the Rationale, ever-shifting, always the same. The object was sacred to the sacerdotes, and served as a source of revelation.

There was never an end to the study of the *tand*: new intuitions were continually derived from some heretofore overlooked relationship of angle and curve. The nomenclature was elaborate: each part, juncture, sweep and twist had its name; each aspect of the relationships between the various parts was likewise categorized. Such was the cult of the *tand*: abstruse, exacting, without compromise. At his puberty rites the young sacerdote might study the original *tand* for as long as he chose; each must construct a duplicate *tand*, relying upon memory alone. Then occurred the most significant event of his lifetime: the viewing of his *tand* by a synod of elders. In awesome stillness, for hours at a time they would ponder his creation, weigh the infinitesimal variations of proportion, radius, sweep and angle. So they would infer the initiate's quality, judge his personal attributes, determine his understanding of Final Sentience, the Rationale and the Basis.

Occasionally the testimony of the *tand* revealed a character so tainted as to be reckoned intolerable; the vile *tand* would be cast into a furnace, the molten metal consigned to a latrine, the unlucky initiate expelled to the face of the planet, to live on his own terms.

The naked white-haired Demie, contemplating his own beautiful *tand*, sighed, moved restlessly. He had been visited by an influence so ardent, so passionate, so simultaneously cruel and tender, that his mind was oppressed. Unbidden, into his mind, came a dark seep of doubt. Can it be, he asked himself, that we have insensibly wandered from the true Rationale? Do we study our *tands* with blinded eyes? ... How to know, oh how to know! All is relative ease and facility in orthodoxy, yet how can it be denied that good is in itself undeniable? Absolutes are the most uncertain of all formulations, while the uncertainties are the most real ...

Twenty miles over the mountains, in the long pale light of the Aerlith afternoon, Ervis Carcolo planned his own plans. 'By daring, by striking hard, by cutting deep can I defeat him! In resolve, in courage, in endurance, I am more than his equal. Not again will he trick me, to slaughter my dragons and kill my men! Oh, Joaz Banbeck, how I will pay you for your deceit!' He raised his arms in wrath. 'Oh Joaz Banbeck, you whey-faced sheep!' Carcolo smote the air with his fist. 'I will crush you like a clod of dry moss!' He frowned, rubbed his round red chin. 'But how? Where? He has every advantage!'

Carcolo pondered his possible stratagems. 'He will expect me to strike, so much is certain. Doubtless he will again wait in ambush. So I will patrol every inch, but this too he will expect and so be wary lest I thunder upon him from above. Will he hide behind Despoire, or along Northguard, to catch me as I cross the Skanse? If so, I must approach by another route – through Maudlin Pass and under Mount Gethron? Then, if he is tardy in his march, I will meet him on Banbeck Verge. And if he is early, I stalk him through the peaks and chasms ...'

CHAPTER EIGHT

With the cold rain of dawn pelting down upon them, with the trail illuminated only by lightning-glare, Ervis Carcolo, his dragons and his men set forth. When the first sparkle of sunlight struck Mount Despoire, they had already traversed Maudlin Pass.

So far, so good, exulted Ervis Carcolo. He stood high in his stirrups to scan Starbreak Fell. No sign of the Banbeck forces. He waited, scanning the far edge of Northguard Ridge, black against the sky. A minute passed. Two minutes. The men beat their hands together, the dragons rumbled and muttered fretfully.

Impatience began to prickle along Carcolo's ribs; he fidgeted and cursed. Could not the simplest of plans be carried through without mistake? But now the flicker of a heliograph from Barch Spike, and another to the south-east from the slopes of Mount Gethron. Carcolo waved forward his army; the way lay clear across Starbreak Fell. Down from Maudlin Pass surged the Happy Valley army: first the Long-horned Murderers, steel-spiked and crested with steel prongs; then the rolling red seethe of the Termagants, darting their heads as they ran; and behind came the balance of the forces.

Starbreak Fell spread wide before them, a rolling slope strewn with flinty meteoric fragments which glinted like flowers on the gray–green moss. To all sides rose majestic peaks, snow blazing white in the clear morning light: Mount Gethron, Mount Despoire, Barch Spike and far to the south, Clew Taw.

The scouts converged from left and right. They brought identical reports: there was no sign of Joaz Banbeck or his troops. Carcolo began to toy with a new possibility. Perhaps Joaz Banbeck had not deigned to take the field. The idea enraged him and filled him with a great joy; if so, Joaz would pay dearly for his neglect.

Halfway across Starbreak Fell they came upon a pen occupied by two hundred of Joaz Banbeck's spratling Fiends. Two old men and a boy tended the pen, and watched the Happy Valley horde advance with manifest terror.

But Carcolo rode past leaving the pen unmolested. If he won the day, it would become part of his spoils; if he lost, the spratling Fiends could do him no harm.

The old men and the boy stood on the roof of their turf hut, watching Carcolo and his troops pass: the men in black uniforms and black peaked caps with back-slanting ear-flaps; the dragons bounding, crawling, loping, plodding, according to their kind, scales glinting: the dull red and maroon of Termagants; the poisonous shine of the Blue Horrors; the black–green Fiends; the gray and brown Juggers and Murderers. Ervis Carcolo rode on the right flank, Bast Givven rode to the rear. And now Carcolo hastened the pace, haunted by the anxiety that Joaz Banbeck might bring his Fiends and Juggers up Banbeck Scarp before he arrived to thrust him back – assuming that Joaz Banbeck in all actuality had been caught napping.

But Carcolo reached Banbeck Verge without challenge. He shouted out in triumph, waved his cap high. 'Joaz Banbeck the sluggard! Let him try now the ascent of Banbeck Scarp!' And Ervis Carcolo surveyed Banbeck Vale with the eye of a conqueror.

Bast Givven seemed to share none of Carcolo's triumph, and kept an uneasy watch to north and south and to the rear.

Carcolo observed him peevishly from the corner of his eye and presently called out, 'Ho, ho, then! What's amiss?'

'Perhaps much, perhaps nothing,' said Bast Givven, searching the landscape.

Carcolo blew out his mustaches. Givven went on, in the cool voice which so completely irritated Carcolo. 'Joaz Banbeck seems to be tricking us as before.'

'Why do you say this?'

'Judge for yourself. Would he allow us advantage without claiming a miser's price?'

'Nonsense!' muttered Carcolo. 'The sluggard is fat with his last victory.' But he rubbed his chin and peered uneasily down into Banbeck Vale. From here it seemed curiously quiet. There was a strange inactivity in the fields and barracks. A chill began to grip Carcolo's heart – then he cried out, 'Look at the brooder: there are the Banbeck dragons!'

Givven squinted down into the vale, glanced sidewise at Carcolo. 'Three Termagants, in egg.' He straightened, abandoned all interest in the vale and scrutinized the peaks and ridges to the north and east. 'Assume that Joaz Banbeck set out before dawn, came up to the Verge, by the Slickenslides, crossed Blue Fell in strength—'

'What of Blue Crevasse?'

'He avoids Blue Crevasse to the north, comes over Barchback, steals across the Skanse and around Barch Spike ...'

Carcolo studied Northguard Ridge with new and startled awareness. A quiver of movement, the glint of scales?

'Retreat!' roared Carcolo. 'Make for Barch Spike! They're behind us!'

Startled, his army broke ranks, fled across Banbeck Verge, up into the harsh spurs of Barch Spike. Joaz, his strategy discovered, launched squads of Murderers to intercept the Happy Valley army, to engage and delay and, if possible, deny them the broken slopes of Barch Spike.

Carcolo calculated swiftly. His own Murderers he considered his finest troops, and held them in great pride. Purposely now he delayed, hoping to engage the Banbeck skirmishers, quickly destroy them and still gain the protection of the Barch declivities.

The Banbeck Murderers, however, refused to close, and scrambled for height up Barch Spike. Carcolo sent forward his Termagants and Blue Horrors; with a horrid snarling the two lines met. The Banbeck Termagants rushed up, to be met by Carcolo's Striding Murderers and forced into humping pounding flight.

The main body of Carcolo's troops, excited at the sight of retreating foes, could not be restrained. They veered off from Barch Spike, plunged down upon Starbreak Fell. The Striding Murderers overtook the Banbeck Termagants, climbed up their backs, toppled them over squealing and kicking, then knifed open the exposed pink bellies.

Banbeck's Long-horned Murderers came circling, struck from the flank into Carcolo's Striding Murderers, goring with steel-tipped horns, impaling on lances. Somehow they overlooked Carcolo's Blue Horrors who sprang down upon them. With axes and maces they laid the Murderers low, performing the rather grisly entertainment of clambering on a subdued Murderer, seizing the horn, stripping back horn, skin and scales, from head to tail. So Joaz Banbeck lost thirty Termagants and perhaps two dozen Murderers. Nevertheless, the attack served its purpose, allowing him to bring his knights, Fiends and Juggers down from Northguard before Carcolo could gain the heights of Barch Spike.

Carcolo retreated in a slantwise line up the pocked slopes, and meanwhile sent six men across the fell to the pen where the spratling Fiends milled in fear at the battle. The men broke the gates, struck down the two old men, herded the young Fiends across the fell toward the Banbeck troops. The hysterical spratlings obeyed their instincts, clasped themselves to the neck of whatever dragon they first encountered; which thereupon became sorely hampered, for its own instincts prevented it from detaching the spratling by force.

This ruse, a brilliant improvisation, created enormous disorder among the Banbeck troops. Ervis Carcolo now charged with all his power directly into the Banbeck center. Two squads of Termagants fanned out to harass the men; his Murderers – the only category in which he outnumbered Joaz Banbeck – were sent to engage Fiends, while Carcolo's own Fiends, pampered, strong, glistening with oily strength, snaked in toward the Banbeck Juggers. Under the great brown hulks they darted, lashing the fifty-pound steel ball at the tip of their tails against the inner side of the Jugger's legs.

A roaring mêlée ensued. Battle lines were uncertain; both men and dragons were crushed, torn apart, hacked to bits. The air sang with bullets, whistled with steel, reverberated to trumpeting, whistles, shouts, screams and bellows.

The reckless abandon of Carcolo's tactics achieved results out of proportion to his numbers. His Fiends burrowed ever deeper into the crazed and almost helpless Banbeck Juggers, while the Carcolo Murderers and Blue Horrors held back the Banbeck Fiends. Joaz Banbeck himself, assailed by Termagants, escaped with his life only by fleeing around behind the battle, where he picked up the support of a squad of Blue Horrors. In a fury he blew a withdrawal signal, and his army backed off down the slopes, leaving the ground littered with struggling and kicking bodies.

Carcolo, throwing aside all restraint, rose in his saddle, signaled to commit his own Juggers, which so far he had treasured like his own children.

Shrilling, hiccuping, they lumbered down into the seethe, tearing away great mouthfuls of flesh to right and left, ripping apart lesser dragons with their brachs, treading on Termagants, seizing Blue Horrors and Murderers, flinging them wailing and clawing through the air. Six Banbeck knights sought to stem the charge, firing their muskets point-blank into the demoniac faces; they went down and were seen no more.

Down on Starbreak Fell tumbled the battle. The nucleus of the fighting became less concentrated, the Happy Valley advantage dissipated. Carcolo hesitated, a long heady instant. He and his troops alike were afire; the intoxication of unexpected success tingled in their brains – but here on Starbreak Fell, could they counter the odds posed by the greater Banbeck forces? Caution dictated that Carcolo withdraw up Barch Spike, to make the most of his limited victory. Already a strong platoon of Fiends had grouped and were maneuvering to charge his meager force of Juggers. Bast Givven approached, clearly expecting the word to retreat. But Carcolo still waited, reveling in the havoc being wrought by his paltry six Juggers.

Bast Givven's saturnine face was stern. 'Withdraw, withdraw! It's annihilation when their flanks bear in on us!'

Carcolo seized his elbow. 'Look! See where those Fiends gather, see where Joaz Banbeck rides! As soon as they charge, send six Striding Murderers from either side; close in on him, kill him!'

Givven opened his mouth to protest, looked where Carcolo pointed, rode to obey the orders.

Here came the Banbeck Fiends, moving with stealthy certainty toward the Happy Valley Juggers. Joaz, rising in his saddle, watched their progress. Suddenly from either side the Striding Murderers were on him. Four of his knights and six young cornets, screaming alarm, dashed back to protect him; there was clanging of steel on steel and steel on scale. The Murderers fought with sword and mace; the knights, their muskets useless, countered with cutlasses, one by one going under. Rearing on hind legs the Murderer corporal hacked down at Joaz, who desperately fended off the blow. The Murderer raised sword and mace together – and from fifty yards a musket pellet smashed into its ear. Crazy with pain, it dropped its weapons, fell forward upon Joaz, writhing and kicking. Banbeck Blue Horrors came to attack; the Murderers darted back and forth over the thrashing corporal, stabbing down at Joaz, kicking at him, finally fleeing the Blue Horrors.

Ervis Carcolo groaned in disappointment; by a half-second only had he fallen short of victory. Joaz Banbeck, bruised, mauled, perhaps wounded, had escaped with his life.

Over the crest of the hill came a rider: an unarmed youth whipping a staggering Spider. Bast Givven pointed him out to Carcolo. 'A messenger from the Valley, in urgency.'

The lad careened down the fell toward Carcolo, shouting ahead, but his message was lost in the din of battle. At last he drew close. 'The Basics, the Basics!'

Carcolo slumped like a half-empty bladder. 'Where?'

'A great black ship, half the valley wide. I was up on the heath, I managed to escape.' He pointed, whimpered.

'Speak, boy!' husked Carcolo. 'What do they do?'

'I did not see; I ran to you.'

Carcolo gazed across the battle field; the Banbeck Fiends had almost reached his Juggers, who were backing slowly, with heads lowered, fangs fully extended.

Carcolo threw up his hands in despair; he ordered Givven, 'Blow a retreat, break clear!'

Waving a white kerchief he rode around the battle to where Joaz Banbeck still lay on the ground, the quivering Murderer only just now being lifted from his legs. Joaz stared up, his face white as Carcolo's kerchief. At the sight of Carcolo his eyes grew wide and dark, his mouth became still.

Carcolo blurted, 'The Basics have come once more; they have dropped into Happy Valley, they are destroying my people.'

Joaz Banbeck, assisted by his knights, gained his feet. He stood swaying, arms limp, looking silently into Carcolo's face.

Carcolo spoke once more. 'We must call truce; this battle is waste! With all our forces let us march to Happy Valley and attack the monsters before they destroy all of us! Ah, think what we could have achieved with the weapons of the sacerdotes!'

Joaz stood silent. Another ten seconds passed. Carcolo cried angrily, 'Come now, what do you say?'

In a hoarse voice Joaz spoke, 'I say no truce. You rejected my warning, you thought to loot Banbeck Vale. I will show you no mercy.'

Carcolo gaped, his mouth a red hole under the sweep of his mustaches. 'But the Basics—'

'Return to your troops. You as well as the Basics are my enemy; why should I choose between you? Prepare to fight for your life; I give you no truce.'

Carcolo drew back, face as pale as Joaz's own. 'Never shall you rest! Even though you win this battle here on Starbreak Fell, yet you shall never know victory. I will persecute you until you cry for relief.'

Banbeck motioned to his knights. 'Whip this dog back to his own.'

Carcolo backed his Spider from the threatening flails, turned, loped away.

The tide of battle had turned. The Banbeck Fiends now had broken past his Blue Horrors; one of his Juggers was gone; another, facing three sidling Fiends, snapped its great jaws, waved its monstrous sword. The Fiends flicked and feinted with their steel balls, scuttled forward. The Jugger chopped, shattered its sword on the rockhard armor of the Fiends; they were underneath, slamming their steel balls into the monstrous legs. It tried to hop clear, toppled majestically. The Fiends slit its belly, and now Carcolo had only five Juggers left.

'Back!' he cried. 'Disengage!'

Up Barch Spike toiled his troops, the battle-front a roaring seethe of scales, armor, flickering metal. Luckily for Carcolo his rear was to the high ground, and after ten horrible minutes he was able to establish an orderly retreat. Two more Juggers had fallen; the three remaining scrambled free. Seizing boulders, they hurled them down into the attackers, who, after a series of sallies and lunges, were well content to break clear. In any event, Joaz, after hearing Carcolo's news, was of no disposition to spend further troops.

Carcolo, waving his sword in desperate defiance, led his troops back around Barch Spike, presently down across the dreary Skanse. Joaz turned back to Banbeck Vale. The news of the Basic raid had spread to all ears. The men rode sober and quiet, looking behind and overhead. Even the dragons seemed infected, and muttered restlessly among themselves.

As they crossed Blue Fell the almost omnipresent wind died; the stillness added to the oppression. Termagants, like the men, began to watch the sky. Joaz wondered, how could they know, how could they sense the Basics? He himself searched the sky, and as his army passed down over the scarp he thought to see, high over Mount Gethron, a flitting little black rectangle, which presently disappeared behind a crag.

CHAPTER NINE

Ervis Carcolo and the remnants of his army raced pell-mell down from the Skanse, through the wilderness of ravines and gulches at the base of Mount Despoire, out on the barrens to the west of Happy Valley. All pretense of military precision had been abandoned. Carcolo led the way, his Spider sobbing with fatigue. Behind in disarray pounded first Murderers and Blue Horrors, with Termagants hurrying along behind, then the Fiends, racing low to the ground, steel balls grinding on rocks, sending up sparks. Far in the rear lumbered the Juggers and their attendants.

Down to the verge of Happy Valley plunged the army and pulled up short, stamping and squealing. Carcolo jumped from his Spider, ran to the brink, stood looking down into the valley.

He had expected to see the ship, yet the actuality of the thing was so immediate and intense as to shock him. It was a tapered cylinder, glossy and black, resting in a field of legumes not far from ramshackle Happy Town. Polished metal disks at either end shimmered and glistened with fleeting films of color. There were three entrance ports: forward, central and aft, and from the central port a ramp had been extended to the ground.

The Basics had worked with ferocious efficiency. From the town straggled a line of people, herded by Heavy Troopers. Approaching the ship they passed through an inspection apparatus controlled by a pair of Basics. A series of instruments and the eyes of the Basics appraised each man, woman and child, classified them by some system not instantly obvious, whereupon the captives were either hustled up the ramp into the ship or prodded into a nearby booth. Peculiarly, no matter how many persons entered, the booth never seemed to fill.

Carcolo rubbed his forehead with trembling fingers, turned his eyes to the ground. When once more he looked up, Bast Givven stood beside him, and together they stared down into the valley.

From behind came a cry of alarm. Starting around, Carcolo saw a black rectangular flyer sliding silently down from above Mount Gethron. Waving his arms Carcolo ran for the rocks, bellowing orders to take cover. Dragons and men scuttled up the gulch. Overhead slid the flyer. A hatch opened, releasing a load of explosive pellets. They struck with a great rattling volley, and up into the air flew pebbles, rock splinters, fragments of bone, scales, skin and flesh. All who failed to reach cover were shredded. The Termagants fared relatively well. The Fiends, though battered and scraped, had all survived. Two of the Juggers had been blinded, and could fight no more till they had grown new eyes.

The flyer slid back once more. Several of the men fired their muskets – an act of apparently futile defiance – but the flyer was struck and damaged. It twisted, veered, soared up in a roaring curve, swooped over on its back, plunged toward the mountainside, crashed in a brilliant orange gush of fire. Carcolo shouted in maniac glee, jumped up and down, ran to the verge of the cliff, shook his fist at the ship below. He quickly quieted, to stand glum and shivering. Then, turning to the ragged cluster of men and dragons who once more had crept down from the gulch, Carcolo cried hoarsely, 'What do you say? Shall we fight? Shall we charge down upon them?'

There was silence; Bast Givven replied in a colorless voice, 'We are helpless. We can accomplish nothing. Why commit suicide?'

Carcolo turned away, heart too full for words. Givven spoke the obvious truth. They would either be killed or dragged aboard the ship; and then, on a world too strange for imagining, be put to uses too dismal to be borne. Carcolo clenched his fists, looked westward with bitter hatred. 'Joaz Banbeck, you brought me to this! When I might yet have fought for my people you detained me!'

'The Basics were here already,' said Givven with unwelcome rationality. 'We could have done nothing since we had nothing to do with.'

'We could have fought!' bellowed Carcolo. 'We might have swept down the Crotch, come upon them with all force! A hundred warriors and four hundred dragons – are these to be despised?'

Bast Givven judged further argument to be pointless. He pointed. 'They now examine our brooders.'

Carcolo turned to look, gave a wild laugh. 'They are astonished! They are awed! And well have they a right to be.'

Givven agreed. 'I imagine the sight of a Fiend or a Blue Horror – not to mention a Jugger – gives them pause for reflection.'

Down in the valley the grim business had ended. The Heavy Troopers marched back into the ship; a pair of enormous men twelve feet high came forth, lifted the booth, carried it up the ramp into the ship. Carcolo and his men watched with protruding eyes. 'Giants!'

Bast Givven chuckled dryly. 'The Basics stare at our Juggers; we ponder their Giants.'

The Basics presently returned to the ship. The ramp was drawn up, the ports closed. From a turret in the bow came a shaft of energy, touching each of the three brooders in succession, and each exploded with a great eruption of black bricks.

Carcolo moaned softly under his breath, but said nothing.

The ship trembled, floated; Carcolo bellowed an order; men and dragons rushed for cover. Flattened behind boulders they watched the black cylinder rise from the valley, drift to the west. 'They make for Banbeck Vale,' said Bast Givven.

Carcolo laughed, a cackle of mirthless glee. Bast Givven looked at him sidelong. Had Ervis Carcolo become addled? He turned away. A matter of no great moment.

Carcolo came to a sudden resolve. He stalked to one of the Spiders, mounted, swung around to face his men. 'I ride to Banbeck Vale. Joaz Banbeck has done his best to despoil me; I shall do my best against him. I give no orders: come or stay as you wish. Only remember! Joaz Banbeck would not allow us to fight the Basics!'

He rode off. The men stared into the plundered valley, turned to look after Carcolo. The black ship was just now slipping over Mount Despoire. There was nothing for them in the valley. Grumbling and muttering they summoned the bone-tired dragons, set off up the dreary mountainside.

Ervis Carcolo rode his Spider at a plunging run across the Skanse. Tremendous crags soared to either side, the blazing sun hung halfway up the black sky. Behind, the Skanse Ramparts; ahead, Barchback, Barch Spike and Northguard Ridge. Oblivious to the fatigue of his Spider, Carcolo whipped it on; gray–green moss pounded back from its wild feet, the narrow head hung low, foam trailed from its gill-vents. Carcolo cared nothing; his mind was empty of all but hate – for the Basics, for Joaz Banbeck, for Aerlith, for man, for human history.

Approaching Northguard the Spider staggered and fell. It lay moaning, neck outstretched, legs trailing back. Carcolo dismounted in disgust, looked back down the long rolling slope of the Skanse to see how many of his troops had followed him. A man riding a Spider at a modest lope turned out to be Bast Givven, who presently came up beside him, inspected the fallen Spider. 'Loosen the surcingle; he will recover the sooner.'

Carcolo glared, thinking to hear a new note in Givven's voice. Nevertheless he bent over the foundered dragon, slipped loose the broad bronze buckle. Givven dismounted, stretched his arms, massaged his thin legs. He pointed. 'The Basic ship descends into Banbeck Vale.'

Carcolo nodded grimly. 'I would be an audience to the landing.' He kicked the Spider. 'Come, get up, have you not rested enough? Do you wish me to walk?'

The Spider whimpered its fatigue, but nevertheless struggled to its feet. Carcolo started to mount, but Bast Givven laid a restraining hand on his shoulder. Carcolo looked back in outrage; here was impertinence! Givven said calmly, 'Tighten the surcingle, otherwise you will fall on the rocks, and once more break your bones.'

Uttering a spiteful phrase under his breath, Carcolo clasped the buckle back into position, the Spider crying out in despair. Paying no heed, Carcolo mounted, and the Spider moved off with trembling steps.

Barch Spike rose ahead like the prow of a white ship, dividing Northguard Ridge from Barchback. Carcolo paused to consider the landscape, tugging his mustaches.

Givven was tactfully silent. Carcolo looked back down the Skanse to the listless straggle of his army, set off to the left.

Passing close under Mount Gethron, skirting the High Jambles, they descended an ancient watercourse to Banbeck Verge. Though perforce they had come without great speed, the Basic ship had moved no faster and had only started to settle into the vale, the disks at bow and stern swirling with furious colors.

Carcolo grunted bitterly. 'Trust Joaz Banbeck to scratch his own itch. Not a soul in sight! He's taken to his tunnels, dragons and all.' Pursing his mouth he rendered a mincing parody of Joaz's voice: "'Ervis Carcolo, my dear friend, there is but one answer to attack: dig tunnels!" And I replied to him, "Am I a sacerdote to live underground? Burrow and delve, Joaz Banbeck, do as you will, I am but an old-time man; I go under the cliffs only when I must."'

Givven gave the faintest of shrugs.

Carcolo went on, 'Tunnels or not, they'll winkle him out. If need be they'll blast open the entire valley. They've no lack of tricks.'

Givven grinned sardonically. 'Joaz Banbeck knows a trick or two – as we know to our sorrow.'

'Let him capture two dozen Basics today,' snapped Carcolo. 'Then I'll concede him a clever man.' He stalked away to the very brink of the cliff, standing in full view of the Basic ship. Givven watched without expression.

Carcolo pointed. 'Aha! Look there!'

'Not I,' said Givven. 'I respect the Basic weapons too greatly.'

'Pah!' spat Carcolo. Nevertheless he moved a trifle back from the brink. 'There are dragons in Kergan's Way. For all Joaz Banbeck's talk of tunnels.' He gazed north along the valley a moment or two, then threw up his hands in frustration. 'Joaz Banbeck will not come up here to me; there is nothing I can do. Unless I walk down into the village, seek him out and strike him down, he will escape me.'

'Unless the Basics captured the two of you and confined you in the same pen,' said Givven.

'Bah!' muttered Carcolo, and moved off to one side.

CHAPTER TEN

The vision-plates which allowed Joaz Banbeck to observe the length and breadth of Banbeck Vale for the first time were being put to practical use. He had evolved the scheme while playing with a set of old lenses, and dismissed it as quickly. Then one day, while trading with the sacerdotes in the cavern under Mount Gethron, he had proposed that they design and supply the optics for such a system.

The blind old sacerdote who conducted the trading gave an ambiguous reply: the possibility of such a project, under certain circumstances, might well deserve consideration. Three months passed; the scheme receded to the back of Joaz Banbeck's mind. Then the sacerdote in the trading-cave inquired if Joaz still planned to install the viewing system; if so he might

take immediate delivery of the optics. Joaz agreed to the barter price, returned to Banbeck Vale with four heavy crates. He ordered the necessary
tunnels driven, installed the lenses, and found that with the study darkened
he could command all quarters of Banbeck Vale.

Now, with the Basic ship darkening the sky, Joaz Banbeck stood in his
study, watching the descent of the great black hulk.

At the back of the chamber maroon portieres parted. Clutching the cloth
with taut fingers stood the minstrel-maiden Phade. Her face was pale, her
eyes bright as opals. In a husky voice she called, 'The ship of death; it has
come to gather souls!'

Joaz turned her a stony glance, turned back to the honed-glass screen.
'The ship is clearly visible.'

Phade ran forward, clasped Joaz's arm, swung around to look into his
face. 'Let us try to escape! Into the mountains, the High Jambles; don't let
them take us so soon!'

'No one deters you,' said Joaz indifferently. 'Escape in any direction you
choose.'

Phade stared at him blankly, then turned her head and watched the
screen. The great black ship sank with sinister deliberation, the disks at bow
and stern now shimmering mother-of-pearl. Phade looked back to Joaz,
licked her lips. 'Are you not afraid?'

Joaz smiled thinly. 'What good to run? Their Trackers are swifter than
Murderers, more vicious than Termagants. They can smell you a mile away,
take you from the very center of the Jambles.'

Phade shivered with superstitious horror. She whispered, 'Let them take
me dead, then; I can't go with them alive.'

Joaz suddenly cursed. 'Look where they land! In our best field of
bellegarde!'

'What is the difference?'

'"Difference"? Must we stop eating because they pay their visit?'

Phade looked at him in a daze, beyond comprehension. She sank slowly
to her knees and began to perform the ritual gestures of the Theurgic cult:
hands palm down to either side, slowly up till the back of the hand touched
the ears, and the simultaneous protrusion of the tongue; over and over
again, eyes staring with hypnotic intensity into emptiness.

Joaz ignored the gesticulations, until Phade, her face screwed up into a
fantastic mask, began to sigh and whimper; then he swung the flaps of his
jacket into her face. 'Give over your folly!'

Phade collapsed moaning to the floor; Joaz's lips twitched in annoyance.
Impatiently he hoisted her erect. 'Look you, these Basics are neither ghouls
nor angels of death; they are no more than pallid Termagants, the basic stock
of our dragons. So now, give over your idiocy, or I'll have Rife take you away.'

'Why do you not make ready? You watch and do nothing.'

'There is nothing more that I can do.'

Phade drew a deep shuddering sigh, stared dully at the screen. 'Will you fight them?'

'Naturally.'

'How can you hope to counter such miraculous power?'

'We will do what we can. They have not yet met our dragons.'

The ship came to rest in a purple and green vine-field across the valley, near the mouth of Clybourne Crevasse. The port slid back, a ramp rolled forth. 'Look,' said Joaz, 'there you see them.'

Phade stared at the queer pale shapes who had come tentatively out on the ramp. 'They seem strange and twisted, like silver puzzles for children.'

'They are the Basics. From their eggs came our dragons. They have done as well with men: look, here are their Heavy Troops.'

Down the ramp, four abreast, in exact cadence, marched the Heavy Troops, to halt fifty yards in front of the ship. There were three squads of twenty: short men with massive shoulders, thick necks, stern down-drawn faces. They wore armor fashioned from overlapping scales of black and blue metal, a wide belt slung with pistol and sword. Black epaulettes extending past their shoulders supported a short ceremonial flap of black cloth ranging down their backs; their helmets bore a crest of sharp spikes, their knee-high boots were armed with kick-knives.

A number of Basics now rode forth. Their mounts, creatures only remotely resembling men, ran on hands and feet, backs high off the ground. Their heads were long and hairless, with quivering loose lips. The Basics controlled them with negligent touches of a quirt, and once on the ground set them cantering smartly through the bellegarde. Meanwhile a team of Heavy Troopers rolled a three-wheeled mechanism down the ramp, directed its complex snout toward the village.

'Never before have they prepared so carefully,' muttered Joaz. 'Here come the Trackers.' He counted. 'Only two dozen? Perhaps they are hard to breed. Generations pass slowly with men; dragons lay a clutch of eggs every year ...'

The Trackers moved to the side and stood in a loose restless group: gaunt creatures seven feet tall, with bulging black eyes, beaked noses, small undershot mouths pursed as if for kissing. From narrow shoulders long arms dangled and swung like ropes. As they waited they flexed their knees, staring sharply up and down the valley, in constant restless motion. After them came a group of Weaponeers – unmodified men wearing loose cloth smocks and cloth hats of green and yellow. They brought with them two more three-wheeled contrivances which they at once began to adjust and test.

The entire group became still and tense. The Heavy Troopers stepped forward with a stumping, heavy-legged gait, hands ready at pistols and swords. 'Here they come,' said Joaz. Phade made a quiet desperate sound, knelt, once more began to perform Theurgic gesticulations. Joaz in disgust ordered her from the study, went to a panel equipped with a bank of six direct-wire communications, the construction of which he had personally supervised. He spoke into three of the telephones, assuring himself that his defenses were alert, then returned to the honed-glass screens.

Across the field of bellegarde came the Heavy Troopers, faces heavy, hard, marked with down-veering creases. Upon either flank the Weaponeers trundled their three-wheeled mechanisms, but the Trackers waited beside the ship. About a dozen Basics rode behind the Heavy Troopers, carrying bulbous weapons on their backs.

A hundred yards from the portal into Kergan's Way, beyond the range of the Banbeck muskets, the invaders halted. A Heavy Trooper ran to one of the Weaponeers' carts, thrust his shoulders under a harness, stood erect. He now carried a gray machine, from which extended a pair of black globes. The Trooper scuttled toward the village like an enormous rat, while from the black globes streamed a flux, intended to interfere with the neural currents of the Banbeck defenders, and so immobilize them.

Explosions sounded, puffs of smoke appeared from nooks and vantages through the crags. Bullets spat into the ground beside the Trooper, several caromed off his armor. At once heat-beams from the ship stabbed against the cliff walls. In his study Joaz Banbeck smiled. The smoke puffs were decoys, the actual shots came from other areas. The Trooper, dodging and jerking, avoided a rain of bullets, ran under the portal, above which two men waited. Affected by the flux, they tottered, stiffened, but nevertheless, they dropped a great stone which struck the Trooper where the neck joined his shoulders, hurled him to the ground. He thrashed his arms and legs up and down, rolled over and over; then bouncing to his feet, he raced back into the valley, soaring and bounding, finally to stumble, plunge headlong to the ground and lie kicking and quivering.

The Basic army watched with no apparent concern or interest.

There was a moment of inactivity. Then from the ship came an invisible field of vibration, traveling across the face of the cliff. Where the focus struck, puffs of dust arose and loose rock became dislodged. A man, lying on a ledge, sprang to his feet, dancing and twisting, plunged two hundred feet to his death. Passing across one of Joaz Banbeck's spy-holes, the vibration was carried into the study where it set up a nerve-grinding howl. The vibration passed along the cliff; Joaz rubbed his aching head.

Meanwhile the Weaponeers discharged one of their instruments: first there came a muffled explosion, then through the air curved a wobbling gray sphere. Inaccurately aimed, it struck the cliff and burst in a great gush of yellow-white gas. The mechanism exploded once more, and this time lobbed the bomb accurately into Kergan's Way – which was now deserted. The bomb produced no effect.

In his study Joaz waited grimly. To now the Basics had taken only tentative, almost playful, steps; more serious efforts would surely follow.

Wind dispersed the gas; the situation remained as before. The casualties so far had been one Heavy Trooper and one Banbeck rifleman.

From the ship now came a stab of red flame, harsh, decisive. The rock at the portal shattered; slivers sang and spun; the Heavy Troopers jogged forward. Joaz spoke into his telephone, bidding his captains caution, lest counter-attacking against a feint, they expose themselves to a new gas bomb.

But the Heavy Troopers stormed into Kergan's Way – in Joaz's mind an act of contemptuous recklessness. He gave a curt order; out from passages and areas swarmed his dragons: Blue Horrors, Fiends, Termagants.

The squat Troopers stared with sagging jaws. Here were unexpected antagonists! Kergan's Way resounded with their calls and orders. First they fell back, then, with the courage of desperation, fought furiously. Up and down Kergan's Way raged the battle. Certain relationships quickly became evident. In the narrow defile neither the Trooper pistols nor the steel-weighted tails of the Fiends could be used effectively. Cutlasses were useless against dragon-scale, but the pincers of the Blue Horrors, the Termagant daggers, the axes, swords, fangs and claws of the Fiends, did bloody work against the Heavy Troopers. A single Trooper and a single Termagant were approximately a match; though the Trooper, gripping the dragon with massive arms, tearing away its brachs, breaking back its neck, won more often than the Termagant. But if two or three Termagants confronted a single Trooper, he was doomed. As soon as he committed himself to one, another would crush his legs, blind him or hack open his throat.

So the Troopers fell back to the valley floor, leaving twenty of their fellows dead in Kergan's Way. The Banbeck men once more opened fire, but once more with minor effect.

Joaz watched from his study, wondering as to the next Basic tactic. Enlightenment was not long in coming. The Heavy Troopers regrouped, stood panting, while the Basics rode back and forth receiving information, admonishing, advising, chiding.

From the black ship came a gush of energy, to strike the cliff above Kergan's Way; the study rocked with the concussion.

Joaz backed away from the vision-plates. What if a ray struck one of his collecting lenses? Might not the energy be guided and reflected directly toward him? He departed his study as it shook to a new explosion.

He ran through a passage, descended a staircase, emerged into one of the central galleries, to find apparent confusion. White-faced women and children, retiring deeper into the mountain, pushed past dragons and men in battle-gear entering one of the new tunnels. Joaz watched for a moment or two to satisfy himself that the confusion held nothing of panic, then joined his warriors in the tunnel leading north.

In some past era an entire section of the cliff at the head of the valley had sloughed off, creating a jungle of piled rock and boulders: the Banbeck Jambles. Here, through a fissure, the new tunnel opened; and here Joaz went with his warriors. Behind them, down the valley, sounded the rumble of explosions as the black ship began to demolish Banbeck Village.

Joaz, peering around a boulder, watched in a fury as great slabs of rock began to scale away from the cliff. Then he stared in astonishment, for to the Basic troops had come an extraordinary reinforcement: eight Giants twice an ordinary man's stature – barrel-chested monsters, gnarled of arm and leg, with pale eyes, shocks of tawny hair. They wore brown and red armor with black epaulettes, and carried swords, maces and blast-cannon slung over their backs.

Joaz considered. The presence of the Giants gave him no reason to alter his central strategy, which in any event was vague and intuitive. He must be prepared to suffer losses, and could only hope to inflict greater losses on the Basics. But what did they care for the lives of their troops? Less than he cared for his dragons. And if they destroyed Banbeck Village, ruined the Vale, how could he do corresponding damage to them?

He looked over his shoulder at the tall white cliffs, wondering how closely he had estimated the position of the sacerdotes' hall. And now he must act; the time had come. He signaled to a small boy, one of his own sons, who took a deep breath, hurled himself blindly away from the shelter of the rocks, ran helter-skelter out to the valley floor. A moment later his mother ran forth to snatch him up and dash back into the Jambles.

'Done well,' Joaz commended them. 'Done well indeed.' Cautiously he again looked forth through the rocks. The Basics were gazing intently in his direction.

For a long moment, while Joaz tingled with suspense, it seemed that they had ignored his ploy. They conferred, came to a decision, flicked the leathery buttocks of their mounts with their quirts. The creatures pranced sidewise, then loped north up the valley. The Trackers fell in behind, then came the Heavy Troopers moving at a humping quick-step. The Weaponeers followed with their three-wheeled mechanisms, and ponderously at the rear came the eight Giants. Across the fields of bellegarde and vetch, over vines, hedges, beds of berries and stands of oil-pod tramped the raiders, destroying with a certain morose satisfaction.

The Basics prudently halted before the Banbeck Jambles while the Trackers ran ahead like dogs, clambering over the first boulders, rearing high to test the air for odor, peering, listening, pointing, twittering doubtfully to each other. The Heavy Troopers moved in carefully, and their near presence spurred on the Trackers. Abandoning caution they bounded into the heart of the Jambles, emitting squeals of horrified consternation when a dozen Blue Horrors dropped among them. They clawed out heat-guns, in their excitement burning friend and foe alike. With silken ferocity the Blue Horrors ripped them apart. Screaming for aid, kicking, flailing, thrashing, those who were able fled as precipitously as they had come. Only twelve from the original twenty-four regained the valley floor; and even as they did so, even as they cried out in relief at winning free from death, a squad of Long-horned Murderers burst out upon them, and these surviving Trackers were knocked down, gored, hacked.

The Heavy Troopers charged forward with hoarse calls of rage, aiming pistols, swinging swords; but the Murderers retreated to the shelter of the boulders.

Within the Jambles the Banbeck men had appropriated the heat-guns dropped by the Trackers, and warily coming forward, tried to burn the Basics. But, unfamiliar with the weapons, the men neglected either to focus or condense the flame and the Basics, no more than mildly singed, hastily whipped their mounts back out of range. The Heavy Troopers, halting not a hundred feet in front of the Jambles, sent in a volley of explosive pellets, which killed two of the Banbeck knights and forced the others back.

At a discreet distance the Basics appraised the situation. The Weaponeers came up and while awaiting instructions, conferred in low tones with the mounts. One of these Weaponeers was now summoned and given orders. He divested himself of all his weapons and holding his empty hands in the air marched forward to the edge of the Jambles. Choosing a gap between a pair of ten-foot boulders, he resolutely entered the rock-maze.

A Banbeck knight escorted him to Joaz. Here, by chance, were also half a dozen Termagants. The Weaponeer paused uncertainly, made a mental readjustment, approached the Termagants. Bowing respectfully he started to speak. The Termagants listened without interest, and presently one of the knights directed him to Joaz.

'Dragons do not rule men on Aerlith,' said Joaz dryly. 'What is your message?'

The Weaponeer looked dubiously toward the Termagants, then somberly back to Joaz. 'You are authorized to act for the entire warren?' He spoke slowly in a dry bland voice, selecting his words with conscientious care.

Joaz repeated shortly, 'What is your message?'

'I bring an integration from my masters.'

'"Integration"? I do not understand you.'

'An integration of the instantaneous vectors of destiny. An interpretation of the future. They wish the sense conveyed to you in the following terms: "Do not waste lives, both ours and your own. You are valuable to us and will be given treatment in accordance with this value. Surrender to the Rule. Cease the wasteful destruction of enterprise.'"

Joaz frowned. 'Destruction of enterprise?'

'The reference is to the content of your genes. The message is at its end. I advise you to accede. Why waste your blood, why destroy yourselves? Come forth now with me; all will be for the best.'

Joaz gave a brittle laugh. 'You are a slave. How can you judge what is best for us?'

The Weaponeer blinked. 'What choice is there for you? All residual pockets of disorganized life are to be expunged. The way of facility is best.' He inclined his head respectfully toward the Termagants. 'If you doubt me, consult your own Revered Ones. They will advise you.'

'There are no Revered Ones here,' said Joaz. 'The dragons fight with us and for us; they are our fellow-warriors. But I have an alternate proposal. Why do not you and your fellows join us? Throw off your slavery, become free men! We will take the ship and go searching for the old worlds of men.'

The Weaponeer exhibited only polite interest. '"Worlds of men"? There are none of them. A few residuals such as yourself remain in the desolate regions. All are to be expunged. Would you not prefer to serve the Rule?'

'Would you not prefer to be a free man?'

The Weaponeer's face showed mild bewilderment. 'You do not understand me. If you choose—'

'Listen carefully,' said Joaz. 'You and your fellows can be your own masters, live among other men.'

The Weaponeer frowned. 'Who would wish to be a wild savage? To whom would we look for law, control, direction, order?'

Joaz threw up his hands in disgust, but made one last attempt. 'I will provide all these; I will undertake such a responsibility. Go back, kill all the Basics – the Revered Ones, as you call them. These are my first orders.'

'Kill them?' The Weaponeer's voice was soft with horror.

'Kill them.' Joaz spoke as if to a child. 'Then we men will possess the ship. We will go to find the worlds where men are powerful—'

'There are no such worlds.'

'Ah, but there must be! At one time men roamed every star in the sky.'

'No longer.'

'What of Eden?'

'I know nothing of it.'

Joaz threw up his hands. 'Will you join us?'

'What would be the meaning of such an act?' said the Weaponeer gently. 'Come then, lay down your arms, submit to the Rule.' He glanced doubtfully toward the Termagants. 'Your own Revered Ones will receive fitting treatment, have no fear on this account.'

'You fool! These "Revered Ones" are slaves, just as you are a slave to the Basics! We breed them to serve us, just as you are bred! Have at least the grace to recognize your own degradation!'

The Weaponeer blinked. 'You speak in terms I do not completely understand. You will not surrender then?'

'No. We will kill all of you, if our strength holds out.'

The Weaponeer bowed, turned, departed through the rocks. Joaz followed, peered out over the valley floor.

The Weaponeer made his report to the Basics, who listened with characteristic detachment. They gave an order, and the Heavy Troopers, spreading out in a skirmish line, moved slowly in toward the rocks. Behind lumbered the Giants, blasters slung forward at the ready, and about twenty Trackers, survivors of the first foray. The Heavy Troopers reached the rocks, peered in. The Trackers clambered above, searching for ambushes, and finding none, signaled back. With great caution the Heavy Troopers entered the Jambles, necessarily breaking formation. Twenty feet they advanced, fifty feet, a hundred feet. Emboldened, the vengeful Trackers sprang forward over the rocks and up surged the Termagants.

Screaming and cursing, the Trackers scrambled back pursued by the dragons. The Heavy Troopers recoiled, then swung up their weapons, fired. Two Termagants were struck under the lower armpits, their most vulnerable spot. Floundering, they tumbled down among the rocks. Others, maddened, jumped squarely down upon the Troopers. There was roaring, squealing, cries of shock and pain. The Giants lumbered up, and grinning vastly plucked away the Termagants, wrenched off their heads, flung them high over the rocks. Those Termagants who were able scuttled back, leaving half a dozen Heavy Troopers wounded, two with their throats torn open.

Again the Heavy Troopers moved forward, with the Trackers reconnoitering above, but more warily. The Trackers froze, yelled a warning. The Heavy Troopers stopped short, calling to each other, swinging their guns nervously. Overhead the Trackers scrambled back, and through the rocks, over the rocks, came dozens of Fiends and Blue Horrors. The Heavy Troopers, grimacing dourly, fired their pistols; and the air reeked with the stench of burning scale, exploded viscera. The dragons surged in upon the men, and now began a terrible battle among the rocks, with the pistols, the maces, even the swords useless for lack of room. The Giants lumbered forward and in turn were attacked by Fiends. Astonished, the idiotic grins faded from their faces; they hopped awkwardly back from the steel-weighted tails, but among the rocks the Fiends were also at a disadvantage, their steel balls clattering and jarring away from rock more often than flesh.

The Giants, recovering, discharged their chest-projectors into the mêlée; Fiends were torn apart as well as Blue Horrors and Heavy Troopers, the Giants making no distinction.

Over the rocks came another wave of dragons: Blue Horrors. They slid down on the heads of the Giants, clawing, stabbing, tearing. In a frenzy the Giants tore at the creatures, flung them to the ground, stamped on them, and the Heavy Troopers burnt them with their pistols.

From nowhere, for no reason, there came a lull. Ten seconds, fifteen seconds passed, with no sound but whimpering and moaning from wounded dragons and men. A sense of imminence weighted the air, and here came the Juggers, looming through the passages. For a brief period Giants and Juggers looked each other face to face. Then Giants groped for their blast-projectors, while Blue Horrors sprang down once more, grappling the Giant arms. The Juggers stumped quickly forward. Dragon brachs grappled Giant arms; bludgeons and maces swung, dragon armor and man armor crushed and ground apart. Man and dragon tumbled over and over, ignoring pain, shock, mutilation.

The struggle became quiet; sobbing and wheezing replaced the roars, and presently eight Juggers, superior in mass and natural armament, staggered away from eight destroyed Giants.

The Troopers meanwhile had drawn together, standing back to back in clots. Step by step, burning with heat-beams the screaming Horrors, Termagants and Fiends who lunged after them, they retreated toward the valley floor, and finally won free of the rocks. The pursuing Fiends, anxious to fight in the open, sprang into their midst, while from the flanks came Long-horned Murderers and Striding Murderers. In a spirit of reckless jubilation, a dozen men riding Spiders, carrying blast-cannon taken from the fallen Giants, charged the Basics and Weaponeers, who waited beside the rather casual emplacement of three-wheeled weapons. The Basics, without shame, jerked their man-mounts around and fled toward the black ship. The Weaponeers swiveled their mechanisms, aimed, discharged bursts of energy. One man fell, two men, three men – then the others were among the Weaponeers, who were soon hacked to pieces … including the one who had served as envoy.

Several of the men, whooping and hooting, set out in chase of the Basics, but the human mounts, springing along like monstrous rabbits, carried the Basics as fast as the Spiders carried the men. From the Jambles came a horn signal; the mounted men halted, wheeled back; the entire Banbeck force turned and retreated full speed into the Jambles.

The Troopers stumbled a few defiant steps in pursuit, then halted in sheer fatigue. Of the original three squads, not enough men to make up a single squad survived. The eight Giants had perished, all Weaponeers and almost the entire group of Trackers.

The Banbeck forces gained the Jambles with seconds only to spare. From the black ship came a volley of explosive pellets, to shatter the rocks at the spot where they had disappeared.

CHAPTER ELEVEN

On a wind-polished cape of rock above Banbeck Vale Ervis Carcolo and Bast Givven had watched the battle. The rocks hid the greater part of the fighting; the cries and clangor rose faint and tinny, like insect noise. There would be the glint of dragon scale, glimpses of running men, the shadow and flicker of movement, but not until the mangled forces of the Basics staggered forth did the outcome of the battle reveal itself. Carcolo shook his head in sour bewilderment. 'The crafty devil, Joaz Banbeck! He's turned them back, he's slaughtered their best!'

'It would appear,' said Bast Givven, 'that dragons armed with fangs, swords and steel balls are more effective than men with guns and heat-beams – at least in close quarters.'

Carcolo grunted. 'I might have done as well myself, under like circumstances.' He turned Bast Givven a waspish glance. 'Do you not agree?'

'Certainly. Beyond all question.'

'Of course,' Carcolo went on, 'I had not the advantage of preparation. The Basics surprised me, but Joaz Banbeck labored under no such handicap.' He looked back down into Banbeck Vale, where the Basic ship was bombarding the Jambles, shattering rocks into splinters. 'Do they plan to blast the Jambles out of the valley? In which case, of course, Joaz Banbeck would have no further refuge. Their strategy is clear. And as I suspected: reserve forces!'

Another thirty Troopers had marched down the ramp to stand immobile in the trampled field before the ship.

Carcolo pounded his fist into his palm. 'Bast Givven, listen now, listen carefully! For it is in our power to do a great deed, to reverse our fortunes! Notice Clybourne Crevasse, how it opens into the Vale, directly behind the Basic ship.'

'Your ambition will yet cost us our lives.'

Carcolo laughed. 'Come, Givven, how many times does a man die? What better way to lose a life than in the pursuit of glory?'

Bast Givven turned, surveyed the meager remnants of the Happy Valley army. 'We could win glory by trouncing a dozen sacerdotes. Flinging ourselves upon a Basic ship is hardly needful.'

'Nevertheless,' said Ervis Carcolo, 'that is how it must be. I ride ahead, you marshal the forces and follow. We meet at the head of Clybourne Crevasse, on the west edge of the Vale!'

CHAPTER TWELVE

Stamping his feet, muttering nervous curses, Ervis Carcolo waited at the head of Clybourne Crevasse. Unlucky chance after chance paraded before his imagination. The Basics might surrender to the difficulties of Banbeck Vale and depart. Joaz Banbeck might attack across the open fields to save Banbeck Village from destruction and so destroy himself. Bast Givven might be unable to control the disheartened men and mutinous dragons of Happy Valley. Any of these situations might occur; any would expunge Carcolo's dreams of glory and leave him a broken man. Back and forth he paced the scarred granite; every few seconds he peered down into Banbeck Vale; every few seconds he turned to scan the bleak skylines for the dark shapes of his dragons, the taller silhouettes of his men.

Beside the Basic ship waited a scanty two squads of Heavy Troopers: those who had survived the original attack and the reserves. They squatted in silent groups, watching the leisurely destruction of Banbeck Village. Fragment by fragment, the spires, towers and cliffs which had housed the Banbeck folk cracked off, slumped down into an ever-growing mound of rubble. An even heavier barrage poured against the Jambles. Boulders broke like eggs; rock splinters drifted down the valley.

A half hour passed. Ervis Carcolo seated himself glumly on a rock.

A jingle, the pad of feet. Carcolo bounded to his feet. Winding across the skyline came the sorry remnants of his forces, the men dispirited, the Termagants surly and petulant, a mere handful each of Fiends, Blue Horrors and Murderers.

Carcolo's shoulders sagged. What could be accomplished with a force so futile as this? He took a deep breath. Show a brave front! Never say die! He assumed his bluffest mien. Stepping forward, he cried out, 'Men, dragons! Today we have known defeat, but the day is not over. The time of redemption is at hand; we shall revenge ourselves on both the Basics and Joaz Banbeck!'

He searched the faces of his men, hoping for enthusiasm. They looked back at him without interest. The dragons, their understanding less complete, snorted softly, hissed and whispered. 'Men and dragons!' bawled Carcolo. 'You ask me, how shall we achieve these glories? I answer, follow where I lead! Fight where I fight! What is death to us, with our valley despoiled?'

Again he inspected his troops, once more finding only listlessness and apathy. Carcolo stifled the roar of frustration which rose into his throat, and turned away. 'Advance!' he called gruffly over his shoulder. Mounting his drooping Spider, he set off down Clybourne Crevasse.

The Basic ship pounded the Jambles and Banbeck Village with equal vehemence. From a vantage on the west rim of the valley Joaz Banbeck watched the blasting of corridor after familiar corridor. Apartments and halls hewn earnestly from the rock, carved, tooled, polished across the generations – all opened, destroyed, pulverized. Now the target became that spire which contained Joaz Banbeck's private apartments, with his study, his workroom, the Banbeck reliquarium.

Joaz clenched and unclenched his fists, furious at his own helplessness. The goal of the Basics was clear. They intended to destroy Banbeck Vale, to exterminate as completely as possible the men of Aerlith – and what could prevent them? Joaz studied the Jambles. The old talus had been splintered away almost to the sheer face of the cliff. Where was the opening into the Great Hall of the sacerdotes? His farfetched hypotheses were diminishing to futility. Another hour would see the utter devastation of Banbeck Village.

Joaz tried to control a sickening sense of frustration. How to stop the destruction? He forced himself to calculate. Clearly, an attack across the valley floor was equivalent to suicide. But behind the black ship opened a ravine similar to that in which Joaz stood concealed: Clybourne Crevasse. The ship's entry gaped wide, Heavy Troopers squatted listlessly to the side. Joaz shook his head with a sour grimace. Inconceivable that the Basics could neglect so obvious a threat.

Still – in their arrogance might they not overlook the possibility of so insolent an act?

Indecision tugged Joaz forward and backward. And now a barrage of explosive pellets split open the spire which housed his apartments. The reliquarium, the ancient trove of the Banbecks, was about to be destroyed. Joaz made a blind gesture, jumped to his feet, called the closest of his dragon masters. 'Assemble the Murderers, three squads of Termagants, two dozen Blue Horrors, ten Fiends, all the riders. We climb to Banbeck Verge, we descend Clybourne Crevasse, we attack the ship!'

The dragon master departed; Joaz gave himself to gloomy contemplation. If the Basics intended to draw him into a trap, they were about to succeed.

The dragon master returned. 'The force is assembled.'

'We ride.'

Up the ravine surged men and dragons, emerging upon Banbeck Verge. Swinging south, they came to the head of Clybourne Crevasse.

A knight at the head of the column suddenly signaled a halt. When Joaz approached he pointed out marks on the floor of the crevasse. 'Dragons and men have passed here recently.'

Joaz studied the tracks. 'Heading down the crevasse.'

'Yes.'

Joaz dispatched a party of scouts who presently came galloping wildly back. 'Ervis Carcolo, with men and dragons, is attacking the ship!'

Joaz wheeled his Spider, plunged headlong down the dim passage, followed by his army.

Outcries and screams of battle reached their ears as they approached the mouth of the crevasse. Bursting out on the valley floor Joaz came upon a scene of desperate carnage, with dragon and Heavy Trooper hacking, stabbing, burning, blasting. Where was Ervis Carcolo? Joaz recklessly rode to look into the entry port which hung wide. Ervis Carcolo then had forced his way into the ship! A trap? Or had he effectuated Joaz's own plan of seizing the ship? What of the Heavy Troopers? Would the Basics sacrifice forty warriors to capture a handful of men? Unreasonable – but now the Heavy Troopers were holding their own. They had formed a phalanx, they now concentrated the energy of their weapons on those dragons who yet opposed them. A trap? If so, it was sprung – unless Ervis Carcolo already had captured the ship. Joaz rose in his saddle, signaled his company. 'Attack!'

The Heavy Troopers were doomed. Striding Murderers hewed from above, Long-horned Murderers thrust from below, Blue Horrors pinched, clipped, dismembered. The battle was done, but Joaz, with men and Termagants, had already charged up the ramp. From within came the hum and throb of power, and also human sounds – cries, shouts of fury.

The sheer ponderous bulk struck at Joaz; he stopped short, peered uncertainly into the ship. Behind him his men waited, muttering under their breath. Joaz asked himself, 'Am I as brave as Ervis Carcolo? What is bravery, in any case? I am completely afraid: I dare not enter, I dare not stay outside.' He put aside all caution, rushed forward, followed by his men and a horde of scuttling Termagants.

Even as Joaz entered the ship he knew Ervis Carcolo had not succeeded; above him the guns still sang and hissed. Joaz's apartments splintered apart. Another tremendous volley struck into the Jambles, laying bare the naked stone of the cliff, and what was hitherto hidden: the edge of a tall opening.

Joaz, inside the ship, found himself in an antechamber. The inner port was closed. He sidled forward, peered through a rectangular pane into what seemed a lobby or staging chamber. Ervis Carcolo and his knights crouched against the far wall, casually guarded by about twenty Weaponeers. A group of Basics rested in an alcove to the side, relaxed, quiet, their attitude one of contemplation.

Carcolo and his men were not completely subdued; as Joaz watched Carcolo lunged furiously forward. A purple crackle of energy punished him, hurled him back against the wall.

From the alcove one of the Basics, staring across the inner chamber, took note of Joaz Banbeck; he flicked out with his brach, touched a rod. An alarm whistle sounded, the outer port slid shut. A trap? An emergency process? The result was the same. Joaz motioned to four men, heavily burdened. They came forward, kneeled, placed on the deck four of the blast cannon which the Giants had carried into the Jambles.

Joaz swung his arm. Cannon belched; metal creaked, melted; acrid odors permeated the room. The hole was still too small. 'Again!' The cannon flamed; the inner port vanished. Into the gap sprang Weaponeers, firing their energy guns. Purple fire cut into the Banbeck ranks. Men curled, twisted, wilted, fell with clenched fingers and contorted faces. Before the cannon could respond, red-scaled shapes scuttled forward: Termagants. Hissing and wailing they swarmed over the Weaponeers, on into the staging chamber. In front of the alcove occupied by the Basics they stopped short, as if in astonishment. The men crowding after fell silent: even Carcolo watched in fascination. Basic stock confronted its derivative, each seeing in the other its caricature. The Termagants crept forward with sinister deliberation; the Basics waved their brachs, whistled, fluted. The Termagants scuttled forward, sprang into the alcove. There was a horrid tumbling and croaking; Joaz, sickened at some elementary level, was forced to look away. The struggle was soon over; there was silence in the alcove. Joaz turned to examine Ervis Carcolo, who stared back, rendered inarticulate by anger, humiliation, pain and fright.

Finally finding his voice Carcolo made an awkward gesture of menace and fury. 'Be off with you,' he croaked. 'I claim this ship. Unless you would lie in your own blood, leave me to my conquest!'

Joaz snorted contemptuously, turned his back on Carcolo, who sucked in his breath, and with a whispered curse, lurched forward. Bast Givven seized him, drew him back. Carcolo struggled, Givven talked earnestly into his ear, and Carcolo at last relaxed, half-weeping.

Joaz meanwhile examined the chamber. The walls were blank, gray; the deck was covered with resilient black foam. There was no obvious illumination, but light was everywhere, exuding from the walls. The air chilled the skin, and smelled unpleasantly acrid: an odor which Joaz had not previously noticed. He coughed, his eardrums rang. A frightening suspicion became certainty; on heavy legs he lunged for the port, beckoning to his troops. 'Outside, they poison us!' He stumbled out on the ramp, gulped fresh air; his men and Termagants followed, and then in a stumbling rush came Ervis Carcolo and his men. Under the hulk of the great ship the group stood gasping, tottering on limp legs, eyes dim and swimming.

Above them, oblivious or careless of their presence, the ship's guns sent forth another barrage. The spire housing Joaz's apartments tottered, collapsed; the Jambles were no more than a heap of rock splinters drifting into a high arched opening. Inside the opening Joaz glimpsed a dark shape, a glint, a shine, a structure – then he was distracted by an ominous sound at his back. From a port at the other end of the ship, a new force of Heavy Troopers had alighted – three new squads of twenty men each, accompanied by a dozen Weaponeers with four of the rolling projectors.

Joaz sagged back in dismay. He glanced along his troops; they were in no condition either to attack or defend. A single alternative remained: flight. 'Make for Clybourne Crevasse,' he called thickly.

Stumbling, lurching, the remnants of the two armies fled under the brow of the great black ship. Behind them Heavy Troopers swung smartly forward, but without haste.

Rounding the ship, Joaz stopped short. In the mouth of Clybourne Crevasse waited a fourth squad of Heavy Troopers, with another Weaponeer and his weapon.

Joaz looked to right and left, up and down the valley. Which way to run, where to turn? The Jambles? They were nonexistent. Motion, slow and ponderous in the opening, previously concealed by tumbled rock, caught his attention. A dark object moved forth; a shutter drew back, a bright disk glittered. Almost instantly a pencil of milky-blue radiance lanced at, into, through the end disk of the Basic ship.

Within, tortured machinery whined, simultaneously up and down the scale, to inaudibility at either end. The luster of the end disks vanished; they became gray, dull; the whisper of power and life previously pervading the ship gave way to dead quiet; the ship itself was dead, and its mass, suddenly unsupported, crushed groaning into the ground.

The Heavy Troopers gazed up in consternation at the hulk which had brought them to Aerlith. Joaz, taking advantage of their indecision, called, 'Retreat! North – up the valley!'

The Heavy Troopers doggedly followed; the Weaponeers however cried out an order to halt. They emplaced their weapons, brought them to bear on the cavern behind the Jambles. Within the opening naked shapes moved with frantic haste; there was slow shifting of massive machinery, a change of lights and shadows, and the milky-blue shaft of radiance struck forth once more. It flicked down; Weaponeers, weapons, two-thirds of the Heavy Troopers vanished like moths in a furnace. The surviving Heavy Troopers halted, retreated uncertainly toward the ship.

In the mouth of Clybourne Crevasse waited the remaining squad of Heavy Troopers. The single Weaponeer crouched over his three-wheeled mechanism. With fateful care he made his adjustments; within the dark opening the naked sacerdotes worked furiously, thrusting, wedging, the strain of their sinews and hearts and minds communicating itself to every man in the valley. The shaft of milky-blue light sprang forth, but too soon: it melted the rock a hundred yards south of Clybourne Crevasse, and now from the Weaponeer's gun came a splash of orange and green flame. Seconds later the mouth of the sacerdotes' cavern erupted. Rocks, bodies, fragments of metal, glass, rubber arched through the air.

The sound of the explosion reverberated through the valley. And the dark object in the cavern was destroyed, was no more than tatters and shreds of metal.

Joaz took three deep breaths, throwing off the effects of the narcotic gas by sheer power of will. He signaled to his Murderers. 'Charge! Kill!'

The Murderers loped forward; the Heavy Troopers threw themselves flat, aimed their weapons, but soon died. In the mouth of Clybourne Crevasse the final squad of Troopers charged wildly forth, to be instantly attacked by Termagants and Blue Horrors who had sidled along the face of the cliff. The Weaponeer was gored by a Murderer; there was no further resistance in the valley, and the ship lay open to attack.

Joaz led the way back up the ramp, through the entry into the now dim staging-chamber. The blast-cannon captured from the Giants lay where his men had dropped them.

Three portals led from the chamber, and these were swiftly burned down. The first revealed a spiral ramp; the second, a long empty hall lined with tiers of bunks; the third, a similar hall in which the bunks were occupied. Pale faces peered from the tiers, pallid hands flickered. Up and down the central corridor marched squat matrons in gray gowns. Ervis Carcolo rushed forward, buffeting the matrons to the deck, peering into the bunks. 'Outside,' he bellowed. 'You are rescued, you are saved. Outside quickly, while there is opportunity.'

But there was only meager resistance to overcome from a half-dozen Weaponeers and Trackers, none whatever from twenty Mechanics – these, short thin men with sharp features and dark hair – and none from the sixteen remaining Basics. All were marched off the ship as prisoners.

CHAPTER THIRTEEN

Quiet filled the valley floor, the silence of exhaustion. Men and dragons sprawled in the trampled fields; the captives stood in a dejected huddle beside the ship. Occasionally an isolated sound came to emphasize the silence: the creak of cooling metal within the ship, the fall of a loose rock from the shattered cliffs; an occasional murmur from the liberated Happy Valley folk, who sat in a group apart from the surviving warriors.

Ervis Carcolo alone seemed restless. For a space he stood with his back to Joaz, slapping his thigh with his scabbard tassel. He contemplated the sky where Skene, a dazzling atom, hung close over the western cliffs, then turned, studied the shattered gap at the north of the valley, filled with the twisted remains of the sacerdotes' construction. He gave his thigh a final slap, looked toward Joaz Banbeck, turned to stalk through the huddle of Happy Valley folk, making brusque motions of no particular significance, pausing here and there to harangue or cajole, apparently attempting to instill spirit and purpose into his defeated people.

In this purpose he was unsuccessful. Presently he swung sharply about, marched across the field to where Joaz Banbeck lay outstretched. Carcolo stared down. 'Well then,' he said bluffly, 'the battle is over, the ship is won.'

Joaz raised himself up on one elbow. 'True.'

'Let us have no misunderstanding on one point,' said Carcolo. 'Ship and contents are mine. An ancient rule defines the rights of him who is first to attack. On this rule I base my claim.'

Joaz looked up in surprise, and seemed almost amused. 'By a rule even more ancient, I have already assumed possession.'

'I dispute this assertion,' said Carcolo hotly. 'Who—'

Joaz held up his hand wearily. 'Silence, Carcolo! You are alive now only because I am sick of blood and violence. Do not test my patience!'

Carcolo turned away, twitching his scabbard tassel with restrained fury. He looked up the valley, turned back to Joaz. 'Here come the sacerdotes, who in fact demolished the ship. I remind you of my proposal, by which we might have prevented this destruction and slaughter.'

Joaz smiled. 'You made your proposal only two days ago. Further, the sacerdotes possess no weapons.'

Carcolo stared as if Joaz had taken leave of his wits. 'How then did they destroy the ship?'

Joaz shrugged. 'I can only make conjectures.'

Carcolo asked sarcastically, 'And what direction do these conjectures lead?'

'I wonder if they had constructed the frame of a spaceship. I wonder if they turned the propulsion beam against the Basic ship.'

Carcolo pursed his mouth dubiously. 'Why should the sacerdotes build themselves a spaceship?'

'The Demie approaches. Why do you not put your question to him?'

'I will do so,' said Carcolo with dignity.

But the Demie, followed by four younger sacerdotes and walking with the air of a man in a dream, passed without speaking.

Joaz rose to his knees, watched after him. The Demie apparently planned to mount the ramp and enter the ship. Joaz jumped to his feet, followed, barred the way to the ramp. Politely he asked, 'What do you seek, Demie?'

'I seek to board the ship.'

'To what end? I ask, of course, from sheer curiosity.'

The Demie inspected him a moment without reply. His face was haggard and tight; his eyes gleamed like frost-stars. Finally he replied, in a voice hoarse with emotion. 'I wish to determine if the ship can be repaired.'

Joaz considered a moment, then spoke in a gentle rational voice. 'The information can be of little interest to you. Would the sacerdotes place themselves so completely under my command?'

'We obey no one.'

'In that case, I can hardly take you with me when I leave.'

The Demie swung around, and for a moment seemed as if he would walk away. His eyes fell on the shattered opening at the end of the vale, and he turned back. He spoke, not in the measured voice of a sacerdote, but in a burst of grief and fury. 'This is your doing! You preen yourself, you count yourself resourceful and clever; you forced us to act, and thereby violate ourselves and our dedication!'

Joaz nodded, with a faint grim smile. 'I knew the opening must lie behind the Jambles; I wondered if you might be building a spaceship; I hoped that you might protect yourselves against the Basics, and so serve my purposes. I admit your charges. I used you and your construction as a weapon, to save myself and my people. Did I do wrong?'

'Right or wrong – who can weigh? You wasted our effort across more than eight hundred Aerlith years! You destroyed more than you can ever replace.'

'I destroyed nothing, Demie. The Basics destroyed your ship. If you had cooperated with us in the defense of Banbeck Vale this disaster would have never occurred. You chose neutrality, you thought yourselves immune from our grief and pain. As you see, such is not the case.'

'And meanwhile our labor of eight hundred and twelve years goes for naught.'

Joaz asked with feigned innocence, 'Why did you need a spaceship? Where do you plan to travel?'

The Demie's eyes burst with flames as intense as those of Skene. 'When the race of men is gone, then we go abroad. We move across the galaxy, we repopulate the terrible old worlds, and the new universal history starts from that day, with the past wiped clean as if it never existed. If the grephs destroy you, what is it to us? We await only the death of the last man in the universe.'

'Do you not consider yourselves men?'

'We are as you know us – Above Men.'

At Joaz's shoulder someone laughed coarsely. Joaz turned his head to see Ervis Carcolo. '"Above Men"?' mocked Carcolo. 'Poor naked waifs of the caves! What can you display to prove your superiority?'

The Demie's mouth drooped, the lines of his face deepened. 'We have our *tands*. We have our knowledge. We have our strength.'

Carcolo turned away with another coarse laugh. Joaz said in a subdued voice, 'I feel more pity for you than you ever felt for us.'

Carcolo returned. 'And where did you learn to build a spaceship? From your own efforts? Or from the work of men before you, men of the old times?'

'We are the ultimate men,' said the Demie. 'We know all that men have ever thought, spoken or devised. We are the last and the first. And when the under-folk are gone, we shall renew the cosmos as innocent and fresh as rain.'

'But men have never gone and will never go,' said Joaz. 'A setback yes, but is not the universe wide? Somewhere are the worlds of men. With the help of the Basics and their Mechanics, I will repair the ship and go forth to find these worlds.'

'You will seek in vain,' said the Demie.

'These worlds do not exist?'

'The Human Empire is dissolved; men exist only in feeble groups.'

'What of Eden, old Eden?'

'A myth, no more.'

'My marble globe, what of that?'

'A toy, an imaginative fabrication.'

'How can you be sure?' asked Joaz, troubled in spite of himself.

'Have I not said that we know all of history? We can look into our *tands* and see deep into the past, until the recollections are dim and misty, and never do we remember planet Eden.'

Joaz shook his head stubbornly. 'There must be an original world from which men came. Call it Earth or Tempe or Eden – somewhere it exists.'

The Demie started to speak, then in a rare show of irresolution held his tongue. Joaz said, 'Perhaps you are right, perhaps we are the last men. But I shall go forth to look.'

'I shall come with you,' said Ervis Carcolo.

'You will be fortunate to find yourself alive tomorrow,' said Joaz.

Carcolo drew himself up. 'Do not dismiss my claim to the ship so carelessly!'

Joaz struggled for words, but could find none. What to do with the unruly Carcolo? He could not find in himself enough harshness to do what he knew should be done. He temporized, turned his back on Carcolo. 'Now you know my plans,' he told the Demie. 'If you do not interfere with me, I shall not interfere with you.'

The Demie moved slowly back. 'Go then. We are a passive race; we despise ourselves for our activity of today. Perhaps it was our greatest mistake ... But go, seek your forgotten world. You will only perish somewhere among the stars. We will wait, as already we have waited.' He turned and walked away, followed by the four younger sacerdotes, who had all the time stood gravely to the side.

Joaz called after him. 'And if the Basics come again? Will you fight with us? Or against us?'

The Demie made no response, but walked to the north, the long white hair swinging down his thin shoulder blades.

Joaz watched him a moment, gazed up and down the ruined valley, shook his head in wonder and puzzlement, turned back to study the great black ship.

Skene touched the western cliffs; there was an instant dimming of light, a sudden chill. Carcolo approached him. 'Tonight I shall hold my folk here in Banbeck Vale, and send them home on the morrow. Meanwhile, I suggest that you board the ship with me and make a preliminary survey.'

Joaz took a deep breath. Why could it not come easier for him? Carcolo had twice sought his life, and, had positions been reversed, would have shown him no mercy. He forced himself to act. His duty to himself, to his people, to his ultimate goal was clear.

He called to those of his knights who carried the captured heat-guns. They approached.

Joaz said, 'Take Carcolo into Clybourne Crevasse. Execute him. Do this at once.'

Protesting, bellowing, Carcolo was dragged off. Joaz turned away with a heavy heart, and sought Bast Givven. 'I take you for a sensible man.'

'I regard myself so.'

'I set you in charge of Happy Valley. Take your folk home, before darkness falls.'

Bast Givven silently went to his people. They stirred, and presently departed Banbeck Vale.

Joaz crossed the valley floor to the tumble of rubble which choked Kergan's Way. He choked with fury as he looked upon the destruction, and for a moment almost wavered in his resolve. Might it not be fit to fly the black ship to Coralyne and take revenge on the Basics? He walked around to stand under the spire which had housed his apartments, and by some strange freak of chance came upon a rounded fragment of yellow marble.

Weighing this in his palm he looked up into the sky where Coralyne already twinkled red, and tried to bring order to his mind.

The Banbeck folk had emerged from the deep tunnels. Phade the minstrel-maiden came to find him. 'What a terrible day,' she murmured. 'What awful events; what a great victory.'

Joaz tossed the bit of yellow marble back into the rubble. 'I feel much the same way. And where it all ends, no one knows less than I.'

The Last Castle

CHAPTER ONE

1

Toward the end of a stormy summer afternoon, with the sun finally breaking out under ragged black rain-clouds, Castle Janeil was overwhelmed and its population destroyed. Until almost the last moment factions among the castle clans contended as to how Destiny properly should be met. The gentlemen of most prestige and account elected to ignore the entire undignified circumstance and went about their normal pursuits, with neither more nor less punctilio than usual. A few cadets, desperate to the point of hysteria, took up weapons and prepared to resist the final assault. Still others, perhaps a quarter of the total population, waited passively, ready – almost happy – to expiate the sins of the human race. In the end, death came uniformly to all, and all extracted as much satisfaction from their dying as this essentially graceless process could afford. The proud sat turning the pages of their beautiful books, discussing the qualities of a century-old essence, or fondling a favorite Phane, and died without deigning to heed the fact. The hotheads raced up the muddy slope which, outraging all normal rationality, loomed above the parapets of Janeil. Most were buried under sliding rubble, but a few gained the ridge to gun, hack and stab, until they themselves were shot, crushed by the half-alive power-wagons, hacked or stabbed. The contrite waited in the classic posture of expiation – on their knees, heads bowed – and perished, so they believed, by a process in which the Meks were symbols and human sin the reality. In the end all were dead: gentlemen, ladies, Phanes in the pavilions; Peasants in the stables. Of all those who had inhabited Janeil, only the Birds survived, creatures awkward, gauche and raucous, oblivious to pride and faith, more concerned with the wholeness of their hides than the dignity of their castle. As the Meks swarmed down over the parapets, the Birds departed their cotes and, screaming strident insults, flapped east toward Hagedorn, now the last castle of Earth.

2

Four months before, the Meks had appeared in the park before Janeil, fresh from the Sea Island massacre. Climbing to the turrets and balconies, sauntering the Sunset Promenade, from ramparts and parapets, the gentlemen and ladies of Janeil, some two thousand in all, looked down at the brown-gold warriors. Their mood was complex: amused indifference, flippant disdain, and a substratum of doubt and foreboding – all the product of three basic circumstances: their own exquisitely subtle civilization, the security provided by Janeil's walls, and the fact that they could conceive no recourse, no means for altering circumstances.

The Janeil Meks had long since departed to join the revolt; there only remained Phanes, Peasants and Birds from which to fashion what would have been the travesty of a punitive force. At the moment there seemed no need for such a force. Janeil was deemed impregnable. The walls, two hundred feet tall, were black rock-melt contained in the meshes of a silver-blue steel alloy. Solar cells provided energy for all the needs of the castle, and in the event of emergency food could be synthesized from carbon dioxide and water vapor, as well as syrup for Phanes, Peasants and Birds. Such a need was not envisaged. Janeil was self-sufficient and secure, though inconveniences might arise when machinery broke down and there were no Meks to repair it. The situation then was disturbing but hardly desperate. During the day the gentlemen so inclined brought forth energy-guns and sport-rifles and killed as many Meks as the extreme range allowed.

After dark the Meks brought forward power-wagons and earth-movers, and began to raise a dike around Janeil. The folk of the castle watched without comprehension until the dike reached a height of fifty feet and dirt began to spill down against the walls. Then the dire purpose of the Meks became apparent, and insouciance gave way to dismal foreboding. All the gentlemen of Janeil were erudite in at least one realm of knowledge; certain were mathematical theoreticians, while others had made a profound study of the physical sciences. Some of these, with a detail of Peasants to perform the sheerly physical exertion, attempted to restore the energy-cannon to functioning condition. Unluckily, the cannon had not been maintained in good order. Various components were obviously corroded or damaged. Conceivably these components might have been replaced from the Mek shops on the second sub-level, but none of the group had any knowledge of the Mek nomenclature or warehousing system. Warrick Madency Arban* suggested that a work-force of Peasants search the warehouse, but in view of the limited mental capacity of the Peasants, nothing was done and the whole plan to restore the energy-cannon came to naught.

The gentlefolk of Janeil watched in fascination as the dirt piled higher

---

* Arban of the Madency family in the Warrick clan.

and higher around them, in a circular mound like a crater. Summer neared its end, and on one stormy day dirt and rubble rose above the parapets, and began to spill over into the courts and piazzas: Janeil must soon be buried and all within suffocated. It was then that a group of impulsive young cadets, with more élan than dignity, took up weapons and charged up the slope. The Meks dumped dirt and stone upon them, but a handful gained the ridge where they fought in a kind of dreadful exaltation.

Fifteen minutes the fight raged and the earth became sodden with rain and blood. For one glorious moment the cadets swept the ridge clear and, had not most of their fellows been lost under the rubble anything might have occurred. But the Meks regrouped and thrust forward. Ten men were left, then six, then four, then one, then none. The Meks marched down the slope, swarmed over the battlements, and with somber intensity killed all within. Janeil, for seven hundred years the abode of gallant gentlemen, and gracious ladies, had become a lifeless hulk.

3

The Mek, standing as if a specimen in a museum case, was a man-like creature, native, in his original version, to a planet of Etamin. His tough rusty-bronze hide glistened metallically as if oiled or waxed; the spines thrusting back from scalp and neck shone like gold, and indeed were coated with a conductive copper–chrome film. His sense organs were gathered in clusters at the site of a man's ears; his visage – it was often a shock, walking the lower corridors, to come suddenly upon a Mek – was corrugated muscle, not dissimilar to the look of an uncovered human brain. His maw, a vertical irregular cleft at the base of this 'face', was an obsolete organ by reason of the syrup sac which had been introduced under the skin of the shoulders; the digestive organs, originally used to extract nutrition from decayed swamp vegetation and coelenterates, had atrophied. The Mek typically wore no garment except possibly a work-apron or a tool-belt, and in the sunlight his rust-bronze skin made a handsome display. This was the Mek solitary, a creature intrinsically as effective as man – perhaps more by virtue of his superb brain which also functioned as a radio transceiver. Working in the mass, by the teeming thousands, he seemed less admirable, less competent: a hybrid of sub-man and cockroach.

Certain savants, notably Morninglight's D.R. Jardine and Salonson of Tuang, considered the Mek bland and phlegmatic, but the profound Claghorn of Castle Hagedorn asserted otherwise. The emotions of the Mek, said Claghorn, were different from human emotions, and only vaguely comprehensible to man. After diligent research Claghorn isolated over a dozen Mek emotions.

In spite of such research, the Mek revolt came as an utter surprise, no less to Claghorn, D.R. Jardine and Salonson than to anyone else. Why? asked everyone. How could a group so long submissive have contrived so murderous a plot?

The most reasonable conjecture was also the simplest: the Mek resented servitude and hated the Earthmen who had removed him from his natural environment. Those who argued against this theory claimed that it projected human emotions and attitudes into a non-human organism, that the Mek had every reason to feel gratitude toward the gentlemen who had liberated him from the conditions of Etamin Nine. To this, the first group would inquire, 'Who projects human attitudes now?' And the retort of their opponents was often: 'Since no one knows for certain, one projection is no more absurd than another.'

CHAPTER TWO

1

Castle Hagedorn occupied the crest of a black diorite crag overlooking a wide valley to the south. Larger, more majestic than Janeil, Hagedorn was protected by walls a mile in circumference and three hundred feet tall. The parapets stood a full nine hundred feet above the valley, with towers, turrets and observation eyries rising even higher. Two sides of the crag, at east and west, dropped sheer to the valley. The north and south slopes, a trifle less steep, were terraced and planted with vines, artichokes, pears and pomegranates. An avenue rising from the valley circled the crag and passed through a portal into the central plaza. Opposite stood the great Rotunda, with at either side the tall Houses of the twenty-eight families.

The original castle, constructed immediately after the return of men to Earth, stood on the site now occupied by the plaza. The tenth Hagedorn, assembling an enormous force of Peasants and Meks, had built the new walls, after which he demolished the old castle. The twenty-eight Houses dated from this time, five hundred years before.

Below the plaza were three service levels: the stables and garages at the bottom, next the Mek shops and Mek living quarters, then the various storerooms, warehouses and special shops: bakery, brewery, lapidary, arsenal, repository, and the like.

The current Hagedorn*, twenty-sixth of the line, was a Claghorn of the Overwheles. His selection had occasioned general surprise, because O.C. Charle, as he had been before his elevation, was a gentleman of no remarkable presence. His elegance, flair, and erudition were only ordinary; he had never been notable for any significant originality of thought. His physical proportions were good; his face was square and bony, with a short straight nose, a benign brow, and narrow gray eyes. His expression, normally a trifle abstracted – his detractors used the word 'vacant' – by a simple lowering of the eyelids, a downward twitch of the coarse blond eyebrows, at once became stubborn and surly, a fact of which O.C. Charle, or Hagedorn, was unaware.

The office, while exerting little or no formal authority, exerted a pervasive influence, and the style of the gentleman who was Hagedorn affected everyone. For this reason the selection of Hagedorn was a matter of no small importance, subject to hundreds of considerations, and it was the rare candidate who failed to have some old solecism or gaucherie discussed with embarrassing candor. While the candidate might never take overt umbrage, friendships were inevitably sundered, rancors augmented, reputations blasted. O.C. Charle's elevation represented a compromise between two factions among the Overwheles, to which clan the privilege of selection had fallen.

The gentlemen between whom O.C. Charle represented a compromise were both highly respected, but distinguished by basically different attitudes toward existence. The first was the talented Garr of the Zumbeld family. He exemplified the traditional virtues of Castle Hagedorn: he was a notable connoisseur of essences, and he dressed with absolute savoir, with never so much as a pleat nor a twist of the characteristic Overwhele rosette awry. He combined insouciance and flair with dignity; his repartee coruscated with brilliant allusions and turns of phrase; when aroused his wit was utterly

---

* The clans of Hagedorn, their colors and associated families:
CLANS COLORS FAMILIES Xanten yellow; black piping Haude, Quay, Idelsea, Esledune, Salonson, Roseth. Beaudry dark blue; white piping Onwane, Zadig, Prine, Fer, Sesune. Overwhele gray, green; red rosettes Claghorn, Abreu, Woss, Hinken, Zumbeld. Aure brown, black Zadhause, Fotergil, Marune, Baudune, Godalming, Lesmanic. Isseth purple, dark red Mazeth, Floy, Luder-Hepman, Uegus, Kerrithew, Bethune. The first gentleman of the castle, elected for life, is known as 'Hagedorn'.
The clan chief, selected by the family elders, bears the name of his clan, thus: 'Xanten', 'Beaudry', 'Overwhele', 'Aure', 'Isseth' – both clans and clan chiefs.
The family elder, selected by household heads, bears the name of his family. Thus 'Idelsea', 'Zadhause', 'Bethune' and 'Claghorn' are both families and family elders.
The remaining gentlemen and ladies bear first the clan, then the family, then the personal name. Thus: Aure Zadhause Ludwick, abbreviated to A.Z. Ludwick, and Beaudry Fer Dariane, abbreviated to B.F. Dariane.

mordant. He could quote every literary work of consequence; he performed expertly upon the nine-stringed lute, and was thus in constant demand at the Viewing of Antique Tabards. He was an antiquarian of unchallenged erudition and knew the locale of every major city of Old Earth, and could discourse for hours upon the history of the ancient times. His military expertise was unparalleled at Hagedorn, and challenged only by D.K. Magdah of Castle Delora and perhaps Brusham of Tuang. Faults? Flaws? Few could be cited: over-punctilio which might be construed as waspishness; an intrepid pertinacity which could be considered ruthlessness. O.Z. Garr could never be dismissed as insipid or indecisive, and his personal courage was beyond dispute. Two years before, a stray band of Nomads had ventured into Lucerne Valley, slaughtering Peasants, stealing cattle, and going so far as to fire an arrow into the chest of an Isseth cadet. O.Z. Garr instantly assembled a punitive company of Meks, loaded them aboard a dozen power-wagons, and set forth in pursuit of the Nomads, finally overtaking them near Drene River, by the ruins of Worster Cathedral. The Nomads were unexpectedly strong, unexpectedly crafty, and were not content to turn tail and flee. During the fighting, O.Z. Garr displayed the most exemplary demeanor, directing the attack from the seat of his power-wagon, a pair of Meks standing by with shields to ward away arrows. The conflict ended in a rout of the Nomads; they left twenty-seven lean black-cloaked corpses strewn on the field, while only twenty Meks lost their lives.

O.Z. Garr's opponent in the election was Claghorn, elder of the Claghorn family. As with O.Z. Garr, the exquisite discriminations of Hagedorn society came to Claghorn as easily as swimming to a fish. He was no less erudite than O.Z. Garr, though hardly so versatile, his principal field of study being the Meks, their physiology, linguistic modes, and social patterns. Claghorn's conversation was more profound, but less entertaining and not so trenchant as that of O.Z. Garr; he seldom employed the extravagant tropes and allusions which characterized Garr's discussions, preferring a style of speech which was unadorned. Claghorn kept no Phanes; O.Z. Garr's four matched Gossamer Dainties were marvels of delight, and at the Viewing of Antique Tabards Garr's presentations were seldom outshone. The important contrast between the two men lay in their philosophic outlook. O.Z. Garr, a traditionalist, a fervent exemplar of his society, subscribed to its tenets without reservation. He was beset by neither doubt nor guilt; he felt no desire to alter the conditions which afforded more than two thousand gentlemen and ladies lives of great richness. Claghorn, while by no means an Expiationist, was known to feel dissatisfaction with the general tenor of life at Castle Hagedorn, and argued so plausibly that many folk refused to listen to him, on the grounds that they became uncomfortable. But an indefinable malaise ran deep, and Claghorn had many influential supporters.

When the time came for ballots to be cast, neither O.Z. Garr nor Claghorn could muster sufficient support. The office finally was conferred upon a gentleman who never in his most optimistic reckonings had expected it: a gentleman of decorum and dignity but no great depth; without flippancy, but likewise without vivacity; affable but disinclined to force an issue to a disagreeable conclusion: O.C. Charle, the new Hagedorn.

Six months later, during the dark hours before dawn, the Hagedorn Meks evacuated their quarters and departed, taking with them power-wagons, tools, weapons and electrical equipment. The act had clearly been long in the planning, for simultaneously the Meks at each of the eight other castles made a similar departure.

The initial reaction at Castle Hagedorn, as elsewhere, was incredulity, then shocked anger, then – when the implications of the act were pondered – a sense of foreboding and calamity.

The new Hagedorn, the clan chiefs, and certain other notables appointed by Hagedorn met in the formal council chamber to consider the matter. They sat around a great table covered with red velvet: Hagedorn at the head; Xanten and Isseth at his left; Overwhele, Aure and Beaudry at his right; then the others, including O.Z. Garr, I.K. Linus, A.G. Bernal, a mathematical theoretician of great ability, and B.F. Wyas, an equally sagacious antiquarian who had identified the sites of many ancient cities: Palmyra, Lübeck, Eridu, Zanesville, Burton-on-Trent, and Massilia among others. Certain family elders filled out the council: Marune and Baudune of Aure; Quay, Roseth and Idelsea of Xanten; Uegus of Isseth, Claghorn of Overwhele.

All sat silent for a period of ten minutes, arranging their minds and performing the silent act of psychic accommodation known as 'intression'.

At last Hagedorn spoke. 'The castle is suddenly bereft of its Meks. Needless to say, this is an inconvenient condition to be adjusted as swiftly as possible. Here, I am sure, we find ourselves of one mind.'

He looked around the table. All thrust forward carved ivory tablets to signify assent – all save Claghorn, who however did not stand it on end to signify dissent.

Isseth, a stern white-haired gentleman magnificently handsome in spite of his seventy years, spoke in a grim voice. 'I see no point in cogitation or delay. What we must do is clear. Admittedly the Peasants are poor material from which to recruit an armed force. Nonetheless, we must assemble them, equip them with sandals, smocks and weapons so that they do not discredit us, and put them under good leadership: O.Z. Garr or Xanten. Birds can locate the vagrants, whereupon we will track them down, order the Peasants to give them a good drubbing, and herd them home on the double.'

Xanten, thirty-five years old – extraordinarily young to be a clan chief

– and a notorious firebrand, shook his head. 'The idea is appealing but impractical. Peasants simply could not stand up to the Meks, no matter how we trained them.'

The statement was manifestly accurate. The Peasants, small andromorphs originally of Spica Ten, were not so much timid as incapable of performing a vicious act.

A dour silence held the table. O.Z. Garr finally spoke. 'The dogs have stolen our power-wagons, otherwise I'd be tempted to ride out and chivy the rascals home with a whip.'*

'A matter of perplexity,' said Hagedorn, 'is syrup. Naturally they carried away what they could. When this is exhausted – what then? Will they starve? Impossible for them to return to their original diet. What was it? Swamp mud? Eh, Claghorn, you're the expert in these matters. Can the Meks return to a diet of mud?'

'No,' said Claghorn. 'The organs of the adult are atrophied. If a cub were started on the diet, he'd probably survive.'

'Just as I assumed.' Hagedorn scowled portentously down at his clasped hands to conceal his total lack of any constructive proposal.

A gentleman in the dark blue of the Beaudrys appeared in the doorway: he poised himself, held high his right arm, and bowed so that the fingers swept the floor.

Hagedorn rose to his feet. 'Come forward, B.F. Robarth; what is your news?' For this was the significance of the newcomer's genuflection.

'The news is a message broadcast from Halcyon. The Meks have attacked; they have fired the structure and are slaughtering all. The radio went dead one minute ago.'

All swung around, some jumped to their feet. 'Slaughter?' croaked Claghorn.

'I am certain that by now Halcyon is no more.'

Claghorn sat staring with eyes unfocused. The others discussed the dire news in voices heavy with horror.

Hagedorn once more brought the council back to order. 'This is clearly an

---

* This, only an approximate translation, fails to capture the pungency of the language. Several words have no contemporary equivalents. 'Skirkling', as in 'to send skirkling', denotes a frantic pell-mell flight in all directions, accompanied by a vibration or twinkling or jerking motion. To 'volith' is to toy idly with a matter, the implication being that the person involved is of such Jovian potency that all difficulties dwindle to contemptible triviality. 'Raudlebogs' are the semi-intelligent beings of Etamin Four, who were brought to Earth, trained first as gardeners, then construction laborers, then sent home in disgrace because of certain repulsive habits they refused to forgo.

The statement of O.Z. Garr, therefore, becomes something like this: 'Were power-wagons at hand, I'd volith riding forth with a whip to send the raudlebogs skirkling home.'

extreme situation – the gravest, perhaps, of our entire history. I am frank to state that I can suggest no decisive counter-act.'

Overwhele inquired, 'What of the other castles? Are they secure?'

Hagedorn turned to B.F. Robarth. 'Will you be good enough to make general radio contact with all other castles, and inquire as to their condition?'

Xanten said, 'Others are as vulnerable as Halcyon: Sea Island and Delora, in particular, and Maraval as well.'

Claghorn emerged from his reverie. 'The gentlemen and ladies of these places, in my opinion, should consider taking refuge at Janeil or here, until the uprising is quelled.'

Others around the table looked at him in surprise and puzzlement. O.Z. Garr inquired in the silkiest of voices: 'You envision the gentlefolk of these castles scampering to refuge at the cock-a-hoop swaggering of the lower orders?'

'Indeed, should they wish to survive,' responded Claghorn politely. A gentleman of late middle age, Claghorn was stocky and strong, with black–gray hair, magnificent green eyes, and a manner which suggested great internal force under stern control. 'Flight by definition entails a certain diminution of dignity,' he went on to say. 'If O.Z. Garr can propound an el-egant manner of taking to one's heels, I will be glad to learn it, and everyone else should likewise heed, because in the days to come the capability may be of comfort to all.'

Hagedorn interposed before O.Z. Garr could reply. 'Let us keep to the issues. I confess I cannot see to the end of all this. The Meks have demon-strated themselves to be murderers: how can we take them back into our service? But if we don't – well, to say the least, conditions will be austere until we can locate and train a new force of technicians. We must consider along these lines.'

'The spaceships!' exclaimed Xanten. 'We must see to them at once!'

'What's this?' inquired Beaudry, a gentleman of rock-hard face. 'How do you mean, "see to them"?'

'They must be protected from damage! What else? They are our link to the Home Worlds. The maintenance Meks probably have not deserted the hangars, since, if they propose to exterminate us, they will want to deny us the spaceships.'

'Perhaps you care to march with a levy of Peasants to take the hangars under firm control?' suggested O.Z. Garr in a somewhat supercilious voice. A long history of rivalry and mutual detestation existed between himself and Xanten.

'It may be our only hope,' said Xanten. 'Still – how does one fight with a levy of Peasants? Better that I fly to the hangars and reconnoiter. Meanwhile, perhaps you, and others with military expertise, will take in hand the recruitment and training of a Peasant militia.'

'In this regard,' stated O.Z. Garr, 'I await the outcome of our current deliberations. If it develops that there lies the optimum course, I naturally will apply my competences to the fullest degree. If your own capabilities are best fulfilled by spying out the activities of the Meks, I hope that you will be largehearted enough to do the same.'

The two gentlemen glared at each other. A year previously their enmity had almost culminated in a duel. Xanten, a gentleman tall, clean-limbed, and nervously active, was gifted with great natural flair, but likewise evinced a disposition too easy for absolute elegance. The traditionalists considered him "sthross", indicating a manner flawed by an almost imperceptible slackness and lack of punctilio: not the best possible choice for clan chief.

Xanten's response to O.Z. Garr was blandly polite. 'I shall be glad to take this task upon myself. Since haste is of the essence I will risk the accusation of precipitousness and leave at once. Hopefully I return to report tomorrow.' He rose, performed a ceremonious bow to Hagedorn, another all-inclusive salute to the council, and departed.

He crossed to Esledune House, where he maintained an apartment on the thirteenth level: four rooms furnished in the style known as Fifth Dynasty, after an epoch in the history of the Altair Home Planets, from which the human race had returned to Earth. His current consort, Araminta, a lady of the Onwane family, was absent on affairs of her own, which suited Xanten well enough. After plying him with questions she would have discredited his simple explanation, preferring to suspect an assignation at his country place. Truth to tell, he had become bored with Araminta and had reason to believe that she felt similarly – or perhaps his exalted rank had provided her less opportunity to preside at glittering social functions than she had expected. They had bred no children. Araminta's daughter by a previous connection had been tallied to her. Her second child must then be tallied to Xanten, preventing him from siring another child.*

Xanten doffed his yellow council vestments and, assisted by a young Peasant buck, donned dark yellow hunting-breeches with black trim, a black jacket, black boots. He drew a cap of soft black leather over his head and slung a pouch over his shoulder, into which he loaded weapons: a coiled blade, an energy gun.

Leaving the apartment, he summoned the lift and descended to the first

---

* The population of Castle Hagedorn was fixed; each gentleman and each lady was permitted a single child. If by chance another were born the parent must either find someone who had not yet sired to sponsor it, or dispose of it another way. The usual procedure was to give the child into the care of the Expiationists.

level armory, where normally a Mek clerk would have served him. Now Xanten, to his vast disgust, was forced to take himself behind the counter and rummage here and there. The Meks had removed most of the sporting rifles, all the pellet ejectors and heavy energy-guns: an ominous circumstance, thought Xanten. At last he found a steel sling-whip, spare power slugs for his gun, a brace of fire grenades and a high-powered monocular.

He returned to the lift and rode to the top level, ruefully considering the long climb when eventually the mechanism broke down, with no Meks at hand to make repairs. He thought of the apoplectic furies of rigid traditionalists such as Beaudry and chuckled: eventful days lay ahead!

Stopping at the top level, he crossed to the parapets and proceeded around to the radio room. Customarily three Mek specialists connected into the apparatus by wires clipped to their quills sat typing messages as they arrived; now B.F. Robarth stood before the mechanism, uncertainly twisting the dials, his mouth wry with deprecation and distaste for the job.

'Any further news?' Xanten asked.

B.F. Robarth gave him a sour grin. 'The folk at the other end seem no more familiar with this cursed tangle than I. I hear occasional voices. I believe that the Meks are attacking Castle Delora.'

Claghorn had entered the room behind Xanten. 'Did I hear you correctly? Delora Castle is gone?'

'Not gone yet, Claghorn. But as good as gone. The Delora walls are little better than a picturesque crumble.'

'Sickening situation!' muttered Xanten. 'How can sentient creatures perform such evil? After all these centuries, how little we actually knew of them!' As he spoke he recognized the tactlessness of his remark; Claghorn had devoted much time to a study of the Meks.

'The act itself is not astounding,' said Claghorn shortly. 'It has occurred a thousand times in human history.'

Mildly surprised that Claghorn should use human history in reference to a case involving the sub-orders, Xanten asked, 'You were never aware of this vicious aspect to the Mek nature?'

'No. Never. Never indeed.'

Claghorn seemed unduly sensitive, thought Xanten. Understandable, all in all. Claghorn's basic doctrine as set forth during the Hagedorn selection was by no means simple, and Xanten neither understood it nor completely endorsed what he conceived to be its goals; but it was plain that the revolt of the Meks had cut the ground out from under Claghorn's feet. Probably to the somewhat bitter satisfaction of O.Z. Garr, who must feel vindicated in his traditionalist doctrines.

Claghorn said tersely, 'The life we've been leading couldn't last forever. It's a wonder it lasted as long as it did.'

'Perhaps so,' said Xanten in a soothing voice. 'Well, no matter. All things change. Who knows? The Peasants may be planning to poison our food … I must go.' He bowed to Claghorn, who returned him a crisp nod, and to B.F. Robarth, then departed the room.

He climbed the spiral staircase – almost a ladder – to the cotes, where the Birds lived in an invincible disorder, occupying themselves with gambling, quarrels, and a version of chess, with rules incomprehensible to every gentleman who had tried to understand it.

Castle Hagedorn maintained a hundred Birds, tended by a gang of long-suffering Peasants, whom the Birds held in vast disesteem. The Birds were garish garrulous creatures, pigmented red, yellow or blue, with long necks, jerking inquisitive heads and an inherent irreverence which no amount of discipline or tutelage could overcome. Spying Xanten, they emitted a chorus of rude jeers: 'Somebody wants a ride! Heavy thing!' 'Why don't the self-anointed two-footers grow wings for themselves?' 'My friend, never trust a Bird! We'll sky you, then fling you down on your fundament!'

'Quiet!' called Xanten. 'I need six fast silent Birds for an important mission. Are any capable of such a task?'

'Are any capable, he asks!' '*A ros ros ros!* When none of us have flown for a week!' 'Silence? We'll give you silence, yellow and black!'

'Come then. You. You. You of the wise eye. You there. You with the cocked shoulder. You with the green pompon. To the basket.'

The Birds designated, jeering, grumbling, reviling the Peasants, allowed their syrup sacs to be filled, then flapped to the wicker seat where Xanten waited. 'To the space depot at Vincenne,' he told them. 'Fly high and silently. Enemies are abroad. We must learn what harm if any has been done to the spaceships.'

'To the depot then!' Each Bird seized a length of rope tied to an overhead framework; the chair was yanked up with a jerk calculated to rattle Xanten's teeth, and off they flew, laughing, cursing each other for not supporting more of the load, but eventually all accommodating themselves to the task and flying with a coordinated flapping of the thirty-six sets of wings. To Xanten's relief, their garrulity lessened; silently they flew south, at a speed of fifty or sixty miles per hour.

The afternoon was already waning. The ancient countryside, scene to so many comings and goings, so much triumph and so much disaster, was laced with long black shadows. Looking down, Xanten reflected that though the human stock was native to this soil, and though his immediate ancestors had maintained their holdings for seven hundred years, Earth still seemed an alien world. The reason of course was by no means mysterious or rooted in paradox. After the Six-Star War, Earth had lain fallow for three thousand years, unpopulated save for a handful of anguished wretches who somehow had survived the cataclysm and who had become semi-barbaric Nomads. Then seven hundred years ago certain rich lords of Altair, motivated to some extent by political disaffection, but no less by caprice, had decided to return to Earth. Such was the origin of the nine great strongholds, the resident gentlefolk and the staffs of specialized andromorphs ... Xanten flew over an area where an antiquarian had directed excavations, revealing a plaza flagged with white stone, a broken obelisk, a tumbled statue ... The sight, by some trick of association, stimulated Xanten's mind to an astonishing vision, so simple and yet so grand that he looked around, in all directions, with new eyes. The vision was Earth re-populated with men, the land cultivated, Nomads driven back into the wilderness.

At the moment the image was farfetched. And Xanten, watching the soft contours of Old Earth slide below, pondered the Mek revolt which had altered his life with such startling abruptness.

Claghorn had long insisted that no human condition endured forever, with the corollary that the more complicated such a condition, the greater its susceptibility to change. In which case the seven-hundred-year continuity at Castle Hagedorn – as artificial, extravagant and intricate as life could be – became an astonishing circumstance in itself. Claghorn had pushed his thesis further. Since change was inevitable, he argued that the gentlefolk should soften the impact by anticipating and controlling the changes – a doctrine which had been attacked with great fervor. The traditionalists labeled all of Claghorn's ideas demonstrable fallacy, and cited the very stability of castle life as proof of its viability. Xanten had inclined first one way, then the other, emotionally involved with neither cause. If anything, the fact of O.Z. Garr's traditionalism had nudged him toward Claghorn's views, and now it seemed as if events had vindicated Claghorn. Change had come, with an impact of the maximum harshness and violence.

There were still questions to be answered, of course. Why had the Meks chosen this particular time to revolt? Conditions had not altered appreciably for five hundred years, and the Meks had never previously hinted dissatisfaction. In fact they had revealed nothing of their feelings, though no one had ever troubled to ask them – save Claghorn.

The Birds were veering east to avoid the Ballarat Mountains, to the west of which were the ruins of a great city, never satisfactorily identified. Below lay the Lucerne Valley, at one time a fertile farm land. If one looked with great concentration, the outline of the various holdings could sometimes be distinguished. Ahead, the spaceship hangars were visible, where Mek technicians maintained four spaceships jointly the property of Hagedorn, Janeil, Tuang, Morninglight and Maraval, though, for a variety of reasons, the ships were never used.

The sun was setting. Orange light twinkled and flickered on the metal walls. Xanten called instructions up to the Birds: 'Circle down. Alight behind that line of trees, but fly low so that none will see.'

Down on stiff wings curved the Birds, six ungainly necks stretched toward the ground. Xanten was ready for the impact; the Birds never seemed able to alight easily when they carried a gentleman. When the cargo was something in which they felt a personal concern, dandelion fluff would never have been disturbed by the jar.

Xanten expertly kept his balance, instead of tumbling and rolling in the manner preferred by the Birds. 'You all have syrup,' he told them. 'Rest; make no noise; do not quarrel. By tomorrow's sunset, if I am not here, return to Castle Hagedorn and say that Xanten was killed.'

'Never fear!' cried the Birds. 'We will wait forever!' 'At any rate till tomorrow's sunset!' 'If danger threatens, if you are pressed – *a ros ros ros!* Call for the Birds.' *'A ros!* We are ferocious when aroused!'

'I wish it were true,' said Xanten. 'The Birds are arrant cowards; this is well-known. Still I value the sentiment. Remember my instructions, and quiet above all! I do not wish to be set upon and stabbed because of your clamor.'

The Birds made indignant sounds. 'Injustice, injustice! We are quiet as the dew!'

'Good.' Xanten hurriedly moved away lest they should bellow new advice or reassurances after him.

Passing through the forest, he came to an open meadow at the far edge of which, perhaps a hundred yards distant, was the rear of the first hangar. He stopped to consider. Several factors were involved. First: the maintenance Meks, with the metal structure shielding them from radio contact, might still be unaware of the revolt. Hardly likely, he decided, in view of the otherwise careful planning. Second: the Meks, in continuous communication with their fellows, acted as a collective organism. The aggregate functioned more competently than its parts, and the individual was not prone to initiative. Hence, vigilance was likely to be extreme. Third: if they expected anyone to attempt a discreet approach, they would necessarily scrutinize most closely the route which he proposed to take.

Xanten decided to wait in the shadows another ten minutes, until the setting sun shining over his shoulder should most effectively blind any who might watch.

Ten minutes passed. The hangars, burnished by the dying sunlight, bulked long, tall, completely quiet. In the intervening meadow long golden grass waved and rippled in a cool breeze ... Xanten took a deep breath, hefted his pouch, arranged his weapons, and strode forth. It did not occur to him to crawl through the grass.

He reached the back of the nearest hangar without challenge. Pressing his ear to the metal he heard nothing. He walked to the corner, looked down the side: no sign of life. Xanten shrugged. Very well then; to the door.

He walked beside the hangar, the setting sun casting a long black shadow ahead of him. He came to a door opening into the hangar administrative office. Since there was nothing to be gained by trepidation, Xanten thrust the door aside and entered.

The offices were empty. The desks, where centuries before underlings had sat, calculating invoices and bills of lading, were bare, polished free of dust. The computers and information banks, black enamel, glass, white and red switches, looked as if they had been installed only the day before.

Xanten crossed to the glass pane overlooking the hangar floor, shadowed under the bulk of the ship.

He saw no Meks. But on the floor of the hangar, arranged in neat rows and heaps, were elements and assemblies of the ship's control mechanism. Service panels gaped wide into the hull to show where the devices had been detached.

Xanten stepped from the office out into the hangar. The spaceship had been disabled, put out of commission. Xanten looked along the neat rows of parts. Certain savants of various castles were expert in the theory of space-time transfer; S.X. Rosenbox of Maraval had even derived a set of equations which, if translated into machinery, eliminated the troublesome Hamus effect. But not one gentleman, even were he so oblivious to personal honor as to touch a hand to a tool, would know how to replace, connect and tune the mechanisms heaped upon the hangar floor.

The malicious work had been done – when? Impossible to say.

Xanten returned to the office, stepped back out into the twilight, and walked to the next hangar. Again no Meks; again the spaceship had been gutted of its control mechanisms. Xanten proceeded to the third hangar, where conditions were the same.

At the fourth hangar he discerned the faint sounds of activity. Stepping into the office, looking through the glass wall into the hangar, he found Meks working with their usual economy of motion, in a near-silence which was uncanny.

Xanten, already uncomfortable from skulking through the forest, became enraged by the cool destruction of his property. He strode forth into the hangar. Slapping his thigh to attract attention he called in a harsh voice, 'Return the components to place! How dare you vermin act in such a manner!'

The Meks turned about their blank countenances to study him through black beaded lens-clusters at each side of their heads.

'What!' bellowed Xanten. 'You hesitate?' He brought forth his steel whip, usually more of a symbolic adjunct than a punitive instrument, and slashed it against the ground. 'Obey! This ridiculous revolt is at its end!'

The Meks still hesitated, and events wavered in the balance. None made a sound, though messages were passing among them, appraising the circumstances, establishing a consensus. Xanten could allow them no such leisure. He marched forward, wielding the whip, striking at the only area where the Meks felt pain: the ropy face. 'To your duties,' he roared. 'A fine maintenance crew are you! A destruction crew is more like it!'

The Meks made the soft blowing sound which might mean anything. They fell back, and now Xanten noted one standing at the head of the companionway leading into the ship: a Mek larger than any he had seen before and one in some fashion different. This Mek was aiming a pellet gun at his head. With an unhurried flourish, Xanten whipped away a Mek who had leaped forward with a knife, and without deigning to aim, fired at and destroyed the Mek who stood on the companionway, even as the slug sang past his head.

The other Meks were nevertheless committed to an attack. All surged forward. Lounging disdainfully against the hull, Xanten shot them as they came, moving his head once to avoid a chunk of metal, again reaching to catch a throw-knife and hurl it into the face of him who had thrown it.

The Meks drew back, and Xanten guessed that they had agreed on a new tactic: either to withdraw for weapons or perhaps to confine him within the hangar. In any event no more could be accomplished here. He made play with the whip and cleared an avenue to the office. With tools, metal bars and forgings striking the glass behind him, he sauntered through the office and out into the night.

The full moon was rising: a great yellow globe casting a smoky saffron glow, like an antique lamp. Mek eyes were not well-adapted for night-seeing, and Xanten waited by the door. Presently Meks began to pour forth, and Xanten hacked at their necks as they came.

The Meks drew back inside the hangar. Wiping his blade, Xanten strode off the way he had come, looking neither right nor left. He stopped short. The night was young. Something tickled his mind: the recollection of the Mek who had fired the pellet gun. He had been larger, possibly a darker bronze, but, more significantly, he had displayed an indefinable poise, almost authority – though such a word, when used in connection with the Meks, was anomalous. On the other hand, someone must have planned the revolt, or at least originated the concept. It might be worthwhile to extend the reconnaissance, though his primary information had been secured.

Xanten turned back and crossed the landing area to the barracks and garages. Once more, frowning in discomfort, he felt the need for discretion. What times these were! when a gentleman must skulk to avoid such as the Meks! He stole up behind the garages, where a half-dozen power-wagons* lay dozing.

Xanten looked them over. All were of the same sort, a metal frame with four wheels, an earth-moving blade at the front. Nearby must be the syrup stock. Xanten presently found a bin containing a number of cannisters. He loaded a dozen on a nearby wagon, slashed the rest with his knife, so that the syrup gushed across the ground. The Meks used a somewhat different formulation; their syrup would be stocked at a different locale, presumably inside the barracks.

Xanten mounted a power-wagon, twisted the *awake* key, tapped the *go* button, and pulled a lever which set the wheels into reverse motion. The power-wagon lurched back. Xanten halted it, turned it so that it faced the barracks. He did likewise with three others, then set them all into motion, one after the other. They trundled forward; the blades cut open the metal wall of the barracks, the roof sagged. The power-wagons continued, pushing the length of the interior, crushing all in their way.

Xanten nodded in profound satisfaction and returned to the power-wagon he had reserved for his own use. Mounting to the seat, he waited. No Meks issued from the barracks. Apparently they were deserted, with the entire crew busy at the hangars. Still, hopefully, the syrup stocks had been destroyed, and many might perish by starvation.

From the direction of the hangars came a single Mek, evidently attracted by the sounds of destruction. Xanten crouched on the seat and as it passed, coiled his whip around the stocky neck. He heaved; the Mek spun to the ground.

Xanten leaped down, seized its pellet-gun. Here was another of the larger Meks, and now Xanten saw it to be without a syrup sac, a Mek in the original state. Astounding! How did the creature survive? Suddenly there were many new questions to be asked – hopefully a few to be answered. Standing on the creature's head, Xanten hacked away the long antenna quills which protruded from the back of the Mek's scalp. It was now insulated, alone, on its own resources – a situation to reduce the most stalwart Mek to apathy.

---

* Power-wagons, like the Meks, originally swamp-creatures from Etamin Nine, were great rectangular slabs of muscle, slung into a rectangular frame and protected from sunlight, insects and rodents by a synthetic pelt. Syrup sacs communicated with their digestive apparatus, wires led to motor nodes in the rudimentary brain. The muscles were clamped to rocker arms which actuated rotors and drive-wheels. The power-wagons, economical, long-lived and docile, were principally used for heavy cartage, earth-moving, heavy-tillage, and other arduous jobs.

'Up!' ordered Xanten. 'Into the back of the wagon!' He cracked the whip for emphasis.

The Mek at first seemed disposed to defy him, but after a blow or two obeyed. Xanten climbed into the seat and started the power-wagon, directed it to the north. The Birds would be unable to carry both himself and the Mek – or in any event they would cry and complain so raucously that they might as well be believed at first. They might or might not wait until the specified hour of tomorrow's sunset; as likely as not they would sleep the night in a tree, awake in a surly mood and return at once to Castle Hagedorn.

All through the night the power-wagon trundled, with Xanten on the seat and his captive huddled in the rear.

CHAPTER THREE

1

The gentlefolk of the castles, for all their assurance, disliked to wander the countryside by night, by reason of what some derided as superstitious fear. Others cited travelers benighted beside moldering ruins and their subsequent visions: the eldritch music they had heard, or the whimper of moon-mirkins, or the far horns of spectral huntsmen. Others had seen pale lavender and green lights, and wraiths which ran with long strides through the forest; and Hode Abbey, now a dank tumble, was notorious for the White Hag and the alarming toll she exacted.

A hundred such cases were known, and while the hardheaded scoffed, none needlessly traveled the countryside by night. Indeed, if ghosts truly haunt the scenes of tragedy and heartbreak, then the landscape of Old Earth must be home to ghosts and specters beyond all numbering – especially that region across which Xanten rolled in the power-wagon, where every rock, every meadow, every vale and swale was crusted thick with human experience.

The moon rose high; the wagon trundled north along an ancient road, the cracked concrete slabs shining pale in the moonlight. Twice Xanten saw flickering orange lights off to the side, and once, standing in the shade of a cypress tree, he thought he saw a tall, quiet shape, silently watching him pass. The captive Mek sat plotting mischief, Xanten well knew. Without its quills it must feel depersonified, bewildered, but Xanten told himself that it would not do to doze.

The road led through a town, certain structures of which still stood. Not even the Nomads took refuge in these old towns, fearing either miasma or perhaps the redolence of grief.

The moon reached the zenith. The landscape spread away in a hundred tones of silver, black and gray. Looking about, Xanten thought that for all the notable pleasures of civilized life, there was yet something to be said for the spaciousness and simplicity of Nomadland. The Mek made a stealthy movement. Xanten did not so much as turn his head. He cracked his whip in the air. The Mek became quiet.

All through the night the power-wagon rolled along the old road, with the moon sinking into the west. The eastern horizon glowed green and lemon-yellow, and presently, as the pallid moon disappeared, the sun rose over the distant line of the mountains. At this moment, off to the right, Xanten spied a drift of smoke.

He halted the wagon. Standing up on the seat, he craned his neck to spy a Nomad encampment about a quarter-mile distant. He could distinguish three or four dozen tents of various sizes and a dozen dilapidated power-wagons. On the hetman's tall tent he thought he saw a black ideogram that he recognized. If so, this would be the tribe which not long before had trespassed on the Hagedorn domain, and which O.Z. Garr had repulsed.

Xanten settled himself upon the seat, composed his garments, set the power-wagon in motion, and guided it toward the camp.

A hundred black-cloaked men, tall and lean as ferrets, watched his approach. A dozen sprang forward and whipping arrows to bows, aimed them at his heart. Xanten turned them a glance of supercilious inquiry, drove the wagon up to the hetman's tent, halted. He rose to his feet. 'Hetman,' he called. 'Are you awake?'

The hetman parted the canvas which closed off his tent, peered out, and after a moment came forth. Like the others he wore a garment of limp black cloth, swathing head and body alike. His face thrust through a square opening: narrow blue eyes, a grotesquely long nose, a chin long, skewed and sharp.

Xanten gave him a curt nod. 'Observe this.' He jerked his thumb toward the Mek in the back of the wagon. The hetman flicked aside his eyes, studied the Mek a tenth-second, and returned to a scrutiny of Xanten. 'His kind have revolted against the gentlemen,' said Xanten. 'In fact they massacre all the men of Earth. Hence we of Castle Hagedorn make this offer to the Nomads. Come to Castle Hagedorn. We will feed, clothe and arm you. We will train you to discipline and the arts of formal warfare. We will provide the most expert leadership within our power. We will then annihilate the Meks, expunge them from Earth. After the campaign, we will train you to technical skills, and you may pursue profitable and interesting careers in the service of the castles.'

The hetman made no reply for a moment. Then his weathered face split into a ferocious grin. He spoke in a voice which Xanten found surprisingly well-modulated. 'So your beasts have finally risen up to rend you! A pity they forebore so long! Well, it is all one to us. You are both alien folk and sooner or later your bones must bleach together.'

Xanten pretended incomprehension. 'If I understand you aright, you assert that in the face of alien assault, all men must fight a common battle; and then, after the victory, cooperate still to their mutual advantage. Am I correct?'

The hetman's grin never wavered. 'You are not men. Only we of Earth soil and Earth water are men. You and your weird slaves are strangers together. We wish you success in your mutual slaughter.'

'Well, then,' declared Xanten, 'I heard you aright after all. Appeals to your loyalty are ineffectual, so much is clear. What of self-interest, then? The Meks, failing to expunge the gentlefolk of the castles, will turn upon the Nomads and kill them as if they were so many ants.'

'If they attack us, we will war on them,' said the hetman. 'Otherwise let them do as they will.'

Xanten glanced thoughtfully at the sky. 'We might be willing, even now, to accept a contingent of Nomads into the service of Castle Hagedorn, this to form a cadre from which a larger, more versatile, group may be formed.'

From the side, another Nomad called in an offensively jeering voice, 'You will sew a sac on our backs where you can pour your syrup, hey?'

Xanten replied in an even voice, 'The syrup is highly nutritious and supplies all bodily needs.'

'Why then do you not consume it yourself?'

Xanten disdained reply.

The hetman spoke. 'If you wish to supply us weapons, we will take them, and use them against whomever threatens us. But do not expect us to defend you. If you fear for your lives, desert your castles and become Nomads.'

'Fear for our lives?' exclaimed Xanten. 'What nonsense! Never! Castle Hagedorn is impregnable, as is Janeil, and most of the other castles as well.'

The hetman shook his head. 'Any time we choose we could take Hagedorn, and kill all you popinjays in your sleep.'

'What!' cried Xanten in outrage. 'Are you serious?'

'Certainly. On a black night we would send a man aloft on a great kite and drop him down on the parapets. He would lower a line, haul up ladders and in fifteen minutes the castle is taken.'

Xanten pulled at his chin. 'Ingenious, but impractical. The Birds would detect such a kite. Or the wind would fail at a critical moment ... All this is beside the point. The Meks fly no kites. They plan to make a display against Janeil and Hagedorn, then, in their frustration, go forth and hunt Nomads.'

The hetman moved back a step. 'What then? We have survived similar attempts by the men of Hagedorn. Cowards all. Hand to hand, with equal weapons, we would make you eat the dirt like the dogs you are.'

Xanten raised his eyebrows in elegant disdain. 'I fear that you forget yourself. You address a clan chief of Castle Hagedorn. Only fatigue and boredom restrain me from punishing you with this whip.'

'Bah,' said the hetman. He crooked a finger to one of his archers. 'Spit this insolent lordling.'

The archer discharged his arrow, but Xanten, who had been expecting some such act, fired his energy gun, destroying arrow, bow, and the archer's hands. He said, 'I see I must teach you common respect for your betters; so it means the whip after all.' Seizing the hetman by the scalp, he coiled the whip smartly once, twice, thrice around the narrow shoulders. 'Let this suffice. I cannot compel you to fight, but at least I can demand decent respect.' He leaped to the ground, and seizing the hetman, pitched him into the back of the wagon alongside the Mek. Then, backing the power-wagon around, he departed the camp without so much as a glance over his shoulder, the thwart of the seat protecting his back from arrows.

The hetman scrambled erect, drew his dagger. Xanten turned his head slightly. 'Take care! Or I will tie you to the wagon and you shall run behind in the dust.'

The hetman hesitated, made a spitting sound between his teeth, drew back. He looked down at his blade, turned it over, and sheathed it with a grunt. 'Where do you take me?'

Xanten halted the wagon. 'No farther. I merely wished to leave your camp with dignity, without dodging and ducking a hail of arrows. You may alight. I take it you still refuse to bring your men into the service of Castle Hagedorn?'

The hetman once more made the spitting sound between his teeth. 'When the Meks have destroyed the castles, we shall destroy the Meks, and Earth will be cleared of star-things.'

'You are a gang of intractable savages. Very well, alight, return to your encampment. Reflect well before you again show disrespect to a Castle Hagedorn clan chief.'

'Bah,' muttered the hetman. Leaping down from the wagon, he stalked back down the track toward his camp.

2

About noon Xanten came to Far Valley, at the edge of the Hagedorn lands. Nearby was a village of Expiationists: malcontents and neurasthenics in the opinion of castle gentlefolk, and a curious group by any standards. A few had held enviable rank; certain others were savants of recognized erudition; but others yet were persons of neither dignity nor reputation, subscribing to the most bizarre and extreme of philosophies. All now performed toil no different from that relegated to the Peasants, and all seemed to take a perverse satisfaction in what – by castle standards – was filth, poverty and degradation.

As might be expected, their creed was by no means homogeneous. Some might better have been described as 'nonconformists' or 'disassociationists'; another group were 'passive expiationists', and others still, a minority, argued for a dynamic program.

Between castle and village was little intercourse. Occasionally the Expiationists bartered fruit or polished wood for tools, nails, medicaments; or the gentlefolk might make up a party to watch the Expiationists at their dancing and singing. Xanten had visited the village on many such occasions and had been attracted by the artless charm and informality of the folk at their play. Now, passing near the village, Xanten turned aside to follow a lane which wound between tall blackberry hedges and out upon a little common where goats and cattle grazed. Xanten halted the wagon in the shade and saw that the syrup sac was full. He looked back at his captive. 'What of you? If you need syrup, pour yourself full. But no, you have no sac. What then do you feed upon? Mud? Unsavory fare. I fear none here is rank enough for your taste. Ingest syrup or munch grass, as you will; only do not stray overfar from the wagon, for I watch with an intent eye.'

The Mek, sitting hunched in a corner, gave no signal that it comprehended, nor did it move to take advantage of Xanten's offer.

Xanten went to a watering trough and, holding his hands under the trickle which issued from a lead pipe, rinsed his face, then drank a swallow or two from his cupped hand.

Turning, he found that a dozen folk of the village had approached. One he knew well, a man who might have become Godalming, or even Aure, had he not become infected with expiationism.

Xanten performed a polite salute. 'A.G. Philidor: it is I, Xanten.'

'Xanten, of course. But here I am A.G. Philidor no longer, merely Philidor.'

Xanten bowed. 'My apologies; I have neglected the full rigor of your informality.'

'Spare me your wit,' said Philidor. 'Why do you bring us a shorn Mek? For adoption, perhaps?' This last alluded to the gentlefolk practice of bringing over-tally babies to the village.

'Now who flaunts his wit? But you have not heard the news?'

'News arrives here last of all. The Nomads are better informed.'

'Prepare yourself for surprise. The Meks have revolted against the castles.

Halcyon and Delora are demolished, and all killed; perhaps others by this time.'

Philidor shook his head. 'I am not surprised.'

'Well then, are you not concerned?'

Philidor considered. 'To this extent. Our own plans, never very feasible, become more farfetched than ever.'

'It appears to me,' said Xanten, 'that you face grave and immediate danger. The Meks surely intend to wipe out every vestige of humanity. You will not escape.'

Philidor shrugged. 'Conceivably the danger exists ... We will take counsel and decide what to do.'

'I can put forward a proposal which you may find attractive,' said Xanten. 'Our first concern, of course, is to suppress the revolt. There are at least a dozen Expiationist communities, with an aggregate population of two or three thousand – perhaps more. I propose that we recruit and train a corps of highly disciplined troops, supplied from the Castle Hagedorn armory, led by Hagedorn's most expert military theoreticians.'

Philidor stared at him incredulously. 'You expect us, the Expiationists, to become your soldiers?'

'Why not?' asked Xanten ingenuously. 'Your life is at stake no less than ours.'

'No one dies more than once.'

Xanten in his turn evinced shock. 'What? Can this be a former gentleman of Hagedorn speaking? Is this the face a man of pride and courage turns to danger? Is this the lesson of history? Of course not! I need not instruct you in this; you are as knowledgeable as I.'

Philidor nodded. 'I know that the history of man is not his technical triumphs, his kills, his victories. It is a composite, a mosaic of a trillion pieces, the account of each man's accommodation with his conscience. This is the true history of the race.'

Xanten made an airy gesture. 'A.G. Philidor, you over-simplify grievously. Do you consider me obtuse? There are many kinds of history. They interact. You emphasize morality. But the ultimate basis of morality is survival. What promotes survival is good, what induces mortifaction is bad.'

'Well spoken!' declared Philidor. 'But let me propound a parable. May a nation of a million beings destroy a creature who otherwise will infect all with a fatal disease? Yes, you will say. Once more: ten starving beasts hunt you, that they may eat. Will you kill them to save your life? Yes, you will say again, though here you destroy more than you save. Once more: a man inhabits a hut in a lonely valley. A hundred spaceships descend from the sky and attempt to destroy him. May he destroy these ships in self-defense, even though he is one and they are a hundred thousand? Perhaps you say yes. What then if a whole world, a whole race of beings, pits itself against this single man? May he kill all? What if the attackers are as human as himself? What if he were the creature of the first instance, who otherwise will infect a world with disease? You see, there is no area where a simple touchstone avails. We have searched and found none. Hence, at the risk of sinning against Survival, we – I, at least; I can only speak for myself – have chosen a morality which at least allows me calm. I kill – nothing. I destroy – nothing.'

'Bah,' said Xanten contemptuously. 'If a Mek platoon entered this valley and began to kill your children, you would not defend them?'

Philidor compressed his lips, turned away. Another man spoke. 'Philidor has defined morality. But who is absolutely moral? Philidor, or I, or you, might desert his morality in such a case.'

Philidor said, 'Look about you. Is there anyone here you recognize?'

Xanten scanned the group. Nearby stood a girl of extraordinary beauty. She wore a white smock and in the dark hair curling to her shoulders she wore a red flower. Xanten nodded. 'I see the maiden O.Z. Garr wished to introduce into his ménage at the castle.'

'Exactly,' said Philidor. 'Do you recall the circumstances?'

'Very well indeed,' said Xanten. 'There was vigorous objection from the Council of Notables – if for no other reason than the threat to our laws of population control. O.Z. Garr attempted to sidestep the law in this fashion. "I keep Phanes," he said. "At times I maintain as many as six, or even eight, and no one utters a word of protest. I will call this girl Phane and keep her among the rest." I and others protested. There was almost a duel over this matter. O.Z. Garr was forced to relinquish the girl. She was given into my custody and I conveyed her to Far Valley.'

Philidor nodded. 'All this is correct. Well – we attempted to dissuade Garr. He refused to be dissuaded, and threatened us with his hunting force of perhaps thirty Meks. We stood aside. Are we moral? Are we strong or weak?'

'Sometimes it is better,' said Xanten, 'to ignore morality. Even though O.Z. Garr is a gentleman and you are but Expiationists ... Likewise in the case of the Meks. They are destroying the castles, and all the men of Earth. If morality means supine acceptance, then morality must be abandoned!'

Philidor gave a sour chuckle. 'What a remarkable situation! The Meks are here, likewise Peasants and Birds and Phanes, all altered, transported and enslaved for human pleasure. Indeed, it is this fact that occasions our guilt, for which we must expiate, and now you want us to compound this guilt!'

'It is a mistake to brood overmuch about the past,' said Xanten. 'Still, if you wish to preserve your option to brood, I suggest that you fight Meks now, or at the very least take refuge in the castle.'

'Not I,' said Philidor. 'Perhaps others may choose to do so.'

'You will wait to be killed?'

'No. I and no doubt others will take refuge in the remote mountains.'

Xanten clambered back aboard the power-wagon. 'If you change your mind, come to Castle Hagedorn.'

He departed.

The road continued along the valley, wound up a hillside, crossed a ridge. Far ahead, silhouetted against the sky, stood Castle Hagedorn.

CHAPTER FOUR

1

Xanten reported to the council.

'The spaceships cannot be used. The Meks have rendered them inoperative. Any plan to solicit assistance from the Home Worlds is pointless.'

'This is sorry news,' said Hagedorn with a grimace. 'Well then, so much for that.'

Xanten continued. 'Returning by power-wagon I encountered a tribe of Nomads. I summoned the hetman and explained to him the advantages of serving Castle Hagedorn. The Nomads, I fear, lack both grace and docility. The hetman gave so surly a response that I departed in disgust.

'At Far Valley I visited the Expiationist village and made a similar proposal, but with no great success. They are as idealistic as the Nomads are churlish. Both are of a fugitive tendency. The Expiationists spoke of taking refuge in the mountains. The Nomads presumably will retreat into the steppes.'

Beaudry snorted. 'How will flight help them? Perhaps they gain a few years – but eventually the Meks will find every last one of them; such is their methodicity.'

'In the meantime,' O.Z. Garr declared peevishly, 'we might have organized them into an efficient combat corps, to the benefit of all. Well then, let them perish; we are secure.'

'Secure, yes,' said Hagedorn gloomily. 'But what when the power fails? When the lifts break down? When air circulation cuts off so that we either stifle or freeze? What then?'

O.Z. Garr gave his head a grim shake. 'We must steel ourselves to undignified expedients, with as good grace as possible. But the machinery of the castle is sound, and I expect small deterioration or failure for conceivably five or ten years. By that time anything may occur.'

Claghorn, who had been leaning indolently back in his seat, spoke at last: 'This essentially is a passive program. Like the defection of the Nomads and Expiationists, it looks very little beyond the immediate moment.'

O.Z. Garr spoke in a voice carefully polite. 'Claghorn is well aware that I yield to none in courteous candor, as well as optimism and directness: in short the reverse of passivity. But I refuse to dignify a stupid little inconvenience by extending it serious attention. How can he label this procedure passivity? Does the worthy and honorable head of the Claghorns have a proposal which more effectively maintains our status, our standards, our self-respect?'

Claghorn nodded slowly, with a faint half-smile which O.Z. Garr found odiously complacent. 'There is a simple and effective method by which the Meks might be defeated.'

'Well, then!' cried Hagedorn. 'Why hesitate? Let us hear it!'

Claghorn looked around the red velvet-covered table, considering the faces of all: the dispassionate Xanten; Beaudry, burly, rigid, face muscles clenched in an habitual expression unpleasantly like a sneer; old Isseth, as handsome, erect and vital as the most dashing cadet; Hagedorn, troubled, glum, his inward perplexity all too evident; the elegant Garr; Overwhele, thinking savagely of the inconveniences of the future; Aure, toying with his ivory tablet, either bored, morose or defeated; the others displaying various aspects of doubt, foreboding, hauteur, dark resentment, impatience; and in the case of Floy, a quiet smile – or as Isseth later characterized it, an imbecilic smirk – intended to convey his total disassociation from the entire irksome matter.

Claghorn took stock of the faces, and shook his head. 'I will not at the moment broach this plan, as I fear it is unworkable. But I must point out that under no circumstances can Castle Hagedorn be as before, even should we survive the Mek attack.'

'Bah!' exclaimed Beaudry. 'We lose dignity, we become ridiculous, by even so much as discussing the beasts.'

Xanten stirred himself. 'A distasteful subject, but remember! Halcyon is destroyed, and Delora, and who knows what others? Let us not thrust our heads in the sand! The Meks will not waft away merely because we ignore them.'

'In any event,' said O.Z. Garr, 'Janeil is secure and we are secure. The other folk, unless they are already slaughtered, might do well to visit us during the inconvenience, if they can justify the humiliation of flight to themselves. I myself believe that the Meks will soon come to heel, anxious to return to their posts.'

Hagedorn shook his head gloomily. 'I find this hard to believe. But very well then, we shall adjourn.'

2

The radio communication system was the first of the castle's vast array of electrical and mechanical devices to break down. The failure occurred so soon and so decisively that certain of the theoreticians, notably I.K. Harde and Uegus, postulated sabotage by the departing Meks. Others remarked that the system had never been absolutely dependable, that the Meks themselves had been forced to tinker continuously with the circuits, that the failure was simply a result of faulty engineering. I.K. Harde and Uegus inspected the unwieldy apparatus, but the cause of failure was not obvious. After a half-hour of consultation they agreed that any attempt to restore the system would necessitate complete re-design and re-engineering, with consequent construction of testing and calibration devices and the fabrication of a complete new family of components. 'This is manifestly impossible,' stated Uegus in his report to the council. 'Even the simplest useful system would require several technician-years. There is not even one single technician to hand. We must therefore await the availability of trained and willing labor.'

'In retrospect,' stated Isseth, the oldest of the clan chiefs, 'it is clear that in many ways we have been less than provident. No matter that the men of the Home Worlds are vulgarians! Men of shrewder calculation than our own would have maintained inter-world connection.'

'Lack of shrewdness and providence were not the deterring factors,' stated Claghorn. 'Communication was discouraged simply because the early lords were unwilling that Earth should be overrun with Home-World parvenus. It is as simple as that.'

Isseth grunted, and started to make a rejoinder, but Hagedorn said hastily, 'Unluckily, as Xanten tells us, the spaceships have been rendered useless, and while certain of our number have a profound knowledge of the theoretical considerations, again who is there to perform the toil? Even were the hangars and spaceships themselves under our control.'

O.Z. Garr declared, 'Give me six platoons of Peasants and six power-wagons equipped with high-energy cannon, and I'll regain the hangars; no difficulties there!'

Beaudry said, 'Well, here's a start, at least. I'll assist in the training of the Peasants, and though I know nothing of cannon operation, rely on me for any advice I can give.'

Hagedorn looked around the group, frowned, pulled at his chin. 'There are difficulties to this program. First, we have at hand only the single power-wagon in which Xanten returned from his reconnaissance. Then, what of our energy cannons? Has anyone inspected them? The Meks were entrusted with maintenance, but it is possible, even likely, that they wrought mischief here as well. O.Z. Garr, you are reckoned an expert military theoretician; what can you tell us in this regard?'

'I have made no inspection to date,' stated O.Z. Garr. 'Today the Display of Antique Tabards will occupy us all until the Hour of Sundown Appraisal.'* He looked at his watch. 'Perhaps now is as good a time as any to adjourn, until I am able to provide detailed information in regard to the cannons.'

Hagedorn nodded his heavy head. 'The time indeed grows late. Your Phanes appear today?'

'Only two,' replied O.Z. Garr. 'The Lazule and the Eleventh Mystery. I can find nothing suitable for the Gossamer Delights nor my little Blue Fay, and the Gloriana still requires tutelage. Today B.Z. Maxelwane's Variflors should repay the most attention.'

'Yes,' said Hagedorn. 'I have heard other remarks to this effect. Very well then, until tomorrow. Eh, Claghorn, you have something to say?'

'Yes, indeed,' said Claghorn mildly. 'We have all too little time at our disposal. Best that we make the most of it. I seriously doubt the efficacy of Peasant troops; to pit Peasants against Meks is like sending rabbits against wolves. What we need, rather than rabbits, are panthers.'

'Ah, yes,' said Hagedorn vaguely. 'Yes, indeed.'

'Where, then, are panthers to be found?' Claghorn looked inquiringly around the table. 'Can no one suggest a source? A pity. Well then, if panthers fail to appear, I suppose rabbits must do. Let us go about the business of converting rabbits into panthers, and instantly. I suggest that we postpone all fêtes and spectacles until the shape of our future is more certain.'

Hagedorn raised his eyebrows, opened his mouth to speak, closed it again. He looked intently at Claghorn to ascertain whether or not he joked. Then he looked dubiously around the table.

Beaudry gave a rather brassy laugh. 'It seems that erudite Claghorn cries panic.'

O.Z. Garr stated: 'Surely, in all dignity, we cannot allow the impertinence of our servants to cause us such eye-rolling alarm. I am embarrassed even to bring the matter forward.'

'I am not embarrassed,' said Claghorn, with the full-faced complacence

---

* Display of Antique Tabards; Hour of Sundown Appraisal: the literal sense of the first term was yet relevant; that of the second had become lost and the phrase was a mere formalism, connoting that hour of late afternoon when visits were exchanged, and wines, liqueurs and essences tasted: in short, a time of relaxation and small talk before the more formal convivialities of dining.

which so exasperated O.Z. Garr. 'I see no reason why you should be. Our lives are threatened, in which case a trifle of embarrassment, or anything else, becomes of secondary importance.'

O.Z. Garr rose to his feet, performed a brusque salute in Claghorn's direction, of such a nature as to constitute a calculated affront. Claghorn, rising, performed a similar salute, so grave and overly complicated as to invest Garr's insult with burlesque overtones. Xanten, who detested O.Z. Garr, laughed aloud.

O.Z. Garr hesitated, then, sensing that under the circumstances taking the matter further would be regarded as poor form, strode from the chamber.

3

The Viewing of Antique Tabards, an annual pageant of Phanes wearing sumptuous garments, took place in the Great Rotunda to the north of the central plaza. Possibly half of the gentlemen, but less than a quarter of the ladies, kept Phanes. These were creatures native to the caverns of Albireo Seven's moon: a docile race, both playful and affectionate, which after several thousand years of selective breeding had become sylphs of piquant beauty. Clad in a delicate gauze which issued from pores behind their ears, along their upper arms and down their backs, they were the most inoffensive of creatures, anxious always to please, innocently vain. Most gentlemen regarded them with affection, but rumors sometimes told of ladies drenching an especially hated Phane in tincture of ammonia, which matted her pelt and destroyed her gauze forever.

A gentleman besotted by a Phane was considered a figure of fun. The Phane, though so carefully bred as to seem a delicate girl, if used sexually became crumpled and haggard, with gauzes drooping and discolored, and everyone would know that such and such a gentleman had misused his Phane. In this regard, at least, the women of the castles might exert their superiority, and did so by conducting themselves with such extravagant provocation that the Phanes in contrast seemed the most ingenuous and fragile of nature sprites. Their life span was perhaps thirty years, during the last ten of which, after they had lost their beauty, they encased themselves in mantles of gray gauze and performed menial tasks in boudoirs, kitchens, pantries, nurseries and dressing rooms.

The Viewing of Antique Tabards was an occasion more for the viewing of Phanes than the tabards, though these, woven of Phane-gauze, were of great intrinsic beauty in themselves.

The Phane owners sat in a lower tier, tense with hope and pride, exulting when one made an especially splendid display, plunging into black depths when the ritual postures were performed with other than grace and elegance. During each display, highly formal music was plucked from a lute by a gentleman from a clan different to that of the Phane owner, the owner never playing the lute to the performance of his own Phane. The display was never overtly a competition and no formal acclamation was allowed, but all watching made up their minds as to which was the most entrancing and graceful of the Phanes, and the repute of the owner was thereby exalted.

The current Viewing was delayed almost half an hour by reason of the defection of the Meks, and certain hasty improvisations had been necessary. But the gentlefolk of Castle Hagedorn were in no mood to be critical and took no heed of the occasional lapses as a dozen young Peasant bucks struggled to perform unfamiliar tasks. The Phanes were as entrancing as ever, bending, twisting, swaying to plangent chords of the lute, fluttering their fingers as if feeling for raindrops, crouching suddenly and gliding, then springing upright as straight as wands, finally bowing and skipping from the platform.

Halfway through the program a Peasant sidled awkwardly into the Rotunda, and mumbled in an urgent manner to the cadet who came to inquire his business. The cadet at once made his way to Hagedorn's polished jet booth. Hagedorn listened, nodded, spoke a few terse words and settled calmly back in his seat as if the message had been of no consequence, and the gentlefolk of the audience were reassured.

The entertainment proceeded. O.Z. Garr's delectable pair made a fine show, but it was generally felt that Lirlin, a young Phane belonging to Isseth Floy Gazuneth, for the first time at a formal showing, made the most captivating display.

The Phanes appeared for a last time, moving all together through a half-improvised minuet, then performing a final half-gay, half-regretful salute, departed the rotunda. For a few moments more the gentlemen and ladies would remain in their booths, sipping essences, discussing the display, arranging affairs and assignations. Hagedorn sat frowning, twisting his hands. Suddenly he rose to his feet. The rotunda instantly became silent.

'I dislike intruding an unhappy note at so pleasant an occasion,' said Hagedorn. 'But the news has just been given to me, and it is fitting that all should know. Janeil Castle is under attack. The Meks are there in great force, with hundreds of power-wagons. They have circled the castle with a dike which prevents any effective use of the Janeil energy-cannon.

'There is no immediate danger to Janeil, and it is difficult to comprehend what the Meks hope to achieve, the Janeil walls being all of two hundred feet high.

'The news, nevertheless, is somber, and it means that eventually we must expect a similar investment – though it is even more difficult to comprehend how Meks could hope to inconvenience us. Our water derives from four wells sunk deep into the earth. We have great stocks of food. Our energy is derived from the sun. If necessary, we could condense water and synthesize food from the air – at least I have been so assured by our great biochemical theoretician, X.B. Ladisname. Still – this is the news. Make of it what you will. Tomorrow the Council of Notables will meet.'

CHAPTER FIVE

1

'Well then,' said Hagedorn to the council, 'for once let us dispense with formality. O.Z. Garr: what of our cannon?'

O.Z. Garr, wearing the magnificent gray and green uniform of the Overwhele Dragoons, carefully placed his morion on the table, so that the panache stood erect. 'Of twelve cannon, four appear to be functioning correctly. Four have been sabotaged by excision of the power-leads. Four have been sabotaged by some means undetectable to careful investigation. I have commandeered a half-dozen Peasants who demonstrate a modicum of mechanical ability, and have instructed them in detail. They are currently engaged in splicing the leads. This is the extent of my current information in regard to the cannon.'

'Moderately good news,' said Hagedorn. 'What of the proposed corps of armed Peasants?'

'The project is under way. A.F. Mull and I.A. Berzelius are now inspecting Peasants with a view to recruitment and training. I can make no sanguine projection as to the military effectiveness of such a corps, even if trained and led by such as A.F. Mull, I.A. Berzelius and myself. The Peasants are a mild, ineffectual race, admirably suited to the grubbing of weeds, but with no stomach whatever for fighting.'

Hagedorn glanced around the council. 'Are there any other suggestions?'

Beaudry spoke in a harsh, angry voice. 'Had the villains but left us our power-wagons, we might have mounted the cannon aboard – the Peasants are equal to this, at least. Then we could roll to Janeil and blast the dogs from the rear.'

'These Meks seem utter fiends!' declared Aure. 'What conceivably do they have in mind? Why, after all these centuries, must they suddenly go mad?'

'We all ask ourselves the same questions,' said Hagedorn. 'Xanten, you returned from reconnaissance with a captive. Have you attempted to question him?'

'No,' said Xanten. 'Truth to tell, I haven't thought of him since.'

'Why not attempt to question him? Perhaps he can provide a clue or two.'

Xanten nodded assent. 'I can try. Candidly, I expect to learn nothing.'

'Claghorn, you are the Mek expert,' said Beaudry. 'Would you have thought the creatures capable of so intricate a plot? What do they hope to gain? Our castles?'

'They are certainly capable of precise and meticulous planning,' said Claghorn. 'Their ruthlessness surprises me – more, possibly, than it should. I have never known them to covet our material possessions, and they show no tendency toward what we consider the concomitants of civilization: fine discriminations of sensation and the like. I have often speculated – I won't dignify the conceit with the status of a theory – that the structural logic of a brain is of rather more consequence than we reckon with. Our own brains are remarkable for their utter lack of rational structure. Considering the haphazard manner in which our thoughts are formed, registered, indexed and recalled, any single rational act becomes a miracle. Perhaps we are incapable of rationality; perhaps all thought is a set of impulses generated by one emotion, monitored by another, ratified by a third. In contrast, the Mek brain is a marvel of what seems to be careful engineering. It is roughly cubical and consists of microscopic cells interconnected by organic fibrils, each a monofilament molecule of negligible electrical resistance. Within each cell is a film of silica, a fluid of variable conductivity and dielectric properties, a cusp of a complex mixture of metallic oxides. The brain is capable of storing great quantities of information in an orderly pattern. No fact is lost, unless it is purposely forgotten, a capacity which the Meks possess. The brain also functions as a radio transceiver, possibly as a radar transmitter and detector, though this again is speculation.

'Where the Mek brain falls short is in its lack of emotional color. One Mek is precisely like another, without any personality differentiation perceptible to us. This, clearly, is a function of their communicative system: unthinkable for a unique personality to develop under these conditions. They served us efficiently and – so we thought – loyally, because they felt nothing about their condition, neither pride in achievement, nor resentment, nor shame. Nothing whatever. They neither loved us nor hated us, nor do they now. It is hard for us to conceive this emotional vacuum, when each of us feels something about everything. We live in a welter of emotions. They are as devoid of emotion as an ice-cube. They were fed, housed, and maintained in a manner they found satisfactory. Why did they revolt? I have speculated at length, but the single reason which I can formulate seems so grotesque and unreasonable that I refuse to take it seriously. If this after all is the correct explanation ...' His voice drifted away.

'Well?' demanded O.Z. Garr peremptorily. 'What, then?'

'Then – it is all the same. They are committed to the destruction of the human race. My speculation alters nothing.'

Hagedorn turned to Xanten. 'All this should assist you in your inquiries.'

'I was about to suggest that Claghorn assist me, if he is so inclined,' said Xanten.

'As you like,' said Claghorn, 'though in my opinion the information, no matter what, is irrelevant. Our single concern should be a means to repel them and to save our lives.'

'And – except the force of "panthers" you mentioned at our previous session – you can conceive of no subtle weapon?' asked Hagedorn wistfully. 'A device to set up electrical resonances in their brains, or something similar?'

'Not feasible,' said Claghorn. 'Certain organs in the creatures' brains function as overload switches. Though it is true that during this time they might not be able to communicate.' After a moment's reflection he added thoughtfully, 'Who knows? A.G. Bernal and Uegus are theoreticians with a profound knowledge of such projections. Perhaps they might construct such a device, or several, against a possible need.'

Hagedorn nodded dubiously, and looked toward Uegus. 'Is this possible?'

Uegus frowned. '"Construct"? I can certainly design such an instrument. But the components – where? Scattered through the storerooms helter-skelter, some functioning, others not. To achieve anything meaningful I must become no better than an apprentice, a Mek.' He became incensed, and his voice hardened. 'I find it hard to believe that I should be forced to point out this fact. Do you hold me and my talents then of such small worth?'

Hagedorn hastened to reassure him. 'Of course not! I for one would never think of impugning your dignity.'

'Never!' agreed Claghorn. 'Nevertheless, during this present emergency, we will find indignities imposed upon us by events, unless now we impose them upon ourselves.'

'Very well,' said Uegus, a humorless smile trembling at his lips. 'You shall come with me to the storeroom. I will point out the components to be brought forth and assembled, you shall perform the toil. What do you say to that?'

'I say yes, gladly, if it will be of real utility. However, I can hardly perform the labor for a dozen different theoreticians. Will any others serve beside myself?'

No one responded. Silence was absolute, as if every gentleman present held his breath.

Hagedorn started to speak, but Claghorn interrupted. 'Pardon, Hagedorn, but here, finally, we are stuck upon a basic principle, and it must be settled now.'

Hagedorn looked desperately around the council. 'Has anyone relevant comment?'

'Claghorn must do as his innate nature compels,' declared O.Z. Garr in the silkiest of voices. 'I cannot dictate to him. As for myself, I can never demean my status as a gentleman of Hagedorn. This creed is as natural to me as drawing breath; if ever it is compromised I become a travesty of a gentleman, a grotesque mask of myself. This is Castle Hagedorn, and we represent the culmination of human civilization. Any compromise therefore becomes degradation; any expedient diminution of our standards becomes dishonor. I have heard the word "emergency" used. What a deplorable sentiment! To dignify the rat-like snappings and gnashings of such as the Meks with the word "emergency" is to my mind unworthy of a gentleman of Hagedorn!'

A murmur of approval went around the council table.

Claghorn leaned far back in his seat, chin on his chest, as if in relaxation. His clear green eyes went from face to face, then returned to O.Z. Garr whom he studied with dispassionate interest. 'Obviously you direct your words to me,' he said, 'and I appreciate their malice. But this is a small matter.' He looked away from O.Z. Garr, to stare up at the massive diamond and emerald chandelier. 'More important is the fact that the council as a whole, in spite of my earnest persuasion, seems to endorse your viewpoint. I can urge, expostulate, insinuate no longer, and I will now leave Castle Hagedorn. I find the atmosphere stifling. I trust that you survive the attack of the Meks, though I doubt that you will. They are a clever, resourceful race, untroubled by qualms or preconceptions, and we have long underestimated their quality.'

Claghorn rose from his seat, inserted the ivory tablet into its socket. 'I bid you all farewell.'

Hagedorn hastily jumped to his feet and held forth his arms imploringly. 'Do not depart in anger, Claghorn! Reconsider! We need your wisdom, your expertise!'

'Assuredly you do,' said Claghorn. 'But even more, you need to act upon the advice I have already extended. Until then, we have no common ground, and any further interchange is futile and tiresome.' He made a brief, all-inclusive salute and departed the chamber.

Hagedorn slowly resumed his seat. The others made uneasy motions, coughed, looked up at the chandelier, studied their ivory tablets. O.Z. Garr muttered something to B.F. Wyas who sat beside him, who nodded solemnly. Hagedorn spoke in a subdued voice: 'We will miss the presence of Claghorn, his penetrating if unorthodox insights ... We have accomplished little. Uegus, perhaps you will give thought to the projector under discussion. Xanten, you were to question the captive Mek. O.Z. Garr, you undoubtedly will see to the repair of the energy cannon ... Aside from these small matters, it appears that we have evolved no general plan of action, to help either ourselves or Janeil.'

Marune spoke. 'What of the other castles? Are they still extant? We have had no news. I suggest that we send Birds to each castle, to learn their condition.'

Hagedorn nodded. 'Yes, this is a wise motion. Perhaps you will see to this, Marune?'

'I will do so.'

'Good. We will now adjourn.'

2

The Birds dispatched by Marune of Aure, one by one returned. Their reports were similar:

'Sea Island is deserted. Marble columns are tumbled along the beach. Pearl Dome is collapsed. Corpses float in the Water Garden.'

'Maraval reeks of death. Gentlemen, Peasants, Phanes – all dead. Alas! Even the Birds have departed!'

'Delora: *a ros ros ros!* A dismal scene! No sign of life!'

'Alume is desolate. The great wooden door is smashed. The Green Flame is extinguished.'

'There is nothing at Halcyon. The Peasants were driven into a pit.'

'Tuang: silence.'

'Morninglight: death.'

CHAPTER SIX

1

Three days later, Xanten constrained six Birds to a lift chair, directed them first on a wide sweep around the castle, then south to Far Valley.

The Birds aired their usual complaints, then bounded down the deck in great ungainly hops which threatened to throw Xanten immediately to the pavement. At last gaining the air, they flew up in a spiral; Castle Hagedorn became an intricate miniature far below, each House marked by its unique cluster of turrets and eyries, its own eccentric roof line, its long streaming pennon.

The Birds performed the prescribed circle, skimming the crags and pines of North Ridge; then, setting wings aslant the upstream, they coasted away toward Far Valley.

Over the pleasant Hagedorn domain flew the Birds and Xanten: over orchards, fields, vineyards, Peasant villages. They crossed Lake Maude with its pavilions and docks, the meadows beyond where the Hagedorn cattle and sheep grazed, and presently came to Far Valley, at the limit of Hagedorn lands.

Xanten indicated where he wished to alight; the Birds, who would have preferred a site closer to the village where they could have watched all that transpired, grumbled and cried out in wrath and set Xanten down so roughly that had he not been alert the shock would have pitched him head over heels.

Xanten alighted without elegance but at least remained on his feet. 'Await me here!' he ordered. 'Do not stray; attempt no flamboyant tricks among the lift-straps. When I return I wish to see six quiet Birds, in neat formation, lift-straps untwisted and untangled. No bickering, mind you! No loud caterwauling, to attract unfavorable comment! Let all be as I have ordered!'

The Birds sulked, stamped their feet, ducked aside their necks, made insulting comments just under the level of Xanten's hearing. Xanten, turning them a final glare of admonition, walked down the lane which led to the village.

The vines were heavy with ripe blackberries and a number of the girls of the village filled baskets. Among them was the girl O.Z. Garr had thought to preempt for his personal use. As Xanten passed, he halted and performed a courteous salute. 'We have met before, if my recollection is correct.'

The girl smiled, a half-rueful, half-whimsical smile. 'Your recollection serves you well. We met at Hagedorn, where I was taken a captive. And later, when you conveyed me here, after dark, though I could not see your face.' She extended her basket. 'Are you hungry? Will you eat?'

Xanten took several berries. In the course of the conversation he learned that the girl's name was Glys Meadowsweet, that her parents were not known to her, but were presumably gentlefolk of Castle Hagedorn who had exceeded their birth tally. Xanten examined her even more carefully than before but could see resemblance to none of the Hagedorn families. 'You might derive from Castle Delora. If there is any family resemblance I can detect, it is to the Cosanzas of Delora – a family noted for the beauty of its ladies.'

'You are not married?' she asked artlessly.

'No,' said Xanten, and indeed he had dissolved his relationship with Araminta only the day before. 'What of you?'

She shook her head. 'I would never be gathering blackberries otherwise; it is work reserved for maidens ... Why do you come to Far Valley?'

'For two reasons. The first to see you.' Xanten heard himself say this with surprise. But it was true, he realized with another small shock of surprise. 'I have never spoken with you properly and I have always wondered if you were as charming and gay as you are beautiful.'

The girl shrugged and Xanten could not be sure whether she were pleased or not, compliments from gentlemen sometimes setting the stage for a sorry aftermath. 'Well, no matter. I came also to speak to Claghorn.'

'He is yonder,' she said in a voice toneless, even cool, and pointed. 'He occupies that cottage.' She returned to her blackberry picking. Xanten bowed and proceeded to the cottage the girl had indicated.

Claghorn, wearing loose knee-length breeches of gray homespun, worked with an axe chopping faggots into stove-lengths. At the sight of Xanten he halted his toil, leaned on the axe and mopped his forehead. 'Ah, Xanten. I am pleased to see you. How are the folk of Castle Hagedorn?'

'As before. There is little to report, even had I come to bring you news.'

'Indeed, indeed?' Claghorn leaned on the axe handle, surveying Xanten with a bright green gaze.

'At our last meeting,' went on Xanten, 'I agreed to question the captive Mek. After doing so I am distressed that you were not at hand to assist, so that you might have resolved certain ambiguities in the responses.'

'Speak on,' said Claghorn. 'Perhaps I shall be able to do so now.'

'After the council meeting I descended immediately to the storeroom where the Mek was confined. It lacked nutriment; I gave it syrup and a pail of water, which it sipped sparingly, then evinced a desire for minced clams. I summoned kitchen help and sent them for this commodity and the Mek ingested several pints. As I have indicated, it was an unusual Mek, standing as tall as myself and lacking a syrup sac. I conveyed it to a different chamber, a storeroom for brown plush furniture, and ordered it to a seat.

'I looked at the Mek and it looked at me. The quills which I removed were growing back; probably it could at least receive from Meks elsewhere. It seemed a superior beast, showing neither obsequiousness nor respect, and answered my questions without hesitation.

'First I remarked: "The gentlefolk of the castles are astounded by the revolt of the Meks. We had assumed that your life was satisfactory. Were we wrong?"

'"Evidently." I am sure that this was the word signaled, though never had I suspected the Meks of dryness or wit of any sort.

'"Very well then," I said. "In what manner?"

"'Surely it is obvious," he said. "We no longer wished to toil at your behest. We wished to conduct our lives by our own traditional standards."

'The response surprised me. I was unaware that the Meks possessed standards of any kind, much less traditional standards.'

Claghorn nodded. 'I have been similarly surprised by the scope of the Mek mentality.'

'I reproached the Mek: "Why kill? Why destroy our lives in order to augment your own?" As soon as I had put the question I realized that it had been unhappily phrased. The Mek, I believe, realized the same; however, in reply he signaled something very rapidly which I believe was: "We knew we must act with decisiveness. Your own protocol made this necessary. We might have returned to Etamin Nine, but we prefer this world Earth, and will make it our own, with our own great slipways, tubs and basking ramps."

'This seemed clear enough, but I sensed an adumbration extending yet beyond. I said, "Comprehensible. But why kill, why destroy? You might have taken yourself to a different region. We could not have molested you."

"'Infeasible, by your own thinking. A world is too small for two competing races. You intended to send us back to dismal Etamin Nine."

"'Ridiculous!" I said. "Fantasy, absurdity. Do you take me for a mooncalf?"

"'No," the creature insisted. "Two of Castle Hagedorn's notables were seeking the highest post. One assured us that, if elected, this would become his life's aim."

"'A grotesque misunderstanding," I told him. "One man, a lunatic, can not speak for all men!"

"'No? One Mek speaks for all Meks. We think with one mind. Are not men of a like sort?"

"'Each thinks for himself. The lunatic who assured you of this tomfoolery is an evil man. But at least matters are clear. We do not propose to send you to Etamin Nine. Will you withdraw from Janeil, take yourselves to a far land and leave us in peace?"

"'No," he said. "Affairs have proceeded too far. We will now destroy all men. The truth of the statement is clear: one world is too small for two races."

"'Unluckily, then, I must kill you," I told him. "Such acts are not to my liking, but, with opportunity, you would kill as many gentlemen as possible!" At this the creature sprang upon me, and I killed it with an easier mind than had it sat staring.

'Now, you know all. It seems that either you or O.Z. Garr stimulated the cataclysm. O.Z. Garr? Unlikely. Impossible. Hence, you, Claghorn, you! have this weight upon your soul!'

Claghorn frowned down at the axe. 'Weight, yes. Guilt, no. Ingenuousness, yes; wickedness, no.'

Xanten stood back. 'Claghorn, your coolness astounds me! Before, when rancorous folk like O.Z. Garr conceived you a lunatic—'

'Peace, Xanten!' exclaimed Claghorn. 'This extravagant breast-beating becomes maladroit. What have I done wrong? My fault is that I tried too much. Failure is tragic, but a phthisic face hanging over the cup of the future is worse. I meant to become Hagedorn, I would have sent the slaves home. I failed, the slaves revolted. So do not speak another word. I am bored with the subject. You can not imagine how your bulging eyes and your concave spine oppress me.'

'Bored you may be,' cried Xanten. 'You decry my eyes, my spine – but what of the thousands dead?'

'How long would they live in any event? Lives as cheap as fish in the sea. I suggest that you put by your reproaches and devote a similar energy to saving yourself. Do you realize that a means exists? You stare at me blankly. I assure you that what I say is true, but you will never learn the means from me.'

'Claghorn,' said Xanten, 'I flew to this spot intending to blow your arrogant head from your body—' Claghorn, no longer heeding, had returned to his wood-chopping.

'Claghorn!' cried Xanten. 'Attend me!'

'Xanten, take your outcries elsewhere, if you please. Remonstrate with your Birds.'

Xanten swung on his heel and marched back down the lane. The girls picking berries looked at him questioningly and moved aside. Xanten halted to look up and down the lane. Glys Meadowsweet was nowhere to be seen. In a new fury he continued. He stopped short. On a fallen tree a hundred feet from the Birds sat Glys Meadowsweet, examining a blade of grass as if it had been an astonishing artifact of the past. The Birds, for a marvel, had actually obeyed him and waited in a fair semblance of order.

Xanten looked up toward the heavens, kicked at the turf. He drew a deep breath and approached Glys Meadowsweet. He noted that she had tucked a flower into her long loose hair.

After a second or two she looked up and searched his face. 'Why are you so angry?'

Xanten slapped his thigh, then seated himself beside her. '"Angry"? No. I am out of my mind with frustration. Claghorn is as obstreperous as a sharp rock. He knows how Castle Hagedorn can be saved but he will not divulge his secret.'

Glys Meadowsweet laughed – an easy, merry sound, like nothing Xanten had ever heard at Castle Hagedorn. '"Secret"? When even I know it?'

'It must be a secret,' said Xanten. 'He will not tell me.'

'Listen. If you fear the Birds will hear, I will whisper.' She spoke a few words into his ear.

Perhaps the sweet breath befuddled Xanten's mind. But the explicit essence of the revelation failed to strike home into his consciousness. He made a sound of sour amusement. 'No secret there. Only what the prehistoric Scythians termed *bathos*. Dishonor to the gentlemen! Do we dance with the Peasants? Do we serve the Birds essences and discuss with them the sheen of our Phanes?'

'"Dishonor", then?' She jumped to her feet. 'Then it is also dishonor for you to talk to me, to sit here with me, to make ridiculous suggestions—'

'I made no suggestions!' protested Xanten. 'I sit here in all decorum—'

'Too much decorum, too much honor!' With a display of passion which astounded Xanten, Glys Meadowsweet tore the flower from her hair and hurled it at the ground.

'There. Hence!'

'No,' said Xanten in sudden humility. He bent, picked up the flower, kissed it, replaced it in her hair. 'I am not over-honorable. I will try my best.' He put his arms on her shoulders, but she held him away.

'Tell me,' she inquired with a very mature severity, 'do you own any of those peculiar insect-women?'

'I? Phanes? I own no Phanes.'

With this Glys Meadowsweet relaxed and allowed Xanten to embrace her, while the Birds clucked, guffawed and made vulgar scratching sounds with their wings.

CHAPTER SEVEN

1

The summer waxed warm. On June 30 Janeil and Hagedorn celebrated the Fête of Flowers, even though the dike was rising high around Janeil. Shortly after, Xanten flew six select Birds into Castle Janeil by night, and proposed to the council that the population be evacuated by Bird-lift – as many as possible, as many who wished to leave. The council listened with stony faces and without comment passed on to a consideration of other affairs.

Xanten returned to Castle Hagedorn. Using the most careful methods, speaking only to trusted comrades, Xanten enlisted thirty or forty cadets

THE DRAGON MASTERS AND OTHER STORIES

and gentlemen to his persuasion, though inevitably he could not keep the doctrinal thesis of his program secret.

The first reaction of the traditionalists was mockery and charges of poltroonery. At Xanten's insistence, challenges were neither issued nor accepted by his hot-blooded associates.

On the evening of September 9 Castle Janeil fell. The news was brought to Castle Hagedorn by excited Birds who told the grim tale again and again in voices ever more hysterical.

Hagedorn, now gaunt and weary, automatically called a council meeting; it took note of the gloomy circumstances. 'We, then, are the last castle! The Meks cannot conceivably do us harm; they can build dikes around our castle walls for twenty years and only work themselves to distraction. We are secure; but yet it is a strange and portentous thought to realize that at last, here at Castle Hagedorn, live the last gentlemen of the race!'

Xanten spoke in a voice strained with earnest conviction: 'Twenty years – fifty years – what difference to the Meks? Once they surround us, once they deploy, we are trapped. Do you comprehend that now is our last opportunity to escape the great cage that Castle Hagedorn is to become?'

'"Escape", Xanten? What a word! For shame!' hooted O.Z. Garr. 'Take your wretched band, escape! To steppe or swamp or tundra! Go as you like, with your poltroons, but be good enough to give over these incessant alarms!'

'Garr, I have found conviction since I became a "poltroon". Survival is good morality. I have this from the mouth of a noted savant.'

'Bah! Such as whom?'

'A.G. Philidor, if you must be informed of every detail.'

O.Z. Garr clapped his hand to his forehead. 'Do you refer to Philidor, the Expiationist? He is of the most extreme stripe, an Expiationist to out-expiate all the rest! Xanten, be sensible, if you please!'

'There are years ahead for all of us,' said Xanten in a wooden voice, 'if we free ourselves from the castle.'

'But the castle is our life!' declared Hagedorn. 'In essence, Xanten, what would we be without the castle? Wild animals? Nomads?'

'We would be alive.'

O.Z. Garr gave a snort of disgust and turned away to inspect a wall-hanging.

Hagedorn shook his head in doubt and perplexity. Beaudry threw his hands up into the air. 'Xanten, you have the effect of unnerving us all. You come in here and inflict this dreadful sense of urgency – but why? In Castle Hagedorn we are as safe as in our mothers' arms. What do we gain by throwing aside all – honor, dignity, comfort, civilized niceties – for no other reason than to slink through the wilderness?'

'Janeil was safe,' said Xanten. 'Today where is Janeil? Death, mildewed cloth, sour wine. What we gain by *slinking* is the assurance of survival. And I plan much more than simple *slinking*.'

'I can conceive of a hundred occasions when death is better than life!' snapped Isseth. 'Must I die in dishonor and disgrace? Why may my last years not be passed in dignity?'

Into the room came B.F. Robarth. 'Councilmen, the Meks approach Castle Hagedorn.'

Hagedorn cast a wild look around the chamber. 'Is there a consensus? What must we do?'

Xanten threw up his hands. 'Everyone must do as he thinks best! I argue no more: I am done. Hagedorn, will you adjourn the council so that we may be about our affairs? I to my *slinking*?'

'Council is adjourned,' said Hagedorn, and all went to stand on the ramparts.

Up the avenue into the castle trooped Peasants from the surrounding countryside, packets slung over their shoulders. Across the valley, at the edge of Bartholomew Forest, was a clot of power-wagons and an amorphous brown–gold mass: Meks.

Aure pointed west. 'Look – there they come, up the Long Swale.' He turned, peered east. 'And look, there at Bambridge: Meks!'

By common consent, all swung about to scan North Ridge. O.Z. Garr pointed to a quiet line of brown–gold shapes. 'There they wait, the vermin! They have penned us in! Well then, let them wait!' He swung away, rode the lift down to the plaza, and crossed swiftly to Zumbeld House, where he worked the rest of the afternoon with his Gloriana, of whom he expected great things.

2

The following day the Meks formalized the investment. Around Castle Hagedorn a great circle of Mek activity made itself apparent: sheds, warehouses, barracks. Within this periphery, just beyond the range of the energy cannon, power-wagons thrust up mounds of dirt.

During the night these mounds lengthened toward the castle, similarly the night after. At last the purpose of the mounds became clear: they were a protective cover above passages or tunnels leading toward the crag on which Castle Hagedorn rested.

The following day several of the mounds reached the base of the crag. Presently a succession of power-wagons loaded with rubble began to flow from the far end. They issued, dumped their loads, and once again entered the tunnels.

Eight of these above-ground tunnels had been established. From each trundled endless loads of dirt and rock, gnawed from the crag on which Castle Hagedorn sat. To the gentlefolk who crowded the parapets the meaning of the work at last became clear.

'They make no attempt to bury us,' said Hagedorn. 'They merely mine out the crag from below us!'

On the sixth day of the siege, a great segment of the hillside shuddered, slumped, and a tall pinnacle of rock reaching almost up to the base of the walls collapsed.

'If this continues,' muttered Beaudry, 'our time will be less than that of Janeil.'

'Come then,' called O.Z. Garr, suddenly active. 'Let us try our energy cannon. We'll blast open their wretched tunnels, and then what will the rascals do?' He went to the nearest emplacement and shouted down for Peasants to remove the tarpaulin.

Xanten, who happened to be standing nearby, said, 'Allow me to assist you.' He jerked away the tarpaulin. 'Shoot now, if you will.'

O.Z. Garr stared at him uncomprehendingly, then leaped forward and swiveled the great projector about so that it aimed at a mound. He pulled the switch; the air crackled in front of the ringed snout, rippled, flickered with purple sparks. The target area steamed, became black, then dark red, then slumped into an incandescent crater. But the underlying earth, twenty feet in thickness, afforded too much insulation; the molten puddle became white-hot but failed to spread or deepen. The energy cannon gave a sudden chatter, as electricity short-circuited through corroded insulation. The cannon went dead. O.Z. Garr inspected the mechanism in anger and disappointment; then, with a gesture of repugnance, he turned away. The cannons were clearly of limited effectiveness.

Two hours later, on the east side of the crag, another great sheet of rock collapsed, and just before sunset a similar mass sheared from the western face, where the wall of the castle rose almost in an uninterrupted line from the cliff below.

At midnight Xanten and those of his persuasion, with their children and consorts, departed Castle Hagedorn. Six teams of Birds shuttled from the flight deck to a meadow near Far Valley, and long before dawn had transported the entire group. There were none to bid them farewell.

3

A week later another section of the east cliff fell away, taking a length of rock-melt buttress with it. At the tunnel mouths the piles of excavated rubble had become alarmingly large.

The terraced south face of the crag was the least disturbed, the most spectacular damage having occurred to east and west. Suddenly, a month after the initial assault, a great section of the terrace slumped forward, leaving an irregular crevasse which interrupted the avenue and hurled down the statues of former notables emplaced at intervals along the avenue's balustrade.

Hagedorn called a council meeting. 'Circumstances,' he said in a wan attempt at facetiousness, 'have not bettered themselves. Our most pessimistic expectations have been exceeded: a dismal situation. I confess that I do not relish the prospect of toppling to my death among all my smashed belongings.'

Aure made a desperate gesture. 'A similar thought haunts me! Death – what of that? All must die! But when I think of my precious belongings I become sick. My books trampled! My fragile vases smashed! My tabards ripped! My rugs buried! My Phanes strangled! My heirloom chandeliers flung aside! These are my nightmares.'

'Your possessions are no less precious than any others,' said Beaudry shortly. 'Still, they have no life of their own; when we are gone, who cares what happens to them?'

Marune winced. 'A year ago I put down eighteen dozen flasks of prime essence; twelve dozen Green Rain; three each of Balthazar and Faidor. Think of these, if you would contemplate tragedy!'

'Had we only known!' groaned Aure. 'I would have – I would have ...' His voice trailed away.

O.Z. Garr stamped his foot in impatience. 'Let us avoid lamentation at all costs! We had a choice, remember? Xanten beseeched us to flee; now he and his like go skulking and foraging through the north mountains with the Expiationists. We chose to remain, for better or worse, and unluckily the worse is occurring. We must accept the fact like gentlemen.'

To this the council gave melancholy assent. Hagedorn brought forth a flask of priceless Rhadamanth and poured with a prodigality which previously would have been unthinkable. 'Since we have no future – to our glorious past!'

That night disturbances were noted here and there around the ring of Mek investment: flames at four separate points, a faint sound of hoarse shouting. On the following day it seemed that the tempo of activity had lessened a trifle.

During the afternoon, however, a vast segment of the east cliff fell away. A moment later, as if after majestic deliberation, the tall east wall split off and toppled, leaving the backs of six great houses exposed to the open sky.

An hour after sunset a team of Birds settled to the flight-deck. Xanten jumped from the seat. He ran down the circular staircase to the ramparts and came down to the plaza by Hagedorn's palace.

Hagedorn, summoned by a kinsman, came forth to stare at Xanten in surprise. 'What do you do here? We expected you to be safely north with the Expiationists!'

'The Expiationists are not safely north,' said Xanten. 'They have joined the rest of us. We are fighting.'

Hagedorn's jaw dropped. 'Fighting? The gentlemen are fighting Meks?'

'As vigorously as possible.'

Hagedorn shook his head in wonder. 'The Expiationists too? I understood that they had planned to flee north.'

'Some have done so, including A.G. Philidor. There are factions among the Expiationists just as here. Most are not ten miles distant. The same with the Nomads. Some have taken their power-wagons and fled. The rest kill Meks with fanatic fervor. Last night you saw our work. We fired four storage warehouses, destroyed syrup tanks, killed a hundred or more Meks, as well as a dozen power-wagons. We suffered losses, which hurt us because there are few of us and many Meks. This is why I am here. We need more men. Come fight beside us!'

Hagedorn turned, motioning to the great central plaza. 'I will call forth the folk from their Houses. Talk to everyone.'

4

The Birds, complaining bitterly at the unprecedented toil, worked all night, transporting the gentlemen who, sobered by the imminent destruction of Castle Hagedorn, were now willing to abandon all scruples and fight for their lives. The staunch traditionalists still refused to compromise their honor, but Xanten gave them cheerful assurance: 'Remain here, then, prowling the castle like so many furtive rats. Take what comfort you can in the fact that you are being protected; the future holds little else for you.'

And many who heard him stalked away in disgust.

Xanten turned to Hagedorn. 'What of you? Do you come or do you stay?'

Hagedorn heaved a deep sigh, almost a groan. 'Castle Hagedorn is at an end. No matter what the eventuality. I come with you.'

5

The situation had suddenly altered. The Meks, established in a loose ring around Castle Hagedorn, had calculated upon no resistance from the countryside and little from the castle. They had established their barracks and syrup depots with thought only for convenience and none for defense; raiding parties, consequently, were able to approach, inflict damages and withdraw before sustaining serious losses of their own. Those Meks posted along North Ridge were harassed almost continuously, and finally were driven down with many losses. The circle around Castle Hagedorn became a cusp; then two days later, after the destruction of five more syrup depots, the Meks drew back even farther. Throwing up earthworks before the two tunnels leading under the south face of the crag, they established a more or less tenable defensive position, but now instead of beleaguering, they became the beleaguered, even though power-wagons of broken rock still issued from the crag.

Within the area thus defended the Meks concentrated their remaining syrup stocks, tools, weapons, ammunition. The area outside the earthworks was floodlit after dark and guarded by Meks armed with pellet guns, making any frontal assault impractical.

For a day the raiders kept to the shelter of the surrounding orchards, appraising the new situation. Then a new tactic was attempted. Six light carriages were improvised and loaded with bladders of a light inflammable oil, with a fire grenade attached. To each of these carriages ten Birds were harnessed, and at midnight sent aloft, with a man for each carriage. Flying high, the Birds then glided down through the darkness over the Mek position, where the fire bombs were dropped. The area instantly seethed with flame. The syrup depot burned; the power-wagons, awakened by the flames, rolled frantically back and forth, crushing Meks and stores, colliding with each other, adding vastly to the terror of the fire. The Meks who survived took shelter in the tunnels. Certain of the floodlights were extinguished and, taking advantage of the confusion, the men attacked the earthworks. After a short, bitter battle, the men killed all the sentinels and took up positions commanding the mouths of the tunnels, which now contained all that remained of the Mek army. It seemed as if the Mek uprising had been put down.

CHAPTER EIGHT

1

The flames died. The human warriors – three hundred men from the castle, two hundred Expiationists and about three hundred Nomads – gathered about the tunnel mouth and, during the balance of the night, considered methods to deal with the immured Meks. At sunrise those men of Castle Hagedorn whose children and consorts were yet inside went to bring them forth. With them, upon their return, came a group of castle gentlemen: among them Beaudry, O.Z. Garr, Isseth, and Aure. They greeted their one-time peers, Hagedorn, Xanten, Claghorn and others, crisply, but with a certain austere detachment which recognized that loss of prestige incurred by those who fought Meks as if they were equals.

'Now what is to happen?' Beaudry inquired of Hagedorn. 'The Meks are trapped but you can't bring them forth. Not impossibly they have syrup stored within for the power-wagons; they may well survive for months.'

O.Z. Garr, assessing the situation from the standpoint of a military theoretician, came forward with a plan of action. 'Fetch down the cannon – or have your underlings do so – and mount them on power-wagons. When the vermin are sufficiently weak, roll the cannon in and wipe out all but a labor force for the castle: we formerly worked four hundred, and this should suffice.'

'Ha!' exclaimed Xanten. 'It gives me great pleasure to inform you that this will never be. If any Meks survive they will repair the spaceships and in-struct us in the maintenance and we will then transport them and Peasants back to their native worlds.'

'How then do you expect us to maintain our lives?' demanded Garr coldly.

'You have the syrup generator. Fit yourself with sacs and drink syrup.'

Garr tilted back his head, stared coldly down his nose. 'This is your voice, yours alone, and your insolent opinion. Others are to be heard from. Hagedorn – you were once a gentleman. Is this also your philosophy, that civilization should wither?'

'It need not wither,' said Hagedorn, 'provided that all of us – you as well as we – toil for it. There can be no more slaves. I have become convinced of this.'

O.Z. Garr turned on his heel, swept back up the avenue into the castle, fol-lowed by the most traditional-minded of his comrades. A few moved aside and talked among themselves in low tones, with one or two black looks for Xanten and Hagedorn.

From the ramparts of the castle came a sudden outcry: 'The Meks! They are taking the castle! They swarm up the lower passages! Attack, save us!'

The men below stared up in consternation. Even as they looked, the castle portals swung shut.

'How is this possible?' demanded Hagedorn. 'I swear all entered the tunnels!'

'It is only too clear,' said Xanten bitterly. 'While they undermined, they drove a tunnel up to the lower levels!'

Hagedorn started forward as if he would charge up the crag alone, then halted. 'We must drive them out. Unthinkable that they pillage our castle!'

'Unfortunately,' said Claghorn, 'the walls bar us as effectually as they did the Meks.'

'We can send up a force by Bird-car! Once we consolidate, we can hunt them down, exterminate them.'

Claghorn shook his head. 'They can wait on the ramparts and flight-deck and shoot down the Birds as they approach. Even if we secured a foothold there would be great bloodshed: one of us killed for every one of them. And they still outnumber us three or four to one.'

Hagedorn groaned. 'The thought of them reveling among my possessions, strutting about in my clothes, swilling my essences – it sickens me!'

'Listen!' said Claghorn. From on high they heard the hoarse yells of men, the crackle of energy-cannon. 'Some of them, at least, hold out on the ramparts!'

Xanten went to a nearby group of Birds who were for once awed and subdued by events. 'Lift me up above the castle, out of range of the pellets, but where I can see what the Meks do!'

'Care, take care!' croaked one of the Birds. 'Ill things occur at the castle.'

'Never mind; convey me up, above the ramparts!'

The Birds lifted him, swung in a great circle around the crag and above the castle, sufficiently distant to be safe from the Mek pellet-guns. Beside those cannon which yet operated stood thirty men and women. Between the great Houses, the Rotunda and the Palace, everywhere the cannon could not be brought to bear, swarmed Meks. The plaza was littered with corpses: gentlemen, ladies and their children – all those who had elected to remain at Castle Hagedorn.

At one of the cannon stood O.Z. Garr. Spying Xanten he gave a shout of hysterical rage, swung up the cannon, fired a bolt. The Birds, screaming, tried to swerve aside, but the bolt smashed two. Birds, car, Xanten fell in a great tangle. By some miracle, the four yet alive caught their balance and a hundred feet from the ground, with a frenzied groaning effort, they slowed their fall, steadied, hovered an instant, sank to the ground. Xanten staggered free of the tangle. Men came running. 'Are you safe?' called Claghorn.

'Safe, yes. Frightened as well.' Xanten took a deep breath and went to sit on an outcrop of rock.

'What's happening up there?' asked Claghorn.

'All dead,' said Xanten, 'all but a score. Garr has gone mad. He fired on me.'

'Look! Meks on the ramparts!' cried A.L. Morgan.

'There!' cried someone else. 'Men! They jump! ... No, they are flung!'

Some were men, some were Meks whom they had dragged with them;

with awful slowness they toppled to their deaths. No more fell. Castle Hagedorn was in the hands of the Meks.

Xanten considered the complex silhouette, at once so familiar and so strange. 'They can't hope to hold out. We need only destroy the sun-cells, and they can synthesize no syrup.'

'Let us do it now,' said Claghorn, 'before they think of this and man the cannon! Birds!'

He went off to give the orders, and forty Birds, each clutching two rocks the size of a man's head, flapped up, circled the castle and presently returned to report the sun-cells destroyed.

Xanten said, 'All that remains is to seal the tunnel entrances against a sudden eruption, which might catch us off guard – then patience.'

'What of the Peasants in the stables – and the Phanes?' asked Hagedorn in a forlorn voice.

Xanten gave his head a slow shake. 'He who was not an Expiationist before must become one now.'

Claghorn muttered, 'They can survive two months – no more.'

But two months passed, and three months, and four months: then one morning the great portals opened and a haggard Mek stumbled forth. He signaled: 'Men: we starve. We have maintained your treasures. Give us our lives or we destroy all before we die.'

Claghorn responded: 'These are our terms. We give you your lives. You must clean the castle, remove and bury the corpses. You must repair the spaceships and teach us all you know regarding them. We will then transport you to Etamin Nine.'

2

Five years later Xanten and Glys Meadowsweet, with their two children, had reason to travel north from their home near Sande River. They took occasion to visit Castle Hagedorn, where now lived only two or three dozen folk, among them Hagedorn.

He had aged, so it seemed to Xanten. His hair was white; his face, once bluff and hearty, had become thin, almost waxen. Xanten could not determine his mood.

They stood in the shade of a walnut tree, with castle and crag looming above them. 'This is now a great museum,' said Hagedorn. 'I am curator, and this will be the function of all the Hagedorns who come after me, for there is incalculable treasure to guard and maintain. Already the feeling of antiquity has come to the castle. The Houses are alive with ghosts. I see them often, especially on the nights of the fêtes ... Ah, those were the times, were they not, Xanten?'

'Yes, indeed,' said Xanten. He touched the heads of his two children. 'Still, I have no wish to return to them. We are men now, on our own world, as we never were before.'

Hagedorn gave a somewhat regretful assent. He looked up at the vast structure, as if now were the first occasion he had laid eyes on it. 'The folk of the future – what will they think of Castle Hagedorn? Its treasures, its books, its tabards?'

'They will come, they will marvel,' said Xanten. 'Almost as I do today.'

'There is much at which to marvel. Will you come within, Xanten? There are still flasks of noble essence laid by.'

'Thank you, no,' said Xanten. 'There is too much to stir old memories. We will go our way, and I think immediately.'

Hagedorn nodded sadly. 'I understand very well. I myself am often given to reverie these days. Well then, goodbye, and journey home with pleasure.'

'We will do so, Hagedorn. Thank you and goodbye.'

If you've enjoyed these books and would
like to read more, you'll find literally thousands
of classic Science Fiction & Fantasy titles
through the **SF Gateway**

✱

*For the new home of
Science Fiction & Fantasy . . .*

✱

*For the most comprehensive collection
of classic SF on the internet . . .*

✱

Visit the SF Gateway

www.sfgateway.com

Jack Vance (1916–)

Jack Vance was born in 1916 and studied mining, engineering and journalism at the University of California. During the Second World War he served in the merchant navy and was torpedoed twice. He started contributing stories to the pulp magazines in the mid-1940s and published his first book, *The Dying Earth*, in 1950. Among his many books are *The Dragon Masters*, for which he won his first Hugo Award, *Big Planet*, *The Anome*, and the Lyonesse sequence. He has won the Hugo, Nebula and World Fantasy Awards, amongst others, and in 1997 was named a Grand Master by the Science Fiction Writers of America.